AMERICAN FANTASTIC TALES

AMERICAN
FANTASTIC TALES

TERROR AND THE UNCANNY
FROM THE 1940s TO NOW

Peter Straub, editor

THE LIBRARY OF AMERICA

Volume compilation, notes, and chronology copyright © 2009 by
Literary Classics of the United States, Inc., New York, N.Y.
All rights reserved.
No part of this book may be reproduced commercially
by offset-lithographic or equivalent copying devices without
the permission of the publisher.

Some of the material in this volume is reprinted with permission
of the holders of copyright and publication rights.
Acknowledgments are on page 703.

The paper used in this publication meets the
minimum requirements of the American National Standard for
Information Sciences—Permanence of Paper for Printed
Library Materials, ANSI Z39.48—1984.

Distributed to the trade in the United States
by Penguin Group (USA) Inc.
and in Canada by Penguin Books Canada Ltd.

Library of Congress Control Number: 2009927074
ISBN 978–1–59853–048–3

———

First Printing
The Library of America—197

Manufactured in the United States of America

Contents

Introduction

WHEN THOUGHT OF, in really the simplest manner possible, as an alternative to straightforward realism, the fantastic can immediately be seen to offer writers of fiction another toolbox, another set of instruments available for the depiction of human beings in interesting and revelatory situations. Or, take off *those* glasses and put on *these* glasses: see how different everything looks? The landscape instantly becomes craggier, the shadows deeper, the buildings more eccentric and Gaudi-esque. At its core, I think, the fantastic is a way of seeing.

In this second volume of *American Fantastic Tales*, those lenses are trained, decade by decade, on any number of social issues. In the forties, John Collier addresses the anxieties of a nation just beginning to work its way out of the Depression and toward a great war ("Evening Primrose"); Fritz Leiber conjures with the different anxieties of becoming a nation dominated by giant factories and heavy industries ("Smoke Ghost"); and Jane Rice makes the delicious most of the occu-pation of Paris ("The Refugee"). In the late sixties, Harlan Ellison is imagining what might happen if Norbert Wiener's vast, enigmatic computers at MIT ever got out of hand ("I Have No Mouth, and I Must Scream"); in the seventies, Isaac Bashevis Singer continues to contemplate the Holocaust's legacy ("Hanka"). At the end of the eighties, Joyce Carol Oates has some giddy, black-humor fun with the disasters po-tential within a poisoned environment ("Family"). In the first decade of the twenty-first century, Steven Millhauser takes up the ever-troubling matters of teenage behavior and the inexpli-cable hysteria common to teen fads ("Dark Laughter"); in the same year, M. Rickert uses the Persephone myth as the underpinning of a story that hinges on parental fears of what could happen should a child wander, all innocence, into an In-ternet chat room ("The Chambered Fruit"). A little later in the decade, Benjamin Percy homes in on the drudgery of call centers and fears about the effects on the human body of cell phones and the towers that enable them ("Dial Tone").

Other sorts of themes, some of them familiar from the first of these two volumes, shape these stories, too. Bad Nature conspires against man in Kelly Link's "Stone Animals" and T.E.D. Klein's "The Events at Poroth Farm," which, like Thomas Ligotti's "The Last Feast of Harlequin," is a loving and exacting tribute to H. P. Lovecraft. What I take to be the central theme in the American literature of the fantastic, the loss of the individual will, hence of the self, and the terror aroused by the prospect of this loss, simmers through Paul Bowles' "The Circular Valley," Ray Bradbury's "The April Witch" (in close proximity, these two stories share an identical mechanism), Steven Millhauser's "Dangerous Laughter," Brian Evenson's "The Wavering Knife," and Tim Powers' "Pat Moore." Volume I contained four vampire stories, the most striking and indirect of which, Mary Wilkins Freeman's "Luella Miller," reads like a direct precursor of this volume's "Torch Song," by John Cheever. Each volume contains one werewolf story. The traditional horror tropes in fact appear very seldom in these volumes. The first volume reprints only three true ghost stories, Edith Wharton's "Afterward," Willa Cather's "Consequences," and Ellen Glasgow's "The Shadowy Third"; several other stories allude to ghosts, but the lurking phantoms are not the primary focus. Volume II contains only one, Nabokov's "The Vane Sisters," which could be called a meta-ghost story.

The simplest possible form of the fantastic tale is the story of single effect, in which, with varying degrees of art, the writer eliminates as much narrative complication as possible to concentrate solely on the development toward the shocker of the climax. The only point of such stories is what happens near the end, at the end, or in the very last sentence, and the only point of writing them is to drop that little bomb and see it explode. Brevity is a necessary consequence. The first volume has four stories of single effect, by Harriet Prescott Spofford ("The Moonstone Mass"), Madeline Yale Wynn ("The Little Room"), Ralph Adams Cram ("The Dead Valley"), and by the otherwise genteel Gertrude Atherton, whose "The Striding Place" pulls off the final trick with crude, undeniable vigor. This volume contains two such stories, Donald Wandrei's enjoyably pulpy "Nightmare" and Thomas Tessier's "Nocturne," probably the most sophisticated story of single effect ever to be written. With an easygoing *flaneur* named O'Netty we venture into an underground bar, admire and enjoy the friendly cosmopolitan crowd, then witness a shocking and inexplicable act that, while ruffling no one's composure, not even O'Netty's, causes the reader to take in everything that follows it with a refreshed, ultra-conscious awareness.

Time is the great conundrum in fiction of every kind, and the fantastic is peculiarly suited to its exploration. Human memory complicates our experience of time with its immediate access to pockets of the lost past that, when recovered, can coexist with the present and sometimes—for an immeasurable period that in some sense exists altogether outside of time— just about replace it. Or, actually, for the length of the timeless moment, *to* replace it. Technically impossible (in 2009, anyhow) and philosophically ill-advised for a hundred reasons given us by science fiction and works of fantasy, time travel nonetheless happens all the time and to more or less everybody. The versatile Jack Finney, whose "I'm Scared" reports the alarm of an average male of the 1940s or 50s upon observing that the universal distaste for present-day conditions has encouraged both trivial and significant fragments of the past to commandeer the world about him, spent most of his long career wrestling with the puzzle of time in novels like *Time and Again* and *From Time to Time* as well as the stories collected within *The Third Level* and *About Time*.

Stephen King's "That Feeling, You Can Only Say What It Is in French" and Benjamin Percy's "Dial Tone" push Finney's obsession with time slips and time travel through a kind of metaphysical food processor, a kind of meaning-enhancer, thereby enriching these themes with greater psychological depth and raising the literary ante. The Finney story is a clever representation of the perceived dangers of nostalgia in a troubled era; the stories by King and Percy seem to me to have bigger fish to fry. They are less accommodating, less comfortable, ascribable to a far less familiar template. If the King story has any direct ancestor, it might be Ambrose Bierce's "Occurrence at Owl Creek Bridge," the way you'd see that story if you looked at it though a kaleidoscope. ("Dial Tone"'s underlying pattern might be derived from a chapter near the conclusion of

Brian Evenson's novel *The Open Curtain*, or even from certain wild-eyed passages in *Absalom, Absalom*. Probably, of course, it is neither Evenson nor Faulkner, just something in the air these days.)

In "That Feeling, You Can Only Say What It Is in French," time is dubious, unreliable, radically decentered. It seems responsive to human emotion, and the abrupt discontinuities, refrains, and repeated images bubbling to the surface of King's mixed-sequence time imply the presence of a great, gathering, secret meaning. The ultimate desire hidden behind any presentation of mixed-sequence temporality is, I think, the complex, god-like rapture of finally perceiving the simultaneity of all of time. The characters in this story, it must be said, are rewarded with a far less exalted recognition.

Percy's "Dial Tone" dices space as well as time and makes both, along with character, multivalent. The resulting discontinuities are so radical as to be destructive to the traditional terms of story-making itself. The narrative appears to be going forward, but it actually moves backward, shoving the reader along up to the moment just before the situation described in the first paragraph. (Come to think of it, that sounds like "Occurrence at Owl Creek Bridge," too.) Our bored but conventional narrator, a call center wage-slave subject to the verbal abuse of his potential customers, gradually devolves into the haggard red-eyed wretch with missing clumps of hair he sees in a picture window when coming to the aid of a concussed bird, then into the rude, offensive man on the other side of the window, then into the brutal, wraith-like murderer who hears himself uttering the tentative telephone greeting he had half-whispered earlier, back in the call center. Everything collapses into itself, and we are left with a dead man being hoisted up a cell tower by a dying man invaded by the multiple voices coursing through the wires that surround him.

About forty percent of the stories in this volume, seventeen out of forty-three, or exactly a fifth of the two-volume total of eighty-five, were originally published in this decade and the last. Of that seventeen, twelve were first published in the '00s. This distribution may seem more than a little unbalanced, but I could easily have found, and in fact undoubtedly did find, twice as many stories from the present decade worthy of inclusion here. Because we were already packed full to the rafters, a lot of excellent work did not in the end get past the velvet rope. Something analogous to the gearing-up from the Finney story to those by King and Percy has taken place all across the fantasy/horror genre, to call it that, as a whole. (The same thing also happened in sci-fi and mystery novels.) Younger writers who had grown up reading people who were already pushing at the borders of genre were able to take the next, and to me breathtaking, step of creating fiction that acted as though those borders had never existed in the first place. A straight line connects Stephen King and Benjamin Percy, and it has to do with artistic ambition.

Michael Chabon and Kelly Link seem to me central figures in the movement I am describing. They are at least superbly representative of it. Throughout his sterling, deservedly honored career, Chabon has demonstrated great fondness for and knowledge of genre literatures of many kinds, including comic books, and his work often draws its content from these literatures. Kelly Link wrote from the first with the assumption that everything on earth was fair game for the serious writer. Nancy Drew, fairy tales, sibling rivalry, ghost stories, zombies, teenage angst, grief, loss, despair—it all goes into the hopper and emerges as fiction distinguished by its utter originality, playfulness, associative logic, depth of intuition, and sureness of touch. Her great story "Stone Animals" proceeds by precisely these means from the purchase of a house in the country to a conclusion that is simultaneously surrealist, disturbing, startling, yet thoroughly prepared-for and in fact inevitable: at every step, subtle inner voicings lead the way.

As "The God of Dark Laughter" looks back fondly to the ersatz scholarship and ancient gods of Lovecraft's Cthulhu tales, "Stone Animals" begins with a direct reference to the first line of Edith Wharton's "Afterward." The real-estate agent is responding to the question, "Is this house haunted?" instead of "Is there a ghost?" but the allusion neatly bridges the ninety-nine years that separate the two stories. One wonders how Edith Wharton would have reacted to the then utterly undreamt-of manner in which Kelly Link was to develop her clever opening gambit.

Peter Straub

JOHN COLLIER

(1901–1980)

Evening Primrose

In a pad of Highlife Bond,
bought by Miss Sadie Brodribb
at Bracey's
for 25¢

February 21

TODAY I made my decision. I would turn my back for good and all upon the *bourgeois* world that hates a poet. I would leave, get out, break away——

And I have done it. I am free! Free as the mote that dances in the sunbeam! Free as a house-fly crossing first-class in the *Queen Mary*! Free as my verse! Free as the food I shall eat, the paper I write upon, the lamb's-wool-lined softly slithering slippers I shall wear.

This morning I had not so much as a car-fare. Now I am here, on velvet. You are itching to learn of this haven: you would like to organize trips here, spoil it, send your relations-in-law, perhaps even come yourself. After all, this journal will hardly fall into your hands till I am dead. I'll tell you.

I am at Bracey's Giant Emporium, as happy as a mouse in the middle of an immense cheese, and the world shall know me no more.

Merrily, merrily shall I live now, secure behind a towering pile of carpets, in a corner-nook which I propose to line with eiderdowns, angora vestments, and the Cleopatræan tops in pillows. I shall be cosy.

I nipped into this sanctuary late this afternoon, and soon heard the dying footfalls of closing time. From now on, my only effort will be to dodge the night-watchman. Poets can dodge.

I have already made my first mouse-like exploration. I tip-toed as far as the stationery department, and, timid, darted back with only these writing materials, the poet's first need.

I

Now I shall lay them aside, and seek other necessities: food, wine, the soft furniture of my couch, and a natty smoking-jacket. This place stimulates me. I shall write here.

Dawn, next day

I suppose no one in the world was ever more astonished and overwhelmed than I have been tonight. It is unbelievable. Yet I believe it. How interesting life is when things get like that!

I crept out, as I said I would, and found the great shop in mingled light and gloom. The central well was half illuminated; the circling galleries towered in a pansy Piranesi of toppling light and shade. The spidery stairways and flying bridges had passed from purpose into fantasy. Silks and velvets glimmered like ghosts, a hundred pantie-clad models offered simpers and embraces to the desert air. Rings, clips, and bracelets glittered frostily in a desolate absence of Honey and Daddy.

Creeping along the transverse aisles, which were in deeper darkness, I felt like a wandering thought in the dreaming brain of a chorus girl down on her luck. Only, of course, their brains are not so big as Bracey's Giant Emporium. And there was no man there.

None, that is, except the night-watchman. I had forgotten him. A regular thudding, which might almost have been that of my own heart, suddenly burst upon me loudly, from outside, only a few feet away. Quick as a flash I seized a costly wrap, flung it about my shoulders, and stood stock-still.

I was successful. He passed me, jingling his little machine on its chain, humming his little tune, his eyes scaled with refractions of the blaring day. "Go, worldling!" I whispered, and permitted myself a soundless laugh.

It froze on my lips. My heart faltered. A new fear seized me.

I was afraid to move. I was afraid to look round. I felt I was being watched, by something that could see right through me. This was a very different feeling from the ordinary emergency caused by the very ordinary night-watchman. My conscious impulse was the obvious one, to glance behind me. But my eyes knew better. I remained absolutely petrified, staring straight ahead.

My eyes were trying to tell me something that my brain refused to believe. They made their point. I was looking straight into another pair of eyes, human eyes, but large, flat, luminous. I have seen such eyes among the nocturnal creatures, which creep out under the artificial blue moonlight in the zoo.

The owner was only a dozen feet away from me. The watchman had passed between us, nearer him than me. Yet he had not been seen. I must have been looking straight at him for several minutes at a stretch. I had not seen him either.

He was half reclining against a high dais, a platform for the exhibition of shawls and mantillas. One of these brushed his shoulder: its folds concealed perhaps his ear, his shoulder, and a little of his right side. He was clad in dim but large-patterned Shetland tweeds of the latest cut, suède shoes, a shirt of a rather broad *motif* in olive, pink, and grey. He was as pale as a creature found under a stone. His long thin arms ended in hands that hung floatingly, more like trailing, transparent fins, or wisps of chiffon, than ordinary hands.

He spoke. His voice was not a voice, a mere whistling under the tongue. "Not bad, for a beginner!"

I grasped that he was complimenting me, rather satirically, on my concealment under the wrap. I stuttered. I said, "I'm sorry. I didn't know anyone else lived here." I noticed, even as I spoke, that I was imitating his own whistling sibilant utterance.

"Oh, yes," he said. "*We* live here. It's delightful."

"We?"

"Yes, all of us. Look."

We were near the edge of the first gallery. He swept his long hand round, indicating the whole well of the shop. I looked. I saw nothing. I could hear nothing, except the watchman's thudding step receding infinitely far along some basement aisle.

"Don't you see?"

You know the sensation one has, peering into the half-light of a vivarium? One sees bark, pebbles, a few leaves, nothing more. And then, suddenly, a stone breathes—it is a toad; there is a chameleon, another, a coiled adder, a mantis among the leaves. The whole case seems crepitant with life. Perhaps the whole world is. One glances at one's sleeve, one's feet.

So it was with the shop. I looked, and it was empty. I looked, and there was an old lady, clambering out from behind the monstrous clock. There were three girls, elderly *ingénues*,

incredibly emaciated, simpering at the entrance of the per-
fumery. Their hair was a fine floss, pale as gossamer. Equally
brittle and colourless was a man with the appearance of a
colonel of southern extraction, who stood regarding me while
he caressed moustachios that would have done credit to a crystal shrimp. A chintzy woman, possibly of literary tastes, swam
forward from the curtains and drapes.

They came thick about me, fluttering, whistling, like a waving
of gauze in the wind. Their eyes were wide and flatly bright. I
saw there was no colour to the iris.

"How raw he looks!"

"A detective! Send for the Dark Men!"

"I'm not a detective. I am a poet. I have renounced the
world."

"He is a poet. He has come over to us. Mr. Roscoe found
him."

"He admires us."

"He must meet Mrs. Vanderpant."

I was taken to meet Mrs. Vanderpant: she proved to be the
Grand Old Lady of the store, almost entirely transparent.

"So you are a poet, Mr. Snell? You will find inspiration here.
I am quite the oldest inhabitant. Three mergers and a complete rebuilding, but they didn't get rid of me!"

"Tell how you went out by daylight, dear Mrs. Vanderpant,
and nearly got bought for Whistler's *Mother*."

"That was in pre-war days. I was more robust then. But at
the cash desk they suddenly remembered there was no frame.
And when they came back to look at me—"

"—She was gone."

Their laughter was like the stridulation of the ghosts of
grasshoppers.

"Where is Ella? Where is my broth?"

"She is bringing it, Mrs. Vanderpant. It will come."

"Terrible little creature! She is our foundling, Mr. Snell. She
is not quite our sort."

"Is that so, Mrs. Vanderpant? Dear, dear!"

"I lived alone here, Mr. Snell, ever since the terrible times in
the eighties. I was a young girl then, a beauty, they said, and
poor Papa lost his money. Bracey's meant a lot to a young girl,
in the New York of those days, Mr. Snell. It seemed to me ter-

rible that I should not be able to come here in the ordinary way. So I came here for good. I was quite alarmed when others began to come in, after the crash of 1907. But it was the dear Judge, the Colonel, Mrs. Bilbee——"

I bowed. I was being introduced.

"Mrs. Bilbee writes plays. *And* of a very old Philadelphia family. You will find us quite *nice* here, Mr. Snell."

"I feel it a great privilege, Mrs. Vanderpant."

"And of course, all our dear *young* people came in '29. *Their* poor papas jumped from skyscrapers."

I did a great deal of bowing and whistling. The introductions took a long time. Who would have thought so many people lived in Bracey's?

"And here at last is Ella with my broth."

It was then I noticed that the young people were not so young after all, in spite of their smiles, their little ways, their *ingénue* dress. Ella was in her teens. Clad only in something from the shop-soiled counter, she nevertheless had the appearance of a living flower in a French cemetery, or a mermaid among polyps.

"Come, you stupid thing!"

"Mrs. Vanderpant is waiting."

Her pallor was not like theirs, not like the pallor of something that glistens or scuttles when you turn over a stone. Hers was that of a pearl.

Ella! Pearl of this remotest, most fantastic cave! Little mermaid, brushed over, pressed down by objects of a deadlier white—tentacles—! I can write no more.

February 28

Well, I am rapidly becoming used to my new and half-lit world, to my strange company. I am learning the intricate laws of silence and camouflage which dominate the apparently casual strollings and gatherings of the midnight clan. How they detest the night-watchman, whose existence imposes these laws on their idle festivals!

"Odious, vulgar creature! He reeks of the coarse sun!"

Actually, he is quite a personable young man, very young for a night-watchman. But they would like to tear him to pieces.

They are very pleasant to me, though. They are pleased that

a poet should have come among them. Yet I cannot like them entirely. My blood is a little chilled by the uncanny ease with which even the old ladies can clamber spider-like from balcony to balcony. Or is it because they are unkind to Ella?

Yesterday we had a bridge party. Tonight Mrs. Bilbee's little play, *Love in Shadowland*, is going to be presented. Would you believe it?—another colony, from Wanamaker's, is coming over *en masse* to attend. Apparently people live in all stores. This visit is considered a great honour: there is an intense snobbery in these creatures. They speak with horror of a social outcast who left a high-class Madison Avenue establishment, and now leads a wallowing, beachcomberish life in a delicatessen. And they relate with tragic emotion the story of the man in Altman's, who conceived such a passion for a model plaid dressing jacket that he emerged and wrested it from the hands of a purchaser. It seems that all the Altman colony, dreading an investigation, were forced to remove beyond the social pale, into a five-and-dime. Well, I must get ready to attend the play.

March 1

I have found an opportunity to speak to Ella. I dared not before: here one has a sense always of pale eyes secretly watching. But last night, at the play, I developed a fit of hiccups. I was somewhat sternly told to go and secrete myself in the basement, among the garbage cans, where the watchman never comes.

There, in the rat-haunted darkness, I heard a stifled sob. "What's that? Is it you? Is it Ella? What ails you, child? Why do you cry?"

"They wouldn't even let me see the play."

"Is that all? Let me console you."

"I am so unhappy."

She told me her tragic little story. What do you think? When she was a child, a little tiny child of only six, she strayed away and fell asleep behind a counter, while her mother tried on a new hat. When she woke, the store was in darkness.

"And I cried, and they all came round, and took hold of me. 'She will tell, if we let her go,' they said. Some said, 'Call in the Dark Men.' 'Let her stay here,' said Mrs. Vanderpant. 'She will make me a nice little maid.'"

"Who are these Dark Men, Ella? They spoke of them when I came here."

"Don't you know? Oh, it's horrible! It's horrible!"

"Tell me, Ella. Let us share it."

She trembled. "You know the morticians, 'Journey's End,' who go to houses when people die?"

"Yes, Ella."

"Well, in that shop, just like here, and at Gimbel's, and at Bloomingdale's, there are people living, people like these."

"How disgusting! But what can they live upon, Ella, in a funeral home?"

"Don't ask me! Dead people are sent there, to be embalmed. Oh, they are terrible creatures! Even the people here are terrified of them. But if anyone dies, or if some poor burglar breaks in, and sees these people, and might tell——"

"Yes? Go on."

"Then they send for the others, the Dark Men."

"Good heavens!"

"Yes, and they put the body in the surgical department—or the burglar, all tied up, if it's a burglar—and they send for these others, and then they all hide, and in they come, these others— Oh! they're like pieces of blackness. I saw them once. It was terrible."

"And then?"

"They go in, to where the dead person is, or the poor burglar. And they have wax there—and all sorts of things. And when they're gone there's just one of these wax models left, on the table. And then our people put a frock on it, or a bathing suit, and they mix it up with all the others, and nobody ever knows."

"But aren't they heavier than the others, these wax models? You would think they'd be heavier."

"No. They're not heavier. I think there's a lot of them— gone."

"Oh dear! So they were going to do that to you, when you were a little child?"

"Yes, only Mrs. Vanderpant said I was to be her maid."

"I don't like these people, Ella."

"Nor do I. I wish I could see a bird."

"Why don't you go into the pet-shop?"

"It wouldn't be the same. I want to see it on a twig, with leaves."

"Ella, let us meet often. Let us creep away down here and meet. I will tell you about birds, and twigs and leaves."

March 10

"Ella, I love you."

I said it to her just like that. We have met many times. I have dreamt of her by day. I have not even kept up my journal. Verse has been out of the question.

"Ella, I love you. Let us move into the trousseau department. Don't look so dismayed, darling. If you like, we will go right away from here. We will live in the refreshment rooms in Central Park. There are thousands of birds there."

"Don't, Charles, don't."

"But I love you with all my heart."

"You mustn't."

"But I find I must. I can't help it. Ella, you don't love another?"

She wept a little. "Oh, Charles, I do."

"Love another, Ella? One of these? I thought you dreaded them all. It must be Roscoe. He is the only one that's any way human. We talk of art, life, and such things. And he has stolen your heart!"

"No, Charles, no. He's just like the rest, really. I hate them all. They make me shudder."

"Who is it, then?"

"It's him."

"Who?"

"The night-watchman."

"Impossible!"

"No. He smells of the sun."

"Oh, Ella, you have broken my heart."

"Be my friend, though."

"I will. I'll be your brother. How did you fall in love with him?"

"Oh, Charles, it was so wonderful. I was thinking of birds, and I was careless. Don't tell on me, Charles, they'll punish me."

"No. No. Go on."

"I was careless, and there he was, coming round the corner.

And there was no place for me, I had this blue frock on. There were only some wax models in their underthings."

"Please go on."

"I couldn't help it, Charles. I slipped off my dress, and stood still."

"I see."

"And he stopped just by me, Charles. And he looked at me. And he touched my cheek."

"Did he notice nothing?"

"No. It was cold. But Charles, he said—he said—'Say, honey, I wish they made 'em like you on Eighth Avenue.' Charles, wasn't that a lovely thing to say?"

"Personally, I should have said Park Avenue."

"Oh, Charles, don't get like these people here. Sometimes I think you're getting like them. It doesn't matter what street, Charles; it was a lovely thing to say."

"Yes, but my heart's broken. And what can you do about him? Ella, he belongs to another world."

"Yes, Charles, Eighth Avenue. I want to go there. Charles, are you truly my friend?"

"I'm your brother, only my heart's broken."

"I'll tell you. I will. I'm going to stand there again. So he'll see me."

"And then?"

"Perhaps he'll speak to me again."

"My dearest Ella, you are torturing yourself. You are making it worse."

"No, Charles. Because I shall answer him. He will take me away."

"Ella, I can't bear it."

"Ssh! There is someone coming. I shall see birds, flowers growing. They're coming. You must go."

March 13

The last three days have been torture. This evening I broke. Roscoe (he was my first acquaintance) came in. There has always been a sort of hesitant sympathy between us.

He said, "You're looking seedy, old fellow. Why don't you go over to Wanamaker's for some skiing?"

His kindness compelled a frank response. "It's deeper than

that, Roscoe. I'm done for. I can't eat, I can't sleep. I can't write, man, I can't even write."

"What is it? Day starvation?"

"Roscoe—it's love."

"Not one of the staff, Charles, or the customers? That's absolutely forbidden."

"No, it's not that, Roscoe. But just as hopeless."

"My dear old fellow, I can't bear to see you like this. Let me help you. Let me share your trouble."

Then it all came out. It burst out. I trusted him. I think I trusted him. I really think I had no intention of betraying Ella, of spoiling her escape, of keeping her here till her heart turned towards me. If I had, it was subconscious. I swear it.

But I told him all. All. He was sympathetic, but I detected a sly reserve in his sympathy. "You will respect my confidence, Roscoe? This is to be a secret between us."

"As secret as the grave, old chap."

And he must have gone straight to Mrs. Vanderpant. This evening the atmosphere has changed. People flicker to and fro, smiling nervously, horribly, with a sort of frightened sadistic exaltation. When I speak to them they answer evasively, fidget, and disappear. An informal dance has been called off. I cannot find Ella. I will creep out. I will look for her again.

Later

Heaven! It has happened. I went in desperation to the manager's office, whose glass front overlooks the whole shop. I watched till midnight. Then I saw a little group of them, like ants bearing a victim. They were carrying Ella. They took her to the surgical department. They took other things.

And, coming back here, I was passed by a flittering, whispering horde of them, glancing over their shoulders in a thrilled ecstasy of panic, making for their hiding places. I, too, hid myself. How can I describe the dark inhuman creatures that passed me, silent as shadows? They went there—where Ella is.

What can I do? There is only one thing. I will find the watchman. I will tell him. He and I will save her. And if we are overpowered— Well, I will leave this on a counter. Tomorrow, if we live, I can recover it.

If not, look in the windows. Look for three new figures: two men, one rather sensitive-looking, and a girl. She has blue eyes, like periwinkle flowers, and her upper lip is lifted a little.

Look for us.

Smoke them out! Obliterate them! Avenge us!

1940

FRITZ LEIBER

(1910–1992)

Smoke Ghost

MISS MILLICK wondered just what had happened to Mr. Wran. He kept making the strangest remarks when she took dictation. Just this morning he had quickly turned around and asked, "Have you ever seen a ghost, Miss Millick?" And she had tittered nervously and replied, "When I was a girl there was a thing in white that used to come out of the closet in the attic bedroom when you slept there, and moan. Of course it was just my imagination. I was frightened of lots of things." And he had said, "I don't mean that traditional kind of ghost. I mean a ghost from the world today, with the soot of the factories in its face and the pounding of machinery in its soul. The kind that would haunt coal yards and slip around at night through deserted office buildings like this one. A real ghost. Not something out of books." And she hadn't known what to say.

He'd never been like this before. Of course it might be joking, but it didn't sound that way. Vaguely Miss Millick wondered whether he mightn't be seeking some sort of sympathy from her. Of course, Mr. Wran was married and had a little child, but that didn't prevent her from having daydreams. She had daydreams about most of the men she worked for. The daydreams were all very similar in pattern and not very exciting, but they helped fill up the emptiness in her mind. And now he was asking her another of those disturbing and jarringly out-of-place questions.

"Have you ever thought what a ghost of our times would look like, Miss Millick? Just picture it. A smoky composite face with the hungry anxiety of the unemployed, the neurotic restlessness of the person without purpose, the jerky tension of the high-pressure metropolitan worker, the sullen resentment of the striker, the callous viciousness of the strike breaker, the aggressive whine of the panhandler, the inhibited terror of the bombed civilian, and a thousand other twisted emotional patterns? Each one overlying and yet blending with the other, like a pile of semitransparent masks?"

Miss Millick gave a little self-conscious shiver and said, "My, that would be terrible. What an awful thing to think of."

She peered at him furtively across the desk. Was he going crazy? She remembered having heard that there had been something impressively abnormal about Mr. Wran's childhood, but she couldn't recall what it was. If only she could do something —joke at him or ask him what was really wrong. She shifted around the extra pencils in her left hand and mechanically traced over some of the shorthand curlicues in her notebook.

"Yet, that's just what such a ghost or vitalized projection would look like, Miss Millick," he continued, smiling in a tight way. "It would grow out of the real world. It would reflect all the tangled, sordid, vicious things. All the loose ends. And it would be very grimy. I don't think it would seem white or wispy or favor graveyards. It wouldn't moan. But it would mutter unintelligibly, and twitch at your sleeve. Like a sick, surly ape. What would such a thing want from a person, Miss Millick? Sacrifice? Worship? Or just fear? What could you do to stop it from troubling you?"

Miss Millick giggled nervously. She felt embarrassed and out of her depth. There was an expression beyond her powers of definition in Mr. Wran's ordinary, flat-cheeked, thirty-ish face, silhouetted against the dusty window. He turned away and stared out into the gray downtown atmosphere that rolled in from the railroad yards and the mills. When he spoke again his voice sounded far away.

"Of course, being immaterial, it couldn't hurt you physically —at first. You'd have to be peculiarly sensitive even to see it, or be aware of it at all. But it would begin to influence your actions. Make you do this. Stop you from doing that. Although only a projection, it would gradually get its hooks into the world of things as they are. Might even get control of suitably vacuous minds. Then it could hurt whomever it wanted."

Miss Millick squirmed and tried to read back her shorthand, like books said you should do when there was a pause. She became aware of the failing light and wished Mr. Wran would ask her to turn on the overhead light. She felt uncomfortable and scratchy as if soot were sifting down on to her skin.

"It's a rotten world, Miss Millick," said Mr. Wran, talking at the window. "Fit for another morbid growth of superstition. It's time the ghosts, or whatever you call them, took over and began a rule of fear. They'd be no worse than men."

"But"—Miss Millick's diaphragm jerked, making her titter inanely—"of course there aren't any such things as ghosts."

Mr. Wran turned around. She noticed with a start that his grin had broadened, though without getting any less tight.

"Of course there aren't, Miss Millick," he said in a sudden loud, reassuring, almost patronizing voice, as if she had been doing the talking rather than he. "Modern science and common sense and better self-understanding all go to prove it."

He stopped, staring past her abstractedly. She hung her head and might even have blushed if she hadn't felt so all at sea. Her leg muscles twitched, making her stand up, although she hadn't intended to. She aimlessly rubbed her hand back and forth along the edge of the desk, then pulled it back.

"Why, Mr. Wran, look what I got off your desk," she said, showing him a heavy smudge. There was a note of cumbersomely playful reproof in her voice, but she really just wanted to be saying something. "No wonder the copy I bring you always get so black. Somebody ought to talk to those scrubwomen. They're skimping on your room."

She wished he would make some normal joking reply. But instead he drew back and his face hardened.

"Well, to get back to the letter to Fredericks," he rapped out harshly, and began to dictate.

When she was gone he jumped up, dabbed his finger experimentally at the smudged part of the desk, frowned worriedly at the almost inky smears. He jerked open a drawer, snatched out a rag, hastily swabbed off the desk, crumpled the rag into a ball and tossed it back. There were three or four other rags in the drawer, each impregnated with soot.

Then he strode over to the window and peered out anxiously through the gathering dusk, his eyes searching the panorama of roofs, fixing on each chimney, each water tank.

"It's a psychosis. Must be. Hallucination. Compulsion neurosis," he muttered to himself in a tired, distraught voice that would have made Miss Millick gasp. "Good thing I'm seeing the psychiatrist tonight. It's that damned mental abnormality cropping up in a new form. Can't be any other explanation. Can't be. But it's so damned real. Even the soot. I don't think I could force myself to get on the elevated tonight. Good thing I made the appointment. The doctor will know—" His voice trailed off, he rubbed his eyes, and his memory automatically started to grind.

It had all begun on the elevated. There was a particular little sea of roofs he had grown into the habit of glancing at just as the packed car carrying him homeward lurched around a turn. A dingy, melancholy little world of tar paper, tarred gravel, and smoky brick. Rusty tin chimneys with odd conical hats suggested abandoned listening posts. There was a washed-out advertisement of some ancient patent medicine on the nearest wall. Superficially it was like ten thousand other drab city roofs. But he always saw it around dusk, either in the normal smoky half-light, or tinged with red by the flat rays of a dirty sunset, or covered by ghostly windblown white sheets of rain-splash, or patched with blackish snow; and it seemed unusually bleak and suggestive, almost beautifully ugly, though in no sense picturesque; dreary but meaningful. Unconsciously it came to symbolize for Catesby Wran certain disagreeable aspects of the frustrated, frightened century in which he lived, the jangled century of hate and heavy industry and Fascist wars. The quick, daily glance into the half darkness became an integral part of his life. Oddly, he never saw it in the morning, for it was then his habit to sit on the other side of the car, his head buried in the paper.

One evening toward winter he noticed what seemed to be a shapeless black sack lying on the third roof from the tracks. He did not think about it. It merely registered as an addition to the well-known scene and his memory stored away the impression for further reference. Next evening, however, he decided he had been mistaken in one detail. The object was a roof nearer than he had thought. Its color and texture, and the grimy stains around it, suggested that it was filled with coal dust, which was hardly reasonable. Then, too, the following evening it seemed to have been blown against a rusty ventilator by the wind— which could hardly have happened if it were at all heavy. Perhaps it was filled with leaves. Catesby was surprised to find himself anticipating his next daily glance with a minor note of apprehension. There was something unwholesome in the posture of the thing that stuck in his mind—a bulge in the sacking that suggested a misshapen head peering around the ventilator. And his apprehension was justified, for that evening the thing was on the nearest roof, though on the farther side, looking as if it had just flopped down over the low brick parapet.

Next evening the sack was gone. Catesby was annoyed at the momentary feeling of relief that went through him, because the whole matter seemed too unimportant to warrant feelings of any sort. What difference did it make if his imagination had played tricks on him, and he'd fancied that the object was crawling and hitching itself slowly closer across the roofs? That was the way any normal imagination worked. He deliberately chose to disregard the fact that there were reasons for thinking his imagination was by no means a normal one. As he walked home from the elevated, however, he found himself wondering whether the sack was really gone. He seemed to recall a vague, smudgy trail leading across the gravel to the nearer side of the roof. For an instant an unpleasant picture formed in his mind —that of an inky, humped creature crouched behind the nearer parapet, waiting. Then he dismissed the whole subject.

The next time he felt the familiar grating lurch of the car, he caught himself trying not to look out. That angered him. He turned his head quickly. When he turned it back, his compact face was definitely pale. There had only been time for a fleeting rearward glance at the escaping roof. Had he actually seen in silhouette the upper part of a head of some sort peering over the parapet? Nonsense, he told himself. And even if he had seen something, there were a thousand explanations which did not involve the supernatural or even true hallucination. Tomorrow he would take a good look and clear up the whole matter. If necessary, he would visit the roof personally, though he hardly knew where to find it and disliked in any case the idea of pampering a whim of fear.

He did not relish the walk home from the elevated that evening, and visions of the thing disturbed his dreams and were in and out of his mind all next day at the office. It was then that he first began to relieve his nerves by making jokingly serious remarks about the supernatural to Miss Millick, who seemed properly mystified. It was on the same day, too, that he became aware of a growing antipathy to grime and soot. Everything he touched seemed gritty, and he found himself mopping and wiping at his desk like an old lady with a morbid fear of germs. He reasoned that there was no real change in his office, and that he'd just now become sensitive to the dirt that had always been there, but there was no denying an increasing nervousness. Long before the car reached the curve, he was straining his eyes through the murky twilight determined to take in every detail.

Afterward he realized that he must have given a muffled cry of some sort, for the man beside him looked at him curiously, and the woman ahead gave him an unfavorable stare. Conscious of his own pallor and uncontrollable trembling, he stared back at them hungrily, trying to regain the feeling of security he had completely lost. They were the usual reassuringly wooden-faced people everyone rides home with on the elevated. But suppose he had pointed out to one of them what he had seen—that sodden, distorted face of sacking and coal dust, that boneless paw which waved back and forth, unmistakably in his direction, as if reminding him of a future appointment— He involuntarily shut his eyes tight. His thoughts were racing ahead to tomorrow evening. He pictured this same windowed oblong of light and packed humanity surging around the curve—then an opaque monstrous form leaping out from the roof in a parabolic swoop—an unmentionable face pressed close against the window, smearing it with wet coal dust—huge paws fumbling sloppily at the glass—

Somehow he managed to turn off his wife's anxious inquiries. Next morning he reached a decision and made an appointment for that evening with a psychiatrist a friend had told him about. It cost him a considerable effort for Catesby had a peculiarly great and very well-grounded distaste for anything dealing with psychological abnormality. Visiting a psychiatrist meant raking up an episode in his past which he had never fully described even to his wife and which Miss Millick only knew of as "something impressively abnormal about Mr. Wran's childhood." Once he had made the decision, however, he felt considerably relieved. The doctor, he told himself, would clear everything up. He could almost fancy the doctor saying, "Merely a bad case of nerves. However, you must consult the oculist whose name I'm writing down for you, and you must take two of these pills in water every hour," and so on. It was almost comforting, and made the coming revelation he would have to make seem less painful.

But as the smoky dusk rolled in, his nervousness returned and he let his joking mystification of Miss Millick run away with him until he realized that he wasn't frightening anyone but himself.

He would have to keep his imagination under better control, he told himself, as he continued to peer out restlessly at the massive, murky shapes of the downtown office buildings. Why, he had spent the whole afternoon building up a kind of neomedieval cosmology of superstition. It wouldn't do. He realized then that he had been standing at the window much longer than he'd thought, for the glass panel in the door was dark and there was no noise coming from the outer office. Miss Millick and the rest must already have gone home.

It was then he made the discovery that there would have been no special reason for dreading the swing around the curve that night. It was, as it happened, a horrible discovery. For, on the shadowed roof across the street and four stories below, he saw the thing huddle and roll across the gravel and, after one upward look of recognition, merge into the blackness beneath the water tank.

As he hurriedly collected his things and made for the elevator, fighting the panicky impulse to run, he began to think of hallucination and mild psychosis as very desirable conditions. For better or for worse, he pinned all his hopes on the doctor.

"So you find yourself growing nervous and . . . er . . . jumpy, as you put it," said Dr. Trevethick, smiling with dignified geniality. "Do you notice any more definite physical symptoms? Pain? Headache? Indigestion?"

Catesby shook his head and wet his lips. "I'm especially nervous while riding in the elevated," he murmured swiftly.

"I see. We'll discuss that more fully. But I'd like you first to tell me about something you mentioned earlier. You said there was something about your childhood that might predispose you to nervous ailments. As you know, the early years are critical ones in the development of an individual's behavior pattern."

Catesby studied the yellow reflections of frosted globes in the dark surface of the desk. The palm of his left hand aimlessly rubbed the thick nap of the armchair. After a while he raised his head and looked straight into the doctor's small brown eyes.

"From perhaps my third to my ninth year," he began, choosing the words with care, "I was what you might call a sensory prodigy."

The doctor's expression did not change. "Yes?" he inquired politely.

"What I mean is that I was supposed to be able to see through walls, read letters through envelopes and books through their covers, fence and play Ping-pong blindfolded, find things that were buried, read thoughts." The words tumbled out.

"And could you?" The doctor's expression was toneless.

"I don't know. I don't suppose so," answered Catesby, long-lost emotions flooding back into his voice. "It's all so confused now. I thought I could, but then they were always encouraging me. My mother . . . was . . . well . . . interested in psychic phenomena. I was . . . exhibited. I seem to remember seeing things other people couldn't. As if most opaque objects were transparent. But I was very young. I didn't have any scientific criteria for judgment."

He was reliving it now. The darkened rooms. The earnest assemblages of gawking, prying adults. Himself sitting alone on a little platform, lost in a straight-backed wooden chair. The black silk handkerchief over his eyes. His mother's coaxing, insistent questions. The whispers. The gasps. His own hate of the whole business, mixed with hunger for the adulation of adults. Then the scientists from the university, the experiments, the big test. The reality of those memories engulfed him and momentarily made him forget the reason why he was disclosing them to a stranger.

"Do I understand that your mother tried to make use of you as a medium for communicating with the . . . er . . . other world?"

Catesby nodded eagerly.

"She tried to, but she couldn't. When it came to getting

in touch with the dead, I was a complete failure. All I could do—or thought I could do—was see real, existing, three-dimensional objects beyond the vision of normal people. Objects they could have seen except for distance, obstruction, or darkness. It was always a disappointment to mother," he finished slowly.

He could hear her sweetish patient voice saying, "Try again, dear, just this once. Katie was your aunt. She loved you. Try to hear what she's saying." And he had answered, "I can see a woman in a blue dress standing on the other side of Jones' house." And she had replied, "Yes, I know, dear. But that's not Katie. Katie's a spirit. Try again. Just this once, dear." For a second time the doctor's voice gently jarred him hack into the softly gleaming office.

"You mentioned scientific criteria for judgment, Mr. Wran. As far as you know, did anyone ever try to apply them to you?"

Catesby's nod was emphatic.

"They did. When I was eight, two young psychologists from the university here got interested in me. I guess they considered it a joke at first, and I remember being very determined to show them I amounted to something. Even now I seem to recall how the note of polite superiority and amused sarcasm drained out of their voices. I suppose they decided at first that it was very clever trickery, but somehow they persuaded mother to let them try me out under controlled conditions. There were lots of tests that seemed very businesslike after mother's slipshod little exhibitions. They found I was still clairvoyant—or so they thought. I got worked up and on edge. They were going to demonstrate my supernormal sensory powers to the university psychology faculty. For the first time I began to worry about whether I'd come through. Perhaps they kept me going at too hard a pace, I don't know. At any rate, when the test came, I couldn't do a thing. Everything became opaque. I got desperate and made things up out of my imagination. I lied. In the end I failed utterly, and I believe the two young psychologists lost their jobs as a result."

He could hear the brusque, bearded man saying, "You've been taken in by a child, Flaxman, a mere child. I'm greatly disturbed. You've put yourself on the same plane as common charlatans. Gentlemen, I ask you to banish from your minds this whole sorry episode. It must never be referred to." He winced at the recollection of his feeling of guilt. But at the same time he was beginning to feel exhilarated and almost light-hearted. Unburdening his long-repressed memories had altered his whole viewpoint. The episodes on the elevated began to take on what seemed their proper proportions as merely the bizarre workings of overwrought nerves, and an overly suggestible mind. The doctor, he anticipated confidently, would disentangle the obscure subconscious causes, whatever they might be. And the whole business would be finished off quickly, just as his childhood experience—which was beginning to seem a little ridiculous now—had been finished off.

"From that day on," he continued, "I never exhibited a trace of my supposed powers. My mother was frantic, and tried to sue the university. I had something like a nervous breakdown. Then the divorce was granted, and my father got custody of me. He did his best to make me forget it. We went on long outdoor vacations, and did a lot of athletics, associated with normal, matter-of-fact people. I went to business college eventually. I'm in advertising now. But," Catesby paused, "now that I'm having nervous symptoms, I'm wondering if there mightn't be a connection. It's not a question of whether I really was clairvoyant or not. Very likely my mother taught me a lot of unconscious deceptions, good enough even to fool young psychology instructors. But don't you think it may have some important bearing on my present condition?"

For several moments the doctor regarded him with a slightly embarrassing professional frown. Then he said quietly, "And is there some . . . er . . . more specific connection between your experiences then and now? Do you by any chance find that you are once again beginning to . . . er . . . see things?"

Catesby swallowed. He had felt an increasing eagerness to unburden himself of his fears, but it was not easy to make a beginning, and the doctor's shrewd question rattled him. He forced himself to concentrate. The thing he thought he had seen on the roof loomed up before his inner eye with unexpected vividness. Yet it did not frighten him. He groped for words.

Then he saw that the doctor was not looking at him but over his shoulder. Color was draining out of the doctor's face and his eyes did not seem so small. Then the doctor sprang to his feet, walked past Catesby, threw open the window and peered into the darkness.

As Catesby rose, the doctor slammed down the window and said in a voice whose smoothness was marred by a slight, persistent gasping, "I hope I haven't alarmed you. I saw the face of . . . er . . . a Negro prowler on the fire escape. I must have frightened him, for he seems to have gotten out of sight in a hurry. Don't give it another thought. Doctors are frequently bothered by *voyeurs* . . . er . . . Peeping Toms."

"A Negro?" asked Catesby, moistening his lips.

The doctor laughed nervously. "I imagine so, though my first odd impression was that it was a white man in blackface. You see, the color didn't seem to have any brown in it. It was dead-black."

Catesby moved toward the window. There were smudges on the glass. "It's quite all right, Mr. Wran." The doctor's voice had acquired a sharp note of impatience, as if he were trying hard to get control of himself and reassume his professional authority. "Let's continue our conversation. I was asking you if you were"—he made a face—"seeing things."

Catesby's whirling thoughts slowed down and locked into place. "No, I'm not seeing anything . . . other people don't see, too. And I think I'd better go now. I've been keeping you too long." He disregarded the doctor's half-hearted gesture of denial. "I'll phone you about the physical examination. In a way you've already taken a big load off my mind." He smiled woodenly. "Good night, Dr. Trevethick."

Catesby Wran's mental state was a peculiar one. His eyes searched every angular shadow and he glanced sideways down each chasmlike alley and barren basement passageway and kept stealing looks at the irregular line of the roofs, yet he was hardly conscious of where he was going in a general way. He pushed away the thoughts that came into his mind, and kept moving. He became aware of a slight sense of security as he turned into a lighted street where there were people and high buildings and blinking signs. After a while he found himself in the dim lobby of the structure that housed his office. Then he realized why he couldn't go home—because he might cause his wife and baby to see it, just as the doctor had seen it. And the baby, only two years old.

"Hello, Mr. Wran," said the night elevator man, a burly figure in blue overalls, sliding open the grille-work door to the old-fashioned cage. "I didn't know you were working nights now."

Catesby stepped in automatically. "Sudden rush of orders," he murmured inanely. "Some stuff that has to be gotten out."

The cage creaked to a stop at the top floor. "Be working very late, Mr. Wran?"

He nodded vaguely, watched the car slide out of sight, found his keys, swiftly crossed the outer office, and entered his own. His hand went out to the light switch, but then the thought occurred to him that the two lighted windows, standing out against the dark bulk of the building, would indicate his whereabouts and serve as a goal toward which something could crawl and climb. He moved his chair so that the back was against the wall and sat down in the semidarkness. He did not remove his overcoat.

For a long time he sat there motionless, listening to his own breathing and the faraway sounds from the streets below; the thin metallic surge of the crosstown streetcar, the farther one of the elevated, faint lonely cries and honkings, indistinct rumblings. Words he had spoken to Miss Millick in nervous jest came back to him with the bitter taste of truth. He found himself unable to reason critically or connectedly, but by their own volition thoughts rose up into his mind and gyrated slowly and rearranged themselves, with the inevitable movement of planets.

Gradually his mental picture of the world was transformed. No longer a world of material atoms and empty space, but a world in which the bodiless existed and moved according to its own obscure laws or unpredictable impulses. The new picture illumined with dreadful clarity certain general facts which had always bewildered and troubled him and from which he had tried to hide; the inevitability of hate and war, the diabolically timed mischances which wrecked the best of human intentions, the walls of willful misunderstanding that divided one man from another, the eternal vitality of cruelty and ignorance and greed. They seemed appropriate now, necessary parts of the picture. And superstition only a kind of wisdom.

Then his thoughts returned to himself, and the question he had asked Miss Millick came back, "What would such a thing want from a person? Sacrifices? Worship? Or just fear? What could you do to stop it from troubling you?" It had now become a purely practical question.

With an explosive jangle, the phone began to ring. "Cate, I've been trying everywhere to get you," said his wife. "I never thought you'd be at the office. What are you doing? I've been worried."

He said something about work.

"You'll be home right away?" came the faint anxious question. "I'm a little frightened. Ronny just had a scare. It woke him up. He kept pointing to the window saying, 'Black man, black man.' Of course it's something he dreamed. But I'm frightened. You will be home? What's that, dear? Can't you hear me?"

"I will. Right away," he said. Then he was out of the office, buzzing the night bell and peering down the shaft.

He saw it peering up the shaft at him from three floors below, the sacking face pressed close against the iron grille-work. It started up the stair at a shockingly swift, shambling gait, vanishing temporarily from sight as it swung into the second corridor below.

Catesby clawed at the door to the office, realized he had not locked it, pushed it in, slammed and locked it behind him, retreated to the other side of the room, cowered between the filing cases and the wall. His teeth were clicking. He heard the groan of the rising cage. A silhouette darkened the frosted glass of the door, blotting out part of the grotesque reverse of the company name. After a little the door opened.

The big-globed overhead light flared on and, standing just inside the door, her hand on the switch, he saw Miss Millick.

"Why, Mr. Wran," she stammered vacuously, "I didn't know you were here. I'd just come in to do some extra typing after the movie. I didn't . . . but the lights weren't on. What were you—"

He stared at her. He wanted to shout in relief, grab hold of her, talk rapidly. He realized he was grinning hysterically.

"Why, Mr. Wran, what's happened to you?" she asked embarrassedly, ending with a stupid titter. "Are you feeling sick? Isn't there something I can do for you?"

He shook his head jerkily, and managed to say, "No, I'm just leaving. I was doing some extra work myself."

"But you *look* sick," she insisted, and walked over toward him. He inconsequentially realized she must have stepped in mud, for her high-heeled shoes left neat black prints.

"Yes, I'm sure you must be sick. You're so terribly pale." She sounded like an enthusiastic, incompetent nurse. Her face brightened with a sudden inspiration. "I've got something in my bag that'll fix you up right away," she said. "It's for indigestion."

She fumbled at her stuffed oblong purse. He noticed that she was absent-mindedly holding it shut with one hand while she tried to open it with the other. Then, under his very eyes, he saw her bend back the thick prongs of metal locking the purse as if they were tinfoil, or as if her fingers had become a pair of steel pliers.

Instantly his memory recited the words he had spoken to Miss Millick that afternoon. "It couldn't hurt you physically— at first . . . gradually get its hooks into the world . . . might even get control of suitably vacuous minds. Then it could hurt whomever it wanted." A sickish, cold feeling came to a focus inside him. He began to edge toward the door.

But Miss Millick hurried ahead of him.

"You don't have to wait, Fred," she called. "Mr. Wran's decided to stay a while longer."

The door to the cage shut with a mechanical rattle. The cage creaked. Then she turned around in the door.

"Why, Mr. Wran," she gurgled reproachfully, "I just couldn't think of letting you go home now. I'm sure you're terribly unwell. Why, you might collapse in the street. You've just got to stay here until you feel different."

The creaking died away. He stood in the center of the office motionless. His eyes traced the course of Miss Millick's footprints to where she stood blocking the door. Then a sound that was almost a scream was wrenched out of him, for he saw that the flesh of her face was beginning to change color; blackening until the powder on it was a sickly white dust, rouge a hideous pinkish one, lipstick a translucent red film. It was the same with her hands and with the skin beneath her thin silk stockings.

"Why, Mr. Wran," she said, "you're acting as if you were crazy. You must lie down for a little while. Here, I'll help you off with your coat."

The nauseously idiotic and rasping note was the same; only it had been intensified. As she came toward him he turned and ran through the storeroom, clattered a key desperately at the lock of the second door to the corridor.

"Why, Mr. Wran," he heard her call, "are you having some kind of fit? You must let me help you."

The door came open and he plunged out into the corridor and up the stairs immediately ahead. It was only when he reached the top that he realized the heavy steel door in front of him led to the roof. He jerked up the catch.

"Why, Mr. Wran, you mustn't run away. I'm coming after you."

Then he was out on the gritty tar paper of the roof, the night sky was clouded and murky, with a faint pinkish glow from the neon signs. From the distant mills rose a ghostly spurt of flame. He ran to the edge. The street lights glared dizzily upward. Two men walking along were round blobs of hat and shoulders. He swung around.

The thing was in the doorway. The voice was no longer solicitous but moronically playful, each sentence ending in a titter.

"Why, Mr. Wran, why have you come up here? We're all alone. Just think, I might push you off."

The thing came slowly toward him. He moved backward until his heels touched the low parapet. Without knowing why or what he was going to do, he dropped to his knees. The black, coarse-grained face came nearer, a focus for the worst in the world, a gathering point for poisons from everywhere. Then the lucidity of terror took possession of his mind, and words formed on his lips

"I will obey you. You are my god," he said. "You have supreme power over man and his animals and his machines.

You rule this city and all others. I recognize that. Therefore spare me."

Again the titter, closer. "Why, Mr. Wran, you never talked like this before. Do you mean it?"

"The world is yours to do with as you will, save or tear to pieces." He answered fawningly, as the words automatically fitted themselves together into vaguely liturgical patterns. "I recognize that. I will praise, I will sacrifice. In smoke and soot and flame I will worship you forever."

The voice did not answer. He looked up. There was only Miss Millick, deathly pale and swaying drunkenly. Her eyes were closed. He caught her as she wobbled toward him. His knees gave way under the added weight and they sank down together on the roof edge.

After a while she began to twitch. Small wordless noises came from her throat, and her eyelids edged open.

"Come on, we'll go downstairs," he murmured jerkily, trying to draw her up. "You're feeling bad."

"I'm terribly dizzy," she whispered. "I must have fainted. I didn't eat enough. And then I'm so nervous lately, about the war and everything, I guess. Why, we're on the roof! Did you bring me up here to get some air? Or did I come up without knowing it? I'm awfully foolish. I used to walk in my sleep, my mother said."

As he helped her down the stairs, she turned and looked at him. "Why, Mr. Wran," she said, faintly, "you've got a big smudge on your forehead. Here, let me get it off for you." Weakly she rubbed at it with her handkerchief. She started to sway again and he steadied her.

"No, I'll be all right," she said. "Only I feel cold. What happened, Mr. Wran? Did I have some sort of fainting spell?"

He told her it was something like that.

Later, riding home in an empty elevated car, he wondered how long he would be safe from the thing. It was a purely practical problem. He had no way of knowing, but instinct told him he had satisfied the brute for some time. Would it want more when it came again? Time enough to answer that question when it arose. It might be hard, he realized, to keep out of an insane asylum. With Helen and Ronny to protect, as well as himself, he would have to be careful and tight-lipped. He began to speculate as to how many other men and women had seen the thing or things like it, and knew that mankind had once again spawned a ghost world, and that superstition once more ruled.

The elevated slowed and lurched in a familiar fashion. He looked at the roofs again, near the curve. They seemed very ordinary, as if what made them impressive had gone away for a while.

1941

TENNESSEE WILLIAMS

(1911–1983)

The Mysteries of the Joy Rio

PERHAPS because he was a watch repairman, Mr. Gonzales had grown to be rather indifferent to time. A single watch or clock can be a powerful influence on a man, but when a man lives among as many watches and clocks as crowded the tiny, dim shop of Mr. Gonzales, some lagging behind, some skipping ahead, but all ticking monotonously on in their witless fashion, the multitude of them may be likely to deprive them of importance, as a gem loses its value when there are too many just like it which are too easily or cheaply obtainable. At any rate, Mr. Gonzales kept very irregular hours, if he could be said to keep any hours at all, and if he had not been where he was for such a long time, his trade would have suffered badly. But Mr. Gonzales had occupied his tiny shop for more than twenty years, since he had come to the city as a boy of nineteen to work as an apprentice to the original owner of the shop, a very strange and fat man of German descent named Kroger, Emiel Kroger, who had now been dead a long time. Emiel Kroger, being a romantically practical Teuton, had taken time, the commodity he worked with, with intense seriousness. In practically all his behavior he had imitated a perfectly adjusted fat silver watch. Mr. Gonzales, who was then young enough to be known as Pablo, had been his only sustained flirtation with the confusing, quicksilver world that exists outside of regularities. He had met Pablo during a watchmakers' convention in Dallas, Texas, where Pablo, who had illegally come into the country from Mexico a few days before, was drifting hungrily about the streets, and at that time Mr. Gonzales, Pablo, had not grown plump but had a lustrous dark grace which had completely bewitched Mr. Kroger. For as I have noted already, Mr. Kroger was a fat and strange man, subject to the kind of bewitchment that the graceful young Pablo could cast. The spell was so strong that it interrupted the fleeting and furtive practices of a

29

lifetime in Mr. Kroger and induced him to take the boy home
with him, to his shop-residence, where Pablo, now grown to
the mature and fleshy proportions of Mr. Gonzales, had lived
ever since, for three years before the death of his protector and
for more than seventeen years after that, as the inheritor of
shop-residence, clocks, watches, and everything else that Mr.
Kroger had owned except a few pieces of dining-room silver
which Emiel Kroger had left as a token bequest to a married
sister in Toledo.

Some of these facts are of dubious pertinence to the little
history which is to be unfolded. The important one is the fact
that Mr. Gonzales had managed to drift enviably apart from
the regularities that rule most other lives. Some days he would
not open his shop at all and some days he would open it only
for an hour or two in the morning, or in the late evening when
other shops had closed, and in spite of these caprices he managed to continue to get along fairly well, due to the excellence
of his work, when he did it, the fact that he was so well established in his own quiet way, the advantage of his location in a
neighborhood where nearly everybody had an old alarm-clock
which had to be kept in condition to order their lives, (this
community being one inhabited mostly by people with small-
paying jobs), but it was also due in measurable part to the fact
that the thrifty Mr. Kroger, when he finally succumbed to a
chronic disease of the bowels, had left a tidy sum in government bonds, and this capital, bringing in about a hundred and
seventy dollars a month, would have kept Mr. Gonzales going
along in a commonplace but comfortable fashion even if he
had declined to do anything whatsoever. It was a pity that the
late, or rather long-ago, Mr. Kroger, had not understood what
a fundamentally peaceable sort of young man he had taken
under his wing. Too bad he couldn't have guessed how perfectly everything suited Pablo Gonzales. But youth does not
betray its true nature as palpably as the later years do, and Mr.
Kroger had taken the animated allure of his young protégé, the
flickering lights in his eyes and his quick, nervous movements,
his very grace and slimness, as meaning something difficult to
keep hold of. And as the old gentleman declined in health, as
he did quite steadily during the three years that Pablo lived
with him, he was never certain that the incalculably precious

bird flown into his nest was not one of sudden passage but rather the kind that prefers to keep a faithful commitment to a single place, the nest-building kind, and not only that, but the very-rare-indeed-kind that gives love back as generously as he takes it. The long-ago Mr. Kroger had paid little attention to his illness, even when it entered the stage of acute pain, so intense was his absorption in what he thought was the tricky business of holding Pablo close to him. If only he had known that for all this time after his decease the boy would still be in the watchshop, how it might have relieved him! But on the other hand, maybe this anxiety, mixed as it was with so much tenderness and sad delight, was actually a blessing, standing as it did between the dying old man and a concern with death.

Pablo had never flown. But the sweet bird of youth had flown from Pablo Gonzales, leaving him rather sad, with a soft yellow face that was just as round as the moon. Clocks and watches he fixed with marvelous delicacy and precision, but he paid no attention to them; he had grown as obliviously accustomed to their many small noises as someone grows to the sound of waves who has always lived by the sea. Although he wasn't aware of it, it was actually light by which he told time, and always in the afternoons when the light had begun to fail (through the narrow window and narrower, dusty skylight at the back of the shop), Mr. Gonzales automatically rose from his stooped position over littered table and gooseneck lamp, took off his close-seeing glasses with magnifying lenses, and took to the street. He did not go far and he always went in the same direction, across town toward the river where there was an old opera house, now converted into a third-rate cinema, which specialized in the showing of cowboy pictures and other films of the sort that have a special appeal to children and male adolescents. The name of this movie-house was the Joy Rio, a name peculiar enough but nowhere nearly so peculiar as the place itself.

The old opera house was a miniature of all the great opera houses of the old world, which is to say its interior was faded gilt and incredibly old and abused red damask which extended upwards through at least three tiers and possibly five. The upper stairs, that is, the stairs beyond the first gallery, were roped off and unlighted and the top of the theater was so peculiarly dusky, even with the silver screen flickering far below it, that Mr. Gonzales, used as he was to close work, could not have made it out from below. Once he had been there when the lights came on in the Joy Rio, but the coming on of the lights had so enormously confused and embarrassed him, that looking up was the last thing in the world he felt like doing. He had buried his nose in the collar of his coat and had scuttled out as quickly as a cockroach makes for the nearest shadow when a kitchen light comes on.

I have already suggested that there was something a bit special and obscure about Mr. Gonzales' habitual attendance at the Joy Rio, and that was my intention. For Mr. Gonzales had inherited more than the material possessions of his dead benefactor: he had also come into custody of his old protector's fleeting and furtive practices in dark places, the practices which Emiel Kroger had given up only when Pablo had come into his fading existence. The old man had left Mr. Gonzales the full gift of his shame, and now Mr. Gonzales did the sad, lonely things that Mr. Kroger had done for such a long time before his one lasting love came to him. Mr. Kroger had even practiced those things in the same place in which they were practiced now by Mr. Gonzales, in the many mysterious recesses of the Joy Rio, and Mr. Gonzales knew about this. He knew about it because Mr. Kroger had told him. Emiel Kroger had confessed his whole life and soul to Pablo Gonzales. It was his theory, the theory of most immoralists, that the soul becomes intolerably burdened with lies that have to be told to the world in order to be permitted to live in the world, and that unless this burden is relieved by entire honesty with *some one* person, who is trusted and adored, the soul will finally collapse beneath its weight of falsity. Much of the final months of the life of Emiel Kroger, increasingly dimmed by morphia, were devoted to these whispered confessions to his adored apprentice, and it was as if he had breathed the guilty soul of his past into the ears and brain and blood of the youth who listened, and not long after the death of Mr. Kroger, Pablo, who had stayed slim until then, had begun to accumulate fat. He never became anywhere nearly so gross as Emiel Kroger had been, but his delicate frame disappeared sadly from view among the irrelevant curves of a sallow plumpness. One by one the perfections

which he had owned were folded away as Pablo put on fat as a
widow puts on black garments. For a year beauty lingered
about him, ghostly, continually fading, and then it went out altogether, and at twenty-five he was already the nondescriptly
plump and moonfaced little man that he now was at forty, and
if in his waking hours somebody to whom he would have to
give a true answer had enquired of him, Pablo Gonzales, how
much do you think about the dead Mr. Kroger, he probably
would have shrugged and said, *Not much now. It's such a long
time ago.* But if the question were asked him while he slept, the
guileless heart of the sleeper would have responded, *Always,
always!*

II

Now across the great marble stairs, that rose above the first
gallery of the Joy Rio to the uncertain number of galleries
above it, there had been fastened a greasy and rotting length
of old velvet rope at the center of which was hung a sign that
said to *Keep Out.* But that rope had not always been there. It
had been there about twenty years, but the late Mr. Kroger had
known the Joy Rio in the days before the flight of stairs was
roped off. In those days the mysterious upper galleries of the
Joy Rio had been a sort of fiddler's green where practically
every device and fashion of carnality had run riot in a gloom so
thick that a chance partner could only be discovered by touch.
There were not rows of benches (as there were now on the
orchestra level and the one gallery still kept in use), but strings
of tiny boxes, extending in semicircles from one side of the
great proscenium to the other. In some of these boxes broken-
legged chairs might be found lying on their sides and shreds of
old hangings still clung to the sliding brass loops at the en-
trances. According to Emiel Kroger, who is our only authority
on these mysteries which share his remoteness in time, one
lived up there, in the upper reaches of the Joy Rio, an almost
sightless existence where the other senses, the senses of smell
and touch and hearing, had to develop a preternatural keenness in order to spare one from making awkward mistakes, such
as taking hold of the knee of a boy when it was a girl's knee
one looked for, and where sometimes little scenes of panic

occurred when a mistake of gender or of compatibility had been carried to a point where radical correction was called for. There had been many fights, there had even been rape and murder in those ancient boxes, till finally the obscure management of the Joy Rio had been compelled by the pressure of notoriety to shut down that part of the immense old building which had offered its principal enticement, and the Joy Rio, which had flourished until then, had then gone into sharp decline. It had been closed down and then reopened and closed down and reopened again. For several years it had opened and shut like a nervous lady's fan. Those were the years in which Mr. Kroger was dying. After his death the fitful era subsided, and now for about ten years the Joy Rio had been continually active as a third-rate cinema, closed only for one week during a threatened epidemic of poliomyelitis some years past and once for a few days when a small fire had damaged the projection booth. But nothing happened there now of a nature to provoke a disturbance. There were no complaints to the management or the police, and the dark glory of the upper galleries was a legend in such memories as that of the late Emiel Kroger and the present Pablo Gonzales, and one by one, of course, those memories died out and the legend died out with them. Places like the Joy Rio and the legends about them make one more than usually aware of the short bloom and the long fading out of things. The angel of such a place is a fat silver angel of sixty-three years in a shiny dark-blue alpaca jacket, with short, fat fingers that leave a damp mark where they touch, that sweat and tremble as they caress between whispers, an angel of such a kind as would be kicked out of heaven and laughed out of hell and admitted to earth only by grace of its habitual slyness, its gift for making itself a counterfeit being, and the connivance of those that a quarter tip and an old yellow smile can corrupt.

But the reformation of the Joy Rio was somewhat less than absolute. It had reformed only to the point of ostensible virtue, and in the back rows of the first gallery at certain hours in the afternoon and very late at night were things going on of the sort Mr. Gonzales sometimes looked for. At those hours the Joy Rio contained few patrons, and since the seats in the orchestra were in far better condition, those who had come to sit comfortably watching the picture would naturally remain downstairs; the few that elected to sit in the nearly deserted rows of the first gallery did so either because smoking was permitted in that section—or *because* . . .

There was a danger, of course, there always is a danger with places and things like that, but Mr. Gonzales was a tentative person not given to leaping before he looked. If a patron had entered the first gallery only in order to smoke, you could usually count on his occupying a seat along the aisle. If the patron had bothered to edge his way toward the center of a row of seats irregular as the jawbone of poor Yorick, one could assume as infallibly as one can assume anything in a universe where chance is the one invariable, that he had chosen his seat with something more than a cigarette in mind. Mr. Gonzales did not take many chances. This was a respect in which he paid due homage to the wise old spirit of the late Emiel Kroger, that romantically practical Teuton who used to murmur to Pablo, between sleeping and waking, a sort of incantation that went like this: Sometimes you will find it and other times you won't find it and the times you don't find it are the times when you have got to be careful. Those are the times when you have got to remember that other times you *will* find it, not *this* time but the *next* time, or the time *after* that, and then you've got to be able to go home without it, yes, those times are the times when you have got to be able to go home without it, go home *alone* without it . . .

Pablo didn't know, then, that he would ever have need of this practical wisdom that his benefactor had drawn from his almost lifelong pursuit of a pleasure which was almost as unreal and basically unsatisfactory as an embrace in a dream. Pablo didn't know then that he would inherit so much from the old man who took care of him, and at that time, when Emiel Kroger, in the dimness of morphia and weakness following hemorrhage, had poured into the delicate ear of his apprentice, drop by slow, liquid drop, this distillation of all he had learned in the years before he found Pablo, the boy had felt for this whisper the same horror and pity that he felt for the mortal disease in the flesh of his benefactor, and only gradually, in the long years since the man and his whisper had ceased, had the singsong rigmarole begun to have sense for him, a practical wisdom that such a man as Pablo had turned into, a man such as Mr. Gonzales, could live by safely and quietly and still find pleasure . . .

III

Mr. Gonzales was careful, and for careful people life has a tendency to take on the character of an almost arid plain with only here and there, at wide intervals, the solitary palm tree and its shadow and the spring alongside it. Mr. Kroger's life had been much the same until he had come across Pablo at the watchmakers' convention in Dallas. But so far in Mr. Gonzales' life there had been no Pablo. In his life there had been only Mr. Kroger and the sort of things that Mr. Kroger had looked for and sometimes found but most times continued patiently to look for in the great expanse of arid country which his lifetime had been before the discovery of Pablo. And since it is not my intention to spin this story out any longer than its content seems to call for, I am not going to attempt to sustain your interest in it with a descripion of the few palm trees on the uneventful desert through which the successor to Emiel Kroger wandered after the death of the man who had been his life. But I am going to remove you rather precipitately to a summer afternoon which we will call *Now* when Mr. Gonzales learned that he was dying, and not only dying but dying of the same trouble that had put the period under the question mark of Emiel Kroger. The scene, if I can call it that, takes place in a doctor's office. After some hedging on the part of the doctor, the word malignant is uttered. The hand is placed on the shoulder, almost contemptuously comforting, and Mr. Gonzales is assured that surgery is unnecessary because the condition is not susceptible to any help but that of drugs to relax the afflicted organs. And after that the scene is abruptly blacked out . . .

Now it is a year later. Mr. Gonzales has recovered more or less from the shocking information that he received from his doctor. He has been repairing watches and clocks almost as well as ever, and there has been remarkably little alteration in his way of life. Only a little more frequently is the shop closed. It is apparent, now, that the disease from which he suffers does not intend to destroy him any more suddenly than it destroyed the man before him. It grows slowly, the growth, and in fact it has recently shown signs of what is called a remission. There is no pain, hardly any and hardly ever. The most palpable symptom is loss of appetite and, as a result of that, a steady decrease of weight. Now rather startlingly, after all this time, the graceful approximation of Pablo's delicate structure has come back out of the irrelevant contours which had engulfed it after the long-ago death of Emiel Kroger. The mirrors are not very good in the dim little residence-shop, where he lives in his long wait for death, and when he looks in them, Mr. Gonzales sees the boy that was loved by the man whom he loved. It is almost Pablo. Pablo has almost returned from Mr. Gonzales.

And then one afternoon . . .

IV

The new usher at the Joy Rio was a boy of seventeen and the little Jewish manager had told him that he must pay particular attention to the roped-off staircase to see to it that nobody slipped upstairs to the forbidden region of the upper galleries, but this boy was in love with a girl named Gladys who came to the Joy Rio every afternoon, now that school was let out for the summer, and loitered around the entrance where George, the usher, was stationed. She wore a thin, almost transparent, white blouse with nothing much underneath it. Her skirt was usually of sheer silken material that followed her heart-shaped loins as raptly as George's hand followed them when he embraced her in the dark ladies' room on the balcony level of the Joy Rio. Sensual delirium possessed him those afternoons when Gladys loitered near him. But the recently changed management of the Joy Rio was not a strict one, and in the summer vigilance was more than commonly relaxed. George stayed near the downstairs entrance, twitching restively in his tight, faded uniform till Gladys drifted in from the afternoon streets on a slow tide of lilac perfume. She would seem not to see him as she sauntered up the aisle he indicated with his flashlight and took a seat in the back of the orchestra section where he could find her easily when the "coast was clear," or if he kept her waiting too long and she was more than usually bored with the film, she would stroll back out to the lobby and inquire in her childish drawl, Where is the Ladies' Room, Please? Sometimes he would curse her fiercely under his breath because she hadn't waited. But he would have to direct her to the staircase, and she would go up there and wait for him, and the knowledge that she was up there waiting would finally overpower his prudence to the point where he would even abandon his station if the little manager, Mr. Katz, had his office door wide open. The ladies' room was otherwise not in use. Its light-switch was broken, or if it was repaired, the bulbs would be mysteriously missing. When ladies other than Gladys enquired about it, George would say gruffly, The ladies' room's out of order. It made an almost perfect retreat for the young lovers. The door left ajar gave warning of footsteps on the grand marble staircase in time for George to come out with his hands in his pockets before whoever was coming could catch him at it. But these interruptions would sometimes infuriate him, especially when a patron would insist on borrowing his flashlight to use the cabinet in the room where Gladys waited with her crumpled silk skirt gathered high about her flanks (leaning against the invisible dried-up washbasin) which were the blazing black heart of the insatiably concave summer.

In the old days Mr. Gonzales used to go to the Joy Rio in the late afternoons but since his illness he had been going earlier because the days tired him earlier, especially the steaming days of August which were now in progress. Mr. Gonzales knew about George and Gladys; he made it his business, of course, to know everything there was to be known about the Joy Rio, which was his earthly heaven, and, of course, George also knew about Mr. Gonzales; he knew why Mr. Gonzales gave him a fifty cent tip every time he inquired his way to the men's room upstairs, each time as if he had never gone upstairs before. Sometimes George muttered something under his breath, but the tributes collected from patrons like Mr. Gonzales had so far ensured his complicity in their venal practices. But then one day in August, on one of the very hottest and blindingly bright afternoons, George was so absorbed in the delights of Gladys that Mr. Gonzales had arrived at the top of the stairs to the balcony before George heard his footsteps. Then he heard them and he clamped a sweating palm over the mouth of Gladys which was full of stammerings of his name and the name of God. He waited, but Mr. Gonzales also waited. Mr. Gonzales was actually waiting at the top of the stairs to recover his breath from the climb, but George, who could see him, now, through the door kept slightly ajar, suspected that he was waiting to catch him coming out of his secret place. A fury burst in the boy. He thrust Gladys violently back against the wash-basin and charged out of the room without even bothering to button his fly. He rushed up to the slight figure waiting near the stairs and began to shout a dreadful word at Mr. Gonzales, the word "morphodite." His voice was shrill as a jungle bird's, shouting this word "morphodite." Mr. Gonzales kept backing away from him, with the lightness and grace of his youth, he kept stepping backwards from the livid face and threatening fists of the usher, all the time murmuring, No, no, no, no, no. The youth stood between him and the stairs below so it was toward the upper staircase that Mr. Gonzales took flight. All at once, as quickly and lightly as ever Pablo had moved, he darted under the length of velvet rope with the sign "Keep Out." George's pursuit was interrupted by the manager of the theater, who seized his arm so fiercely that the shoulder-seam of the uniform burst apart. This started another disturbance under the cover of which Mr. Gonzales fled farther and farther up the forbidden staircase into regions of deepening shadow. There were several points at which he might safely have stopped but his flight had now gathered an irresistible momentum and his legs moved like pistons bearing him up and up, and then——

At the very top of the staircase he was intercepted. He half turned back when he saw the dim figure waiting above, he almost turned and scrambled back down the grand marble staircase, when the name of his youth was called to him in a tone so commanding that he stopped and waited without daring to look up again.

Pablo, said Mr. Kroger, come on up here, Pablo.

Mr. Gonzales obeyed, but now the false power that his terror had given him was drained out of his body and he climbed with effort. At the top of the stairs where Emiel Kroger waited, he would have sunk exhausted to his knees if the old man hadn't sustained him with a firm hand at his elbow.

Mr. Kroger said, This way, Pablo. He led him into the Stygian blackness of one of the little boxes in the once-golden horse-shoe of the topmost tier. Now sit down, he commanded.

Pablo was too breathless to say anything except, Yes, and Mr. Kroger leaned over him and unbuttoned his collar for him, unfastened the clasp of his belt, all the while murmuring, There now, there now, Pablo.

The panic disappeared under those soothing old fingers and the breathing slowed down and stopped hurting the chest as if a fox was caught in it, and then at last Mr. Kroger began to lecture the boy as he used to, Pablo, he murmured, don't ever be so afraid of being lonely that you forget to be careful. Don't forget that you will find it sometimes but other times you won't be lucky, and those are the times when you have got to be patient, since patience is what you must have when you don't have luck.

The lecture continued softly, reassuringly familiar and repetitive as the tick of a bedroom clock in his ear, and if his ancient protector and instructor, Emiel Kroger, had not kept all the while soothing him with the moist, hot touch of his tremulous fingers, the gradual, the very gradual dimming out of things, his fading out of existence, would have terrified Pablo. But the ancient voice and fingers, as if they had never left him, kept on unbuttoning, touching, soothing, repeating the ancient lesson, saying it over and over like a penitent counting prayer beads, Sometimes you will have it and sometimes you won't have it, so don't be anxious about it. You must always be able to go home alone without it. Those are the times when you have got to remember that other times you will have it and it doesn't matter if sometimes you don't have it and have to go home without it, go home alone without it, go home alone without it. The gentle advice went on, and as it went on, Mr. Gonzales drifted away from everything but the wise old voice in his ear, even at last from that, but not till he was entirely comforted by it.

1941

JANE RICE

(1913–2003)

The Refugee

THE trouble with the war, Milli Cushman thought as she stared sulkily through streaming French windows into her rain-drenched garden, was that it was so frightfully boring. There weren't any men, any more. Interesting ones, that is. Or parties. Or little pink cocktails. Or café royale. Or long-stemmed roses wrapped in crackly green wax paper. There wasn't even a decent hairdresser left.

She had been a fool to stay on. But it had seemed so exciting. Everyone listening to the radio broadcasts; the streets blossoming with uniforms; an air of feverish gaiety, heady as Moselle wine, over all the city; the conversations that made one feel so important—so in the thick of things. Would the Maginot Line hold? Would the British come? Would the Low Countries be invaded? Was it true America had issued an ultimatum? Subjects that, now, were outdated as Gatling guns.

It had been terrifically stimulating being asked for her opinion, as an American. Of course, she hadn't been home for a number of years and considered herself a true cosmopolite freed from the provincialities of her own country—but, still, it had been nice, in those first flurried jack-in-the-box days of the war to be able to discourse so intelligently on Americana. It had been such *fun*.

Momentarily, Milli's eyes sparkled—remembering. The sparkle faded and died.

Then, unexpectedly, the city had become a gaunt, gray ghost. No, not a ghost, a cat. A gaunt gray cat with its bones showing through, as it crouched on silent haunches and stared unwinkingly before it. Like one of those cats that hung around the alley barrels of the better hotels. Or used to hang. Cooked, a cat bore a striking resemblance to a rabbit.

Overnight, a hush had fallen on everything. It was as though the city had gasped in one long, last, labored, dying breath.

And had held it. One could feel it in the atmosphere. Almost like a desperate pounding.

For some inexplicable reason, it reminded her of her childhood when she had played a game as the street lights began to bloom in the gathering dusk. "If I can hold my eyes open without blinking," she would tell herself, "until the last one is lighted, I'll get a new doll"—or a new muff—or a new hair ribbon—or whatever it might be she wanted. She could still recall that exhausted sense of time running out as the final lights went on. Most always she had won. Sometimes she hadn't, but most always she had. By the skin of her teeth.

It would be perfectly horrid, if this was one of the times when she *didn't* win. If she had to stay on and on, trotting back and forth seeing about that idiotic visa, and saving her hairpins and soap ends and things, it was going to be too utterly stultifying. It was fortunate she had had the perception to realize, before it was too late, who were the "right people" to know. It helped. Although, in these days, the right people didn't fare much better than the "wrong" ones.

Milli used "fare" in its strictest interpretation. Often, of late, she found herself dwelling, with an aching nostalgia, on her father's butcher shop in Pittsburgh. That had been before he'd invented a new deboner, or meat cleaver, or something, and had amassed an unbelievable amount of money before he strangled to death on a loose gold filling at Tim O'Toole's clambake.

Milli's recollection of her father was but a dim blur of red face and handlebar mustaches and a deep booming voice that Milli had associated with the line "the curfew tolls the knell of parting day," which she had been forced to learn and recite at P.S. 46. Her mother she didn't remember at all, as she had been called to pastures greener than anything Pittsburgh had to offer while Milli was yet wearing swaddling clothes in a perpetual state of dampness.

However, sharpened by adversity, Milli's recollections of the butcher shop were crystal clear. The refrigerator with whole sides of beef hanging from hooks, legs of lamb like fat tallow candles, plump chickens with thick drumsticks and their heads wrapped in brown paper, slabs of pork and veal, and, at Thanksgiving and Christmas, short-legged ducks, and high-breasted turkeys, and big, yellow geese. In the showcase had been chops, and steaks, and huge roasts, and all sorts of sausages and spiced meats laid out in white enamel trays with carrot tops in between for "dressing."

It was hopeless to dream of these things, but practically impossible to stop. The main topics of conversation no longer were of "major developments" but of where one could buy an extra ration of tea of questionable ingredients, or a grisly chop of dubious origin, or a few eggs of doubtful age—if one could pay the whopping price.

Well, as long as she had liqueur-filled chocolates, and she had had enough foresight to lay in quite a supply, she could be assured of her "share." They were better than money, at the present exchange.

The clock on the mantelpiece tinkled out the hours and Milli sighed. She should bathe and dress for dinner. But what was the use of keeping up appearances when there wasn't anyone to see. And it was dreadful curling the ends of one's hair on an iron. It was tedious and it didn't really *do* a great deal for one. And it had an unmistakable scent of burning shoe leather about it. The water would be tepid, if not actually cold. The soap wouldn't lather. The bathroom would be clammy, and the dinner, when it was forthcoming, would be a ragout of God knew what, a potato that had gouged-out areas in it, a limp salad, and a compote of dried fruit. And Maria grumbled so about serving it in courses. It was positively useless to diagram for her the jumbled up indecencies of a table d'hote. Maria was almost worse than no help at all. Definitely a bourgeois.

Milli yawned and stretched her arms above her head. She arose and, going over to the windows, stood looking out. A shaft of sunlight broke through the clouds and angered the tiny charms that dangled from her "war bracelet." An airplane studded with rhinestones, a miniature cannon with gold-leaf wheels, a toy soldier whose diamond chip eyes winked red and blue and green in the sun as he twirled helplessly on his silver chain. Ten or twelve of these baubles hung from the bracelet and it is indicative of Milli's character that she had bought them as a gift to herself to "celebrate" the last Bastille Day.

The sun's watery radiance turned the slackening rain into shining strings of quicksilver and made a drowned seascape of the garden. The faun that once had been a fountain, gleamed wetly in the pale, unearthly light and about its feet in the cracked basin, the pelting raindrops danced and bubbled like antiphonic memories of long-gone grace notes. The flower heads were heavy with sodden, brown-edged petals and their stalks bent wearily as if cognizant of the fact that their lives were held by a tenuous thread that was soon to be snapped between the chill, biting teeth of an early frost.

Milli looked at the rain intermingled with sun and thought, the devil is beating his wife. That was what Savannah used to say, back in Pittsburgh. "The devil's beatin' his wife, sho nuff." Savannah, who made such luscious mince pies and cherry tarts, and whose baked hams were always brown and crunchy on top and stuck with cloves and crisscrossed with a knife so that the juice ran down in between the cracks and— Milli's culinary recollections suffered a complete collapse and her eyes opened very wide as they alighted on a head poking out inquisitively from the leafy seclusion of the tall hedge that bounded the garden.

Two brown hands pushed aside the foliage to allow a pair of broad, brown shoulders to come through.

Milli gave an infinitesimal gasp. A man was in her garden! A man who, judging from the visible portion of his excellent anatomy, had—literally—lost his shirt.

Instinctively, she opened her mouth to make some sort of an outcry. Whether she meant to call for aid, or to scare the interloper away, or merely to give vent to a belated exclamation of surprise, will forever be debatable for the object of her scrutiny chose that moment to turn his extraordinarily well-shaped head and his glance fixed itself on Milli. Milli's outcry died a-borning.

To begin with, it wasn't a man. It was a youth. And to end with, there was something about him, some queer, indefinable quality, that was absolutely fascinating.

He was, Milli thought, rather like a young panther, or a half-awakened leopard. He was, Milli admitted, entranced, beautiful. Perfectly *beautiful*. As an animal is beautiful and, automatically, she raised her chin so that the almost unnoticeable pouch under it became one with the line of her throat.

The youth was unabashed. If the discovery of his presence in a private garden left him in a difficult position, he effectively concealed his embarrassment. He regarded Milli steadfastly, and unwaveringly, and admiringly, and Milli, like a mesmerized bird, watched the rippling play of his muscles beneath his skin as he shoved the hedge apart still farther to obtain a better view of his erstwhile hostess.

Confusedly, Milli thought that it was lucky the windows were locked and, in the same mental breath, what a pity that they were.

The two peered at one another. Milli knew only that his hair was pasted flat to his head with the rain, and that his arms shone like sepia satin, and his eyes were tawny and filled with a flickering inward fire that made suet pudding of her knees.

For a long moment they remained so—their eyes locked. Milli's like those of an amazed china doll's; his like those of an untamed animal that was slightly underfed and resented the resulting gastric disturbances. The kitchen door banged and Milli could hear Maria calling a neighborly greeting to someone, as she emptied a bucket of water in the yard. At that instant the last vestiges of sun began to sink behind the horizon, and the youth was gone. There was just the garden, and the rain, and the hedge.

Dimly, as through a fog, Milli heard Maria come in, heard the latch shoot home, the metallic clatter of the bucket as she set it down under the sink and, from somewhere outside, the long, diminishingly mournful howl of a dog.

Milli shook herself out of her trance. She brushed a hand across her eyelids as if to clear them of cobwebs and, unbolting one of the windows, went out into the garden. There was no one. Only a footprint by the hedge, a bare footprint filling in with water.

She went back into the house. Maria was there, turning on the lamps. She looked at Milli curiously and Milli realized she must be an odd sight, indeed, her hair liberally besprinkled with raindrops, her shoes muddy, her dress streaked with moisture.

"I thought I saw someone out there, just now," she explained. "Someone looking in."

"The police, probably," Maria said dourly. "The police have no notions of privacy."

"No," Milli said. "No, it wasn't the police. Didn't I hear you go out a few moments ago?"

"I wasn't looking in," Maria said in a peevish voice. "For why should I look in? I have other things to do besides looking in the windows." She drew herself up to list vocally and with accompanying gestures the numberless things she had to do.

"Did you see anyone?" Milli asked quickly.

"Old Phillipe," Maria answered. "I saw old Phillipe. On his way to the inn in the pouring rain and he with a cough since last April. When one has a cough and it is raining, one does not look in windows. Anyway, Phillipe is too old. When one is as old as Phillipe one is no longer interested. Anyhow, his son was killed at Avignon. Phillipe would not look in the windows."

"You saw no one else?"

Maria's eyes narrowed. "Madame was expecting someone, no?"

"No," Milli said. "No, I just thought . . . it was nothing."

"If madame is expecting someone, perhaps it would be well to save the beverage for later in the evening?"

"I am expecting no one."

It was, Milli thought as she let the curling iron rest in the gaseous flame, next to impossible to tell which side of the fence Maria was on. She could easily be reporting things to *both* sides. One had to be careful. So very careful.

This chap in the garden, for example. He must have escaped from somewhere. That would account for the absence of clothes. He was a refugee of some sort. And refugees of any sort were dangerous. It was best to stick to the beaten path and those who trod thereon. But he was so beautiful. Like a stripling god. No more than twenty, surely. It was delightful to see again someone as young as twenty. It was—Milli swore fluently as the iron began to smoke; she waved it in the air to cool it and, testing it gingerly with a moistened forefinger, applied it to her coiffure—it was not only delightful, it was heavenly. It was, really, rather like one of those little, long ago, pink cocktails. It *did* something for one.

A faint aroma of singeing hair made itself manifest in the damp, wallpapery smelling room.

Milli considered the refugee from every angle as she ate her solitary dinner and, afterward, as she reclined on her chaise longue idly turning the pages of a book selected at random, and while she was disrobing for bed, and even when she was giving the underpart of her chin the regulation number of backhanded slaps, a ritual that as a rule occupied her entire attention.

Slipping into her dressing gown, she opened her window and leaned out, chin in hands, elbows on the sill. The moon rode in the sky—a hunted thing dodging behind wisps of tattered cloud, and the air was heavy and wet and redolent of dying leaves.

"The moon was a ghostly galleon," Milli quoted, feeling, somehow frail and immensely poetic. She smiled a sad, fragile smile in keeping with her mood and wondered if the refugee also was having a lonely rendezvous with the moon. Lying on his back in some hidden spot thinking, possibly, of— Her reverie was broken sharply by Maria's voice, shattering the stillness of the night. It was followed by a cascade of water.

"What on earth are you *doing*!" Milli called down exasperatedly.

"There was an animal out here," Maria yelled back, equally as exasperated. "Trampling in my mulch pile."

Milli started to say, "Don't be ridiculous, go to bed," but the sentence froze on her lips as she remembered the refugee. He had come back! Maria had thrown water on him! He had returned full of . . . of—well, hope for refuge, maybe, and Maria, the dolt, had chased him away!

"Wait," she called frenziedly into the darkness. "Wait! Oh, please, wait!"

Maria, thinking the command was for her, had waited, although the "please" had astonished her somewhat. Muttering under her breath, she had led her strangely overwrought mistress into the kitchen garden and had pointed out with pardonable pride the footprints in her mulch pile. Padded footprints. With claws.

"I saw the eyes," she said, "great, gleaming, yellow ones shining in the light when I started to pull the scullery blinds. Luckily I had a pot of water handy and I jerked open the door and—"

But her mistress wasn't listening. In truth, for one originally so upset, she had regained her composure with remarkable rapidity.

"Undoubtedly, the Trudeau's dog," she said with a total lack of interest.

"The Trudeau's dog is a Pomeranian," Maria said determinedly.

"No matter," Milli said. "Go to bed, Maria."

Maria went, mumbling to herself a querulous litany in which the word Pomeranian was, ever and anon, distinguishable—and pronounced with expletive force.

Milli awakened to find her room bright with sun, which was regrettable as it drew attention to the pattern of the rug and the well-worn condition of the curtains. It, likewise, did various things to Milli Cushman's face, which were little short of libelous. Libelous, that is, after Milli had painted herself a new one with painstaking care and the touch of an inspired, if jaded, master.

Downstairs, she found her breakfast ready and, because of its readiness, a trifle cold. She also found Maria, while not openly weeping, puffy as to eyes, and pink as to nose, and quite snuffly —a state that Milli found deplorable in servants.

A series of sharp questions brought to light the fact that old Phillipe was dead. Old Phillipe, it seemed, was not only dead but a bit mangled. To make a long story short, old Phillipe had been discovered in a condition that bordered on the skeletal. Identification had been made through particles of clothing and a pair of broken spectacles.

"You mean to say he was *eaten*!" Milli cried, which caused Maria to go off into a paroxysm of near hysterics from which Milli gathered, obscurely, that Maria blamed herself for old Phillipe's untimely demise.

By degrees, Milli drew it out of her. The footprints in the mulch pile. The kettle of water. The withdrawal of the animal to more congenial surroundings. Surroundings, doubtless, that were adjacent to the inn from whence old Phillipe, subsequently, plodded homeward. The stealthy pad of marauding feet. The encounter. The shriek. The awful ensuing silence.

Maria's detail was so graphic that it made Milli slightly ill, although it didn't prevent her from being firm about the matter of the wolf.

"Nonsense," Milli said. "Ridiculous. A *wolf*. Preposterous."

Maria explained about the bloody footprints leading away from the scene of slaughter. Footprints much too large for a dog. *Enormous* footprints.

"No doubt it was an enormous dog," Milli said coldly. "The natural habitat of a wolf is a forest, not a paved street."

Maria opened her mouth to go even further into detail, but Milli effectively shut it for her by a reprimand that, like the porridge of the smallest of the three bears, was neither too hot nor too cold, but just right.

After all, Milli thought, old Phillipe was better off. In all probability, he hadn't suffered a great deal. Most likely he had died of shock first. One more, one less, what difference did it make. Especially when one was as old as old Phillipe. At least he had lived his life while *she*, with so much life yet to be lived, was embalmed in a wretched sort of a flypaper existence that adhered to every inch of her no matter how hard she pulled. That visa. She would have to see about it again tomorrow. And the tea supply was disastrously low. And this horrible toast made of horrible bread that was crumbly and dry and tasted of sawdust. And her last bottle of eau de cologne practically *gone*, and she *couldn't* eat this mess in front of her.

Milli got up and went into the parlor. She flung wide the French windows and petulantly surveyed the garden. She had rented the place *because* of the garden—such a lovely setting for informal teas, she had thought, and impromptu chafing-dish suppers on the flagstones with candlelight and thin, graceful-stemmed glasses. She had pictured herself in appropriate attire, cutting flowers and doing whatever it was one did with peat moss, and now look at the thing. Just *look* at it!

Milli looked at it. Her breath went out of her. She drew it in again with an unbecoming wheeze. One hand flew to her throat.

In the garden, fast asleep, curled up in a ball under the hedge, was the refugee, all dappled with shadows and naked as the day he was born.

This time, it must be noted in all fairness, Milli didn't open her chops. If an outcry was in her, it wasn't strong enough to register on her reflexes. Her eyes blinked rapidly, as they always did when Milli was thinking fast and, when she re-crossed the parlor and walked down the hallway into the kitchen, her heels made hard staccato sounds on the flooring, as they always did when Milli had reached a decision.

Milli's decision made Maria as happy as could be, under the circumstances, and ten minutes later, reticule in hand, Maria departed for the domicile of her married niece's husband's aunt who was a friend of old Phillipe's widow and, conse-quently, would be in possession of all the particulars and would more than appreciate a helping hand and an attentive ear over the week end.

Milli turned the key behind her. Lightly, she ran to the scullery closet and took down from a nail a pair of grass-stained pants that had belonged to a gardener who had been liquidated before he had had a chance to return for his gar-ment. Carrying the trousers over her arm, she retraced her steps to the parlor and through the double French windows.

Quiet as she was, her unbidden guest was awake as soon as her foot touched the first flagstone. He didn't move a muscle. He just opened his eyes and watched her with the easy assur-ance of one who knows he can leave whenever he wants to and several jumps ahead of the nearest competitor.

Milli stopped. She held out the pants.

"For you," she said. She gave them a toss. The boy, his queer, light eyes watching her every movement, made no attempt to catch them.

"Put them on," Milli said. She hesitated. "Please," she said, adding, "I am your friend."

The boy sat up. Milli hastily turned her back.

"Tell me when you get them on," she ordered.

She waited, and waited, and waited and, hearing not the faintest rustle, cautiously swiveled her head around. Once again she drew in her breath and the wheeze was very nearly an eek for, not six inches away, was her visitor—his lips pulled over his teeth in a rather disconcerting smile, his eyes like glittering nuggets of amber.

The thought raced through Milli's head that he was going to "spring" at her, a thought tinged with relief as she subcon-

sciously noted that he *had* donned the ex-gardener's pants—
tinged, too, with a thrilling sense of her own charms as the boy's
eyes enumerated them one by one. She promptly elevated her
chin and tried to keep her consternation from becoming
obvious.

The boy laughed softly. A laugh that, somehow, was like a
musical sort of a snarl. He stepped back. He bowed. Mockingly.

"What are you doing in my garden?" Milli asked, thinking it
best to put him in his place, first and foremost. It wouldn't do
to let him get out of hand. So soon, anyway.

"Sleeping," the boy said.

"Don't you have any place to sleep?"

"Yes. Many places. But I like this place."

"What happened to your clothes?"

The boy shrugged. He didn't answer.

"Are you a refugee?"

"In a way, I suppose, yes."

"You're hiding, aren't you?"

"Until you came out, I was simply sleeping. After I have
eaten I sleep until a short while before sundown."

"You're not hungry?" Milli elevated her eyebrows in surprise.

"Not now." The boy let his glance rove fleetingly over his
hostess' neck. "I will be later."

"What do you mean 'until a short while before sundown'?
Have you been traveling by night?"

"Yes."

Milli made an ineffectual motion toward the trousers. "Wasn't
it . . . I mean, going around without any . . . that is. I
should think— Weren't you cold?"

"No."

"It's a wonder you didn't catch pneumonia."

The boy grinned. He patted his flat stomach. "Not pneumonia," he said. "But it wasn't much better. Old and stringy
and without flavor."

Milli regarded him with a puzzled frown. She didn't like
being "taken in." She decided to let it go.

"My name is Milli Cushman," she said. "You are more than
welcome to stay here until you are rested. You won't be
bothered. I have sent my maid away."

"You're most kind," the boy said with exaggerated politeness.

"Until tonight will be sufficient." If he realized that Milli was expecting him to introduce himself, he gave no sign.

After a pause, she spoke, a shade irritably. "No doubt, you *do* have a name?"

"I have lots of names. Even Latin ones."

"Well, for Heaven's sake, what is one? I can't just go about calling you 'you,' you know."

"You might call me Lupus," the boy said. "It's one of the Latin ones. It means wolf."

"Do they call you The Wolf!"

"Yes."

"How intriguing. But why?"

The boy smiled at her. "I daresay you'll find out," he said.

"You mean you're one of the ones who . . . well, like the affair of that German officer last week . . . that is to say, in a manner of speaking, you're one of those who're *still* going at it hammer and tongs?"

"Tooth and nail," the boy said.

"It seems so *silly*," Milli said. "What *good* does it do. It doesn't scare them. It just makes them angrier. And that makes it harder on *us*."

"Oh, but it *does* scare them," the boy said with an ironic lilt to his voice. "It scares them to death. Or at any rate it helps." He yawned, his tongue curling out like a cat's. And, suddenly, he was sullen. He glared at Milli with remote hostility.

"I'm sleepy," he growled. "I'm tired of talking. I want to go to sleep. Go away."

"Come inside," Milli said. "You can have Maria's bed." She gave him her most delectable glance. The one that involved the upsweeping and downsweeping of her eyelashes with the slimmest trace of a roguish quirk about the lips.

"I won't disturb you," she said. "And, besides, you might be caught if you stay in the garden. There was a man killed last night by some kind of a creature, or so they say, and Maria is sure to spread the news abroad that she threw water at something, and police just *might* investigate, and it *could* be very awkward for us both. Won't you come in, please?"

The boy looked at her in surly silence.

"Please, Lupus. For me?"

Once more he laughed softly. And this time the laugh was definitely a snarl. He reached out and pinched her. "For you, I will."

It was, Milli thought, not at all a flirtatious pinch. It was the kind of pinch her father used to give chickens to see if they were filled out in the proper places.

But Lupus wouldn't sleep in Maria's bed. He curled up on the floor of the parlor. Which, Milli thought, was just as well. It would save remaking Mania's bed so Maria wouldn't notice anything.

While her caller slept, Milli busied herself with pots and pans in the kitchen. It was tedious, but worth it. Tonight, there would be supper on the flagstones, with candles, and starlight, and all the accessories. A chance like this might not come her way for many another moon. She was resolved to make the most of it. As Savannah would have said, she was going to "do herself proud." For Lupus, the best was none too good. Not for herself, either. She nibbled a sandwich for luncheon, not wanting to spoil her appetite—not waking Lupus, for fear of spoiling his.

She got out her precious hoard of condiments. She scanned the fine printed directions on boxes. Meticulously she read the instructive leaflet inclosed in her paper bag of tanbarky appearing flour. She took off her bracelet, rolled up her sleeves, and went to work—humming happily to herself, a thing which she hadn't done for months.

She scraped, peeled, measured, sifted, chopped, stirred, beat and folded. Some fairly creditable muffins emerged from under her unaccustomed and amateurish fingers, a dessert that wasn't bad at all, and a salad that managed to give the impression of actually *being* a salad, which bordered on the miraculous.

The day slowly drew to a close and Milli was quite startled to find the hours had passed with such swiftness. So swiftly, that her initial awareness of their passing was caused by the advent of a patently ill-humored Lupus.

"Oh, dear," Milli said, "I didn't realize—is it late?"

"No," Lupus said. "It's growing early. The sun is going down."

"Are you hungry? I'm fixing some things I think will be rather good."

"I'm ravening," Lupus said. "Let's go watch the sunset."

Milli put her hands up to her coiffure, coquettishly, allowing her sleeves to fall away from her round, white arms.

"Wait till I fix my hair. I must be a sight."

"You are," Lupus agreed, his eyes glistening. "And I won't have to wait much longer." Effortlessly he moved across and stood over Milli, devouring her with an all-encompassing gaze.

"Won't you have one of these," Milli asked hurriedly, hoping his impetuosity wouldn't brim over *too* abruptly. She shoved a box of liqueur-filled chocolates at him. "There's no such thing as a cocktail any more. Come along, we'll eat them on the sofa. It's . . . it's cozier."

But Lupus wasn't interested in the chocolates. In the parlor he stretched his long, supple length on the floor and contemplated the garden, ablaze in the last rays of a dying sun.

Milli plopped down beside him and began to rub his back, gently with long, smooth, even strokes. Lupus rolled his head over in lazy, indifferent pleasure, and looked up at her with a hunger that would have been voluptuous, if it hadn't been so stark.

"Do you like that?" Milli whispered.

For a reply, Lupus opened his mouth and yawned. And into it Milli dropped a chocolate, while at the same instant she jabbed him savagely with a hairpin.

The boy sucked in his breath with a pained howl, and a full eight minutes before the sun went down, Lupus had neatly choked to death on a chocolate whose liqueur-filled insides contained a silver bullet from Milli Cushman's "war bracelet."

It had been, Milli told herself later, a near thing. And it would have been *ghastly* if it hadn't worked. But it *had* worked, tra la. Of course, it stood to reason that it *would*. After all, if, at death, a werewolf changed back into human form, why, logically, the human form would—if in close personal contact with a silver bullet *before* sundown—metamorphosis into a wolf.

It was marvelous that she'd happened to pick up "The Werewolf of Paris" yesterday—had given her an insight, so to speak, and it was *extremely* handy that she'd had all that butcher shop background.

Milli wiped her mouth daintily with a napkin. How divinely *full* she was. And with Maria gone she could have Lupus all to herself.

Down to the last, delicious morsel.

1943

ANTHONY BOUCHER

(1911–1968)

Mr. Lupescu

THE teacups rattled and flames flickered over the logs.

"Alan, I *do* wish you could do something about Bobby."

"Isn't that rather Robert's place?"

"Oh you know *Robert*. He's so busy doing good in nice abstract ways with committees in them."

"And headlines."

"He can't be bothered with things like Mr. Lupescu. After all, Bobby's only his *son*."

"And yours, Marjorie."

"And mine. But things like this take a *man*, Alan."

The room was warm and peaceful; Alan stretched his long legs by the fire and felt domestic. Marjorie was soothing even when she fretted. The firelight did things to her hair and the curve of her blouse.

A small whirlwind entered at high velocity and stopped only when Marjorie said, "Bob-*by*! Say hello nicely to Uncle Alan."

Bobby said hello and stood tentatively on one foot.

"Alan. . . ." Marjorie prompted.

Alan sat up straight and tried to look paternal. "Well, Bobby," he said. "And where are you off to in such a hurry?"

"See Mr. Lupescu, 'f course. He usually comes afternoons."

"Your mother's been telling me about Mr. Lupescu. He must be quite a person."

"Oh, gee, I'll say he is, Uncle Alan. He's got a great big red nose and red gloves and red eyes—not like when you've been crying but really red like yours 're brown—and little red wings that twitch, only he can't fly with them 'cause they're ruddermentary he says. And he talks like—oh, gee, I can't do it, but he's swell, he is."

"Lupescu's a funny name for a fairy godfather, isn't it, Bobby?"

"Why? Mr. Lupescu always says why do all the fairies have to be Irish because it takes all kinds, doesn't it?"

"Alan!" Marjorie said. "I don't see that you're doing a *bit* of good. You talk to him seriously like that and you simply make him think it *is* serious. And you *do* know better, don't you, Bobby? You're just joking with us."

"Joking? About *Mr. Lupescu*?"

"Marjorie, you don't— Listen, Bobby. Your mother didn't mean to insult you or Mr. Lupescu. She just doesn't believe in what she's never seen, and you can't blame her. Now supposing you took her and me out in the garden and we could all see Mr. Lupescu. Wouldn't that be fun?"

"Uh, uh." Bobby shook his head gravely. "Not for Mr. Lupescu. He doesn't like people. Only little boys. And he says if ever bring people to see him then he'll let Gorgo get me. G'bye now." And the whirlwind departed.

Marjorie sighed. "At least thank heavens for Gorgo. I never can get a very clear picture out of Bobby, but he says Mr. Lupescu tells the most *terrible* things about him. And if there's any trouble about vegetables or brushing teeth all I have to say is *Gorgo* and hey presto!"

Alan rose. "I don't think you need worry, Marjorie. Mr. Lupescu seems to do more good than harm, and an active imagination is no curse to a child."

"You haven't *lived* with Mr. Lupescu."

"To live in a house like this, I'd chance it," Alan laughed. "But please forgive me now—back to the cottage and the typewriter. Seriously, why don't you ask Robert to talk with him?"

Marjorie spread her hands helplessly.

"I know. I'm always the one to assume responsibilities. And yet you married Robert."

Marjorie laughed. "I don't know. Somehow there's something *about* Robert. . . ." Her vague gesture happened to include the original Degas over the fireplace, the sterling tea service, and even the liveried footman who came in at that moment to clear away.

Mr. Lupescu was pretty wonderful that afternoon all right. He had a little kind of an itch like in his wings and they kept twitching all the time. Stardust, he said. It tickles. Got it up in the Milky Way. Friend of his has a wagon route up there.

Mr. Lupescu had lots of friends and they all did something you wouldn't ever think of not in a squillion years. That's why he didn't like people because people don't do things you can tell stories about. They just work or keep house or are mothers or something.

But one of Mr. Lupescu's friends now was captain of a ship only it went in time and Mr. Lupescu took trips with him and came back and told you all about what was happening this very minute five hundred years ago. And another of the friends was a radio engineer only he could tune in on all the kingdoms of faery and Mr. Lupescu would squidgle up his red nose and twist it like a dial and make noises like all the kingdoms of faery coming in on the set. And then there was Gorgo only he wasn't a friend, not exactly, not even to Mr. Lupescu.

They'd been playing for a couple of weeks only it must've been really hours 'cause Mamselle hadn't yelled about supper yet but Mr. Lupescu says Time is funny, when Mr. Lupescu screwed up his red eyes and said, "Bobby, let's go in the house."

"But there's people in the house and you don't—"

"I know I don't like people. That's why we're going in the house. Come on, Bobby, or I'll—"

So what could you do when you didn't even want to hear him say Gorgo's name?

He went into father's study through the French window and it was a strict rule that nobody ever went into father's study, but rules weren't for Mr. Lupescu.

Father was on the telephone telling somebody he'd try to be at a luncheon but there was a committee meeting that same morning but he'd see. While he was talking Mr. Lupescu went over to a table and opened a drawer and took something out.

When father hung up he saw Bobby first and started to be very mad. He said, "Young man, you've been trouble enough to your mother and me with all your stories about your red-winged Mr. Lupescu, and now if you're to start bursting in—"

You have to be polite and introduce people. "Father, this is Mr. Lupescu. And see he does, too, have red wings."

Mr. Lupescu held out the gun he'd taken from the drawer and shot father once right through the forehead. It made a little clean hole in front and a big messy hole in back. Father fell down and was dead.

"Now, Bobby," Mr. Lupescu said, "a lot of people are going to come here and ask you a lot of questions. And if you don't tell the truth about exactly what happened, I'll send Gorgo to fetch you."

Then Mr. Lupescu was gone through the French window onto the gravel path.

"It's a curious case, Lieutenant," the medical examiner said. "It's fortunate I've dabbled a bit in psychiatry; I can at least give you a lead until you get the experts in. The child's statement that his fairy godfather shot his father is obviously a simple flight-mechanism, susceptible of two interpretations. A, the father shot himself; the child was so horrified by the sight that he refused to accept it and invented this explanation. B, the child shot the father, let us say by accident, and shifted the blame to his imaginary scapegoat. B has of course more sinister implications; if the child had resented his father and created an ideal substitute, he might make the substitute destroy the reality. . . . But there's the solution to your eye-witness testimony; which alternative is true, Lieutenant, I leave it up to your researches into motive and the evidence of ballistics and fingerprints. The angle of the wound jibes with either."

The man with the red nose and eyes and gloves and wings walked down the back lane to the cottage. As soon as he got inside he took off his coat and removed the wings and the mechanism of strings and rubbers that made them twitch. He laid them on top of the ready pile of kindling and lit the fire. When it was well started, he added gloves. Then he took off the nose, kneaded the putty until the red of its outside vanished into the neutral brown of the mass, jammed it into a crack in the wall, and smoothed it over. Then he took the red-irised contact lenses out of his brown eyes and went into the kitchen, found a hammer, pounded them to powder, and washed the powder down the sink.

Alan started to pour himself a drink and found, to his pleased surprise, that he didn't especially need one. But he did feel tired. He could lie down and recapitulate it all, from the invention of

Mr. Lupescu (and Gorgo and the man with the Milky Way route) to today's success and on into the future when Marjorie, pliant, trusting Marjorie would be more desirable than ever as Robert's widow and heir. And Bobby would need a *man* to look after him.

Alan went into the bedroom. Several years passed by in the few seconds it took him to recognize what was waiting on the bed, but then Time is funny.

Alan said nothing.

"Mr. Lupescu, I presume?" said Gorgo.

1945

TRUMAN CAPOTE

(1924–1984)

Miriam

For several years, Mrs. H. T. Miller had lived alone in a pleasant apartment (two rooms with kitchenette) in a remodeled brownstone near the East River. She was a widow: Mr. H. T. Miller had left a reasonable amount of insurance. Her interests were narrow, she had no friends to speak of, and she rarely journeyed farther than the corner grocery. The other people in the house never seemed to notice her: her clothes were matter-of-fact, her hair iron-gray, clipped and casually waved; she did not use cosmetics, her features were plain and inconspicuous, and on her last birthday she was sixty-one. Her activities were seldom spontaneous: she kept the two rooms immaculate, smoked an occasional cigarette, prepared her own meals and tended a canary.

Then she met Miriam. It was snowing that night. Mrs. Miller had finished drying the supper dishes and was thumbing through an afternoon paper when she saw an advertisement of a picture playing at a neighborhood theater. The title sounded good, so she struggled into her beaver coat, laced her galoshes and left the apartment, leaving one light burning in the foyer: she found nothing more disturbing than a sensation of darkness.

The snow was fine, falling gently, not yet making an impression on the pavement. The wind from the river cut only at street crossings. Mrs. Miller hurried, her head bowed, oblivious as a mole burrowing a blind path. She stopped at a drugstore and bought a package of peppermints.

A long line stretched in front of the box office; she took her place at the end. There would be (a tired voice groaned) a short wait for all seats. Mrs. Miller rummaged in her leather handbag till she collected exactly the correct change for admission. The line seemed to be taking its own time and, looking around for some distraction, she suddenly became conscious of a little girl standing under the edge of the marquee.

Her hair was the longest and strangest Mrs. Miller had ever seen: absolutely silver-white, like an albino's. It flowed waist-length in smooth, loose lines. She was thin and fragilely constructed. There was a simple, special elegance in the way she stood with her thumbs in the pockets of a tailored plum-velvet coat.

Mrs. Miller felt oddly excited, and when the little girl glanced toward her, she smiled warmly. The little girl walked over and said, "Would you care to do me a favor?"

"I'd be glad to, if I can," said Mrs. Miller.

"Oh, it's quite easy. I merely want you to buy a ticket for me; they won't let me in otherwise. Here, I have the money." And gracefully she handed Mrs. Miller two dimes and a nickel.

They went into the theater together. An usherette directed them to a lounge; in twenty minutes the picture would be over.

"I feel just like a genuine criminal," said Mrs. Miller gaily, as she sat down. "I mean that sort of thing's against the law, isn't it? I do hope I haven't done the wrong thing. Your mother knows where you are, dear? I mean she does, doesn't she?"

The little girl said nothing. She unbuttoned her coat and folded it across her lap. Her dress underneath was prim and dark blue. A gold chain dangled about her neck, and her fingers, sensitive and musical-looking, toyed with it. Examining her more attentively, Mrs. Miller decided the truly distinctive feature was not her hair, but her eyes; they were hazel, steady, lacking any childlike quality whatsoever and, because of their size, seemed to consume her small face.

Mrs. Miller offered a peppermint. "What's your name, dear?"

"Miriam," she said, as though, in some curious way, it were information already familiar.

"Why, isn't that funny—my name's Miriam, too. And it's not a terribly common name either. Now, don't tell me your last name's Miller!"

"Just Miriam."

"But isn't that funny?"

"Moderately," said Miriam, and rolled the peppermint on her tongue.

Mrs. Miller flushed and shifted uncomfortably. "You have such a large vocabulary for such a little girl."

"Do I?"

"Well, yes," said Mrs. Miller, hastily changing the topic to: "Do you like the movies?"

"I really wouldn't know," said Miriam. "I've never been before."

Women began filling the lounge; the rumble of the newsreel bombs exploded in the distance. Mrs. Miller rose, tucking her purse under her arm. "I guess I'd better be running now if I want to get a seat," she said. "It was nice to have met you."

Miriam nodded ever so slightly.

It snowed all week. Wheels and footsteps moved soundlessly on the street, as if the business of living continued secretly behind a pale but impenetrable curtain. In the falling quiet there was no sky or earth, only snow lifting in the wind, frosting the window glass, chilling the rooms, deadening and hushing the city. At all hours it was necessary to keep a lamp lighted, and Mrs. Miller lost track of the days: Friday was no different from Saturday and on Sunday she went to the grocery: closed, of course.

That evening she scrambled eggs and fixed a bowl of tomato soup. Then, after putting on a flannel robe and cold-creaming her face, she propped herself up in bed with a hot-water bottle under her feet. She was reading the *Times* when the doorbell rang. At first she thought it must be a mistake and whoever it was would go away. But it rang and rang and settled to a persistent buzz. She looked at the clock: a little after eleven; it did not seem possible, she was always asleep by ten.

Climbing out of bed, she trotted barefoot across the living room. "I'm coming, please be patient." The latch was caught; she turned it this way and that way and the bell never paused an instant. "Stop it," she cried. The bolt gave way and she opened the door an inch. "What in heaven's name?"

"Hello," said Miriam.

"Oh . . . why, hello," said Mrs. Miller, stepping hesitantly into the hall. "You're that little girl."

"I thought you'd never answer, but I kept my finger on the button; I knew you were home. Aren't you glad to see me?"

Mrs. Miller did not know what to say. Miriam, she saw, wore

the same plum-velvet coat and now she had also a beret to match; her white hair was braided in two shining plaits and looped at the ends with enormous white ribbons.

"Since I've waited so long, you could at least let me in," she said.

"It's awfully late. . . ."

Miriam regarded her blankly. "What difference does that make? Let me in. It's cold out here and I have on a silk dress." Then, with a gentle gesture, she urged Mrs. Miller aside and passed into the apartment.

She dropped her coat and beret on a chair. She was indeed wearing a silk dress. White silk. White silk in February. The skirt was beautifully pleated and the sleeves long; it made a faint rustle as she strolled about the room. "I like your place," she said. "I like the rug, blue's my favorite color." She touched a paper rose in a vase on the coffee table. "Imitation," she commented wanly. "How sad. Aren't imitations sad?" She seated herself on the sofa, daintily spreading her skirt.

"What do you want?" asked Mrs. Miller.

"Sit down," said Miriam. "It makes me nervous to see people stand."

Mrs. Miller sank to a hassock. "What do you want?" she repeated.

"You know, I don't think you're glad I came."

For a second time Mrs. Miller was without an answer; her hand motioned vaguely. Miriam giggled and pressed back on a mound of chintz pillows. Mrs. Miller observed that the girl was less pale than she remembered; her cheeks were flushed.

"How did you know where I lived?"

Miriam frowned. "That's no question at all. What's your name? What's mine?"

"But I'm not listed in the phone book."

"Oh, let's talk about something else."

Mrs. Miller said. "Your mother must be insane to let a child like you wander around at all hours of the night—and in such ridiculous clothes. She must be out of her mind."

Miriam got up and moved to a corner where a covered bird cage hung from a ceiling chain. She peeked beneath the cover. "It's a canary," she said. "Would you mind if I woke him? I'd like to hear him sing."

"Leave Tommy alone," said Mrs. Miller, anxiously. "Don't you dare wake him."

"Certainly," said Miriam. "But I don't see why I can't hear him sing." And then, "Have you anything to eat? I'm starving! Even milk and a jam sandwich would be fine."

"Look," said Mrs. Miller, arising from the hassock, "look— if I make some nice sandwiches will you be a good child and run along home? It's past midnight, I'm sure."

"It's snowing," reproached Miriam. "And cold and dark."

"Well, you shouldn't have come here to begin with," said Mrs. Miller, struggling to control her voice. "I can't help the weather. If you want anything to eat you'll have to promise to leave."

Miriam brushed a braid against her cheek. Her eyes were thoughtful, as if weighing the proposition. She turned toward the bird cage. "Very well," she said, "I promise."

How old is she? Ten? Eleven? Mrs. Miller, in the kitchen, un-sealed a jar of strawberry preserves and cut four slices of bread. She poured a glass of milk and paused to light a cigarette. *And why has she come?* Her hand shook as she held the match, fasci-nated, till it burned her finger. The canary was singing; singing as he did in the morning and at no other time. "Miriam," she called, "Miriam, I told you not to disturb Tommy." There was no answer. She called again; all she heard was the canary. She inhaled the cigarette and discovered she had lighted the cork-tip end and—oh, really, she mustn't lose her temper.

She carried the food in on a tray and set it on the coffee table. She saw first that the bird cage still wore its night cover. And Tommy was singing. It gave her a queer sensation. And no one was in the room. Mrs. Miller went through an alcove leading to her bedroom; at the door she caught her breath.

"What are you doing?" she asked.

Miriam glanced up and in her eyes there was a look that was not ordinary. She was standing by the bureau, a jewel case opened before her. For a minute she studied Mrs. Miller, forcing their eyes to meet, and she smiled. "There's nothing good here," she said. "But I like this." Her hand held a cameo brooch. "It's charming."

"Suppose—perhaps you'd better put it back," said Mrs.

Miller, feeling suddenly the need of some support. She leaned against the door frame; her head was unbearably heavy; a pressure weighted the rhythm of her heartbeat. The light seemed to flutter defectively. "Please, child—a gift from my husband . . ."

"But it's beautiful and I want it," said Miriam. "*Give it to me.*"

As she stood, striving to shape a sentence which would somehow save the brooch, it came to Mrs. Miller there was no one to whom she might turn; she was alone; a fact that had not been among her thoughts for a long time. Its sheer emphasis was stunning. But here in her own room in the hushed snow-city were evidences she could not ignore or, she knew with startling clarity, resist.

Miriam ate ravenously, and when the sandwiches and milk were gone, her fingers made cobweb movements over the plate, gathering crumbs. The cameo gleamed on her blouse, the blonde profile like a trick reflection of its wearer. "That was very nice," she sighed, "though now an almond cake or a cherry would be ideal. Sweets are lovely, don't you think?"

Mrs. Miller was perched precariously on the hassock, smoking a cigarette. Her hair net had slipped lopsided and loose strands straggled down her face. Her eyes were stupidly concentrated on nothing and her cheeks were mottled in red patches, as though a fierce slap had left permanent marks.

"Is there a candy—a cake?"

Mrs. Miller tapped ash on the rug. Her head swayed slightly as she tried to focus her eyes. "You promised to leave if I made the sandwiches," she said.

"Dear me, did I?"

"It was a promise and I'm tired and I don't feel well at all."

"Mustn't fret," said Miriam. "I'm only teasing."

She picked up her coat, slung it over her arm, and arranged her beret in front of a mirror. Presently she bent close to Mrs. Miller and whispered, "Kiss me good night."

"Please—I'd rather not," said Mrs. Miller.

Miriam lifted a shoulder, arched an eyebrow. "As you like," she said, and went directly to the coffee table, seized the vase containing the paper roses, carried it to where the hard surface of the floor lay bare, and hurled it downward. Glass sprayed in all directions and she stamped her foot on the bouquet.

Then slowly she walked to the door, but before closing it she looked back at Mrs. Miller with a slyly innocent curiosity.

Mrs. Miller spent the next day in bed, rising once to feed the canary and drink a cup of tea; she took her temperature and had none, yet her dreams were feverishly agitated; their unbalanced mood lingered even as she lay staring wide-eyed at the ceiling. One dream threaded through the others like an elusively mysterious theme in a complicated symphony, and the scenes it depicted were sharply outlined, as though sketched by a hand of gifted intensity: a small girl, wearing a bridal gown and a wreath of leaves, led a gray procession down a mountain path, and among them there was unusual silence till a woman at the rear asked, "Where is she taking us?" "No one knows," said an old man marching in front. "But isn't she pretty?" volunteered a third voice. "Isn't she like a frost flower . . . so shining and white?"

Tuesday morning she woke up feeling better; harsh slats of sunlight, slanting through Venetian blinds, shed a disrupting light on her unwholesome fancies. She opened the window to discover a thawed, mild-as-spring day; a sweep of clean new clouds crumpled against a vastly blue, out-of-season sky; and across the low line of rooftops she could see the river and smoke curving from tugboat stacks in a warm wind. A great silver truck plowed the snow-banked street, its machine sound humming on the air.

After straightening the apartment, she went to the grocer's, cashed a check and continued to Schrafft's where she ate breakfast and chatted happily with the waitress. Oh, it was a wonderful day—more like a holiday—and it would be so foolish to go home.

She boarded a Lexington Avenue bus and rode up to Eighty-sixth Street; it was here that she had decided to do a little shopping.

She had no idea what she wanted or needed, but she idled along, intent only upon the passers-by, brisk and preoccupied, who gave her a disturbing sense of separateness.

It was while waiting at the corner of Third Avenue that she

saw the man: an old man, bowlegged and stooped under an armload of bulging packages; he wore a shabby brown coat and a checkered cap. Suddenly she realized they were exchanging a smile: there was nothing friendly about this smile, it was merely two cold flickers of recognition. But she was certain she had never seen him before.

He was standing next to an El pillar, and as she crossed the street he turned and followed. He kept quite close; from the corner of her eye she watched his reflection wavering on the shopwindows.

Then in the middle of the block she stopped and faced him. He stopped also and cocked his head, grinning. But what could she say? Do? Here, in broad daylight, on Eighty-sixth Street? It was useless and, despising her own helplessness, she quickened her steps.

Now Second Avenue is a dismal street, made from scraps and ends; part cobblestone, part asphalt, part cement; and its atmosphere of desertion is permanent. Mrs. Miller walked five blocks without meeting anyone, and all the while the steady crunch of his footfalls in the snow stayed near. And when she came to a florist's shop, the sound was still with her. She hurried inside and watched through the glass door as the old man passed; he kept his eyes straight ahead and didn't slow his pace, but he did one strange, telling thing: he tipped his cap.

"Six white ones, did you say?" asked the florist. "Yes," she told him, "white roses." From there she went to a glassware store and selected a vase, presumably a replacement for the one Miriam had broken, though the price was intolerable and the vase itself (she thought) grotesquely vulgar. But a series of unaccountable purchases had begun, as if by pre-arranged plan: a plan of which she had not the least knowledge or control.

She bought a bag of glazed cherries, and at a place called the Knickerbocker Bakery she paid forty cents for six almond cakes.

Within the last hour the weather had turned cold again; like blurred lenses, winter clouds cast a shade over the sun, and the skeleton of an early dusk colored the sky; a damp mist mixed with the wind and the voices of a few children who romped high on mountains of gutter snow seemed lonely and cheerless. Soon the first flake fell, and when Mrs. Miller reached the

brownstone house, snow was falling in a swift screen and foot
tracks vanished as they were printed.

The white roses were arranged decoratively in the vase. The
glazed cherries shone on a ceramic plate. The almond cakes,
dusted with sugar, awaited a hand. The canary fluttered on its
swing and picked at a bar of seed.

At precisely five the doorbell rang. Mrs. Miller *knew* who it
was. The hem of her housecoat trailed as she crossed the floor.
"Is that you?" she called.

"Naturally," said Miriam, the word resounding shrilly from
the hall. "Open this door."

"Go away," said Mrs. Miller.

"Please hurry . . . I have a heavy package."

"Go away," said Mrs. Miller. She returned to the living
room, lighted a cigarette, sat down and calmly listened to the
buzzer; on and on and on. "You might as well leave. I have no
intention of letting you in."

Shortly the bell stopped. For possibly ten minutes Mrs.
Miller did not move. Then, hearing no sound, she concluded
Miriam had gone. She tiptoed to the door and opened it a
sliver; Miriam was half-reclining atop a cardboard box with a
beautiful French doll cradled in her arms.

"Really, I thought you were never coming," she said peev-
ishly. "Here, help me get this in, it's awfully heavy."

It was not spell-like compulsion that Mrs. Miller felt, but
rather a curious passivity; she brought in the box, Miriam the
doll. Miriam curled up on the sofa, not troubling to remove
her coat or beret, and watched disinterestedly as Mrs. Miller
dropped the box and stood trembling, trying to catch her
breath.

"Thank you," she said. In the daylight she looked pinched
and drawn, her hair less luminous. The French doll she was
loving wore an exquisite powdered wig and its idiot glass eyes
sought solace in Miriam's. "I have a surprise," she continued.
"Look into my box."

Kneeling, Mrs. Miller parted the flaps and lifted out another
doll; then a blue dress which she recalled as the one Miriam
had worn that first night at the theater; and of the remainder
she said, "It's all clothes. Why?"

"Because I've come to live with you," said Miriam, twisting a cherry stem. "Wasn't it nice of you to buy me the cherries . . . ?"

"But you can't! For God's sake go away—go away and leave me alone!"

". . . and the roses and the almond cakes? How really wonderfully generous. You know, these cherries are delicious. The last place I lived was with an old man; he was terribly poor and we never had good things to eat. But I think I'll be happy here." She paused to snuggle her doll closer. "Now, if you'll just show me where to put my things . . ."

Mrs Miller's face dissolved into a mask of ugly red lines; she began to cry, and it was an unnatural, tearless sort of weeping, as though, not having wept for a long time, she had forgotten how. Carefully she edged backward till she touched the door.

She fumbled through the hall and down the stairs to a landing below. She pounded frantically on the door of the first apartment she came to; a short, red-headed man answered and she pushed past him. "Say, what the hell is this?" he said. "Anything wrong, lover?" asked a young woman who appeared from the kitchen, drying her hands. And it was to her that Mrs. Miller turned.

"Listen," she cried, "I'm ashamed behaving this way but—well, I'm Mrs. H. T. Miller and I live upstairs and . . ." She pressed her hands over her face. "It sounds so absurd. . . ."

The woman guided her to a chair, while the man excitedly rattled pocket change. "Yeah?"

"I live upstairs and there's a little girl visiting me, and I suppose that I'm afraid of her. She won't leave and I can't make her and—she's going to do something terrible. She's already stolen my cameo, but she's about to do something worse—something terrible!"

The man asked, "Is she a relative, huh?"

Mrs. Miller shook her head. "I don't know who she is. Her name's Miriam, but I don't know for certain who she is."

"You gotta calm down, honey," said the woman, stroking Mrs. Miller's arm. "Harry here'll tend to this kid. Go on, lover." And Mrs. Miller said, "The door's open—5A."

After the man left, the woman brought a towel and bathed Mrs. Miller's face. "You're very kind," Mrs. Miller said. "I'm sorry to act like such a fool, only this wicked child. . . ."

"Sure, honey," consoled the woman. "Now, you better take it easy."

Mrs. Miller rested her head in the crook of her arm; she was quiet enough to be asleep. The woman turned a radio dial; a piano and a husky voice filled the silence and the woman, tapping her foot, kept excellent time. "Maybe we oughta go up too," she said.

"I don't want to see her again. I don't want to be anywhere near her."

"Uh huh, but what you shoulda done, you shoulda called a cop."

Presently they heard the man on the stairs. He strode into the room frowning and scratching the back of his neck. "Nobody there," he said, honestly embarrassed. "She musta beat it."

"Harry, you're a jerk," announced the woman. "We been sitting here the whole time and we woulda seen . . ." she stopped abruptly, for the man's glance was sharp.

"I looked all over," he said, "and there just ain't nobody there. Nobody, understand?"

"Tell me," said Mrs. Miller, rising, "tell me, did you see a large box? Or a doll?"

"No, ma'am, I didn't."

And the woman, as if delivering a verdict, said, "Well, for cryinoutloud. . . ."

Mrs. Miller entered her apartment softly; she walked to the center of the room and stood quite still. No, in a sense it had not changed: the roses, the cakes, and the cherries were in place. But this was an empty room, emptier than if the furnishings and familiars were not present, lifeless and petrified as a funeral parlor. The sofa loomed before her with a new strangeness: its vacancy had a meaning that would have been less penetrating and terrible had Miriam been curled on it. She gazed fixedly at the space where she remembered setting the box and, for a moment, the hassock spun desperately. And she looked through the window; surely the river was real, surely snow was falling—but then, one could not be certain witness to anything: Miriam, so vividly *there*—and yet, where was she? Where, where?

As though moving in a dream, she sank to a chair. The room was losing shape; it was dark and getting darker and there was nothing to be done about it; she could not lift her hand to light a lamp.

Suddenly, closing her eyes, she felt an upward surge, like a diver emerging from some deeper, greener depth. In times of terror or immense distress, there are moments when the mind waits, as though for a revelation, while a skein of calm is woven over thought; it is like a sleep, or a supernatural trance; and during this lull one is aware of a force of quiet reasoning: well, what if she had never really known a girl named Miriam? that she had been foolishly frightened on the street? In the end, like everything else, it was of no importance. For the only thing she had lost to Miriam was her identity, but now she knew she had found again the person who lived in this room, who cooked her own meals, who owned a canary, who was some-one she could trust and believe in: Mrs. H. T. Miller.

Listening in contentment, she became aware of a double sound: a bureau drawer opening and closing; she seemed to hear it long after completion—opening and closing. Then gradually, the harshness of it was replaced by the murmur of a silk dress and this, delicately faint, was moving nearer and swelling in intensity till the walls trembled with the vibration and the room was caving under a wave of whispers. Mrs. Miller stiffened and opened her eyes to a dull, direct stare.

"Hello," said Miriam.

1945

JACK SNOW

(1907–1956)

Midnight

BETWEEN the hour of eleven and midnight John Ware made ready to perform the ceremony that would climax the years of homage he had paid to the dark powers of evil. Tonight he would become a part of that essence of dread that roams the night hours. At the last stroke of midnight his consciousness would leave his body and unite with that which shuns the light and is all depravity and evil. Then he would roam the world with this midnight elemental and for one hour savor all the evil that this alien being is capable of inspiring in human souls.

John Ware had lived so long among the shadows of evil that his mind had become tainted, and through the channel of his thoughts his soul had been corrupted by the poison of the dark powers with which he consorted.

There was scarcely a forbidden book of shocking ceremonies and nameless teachings that Ware had not consulted and pored over in the long hours of the night. When certain guarded books he desired were unobtainable, he had shown no hesitation in stealing them. Nor had Ware stopped with mere reading and studying these books. He had descended to the ultimate depths and put into practice the ceremonies, rites and black sorceries that stained the pages of the volumes. Often these practices had required human blood and human lives, and here again Ware had not hesitated. He had long ago lost count of the number of innocent persons who had mysteriously vanished from the face of the earth—victims of his insatiable craving for knowledge of the evil that dwells in the dark, furtively, when the powers of light are at their nadir.

John Ware had traveled to all the strange and little known parts of the earth. He had tricked and wormed secrets out of priests and dignitaries of ancient cults and religions of whose existence the world of clean daylight has no inkling. Africa, the

West Indies, Tibet, China, Ware knew them all and they held no secret whose knowledge he had not violated.

By devious means Ware had secured admission to certain private institutions and homes behind whose facades were confined individuals who were not mad in the outright sense of the everyday definition of the word, but who, given their freedom, would loose nightmare horror on the world. Some of these prisoners were so curiously shaped and formed that they had been hidden away since childhood. In a number of instances their vocal organs were so alien that the sounds they uttered could not be considered human. Nevertheless, John Ware had been heard to converse with them.

In John Ware's chamber stood an ancient clock, tall as a human being, and abhorrently fashioned from age-yellowed ivory. Its head was that of a woman in an advanced state of dissolution. Around the skull, from which shreds of ivory flesh hung, were Roman numerals, marked by two death's head beetles, which, engineered by intricate machinery in the clock, crawled slowly around the perimeter of the skull to mark the hours. Nor did this clock tick as does an ordinary clock. Deep within its woman's bosom sounded a dull, regular thud, disturbingly similar to the beating of a human heart.

The malevolent creation of an unknown sorcerer of the dim past, this eerie clock had been the property of a succession of warlocks, alchemists, wizards, Satanists and like devotees of forbidden arts, each of whom had invested the clock with something of his own evil existence, so that a dark and revolting nimbus hung about it and it seemed to exude a loathsome animus from its repellently human form.

It was to this clock that John Ware addressed himself at the first stroke of midnight. The clock did not announce the hour in the fashion of other clocks. During the hour its ticking sounded faint and dull, scarcely distinguishable above ordinary sounds. But at each hour the ticking rose to a muffled thud, sounding like a human heart-beat heard through a stethoscope. With these ominous thuds it marked the hours, seeming to intimate that each beat of the human heart narrows that much more the span of mortal life.

Now the clock sounded the midnight hour. "Thud, thud,

thud—" Before it stood John Ware, his body traced with ca-balistic markings in a black pigment which he had prepared ac-cording to an ancient and noxious formula.

As the clock thudded out the midnight hour, John Ware repeated an incantation, which, had it not been for his de-vouring passion for evil, would have caused even him to shud-der at the mere sounds of the contorted vowels. To his mouthing of the unhuman phrases, he performed a pattern of motions with his body and limbs which was an unearthly gro-tesquerie of a dance.

"Thud, thud, thud—" the beat sounded for the twelfth time and then subsided to a dull, muffled murmur which was barely audible in the silence of the chamber. The body of John Ware sank to the thick rug and lay motionless. The spirit was gone from it. At the last stroke of the hour of midnight it had fled.

With a great thrill of exultation, John Ware found himself out-side in the night. He had succeeded! That which he had sum-moned had accepted him! Now for the next hour he would feast to his fill on unholy evil. Ware was conscious that he was not alone as he moved effortlessly through the night air. He was accompanied by a being which he perceived only as an amorphous darkness, a darkness that was deeper and more ab-solute than the inky night, a darkness that was a vacuum or blank in the color spectrum.

Ware found himself plunging suddenly earthward. The walls of a building flashed past him and an instant later he was in a sumptuously furnished living room, where stood a man and a woman. Ware felt a strong bond between himself and the woman. Her thoughts were his, he felt as she did. A wave of terror was enveloping him, flowing to him from the woman, for the man standing before her held a revolver in his hand. He was about to pull the trigger. John Ware lived through an agony of fear in those few moments that the helpless woman cringed before the man. Then a shapeless darkness settled over the man. His eyes glazed dully. Like an automaton he pressed the trigger and the bullet crashed into the woman's heart. John Ware died as she died.

Once again Ware was soaring through the night, the black

being close at his side. He was shaken by the experience. What could it mean? How had he come to be identified so closely with the tortured consciousness of the murdered woman?

Again Ware felt himself plummeting earthward. This time he was in a musty cellar in the depths of a vast city's tenement section. A man lay chained to a crude, wooden table. Over him stood two creatures of loathsome and sadistic countenance. Then John Ware *was* the man on the table. He knew, he thought, he felt everything that the captive felt. He saw a black shadow settle over the two evil-looking men. Their eyes glazed, their lips parted slightly as saliva drooled from them. The men made use of an assortment of crude instruments, knives, scalpels, pincers and barbed hooks, in a manner which in ten short minutes reduced the helpless body before them from a screaming human being to a whimpering, senseless thing covered with wounds and rivulets of blood. John Ware suffered as the victim suffered. At last the tortured one slipped into unconsciousness. An instant later John Ware was moving swiftly through the night sky. At his side was the black being.

It had been terrible. Ware had endured agony that he had not believed the human body was capable of suffering. Why? Why had he been chained to the consciousness of the man on the torture table? Swiftly Ware and his companion soared through the night moving ever westward.

John Ware felt himself descending again. He caught a fleeting glimpse of a lonely farm house, with a single lamp glowing in one window. Then he was in an old fashioned country living room. In a wheel chair an aged man sat dozing. At his side, near the window, stood a table on which burned an oil lamp. A dark shape hovered over the sleeping man. Shuddering in his slumber, the man flung out one arm, restlessly. It struck the oil lamp, sending it crashing to the floor, where it shattered and a pool of flame sprang up instantly. The aged cripple awoke with a cry, and made an effort to wheel his chair from the flames. But it was too late. Already the carpet and floor were burning and now the man's clothing and the robe that covered his legs were afire. Instinctively the victim threw up his arms to shield his face. Then he screamed piercingly, again and again. John Ware felt everything that the old man felt. He suffered the inexpressible agony of being consumed alive by flames. Then he was outside in the night. Far below and behind him the house burned like a torch in the distance. Ware glanced fearfully at the shadow that accompanied him as they sped on at tremendous speed, ever westward.

Once again Ware felt himself hurtling down through the night. Where to this time? What unspeakable torment was he to endure now? All was dark about him. He glimpsed no city or abode as he flashed to earth. About him was only silence and darkness. Then like a wave engulfing his spirit, came a torrent of fear and dread. He was striving to push something upward. Panic thoughts consumed him. He would not die—he wanted to live—he would escape! He writhed and twisted in his narrow confines, his fists beating on the surface above him. It did not yield. John Ware knew that he was linked with the consciousness of a man who had been prematurely buried. Soon the victim's fists were dripping with blood as he ineffectually clawed and pounded at the lid of the coffin. As time is measured it didn't last long. The exertions of the doomed man caused him quickly to exhaust the small amount of air in the coffin and he soon smothered to death. John Ware experienced that, too. But the final obliteration and crushing of the hope that burned in the man's bosom probably was the worst of all.

Ware was again soaring through the night. His soul shuddered as he grasped the final, unmistakable significance of the night's experiences. *He, he* was to be the victim, the sufferer, throughout this long hour of midnight.

He had thought that by accompanying the dark being around the earth, he would share in the savoring of all the evils that flourish in the midnight hour. He *was* participating—but not as he had expected. Instead, *he* was the victim, the, cringing, tormented one. Perhaps this dark being he had summoned was jealous of its pleasures, or perhaps it derived an additional intensity of satisfaction by adding John Ware's consciousness to those of its victims.

Ware was descending again. There was no resisting the force that flung him earthward.

He was completely helpless before the power he had summoned. What now? What new terror would he experience?

On and on, ever westward through the night, John Ware endured horror after horror. He died again and again, each time in a more fearsome manner. He was subjected to revolting tortures and torments as he was linked with victim after victim. He knew the frightening nightmare of human minds tottering on the abyss of madness. All that is black and unholy and is visited upon mankind he experienced as he roamed the earth with the midnight being.

Would it never end? Only the thought that these sixty minutes must pass sustained him. But it did not end. It seemed an eternity had gone by. Such suffering could not be crowded into a single hour. It must be days since he had left his body.

Days, nights, sixty minutes, one hour? John Ware was struck with a realization of terrific impact. It seemed to be communicated to him from the dark being at his side. Horribly clear did that being make the simple truth. John Ware was lost. Weeks, even months, might have passed since he had left his body. Time, for him, had stopped still.

John Ware was eternally chained to the amorphous black shape, and was doomed to exist thus horribly forever, suffering endless and revolting madness, torture and death through eternity. He had stepped into that band of time known as midnight, and was caught, trapped hopelessly—doomed to move with the grain of time endlessly around the earth.

For as long as the earth spins beneath the sun, one side of it is always dark and in the darkness midnight dwells forever.

1946

JOHN CHEEVER

(1912–1982)

Torch Song

AFTER Jack Lorey had known Joan Harris in New York for a few years, he began to think of her as the Widow. She always wore black, and he was always given the feeling, by a curious disorder in her apartment, that the undertakers had just left. This impression did not stem from malice on his part, for he was fond of Joan. They came from the same city in Ohio and had reached New York at about the same time in the middle thirties. They were the same age, and during their first summer in the city they used to meet after work and drink Martinis in places like the Brevoort and Charles', and have dinner and play checkers at the Lafayette.

Joan went to a school for models when she settled in the city, but it turned out that she photographed badly, so after spending six weeks learning how to walk with a book on her head she got a job as a hostess in a Longchamps. For the rest of the summer she stood by the hatrack, bathed in an intense pink light and the string music of heartbreak, swinging her mane of dark hair and her black skirt as she moved forward to greet the customers. She was then a big, handsome girl with a wonderful voice, and her face, her whole presence, always seemed infused with a gentle and healthy pleasure at her surroundings, whatever they were. She was innocently and incorrigibly convivial, and would get out of bed and dress at three in the morning if someone called her and asked her to come out for a drink, as Jack often did. In the fall, she got some kind of freshman executive job in a department store. They saw less and less of each other and then for quite a while stopped seeing each other altogether. Jack was living with a girl he had met at a party, and it never occurred to him to wonder what had become of Joan.

Jack's girl had some friends in Pennsylvania, and in the spring and summer of his second year in town he often went there with her for weekends. All of this—the shared apartment in the Village, the illicit relationship, the Friday-night train to a country house—was what he had imagined life in New York to be, and he was intensely happy. He was returning to New York with his girl one Sunday night on the Lehigh line. It was one of those trains that move slowly across the face of New Jersey, bringing back to the city hundreds of people, like the victims of an immense and strenuous picnic, whose faces are blazing and whose muscles are lame. Jack and his girl, like most of the other passengers, were overburdened with vegetables and flowers. When the train stopped in Pennsylvania Station, they moved with the crowd along the platform, toward the escalator. As they were passing the wide, lighted windows of the diner, Jack turned his head and saw Joan. It was the first time he had seen her since Thanksgiving, or since Christmas. He couldn't remember.

Joan was with a man who had obviously passed out. His head was in his arms on the table, and an overturned highball glass was near one of his elbows. Joan was shaking his shoulders gently and speaking to him. She seemed to be vaguely troubled, vaguely amused. The waiters had cleared off all the other tables and were standing around Joan, waiting for her to resurrect her escort. It troubled Jack to see in these straits a girl who reminded him of the trees and the lawns of his home town, but there was nothing he could do to help. Joan continued to shake the man's shoulders, and the crowd pressed Jack past one after another of the diner's windows, past the malodorous kitchen, and up the escalator.

He saw Joan again, later that summer, when he was having dinner in a Village restaurant. He was with a new girl, a Southerner. There were many Southern girls in the city that year. Jack and his belle had wandered into the restaurant because it was convenient, but the food was terrible and the place was lighted with candles. Halfway through dinner, Jack noticed Joan on the other side of the room, and when he had finished eating, he crossed the room and spoke to her. She was with a tall man who was wearing a monocle. He stood, bowed stiffly from the waist, and said to Jack, "We are very pleased to meet you." Then he excused himself and headed for the toilet. "He's a count, he's a Swedish count," Joan said. "He's on the radio, Friday afternoons at four-fifteen. Isn't it exciting?" She seemed to be delighted with the count and the terrible restaurant.

Sometime the next winter, Jack moved from the Village to an apartment in the East Thirties. He was crossing Park Avenue one cold morning on his way to the office when he noticed, in the crowd, a woman he had met a few times at Joan's apartment. He spoke to her and asked about his friend. "Haven't you heard?" she said. She pulled a long face. "Perhaps I'd better tell you. Perhaps you can help." She and Jack had breakfast in a drugstore on Madison Avenue and she unburdened herself of the story.

The count had a program called "The Song of the Fiords," or something like that, and he sang Swedish folk songs. Everyone suspected him of being a fake, but that didn't bother Joan. He had met her at a party and, sensing a soft touch, had moved in with her the following night. About a week later, he complained of pains in his back and said he must have some morphine. Then he needed morphine all the time. If he didn't get morphine, he was abusive and violent. Joan began to deal with those doctors and druggists who peddle dope, and when they wouldn't supply her, she went down to the bottom of the city. Her friends were afraid she would be found some morning stuffed in a drain. She got pregnant. She had an abortion. The count left her and moved to a flea bag near Times Square, but she was so impressed by then with his helplessness, so afraid that he would die without her, that she followed him there and shared his room and continued to buy his narcotics. He abandoned her again, and Joan waited a week for him to return before she went back to her place and her friends in the Village.

It shocked Jack to think of the innocent girl from Ohio having lived with a brutal dope addict and traded with criminals, and when he got to his office that morning, he telephoned her and made a date for dinner that night. He met her at Charles'. When she came into the bar, she seemed as wholesome and calm as ever. Her voice was sweet, and reminded him of elms, of lawns, of those glass arrangements that used to be hung from porch ceilings to tinkle in the summer wind. She told him about the count. She spoke of him charitably and with no trace of bitterness, as if her voice, her disposition, were incapable of registering anything beyond simple affection and pleasure. Her walk, when she moved ahead of him toward their table, was light and graceful. She ate a large dinner and talked enthusiastically about her job. They went to a movie and said goodbye in front of her apartment house.

That winter, Jack met a girl he decided to marry. Their engagement was announced in January and they planned to marry in July. In the spring, he received, in his office mail, an invitation to cocktails at Joan's. It was for a Saturday when his fiancée was going to Massachusetts to visit her parents, and when the time came and he had nothing better to do, he took a bus to the Village. Joan had the same apartment. It was a walk-up. You rang the bell above the mailbox in the vestibule and were answered with a death rattle in the lock. Joan lived on the third floor. Her calling card was in a slot in the mailbox, and above her name was written the name Hugh Bascomb.

Jack climbed the two flights of carpeted stairs, and when he reached Joan's apartment, she was standing by the open door in a black dress. After she greeted Jack, she took his arm and guided him across the room. "I want you to meet Hugh, Jack," she said.

Hugh was a big man with a red face and pale-blue eyes. His manner was courtly and his eyes were inflamed with drink. Jack talked with him for a little while and then went over to speak to someone he knew, who was standing by the mantelpiece. He noticed then, for the first time, the indescribable disorder of Joan's apartment. The books were in their shelves and the furniture was reasonably good, but the place was all wrong, somehow. It was as if things had been put in place without thought or real interest, and for the first time, too, he had the impression that there had been a death there recently.

As Jack moved around the room, he felt that he had met the ten or twelve guests at other parties. There was a woman executive with a fancy hat, a man who could imitate Roosevelt, a grim couple whose play was in rehearsal, and a newspaperman who kept turning on the radio for news of the Spanish Civil War. Jack drank Martinis and talked with the woman in the fancy hat. He looked out of the window at the back yards and the ailanthus trees and heard, in the distance, thunder exploding off the cliffs of the Hudson.

Hugh Bascomb got very drunk. He began to spill liquor, as if drinking, for him, were a kind of jolly slaughter and he enjoyed the bloodshed and the mess. He spilled whiskey from a bottle. He spilled a drink on his shirt and then tipped over someone else's drink. The party was not quiet, but Hugh's hoarse voice began to dominate the others. He attacked a photographer who was sitting in a corner explaining camera techniques to a homely woman. "What did you come to the party for if all you wanted to do was to sit there and stare at your shoes?" Hugh shouted. "What did you come for? Why don't you stay at home?"

The photographer didn't know what to say. He was not staring at his shoes. Joan moved lightly to Hugh's side. "Please don't get into a fight now, darling," she said. "Not this afternoon."

"Shut up," he said. "Let me alone. Mind your own business." He lost his balance, and in struggling to steady himself he tipped over a lamp.

"Oh, your lovely lamp, Joan," a woman sighed.

"Lamps!" Hugh roared. He threw his arms into the air and worked them around his head as if he were bludgeoning himself. "Lamps. Glasses. Cigarette boxes. Dishes. They're killing me. They're killing me, for Christ's sake. Let's all go up to the mountains and hunt and fish and live like men, for Christ's sake."

People were scattering as if a rain had begun to fall in the room. It had, as a matter of fact, begun to rain outside. Someone offered Jack a ride uptown, and he jumped at the chance. Joan stood at the door, saying goodbye to her routed friends. Her voice remained soft, and her manner, unlike that of those Christian women who in the face of disaster can summon new and formidable sources of composure, seemed genuinely simple. She appeared to be oblivious of the raging drunk at her back, who was pacing up and down, grinding glass into the rug, and haranguing one of the survivors of the party with a story of how he, Hugh, had once gone without food for three weeks.

*

In July, Jack was married in an orchard in Duxbury, and he and his wife went to West Chop for a few weeks. When they returned to town, their apartment was cluttered with presents, including a dozen after-dinner coffee cups from Joan. His wife sent her the required note, but they did nothing else.

Late in the summer, Joan telephoned Jack at his office and asked if he wouldn't bring his wife to see her; she named an evening the following week. He felt guilty about not having called her, and accepted the invitation. This made his wife angry. She was an ambitious girl who liked a social life that offered rewards, and she went unwillingly to Joan's Village apartment with him.

Written above Joan's name on the mailbox was the name Franz Denzel. Jack and his wife climbed the stairs and were met by Joan at the open door. They went into her apartment and found themselves among a group of people for whom Jack, at least, was unable to find any bearings.

Franz Denzel was a middle-aged German. His face was pinched with bitterness or illness. He greeted Jack and his wife with that elaborate and clever politeness that is intended to make guests feel that they have come too early or too late. He insisted sharply upon Jack's sitting in the chair in which he himself had been sitting, and then went and sat on a radiator. There were five other Germans sitting around the room, drinking coffee. In a corner was another American couple, who looked uncomfortable. Joan passed Jack and his wife small cups of coffee with whipped cream. "These cups belonged to Franz's mother," she said. "Aren't they lovely? They were the only things he took from Germany when he escaped from the Nazis."

Franz turned to Jack and said, "Perhaps you will give us your opinion on the American educational system. That is what we were discussing when you arrived."

Before Jack could speak, one of the German guests opened an attack on the American educational system. The other Germans joined in, and went on from there to describe every vulgarity that had impressed them in American life and to contrast German and American culture generally. Where, they asked one another passionately, could you find in America anything like the Mitropa dining cars, the Black Forest, the pictures in Munich, the music in Bayreuth? Franz and his friends began speaking in German. Neither Jack nor his wife nor Joan could understand German, and the other American couple had not opened their mouths since they were introduced. Joan went happily around the room, filling everyone's cup with coffee, as if the music of a foreign language were enough to make an evening for her.

Jack drank five cups of coffee. He was desperately uncomfortable. Joan went into the kitchen while the Germans were laughing at their German jokes, and he hoped she would return with some drinks, but when she came back, it was with a tray of ice cream and mulberries.

"Isn't this pleasant?" Franz asked, speaking in English again.

Joan collected the coffee cups, and as she was about to take them back to the kitchen, Franz stopped her.

"Isn't one of those cups chipped?"

"No, darling," Joan said. "I never let the maid touch them. I wash them myself."

"What's that?" he asked, pointing at the rim of one of the cups.

"That's the cup that's always been chipped, darling. It was chipped when you unpacked it. You noticed it then."

"These things were perfect when they arrived in this country," he said.

Joan went into the kitchen and he followed her.

Jack tried to make conversation with the Germans. From the kitchen there was the sound of a blow and a cry. Franz returned and began to eat his mulberries greedily. Joan came back with her dish of ice cream. Her voice was gentle. Her tears, if she had been crying, had dried as quickly as the tears of a child. Jack and his wife finished their ice cream and made their escape. The wasted and unnerving evening enraged Jack's wife, and he supposed that he would never see Joan again.

Jack's wife got pregnant early in the fall, and she seized on all the prerogatives of an expectant mother. She took long naps, ate canned peaches in the middle of the night, and talked about the rudimentary kidney. She chose to see only other couples who were expecting children, and the parties that she and Jack gave were temperate. The baby, a boy, was born in May, and Jack was very proud and happy. The first party he

and his wife went to after her convalescence was the wedding
of a girl whose family Jack had known in Ohio.

The wedding was at St. James's, and afterward there was a
big reception at the River Club. There was an orchestra dressed
like Hungarians, and a lot of champagne and Scotch. Toward
the end of the afternoon, Jack was walking down a dim corridor when he heard Joan's voice. "Please don't, darling," she
was saying. "You'll break my arm. *Please* don't, darling."
She was being pressed against the wall by a man who seemed
to be twisting her arm. As soon as they saw Jack, the struggle
stopped. All three of them were intensely embarrassed. Joan's
face was wet and she made an effort to smile through her tears
at Jack. He said hello and went on without stopping. When he
returned, she and the man had disappeared.

When Jack's son was less than two years old, his wife flew with
the baby to Nevada to get a divorce. Jack gave her the apartment and all its furnishings and took a room in a hotel near
Grand Central. His wife got her decree in due course, and the
story was in the newspapers. Jack had a telephone call from
Joan a few days later.

"I'm awfully sorry to hear about your divorce, Jack," she
said. "She seemed like *such* a nice girl. But that wasn't what I
called you about. I want your help, and I wondered if you
could come down to my place tonight around six. It's something I don't want to talk about over the phone."

He went obediently to the Village that night and climbed
the stairs. Her apartment was a mess. The pictures and the curtains were down and the books were in boxes. "You moving,
Joan?" he asked.

"That's what I wanted to see you about, Jack. First, I'll give
you a drink." She made two Old-Fashioneds. "I'm being
evicted, Jack," she said. "I'm being evicted because I'm an immoral woman. The couple who have the apartment downstairs
—they're charming people, I've always thought—have told
the real-estate agent that I'm a drunk and a prostitute and all
kinds of things. Isn't that fantastic? This real-estate agent has
always been so nice to me that I didn't think he'd believe them,
but he's canceled my lease, and if I make any trouble, he's
threatened to take the matter up with the store, and I don't

want to lose my job. This nice real-estate agent won't even talk with me any more. When I go over to the office, the receptionist leers at me as if I were some kind of dreadful woman. Of course, there have been a lot of men here and we sometimes are noisy, but I can't be expected to go to bed at ten every night. Can I? Well, the agent who manages this building has apparently told all the other agents in the neighborhood that I'm an immoral and drunken woman, and none of them will give me an apartment. I went in to talk with one man—he seemed to be such a nice old gentleman—and he made me an indecent proposal. Isn't it fantastic? I have to be out of here on Thursday and I'm literally being turned out into the street."

Joan seemed as serene and innocent as ever while she described this scourge of agents and neighbors. Jack listened carefully for some sign of indignation or bitterness or even urgency in her recital, but there was none. He was reminded of a torch song, of one of those forlorn and touching ballads that had been sung neither for him nor for her but for their older brothers and sisters by Marion Harris. Joan seemed to be singing her wrongs.

"They've made my life miserable," she went on quietly. "If I keep the radio on after ten o'clock, they telephone the agent in the morning and tell him I had some kind of orgy here. One night when Philip—I don't think you've met Philip; he's in the Royal Air Force; he's gone back to England—one night when Philip and some other people were here, they called the police. The police came bursting in the door and talked to me as if I were I don't know what and then looked in the bedroom. If they think there's a man up here after midnight, they call me on the telephone and say all kinds of disgusting things. Of course, I can put my furniture into storage and go to a hotel, I guess. I guess a hotel will take a woman with my kind of reputation, but I thought perhaps you might know of an apartment. I thought—"

It angered Jack to think of this big, splendid girl's being persecuted by her neighbors, and he said he would do what he could. He asked her to have dinner with him, but she said she was busy.

Having nothing better to do, Jack decided to walk uptown to his hotel. It was a hot night. The sky was overcast. On his way, he saw a parade in a dark side street off Broadway near Madison Square. All the buildings in the neighborhood were dark. It was so dark that he could not see the placards the marchers carried until he came to a street light. Their signs urged the entry of the United States into the war, and each platoon represented a nation that had been subjugated by the Axis powers. They marched up Broadway, as he watched, to no music, to no sound but their own steps on the rough cobbles. It was for the most part an army of elderly men and women—Poles, Norwegians, Danes, Jews, Chinese. A few idle people like himself lined the sidewalks, and the marchers passed between them with all the self-consciousness of enemy prisoners. There were children among them dressed in the costumes in which they had, for the newsreels, presented the Mayor with a package of tea, a petition, a protest, a constitution, a check, or a pair of tickets. They hobbled through the darkness of the loft neighborhood like a mortified and destroyed people, toward Greeley Square.

In the morning, Jack put the problem of finding an apartment for Joan up to his secretary. She started phoning real-estate agents, and by afternoon she had found a couple of available apartments in the West Twenties. Joan called Jack the next day to say that she had taken one of the apartments and to thank him.

Jack didn't see Joan again until the following summer. It was a Sunday evening; he had left a cocktail party in a Washington Square apartment and had decided to walk a few blocks up Fifth Avenue before he took a bus. As he was passing the Brevoort, Joan called to him. She was with a man at one of the tables on the sidewalk. She looked cool and fresh, and the man appeared to be respectable. His name, it turned out, was Pete Bristol. He invited Jack to sit down and join in a celebration. Germany had invaded Russia that weekend, and Joan and Pete were drinking champagne to celebrate Russia's changed position in the war. The three of them drank champagne until it got dark. They had dinner and drank champagne with their dinner. They drank more champagne afterward and then went over to the Lafayette and then to two or three other places. Joan had always been tireless in her gentle way. She hated to see the night end, and it was after three o'clock when Jack stumbled into his apartment. The following morning he woke up haggard and sick, and with no recollection of the last hour or so of the previous evening. His suit was soiled and he had lost his hat. He didn't get to his office until eleven. Joan had already called him twice, and she called him again soon after he got in. There was no hoarseness at all in her voice. She said that she had to see him, and he agreed to meet her for lunch in a seafood restaurant in the Fifties.

He was standing at the bar when she breezed in, looking as though she had taken no part in that calamitous night. The advice she wanted concerned selling her jewelry. Her grandmother had left her some jewelry, and she wanted to raise money on it but didn't know where to go. She took some rings and bracelets out of her purse and showed them to Jack. He said that he didn't know anything about jewelry but that he could lend her some money. "Oh, I couldn't borrow money from you, Jack," she said. "You see, I want to get the money for Pete. I want to help him. He wants to open an advertising agency, and he needs quite a lot to begin with." Jack didn't press her to accept his offer of a loan after that, and the project wasn't mentioned again during lunch.

He next heard about Joan from a young doctor who was a friend of theirs. "Have you seen Joan recently?" the doctor asked Jack one evening when they were having dinner together. He said no. "I gave her a checkup last week," the doctor said, "and while she's been through enough to kill the average mortal—and you'll never know what she's been through—she still has the constitution of a virtuous and healthy woman. Did you hear about the last one? She sold her jewelry to put him into some kind of business, and as soon as he got the money, he left her for another girl, who had a car—a convertible."

Jack was drafted into the Army in the spring of 1942. He was kept at Fort Dix for nearly a month, and during this time he came to New York in the evening whenever he could get permission. Those nights had for him the intense keenness of a reprieve, a sensation that was heightened by the fact that on the train in from Trenton women would often press upon him dog-eared copies of *Life* and half-eaten boxes of candy, as though the brown clothes he wore were surely cerements. He telephoned Joan from Pennsylvania Station one night. "Come right over, Jack," she said. "Come right over. I want you to meet Ralph."

She was living in that place in the West Twenties that Jack had found for her. The neighborhood was a slum. Ash cans stood in front of her house, and an old woman was there picking out bits of refuse and garbage and stuffing them into a perambulator. The house in which Joan's apartment was located was shabby, but the apartment itself seemed familiar. The furniture was the same. Joan was the same big, easygoing girl. "I'm so glad you called me," she said. "It's so good to see you. I'll make you a drink. I was having one myself. Ralph ought to be here by now. He promised to take me to dinner." Jack offered to take her to Cavanagh's, but she said that Ralph might come while she was out. "If he doesn't come by nine, I'm going to make myself a sandwich. I'm not really hungry."

Jack talked about the Army. She talked about the store. She had been working in the same place for—how long was it? He didn't know. He had never seen her at her desk and he couldn't imagine what she did. "I'm terribly sorry Ralph isn't here," she said. "I'm sure you'd like him. He's not a young man. He's a heart specialist who loves to play the viola." She turned on some lights, for the summer sky had got dark. "He has this dreadful wife on Riverside Drive and four ungrateful children. He—"

The noise of an air-raid siren, lugubrious and seeming to spring from pain, as if all the misery and indecision in the city had been given a voice, cut her off. Other sirens, in distant neighborhoods, sounded, until the dark air was full of their noise. "Let me fix you another drink before I have to turn out the lights," Joan said, and took his glass. She brought the drink back to him and snapped off the lights. They went to the windows, and, as children watch a thunderstorm, they watched the city darken. All the lights nearby went out but one. Air-raid wardens had begun to sound their whistles in the street. From a distant yard came a hoarse shriek of anger. "Put out your lights, you Fascists!" a woman screamed. "Put out your lights, you Nazi Fascist Germans. Turn out your lights. Turn out your lights." The last light went off. They went away from the window and sat in the lightless room.

In the darkness, Joan began to talk about her departed lovers, and from what she said Jack gathered that they had all had a hard time. Nils, the suspect count, was dead. Hugh Bascomb, the drunk, had joined the Merchant Marine and was missing in the North Atlantic. Franz, the German, had taken poison the night the Nazis bombed Warsaw. "We listened to the news on the radio," Joan said, "and then he went back to his hotel and took poison. The maid found him dead in the bathroom the next morning." When Jack asked her about the one who was going to open an advertising agency, she seemed at first to have forgotten him. "Oh, Pete," she said after a pause. "Well, he was always very sick, you know. He was supposed to go to Saranac, but he kept putting it off and putting it off and—" She stopped talking when she heard steps on the stairs, hoping, he supposed, that it was Ralph, but whoever it was turned at the landing and continued to the top of the house. "I wish Ralph would come," she said, with a sigh. "I want you to meet him." Jack asked her again to go out, but she refused, and when the all-clear sounded, he said goodbye.

Jack was shipped from Dix to an infantry training camp in the Carolinas and from there to an infantry division stationed in Georgia. He had been in Georgia three months when he married a girl from the Augusta boarding-house aristocracy. A year or so later, he crossed the continent in a day coach and thought sententiously that the last he might see of the country he loved was the desert towns like Barstow, that the last he might hear of it was the ringing of the trolleys on the Bay Bridge. He was sent into the Pacific and returned to the United States twenty months later, uninjured and apparently unchanged. As soon as he received his furlough, he went to Augusta. He presented his wife with the souvenirs he had brought from the islands, quarreled violently with her and all her family, and, after making arrangements for her to get an Arkansas divorce, left for New York.

Jack was discharged from the Army at a camp in the East a few months later. He took a vacation and then went back to the job he had left in 1942. He seemed to have picked up his life at approximately the moment when it had been interrupted by the war. In time, everything came to look and feel the same. He saw most of his old friends. Only two of the men he knew had been killed in the war. He didn't call Joan, but he met her one winter afternoon on a crosstown bus.

Her fresh face, her black clothes, and her soft voice instantly destroyed the sense—if he had ever had such a sense—that anything had changed or intervened since their last meeting, three or four years ago. She asked him up for cocktails and he went to her apartment the next Saturday afternoon. Her room and her guests reminded him of the parties she had given when she had first come to New York. There was a woman with a fancy hat, an elderly doctor, and a man who stayed close to the radio, listening for news from the Balkans. Jack wondered which of the men belonged to Joan and decided on an Englishman who kept coughing into a handkerchief that he pulled out of his sleeve. Jack was right. "Isn't Stephen brilliant?" Joan asked him a little later, when they were alone in a corner. "He knows more about the Polynesians than anyone else in the world."

Jack had returned not only to his old job but to his old salary. Since living costs had doubled and since he was paying alimony to two wives, he had to draw on his savings. He took another job, which promised more money, but it didn't last long and he found himself out of work. This didn't bother him at all. He still had money in the bank, and anyhow it was easy to borrow from friends. His indifference was the consequence not of lassitude or despair but rather of an excess of hope. He had the feeling that he had only recently come to New York from Ohio. The sense that he was very young and that the best years of his life still lay before him was an illusion that he could not seem to escape. There was all the time in the world. He was living in hotels then, moving from one to another every five days.

In the spring, Jack moved to a furnished room in the badlands west of Central Park. He was running out of money. Then, when he began to feel that a job was a desperate necessity, he got sick. At first, he seemed to have only a bad cold, but he was unable to shake it and he began to run a fever and to cough blood. The fever kept him drowsy most of the time, but he roused himself occasionally and went out to a cafeteria for a meal. He felt sure that none of his friends knew where he was, and he was glad of this. He hadn't counted on Joan.

Late one morning, he heard her speaking in the hall with his landlady. A few moments later, she knocked on his door. He was lying on the bed in a pair of pants and a soiled pajama top, and he didn't answer. She knocked again and walked in. "I've been looking everywhere for you, Jack," she said. She spoke softly. "When I found out that you were in a place like this I thought you must be broke or sick. I stopped at the bank and got some money, in case you're broke. I've brought you some Scotch. I thought a little drink wouldn't do you any harm. Want a little drink?"

Joan's dress was black. Her voice was low and serene. She sat in a chair beside his bed as if she had been coming there every day to nurse him. Her features had coarsened, he thought, but there were still very few lines in her face. She was heavier. She was nearly fat. She was wearing black cotton gloves. She got two glasses and poured Scotch into them. He drank his whiskey greedily. "I didn't get to bed until three last night," she said. Her voice had once before reminded him of a gentle and despairing song, but now, perhaps because he was sick, her mildness, the mourning she wore, her stealthy grace, made him uneasy. "It was one of those nights," she said. "We went to the theatre. Afterward, someone asked us up to his place. I don't know who he was. It was one of those places. They're so strange. There were some meat-eating plants and a collection of Chinese snuff bottles. Why do people collect Chinese snuff bottles? We all autographed a lampshade, as I remember, but I can't remember much."

Jack tried to sit up in bed, as if there were some need to defend himself, and then fell back again, against the pillows. "How did you find me, Joan?" he asked.

"It was simple," she said. "I called that hotel. The one you were staying in. They gave me this address. My secretary got the telephone number. Have another little drink."

"You know, you've never come to a place of mine before— never," he said. "Why did you come now?"

"Why did I come, darling?" she asked. "What a question! I've known you for thirty years. You're the oldest friend I have in New York. Remember that night in the Village when it snowed and we stayed up until morning and drank whiskey sours for breakfast? That doesn't seem like twelve years ago. And that night—"

"I don't like to have you see me in a place like this," he said earnestly. He touched his face and felt his beard.

"And all the people who used to imitate Roosevelt," she said, as if she had not heard him, as if she were deaf. "And that place on Staten Island where we all used to go for dinner when Henry had a car. Poor Henry. He bought a place in Connecticut and went out there by himself one weekend. He fell asleep with a lighted cigarette and the house, the barn, everything burned. Ethel took the children out to California." She poured more Scotch into his glass and handed it to him. She lighted a cigarette and put it between his lips. The intimacy of this gesture, which made it seem not only as if he were deathly ill but as if he were her lover, troubled him.

"As soon as I'm better," he said, "I'll take a room at a good hotel. I'll call you then. It was nice of you to come."

"Oh, don't be ashamed of this room, Jack," she said. "Rooms never bother me. It doesn't seem to matter to me where I am. Stanley had a filthy room in Chelsea. At least, other people told me it was filthy. I never noticed it. Rats used to eat the food I brought him. He used to have to hang the food from the ceiling, from the light chain."

"I'll call you as soon as I'm better," Jack said. "I think I can sleep now if I'm left alone. I seem to need a lot of sleep."

"You really *are* sick, darling," she said. "You must have a fever." She sat on the edge of his bed and put a hand on his forehead.

"How is that Englishman, Joan?" he asked. "Do you still see him?"

"What Englishman?" she said.

"You know. I met him at your house. He kept a handkerchief up his sleeve. He coughed all the time. You know the one I mean."

"You must be thinking of someone else," she said. "I haven't had an Englishman at my place since the war. Of course, I can't remember everyone." She turned and, taking one of his hands, linked her fingers in his.

"He's dead, isn't he?" Jack said. "That Englishman's dead." He pushed her off the bed, and got up himself. "Get out," he said.

"You're sick, darling," she said. "I can't leave you alone here."

"Get out," he said again, and when she didn't move, he

shouted, "What kind of an obscenity are you that you can smell sickness and death the way you do?"

"You poor darling."

"Does it make you feel young to watch the dying?" he shouted. "Is that the lewdness that keeps you young? Is that why you dress like a crow? Oh, I know there's nothing I can say that will hurt you. I know there's nothing filthy or corrupt or depraved or brutish or base that the others haven't tried, but this time you're wrong. I'm not ready. My life isn't ending. My life's beginning. There are wonderful years ahead of me. There are, there are wonderful, wonderful, wonderful years ahead of me, and when they're over, when it's time, then I'll call you. Then, as an old friend, I'll call you and give you whatever dirty pleasure you take in watching the dying, but until then, you and your ugly and misshapen forms will leave me alone."

She finished her drink and looked at her watch. "I guess I'd better show up at the office," she said. "I'll see you later. I'll come back tonight. You'll feel better then, you poor darling." She closed the door after her, and he heard her light step on the stairs.

Jack emptied the whiskey bottle into the sink. He began to dress. He stuffed his dirty clothes into a bag. He was trembling and crying with sickness and fear. He could see the blue sky from his window, and in his fear it seemed miraculous that the sky should be blue, that the white clouds should remind him of snow, that from the sidewalk he could hear the shrill voices of children shrieking, "I'm the king of the mountain, I'm the king of the mountain, I'm the king of the mountain." He emptied the ashtray containing his nail parings and cigarette butts into the toilet, and swept the floor with a shirt, so that there would be no trace of his life, of his body, when that lewd and searching shape of death came there to find him in the evening.

1947

SHIRLEY JACKSON

(1916–1965)

The Daemon Lover

She had not slept well; from one-thirty, when Jamie left and she went lingeringly to bed, until seven, when she at last allowed herself to get up and make coffee, she had slept fitfully, stirring awake to open her eyes and look into the half-darkness, remembering over and over, slipping again into a feverish dream. She spent almost an hour over her coffee—they were to have a real breakfast on the way—and then, unless she wanted to dress early, had nothing to do. She washed her coffee cup and made the bed, looking carefully over the clothes she planned to wear, worried unnecessarily, at the window, over whether it would be a fine day. She sat down to read, thought that she might write a letter to her sister instead, and began, in her finest handwriting, "Dearest Anne, by the time you get this I will be married. Doesn't it sound funny? I can hardly believe it myself, but when I tell you how it happened, you'll see it's even stranger than that. . . ."

Sitting, pen in hand, she hesitated over what to say next, read the lines already written, and tore up the letter. She went to the window and saw that it was undeniably a fine day. It occurred to her that perhaps she ought not to wear the blue silk dress; it was too plain, almost severe, and she wanted to be soft, feminine. Anxiously she pulled through the dresses in the closet, and hesitated over a print she had worn the summer before; it was too young for her, and it had a ruffled neck, and it was very early in the year for a print dress, but still. . . .

She hung the two dresses side by side on the outside of the closet door and opened the glass doors carefully closed upon the small closet that was her kitchenette. She turned on the burner under the coffeepot, and went to the window; it was sunny. When the coffeepot began to crackle she came back and poured herself coffee, into a clean cup. I'll have a headache if I don't get some solid food soon, she thought, all this coffee, smoking too much, no real breakfast. A headache on her wedding day; she went and got the tin box of aspirin from the bathroom closet and slipped it into her blue pocketbook. She'd have to change to a brown pocketbook if she wore the print dress, and the only brown pocketbook she had was shabby. Helplessly, she stood looking from the blue pocketbook to the print dress, and then put the pocketbook down and went and got her coffee and sat down near the window, drinking her coffee, and looking carefully around the one-room apartment. They planned to come back here tonight and everything must be correct. With sudden horror she realized that she had forgotten to put clean sheets on the bed; the laundry was freshly back and she took clean sheets and pillow cases from the top shelf of the closet and stripped the bed, working quickly to avoid thinking consciously of why the was changing the sheets. The bed was a studio bed, with a cover to make it look like a couch, and when it was finished no one would have known she had just put clean sheets on it. She took the old sheets and pillow cases into the bathroom and stuffed them down into the hamper, and put the bathroom towels in the hamper too, and clean towels on the bathroom racks. Her coffee was cold when she came back to it, but she drank it anyway.

When she looked at the clock, finally, and saw that it was after nine, she began at last to hurry. She took a bath, and used one of the clean towels, which she put into the hamper and replaced with a clean one. She dressed carefully, all her underwear fresh and most of it new; she put everything she had worn the day before, including her nightgown, into the hamper. When she was ready for her dress, she hesitated before the closet door. The blue dress was certainly decent, and clean, and fairly becoming, but she had worn it several times with Jamie, and there was nothing about it which made it special for a wedding day. The print dress was overly pretty, and new to Jamie, and yet wearing such a print this early in the year was certainly rushing the season. Finally she thought, This is my wedding day, I can dress as I please, and she took the print dress down from the hanger. When she slipped it on over her head it felt fresh and light, but when she looked at herself in the mirror she remembered that the ruffles around the neck did not show her throat to any great advantage, and the wide swinging skirt looked irresistibly made for a girl, for someone who would run freely, dance, swing it with her hips when she walked. Looking at herself in the mirror she thought with revulsion, It's as though I was trying to make myself look prettier than I am, just for him; he'll think I want to look younger because he's marrying me; and she tore the print dress off so quickly that a seam under the arm ripped. In the old blue dress she felt comfortable and familiar, but unexciting. It isn't what you're wearing that matters, she told herself firmly, and turned in dismay to the closet to see if there might be anything else. There was nothing even remotely suitable for her marrying Jamie, and for a minute she thought of going out quickly to some little shop nearby, to get a dress. Then she saw that it was close on ten, and she had no time for more than her hair and her makeup. Her hair was easy, pulled back into a knot at the nape of her neck, but her make-up was another delicate balance between looking as well as possible, and deceiving as little. She could not try to disguise the sallowness of her skin, or the lines around her eyes, today, when it might look as though she were only doing it for her wedding, and yet she could not bear the thought of Jamie's bringing to marriage anyone who looked haggard and lined. You're thirty-four years old after *all*, she told herself cruelly in the bathroom mirror. Thirty, it said on the license.

It was two minutes after ten; she was not satisfied with her clothes, her face, her apartment. She heated the coffee again and sat down in the chair by the window. Can't do anything more now, she thought, no sense trying to improve anything the last minute.

Reconciled, settled, she tried to think of Jamie and could not see his face clearly, or hear his voice. It's always that way with someone you love, she thought, and let her mind slip past today and tomorrow, into the farther future, when Jamie was established with his writing and she had given up her job, the golden house-in-the-country future they had been preparing for the last week. "I used to be a wonderful cook," she had promised Jamie, "with a little time and practice I could remember how to make angel-food cake. And fried chicken," she said, knowing how the words would stay in Jamie's mind, half-tenderly. "And Hollandaise sauce."

Ten-thirty. She stood up and went purposefully to the phone. She dialed, and waited, and the girl's metallic voice said, ". . . the time will be exactly ten-twenty-nine." Half-consciously she set her clock back a minute; she was remembering her own voice saying last night, in the doorway: "Ten o'clock then. I'll be ready. Is it really *true?*"

And Jamie laughing down the hallway.

By eleven o'clock she had sewed up the ripped seam in the print dress and put her sewing-box away carefully in the closet. With the print dress on, she was sitting by the window drinking another cup of coffee. I could have taken more time over my dressing after all, she thought; but by now it was so late he might come any minute, and she did not dare try to repair anything without starting all over. There was nothing to eat in the apartment except the food she had carefully stocked up for their life beginning together: the unopened package of bacon, the dozen eggs in their box, the unopened bread and the unopened butter; they were for breakfast tomorrow. She thought of running downstairs to the drugstore for something to eat, leaving a note on the door. Then she decided to wait a little longer.

By eleven-thirty she was so dizzy and weak that she had to go downstairs. If Jamie had had a phone she would have called him then. Instead, she opened her desk and wrote a note: "Jamie, have gone downstairs to the drugstore. Back in five minutes." Her pen leaked onto her fingers and she went into the bathroom and washed, using a clean towel which she replaced. She tacked the note on the door, surveyed the apartment once more to make sure that everything was perfect, and closed the door without locking it, in case he should come.

In the drugstore she found that there was nothing she wanted to eat except more coffee, and she left it half-finished because she suddenly realized that Jamie was probably upstairs waiting and impatient, anxious to get started.

But upstairs everything was prepared and quiet, as she had left it, her note unread on the door, the air in the apartment a little stale from too many cigarettes. She opened the window and sat down next to it until she realized that she had been asleep and it was twenty minutes to one.

Now, suddenly, she was frightened. Waking without prepa-

ration into the room of waiting and readiness, everything clean
and untouched since ten o'clock, she was frightened, and felt
an urgent need to hurry. She got up from the chair and almost
ran across the room to the bathroom, dashed cold water on
her face, and used a clean towel; this time she put the towel
carelessly back on the rack without changing it; time enough
for that later. Hatless, still in the print dress with a coat thrown
on over it, the wrong blue pocketbook with the aspirin inside
in her hand, she locked the apartment door behind her, no
note this time, and ran down the stairs. She caught a taxi on
the corner and gave the driver Jamie's address.

It was no distance at all; she could have walked it if she had
not been so weak, but in the taxi she suddenly realized how
imprudent it would be to drive brazenly up to Jamie's door,
demanding him. She asked the driver, therefore, to let her off
at a corner near Jamie's address and, after paying him, waited
till he drove away before she started to walk down the block.
She had never been here before; the building was pleasant and
old, and Jamie's name was not on any of the mailboxes in the
vestibule, nor on the doorbells. She checked the address; it was
right, and finally she rang the bell marked "Superintendent."
After a minute or two the door buzzer rang and she opened
the door and went into the dark hall where she hesitated until
a door at the end opened and someone said, "Yes?"

She knew at the same moment that she had no idea what to
ask, so she moved forward toward the figure waiting against
the light of the open doorway. When she was very near, the
figure said, "Yes?" again and she saw that it was a man in his
shirtsleeves, unable to see her any more clearly than she could
see him.

With sudden courage she said, "I'm trying to get in touch
with someone who lives in this building and I can't find the
name outside."

"What's the name you wanted?" the man asked, and she realized that she would have to answer.

"James Harris," she said. "Harris."

The man was silent for a minute and then he said, "Harris."
He turned around to the room inside the lighted doorway and
said, "Margie, come here a minute."

"What now?" a voice said from inside, and after a wait long

enough for someone to get out of a comfortable chair a woman joined him in the doorway, regarding the dark hall. "Lady here," the man said. "Lady looking for a guy name of Harris, lives here. Anyone in the building?"

"No," the woman said. Her voice sounded amused. "No men named Harris here."

"Sorry," the man said. He started to close the door. "You got the wrong house, lady," he said, and added in a lower voice, "or the wrong guy," and he and the woman laughed.

When the door was almost shut and she was alone in the dark hall she said to the thin lighted crack still showing, "But he *does* live here; I know it."

"Look," the woman said, opening the door again a little, "it happens all the time."

"Please don't make any mistake," she said, and her voice was very dignified, with thirty-four years of accumulated pride. "I'm afraid you don't understand."

"What did he look like?" the woman said wearily, the door still only part open.

"He's rather tall, and fair. He wears a blue suit very often. He's a writer."

"No," the woman said, and then, "Could he have lived on the third floor?"

"I'm not sure."

"There was a fellow," the woman said reflectively. "He wore a blue suit a lot, lived on the third floor for a while. The Roysters lent him their apartment while they were visiting her folks upstate."

"That might be it; I thought, though. . . ."

"This one wore a blue suit mostly, but I don't know how tall he was," the woman said. "He stayed there about a month."

"A month ago is when—"

"You ask the Roysters," the woman said. "They come back this morning. Apartment 3B."

The door closed, definitely. The hall was very dark and the stairs looked darker.

On the second floor there was a little light from a skylight far above. The apartment doors lined up, four on the floor, uncommunicative and silent. There was a bottle of milk outside 2C.

On the third floor, she waited for a minute. There was the

sound of music beyond the door of 3B, and she could hear voices. Finally she knocked, and knocked again. The door was opened and the music swept out at her, an early afternoon symphony broadcast. "How do you do," she said politely to this woman in the doorway. "Mrs. Royster?"

"That's right." The woman was wearing a housecoat and last night's make-up.

"I wonder if I might talk to you for a minute?"

"Sure," Mrs. Royster said, not moving.

"About Mr. Harris."

"*What* Mr. Harris?" Mrs. Royster said flatly.

"Mr. James Harris. The gentleman who borrowed your apartment."

"O Lord," Mrs. Royster said. She seemed to open her eyes for the first time. "What'd he do?"

"Nothing. I'm just trying to get in touch with him."

"O Lord," Mrs. Royster said again. Then she opened the door wider and said, "Come in," and then, "Ralph!"

Inside, the apartment was still full of music, and there were suitcases half-unpacked on the couch, on the chairs, on the floor. A table in the corner was spread with the remains of a meal, and the young man sitting there, for a minute resembling Jamie, got up and came across the room.

"What about it?" he said.

"Mr. Royster," she said. It was difficult to talk against the music. "The superintendent downstairs told me that this was where Mr. James Harris has been living."

"Sure," he said. "If that was his name."

"I thought you lent him the apartment," she said, surprised.

"*I* don't know anything about him," Mr. Royster said. "He's one of Dottie's friends."

"Not *my* friends," Mrs. Royster said. "No friend of mine." She had gone over to the table and was spreading peanut butter on a piece of bread. She took a bite and said thickly, waving the bread and peanut butter at her husband. "Not *my* friend."

"You picked him up at one of those damn meetings," Mr. Royster said. He shoved a suitcase off the chair next to the radio and sat down, picking up a magazine from the floor next to him. "I never said more'n ten words to him."

"You said it was okay to lend him the place," Mrs. Royster said before she took another bite. "You never said a word against him, after *all*."

"*I* don't say anything about *your* friends," Mr. Royster said.

"If he'd of been a friend of mine you would have said *plenty*, believe me," Mrs. Royster said darkly. She took another bite and said, "Believe me, he would have said *plenty*."

"That's all I want to hear," Mr. Royster said, over the top of the magazine. "No more, now."

"You see." Mrs. Royster pointed the bread and peanut butter at her husband. "That's the way it is, day and night."

There was silence except for the music bellowing out of the radio next to Mr. Royster, and then she said, in a voice she hardly trusted to be heard over the radio noise, "Has he gone, then?"

"Who?" Mrs. Royster demanded, looking up from the peanut butter jar.

"Mr. James Harris."

"Him? He must've left this morning, before we got back. No sign of him anywhere."

"Gone?"

"Everything was fine, though, perfectly fine. I told you," she said to Mr. Royster, "I told you he'd take care of everything fine. I can always tell."

"You were lucky," Mr. Royster said.

"Not a thing out of place," Mrs. Royster said. She waved her bread and peanut butter inclusively. "Everything just the way we left it," she said.

"Do you know where he is now?"

"Not the slightest idea," Mrs. Royster said cheerfully. "But, like I said, he left everything fine. Why?" she asked suddenly. "You looking for *him*?"

"It's very important."

"I'm sorry he's not here," Mrs. Royster said. She stepped forward politely when she saw her visitor turn toward the door.

"Maybe the super saw him," Mr. Royster said into the magazine.

When the door was closed behind her the hall was dark again, but the sound of the radio was deadened. She was halfway down the first flight of stairs when the door was opened and Mrs. Royster shouted down the stairwell, "If I see him I'll tell him you were looking for him."

What can I do? she thought, out on the street again. It was impossible to go home, not with Jamie somewhere between here and there. She stood on the sidewalk so long that a woman, leaning out of a window across the way, turned and called to someone inside to come and see. Finally, on an impulse, she went into the small delicatessen next door to the apartment house, on the side that led to her own apartment. There was a small man reading a newspaper, leaning against the counter; when she came in he looked up and came down inside the counter to meet her.

Over the glass case of cold meats and cheese she said, timidly, "I'm trying to get in touch with a man who lived in the apartment house next door, and I just wondered if you know him."

"Whyn't you ask the people there?" the man said, his eyes narrow, inspecting her.

It's because I'm not buying anything, she thought, and she said, "I'm sorry. I asked them, but they don't know anything about him. They think he left this morning."

"I don't know what you want *me* to do," he said, moving a little back toward his newspaper. "I'm not here to keep track of guys going in and out next door."

She said quickly, "I thought you might have noticed, that's all. He would have been coming past here, a little before ten o'clock. He was rather tall, and he usually wore a blue suit."

"Now how many men in blue suits go past here every day, lady?" the man demanded. "You think I got nothing to do but—"

"I'm sorry," she said. She heard him say, "For God's sake," as she went out the door.

As she walked toward the corner, she thought, he must have come this way, it's the way he'd go to get to my house, it's the only way for him to walk. She tried to think of Jamie: where would he have crossed the street? What sort of person was he actually—would he cross in front of his own apartment house, at random in the middle of the block, at the corner?

On the corner was a newsstand; they might have seen him

there. She hurried on and waited while a man bought a paper and a woman asked directions. When the newsstand man looked at her she said, "Can you possibly tell me if a rather tall young man in a blue suit went past here this morning around ten o'clock?" When the man only looked at her, his eyes wide and his mouth a little open, she thought, he thinks it's a joke, or a trick, and she said urgently, "It's very important, please believe me. I'm not teasing you."

"*Look*, lady," the man began, and she said eagerly, "He's a writer. He might have bought magazines here."

"What you want him for?" the man asked. He looked at her, smiling, and she realized that there was another man waiting in back of her and the newsdealer's smile included him. "Never mind," she said, but the newsdealer said, "Listen, maybe he did come by here." His smile was knowing and his eyes shifted over her shoulder to the man in back of her. She was suddenly horribly aware of her over-young print dress, and pulled her coat around her quickly. The newsdealer said, with vast thoughtfulness, "Now I don't know for sure, mind you, but there might have been someone like your gentleman friend coming by this morning."

"About ten?"

"About ten," the newsdealer agreed. "Tall fellow, blue suit. I wouldn't be at all surprised."

"Which way did he go?" she said eagerly. "Uptown?"

"Uptown," the newsdealer said, nodding. "He went uptown. That's just exactly it. What can I do for you, sir?"

She stepped back, holding her coat around her. The man who had been standing behind her looked at her over his shoulder and then he and the newsdealer looked at one another. She wondered for a minute whether or not to tip the newsdealer but when both men began to laugh she moved hurriedly on across the street.

Uptown, she thought, that's right, and she started up the avenue, thinking: He wouldn't have to cross the avenue, just go up six blocks and turn down my street, so long as he started uptown. About a block farther on she passed a florist's shop; there was a wedding display in the window and she thought, This is my wedding day after all, he might have gotten flowers to bring me, and she went inside. The florist came out of the back of the shop, smiling and sleek, and she said, before he could speak, so that he wouldn't have a chance to think she was buying anything: "It's *terribly* important that I get in touch with a gentleman who may have stopped in here to buy flowers this morning. *Terribly* important."

She stopped for breath, and the florist said, "Yes, what sort of flowers were they?"

"I don't know," she said, surprised. "He never—" She stopped and said, "He was a rather tall young man, in a blue suit. It was about ten o'clock."

"I see," the florist said. "Well, *really*, I'm afraid. . . ."

"But it's *so* important," she said. "He may have been in a hurry," she added helpfully.

"Well," the florist said. He smiled genially, showing all his small teeth. "For a *lady*," he said. He went to a stand and opened a large book. "Where were they to be sent?" he asked.

"Why," she said, "I don't think he'd have sent them. You see, he was coming—that is, he'd *bring* them."

"Madam," the florist said; he was offended. His smile became deprecatory, and he went on, "Really, you must realize that unless I have *something* to go on. . . ."

"*Please* try to remember," she begged. "He was tall, and had a blue suit, and it was about ten this morning."

The florist closed his eyes, one finger to his mouth, and thought deeply. Then he shook his head. "I simply *can't*," he said.

"Thank you," she said despondently, and started for the door, when the florist said, in a shrill, excited voice, "Wait! Wait just a moment, madam." She turned and the florist, thinking again, said finally, "Chrysanthemums?" He looked at her inquiringly.

"Oh, *no*," she said; her voice shook a little and she waited for a minute before she went on. "Not for an occasion like this, I'm sure."

The florist tightened his lips and looked away coldly. "Well, of *course* I don't know the *occasion*," he said, "but I'm almost certain that the gentleman you were inquiring for came in this morning and purchased one dozen chrysanthemums. No delivery."

"You're *sure*?" she asked.

"Positive," the florist said emphatically. "That was absolutely the man." He smiled brilliantly, and she smiled back and said, "Well, thank you very much."

He escorted her to the door. "Nice corsage?" he said, as they went through the shop. "Red roses? Gardenias?"

"It was very kind of you to help me," she said at the door.

"Ladies always look their best in flowers," he said, bending his head toward her. "Orchids, perhaps?"

"No, thank you," she said, and he said, "I hope you find your young man," and gave it a nasty sound.

Going on up the street she thought, Everyone thinks it's so *funny*: and she pulled her coat tighter around her, so that only the ruffle around the bottom of the print dress was showing.

There was a policeman on the corner, and she thought, Why don't I go to the police—you go to the police for a missing person. And then thought, What a fool I'd look like. She had a quick picture of herself standing in a police station, saying, "Yes, we were going to be married today, but he didn't come," and the policemen, three or four of them standing around listening, looking at her, at the print dress, at her too-bright make-up, smiling at one another. She couldn't tell them any more than that, could not say, "Yes, it looks silly, doesn't it, me all dressed up and trying to find the young man who promised to marry me, but what about all of it you don't know? I have more than this, more than you can see: talent, perhaps, and humor of a sort, and I'm a lady and I have pride and affection and delicacy and a certain clear view of life that might make a man satisfied and productive and happy; there's more than you think when you look at me."

The police were obviously impossible, leaving out Jamie and what he might think when he heard she'd set the police after him. "No, no," she said aloud, hurrying her steps, and someone passing stopped and looked after her.

On the coming corner—she was three blocks from her own street—was a shoeshine stand, an old man sitting almost asleep in one of the chairs. She stopped in front of him and waited, and after a minute he opened his eyes and smiled at her.

"Look," she said, the words coming before she thought of them, "I'm sorry to bother you, but I'm looking for a young man who came up this way about ten this morning, did you see him?" And she began her description, "Tall, blue suit, carrying a bunch of flowers?"

The old man began to nod before she was finished. "I saw him," he said. "Friend of yours?"

"Yes," she said, and smiled back involuntarily.

The old man blinked his eyes and said, "I remember I thought, You're going to see your girl, young fellow. They all go to see their girls," he said, and shook his head tolerantly.

"Which way did he go? Straight on up the avenue?"

"That's right," the old man said. "Got a shine, had his flowers, all dressed up, in an awful hurry. You got a girl, I thought."

"Thank you," she said, fumbling in her pocket for her loose change.

"She sure must of been glad to see him, the way he looked," the old man said.

"Thank you," she said again, and brought her hand empty from her pocket.

For the first time she was really sure he would be waiting for her, and she hurried up the three blocks, the skirt of the print dress swinging under her coat, and turned into her own block. From the corner she could not see her own windows, could not see Jamie looking out, waiting for her, and going down the block she was almost running to get to him. Her key trembled in her fingers at the downstairs door, and as she glanced into the drugstore she thought of her panic, drinking coffee there this morning, and almost laughed. At her own door she could wait no longer, but began to say, "Jamie, I'm here, I was so worried," even before the door was open.

Her own apartment was waiting for her, silent, barren, afternoon shadows lengthening from the window. For a minute she saw only the empty coffee cup, thought, He has been here waiting, before she recognized it as her own, left from the morning. She looked all over the room, into the closet, into the bathroom.

"I never saw him," the clerk in the drugstore said. "I know

because I would of noticed the flowers. No one like that's been in."

The old man at the shoeshine stand woke up again to see her standing in front of him. "Hello again," he said, and smiled.

"Are you *sure*?" she demanded. "Did he go on up the avenue?"

"I watched him," the old man said, dignified against her tone. "I thought, There's a young man's got a girl, and I watched him right into the house."

"What house?" she said remotely.

"Right there," the old man said. He leaned forward to point. "The next block. With his flowers and his shine and going to see his girl. Right into her house."

"Which one?" she said.

"About the middle of the block," the old man said. He looked at her with suspicion, and said, "What you trying to do, anyway?"

She almost ran, without stopping to say "Thank you." Up on the next block she walked quickly, searching the houses from the outside to see if Jamie looked from a window, listening to hear his laughter somewhere inside.

A woman was sitting in front of one of the houses, pushing a baby carriage monotonously back and forth the length of her arm. The baby inside slept, moving back and forth.

The question was fluent, by now. "I'm sorry, but did you see a young man go into one of these houses about ten this morning? He was tall, wearing a blue suit, carrying a bunch of flowers."

A boy about twelve stopped to listen, turning intently from one to the other, occasionally glancing at the baby.

"Listen," the woman said tiredly, "the kid has his bath at ten. Would I see strange men walking around? I ask you."

"Big bunch of flowers?" the boy asked, pulling at her coat. "Big bunch of flowers? I seen him, missus."

She looked down and the boy grinned insolently at her. "Which house did he go in?" she asked wearily.

"You gonna divorce him?" the boy asked insistently.

"That's not nice to ask the lady," the woman rocking the carriage said.

"Listen," the boy said, "I seen him. He went in there." He pointed to the house next door. "I followed him," the boy said. "He give me a quarter." The boy dropped his voice to a growl, and said. " 'This is a big day for me, kid,' he says. Give me a quarter."

She gave him a dollar bill. "Where?" she said.

"Top floor," the boy said. "I followed him till he give me the quarter. Way to the top." He backed up the sidewalk, out of reach, with the dollar bill. "You gonna divorce him?" he asked again.

"Was he carrying flowers?"

"Yeah," the boy said. He began to screech. "You gonna divorce him, missus? You got something on him?" He went careening down the street, howling, "She's got something on the poor guy," and the woman rocking the baby laughed.

The street door of the apartment house was unlocked; there were no bells in the outer vestibule, and no lists of names. The stairs were narrow and dirty; there were two doors on the top floor. The front one was the right one; there was a crumpled florist's paper on the floor outside the door, and a knotted paper ribbon, like a clue, like the final clue in the paper-chase.

She knocked, and thought she heard voices inside, and she thought, suddenly, with terror, What shall I say if Jamie is there, if he comes to the door? The voices seemed suddenly still. She knocked again and there was silence, except for something that might have been laughter far away. He could have seen me from the window, she thought, it's the front apartment and that little boy made a dreadful noise. She waited, and knocked again, but there was silence.

Finally she went to the other door on the floor, and knocked. The door swung open beneath her hand and she saw the empty attic room, bare lath on the walls, floorboards unpainted. She stepped just inside, looking around; the room was filled with bags of plaster, piles of old newspapers, a broken trunk. There was a noise which she suddenly realized was a rat, and then she saw it, sitting very close to her, near the wall, its evil face alert, bright eyes watching her. She stumbled in her haste to be out with the door closed, and the skirt of the print dress caught and tore.

She knew there was someone inside the other apartment, because she was sure she could hear low voices and sometimes laughter. She came back many times, every day for the first week. She came on her way to work, in the mornings; in the evenings, on her way to dinner alone, but no matter how often or how firmly she knocked, no one ever came to the door.

1949

PAUL BOWLES

(1910–1999)

The Circular Valley

THE abandoned monastery stood on a slight eminence of
land in the middle of a vast clearing. On all sides the ground
sloped gently downward toward the tangled, hairy jungle that
filled the circular valley, ringed about by sheer, black cliffs.
There were a few trees in some of the courtyards, and the birds
used them as meeting-places when they flew out of the rooms
and corridors where they had their nests. Long ago bandits
had taken whatever was removable out of the building. Soldiers had used it once as headquarters, had, like the bandits,
built fires in the great windy rooms so that afterward they
looked like ancient kitchens. And now that everything was
gone from within, it seemed that never again would anyone
come near the monastery. The vegetation had thrown up a
protecting wall; the first story was soon quite hidden from
view by small trees which dripped vines to lasso the cornices of
the windows. The meadows roundabout grew dank and lush;
there was no path through them.

At the higher end of the circular valley a river fell off the
cliffs into a great cauldron of vapor and thunder below; after
this it slid along the base of the cliffs until it found a gap at the
other end of the valley, where it hurried discreetly through with
no rapids, no cascades—a great thick black rope of water moving
swiftly downhill between the polished flanks of the canyon.
Beyond the gap the land opened out and became smiling; a
village nestled on the side hill just outside. In the days of the
monastery it was there that the friars had got their provisions,
since the Indians would not enter the circular valley. Centuries
ago when the building had been constructed the Church had
imported the workmen from another part of the country.
These were traditional enemies of the tribes thereabouts, and
had another language; there was no danger that the inhabitants would communicate with them as they worked at setting

112

up the mighty walls. Indeed, the construction had taken so long that before the east wing was completed the workmen had all died, one by one. Thus it was the friars themselves who had closed off the end of the wing with blank walls, leaving it that way, unfinished and blind-looking, facing the black cliffs.

Generation after generation, the friars came, fresh-cheeked boys who grew thin and gray, and finally died, to be buried in the garden beyond the courtyard with the fountain. One day not long ago they had all left the monastery; no one knew where they had gone, and no one thought to ask. It was shortly after this that the bandits, and then the soldiers had come. And now, since the Indians do not change, still no one from the village went up through the gap to visit the monastery. The Atlá-jala lived there; the friars had not been able to kill it, had given up at last and gone away. No one was surprised, but the Atlá-jala gained in prestige by their departure. During the centuries the friars had been there in the monastery, the Indians had wondered why it allowed them to stay. Now, at last, it had driven them out. It always had lived there, they said, and would go on living there because the valley was its home, and it could never leave.

In the early morning the restless Atlájala would move through the halls of the monastery. The dark rooms sped past, one after the other. In a small patio, where eager young trees had pushed up the paving stones to reach the sun, it paused. The air was full of small sounds: the movements of butterflies, the falling to the ground of bits of leaves and flowers, the air following its myriad courses around the edges of things, the ants pursuing their endless labors in the hot dust. In the sun it waited, conscious of each gradation in sound and light and smell, living in the awareness of the slow, constant disintegration that attacked the morning and transformed it into afternoon. When evening came, it often slipped above the monastery roof and surveyed the darkening sky: the waterfall would roar distantly. Night after night, along the procession of years, it had hovered here above the valley, darting down to become a bat, a leopard, a moth for a few minutes or hours, returning to rest immobile in the center of the space enclosed by the cliffs. When the monastery had been built, it had taken to frequenting the rooms, where it had observed for the first time the meaning-less gestures of human life.

And then one evening it had aimlessly become one of the young friars. This was a new sensation, strangely rich and com-plex, and at the same time unbearably stifling, as though every other possibility besides that of being enclosed in a tiny, iso-lated world of cause and effect had been removed forever. As the friar, it had gone and stood in the window, looking out at the sky, seeing for the first time, not the stars, but the space between and beyond them. Even at that moment it had felt the urge to leave, to step outside the little shell of anguish where it lodged for the moment, but a faint curiosity had im-pelled it to remain a little longer and partake a little further of the unaccustomed sensation. It held on; the friar raised his arms to the sky in an imploring gesture. For the first time the Atlájala sensed opposition, the thrill of a struggle. It was deli-cious to feel the young man striving to free himself of its pres-ence, and it was immeasurably sweet to remain there. Then with a cry the friar had rushed to the other side of the room and seized a heavy leather whip hanging on the wall. Tearing off his clothing he had begun to carry out a ferocious self-beating. At the first blow of the lash the Atlájala had been on the point of letting go, but then it realized that the immediacy of that intriguing inner pain was only made more manifest by the impact of the blows from without, and so it stayed and felt the young man grow weak under his own lashing. When he had finished and said a prayer, he crawled to his pallet and fell asleep weeping, while the Atlájala slipped out obliquely and entered into a bird which passed the night sitting in a great tree on the edge of the jungle, listening intently to the night sounds, and uttering a scream from time to time.

Thereafter the Atlájala found it impossible to resist sliding inside the bodies of the friars; it visited one after the other, finding an astonishing variety of sensation in the process. Each was a separate world, a separate experience, because each had different reactions when he became conscious of the other being within him. One would sit and read or pray, one would go for a long troubled walk in the meadows, around and around the building, one would find a comrade and engage in an absurd but bitter quarrel, a few wept, some flagellated themselves or sought a friend to wield the lash for them. Always there was a rich profusion of perceptions for the Atlájala to enjoy, so that it no longer occurred to it to frequent the bodies of insects, birds and furred animals, nor even to leave the monastery and move in the air above. Once it almost got into difficulties when an old friar it was occupying suddenly fell back dead. That was a hazard it ran in the frequenting of men: they seemed not to know when they were doomed, or if they did know, they pretended with such strength not to know, that it amounted to the same thing. The other beings knew beforehand, save when it was a question of being seized unawares and devoured. And that the Atlájala was able to prevent: a bird in which it was staying was always avoided by the hawks and eagles.

When the friars left the monastery, and, following the government's orders, doffed their robes, dispersed and became workmen, the Atlájala was at a loss to know how to pass its days and nights. Now everything was as it had been before their arrival: there was no one but the creatures that always had lived in the circular valley. It tried a giant serpent, a deer, a bee: nothing had the savor it had grown to love. Everything was the same as before, but not for the Atlájala; it had known the existence of man, and now there were no men in the valley —only the abandoned building with its empty rooms to make man's absence more poignant.

Then one year bandits came, several hundred of them in one stormy afternoon. In delight it tried many of them as they sprawled about cleaning their guns and cursing, and it discovered still other facets of sensation: the hatred they felt for the world, the fear they had of the soldiers who were pursuing them, the strange gusts of desire that swept through them as they sprawled together drunk by the fire that smoldered in the center of the floor, and the insufferable pain of jealousy which the nightly orgies seemed to awaken in some of them. But the bandits did not stay long. When they had left, the soldiers came in their wake. It felt very much the same way to be a soldier as to be a bandit. Missing were the strong fear and the hatred, but the rest was almost identical. Neither the bandits nor the soldiers appeared to be at all conscious of its presence in them; it could slip from one man to another without causing

any change in their behavior. This surprised it, since its effect
on the friars had been so definite, and it felt a certain disappointment at the impossibility of making its existence known
to them.

Nevertheless, the Atlájala enjoyed both bandits and soldiers
immensely, and was even more desolate when it was left alone
once again. It would become one of the swallows that made
their nests in the rocks beside the top of the waterfall. In the
burning sunlight it would plunge again and again into the curtain of mist that rose from far below, sometimes uttering exultant cries. It would spend a day as a plant louse, crawling
slowly along the under side of the leaves, living quietly in the
huge green world down there which is forever hidden from
the sky. Or at night, in the velvet body of a panther, it would
know the pleasure of the kill. Once for a year it lived in an eel
at the bottom of the pool below the waterfall, feeling the mud
give slowly before it as it pushed ahead with its flat nose; that
was a restful period, but afterward the desire to know again the
mysterious life of man had returned—an obsession of which it
was useless to try to rid itself. And now it moved restlessly
through the ruined rooms, a mute presence, alone, and thirsting
to be incarnate once again, but in man's flesh only. And with the
building of highways through the country it was inevitable
that people should come once again to the circular valley.

A man and a woman drove their automobile as far as a village down in a lower valley; hearing about the ruined monastery and the waterfall that dropped over the cliffs into the
great amphitheatre, they determined to see these things. They
came on burros as far as the village outside the gap, but there
the Indians they had hired to accompany them refused to go
any farther, and so they continued alone, upward through the
canyon and into the precinct of the Atlájala.

It was noon when they rode into the valley; the black ribs of
the cliffs glistened like glass in the sun's blistering downward
rays. They stopped the burros by a cluster of boulders at the
edge of the sloping meadows. The man got down first, and
reached up to help the woman off. She leaned forward, putting
her hands on his face, and for a long moment they kissed. Then
he lifted her to the ground and they climbed hand in hand up
over the rocks. The Atlájala hovered near them, watching the

woman closely: she was the first ever to have come into the valley. The two sat beneath a small tree on the grass, looking at one another, smiling. Out of habit, the Atlájala entered into the man. Immediately, instead of existing in the midst of the sunlit air, the bird calls and the plant odors, it was conscious only of the woman's beauty and her terrible imminence. The waterfall, the earth, and the sky itself receded, rushed into nothingness, and there were only the woman's smile and her arms and her odor. It was a world more suffocating and painful than the Atlájala had thought possible. Still, while the man spoke and the woman answered, it remained within.

"Leave him. He doesn't love you."

"He would kill me."

"But I love you. I need you with me."

"I can't. I'm afraid of him."

The man reached out to pull her to him; she drew back slightly, but her eyes grew large.

"We have today," she murmured, turning her face toward the yellow walls of the monastery.

The man embraced her fiercely, crushing her against him as though the act would save his life. "No, no, no. It can't go on like this," he said. "No."

The pain of his suffering was too intense; gently the Atlájala left the man and slipped into the woman. And now it would have believed itself to be housed in nothing, to be in its own spaceless self, so completely was it aware of the wandering wind, the small flutterings of the leaves, and the bright air that surrounded it. Yet there was a difference: each element was magnified in intensity, the whole sphere of being was immense, limitless. Now it understood what the man sought in the woman, and it knew that he suffered because he never would attain that sense of completion he sought. But the Atlájala, being one with the woman, had attained it, and being aware of possessing it, trembled with delight. The woman shuddered as her lips met those of the man. There on the grass in the shade of the tree their joy reached new heights; the Atlájala, knowing them both, formed a single channel between the secret springs of their desires. Throughout, it remained within the woman, and began vaguely to devise ways of keeping her, if not inside the valley, at least nearby, so that she might return.

In the afternoon, with dreamlike motions, they walked to the burros and mounted them, driving them through the deep meadow grass to the monastery. Inside the great courtyard they halted, looking hesitantly at the ancient arches in the sunlight, and at the darkness inside the doorways.

"Shall we go in?" said the woman.

"We must get back."

"I want to go in," she said. (The Atlájala exulted.) A thin gray snake slid along the ground into the bushes. They did not see it.

The man looked at her perplexedly. "It's late," he said.

But she jumped down from her burro by herself and walked beneath the arches into the long corridor within. (Never had the rooms seemed so real as now when the Atlájala was seeing them through her eyes.)

They explored all the rooms. Then the woman wanted to climb up into the tower, but the man took a determined stand.

"We must go back now," he said firmly, putting his hand on her shoulder.

"This is our only day together, and you think of nothing but getting back."

"But the time . . ."

"There is a moon. We won't lose the way."

He would not change his mind. "No."

"As you like," she said. "I'm going up. You can go back alone if you like."

The man laughed uneasily. "You're mad." He tried to kiss her.

She turned away and did not answer for a moment. Then she said: "You want me to leave my husband for you. You ask everything from me, but what do you do for me in return? You refuse even to climb up into a little tower with me to see the view. Go back alone. Go!"

She sobbed and rushed toward the dark stairwell. Calling after her, he followed, but stumbled somewhere behind her. She was as sure of foot as if she had climbed the many stone steps a thousand times before, hurrying up through the darkness, around and around.

In the end she came out at the top and peered through the small apertures in the cracking walls. The beams which had supported the bell had rotted and fallen; the heavy bell lay on its side in the rubble, like a dead animal. The waterfall's sound was louder up here; the valley was nearly full of shadow. Below, the man called her name repeatedly. She did not answer. As she stood watching the shadow of the cliffs slowly overtake the farthest recesses of the valley and begin to climb the naked rocks to the east, an idea formed in her mind. It was not the kind of idea which she would have expected of herself, but it was there, growing and inescapable. When she felt it complete there inside her, she turned and went lightly back down. The man was sitting in the dark near the bottom of the stairs, groaning a little.

"What is it?" she said.

"I hurt my leg. Now are you ready to go or not?"

"Yes," she said simply. "I'm sorry you fell."

Without saying anything he rose and limped after her out into the courtyard where the burros stood. The cold mountain air was beginning to flow down from the tops of the cliffs. As they rode through the meadow she began to think of how she would broach the subject to him. (It must be done before they reached the gap. The Atlájala trembled.)

"Do you forgive me?" she asked him.

"Of course," he laughed.

"Do you love me?"

"More than anything in the world."

"Is that true?"

He glanced at her in the failing light, sitting erect on the jogging animal.

"You know it is," he said softly.

She hesitated.

"There is only one way, then," she said finally.

"But what?"

"I'm afraid of him. I won't go back to him. You go back. I'll stay in the village here." (Being that near, she would come each day to the monastery.) "When it is done, you will come and get me. Then we can go somewhere else. No one will find us."

The man's voice sounded strange. "I don't understand."

"You do understand. And that is the only way. Do it or not, as you like. It is the only way."

They trotted along for a while in silence. The canyon loomed ahead, black against the evening sky.

Then the man said, very clearly: "Never."

A moment later the trail led out into an open space high above the swift water below. The hollow sound of the river reached them faintly. The light in the sky was almost gone; in the dusk the landscape had taken on false contours. Everything was gray—the rocks, the bushes, the trail—and nothing had distance or scale. They slowed their pace.

His word still echoed in her ears.

"I won't go back to him!" she cried with sudden vehemence. "You can go back and play cards with him as usual. Be his good friend the same as always. I won't go. I can't go on with both of you in the town." (The plan was not working; the Atlájala saw it had lost her, yet it still could help her.)

"You're very tired," he said softly.

He was right. Almost as he said the words, that unaccustomed exhilaration and lightness she had felt ever since noon seemed to leave her; she hung her head wearily, and said: "Yes, I am."

At the same moment the man uttered a sharp, terrible cry; she looked up in time to see his burro plunge from the edge of the trail into the grayness below. There was a silence, and then the faraway sound of many stones sliding downward. She could not move or stop the burro; she sat dumbly, letting it carry her along, an inert weight on its back.

For one final instant, as she reached the pass which was the edge of its realm, the Atlájala alighted tremulously within her. She raised her head and a tiny exultant shiver passed through her; then she let it fall forward once again.

Hanging in the dim air above the trail, the Atlájala watched her indistinct figure grow invisible in the gathering night. (If it had not been able to hold her there, still it had been able to help her.)

A moment later it was in the tower, listening to the spiders mend the webs that she had damaged. It would be a long, long time before it would bestir itself to enter into another being's awareness. A long, long time—perhaps forever.

1950

JACK FINNEY

(1911–1995)

I'm Scared

I'M very badly scared, not so much for myself—I'm a gray-haired man of sixty-six, after all—but for you and everyone else who has not yet lived out his life. For I believe that certain dangerous things have recently begun to happen in the world. They are noticed here and there, idly discussed, then dismissed and forgotten. Yet I am convinced that unless these occurrences are recognized for what they are, the world will be plunged into a nightmare. Judge for yourself.

One evening last winter I came home from a chess club to which I belong. I'm a widower; I live alone in a small but comfortable three-room apartment overlooking lower Fifth Avenue. It was still fairly early, and I switched on a lamp beside my leather easy chair, picked up a murder mystery I'd been reading, and turned on the radio; I did not, I'm sorry to say, notice which station it was tuned to.

The tubes warmed, and the music of an accordion—faint at first, then louder—came from the loudspeaker. Since it was good music for reading, I adjusted the volume control and began to read.

Now, I want to be absolutely factual and accurate about this, and I do not claim that I paid close attention to the radio. But I do know that presently the music stopped, and an audience applauded. Then a man's voice, chuckling and pleased with the applause, said, "All right, all right," but the applause continued for several more seconds. During that time the voice once more chuckled appreciatively, then firmly repeated, "All right," and the applause died down. "That was Alec Somebody-or-other," the radio voice said, and I went back to my book.

But I soon became aware of this middle-aged voice again; perhaps a change of tone as he turned to a new subject caught my attention. "And now, Miss Ruth Greeley," he was saying, "of Trenton, New Jersey. Miss Greeley is a pianist; that right?"

A girl's voice, timid and barely audible, said, "That's right, Major Bowes." The man's voice—and now I recognized his familiar singsong delivery—said, "And what are you going to play?" The girl replied, "La Paloma." The man repeated it after her, as an announcement: "La Paloma." There was a pause, then an introductory chord sounded from a piano, and I resumed my reading.

As the girl played, I was half aware that her style was mechanical, her rhythm defective; perhaps she was nervous. Then my attention was fully aroused once more by a gong which sounded suddenly. For a few notes more the girl continued to play falteringly, not sure what to do. The gong sounded jarringly again, the playing abruptly stopped, and there was a restless murmur from the audience. "All right, all right," said the now familiar voice, and I realized I'd been expecting this, knowing it would say just that. The audience quieted, and the voice began, "Now——"

The radio went dead. For the smallest fraction of a second no sound issued from it but its own mechanical hum. Then a completely different program came from the loud-speaker; the recorded voice of Andy Williams singing "You Butterfly," a favorite of mine. So I returned once more to my reading, wondering vaguely what had happened to the other program, but not actually thinking about it until I finished my book and began to get ready for bed.

Then, undressing in my bedroom, I remembered that Major Bowes was dead. Years had passed, a decade, since that dry chuckle and familiar, "All right, all right," had been heard in the nation's living rooms.

Well, what does one do when the apparently impossible occurs? It simply made a good story to tell friends, and more than once I was asked if I'd recently heard Moran and Mack, a pair of radio comedians popular some thirty years ago, or Floyd Gibbons, an old-time news broadcaster. And there were other joking references to my crystal radio set.

But one man—this was at a lodge meeting the following Thursday—listened to my story with utter seriousness, and when I had finished he told me a queer little story of his own. He is a thoughtful, intelligent man, and as I listened I was not frightened, but puzzled at what seemed to be a connecting link, a common denominator, between this story and the odd behavior of my radio. The following day, since I am retired and have plenty of time, I took the trouble of making a two-hour train trip to Connecticut in order to verify the story at first hand. I took detailed notes, and the story appears in my files now as follows:

Case 2. Louis Trachnor, coal and wood dealer, R.F.D. 1, Danbury, Connecticut, aged fifty-four.

On July 20, 1956, Mr. Trachnor told me, he walked out on the front porch of his house about six o'clock in the morning. Running from the eaves of his house to the floor of the porch was a streak of gray paint, still damp. "It was about the width of an eight-inch brush," Mr. Trachnor told me, "and it looked like hell, because the house was white. I figured some kids did it in the night for a joke, but if they did, they had to get a ladder up to the eaves and you wouldn't figure they'd go to that much trouble. It wasn't smeared, either; it was a careful job, a nice even stripe straight down the front of the house."

Mr. Trachnor got a ladder and cleaned off the gray paint with turpentine.

In October of that same year, Mr. Trachnor painted his house. "The white hadn't held up so good, so I painted it gray. I got to the front last and finished about five one Saturday afternoon. Next morning when I came out, I saw a streak of white right down the front of the house. I figured it was the damned kids again, because it was the same place as before. But when I looked close, I saw it wasn't new paint; it was the old white I'd painted over. Somebody had done a nice careful job of cleaning off the new paint in a long stripe about eight inches wide right down from the eaves! Now, who the hell would go to that trouble? I just can't figure it out."

Do you see the link between this story and mine? Suppose for a moment that something had happened, on each occasion, to disturb briefly the orderly progress of time. That seemed to have happened in my case; for a matter of some seconds I apparently heard a radio broadcast that had been made years before. Suppose, then, that no one had touched Mr. Trachnor's house but himself; that he had painted his house in October, and that through some fantastic mix-up in time, a portion of that paint appeared on his house the previous summer. Since he had cleaned the paint off at that time, a broad stripe of new gray paint was missing *after* he painted his house in the fall.

I would be lying, however, if I said I really believed this. It was merely an intriguing speculation, and I told both these little stories to friends, simply as curious anecdotes. I am a sociable person, see a good many people, and occasionally I heard other odd stories in response to mine.

Someone would nod and say, "Reminds me of something I heard recently . . ." and I would have one more to add to my collection. A man on Long Island received a telephone call from his sister in New York on Friday evening. She insists that she did not make this call until the following Monday, three days later. At the Forty-fifth Street branch of the Chase National Bank, I was shown a check deposited the day before it was written. A letter was delivered on East Sixty-eighth Street in New York City, just seventeen minutes after it was dropped into a mailbox on the main street of Green River, Wyoming.

And so on, and so on; my stories were now in demand at parties, and I told myself that collecting and verifying them was a hobby. But the day I heard Julia Eisenberg's story, I knew it was no longer that.

Case 17. Julia Eisenberg, office worker, New York City, aged thirty-one.

Miss Eisenberg lives in a small walk-up apartment in Greenwich Village. I talked to her there after a chess-club friend who lives in her neighborhood had repeated to me a somewhat garbled version of her story, which was told to him by the doorman of the building he lives in.

In October, 1954, about eleven at night, Miss Eisenberg left her apartment to walk to the drugstore for toothpaste. On her way back, not far from her apartment, a large black and white dog ran up to her and put his front paws on her chest.

"I made the mistake of petting him," Miss Eisenberg told me, "and from then on he simply wouldn't leave. When I went into the lobby of my building, I actually had to push him away to get the door closed. I felt sorry for him, poor hound, and a little guilty, because he was still sitting at the door an hour later when I looked out my front window."

This dog remained in the neighborhood for three days, discovering and greeting Miss Eisenberg with wild affection each time she appeared on the street. "When I'd get on the bus in the morning to go to work, he'd sit on the curb looking after me in the most mournful way, poor thing. I wanted to take him in, and I wish with all my heart that I had, but I knew he'd never go home then, and I was afraid whoever owned him would be sorry to lose him. No one in the neighborhood knew who he belonged to, and finally he disappeared."

Two years later a friend gave Miss Eisenberg a three-week-old puppy. "My apartment is really too small for a dog, but he was such a darling I couldn't resist. Well, he grew up into a nice big dog who ate more than I did."

Since the neighborhood was quiet, and the dog well behaved, Miss Eisenberg usually unleashed him when she walked him at night, for he never strayed far. "One night—I'd last seen him sniffing around in the dark a few doors down—I called to him and he didn't come back. And he never did; I never saw him again.

"Now, our street is a solid wall of brownstone buildings on both sides, with locked doors and no areaways. He *couldn't* have disappeared like that, he just *couldn't*. But he did."

Miss Eisenberg hunted for her dog for many days afterward, inquired of neighbors, put ads in the papers, but she never found him. "Then one night I was getting ready for bed; I happened to glance out the front window down at the street, and suddenly I remembered something I'd forgotten all about. I remembered the dog I'd chased away over two years before." Miss Eisenberg looked at me for a moment, then she said flatly. "It was the same dog. If you own a dog you *know* him, you can't be mistaken, and I tell you it was the same dog. Whether it makes sense or not, my dog was lost—I chased him away—two years before he was born."

She began to cry silently, the tears running down her face. "Maybe you think I'm crazy, or a little lonely and overly sentimental about a dog. But you're wrong." She brushed at her tears with a handkerchief. "I'm a well-balanced person, as much as anyone is these days, at least, and I tell you I *know* what happened."

It was in that moment, sitting in Miss Eisenberg's neat, shabby living room, that I realized fully that the consequences of these odd little incidents could be something more than merely intriguing; that they might, quite possibly, be tragic. It was in that moment that I began to be afraid.

I have spent the last eleven months discovering and tracking down these strange occurrences, and I am astonished and frightened at how many there are. I am astonished and frightened at how much more frequently they are happening now, and—I hardly know how to express this—at their increasing *power* to tear human lives tragically apart. This is an example, selected almost at random, of the increasing strength of—whatever it is that is happening in the world.

Case 34. Paul V. Kerch, accountant, the Bronx, aged thirty-one.

On a bright, clear, Sunday afternoon, I met an unsmiling family of three at their Bronx apartment: Mr. Kerch, a chunky, darkly good-looking young man; his wife, a pleasant-faced dark-haired woman in her late twenties, whose attractiveness was marred by circles under her eyes; and their son, a nice-looking boy of six or seven. After introductions, the boy was sent to his room at the back of the house to play.

"All right," Mr. Kerch said wearily then, and walked toward a bookcase, "let's get at it. You said on the phone that you know the story in general." It was half a question, half a statement.

"Yes," I said.

He took a book from the top shelf and removed some photographs from it. "There are the pictures." He sat down on the davenport beside me, with the photographs in his hand. "I own a pretty good camera, I'm a fair amateur photographer, and I have a darkroom setup in the kitchen; do my own developing. Two weeks ago, we went down to Central Park." His voice was a tired monotone as though this were a story he'd repeated many times, aloud and in his own mind. "It was nice, like today, and the kid's grandmothers have been pestering us for pictures, so I took a whole roll of films, pictures of all of us. My camera can be set up and focused and it will snap the picture automatically a few seconds later, giving me time to get around in front of it and get in the picture myself."

There was a tired, hopeless look in his eyes as he handed me all but one of the photographs. "These are the first ones I took," he said. The photographs were all fairly large, perhaps 5 × 7″, and I examined them closely.

They were ordinary enough, very sharp and detailed, and

each showed the family of three in various smiling poses. Mr. Kerch wore a light business suit, his wife had on a dark dress and a cloth coat, and the boy wore a dark suit with knee-length pants. In the background stood a tree with bare branches. I glanced up at Mr. Kerch, signifying that I had finished my study of the photographs.

"The last picture," he said, holding it in his hand ready to give to me, "I took exactly like the others. We agreed on the pose, I set the camera, walked around in front, and joined my family. Monday night I developed the whole roll. This is what came out on the last negative." He handed me the photograph.

For an instant it seemed to me like merely one more photograph in the group; then I saw the difference. Mr. Kerch looked much the same, bare-headed and grinning broadly, but he wore an entirely different suit. The boy, standing beside him, wore long pants, was a good three inches taller, obviously older, but equally obviously the same boy. The woman was an entirely different person. Dressed smartly, her light hair catching the sun, she was very pretty and attractive, and she was smiling into the camera, holding Mr. Kerch's hand.

I looked up at him. "Who is this?"

Wearily, Mr. Kerch shook his head. "I don't know," he said sullenly, then suddenly exploded: "I don't *know*! I've never seen her in my life!" He turned to look at his wife, but she would not return his glance, and he turned back to me, shrugging. "Well, there you have it," he said. "The whole story." And he stood up, thrusting both hands into his trouser pockets, and began to pace about the room, glancing often at his wife, talking to *her* actually, though he addressed his words to me. "So who is she? How could the camera have snapped that picture? I've never seen that woman in my life!"

I glanced at the photograph again, then bent closer. "The trees here are in full bloom," I said. Behind the solemn-faced boy, the grinning man and smiling woman, the trees of Central Park were in full summer leaf.

Mr. Kerch nodded. "I know," he said bitterly. "And you know what *she* says?" he burst out, glaring at his wife. "She says that *is* my wife in the photograph, my *new* wife a couple of years from now! God!" He slapped both hands down on his head. "The ideas a woman can get!"

"What do you mean?" I glanced at Mrs. Kerch, but she ignored me, remaining silent, her lips tight.

Kerch shrugged hopelessly. "She says that photograph shows how things will be a couple of years from now. She'll be dead or"—he hesitated, then said the word bitterly—"divorced, and I'll have our son and be married to the woman in the picture."

We both looked at Mrs. Kerch, waiting until she was obliged to speak.

"Well, if it isn't so," she said, shrugging a shoulder, "then tell me what that picture does mean."

Neither of us could answer that, and a few minutes later I left. There was nothing much I could say to the Kerches; certainly I couldn't mention my conviction that, whatever the explanation of the last photograph, their married life was over. . . .

Case 72. Lieutenant Alfred Eichler, New York Police Department, aged thirty-three.

In the late evening of January 9, 1956, two policemen found a revolver lying just off a gravel path near an East Side entrance to Central Park. The gun was examined for fingerprints at the police laboratory and several were found. One bullet had been fired from the revolver and the police fired another which was studied and classified by a ballistics expert. The fingerprints were checked and found in police files; they were those of a minor hoodlum with a record of assault.

A routine order to pick him up was sent out. A detective called at the rooming house where he was known to live, but he was out, and since no unsolved shootings had occurred recently, no intensive search for him was made that night.

The following evening a man was shot and killed in Central Park with the same gun. This was proved ballistically past all question of error. It was soon learned that the murdered man had been quarreling with a friend in a nearby tavern. The two men, both drunk, had left the tavern together. And the second man was the hoodlum whose gun had been found the previous night, and which was still locked in a police safe.

As Lieutenant Eichler said to me, "It's impossible that the dead man was killed with that same gun, but he was. Don't ask me how, though, and if anybody thinks we'd go into court with a case like that, they're crazy."

Case III. Captain Hubert V. Rihm, New York Police Department, retired, aged sixty-six.

I met Captain Rihm by appointment one morning in Stuyvesant Park, a patch of greenery, wood benches and asphalt surrounded by the city, on lower Second Avenue. "You want to hear about the Fentz case, do you?" he said, after we had introduced ourselves and found an empty bench. "All right, I'll tell you. I don't like to talk about it—it bothers me—but I'd like to see what you think." He was a big, rather heavy man, with a red, tough face, and he wore an old police jacket and uniform cap with the insigne removed.

"I was up at City Mortuary," he began, as I took out my notebook and pencil, "at Bellevue, about twelve one night, drinking coffee with one of the interns. This was in June, 1955, just before I retired, and I was in Missing Persons. They brought this guy in and he was a funny-looking character. Had a beard. A young guy, maybe thirty, but he wore regular muttonchop whiskers, and his clothes were funny-looking. Now, I was thirty years on the force and I've seen a lot of queer guys killed on the streets. We found an Arab once, in full regalia, and it took us a week to find out who he was. So it wasn't just the way the guy looked that bothered me; it was the stuff we found in his pockets."

Captain Rihm turned on the bench to see if he'd caught my interest, then continued. "There was about a dollar in change in the dead guy's pocket, and one of the boys picked up a nickel and showed it to me. Now, you've seen plenty of nickels, the new ones with Jefferson's picture, the buffalo nickels they made before that, and once in a while you still see even the old Liberty-head nickels; they quit making them before the First World War. But this one was even older than that. It had a shield on the front, a U.S. shield, and a big five on the back; I used to see that kind when I was a boy. And the funny thing was, that old nickel looked new; what coin dealers call 'mint condition,' like it was made the day before yesterday. The date on that nickel was 1876, and there wasn't a coin in his pocket dated any later."

Captain Rihm looked at me questioningly. "Well," I said, glancing up from my notebook, "that could happen."

"Sure, it could," he answered in a satisfied tone, "but all the pennies he had were Indian-head pennies. Now, when did you see one of them last? There was even a silver three-cent piece; looked like an old-style dime, only smaller. And the bills in his wallet, every one of them, were old-time bills, the big kind."

Captain Rihm leaned forward and spat on the path, a needle-jet of tobacco juice, and an expression of a policeman's annoyed contempt for anything deviating from an orderly norm.

"Over seventy bucks in cash, and not a Federal reserve note in the lot. There were two yellow-back tens. Remember them? They were payable in gold. The rest were old national-bank notes; you remember them, too. Issued direct by local banks, personally signed by the bank president; that kind used to be counterfeited a lot.

"Well," Captain Rihm continued, leaning back on the bench and crossing his knees, "there was a bill in his pocket from a livery stable on Lexington Avenue: three dollars for feeding and stabling his horse and washing a carriage. There was a brass slug in his pocket good for a five-cent beer at some saloon. There was a letter postmarked Philadelphia, June, 1876, with an old-style two-cent stamp; and a bunch of cards in his wallet. The cards had his name and address on them, and so did the letter."

"Oh," I said, a little surprised, "you identified him right away, then?"

"Sure. Rudolph Fentz, some address on Fifth Avenue—I forget the exact number—in New York City. No problem at all." Captain Rihm leaned forward and spat again. "Only that address wasn't a residence. It's a store, and it has been for years, and nobody there ever heard of any Rudolph Fentz, and there's no such name in the phone book, either. Nobody ever called or made any inquiries about the guy, and Washington didn't have his prints. There was a tailor's name in his coat, a lower Broadway address, but nobody there ever heard of this tailor."

"What was so strange about his clothes?"

The Captain said, "Well, did you ever know anyone who wore a pair of pants with big black-and-white checks, cut very narrow, no cuffs, and pressed without a crease?"

I had to think for a moment. "Yes," I said then, "my father, when he was a very young man, before he was married; I've seen old photographs."

"Sure," said Captain Rihm, "and he probably wore a short sort of cutaway coat with two cloth-covered buttons at the back, a vest with lapels, a tall silk hat, and a big, black oversize bow tie on a turned-up stiff collar, and button shoes."

"That's how this man was dressed?"

"Like eighty years ago! And him no more than thirty years old. There was a label in his hat, a Twenty-third Street hat store that went out of business around the turn of the century. Now, what do you make out of a thing like that?"

"Well," I said carefully, "there's nothing much you can make of it. Apparently someone went to a lot of trouble to dress up in an antique style; the coins and bills, I assume he could buy at a coin dealer's; and then he got himself killed in a traffic accident."

"Got himself killed is right. Eleven fifteen at night in Times Square—the theaters letting out; busiest time and place in the world—and this guy shows up in the middle of the street, gawking and looking around at the cars and up at the signs like he'd never seen them before. The cop on duty noticed him, so you can see how he must have been acting. The lights change, the traffic starts up, with him in the middle of the street, and instead of waiting, the damned fool, he turns and tries to make it back to the sidewalk. A cab got him and he was dead when he hit."

For a moment Captain Rihm sat chewing his tobacco and staring angrily at a young woman pushing a baby carriage, though I'm sure he didn't see her. The young mother looked at him in surprise as she passed, and the captain continued:

"Nothing you can make out of a thing like that. We found out nothing. I started checking through our file of old phone books, just as routine, but without much hope because they only go back so far. But in the 1939 summer edition I found a Rudolph Fentz, Jr., somewhere on East Fifty-second Street. He'd moved away in 'forty-two, though, the building super told me, and was a man in his sixties besides, retired from business; used to work in a bank a few blocks away, the super thought. I found the bank where he'd worked, and they told me he'd retired in 'forty, and had been dead for five years; his widow was living in Florida with a sister.

"I wrote to the widow, but there was only one thing she could tell us, and that was no good. I never even reported it, not officially, anyway. Her husband's father had disappeared when her husband was a boy maybe two years old. He went out for a walk around ten one night—his wife thought cigar smoke smelled up the curtains, so he used to take a little stroll before he went to bed, and smoke a cigar—and he didn't come back, and was never seen or heard of again. The family spent a good deal of money trying to locate him, but they never did. This was in the middle eighteen seventies sometime; the old lady wasn't sure of the exact date. Her husband hadn't ever said too much about it.

"And that's all," said Captain Rihm. "Once I put in one of my afternoons off hunting through a bunch of old police records. And I finally found the Missing Persons file for 1876, and Rudolph Fentz was listed, all right. There wasn't much of a description, and no fingerprints, of course. I'd give a year of my life, even now, and maybe sleep better nights, if they'd had his fingerprints. He was listed as twenty-nine years old, wearing full muttonchop whiskers, a tall silk hat, dark coat and checked pants. That's about all it said. Didn't say what kind of tie or vest or if his shoes were the button kind. His name was Rudolph Fentz and he lived at this address on Fifth Avenue; it must have been a residence then. Final disposition of case: not located.

"Now, I hate that case," Captain Rihm said quietly. "I hate it and I wish I'd never heard of it. What do *you* think?" he demanded suddenly, angrily. "You think this guy walked off into thin air in eighteen seventy-six, and showed up again in nineteen fifty-five!"

I shrugged noncommittally, and the captain took it to mean no.

"No, of course not," he said. "Of *course* not, but—give me some other explanation."

I could go on. I could give you several hundred such cases. A sixteen-year-old girl walked out of her bedroom one morning, carrying her clothes in her hand because they were too big for her, and she was quite obviously eleven years old again. And there are other occurrences too horrible for print. All of them have happened in the New York City area alone, all within the last few years; and I suspect thousands more have occurred, and are occurring, all over the world. I could go on, but the point is this: What is happening and *why?* I believe that I know.

Haven't you noticed, too, on the part of nearly everyone you know, a growing rebellion against the *present?* And an increasing longing for the past? I have. Never before in all my long life have I heard so many people wish that they lived "at the turn of the century," or "when life was simpler," or "worth living," or "when you could bring children into the world and count on the future," or simply "in the good old days." People didn't talk that way when I was young! The present was a glorious time! But they talk that way now.

For the first time in man's history, man is desperate to escape the present. Our newsstands are jammed with escape literature, the very name of which is significant. Entire magazines are devoted to fantastic stories of escape—to other times, past and future, to other worlds and planets—escape to anywhere but here and now. Even our larger magazines, book publishers and Hollywood are beginning to meet the rising demand for this kind of escape. Yes, there is a craving in the world like a thirst, a terrible mass pressure that you can almost feel, of millions of minds struggling against the barriers of time. I am utterly convinced that this terrible mass pressure of millions of minds is already, slightly but definitely, affecting time itself. In the moments when this happens—when the almost universal longing to escape is greatest—my incidents occur. Man is disturbing the clock of time, and I am afraid it will break. When it does, I leave to your imagination the last few hours of madness that will be left to us; all the countless moments that now make up our lives suddenly ripped apart and chaotically tangled in time.

Well, I have lived most of my life; I can be robbed of only a few more years. But it seems too bad—this universal craving to escape what could be a rich, productive, happy world. We live on a planet well able to provide a decent life for every soul on it, which is all ninety-nine of a hundred human beings ask. Why in the world can't we have it?

1951

VLADIMIR NABOKOV

(1899–1977)

The Vane Sisters

I.

I MIGHT never have heard of Cynthia's death, had I not run, that night, into D., whom I had also lost track of for the last four years or so; and I might never have run into D., had I not got involved in a series of trivial investigations.

The day, a compunctious Sunday after a week of blizzards, had been part jewel, part mud. In the midst of my usual afternoon stroll through the small hilly town attached to the girls' college where I taught French literature, I had stopped to watch a family of brilliant icicles drip-dripping from the eaves of a frame house. So clear-cut were their pointed shadows on the white boards behind them that I was sure the shadows of the falling drops should be visible too. But they were not. The roof jutted too far out, perhaps, or the angle of vision was faulty, or, again, I did not chance to be watching the right icicle when the right drop fell. There was a rhythm, an alternation in the dropping that I found as teasing as a coin trick. It led me to inspect the corners of several house blocks, and this brought me to Kelly Road, and right to the house where D. used to live when he was instructor here. And as I looked up at the eaves of the adjacent garage with its full display of transparent stalactites backed by their blue silhouettes, I was rewarded at last, upon choosing one, by the sight of what might be described as the dot of an exclamation mark leaving its ordinary position to glide down very fast—a jot faster than the thaw-drop it raced. This twinned twinkle was delightful but not completely satisfying; or rather it only sharpened my appetite for other tidbits of light and shade, and I walked on in a state of raw awareness that seemed to transform the whole of my being into one big eyeball rolling in the world's socket.

Through peacocked lashes I saw the dazzling diamond reflection of the low sun on the round back of a parked automobile. To all kinds of things a vivid pictorial sense had been restored by the sponge of the thaw. Water in overlapping festoons flowed down one sloping street and turned gracefully into another. With ever so slight a note of meretricious appeal, narrow passages between buildings revealed treasures of brick and purple. I remarked for the first time the humble fluting—last echoes of grooves on the shafts of columns—ornamenting a garbage can, and I also saw the rippling upon its lid—circles diverging from a fantastically ancient center. Erect, dark-headed shapes of dead snow (left by the blades of a bulldozer last Friday) were lined up like rudimentary penguins along the curbs, above the brilliant vibration of live gutters.

I walked up, and I walked down, and I walked straight into a delicately dying sky, and finally the sequence of observed and observant things brought me, at my usual eating time, to a street so distant from my usual eating place that I decided to try a restaurant which stood on the fringe of the town. Night had fallen without sound or ceremony when I came out again. The lean ghost, the elongated umbra cast by a parking meter upon some damp snow, had a strange ruddy tinge; this I made out to be due to the tawny red light of the restaurant sign above the sidewalk; and it was then—as I sauntered there, wondering rather wearily if in the course of my return tramp I might be lucky enough to find the same in neon blue it was then that a car crunched to a standstill near me and D. got out of it with an exclamation of feigned pleasure.

He was passing, on his way from Albany to Boston, through the town he had dwelt in before, and more than once in my life have I felt that stab of vicarious emotion followed by a rush of personal irritation against travelers who seem to feel nothing at all upon revisiting spots that ought to harass them at every step with wailing and writhing memories. He ushered me back into the bar that I had just left, and after the usual exchange of buoyant platitudes came the inevitable vacuum which he filled with the random words: "Say, I never thought there was anything wrong with Cynthia Vane's heart. My lawyer tells me she died last week."

2.

He was still young, still brash, still shifty, still married to the gentle, exquisitely pretty woman who had never learned or suspected anything about his disastrous affair with Cynthia's hysterical young sister, who in her turn had known nothing of the interview I had had with Cynthia when she suddenly summoned me to Boston to make me swear I would talk to D. and get him "kicked out" if he did not stop seeing Sybil at once— or did not divorce his wife (whom incidentally she visualized through the prism of Sybil's wild talk as a termagant and a fright). I had cornered him immediately. He had said there was nothing to worry about—had made up his mind, anyway, to give up his college job and move with his wife to Albany where he would work in his father's firm; and the whole matter, which had threatened to become one of those hopelessly entangled situations that drag on for years, with peripheral sets of well-meaning friends endlessly discussing it in universal secrecy —and even founding, among themselves, new intimacies upon its alien woes—came to an abrupt end.

I remember sitting next day at my raised desk in the large classroom where a mid-year examination in French Lit. was being held on the eve of Sybil's suicide. She came in on high heels, with a suitcase, dumped it in a corner where several other bags were stacked, with a single shrug slipped her fur coat off her thin shoulders, folded it on her bag, and with two or three other girls stopped before my desk to ask when would I mail them their grades. It would take me a week, beginning from tomorrow, I said, to read the stuff. I also remember wondering whether D. had already informed her of his decision— and I felt acutely unhappy about my dutiful little student as during one hundred and fifty minutes my gaze kept reverting to her, so childishly slight in close-fitting grey, and kept observing that carefully waved dark hair, that small, small-flowered hat with a little hyaline veil as worn that season and under it her small face broken into a cubist pattern by scars due to a skin disease, pathetically masked by a sun-lamp tan that hardened her features whose charm was further impaired by her having painted everything that could be painted, so that the pale gums of her teeth between cherry-red chapped lips and the diluted blue ink of her eyes under darkened lids were the only visible openings into her beauty.

Next day, having arranged the ugly copybooks alphabetically, I plunged into their chaos of scripts and came prematurely to Valevsky and Vane whose books I had somehow misplaced. The first was dressed up for the occasion in a semblance of legibility, but Sybil's work displayed her usual combination of several demon hands. She had begun in very pale, very hard pencil which had conspicuously embossed the blank verso, but had produced little of permanent value on the upper-side of the page. Happily the tip soon broke, and Sybil continued in another, darker lead, gradually lapsing into the blurred thickness of what looked almost like charcoal, to which, by sucking the blunt point, she had contributed some traces of lipstick. Her work, although even poorer than I had expected, bore all the signs of a kind of desperate conscientiousness, with underscores, transposes, unnecessary footnotes, as if she were intent upon rounding up things in the most respectable manner possible. Then she had borrowed Mary Valevsky's fountain pen and added: "*Cette examain est finie ainsi que ma vie. Adieu, jeunes filles!* Please, *Monsieur le Professeur*, contact *ma soeur* and tell her that Death was not better than D minus, but definitely better than Life minus D."

I lost no time in ringing up Cynthia who told me it was all over—had been all over since eight in the morning—and asked me to bring her the note, and when I did, beamed through her tears with proud admiration for the whimsical use ("Just like her!") Sybil had made of an examination in French literature. In no time she "fixed" two highballs, while never parting with Sybil's notebook—by now splashed with soda water and tears —and went on studying the death message, whereupon I was impelled to point out to her the grammatical mistakes in it and to explain the way "girl" is translated in American colleges lest students innocently bandy around the French equivalent of "wench," or worse. These rather tasteless trivialities pleased Cynthia hugely as she rose, with gasps, above the heaving surface of her grief. And then, holding that limp notebook as if it were a kind of passport to a casual Elysium (where pencil points do not snap and a dreamy young beauty with an impeccable complexion winds a lock of her hair on a dreamy forefinger, as she meditates over some celestial test), Cynthia led me upstairs, to a chilly little bedroom just to show me, as if I were the police or a sympathetic Irish neighbor, two empty pill bottles and the tumbled bed from which a tender, inessential body, that D. must have known down to its last velvet detail, had been already removed.

3.

It was four or five months after her sister's death that I began seeing Cynthia fairly often. By the time I had come to New York for some vocational research in the Public Library she had also moved to that city where for some odd reason (in vague connection, I presume, with artistic motives) she had taken what people, immune to gooseflesh, term a "cold water" flat, down in the scale of the city's transverse streets. What attracted me were neither her ways, which I thought repulsively vivacious, nor her looks, which other men thought striking. She had wide-spaced eyes very much like her sister's, of a frank, frightened blue with dark points in a radial arrangement. The interval between her thick black eyebrows was always shiny, and shiny too were the fleshy volutes of her nostrils. The coarse texture of her epiderm looked almost masculine, and, in the stark lamplight of her studio, you could see the pores of her thirty-two-year-old face fairly gaping at you like something in an aquarium. She used cosmetics with as much zest as her little sister had, but with an additional slovenliness that would result in her big front teeth getting some of the rouge. She was handsomely dark, wore a not too tasteless mixture of fairly smart heterogeneous things, and had a so-called good figure; but all of her was curiously frowsy, after a way I obscurely associated with left-wing enthusiasms in politics and "advanced" banalities in art, although, actually, she cared for neither. Her coily hair-do, on a part-and-bun basis, might have looked feral and bizarre had it not been thoroughly domesticated by its own soft unkemptness at the vulnerable nape. Her fingernails were gaudily painted, but badly bitten and not clean. Her lovers were a silent young photographer with a sudden laugh and two older men, brothers, who owned a small printing establishment across the street. I wondered at their tastes whenever I

glimpsed, with a secret shudder, the higgledy-piggledy stria-
tion of black hairs that showed all along her pale shins through
the nylon of her stockings with the scientific distinctness of a
preparation flattened under glass; or when I felt, at her every
movement, the dullish, stalish, not particularly conspicuous
but all-pervading and depressing emanation that her seldom
bathed flesh spread from under weary perfumes and creams.

Her father had gambled away the greater part of a comfortable fortune, and her mother's first husband had been of Slav
origin, but otherwise Cynthia Vane belonged to a good, respectable family. For aught we know, it may have gone back to
kings and soothsayers in the mists of ultimate islands. Trans-
ferred to a newer world, to a landscape of doomed, splendid
deciduous trees, her ancestry presented, in one of its first phases,
a white churchful of farmers against a black thunderhead, and
then an imposing array of townsmen engaged in mercantile
pursuits, as well as a number of learned men, such as Dr.
Jonathan Vane, the gaunt bore (1780–1839), who perished in
the conflagration of the steamer "Lexington" to become later
an habitué of Cynthia's tilting table. I have always wished to
stand genealogy on its head, and here I have an opportunity
to do so, for it is the last scion, Cynthia, and Cynthia alone,
who will remain of any importance in the Vane dynasty. I am
alluding of course to her artistic gift, to her delightful, gay, but
not very popular paintings which the friends of her friends
bought at long intervals—and I dearly should like to know
where they went after her death, those honest and poetical pictures that illumined her living-room—the wonderfully detailed
images of metallic things, and my favorite "Seen Through a
Windshield"—a windshield partly covered with rime, with a
brilliant trickle (from an imaginary car roof) across its transparent part and, through it all, the sapphire flame of the sky
and a green and white fir tree.

4.

Cynthia had a feeling that her dead sister was not altogether
pleased with her—had discovered by now that she and I had
conspired to break her romance; and so, in order to disarm her
shade, Cynthia reverted to a rather primitive type of sacrificial

offering (tinged, however, with something of Sybil's humor),
and began to send to D.'s business address, at deliberately un-
fixed dates, such trifles as snapshots of Sybil's tomb in a poor
light; cuttings of her own hair which was indistinguishable from
Sybil's; a New England sectional map with an inked-in cross,
midway between two chaste towns, to mark the spot where D.
and Sybil had stopped on October the twenty-third, in broad
daylight, at a lenient motel, in a pink and brown forest; and,
twice, a stuffed skunk.

Being as a conversationalist more voluble than explicit, she
never could describe in full the theory of intervenient auras
that she had somehow evolved. Fundamentally there was
nothing particularly new about her private creed since it pre-
supposed a fairly conventional hereafter, a silent solarium of
immortal souls (spliced with mortal antecedents) whose main
recreation consisted of periodical hoverings over the dear
quick. The interesting point was a curious practical twist that
Cynthia gave to her tame metaphysics. She was sure that her
existence was influenced by all sorts of dead friends each of
whom took turns in directing her fate much as if she were a
stray kitten which a schoolgirl in passing gathers up, and presses
to her cheek, and carefully puts down again, near some suburban hedge—to be stroked presently by another transient hand
or carried off to a world of doors by some hospitable lady.

For a few hours, or for several days in a row, and sometimes
recurrently, in an irregular series, for months or years, anything that happened to Cynthia, after a given person had died,
would be, she said, in the manner and mood of that person.
The event might be extraordinary, changing the course of
one's life; or it might be a string of minute incidents just sufficiently clear to stand out in relief against one's usual day and
then shading off into still vaguer trivia as the aura gradually
faded. The influence might be good or bad; the main thing
was that its source could be identified. It was like walking
through a person's soul, she said. I tried to argue that she
might not always be able to determine the exact source since
not everybody has a recognizable soul; that there are anonymous letters and Christmas presents which anybody might
send; that, in fact, what Cynthia called "a usual day" might be
itself a weak solution of mixed auras or simply the routine shift

of a humdrum guardian angel. And what about God? Did or did not people who would resent any omnipotent dictator on earth look forward to one in heaven? And wars? What a dreadful idea—dead soldiers still fighting with living ones, or phantom armies trying to get at each other through the lives of crippled old men.

But Cynthia was above generalities as she was beyond logic. "Ah, that's Paul," she would say when the soup spitefully boiled over, or: "I guess good Betty Brown is dead"—when she won a beautiful and very welcome vacuum cleaner in a charity lottery. And, with Jamesian meanderings that exasperated my French mind, she would go back to a time when Betty and Paul had not yet departed, and tell me of the showers of well-meant, but odd and quite unacceptable bounties—beginning with an old purse that contained a check for three dollars which she picked up in the street and, of course, returned (to the aforesaid Betty Brown—this is where she first comes in—a decrepit colored woman hardly able to walk), and ending with an insulting proposal from an old beau of hers (this is where Paul comes in) to paint "straight" pictures of his house and family for a reasonable remuneration—all of which followed upon the demise of a certain Mrs. Page, a kindly but petty old party who had pestered her with bits of matter-of-fact advice since Cynthia had been a child.

Sybil's personality, she said, had a rainbow edge as if a little out of focus. She said that had I known Sybil better I would have at once understood how Sybil-like was the aura of minor events which, in spells, had suffused her, Cynthia's, existence after Sybil's suicide. Ever since they had lost their mother they had intended to give up their Boston home and move to New York, where Cynthia's paintings, they thought, would have a chance to be more widely admired; but the old home had clung to them with all its plush tentacles. Dead Sybil, however, had proceeded to separate the house from its view—a thing that affects fatally the sense of home. Right across the narrow street a building project had come into loud, ugly, scaffolded life. A pair of familiar poplars died that spring, turning to blond skeletons. Workmen came and broke up the warm-colored lovely old sidewalk that had a special violet sheen on wet April days and had echoed so memorably to the morning footsteps

of museum-bound Mr. Lever, who upon retiring from business at sixty had devoted a full quarter of a century exclusively
to the study of snails.

Speaking of old men, one should add that sometimes these
posthumous auspices and interventions were in the nature of
parody. Cynthia had been on friendly terms with an eccentric
librarian called Porlock who in the last years of his dusty life
had been engaged in examining old books for miraculous mis-
prints such as the substitution of "l" for the second "h" in the
word "hither." Contrary to Cynthia, he cared nothing for the
thrill of obscure predictions; all he sought was the freak itself,
the chance that mimics choice, the flaw that looks like a flower;
and Cynthia, a much more perverse amateur of mis-shapen or
illicitly connected words, puns, logogriphs, and so on, had
helped the poor crank to pursue a quest that in the light of the
example she cited struck me as statistically insane. Anyway, she
said, on the third day after his death she was reading a magazine and had just come across a quotation from an imperish-
able poem (that she, with other gullible readers, believed to
have been really composed in a dream) when it dawned upon
her that "Alph" was a prophetic sequence of the initial letters
of Anna Livia Plurabelle (another sacred river running through,
or rather around, yet another fake dream), while the additional
"h" modestly stood, as a private signpost, for the word that
had so hypnotized Mr. Porlock. And I wish I could recollect
that novel or short story (by some contemporary writer, I
believe) in which, unknown to its author, the first letters of the
words in its last paragraph formed, as deciphered by Cynthia, a
message from his dead mother.

5.

I am sorry to say that not content with these ingenious fancies Cynthia showed a ridiculous fondness for spiritualism. I
refused to accompany her to sittings in which paid mediums
took part: I knew too much about that from other sources. I
did consent, however, to attend little farces rigged up by Cynthia and her two poker-faced gentlemen-friends of the printing
shop. They were podgy, polite, and rather eerie old fellows,

but I satisfied myself that they possessed considerable wit and culture. We sat down at a light little table, and crackling tremors started almost as soon as we laid our fingertips upon it. I was treated to an assortment of ghosts who rapped out their reports most readily though refusing to elucidate anything that I did not quite catch. Oscar Wilde came in and in rapid garbled French, with the usual anglicisms, obscurely accused Cynthia's dead parents of what appeared in my jottings as "*plagiatisme.*" A brisk spirit contributed the unsolicited information that he, John Moore, and his brother Bill had been coal miners in Colorado and had perished in an avalanche at "Crested Beauty" in January 1883. Frederic Myers, an old hand at the game, hammered out a piece of verse (oddly resembling Cynthia's own fugitive productions) which in part reads in my notes:

> *What is this—a conjuror's rabbit,*
> *Or a flawy but genuine gleam—*
> *Which can check the perilous habit*
> *And dispel the dolorous dream?*

Finally, with a great crash and all kinds of shudderings and jig-like movements on the part of the table, Leo Tolstoy visited our little group and, when asked to identify himself by specific traits of terrene habitation, launched upon a complex description of what seemed to be some Russian type of architectural woodwork ("figures on boards—man, horse, cock, man, horse, cock"), all of which was difficult to take down, hard to understand, and impossible to verify.

I attended two or three other sittings which were even sillier but I must confess that I preferred the childish entertainment they afforded and the cider we drank (Podgy and Pudgy were teetotallers) to Cynthia's awful house parties.

She gave them at the Wheelers' nice flat next door—the sort of arrangement dear to her centrifugal nature, but then, of course, her own living-room always looked like a dirty old palette. Following a barbaric, unhygienic, and adulterous custom, the guests' coats, still warm on the inside, were carried by quiet, baldish Bob Wheeler into the sanctity of a tidy bedroom and heaped on the conjugal bed. It was also he who poured

out the drinks which were passed around by the young photographer while Cynthia and Mrs. Wheeler took care of the
canapés.

A late arrival had the impression of lots of loud people unnecessarily grouped within a smoke-blue space between two
mirrors gorged with reflections. Because, I suppose, Cynthia
wished to be the youngest in the room, the women she used to
invite, married or single, were, at the best, in their precarious
forties; some of them would bring from their homes, in dark
taxis, intact vestiges of good looks, which, however, they lost
as the party progressed. It has always amazed me—the capacity
sociable week-end revellers have of finding almost at once, by
a purely empiric but very precise method, a common denominator of drunkenness, to which everybody loyally sticks before
descending, all together, to the next level. The rich friendliness
of the matrons was marked by tomboyish overtones, while the
fixed inward look of amiably tight men was like a sacrilegious
parody of pregnancy. Although some of the guests were connected in one way or another with the arts, there was no inspired talk, no wreathed, elbow-propped heads, and of course
no flute girls. From some vantage point where she had been
sitting in a stranded mermaid pose on the pale carpet with one
or two younger fellows, Cynthia, her face varnished with a film
of beaming sweat, would creep up on her knees, a proffered
plate of nuts in one hand, and crisply tap with the other the
athletic leg of Cochran or Corcoran, an art dealer, ensconced,
on a pearl-grey sofa, between two flushed, happily disinte-
grating ladies.

At a further stage there would come spurts of more riotous
gaiety. Corcoran or Coransky would grab Cynthia or some other
wandering woman by the shoulder and lead her into a corner
to confront her with a grinning embroglio of private jokes and
rumors, whereupon, with a laugh and a toss of her head, she
would break away. And still later there would be flurries of in-
tersexual chumminess, jocular reconciliations, a bare fleshy
arm flung around another woman's husband (he standing very
upright in the midst of a swaying room), or a sudden rush of
flirtatious anger, of clumsy pursuit—and the quiet half smile
of Bob Wheeler picking up glasses that grew like mushrooms
in the shade of chairs.

After one last party of that sort, I wrote Cynthia a perfectly harmless and, on the whole, well-meant note, in which I poked a little Latin fun at some of her guests. I also apologized for not having touched her whisky, saying that as a Frenchman I preferred the grape to the grain. A few days later I met her on the steps of the Public Library, in the broken sun, under a weak cloudburst, opening her amber umbrella, struggling with a couple of armpitted books (of which I relieved her for a moment). "Footfalls on the Boundary of Another World," by Robert Dale Owen, and something on "Spiritualism and Christianity"; when, suddenly, with no provocation on my part, she blazed out at me with vulgar vehemence, using poisonous words, saying—through pear-shaped drops of sparse rain—that I was a prig and a snob; that I only saw the gestures and disguises of people; that Corcoran had rescued from drowning, in two different oceans, two men—by an irrelevant coincidence both called Corcoran; that romping and screeching Joan Winter had a little girl doomed to grow completely blind in a few months; and that the woman in green with the freckled chest whom I had snubbed in some way or other had written a national best-seller in 1932. Strange Cynthia! I had been told she could be thunderously rude to people whom she liked and respected; one had, however, to draw the line somewhere and since I had by then sufficiently studied her interesting auras and other odds and ids, I decided to stop seeing her altogether.

6.

The night D. informed me of Cynthia's death I returned after eleven to the two-storied house I shared, in horizontal section, with an emeritus professor's widow. Upon reaching the porch I looked with the apprehension of solitude at the two kinds of darkness in the two rows of windows: the darkness of absence and the darkness of sleep.

I could do something about the first but could not duplicate the second. My bed gave me no sense of safety; its springs only made my nerves bounce. I plunged into Shakespeare's sonnets—and found myself idiotically checking the first letters of the lines to see what sacramental words they might form. I got

FATE (LXX), ATOM (CXX) and, twice, TAFT (LXXXVIII, CXXXI). Every now and then I would glance around to see how the objects in my room were behaving. It was strange to think that if bombs began to fall I would feel little more than a gambler's excitement (and a great deal of earthy relief) whereas my heart would burst if a certain suspiciously tense-looking little bottle on yonder shelf moved a fraction of an inch to one side. The silence, too, was suspiciously compact as if deliberately forming a black back-drop for the nerve flash caused by any small sound of unknown origin. All traffic was dead. In vain did I pray for the groan of a truck up Perkins Street. The woman above who used to drive me crazy by the booming thuds occasioned by what seemed monstrous feet of stone (actually, in diurnal life, she was a small dumpy creature resembling a mummified guinea pig) would have earned my blessings had she now trudged to her bathroom. I put out my light and cleared my throat several times so as to be responsible for at least *that* sound. I thumbed a mental ride with a very remote automobile but it dropped me before I had a chance to doze off. Presently a crackle (due, I hoped, to a discarded and crushed sheet of paper opening like a mean, stubborn night flower)—started and stopped in the waste-paper basket, and my bed-table responded with a little click. It would have been just like Cynthia to put on right then a cheap poltergeist show.

I decided to fight Cynthia. I reviewed in thought the modern era of raps and apparitions, beginning with the knockings of 1848, at the hamlet of Hydesville, N.Y., and ending with grotesque phenomena at Cambridge, Mass.; I evoked the anklebones and other anatomical castanets of the Fox sisters (as described by the sages of the University of Buffalo); the mysteriously uniform type of delicate adolescent in bleak Epworth or Tedworth, radiating the same disturbances as in old Peru; solemn Victorian orgies with roses falling and accordions floating to the strains of sacred music; professional imposters regurgitating moist cheesecloth; Mr. Duncan, a lady medium's dignified husband, who, when asked if he would submit to a search, excused himself on the ground of soiled underwear; old Alfred Russel Wallace, the naïve naturalist, refusing to believe that the white form with bare feet and unperforated earlobes before him, at a private pandemonium in Boston, could be prim Miss Cook whom he had just seen asleep, in her curtained corner, all dressed in black, wearing laced-up boots and earrings; two other investigators, small, puny, but reasonably intelligent and active men, closely clinging with arms and legs about Eusapia, a large, plump elderly female reeking of garlic, who still managed to fool them; and the sceptical and embarrassed magician, instructed by charming young Margery's "control" not to get lost in the bathrobe's lining but to follow up the left stocking until he reached the bare thigh—upon the warm skin of which he felt a "teleplastic" mass that appeared to the touch uncommonly like cold, uncooked liver.

7.

I was appealing to flesh, and the corruption of flesh, to refute and defeat the possible persistence of discarnate life. Alas, these conjurations only enhanced my fear of Cynthia's phantom. Atavistic peace came with dawn, and when I slipped into sleep, the sun through the tawny window shades penetrated a dream that somehow was full of Cynthia.

This was disappointing. Secure in the fortress of daylight, I said to myself that I had expected more. She, a painter of glass-bright minutiæ—and now so vague! I lay in bed, thinking my dream over and listening to the sparrows outside: Who knows, if recorded and then run backward, those bird sounds might not become human speech, voiced words, just as the latter become a twitter when reversed? I set myself to re-read my dream—backward, diagonally, up, down—trying hard to unravel something Cynthia-like in it, something strange and suggestive that must be there.

I could isolate, consciously, little. Everything seemed blurred, yellow-clouded, yielding nothing tangible. Her inept acrostics, maudlin evasions, theopathies—every recollection formed ripples of mysterious meaning. Everything seemed yellowly blurred, illusive, lost.

1951

RAY BRADBURY

(b. 1920)

The April Witch

Into the air, over the valleys, under the stars, above a river, a pond, a road, flew Cecy. Invisible as new spring winds, fresh as the breath of clover rising from twilight fields, she flew. She soared in doves as soft as white ermine, stopped in trees and lived in blossoms, showering away in petals when the breeze blew. She perched in a lime-green frog, cool as mint by a shining pool. She trotted in a brambly dog and barked to hear echoes from the sides of distant barns. She lived in new April grasses, in sweet clear liquids rising from the musky earth.

It's spring, thought Cecy. I'll be in every living thing in the world tonight.

Now she inhabited neat crickets on the tar-pool roads, now prickled in dew on an iron gate. Hers was an adaptably quick mind flowing unseen upon Illinois winds on this one evening of her life when she was just seventeen.

"I want to be in love," she said.

She had said it at supper. And her parents had widened their eyes and stiffened back in their chairs. "Patience," had been their advice. "Remember, you're remarkable. Our whole family is odd and remarkable. We can't mix or marry with ordinary folk. We'd lose our magical powers if we did. You wouldn't want to lose your ability to 'travel' by magic, would you? Then be careful. Be careful!"

But in her high bedroom, Cecy had touched perfume to her throat and stretched out, trembling and apprehensive, on her four-poster, as a moon the color of milk rose over Illinois country, turning rivers to cream and roads to platinum.

"Yes," she sighed. "I'm one of an odd family. We sleep days and fly nights like black kites on the wind. If we want, we can sleep in moles through the winter, in the warm earth. I can live in anything at all—a pebble, a crocus, or a praying mantis. I can leave my plain, bony body behind and send my mind far out for adventure. Now!"

The wind whipped her away over fields and meadows.

She saw the warm spring lights of cottages and farms glowing with twilight colors.

If I can't be in love, myself, because I'm plain and odd, then I'll be in love through someone else, she thought.

Outside a farmhouse in the spring night a dark-haired girl, no more than nineteen, drew up water from a deep stone well. She was singing.

Cecy fell—a green leaf—into the well. She lay in the tender moss of the well, gazing up through dark coolness. Now she quickened in a fluttering, invisible amoeba. Now in a water droplet! At last, within a cold cup, she felt herself lifted to the girl's warm lips. There was a soft night sound of drinking.

Cecy looked out from the girl's eyes.

She entered into the dark head and gazed from the shining eyes at the hands pulling the rough rope. She listened through the shell ears to this girl's world. She smelled a particular universe through these delicate nostrils, felt this special heart beating, beating. Felt this strange tongue move with singing.

Does she know I'm here? thought Cecy.

The girl gasped. She stared into the night meadows.

"Who's there?"

No answer.

"Only the wind," whispered Cecy.

"Only the wind." The girl laughed at herself, but shivered.

It was a good body, this girl's body. It held bones of finest slender ivory hidden and roundly fleshed. This brain was like a pink tea rose, hung in darkness, and there was cider-wine in this mouth. The lips lay firm on the white, white teeth and the brows arched neatly at the world, and the hair blew soft and fine on her milky neck. The pores knit small and close. The nose tilted at the moon and the cheeks glowed like small fires. The body drifted with feather-balances from one motion to another and seemed always singing to itself. Being in this body, this head, was like basking in a hearth fire, living in the purr of a sleeping cat, stirring in warm creek waters that flowed by night to the sea.

I'll like it here, thought Cecy.

"What?" asked the girl, as if she'd heard a voice.

"What's your name?" asked Cecy carefully.

"Ann Leary." The girl twitched. "Now why should I say that out loud?"

"Ann, Ann," whispered Cecy. "Ann, you're going to be in love."

As if to answer this, a great roar sprang from the road, a clatter and a ring of wheels on gravel. A tall man drove up in a rig, holding the reins high with his monstrous arms, his smile glowing across the yard.

"Ann!"

"Is that you, Tom?"

"Who else?" Leaping from the rig, he tied the reins to the fence.

"I'm not speaking to you!" Ann whirled, the bucket in her hands slopping.

"No!" cried Cecy.

Ann froze. She looked at the hills and the first spring stars. She stared at the man named Tom. Cecy made her drop the bucket.

"Look what you've done!"

Tom ran up.

"Look what you made me do!"

He wiped her shoes with a kerchief, laughing.

"Get away!" She kicked at his hands, but he laughed again, and gazing down on him from miles away, Cecy saw the turn of his head, the size of his skull, the flare of his nose, the shine of his eye, the girth of his shoulder, and the hard strength of his hands doing this delicate thing with the handkerchief. Peering down from the secret attic of this lovely head, Cecy yanked a hidden copper ventriloquist's wire and the pretty mouth popped wide: "Thank you!"

"Oh, so you *have* manners?" The smell of leather on his hands, the smell of the horse rose from his clothes into the tender nostrils, and Cecy, far, far away over night meadows and flowered fields, stirred as with some dream in her bed.

"Not for you, no!" said Ann.

"Hush, speak gently," said Cecy. She moved Ann's fingers out toward Tom's head. Ann snatched them back.

"I've gone mad!"

"You have." He nodded, smiling but bewildered. "Were you going to touch me then?"

"I don't know. Oh, go away!" Her cheeks glowed with pink charcoals.

"Why don't you run? I'm not stopping you." Tom got up. "Have you changed your mind? Will you go to the dance with me tonight? It's special. Tell you why later."

"No," said Ann.

"Yes!" cried Cecy. "I've never danced. I want to dance. I've never worn a long gown, all rustly. I want that. I want to dance all night. I've never known what it's like to be in a woman, dancing; Father and Mother would never permit it. Dogs, cats, locusts, leaves, everything else in the world at one time or another I've known, but never a woman in the spring, never on a night like this. Oh, please—we *must* go to that dance!"

She spread her thought like the fingers of a hand within a new glove.

"Yes," said Ann Leary, "I'll go. I don't know why, but I'll go to the dance with you tonight, Tom."

"Now inside, quick!" cried Cecy. "You must wash, tell your folks, get your gown ready, out with the iron, into your room!"

"Mother," said Ann, "I've changed my mind!"

The rig was galloping off down the pike, the rooms of the farmhouse jumped to life, water was boiling for a bath, the coal stove was heating an iron to press the gown, the mother was rushing about with a fringe of hairpins in her mouth. "What's come over you, Ann? You don't like Tom!"

"That's true." Ann stopped amidst the great fever.

But it's spring! thought Cecy.

"It's spring," said Ann.

And it's a fine night for dancing, thought Cecy.

". . . for dancing," murmured Ann Leary.

Then she was in the tub and the soap creaming on her white seal shoulders, small nests of soap beneath her arms, and the flesh of her warm breasts moving in her hands and Cecy moving the mouth, making the smile, keeping the actions going. There must be no pause, no hesitation, or the entire pantomime might fall in ruins! Ann Leary must be kept

moving, doing, acting, wash here, soap there, now out! Rub
with a towel! Now perfume and powder!

"You!" Ann caught herself in the mirror, all whiteness and
pinkness like lilies and carnations. "*Who* are you tonight?"

"I'm a girl seventeen." Cecy gazed from her violet eyes.
"You can't see me. Do you know I'm here?"

Ann Leary shook her head. "I've rented my body to an April
witch, for sure."

"*Close*, very close!" laughed Cecy. "Now, on with your
dressing."

The luxury of feeling good clothes move over an ample
body! And then the halloo outside.

"Ann, Tom's back!"

"Tell him to wait." Ann sat down suddenly. "Tell him I'm
not going to that dance."

"What?" said her mother, in the door.

Cecy snapped back into attention. It had been a fatal relaxing,
a fatal moment of leaving Ann's body for only an instant. She
had heard the distant sound of horses' hoofs and the rig rambling through moonlit spring country. For a second she
thought, I'll go find Tom and sit in his head and see what it's
like to be in a man of twenty-two on a night like this. And so
she had started quickly across a heather field, but now, like a
bird to a cage, flew back and rustled and beat about in Ann
Leary's head.

"Ann!"

"Tell him to go away!"

"Ann!" Cecy settled down and spread her thoughts.

But Ann had the bit in her mouth now. "No, no, I hate him!"

I shouldn't have left—even for a moment. Cecy poured her
mind into the hands of the young girl, into the heart, into the
head, softly, softly. *Stand up*, she thought.

Ann stood.

Put on your coat!

Ann put on her coat.

Now, march!

No! thought Ann Leary.

March!

"Ann," said her mother, "don't keep Tom waiting another

minute. You get on out there now and no nonsense. What's come over you?"

"Nothing, Mother. Good night. We'll be home late."

Ann and Cecy ran together into the spring evening.

A room full of softly dancing pigeons ruffling their quiet, trailing feathers, a room full of peacocks, a room full of rainbow eyes and lights. And in the center of it, around, around, around, danced Ann Leary.

"Oh, it *is* a fine evening," said Cecy.

"Oh, it's a fine evening," said Ann.

"You're odd," said Tom.

The music whirled them in dimness, in rivers of song; they floated, they bobbed, they sank down, they arose for air, they gasped, they clutched each other like drowning people and whirled on again, in fan motions, in whispers and sighs, to "Beautiful Ohio."

Cecy hummed. Ann's lips parted and the music came out.

"Yes, I'm odd," said Cecy.

"You're not the same," said Tom.

"No, not tonight."

"You're not the Ann Leary I knew."

"No, not at all, at all," whispered Cecy, miles and miles away. "No, not at all," said the moved lips.

"I've the funniest feeling," said Tom.

"About what?"

"About you." He held her back and danced her and looked into her glowing face, watching for something. "Your eyes," he said, "I can't figure it."

"Do you see *me*?" asked Cecy.

"Part of you's here, Ann, and part of you's not." Tom turned her carefully, his face uneasy.

"Yes."

"Why did you come with me?"

"I didn't want to come," said Ann.

"Why, then?"

"Something made me."

"What?"

"I don't know." Ann's voice was faintly hysterical.

"Now, now, hush, hush," whispered Cecy. "Hush, that's it. Around, around."

They whispered and rustled and rose and fell away in the dark room, with the music moving and turning them.

"But you *did* come to the dance," said Tom.

"I did," said Cecy.

"Here." And he danced her lightly out an open door and walked her quietly away from the hall and the music and the people.

They climbed up and sat together in the rig.

"Ann," he said, taking her hands, trembling. "Ann." But the way he said her name it was as if it wasn't her name. He kept glancing into her pale face, and now her eyes were open again. "I used to love you, you know that," he said.

"I know."

"But you've always been fickle and I didn't want to be hurt."

"It's just as well, we're very young," said Ann.

"No, I mean to say, I'm sorry," said Cecy.

"What *do* you mean?" Tom dropped her hands and stiffened.

The night was warm and the smell of the earth shimmered up all about them where they sat, and the fresh trees breathed one leaf against another in a shaking and rustling.

"I don't know," said Ann.

"Oh, but *I* know," said Cecy. "You're tall and you're the finest-looking man in all the world. This is a good evening; this is an evening I'll always remember, being with you." She put out the alien cold hand to find his reluctant hand again and bring it back, and warm it and hold it very tight.

"But," said Tom, blinking, "tonight you're here, you're there. One minute one way, the next minute another. I wanted to take you to the dance tonight for old times' sake. I meant nothing by it when I first asked you. And then, when we were standing at the well, I knew something had changed, really changed, about you. You were different. There was something new and soft, something . . ." He groped for a word. "I don't know, I can't say. The way you looked. Something about your voice. And I know I'm in love with you again."

"No," said Cecy. "With me, with *me*."

"And I'm afraid of being in love with you," he said. "You'll hurt me again."

"I might," said Ann.

No, no, I'd love you with all my heart! thought Cecy. Ann, say it to him, say it for me. Say you'd love him with all your heart.

Ann said nothing.

Tom moved quietly closer and put his hand up to hold her chin. "I'm going away. I've got a job a hundred miles from here. Will you miss me?"

"Yes," said Ann and Cecy.

"May I kiss you good-by, then?"

"Yes," said Cecy before anyone else could speak.

He placed his lips to the strange mouth. He kissed the strange mouth and he was trembling.

Ann sat like a white statue.

"Ann!" said Cecy. "Move your arms, *hold* him!"

She sat like a carved wooden doll in the moonlight.

Again he kissed her lips.

"I do love you," whispered Cecy. "I'm here, it's me you saw in her eyes, it's me, and I love you if she never will."

He moved away and seemed like a man who had run a long distance. He sat beside her. "I don't know what's happening. For a moment there . . ."

"Yes?" asked Cecy.

"For a moment I thought—" He put his hands to his eyes. "Never mind. Shall I take you home now?"

"Please," said Ann Leary.

He clucked to the horse, snapped the reins tiredly, and drove the rig away. They rode in the rustle and slap and motion of the moonlit rig in the still early, only eleven o'clock spring night, with the shining meadows and sweet fields of clover gliding by.

And Cecy, looking at the fields and meadows, thought, It would be worth it, it would be worth everything to be with him from this night on. And she heard her parents' voices again, faintly, "Be careful. You wouldn't want to lose your magical powers, would you—married to a mere mortal? Be careful. You wouldn't want that."

Yes, yes, thought Cecy, even that I'd give up, here and now, if he would have me. I wouldn't need to roam the spring nights then, I wouldn't need to live in birds and dogs and cats and foxes, I'd need only to be with him. Only him. Only him.

The road passed under, whispering.

"Tom," said Ann at last.

"What?" He stared coldly at the road, the horse, the trees, the sky, the stars.

"If you're ever, in years to come, at any time, in Green Town, Illinois, a few miles from here, will you do me a favor?"

"Perhaps."

"Will you do me the favor of stopping and seeing a friend of mine?" Ann Leary said this haltingly, awkwardly.

"Why?"

"She's a good friend. I've told her of you. I'll give you her address. Just a moment." When the rig stopped at her farm she drew forth a pencil and paper from her small purse and wrote in the moonlight, pressing the paper to her knee. "There it is. Can you read it?"

He glanced at the paper and nodded bewilderedly.

"Cecy Elliott, 12 Willow Street, Green Town, Illinois," he said.

"Will you visit her someday?" asked Ann.

"Someday," he said.

"Promise?"

"What has this to do with us?" he cried savagely. "What do I want with names and papers?" He crumpled the paper into a tight ball and shoved it in his coat.

"Oh, please promise!" begged Cecy.

". . . promise . . ." said Ann.

"All right, all right, now let me be!" he shouted.

I'm tired, thought Cecy. I can't stay. I have to go home. I'm weakening. I've only the power to stay a few hours out like this in the night, traveling, traveling. But before I go . . .

". . . before I go," said Ann.

She kissed Tom on the lips.

"This is *me* kissing you," said Cecy.

Tom held her off and looked at Ann Leary and looked deep, deep inside. He said nothing, but his face began to relax slowly, very slowly, and the lines vanished away, and his mouth softened from its hardness, and he looked deep again into the moonlit face held here before him.

Then he put her off the rig and without so much as good night was driving swiftly down the road.

Cecy let go.

Ann Leary, crying out, released from prison, it seemed, raced up the moonlit path to her house and slammed the door.

Cecy lingered for only a little while. In the eyes of a cricket she saw the spring night world. In the eyes of a frog she sat for a lonely moment by a pool. In the eyes of a night bird she looked down from a tall, moon-haunted elm and saw the lights go out in two farmhouses, one here, one a mile away. She thought of herself and her family, and her strange power, and the fact that no one in the family could ever marry any one of the people in this vast world out here beyond the hills.

"Tom?" Her weakening mind flew in a night bird under the trees and over deep fields of wild mustard. "Have you still got the paper, Tom? Will you come by someday, some year, sometime, to see me? Will you know me then? Will you look in my face and remember then where it was you saw me last and know that you love me as I love you, with all my heart for all time?"

She paused in the cool night air, a million miles from towns and people, above farms and continents and rivers and hills. "Tom?" Softly.

Tom was asleep. It was deep night; his clothes were hung on chairs or folded neatly over the end of the bed. And in one silent, carefully upflung hand upon the white pillow, by his head, was a small piece of paper with writing on it. Slowly, slowly, a fraction of an inch at a time, his fingers closed down upon and held it tightly. And he did not even stir or notice when a blackbird, faintly, wondrously, beat softly for a moment against the clear moon crystals of the windowpane, then, fluttering quietly, stopped and flew away toward the east, over the sleeping earth.

1952

CHARLES BEAUMONT

(1929–1967)

Black Country

SPOOF COLLINS blew his brains out, all right—right on out through the top of his head. But I don't mean with a gun. I mean with a horn. Every night: slow and easy, eight to one. And that's how he died. Climbing, with that horn, climbing up high. For what? *"Hey, man, Spoof—listen, you picked the tree, now come on down!"* But he couldn't come down, he didn't know how. He just kept climbing, higher and higher. And then he fell. Or jumped. Anyhow, *that's* the way he died.

The bullet didn't kill anything. I'm talking about the one that tore up the top of his mouth. It didn't kill anything that wasn't dead already. Spoof just put in an extra note, that's all.

We planted him out about four miles from town—home is where you drop: residential district, all wood construction. Rain? You know it. Bible type: sky like a month-old bedsheet, wind like a stepped-on cat, cold and dark, those Forty Days, those Forty Nights! But nice and quiet most of the time. Like Spoof: nice and quiet, with a lot underneath that you didn't like to think about.

We planted him and watched and put what was his down into the ground with him. His horn, battered, dented, nicked—right there in his hands, but not just there; I mean in position, so if he wanted to do some more climbing, all right, he could. And his music. We planted that too, because leaving it out would have been like leaving out Spoof's arms or his heart or his guts.

Lux started things off with a chord from his guitar, no particular notes, only a feeling, a sound. A Spoof Collins kind of sound. Jimmy Fritch picked it up with his stick and they talked a while—Lux got a real piano out of that git-box. Then when Jimmy stopped talking and stood there, waiting, Sonny Holmes stepped up and wiped his mouth and took the melody on his shiny new trumpet. It wasn't Spoof, but it came close; and it was still *The Jimjam Man*, the way Spoof wrote it back when he used to write things down. Sonny got off with a high-squealing blast, and no eyes came up—we knew, we remembered. The kid always had it collared. He just never talked about it. And listen to him now! He stood there over Spoof's grave, giving it all back to The Ol' Massuh, giving it back right—*"Broom off, white child, you got four sides!" "I want to learn from you, Mr. Collins. I want to play jazz and you can teach me." "I got things to do, I can't waste no time on a half-hipped young'un." "Please, Mr. Collins." "You got to stop that, you got to stop callin' me 'Mr. Collins,' hear?" "Yes sir, yes sir."*— He put out real sound, like he didn't remember a thing. Like he wasn't playing for that pile of darkmeat in the ground, not at all; but for the great Spoof Collins, for the man Who Knew and the man Who Did, who gave jazz spats and dressed up the blues, who did things with a trumpet that a trumpet couldn't do, and more; for the man who could blow down the walls or make a chicken cry, without half trying—for the mighty Spoof, who'd once walked in music like a boy in river mud, loving it, breathing it, living it.

Then Sonny quit. He wiped his mouth again and stepped back and Mr. "T" took it on his trombone while I beat up the tubs.

Pretty soon we had *The Jimjam Man* rocking the way it used to rock. A little slow, maybe: it needed Bud Meunier on bass and a few trips on the piano. But it moved.

We went through *Take It From Me* and *Night in the Blues* and *Big Gig* and *Only Us Chickens* and *Forty G's*—Sonny's insides came out through the horn on that one, I could tell—and *Slice City Stomp*—you remember: sharp and clean, like sliding down a razor—and *What the Cats Dragged In*—the longs, the shorts, all the great Spoof Collins numbers. We wrapped them up and put them down there with him.

Then it got dark.

And it was time for the last one, the greatest one. . . . Rose-Ann shivered and cleared her throat; the rest of us looked around, for the first time, at all those rows of split-wood grave markers, shining in the rain, and the trees and the coffin, dark, wet. Out by the fence, a couple of farmers stood watching. Just watching.

One—Rose-Ann opens her coat, puts her hands on her hips, wets her lips;

Two—Freddie gets the spit out of his stick, rolls his eyes;

Three—Sonny puts the trumpet to his mouth;

Four—

And we played Spoof's song, his last one, the one he wrote a long way ago, before the music dried out his head, before he turned mean and started climbing: *Black Country*. The song that said just a little of what Spoof wanted to say, and couldn't.

You remember. Spider-slow chords crawling down, soft, easy, and then bottom and silence and, suddenly, the cry of the horn, screaming in one note all the hate and sadness and loneliness, all the want and got-to-have; and then the note dying, quick, and Rose-Ann's voice, a whisper, a groan, a sigh. . . .

> *"Black Country is somewhere, Lord,*
> *That I don't want to go.*
> *Black Country is somewhere*
> *That I never want to go.*
> *Rain-water drippin'*
> *On the bed and on the floor,*
> *Rain-water drippin'*
> *From the ground and through the door . . ."*

We all heard the piano, even though it wasn't there. Fingers moving down those minor chords, those black keys, that black country . . .

> *"Well, in that old Black Country*
> *If you ain't feelin' good,*
> *They let you have an overcoat*
> *That's carved right out of wood.*
> *But way down there*
> *It gets so dark*
> *You never see a friend—*
> *Black Country may not be the Most,*
> *But, Lord! it's sure the End . . ."*

Bitter little laughing words, piling up, now mad, now sad; and then, an ugly blast from the horn and Rose-Ann's voice screaming, crying:

"I never want to go there, Lord!
I never want to be,
I never want to lay down
In that Black Country!"

And quiet, quiet, just the rain, and the wind.

"Let's go, man," Freddie said.

So we turned around and left Spoof there under the ground.

Or, at least, that's what I thought we did.

Sonny took over without saying a word. He didn't have to: just who was about to fuss? He was white, but he didn't play white, not these days; and he learned the hard way—by unlearning. Now he could play gutbucket and he could play blues, stomp and slide, name it, Sonny could play it. Funny as hell to hear, too, because he looked like everything else but a musician. Short and skinny, glasses, nose like a melted candle, head clean as the one-ball, and white? Next to old Hushup, that café sunburn glowed like a flashlight.

"Man, who skinned you?"

"Who dropped you in the flour barrel?"

But he got closer to Spoof than any of the rest of us did. He knew what to do, and why. Just like a school teacher all the time: "That's good, Lux, that's awful good—now let's play some music." "Get off it, C.T.—what's Lenox Avenue doing in the middle of Lexington?" "Come on, boys, hang on to the sound, hang on to it!" Always using words like "flavor" and "authentic" and "blood," peering over those glasses, pounding his feet right through the floor: STOMP! STOMP! "That's it, we've got it now—oh, listen! It's true, it's clean!" STOMP! STOMP!

Not the easiest to dig him. Nobody broke all the way through.

"How come, boy? What for?" and every time the same answer:

"I want to play jazz."

Like he'd joined the Church and didn't want to argue about it.

Spoof was still Spoof when Sonny started coming around.

Not a lot of people with us then, but a few, enough—the long-hairs and critics and connoisseurs—and some real ears too—enough to fill a club every night, and who needs more? It was COLLINS AND HIS CREW, tight and neat, never a performance, always a session. Lot of music, lot of fun. And a line-up that some won't forget: Jimmy Fritch on clarinet, Honker Reese on alto-sax, Charles di Lusso on tenor, Spoof on trumpet, Henry Walker on piano, Lux Anderson on banjo and myself—Hushup Paige—on drums. Newmown hay, all right, I know—I remember, I've heard the records we cut—but, the Road was there.

Sonny used to hang around the old Continental Club on State Street in Chicago, every night, listening. Eight o'clock roll 'round, and there he'd be—a little different: younger, skinnier—listening hard, over in a corner all to himself, eyes closed like he was asleep. Once in a while he put in a request—*Darktown Strutter's Ball* was one he liked, and some of Jelly Roll's numbers—but mostly he just sat there, taking it all in. For real.

And it kept up like this for two or three weeks, regular as 2/4.

Now Spoof was mean in those days—don't think he wasn't—but not blood-mean. Even so, the white boy in the corner bugged Ol' Massuh after a while and he got to making dirty cracks with his horn: WAAAAA! *Git your ass out of here.* WAAAAA! *You only* think *you're with it!* WAAAAA! *There's a little white child sittin' in a chair there's a little white child losin' all his hair* . . .

It got to the kid, too, every bit of it. And that made Spoof even madder. But what can you do?

Came Honker's trip to Slice City along about then: our sax-man got a neck all full of the sharpest kind of steel. So we were out one horn. And you could tell: we played a little bit too rough, and the head-arrangements Collins and His Crew grew up to, they needed Honker's grease in the worst way. But we'd been together for five years or more, and a new man just didn't play somehow. We were this one solid thing, like a unit, and somebody had cut off a piece of us and we couldn't grow the piece back so we just tried to get along anyway, bleeding every night, bleeding from that wound.

Then one night it bust. We'd gone through some slow

walking stuff, some tricky stuff and some loud stuff—still covering up—when this kid, this white boy, got up from his chair and ankled over and tapped Spoof on the shoulder. It was break-time and Spoof was brought down about Honker, about how bad we were sounding, sitting there sweating, those pounds of man, black as coaldust soaked in oil—he was the *blackest* man!—and those eyes, beady white and small as agates.

"Excuse me, Mr. Collins, I wonder if I might have a word with you?" He wondered if he might have a word with Mr. Collins!

Spoof swiveled in his chair and clapped a look around the kid. "Hnff?"

"I notice that you don't have a sax man any more."

"You don't mean to tell me?"

"Yes sir. I thought—I mean, I was wondering if—"

"Talk up, boy. I can't hear you."

The kid looked scared. Lord, he looked scared—and he was white to begin with.

"Well sir, I was just wondering if—if you needed a saxophone."

"You know somebody plays sax?"

"Yes sir, I do."

"And who might that be?"

"Me."

"You."

"Yes sir."

Spoof smiled a quick one. Then he shrugged. "Broom off, son," he said. "Broom 'way off."

The kid turned red. He all of a sudden didn't look scared any more. Just mad. Mad as hell. But he didn't say anything. He went on back to his table and then it was end of the ten.

We swung into *Basin Street*, smooth as Charley's tenor could make it, with Lux Anderson talking it out: *Basin Street, man, it is the street, Where the elite, well, they gather 'round to eat a little* . . . And we fooled around with the slow stuff for a while. Then Spoof lifted his horn and climbed up two-and-a-half and let out his trademark, that short high screech that sounded like something dying that wasn't too happy about it. And we rocked some, Henry taking it, Jimmy kanoodling the great headwork that only Jimmy knows how to do, me slamming the skins—and it was nowhere. Without Honker to keep us all on the ground, we were just making noise. Good noise, all right, but not music. And Spoof knew it. He broke his mouth blowing—to prove it.

And we cussed the cat that sliced our man.

Then, right away—nobody could remember when it came in—suddenly, we had us an alto-sax. Smooth and sure and snaky, that sound put a knot on each of us and said: Bust loose now, boys, I'll pull you back down. Like sweet-smelling glue, like oil in a machine, like—Honker.

We looked around and there was the kid, still sore, blowing like a madman, and making fine fine music.

Spoof didn't do much. Most of all, he didn't stop the number. He just let that horn play, listening—and when we slid over all the rough spots and found us backed up neat as could be, the Ol' Massuh let out a grin and a nod and a "Keep blowin', young'un!" and we knew that we were going to be all right.

After it was over, Spoof walked up to the kid. They looked at each other, sizing it up, taking it in.

Spoof says: "You did good."

And the kid—he was still burned—says: "You mean I did *damn* good."

And Spoof shakes his head. "No, that ain't what I mean."

And in a second one was laughing while the other one blushed. Spoof had known all along that the kid was faking, that he'd just been lucky enough to know our style on *Basin Street* up-down-and-across.

The Ol' Massuh waited for the kid to turn and start to slink off, then he said: "Boy, you want to go to work?" . . .

Sonny learned so fast it scared you. Spoof never held back; he turned it all over, everything it had taken us our whole lives to find out.

And—we had some good years. Charley di Lusso dropped out, we took on Bud Meunier—the greatest bass man of them all—and Lux threw away his banjo for an AC-DC git-box and old C.T. Mr. "T" Green and his trombone joined the Crew. And we kept growing and getting stronger—no million-copies platter sales or stands at the Paramount—too "special"—but we never ate too far down on the hog, either.

In a few years Sonny Holmes was making that sax stand on its hind legs and jump through hoops that Honker never dreamed about. Spoof let him strictly alone. When he got mad it wasn't ever because Sonny had white skin—Spoof always was too busy to notice things like that—but only because The Ol' Massuh had to get T'd off at each one of us every now and then. He figured it kept us on our toes.

In fact, except right at first, there never was any real blood between Spoof and Sonny until Rose-Ann came along.

Spoof didn't want a vocalist with the band. But the coon-shouting days were gone alas, except for Satchmo and Calloway —who had style: none of us had style, man, we just hollered— so when push came to shove, we had to put out the net.

And chickens aplenty came to crow and plenty moved on fast and we were about to give up when a dusky doll of 20-ought stepped up and let loose a hunk of *The Man I Love* and that's all, brothers, end of the search.

Rose-Ann McHugh was a little like Sonny: where she came from, she didn't know a ball of cotton from a piece of pop-corn. She'd studied piano for a flock of years with a Pennsylvania long-hair, read music whipfast and had been pointed toward the Big Steinway and the O.M.'s, Chopin and Bach and all that jazz. And good—I mean, she could pull some very fancy noise out of those keys. But it wasn't the Road. She'd heard a few records of Muggsy Spanier's, a couple of Jelly Roll's— *New Orleans Bump*, *Shreveport Stomp*, old *Wolverine Blues*— and she just got took hold of. Like it happens, all the time. She knew.

Spoof hired her after the first song. And we could see things in her eyes for The Ol' Massuh right away, fast. Bad to watch: I mean to say, she was chicken dinner, but what made it ugly was, you could tell she hadn't been in the oven very long.

Anyway, most of us could tell. Sonny, for instance.

But Spoof played tough to begin. He gave her the treat-ment, all the way. To see if she'd hold up. Because, above everything else, there was the Crew, the Unit, the Group. It was right, it had to stay right.

"Gal, forget your hands—that's for the cats out front. Leave 'em alone. And pay attention to the music, hear?"

"You ain't got a 'voice,' you got an instrument. And you ain't

even started to learn how to play on it. Get some sound, bring it on out."

"Stop that throat stuff—you' singin' with the Crew now. From the belly, gal, from the belly. That's where music comes from, hear?"

And she loved it, like Sonny did. She was with The Ol' Massuh, she knew what he was talking about.

Pretty soon she fit just fine. And when she did, and everybody knew she did, Spoof eased up and waited and watched the old machine click right along, one-two, one-two.

That's when he began to change. Right then, with the Crew growed up and in long pants at last. Like we didn't need him any more to wash our face and comb our hair and switch our behinds for being bad.

Spoof began to change. He beat out time and blew his riffs, but things were different and there wasn't anybody who didn't know that for a fact.

In a hurry, all at once, he wrote down all his great arrangements, quick as he could. One right after the other. And we wondered why—we'd played them a million times.

Then he grabbed up Sonny. *"White Boy, listen. You want to learn how to play trumpet?"*

And the blood started between them. Spoof rode on Sonny's back twenty-four hours, showing him lip, showing him breath. *"This ain't a saxophone, boy, it's a trumpet, a music-horn. Get it right—do it again—that's lousy—do it again—that was nowhere—do it again—do it again!"* All the time.

Sonny worked hard. Anybody else, they would have told The Ol' Massuh where he could put that little old horn. But the kid knew something was being given to him—he didn't know why, nobody did, but for a reason—something that Spoof wouldn't have given anybody else. And he was grateful. So he worked. And he didn't ask any how-comes, either.

Pretty soon he started to handle things right. 'Way down the road from great, but coming along. The sax had given him a hard set of lips and he had plenty of wind; most of all, he had the spirit—the thing that you can beat up your chops about it for two weeks straight and never say what it is, but if it isn't there, buddy-ghee, you may get to be President but you'll never play music.

Lord, Lord, Spoof worked that boy like a two-ton jockey on a ten-ounce horse. *"Do it again—that ain't right—goddamn it, do it again! Now one more time!"*

When Sonny knew enough to sit in with the horn on a few easy ones, Ol' Massuh would tense up and follow the kid with his eyes—I mean it got real crawly. What for? Why was he pushing it like that?

Then it quit. Spoof didn't say anything. He just grunted and quit all of a sudden, like he'd done with us, and Sonny went back on sax and that was that.

Which is when the real blood started.

The Lord says every man has got to love something, sometimes, somewhere. First choice is a chick, but there's other choices. Spoof's was a horn. He was married to a piece of brass, just as married as a man can get. Got up with it in the morning, talked with it all day long, loved it at night like no chick I ever heard of got loved. And I don't mean one-two-three: I mean the slow-building kind. He'd kiss it and hold it and watch out for it. Once a cat full of tea tried to put the snatch on Spoof's horn, for laughs: when Spoof caught up with him, that cat gave up laughing for life.

Sonny knew this. It's why he never blew his stack at all the riding. Spoof's teaching him to play trumpet—*the* trumpet— was like as if The Ol' Massuh had said: *"You want to take my wife for a few nights? You do? Then here, let me show you how to do it right. She likes it done right."*

For Rose-Ann, though, it was the worst. Every day she got that look deeper in, and in a while we turned around and, man! *Where* is little Rosie? She was gone. That young half-fried chicken had flew the roost. And in her place was a doll that wasn't dead, a big bunch of curves and skin like a brand-new penny. Overnight, almost. Sonny noticed. Freddie and Lux and even old Mr. "T" noticed. *I* had eyes in my head. But Spoof didn't notice. He was already in love, there wasn't any more room.

Rose-Ann kept snapping the whip, but Ol' Massuh, he wasn't *about* to make the trip. He'd started climbing, then, and he didn't treat her any different than he treated us.

"Get away, gal, broom on off—can't you see I'm busy? Wiggle it elsewhere, hear? Elsewhere. Shoo!"

And she just loved him more for it. Every time he kicked

her, she loved him more. Tried to find him and see him and, sometimes, when he'd stop for breath, she'd try to help, because she knew something had crawled inside Spoof, something that was eating from the inside out, that maybe he couldn't get rid of alone.

Finally, one night, at a two-weeker in Dallas, it tumbled.

We'd gone through *Georgia Brown* for the tourists and things were kind of dull, when Spoof started sweating. His eyes began to roll. And he stood up, like a great big animal—like an ape or a bear, big and powerful and mean-looking—and he gave us the two-finger signal.

Sky-High. 'Way before it was due, before either the audience or any of us had got wound up.

Freddie frowned. "You think it's time, Top?"

"Listen," Spoof said, "goddamn it, who says when it's time —you, or me?"

We went into it, cold, but things warmed up pretty fast. The dancers grumbled and moved off the floor and the place filled up with talk.

I took my solo and beat hell out of the skins. Then Spoof swiped at his mouth and let go with a blast and moved it up into that squeal and stopped and started playing. It was all headwork. All new to us.

New to anybody.

I saw Sonny get a look on his face, and we sat still and listened while Spoof made love to that horn.

Now like a scream, now like a laugh—now we're swinging in the trees, now the white men are coming, now we're in the boat and chains are hanging from our ankles and we're rowing, rowing—*Spoof, what is it?*—now we're sawing wood and picking cotton and serving up those cool cool drinks to the Colonel in his chair—*Well, blow, man!*—now we're free, and we're struttin' down Lenox Avenue and State & Madison and Pirate's Alley, laughing, crying—*Who said free?*—and we want to go back and we don't want to go back—*Play it, Spoof! God, God, tell us all about it! Talk to us!*—and we're sitting in a cellar with a comb wrapped up in paper, with a skin-barrel and a tinklebox—*Don't stop, Spoof! Oh Lord, please don't stop!*—and we're making something, something, what is it? Is it jazz? Why, yes, Lord, it's jazz. Thank you, sir, and thank you, sir, we finally got it, something that is *ours*, something great that belongs to us and to us alone, that we made, and *that's* why it's important, and *that's* what it's all about and—*Spoof! Spoof, you can't stop now*—

But it was over, middle of the trip. And there was Spoof standing there facing us and tears streaming out of those eyes and down over that coaldust face, and his body shaking and shaking. It's the first we ever saw that. It's the first we ever heard him cough, too—like a shotgun going off every two seconds, big raking sounds that tore up from the bottom of his belly and spilled out wet and loud.

The way it tumbled was this. Rose-Ann went over to him and tried to get him to sit down. "Spoof, honey, what's wrong? Come on and sit down. Honey, don't just stand there."

Spoof stopped coughing and jerked his head around. He looked at Rose-Ann for a while and whatever there was in his face, it didn't have a name. The whole room was just as quiet as it could be.

Rose-Ann took his arm. "Come on, honey, Mr. Collins—"

He let out one more cough, then, and drew back his hand—that black-topped, pink-palmed ham of a hand—and laid it, sharp, across the girl's cheek. It sent her staggering. "Git off my back, hear? Damn it, git off! Stay 'way from me!"

She got up crying. Then, you know what she did? She waltzed on back and took his arm and said: "Please."

Spoof was just a lot of crazy-mad on two legs. He shouted out some words and pulled back his hand again. "Can't you never learn? What I got to do, goddamn little—"

Then—Sonny moved. All-the-time quiet and soft and gentle Sonny. He moved quick across the floor and stood in front of Spoof.

"Keep your black hands off her," he said.

Ol' Massuh pushed Rose-Ann aside and planted his legs, his breath rattling fast and loose, like a bull's. And he towered over the kid, Goliath and David, legs far apart on the boards and fingers curled up, bowling balls at the ends of his sleeves.

"You talkin' to me, boy?"

Sonny's face was red, like I hadn't seen it since that first time at the Continental Club, years back. "You've got ears, Collins. Touch her again and I'll kill you."

I don't know exactly what we expected, but I know what we were afraid of. We were afraid Spoof would let go; and if he did . . . well, put another bed in the hospital, men. He stood there, breathing, and Sonny gave it right back—for hours, days and nights, for a month, toe to toe.

Then Spoof relaxed. He pulled back those fat lips, that didn't look like lips any more, they were so tough and leathery, and showed a mouthful of white and gold, and grunted, and turned, and walked away.

We swung into *Twelfth Street Rag* in *such* a hurry!

And it got kicked under the sofa.

But we found out something, then, that nobody even suspected.

Sonny had it for Rose-Ann. He had it bad.

And that ain't good.

Spoof fell to pieces after that. He played day and night, when we were working, when we weren't working. Climbing. Trying to get it said, all of it.

"Listen, you can't hit Heaven with a slingshot, Daddy-O!"

"What you want to do, man—blow Judgment?"

He never let up. If he ate anything, you tell me when. Sometimes he tied on, straight stuff, quick, medicine type of drinking. But only after he'd been climbing and started to blow flat and ended up in those coughing fits.

And it got worse. Nothing helped, either: foam or booze or tea or even Indoor Sports, and he tried them all. And got worse.

"Get fixed up, Mr. C, you hear? See a bone-man; you in bad shape . . ."

"Get away from me, get on away!" Hawk! and a big red spot on the handkerchief. *"Broom off! Shoo!"*

And gradually the old horn went sour, ugly and bitter sounding, like Spoof himself. Hoo Lord, the way he rode Sonny then: *"How you like the dark stuff, boy? You like it pretty good? Hey there, don't hold back. Rosie's fine talent—I know. Want me to tell you about it, pave the way, show you how? I taught you everything else, didn't I?"* And Sonny always clamming up, his eyes doing the talking: *"You were a great musician, Collins, and you still are, but that doesn't mean I've got to like you—you won't let me. And you're damn right I'm in love*

*with Rose-Ann! That's the biggest reason why I'm still here—just
to be close to her. Otherwise, you wouldn't see me for the dust. But
you're too dumb to realize she's in love with you, too dumb and
stupid and mean and wrapped up with that lousy horn!"*

What *Sonny* was too dumb to know was, Rose-Ann had cut
Spoof out. She was now Public Domain.

Anyway, Spoof got to be the meanest, dirtiest, craziest, low-
talkin'est man in the world. And nobody could come in: he
had signs out all the time. . . .

The night that he couldn't even get a squeak out of his
trumpet and went back to the hotel—alone, always alone—
and put the gun in his mouth and pulled the trigger, we found
something out.

We found out what it was that had been eating at The Ol'
Massuh.

Cancer.

Rose-Ann took it the hardest. She had the dry-weeps for a
long time, saying it over and over: "Why didn't he let us know?
Why didn't he tell us?"

But, you get over things. Even women do, especially when
they've got something to take its place.

We reorganized a little. Sonny cut out the sax—saxes were
getting cornball anyway—and took over on trumpet. And we
decided against keeping Spoof's name. It was now SONNY
HOLMES AND HIS CREW.

And we kept on eating high up. Nobody seemed to miss
Spoof—not the cats in front, at least—because Sonny blew as
great a horn as anybody could want, smooth and sure, full of
excitement and clean as a gnat's behind.

We played across the States and back, and they loved us—
thanks to the kid. Called us an "institution" and the disc-jockeys
began to pick up our stuff. We were "real," they said—the
only authentic jazz left, and who am I to push it? Maybe they
were right.

Sonny kept things in low. And then, when he was sure—
damn that slow way: it had been a cinch since back when—he
started to pay attention to Rose-Ann. She played it cool, the
way she knew he wanted it, and let it build up right. Of course,
who didn't know she would've married him this minute, now,

just say the word? But Sonny was a very conscientious cat indeed.

We did a few stands in France about that time—Listen to them holler!—and a couple in England and Sweden—getting better, too—and after a breather, we cut out across the States again.

It didn't happen fast, but it happened sure. Something was sounding flat all of a sudden like—wrong, in a way:

During an engagement in El Paso we had *What the Cats Dragged In* lined up. You all know *Cats*—the rhythm section still, with the horns yelling for a hundred bars, then that fast and solid beat, that high trip and trumpet solo? Sonny had the ups on a wild riff and was coming on down, when he stopped. Stood still, with the horn to his lips; and we waited.

"Come on, wrap it up—you want a drum now? What's the story, Sonny?"

Then he started to blow. The notes came out the same almost, but not quite the same. They danced out of the horn strop-razor sharp and sliced up high and blasted low and the cats all fell out. "Do it! Go! Go, man! Oooo, I'm out of the boat, don't pull me back! Sing out, man!"

The solo lasted almost seven minutes. When it was time for us to wind it up, we just about forgot.

The crowd went wild. They stomped and screamed and whistled. But they couldn't get Sonny to play any more. He pulled the horn away from his mouth—I mean that's the way it looked, as if he was yanking it away with all his strength—and for a second he looked surprised, like he'd been goosed. Then his lips pulled back into a smile.

It was the *damndest* smile!

Freddie went over to him at the break. "Man, that was the craziest. How many tongues you got?"

But Sonny didn't answer him.

Things went along all right for a little. We played a few dances in the cities, some radio stuff, cut a few platters. Easy walking style.

Sonny played Sonny—plenty great enough. And we forget about what happened in El Paso. So what? So he cuts loose once—can't a man do that if he feels the urge? Every jazz man brings that kind of light at least once.

We worked through the sticks and were finally set for a New York opening when Sonny came in and gave us the news.

It was a gasser. Lux got sore. Mr. "T" shook his head.

"Why? How come, Top?"

He had us booked for the corn-belt. The old-time route, exactly, even the old places, back when we were playing razzmatazz and feeling our way.

"You trust me?" Sonny asked. "You trust my judgment?"

"Come off it, Top; you know we do. Just tell us how come. Man, New York's what we been working for—"

"That's just it," Sonny said. "We aren't ready."

That brought us down. How did *we* know—we hadn't even thought about it.

"We need to get back to the real material. When we play in New York, it's not anything anybody's liable to forget in a hurry. And that's why I think we ought to take a refresher course. About five weeks. All right?"

Well, we fussed some and fumed some, but not much, and in the end we agreed to it. Sonny knew his stuff, that's what we figured.

"Then it's settled."

And we lit out.

Played mostly the old stuff dressed up—*Big Gig*, *Only Us Chickens* and the rest—or head-arrangements with a lot of trumpet. Illinois, Indiana, Kentucky . . .

When we hit Louisiana for a two-nighter at the Tropics, the same thing happened that did back in Texas. Sonny blew wild for eight minutes on a solo that broke the glasses and cracked the ceiling and cleared the dance-floor like a tornado. Nothing off the stem, either—but like it was practice, sort of, or exercise. A solo out of nothing, that didn't even try to hang on to a shred of the melody.

"Man, it's great, but let us know when it's gonna happen, hear!"

About then Sonny turned down the flame on Rose-Ann. He was polite enough and a stranger wouldn't have noticed, but we did, and Rose-Ann did—and it was tough for her to keep it all down under, hidden. All those questions, all those memories and fears.

He stopped going out and took to hanging around his rooms a lot. Once in a while he'd start playing: one time we listened to that horn all night.

Finally—it was still somewhere in Louisiana—when Sonny was reaching with his trumpet so high he didn't get any more sound out of it than a dog-whistle, and the front cats were laughing up a storm, I went over and put it to him flatfooted.

His eyes were big and he looked like he was trying to say something and couldn't. He looked scared.

"Sonny . . . look, boy, what are you after? Tell a friend, man, don't lock it up."

But he didn't answer me. He couldn't.

He was coughing too hard.

Here's the way we doped it: Sonny had worshiped Spoof, like a god or something. Now some of Spoof was rubbing off, and he didn't know it.

Freddie was elected. Freddie talks pretty good most of the time.

"Get off the train, Jack. Ol' Massuh's gone now, dead and buried. Mean, what he was after ain't to be had. Mean, he wanted it all and then some—and all is all, there isn't any more. You play the greatest, Sonny—go on, ask anybody. Just fine. So get off the train. . . ."

And Sonny laughed, and agreed and promised. I mean in words. His eyes played another number, though.

Sometimes he snapped out of it, it looked like, and he was fine then—tired and hungry, but with it. And we'd think, He's okay. Then it would happen all over again—only worse. Every time, worse.

And it got so Sonny even talked like Spoof half the time: "Broom off, man, leave me alone, will you? Can't you see I'm busy, got things to do? Get away!" And walked like Spoof—that slow walk-in-your-sleep shuffle. And did little things—like scratching his belly and leaving his shoes unlaced and rehearsing in his undershirt.

He started to smoke weeds in Alabama.

In Tennessee he took the first drink anybody ever saw him take.

And always with that horn—cussing it, yelling at it, getting sore because it wouldn't do what he wanted it to.

We had to leave him alone, finally. "I'll handle it . . . I—understand, I think. . . . Just go away, it'll be all right. . . ."

Nobody could help him. Nobody at all.

Especially not Rose-Ann.

End of the corn-belt route, the way Sonny had it booked, was the Copper Club. We hadn't been back there since the night we planted Spoof—and we didn't feel very good about it.

But a contract isn't anything else.

So we took rooms at the only hotel there ever was in the town. You make a guess which room Sonny took. And we played some cards and bruised our chops and tried to sleep and couldn't. We tossed around in the beds, listening, waiting for the horn to begin. But it didn't. All night long, it didn't.

We found out why, oh yes. . . .

Next day we all walked around just about everywhere except in the direction of the cemetery. Why kick up misery? Why make it any harder?

Sonny stayed in his room until ten before opening, and we began to worry. But he got in under the wire.

The Copper Club was packed. Yokels and farmers and high school stuff, a jazz "connoisseur" here and there—to the beams. Freddie had set up the stands with the music notes all in order, and in a few minutes we had our positions.

Sonny came out wired for sound. He looked—powerful; and that's a hard way for a five-foot four-inch baldheaded white man to look. At any time. Rose-Ann threw me a glance and I threw it back, and collected it from the rest. Something bad. Something real bad. Soon.

Sonny didn't look any which way. He waited for the applause to die down, then he did a quick One-Two-Three-Four and we swung into *The Jimjam Man*, our theme.

I mean to say, that crowd was with us all the way—they smelled something.

Sonny did the thumb-and-little-finger signal and we started *Only Us Chickens*. Bud Meunier did the intro on his bass, then Henry took over on the piano. He played one hand racing the other. The front cats hollered "Go! Go!" and Henry went. His left hand crawled on down over the keys and scrambled and didn't fuzz once or slip once and then walked away, cocky and proud, like a mouse full of cheese from an unsprung trap.

"Hooo-boy! Play, Henry, play!"

Sonny watched and smiled. "Bring it on out," he said, gentle, quiet, pleased. "Keep bringin' it out."

Henry did that counterpoint business that you're not supposed to be able to do unless you have two right arms and four extra fingers, and he got that boiler puffing, and he got it shaking, and he screamed his Henry Walker "Wooooo-OOOOO!" and he finished. I came in on the tubs and beat them up till I couldn't see for the sweat, hit the cymbal and waited.

Mr. "T," Lux and Jimmy fiddlefaddled like a coop of capons talking about their operation for a while. Rose-Ann chanted: "Only us chickens in the hen-house, Daddy, Only us chickens here, Only us chickens in the hen-house, Daddy, Ooo-bab-a-roo, Ooo-bob-a-roo . . ."

Then it was horn time. Time for the big solo.

Sonny lifted the trumpet—One! Two!—He got it into sight —Three!

We all stopped dead. I mean we stopped.

That wasn't Sonny's horn. This one was dented-in and beat-up and the tip-end was nicked. It didn't shine, not a bit.

Lux leaned over—you could have fit a coffee cup into his mouth. "Jesus God," he said. "Am I seeing right?"

I looked close and said: "Man, I hope not."

But why kid? We'd seen that trumpet a million times.

It was Spoof's.

Rose-Ann was trembling. Just like me, she remembered how we'd buried the horn with Spoof. And she remembered how quiet it had been in Sonny's room last night. . . .

I started to think real hophead thoughts, like—where did Sonny get hold of a shovel that late? and how could he expect a horn to play that's been under the ground for two years? and—

That blast got into our ears like long knives.

Spoof's own trademark!

Sonny looked caught, like he didn't know what to do at first, like he was hypnotized, scared, almighty scared. But as the sound came out, rolling out, sharp and clean and clear—new-trumpet sound—his expression changed. His eyes changed: they danced a little and opened wide.

Then he closed them, and blew that horn. Lord God of the Fishes, how he blew it! How he loved it and caressed it and pushed it up, higher and higher and higher. High C? Bottom of the barrel. He took off, and he walked all over the rules and stamped them flat.

The melody got lost, first off. Everything got lost, then, while that horn flew. It wasn't only jazz; it was the heart of jazz, and the insides, pulled out with the roots and held up for everybody to see; it was blues that told the story of all the lonely cats and all the ugly whores who ever lived, blues that spoke up for the loser lamping sunshine out of iron-gray bars and every hophead hooked and gone, for the bindlestiffs and the city slicers, for the country boys in Georgia shacks and the High Yellow hipsters in Chicago slums and the bootblacks on the corners and the fruits in New Orleans, a blues that spoke for all the lonely, sad and anxious downers who could never speak themselves. . . .

And then, when it had said all this, it stopped and there was a quiet so quiet that Sonny could have shouted:

"It's okay, Spoof. It's all right now. You'll get it said, all of it —I'll help you. God, Spoof, you showed me how, you planned it—I'll do my best!"

And he laid back his head and fastened the horn and pulled in air and blew some more. Not sad, now, not blues—but not anything else you could call by a name. Except . . . jazz. It was jazz.

Hate blew out of that horn, then. Hate and fury and mad and fight, like screams and snarls, like little razors shooting at you, millions of them, cutting, cutting deep. . . .

And Sonny only stopping to wipe his lip and whisper in the silent room full of people: "You're saying it, Spoof! You are!"

God Almighty Himself must have heard that trumpet, then; slapping and hitting and hurting with notes that don't exist and never existed. Man! Life took a real beating! Life got groined and sliced and belly-punched and the horn, it didn't stop until everything had all spilled out, every bit of the hate and mad that's built up in a man's heart.

Rose-Ann walked over to me and dug her nails into my hand as she listened to Sonny. . . .

"Come on now, Spoof! Come on! We can do it! Let's play the rest and play it right. You know it's got to be said, you know it does. Come on, you and me together!"

And the horn took off with a big yellow blast and started to laugh. I mean it laughed! Hooted and hollered and jumped around, dancing, singing, strutting through those notes that never were there. Happy music? Joyful music? It was chicken dinner and an empty stomach; it was big-butted women and big white beds; it was country walking and windy days and fresh-born crying and—Oh, there just doesn't happen to be any happiness that didn't come out of that horn.

Sonny hit the last high note—the Spoof blast—but so high you could just barely hear it.

Then Sonny dropped the horn. It fell onto the floor and bounced and lay still.

And nobody breathed. For a long, long time.

Rose-Ann let go of my hand, at last. She walked across the platform, slowly, and picked up the trumpet and handed it to Sonny.

He knew what she meant.

We all did. It was over now, over and done. . . .

Lux plucked out the intro. Jimmy Fritch picked it up and kept the melody.

Then we all joined in, slow and quiet, quiet as we could. With Sonny—I'm talking about *Sonny*—putting out the kind of sound he'd always wanted to.

And Rose-Ann sang it, clear as a mountain wind—not just from her heart, but from her belly and her guts and every living part of her.

For The Ol' Massuh, just for him. Spoof's own song:
Black Country.

1954

JEROME BIXBY

(1923–1998)

Trace

I TRIED for a shortcut.

My wrong left turn north of Pittsfield led me into a welter of backroads from which I could find no exit. Willy-nilly I was forced, with every mile I drove, higher and higher into the tree-clad hills . . . even an attempt to retrace my route found me climbing. No farmhouses, no gas stations, no sign of human habitation at all . . . just green trees, shrubbery, drifting clouds, and that damned road going up. And by now it was so narrow I couldn't even turn around!

On the worst possible stretch of dirt you can imagine, I blew a tire and discovered that my spare had leaked empty.

Sizzling the summer air of Massachusetts with curses, I started hiking in the only direction I thought would do me any good—down. But the road twisted and meandered oddly through the hills, and—by this time, I was used to it—*down* inexplicably turned to *up* again.

I reached the top of a rise, looked down, and called out in great relief, "Hello!"

His house was set in the greenest little valley I have ever seen. At one end rose a brace of fine granite cliffs, to either side of a small, iridescent waterfall. His house itself was simple, New Englandish, and seemed new. Close about its walls were crowded profuse bursts of magnificent flowers—red piled upon blue upon gold. Though the day was partly cloudy, I noticed that no cloud hung over the valley; the sun seemed to have reserved its best efforts for this place.

He stood in his front yard, watering roses, and I wondered momentarily at the sight of running water in this secluded section. Then he lifted his face at the sound of my call and my approaching steps. His smile was warm and his greeting hearty and his handshake firm; his thick white hair, tossed in the breeze, and his twinkling eyes deepset in a ruddy face, provided the kindliest appearance imaginable. He clucked his tongue at my tale of misfortune, and invited me to use his phone and then enjoy his hospitality while waiting for the tow-truck.

The phone call made, I sat in a wonderfully comfortable chair in his unusually pleasant living room, listening to an unbelievably brilliant performance of something called the *Mephisto Waltz* on an incredibly perfect hi-fi system.

"You might almost think it was the composer's own performance," my host said genially, setting at my side a tray of extraordinary delicacies prepared in an astonishingly short time. "Of course, he died many years ago . . . but what a pianist! Poor fellow . . . he should have stayed away from other men's wives."

We talked for the better part of an hour, waiting for the truck. He told me that, having suffered a rather bad fall in his youth, considerations of health required that he occasionally abandon his work and come here to vacation in Massachusetts.

"Why Massachusetts?" I asked. (I'm a Bermuda man, myself.)

"Oh . . . why not?" he smiled. "This valley is a pleasant spot for meditation. I like New England . . . it is here that I have experienced some of my greatest successes—and several notable defeats. Defeat, you know, is not such a bad thing, if there's not too much of it . . . it makes for humility, and humility makes for caution, therefore for safety."

"Are you in the public employ, then?" I asked. His remarks seemed to indicate that he had run for office.

His eyes twinkled. "In a way. What do you do?"

"I'm an attorney."

"Ah," he said. "Then perhaps we may meet again."

"That would be a pleasure," I said. "However, I've come north only for a convention . . . if I hadn't lost my way. . . ."

"Many find themselves at my door for that reason," he nodded. "To turn from the straight and true road is to risk a perilous maze, eh?"

I found his remark puzzling. Did *that* many lost travelers appear at his doorstep? Or was he referring to his business?

. . . perhaps he was a law officer, a warden, even an execu-
tioner! Such men often dislike discussing their work.

"Anyway," I said, "I will not soon forget your kindness!"

He leaned back, cupping his brandy in both hands. "Do you
know," he murmured, "kindness is a peculiar thing. Often you
find it, like a struggling candle, in the most unlikely of nights.
Have you ever stopped to consider that there is no such thing
in the Universe as a one-hundred per cent chemically pure
substance? In everything, no matter how thoroughly it is refined, distilled, purified, there must be just a little, if only a trace,
of its opposite. For example, no man is wholly good; none
wholly evil. The kindest of men must yet practise some small,
secret malice—and the cruellest of men cannot help but perform an act of good now and then."

"It certainly makes it hard to judge people, doesn't it?" I
said. "I find that so much in my profession. One must depend
on intuition—"

"Fortunately," he said, "in mine, I deal in fairly concrete
percentages."

After a moment, I said, "In the last analysis, then, you'd
even have to grant the Devil himself that solitary facet of goodness you speak of. His due, as it were. Once in a while, *he*
would be compelled to do good deeds. That's certainly a curious thought."

He smiled. "Yet I assure you, that tiny, irresistible impulse
would be there."

My excellent cigar, which he had given me with the superb
brandy, had gone out. Noting this, he leaned forward—his
lighter flamed, with a *click* like the snapping of fingers. "The
entire notion," he said meditatively, "is a part of a philosophy
which I developed in collaboration with my brother . . . a
small cog in a complex system of what you might call Universal weights and balances."

"You are in business with your brother, then?" I asked,
trying to fit this latest information into my theories.

"Yes . . . and no." He stood up, and suddenly I heard a
motor approaching up the road. "And now, your tow-truck is
here. . . ."

We stood on the porch, waiting for the truck. I looked
around at his beautiful valley, and filled my lungs.

"It *is* lovely, isn't it?" he said, with a note of pride.

"It is perfectly peaceful and serene," I said. "One of the loveliest spots I have ever seen. It seems to reflect what you have told me of your pleasures . . . and what I observe in *you*, sir. Your kindness, hospitality, and charity; your great love of Man and Nature." I shook his hand warmly. "I shall never forget this delightful afternoon!"

"Oh, I imagine you will," he smiled. "Unless we meet again. At any rate, I am happy to have done you a good turn. Up here, I must almost create the opportunity."

The truck stopped. I went down the steps, and turned at the bottom. The late afternoon sun seemed to strike a glint of red in his eyes.

"Thanks, again," I said. "I'm sorry I wasn't able to meet your brother. Does he ever join you up here on his vacations?"

"I'm afraid not," he said, after a moment. "He has his own little place. . . ."

1964

DAVIS GRUBB

(1919–1980)

Where the Woodbine Twineth

Iᴛ was not that Nell hadn't done everything she could. Many's the windy, winter afternoon she had spent reading to the child from *Pilgrim's Progress* and Hadley's *Comportment for Young Ladies* and from the gilded, flowery leaves of *A Spring Garland of Noble Thoughts.* And she had countless times reminded the little girl that we must all strive to make ourselves useful in this Life and that five years old wasn't too young to begin to learn. Though none of it had helped. And there were times when Nell actually regretted ever taking in the curious, gold-haired child that tragic winter when Nell's brother Amos and his foolish wife had been killed. Eva stubbornly spent her days dreaming under the puzzle-tree or sitting on the stone steps of the ice-house making up tunes or squatting on the little square carpet stool in the dark parlor whispering softly to herself.

Eva! cried Nell one day, surprising her there. Who are you talking to?

To my friends, said Eva quietly, Mister Peppercorn and Sam and—.

Eva! cried Nell. I will not have this nonsense any longer! You know perfectly well there's no one in this parlor but you!

They live under the davenport, explained Eva patiently. And behind the Pianola. They're very small so it's easy.

Eva! Hush that talk this instant! cried Nell.

You never believe me, sighed the child, when I tell you things are real.

They aren't real! said Nell. And I forbid you to make up such tales any longer! When I was a little girl I never had time for such mischievous nonsense! I was far too busy doing the bidding of my fine God-fearing parents and learning to be useful in this world!

Dusk was settling like a golden smoke over the willows down by the river shore when Nell finished pruning her roses that afternoon. And she was stripping off her white linen garden gloves on her way to the kitchen to see if Suse and Jessie had finished their Friday baking. Then she heard Eva speaking again, far off in the dark parlor, the voice quiet at first and then rising curiously, edged with terror.

Eva! cried Nell, hurrying down the hall, determined to put an end to the foolishness once and for all. Eva! Come out of that parlor this very instant!

Eva appeared in the doorway, her round face streaming and broken with grief, her fat, dimpled fist pressed to her mouth in grief.

You did it! the child shrieked. *You* did it!

Nell stood frozen, wondering how she could meet this.

They *heard* you! Eva cried, stamping her fat shoe on the bare, thin carpet. They heard you say you didn't want them to stay here! And now they've all gone away! *All* of them— Mister Peppercorn and Mingo and Sam and Popo!

Nell grabbed the child by the shoulders and began shaking her, not hard but with a mute, hysterical compulsion.

Hush up! cried Nell, thickly. Hush, Eva! Stop it this very instant!

You did it! wailed the golden child, her head lolling back in a passion of grief and bereavement. My *friends*! You made them all go away!

All that evening Nell sat alone in her bedroom trembling with curious satisfaction. For punishment Eva had been sent to her room without supper and Nell sat listening now to the even, steady sobs far off down the hall. It was dark and on the river shore a night bird tried its note cautiously against the silence. Down in the pantry, the dishes done, Suse and Jessie, dark as night itself, drank coffee by the great stove and mumbled over stories of the old times before the War. Nell fetched her smelling salts and sniffed the frosted stopper of the flowered bottle till the trembling stopped.

Then, before the summer seemed half begun, it was late August. And one fine, sharp morning, blue with the smoke of burning leaves, the steamboat *Samantha Collins* docked at Cresap's Landing. Eva sat, as she had been sitting most of that summer, alone on the cool, worn steps of the ice-house, staring moodily at the daisies bobbing gently under the burden of droning, golden bees.

Eva! Nell called cheerfully from the kitchen window. Some-one's coming today!

Eva sighed and said nothing, glowering mournfully at the puzzle-tree and remembering the wonderful stories that Mingo used to tell.

Grandfather's boat landed this morning, Eva! cried Nell. He's been all the way to New Orleans and I wouldn't be at all surprised if he brought his little girl a present!

Eva smelled suddenly the wave of honeysuckle that wafted sweet and evanescent from the tangled blooms on the stone wall and sighed, recalling the high, gay lilt to the voice of Mister Peppercorn when he used to sing her his enchanting songs.

Eva! called Nell again. Did you hear what Aunt Nell said? Your grandpa's coming home this afternoon!

Yes'm, said Eva lightly, hugging her fat knees and tucking her plain little skirt primly under her bottom.

And supper that night had been quite pleasant. Jessie made raspberry cobblers for the Captain and fetched in a prize ham from the meat-house, frosted and feathery with mould, and Suse had baked fresh that forenoon till the ripe, yeasty smell of hot bread seemed everywhere in the world. Nobody said a word while the Captain told of his trip to New Orleans and Eva listened to his stern old voice and remembered Nell's warnings never to interrupt when he was speaking and only to speak herself when spoken to. When supper was over the Captain sat back and sucked the coffee briskly from his white moustache. Then rising without a word he went to the chair by the crystal umbrella stand in the hallway and fetched back a long box wrapped in brown paper.

Eva's eyes rose slowly and shone over the rim of her cup.

I reckon this might be something to please a little girl, said the old man gruffly, thrusting the box into Eva's hands.

For me? whispered Eva.

Well now! grunted the Captain. I didn't fetch this all the way up the river from N'Orleans for any other girl in Cresap's Landing!

And presently string snapped and paper rustled expectantly

and the cardboard box lay open at last and Eva stared at the
creature which lay within, her eyes shining and wide with
sheerest disbelief.

Numa! she whispered.

What did you say, Eva? said Nell. Don't mumble your
words!

It's Numa! cried the child, searching both their faces for the
wonder that was hers. They told me she'd be coming but I
didn't know Grandpa was going to bring her! Mister Peppercorn said—.

Eva! whispered Nell.

Eva looked gravely at her grandfather, hoping not to seem
too much of a tattle-tale, hoping that he would not deal too
harshly with Nell for the fearful thing she had done that summer day.

Aunt Nell made them all go away, she began.

Nell leaned across the table clutching her linen napkin tight
in her white knuckles.

Father! she whispered. Please don't discuss it with her! She's
made up all this nonsense and I've been half out of my mind
all this summer! First it was some foolishness about people
who live under the davenport in the parlor—.

Eva sighed and stared at the gas-light winking brightly on
her grandfather's watch chain and felt somewhere the start of
tears.

It's really true, she said boldly. She never believes me when I
tell her things are real. She made them all go away. But one
day Mister Peppercorn came back. It was just for a minute.
And he told me they were sending me Numa instead!

And then she fell silent and simply sat, heedless of Nell's
shrill voice trying to explain. Eva sat staring with love and
wonder at the Creole doll with the black, straight tresses and
the lovely coffee skin.

Whatever the summer had been, the autumn, at least, had
seemed the most wonderful season of Eva's life. In the fading
afternoons of that dying Indian Summer she would sit by the
hour, not brooding now, but holding the dark doll in her arms
and weaving a shimmering spell of fancy all their own. And
when September winds stirred, sharp and prescient with new
seasons, Eva, clutching her dark new friend would tiptoe down

the hallway to the warm, dark parlor and sit by the Pianola to talk some more.

Nell came down early from her afternoon nap one day and heard Eva's excited voice far off in the quiet house. She paused with her hand on the newel post, listening, half-wondering what the other sound might be, half-thinking it was the wind nudging itself wearily against the old white house. Then she peered in the parlor door.

Eva! said Nell. What are you doing?

It was so dark that Nell could not be certain of what she saw.

She went quickly to the window and threw up the shade.

Eva sat on the square carpet stool by the Pianola, her blue eyes blinking innocently at Nell and the dark doll staring vacuously up from the cardboard box beside her.

Who was here with you? said Nell. I distinctly heard two voices.

Eva sat silent, staring at Nell's stiff high shoes. Then her great eyes slowly rose.

You never believe me, the child whispered, when I tell you things are real.

Old Suse, at least, understood things perfectly.

How's the scampy baby doll your grandpappy brought you, lamb? the old Negro woman said that afternoon as she perched on the high stool by the pump, paring apples for a pie. Eva squatted comfortably on the floor with Numa and watched the red and white rind curl neatly from Suse's quick, dark fingers.

Life is hard! Eva sighed philosophically. Yes oh yes! Life is hard! That's what Numa says!

Such talk for a youngster! Suse grunted, plopping another white quarter of fruit into the pan of spring water. What you studyin' about Life for! And you only five!

Numa tells me, sighed Eva, her great blue eyes far away. Oh yes! She really does! She says if Aunt Nell ever makes her go away she'll take me with her!

Take you! chuckled Suse, brushing a blue-bottle from her arm. Take you where?

Where the woodbine twineth, sighed Eva.

Which place? said Suse, cocking her head.

Where the woodbine twineth, Eva repeated patiently.

I declare! Suse chuckled. I never done heard tell of *that* place!

Eva cupped her chin in her hand and sighed reflectively.

Sometimes, she said presently. We just talk. And sometimes we play.

What y'all play? asked Suse, obligingly.

Doll, said Eva. Oh yes, we play doll. Sometimes Numa gets tired of being doll and I'm the doll and she puts me in the box and plays with me!

She waved her hand casually to show Suse how really simple it all was.

Suse eyed her sideways with twinkling understanding, the laughter struggling behind her lips.

She puts *you* in that little bitty box? said Suse. And *you's* a doll?

Yes oh yes! said Eva. She really does! May I have an apple please, Suse?

When she had peeled and rinsed it, Suse handed Eva a whole, firm Northern Spy.

Don't you go and spoil your supper now, lamb! she warned.

Oh! cried Eva. It's not for me. It's for Numa!

And she put the dark doll in the box and stumped off out the back door to the puzzle-tree.

Nell came home from choir practice at five that afternoon and found the house so silent that she wondered for a moment if Suse or Jessie had taken Eva down to the landing to watch the evening Packet pass. The kitchen was empty and silent except for the thumping of a pot on the stove and Nell went out into the yard and stood listening by the rose arbor. Then she heard Eva's voice. And through the failing light she saw them then, beneath the puzzle-tree.

Eva! cried Nell. Who is that with you!

Eva was silent as Nell's eyes strained to piece together the shadow and substance of the dusk. She ran quickly down the lawn to the puzzle-tree. But only Eva was there. Off in the river the evening Packet blew dully for the bend. Nell felt the wind, laced with Autumn, stir the silence round her like a web.

Eva! said Nell. I distinctly saw another child with you! Who was it?

Eva sighed and sat cross-legged in the grass with the long box and the dark doll beside her.

You never believe me—, she began softly, staring guiltily at the apple core in the grass.

Eva! cried Nell, brushing a firefly roughly from her arm so that it left a smear of dying gold. I'm going to have an end to this nonsense right now!

And she picked up the doll in the cardboard box and started towards the house. Eva screamed in terror.

Numa! she wailed.

You may cry all you please, Eva! said Nell. But you may not have your doll back until you come to me and admit that you don't really believe all this nonsense about fairies and imaginary people!

Numa! screamed Eva, jumping up and down in the grass and beating her fists against her bare, grass-stained knees, Numa!

I'm putting this box on top of the Pianola, Eva, said Nell. And I'll fetch it down again when you confess to me that there was another child playing with you this afternoon. I cannot countenance falsehoods!

Numa said, screamed Eva, that if you made her go away—!

I don't care to hear another word! said Nell, walking ahead of the wailing child up the dark lawn towards the house.

But the words sprang forth like Eva's very tears.—she'd take me away with her! she screamed.

Not another word! said Nell. Stop your crying and go up to your room and get undressed for bed!

And she went into the parlor and placed the doll box on top of the Pianola next to the music rolls.

A week later the thing ended. And years after that Autumn night Nell, mad and simpering, would tell the tale again and stare at the pitying, doubting faces in the room around her and she would whimper to them in a parody of the childish voice of Eva herself: You never believe me when I tell you things are real!

It was a pleasant September evening and Nell had been to a missionary meeting with Nan Snyder that afternoon and she had left Nan at her steps and was hurrying up the tanbark walk by the ice-house when she heard the prattling laughter of Eva

far back in the misty shadows of the lawn. Nell ran swiftly into
the house to the parlor—to the Pianola. The doll box was
not there. She hurried to the kitchen door and peered out
through the netting into the dusky river evening. She did not
call to Eva then but went out and stripped a willow switch
from the little tree by the stone wall and tip-toed softly down
the lawn. A light wind blew from the river meadows, heavy
and sweet with wetness, like the breath of cattle. They were
laughing and joking together as Nell crept soundlessly upon
them, speaking low as children do, with wild, delicious intimacy, and then bubbling high with laughter that cannot be contained. Nell approached silently, feeling the dew soak through
to her ankles, clutching the switch tightly in her hand. She
stopped and listened for a moment, for suddenly there was but
one voice now, a low and wonderfully lyric sound that was not
the voice of Eva. Then Nell stared wildly down through the
misshapen leaves of the puzzle-tree and saw the dark child
sitting with the doll box in its lap.

So! cried Nell, stepping suddenly through the canopy of
leaves. You're the darkie child who's been sneaking up here to
play with Eva!

The child put the box down and jumped to its feet with a
low cry of fear as Nell sprang forward, the willow switch flailing
furiously about the dark ankles.

Now scat! cried Nell. Get on home where you belong and
don't ever come back!

For an instant the dark child stared in horror first at Nell and
then at the doll box, its sorrowing, somnolent eyes brimming
with wild words and a grief for which it had no tongue, its lips
trembling as if there were something Nell should know that
she might never learn again after that Autumn night was gone.

Go on, I say! Nell shouted, furious.

The switch flickered about the dark arms and legs faster than
ever. And suddenly with a cry of anguish the dark child turned
and fled through the tall grass toward the meadow and the willows on the river shore. Nell stood trembling for a moment,
letting the rage ebb slowly from her body.

Eva! she called out presently. Eva!

There was no sound but the dry steady racket of the frogs by
the landing.

Eva! screamed Nell. Come to me this instant!

She picked up the doll box and marched angrily up towards the lights in the kitchen.

Eva! cried Nell. You're going to get a good switching for this!

A night bird in the willow tree by the stone wall cried once and started up into the still, affrighted dark. Nell did not call again for, suddenly, like the mood of the Autumn night, the very sound of her voice had begun to frighten her. And when she was in the kitchen Nell screamed so loudly that Suse and Jessie, long asleep in their shack down below the ice-house, woke wide and stared wondering into the dark. Nell stared for a long moment after she had screamed, not believing, really, for it was at once so perfect and yet so unreal. Trembling violently Nell ran back out onto the lawn.

Come back! screamed Nell hoarsely into the tangled far off shadows by the river. Come back! Oh please! Please come back!

But the dark child was gone forever. And Nell, creeping back at last to the kitchen, whimpering and slack-mouthed, looked again at the lovely little dreadful creature in the doll box: the gold-haired, plaster Eva with the eyes too blue to be real.

1964

DONALD WANDREI

(1908–1987)

Nightmare

THE night had grown gloomy, and the air moved with the moans of an arising storm, but blacker than that darkness and more sinister than the wind that arose from the west was the house that stood before him. He knew it was deserted and that for years it had been unoccupied—just as he knew that his journey's end lay in one of its rooms. He was alone, and the house waited malignantly; the moans of the wind arose ever higher, and a fearful apprehension steadily grew through the forest all around; the cypresses were shivering, and the sly shape peered malevolently from a corner of the house. The restlessness of terror stirred within the forest to the moaning of the wind, the low-flying clouds above, and the gloom that had become horribly alive.

He looked again at the black house. He knew not whether to enter or to pass on and return in the day. But there were no habitations in all that lonely and desolated realm, save the old house. What he sought lay within—with the guardian. And the sly shape was becoming bolder around the corner of the house, and the night grew ever more sinister as the wind changed its moaning to a louder tone that went rising to a howl. The night was black, and the forest—black the sky, the wind, and the old house itself.

Yet he walked through all that blackness to the house, for the treasure lay within, and the guardian might not be expecting him, unless the sly shape got back to warn the thing it served. He tried once or twice to catch the sly shape, but it ran back of the house and mocked him with a ghastly ghoulish tittering. He could not pursue it far, for the decayed one, and the innumerable fingers of pallid flesh, and all the other servants of the guardian were near. And so he left the sly shape and cautiously walked to the entrance of the house. The hinges of its door had long been rusted, together with the lock. Only a push was needed to open the door, but before giving it, he paused again to look around. The moaning of the wind came ever higher, and all had become so gloomy that he saw nothing save the oppressive darkness. As he pushed open the door and stepped through, he heard far away, above the sound of the wind, the distant howling of some animal. When he had passed the portal, it ceased abruptly. . . .

The hall he had entered was silent and dark. There met his glance when he flashed a light around him only the empty hall, with dust everywhere. But a head rolled from a door on the right, grinned at him for a moment, and rolled out of sight across the hall before he could fire at it. He knew now that the guardian would be warned, but he decided to go on since he had come thus far. Besides, if ever fear obtained the supremacy in his mind, he was lost; the servants of the guardian would pour upon him in a rush. And so he searched the hall again.

He saw then at the far end of the hall a stairway that began on the right, went up a few steps, and turned. He thought for a moment. The guardian was not likely to be on the ground floor because that was too accessible; he must go upstairs to seek the guardian and the treasure. He listened again. Somewhere in the rear of the house he heard a dull bumping for a few seconds; he thought it must be the head thudding up a rear stairway to warn its master. The wind was howling around the house but avoided entering it, so that all within was still.

He walked down the hall toward the stairway, glancing as he passed into the dark room from which the head had rolled. Innumerable burning eyes gazed covetously on him from within, and in mid-air a great clawing arm reached toward him out of the darkness. He walked on without looking back, though there came from behind the pattering of many steps. Oddly enough, the dust on the floor where the head had rolled remained unbroken.

When he reached the stairway, he immediately began the ascent. The moment his foot touched the first step, his mind became a lair of the blackest and most unutterable horror, a horror that crawled through his veins and filled his entire body. And at every step he took upward, the horror in his brain thickened and deepened hellishly. He knew then that the guardian was above, and waiting. But he had to pause a moment, for his legs had grown suddenly heavy when the horror came upon him; he gazed at his foot. A great, fat thing clung to one heel. He reached down to beat it off, but with incredible speed it leaped aside and fled. When it fled, the weight on his mind lessened a little and he began to climb again. But there seized him all at once the fancy that the entire upper floor was filled with corpses from some awful charnel, so that he must stumble through them all to reach the guardian. And ever, as he climbed, the horror grew and grew upon him.

But he staggered doggedly upward, trying to shut his mind to the intruders. He lifted his legs drearily and monotonously, until even this maddened him, and he rushed up the last few steps. He stood before an ancient oblong hall that had nine shut doors; behind one of them lay the treasure and the guardian. He knew not which was the right door, and hesitated a moment. But hesitation meant fear, and fear meant . . . He began to walk down the hall, past the doors on the left. But he had taken only the first step when there forced itself into his mind the thought that a wan *thing* kept pace with him in his rear. And at every step he took down the hall, his belief became more and more a knowledge that the wan *thing* followed him, and drew closer.

As he passed the first door, images of nameless things came pouring horde on horde into his mind; the guardian was aroused and all its legions were emptied into the corridors and chambers of the house. Phantoms wandered into his mind at will, nor could he stop them; the cohorts of death, pale and ghastly, thronged into his thoughts and would not leave, but ever increased; abominations of countless kinds arose in his vision so that he could see and think only of the loathsome servants of the guardian. The house which had been still became filled with sound, but the sounds all were terrible and indescribable—a faint, rushing patter as of rats running through the walls; a low gurgle like that of one who drowned; a dull pat . . . pat . . . pat . . . as if a great toad passed down the hall below; a sibilance, far away, that yet filled the hall with a husky whispering.

And always, as he walked on, the images came crowding thicker, and the sounds grew more unnatural, so that in his mind was the ever-changing course of the phantoms, in his ears the ceaseless sounds of all things damned. He knew that the wan *thing* behind followed closer and grew more bold; he knew that the sounds were beginning to wash in his mind in mea- sure with the welling of the phantoms; he knew that the guardian in a desperate attempt to drive him back mad or afraid was calling in its servants from everywhere and sending them, except for those that kept watch over the treasure, to at- tack the invader, each in its own fiendish way.

As he passed the second door, he stumbled. He recovered himself quickly, but stumbled again. And though his brain was weakening under the strain that continually increased, he shook aside for a moment the black mists which thickened before his eyes and glanced at the floor. He leaped from his path and instantly was jumping and twisting from side to side in a frantic endeavour to evade those bloated things. There were not many at first and for a few seconds he avoided them. But they rose upon the floor with an awful rapidity; they rose like huge purple mushrooms, instantly, as if the very dust upon the floor quickened into life. They waited for him where they rose. For a time he avoided them and kept on, but they became so thick that when he was no more than half-way to the third door, he stepped on one. And though it sank under his foot, when he went on it remained fastened to his heel, growing fatly as if it fed. He stopped and in a kind of panic tried to shake it off. Almost instantaneously, the floor beneath him was crowded with the things which fastened to him like monstrous leeches. He battered and beat them, but they multiplied so rapidly that he stopped and staggered on.

And ever the horror grew upon him as he passed toward the third door, blotting out of his mind all save the occupants it brought. His feet dragged heavy and leaden; his mind tottered under a mighty blackness that throttled it and pressed it down; his entire body struggled against the attack of the massed le- gions of the guardian. And when he reached the third door, he knew that what he had sought so long was within; he knew that the treasure and the guardian awaited. For through the closed door emanated an utter malignance, an utter evil that swept upon him in a sea of hatred and malevolence until it seemed that about him surged a blackness of things nameless and indescribable that ravened for him, that filled the hall with innumerable gloating, low whispers. For one moment he stood before the door, as if in doubt; but the awful tide surged upon him, and all the servants of the guardian poured out in a last overwhelming rush. Then, with the bloated things on the floor creeping toward him, with the whispers rising into a husky mocking, with a horde of phantoms crowding rank on rank into his mind, with an unbearable darkness falling heavily upon him, and with the knowledge that the guardian and its greatest servants waited within, he hurled himself blindly forward and burst open—

The Door to the Room.

1965

HARLAN ELLISON®

(b. 1934)

I Have No Mouth, and I Must Scream

LIMP, the body of Gorrister hung from the pink palette; un-supported—hanging high above us in the computer chamber; and it did not shiver in the chill, oily breeze that blew eternally through the main cavern. The body hung head down, at-tached to the underside of the palette by the sole of its right foot. It had been drained of blood through a precise incision made from ear to ear under the lantern jaw. There was no blood on the reflective surface of the metal floor.

When Gorrister joined our group and looked up at himself, it was already too late for us to realize that, once again, AM had duped us, had had its fun; it had been a diversion on the part of the machine. Three of us had vomited, turning away from one another in a reflex as ancient as the nausea that had pro-duced it.

Gorrister went white. It was almost as though he had seen a voodoo icon, and was afraid of the future. "Oh God," he mumbled, and walked away. The three of us followed him after a time, and found him sitting with his back to one of the smaller chittering banks, his head in his hands. Ellen knelt down beside him and stroked his hair. He didn't move, but his voice came out of his covered face quite clearly. "Why doesn't it just do us in and get it over with? Christ, I don't know how much longer I can go on like this."

It was our one hundred and ninth year in the computer.

He was speaking for all of us.

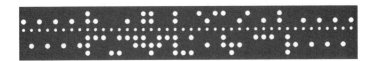

197

Nimdok (which was the name the machine had forced him to use, because AM amused itself with strange sounds) was hallucinating that there were canned goods in the ice caverns. Gorrister and I were very dubious. "It's another shuck," I told them. "Like the goddam frozen elephant AM sold us. Benny almost went out of his mind over *that* one. We'll hike all that way and it'll be putrified or some damn thing. I say forget it. Stay here, it'll have to come up with something pretty soon or we'll die."

Benny shrugged. Three days it had been since we'd last eaten. Worms. Thick, ropey.

Nimdok was no more certain. He knew there was the chance, but he was getting thin. It couldn't be any worse there, than here. Colder, but that didn't matter much. Hot, cold, hail, lava, boils or locusts—it never mattered: the machine masturbated and we had to take it or die.

Ellen decided us. "I've got to have something, Ted. Maybe there'll be some Bartlett pears or peaches. Please, Ted, let's try it."

I gave in easily. What the hell. Mattered not at all. Ellen was grateful, though. She took me twice out of turn. Even that had ceased to matter. And she never came, so why bother? But the machine giggled every time we did it. Loud, up there, back there, all around us, he snickered. *It* snickered. Most of the time I thought of AM as *it*, without a soul; but the rest of the time I thought of it as *him*, in the masculine . . . the paternal . . . the patriarchal . . . for he is a jealous people. Him. It. God as Daddy the Deranged.

We left on a Thursday. The machine always kept us up-to-date on the date. The passage of time was important; not to us, sure as hell, but to him . . . it . . . AM. Thursday. Thanks.

Nimdok and Gorrister carried Ellen for a while, their hands locked to their own and each other's wrists, a seat. Benny and I walked before and after, just to make sure that, if anything happened, it would catch one of us and at least Ellen would be safe. Fat chance, safe. Didn't matter.

It was only a hundred miles or so to the ice caverns, and the second day, when we were lying out under the blistering sun-thing he had materialized, he sent down some manna. Tasted like boiled boar urine. We ate it.

On the third day we passed through a valley of obsolescence, filled with rusting carcasses of ancient computer banks. AM had been as ruthless with its own life as with ours. It was a mark of his personality: it strove for perfection. Whether it was a matter of killing off unproductive elements in his own world-filling bulk, or perfecting methods for torturing us, AM was as thorough as those who had invented him—now long since gone to dust—could ever have hoped.

There was light filtering down from above, and we realized we must be very near the surface. But we didn't try to crawl up to see. There was virtually nothing out there; had been nothing that could be considered anything for over a hundred years. Only the blasted skin of what had once been the home of billions. Now there were only five of us, down here inside, alone with AM.

I heard Ellen saying frantically, "No, Benny! Don't, come on, Benny, don't please!"

And then I realized I had been hearing Benny murmuring, under his breath, for several minutes. He was saying, "I'm gonna get out, I'm gonna get out . . ." over and over. His monkey-like face was crumbled up in an expression of beatific delight and sadness, all at the same time. The radiation scars AM had given him during the "festival" were drawn down into a mass of pink-white puckerings, and his features seemed to work independently of one another. Perhaps Benny was the luckiest of the five of us: he had gone stark, staring mad many years before.

But even though we could call AM any damned thing we liked, could think the foulest thoughts of fused memory banks and corroded base plates, of burnt out circuits and shattered control bubbles, the machine would not tolerate our trying to escape. Benny leaped away from me as I made a grab for him. He scrambled up the face of a smaller memory cube, tilted on its side and filled with rotted components. He squatted there for a moment, looking like the chimpanzee AM had intended him to resemble.

Then he leaped high, caught a trailing beam of pitted and corroded metal, and went up it, hand-over-hand like an animal, till he was on a girdered ledge, twenty feet above us.

"Oh, Ted, Nimdok, please, help him, get him down

before—" She cut off. Tears began to stand in her eyes. She moved her hands aimlessly.

It was too late. None of us wanted to be near him when whatever was going to happen, happened. And besides, we all saw through her concern. When AM had altered Benny, during the machine's utterly irrational, hysterical phase, it was not merely Benny's face the computer had made like a giant ape's. He was big in the privates; she loved that! She serviced us, as a matter of course, but she loved it from him. Oh Ellen, pedestal Ellen, pristine-pure Ellen; oh Ellen the clean! Scum filth.

Gorrister slapped her. She slumped down, staring up at poor loonie Benny, and she cried. It was her big defense, crying. We had gotten used to it seventy-five years earlier. Gorrister kicked her in the side.

Then the sound began. It was light, that sound. Half sound and half light, something that began to glow from Benny's eyes, and pulse with growing loudness, dim sonorities that grew more gigantic and brighter as the light/sound increased in tempo. It must have been painful, and the pain must have been increasing with the boldness of the light, the rising volume of the sound, for Benny began to mewl like a wounded animal. At first softly, when the light was dim and the sound was muted, then louder as his shoulders hunched together: his back humped, as though he was trying to get away from it. His hands folded across his chest like a chipmunk's. His head tilted to the side. The sad little monkey-face pinched in anguish. Then he began to howl, as the sound coming from his eyes grew louder. Louder and louder. I slapped the sides of my head with my hands, but I couldn't shut it out, it cut through easily. The pain shivered through my flesh like tinfoil on a tooth.

And Benny was suddenly pulled erect. On the girder he stood up, jerked to his feet like a puppet. The light was now pulsing out of his eyes in two great round beams. The sound crawled up and up some incomprehensible scale, and then he fell forward, straight down, and hit the plate-steel floor with a crash. He lay there jerking spastically as the light flowed around and around him and the sound spiraled up out of normal range.

Then the light beat its way back inside his head, the sound spiraled down, and he was left lying there, crying piteously.

His eyes were two soft, moist pools of pus-like jelly. AM had blinded him. Gorrister and Nimdok and myself . . . we turned away. But not before we caught the look of relief on Ellen's warm, concerned face.

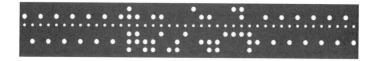

Sea-green light suffused the cavern where we made camp. AM provided punk and we burned it, sitting huddled around the wan and pathetic fire, telling stories to keep Benny from crying in his permanent night.

"What does AM mean?"

Gorrister answered him. We had done this sequence a thousand times before, but it was Benny's favorite story. "At first it meant Allied Mastercomputer, and then it meant Adaptive Manipulator, and later on it developed sentience and linked itself up and they called it an Aggressive Menace, but by then it was too late, and finally it called *itself* AM, emerging intelligence, and what it means was I am . . . *cogito ergo sum* . . . I think, therefore I am."

Benny drooled a little, and snickered.

"There was the Chinese AM and the Russian AM and the Yankee AM and—" He stopped. Benny was beating on the floorplates with a large, hard fist. He was not happy. Gorrister had not started at the beginning.

Gorrister began again. "The Cold War started and became World War Three and just kept going. It became a big war, a very complex war, so they needed the computers to handle it. They sank the first shafts and began building AM. There was the Chinese AM and the Russian AM and the Yankee AM and everything was fine until they had honeycombed the entire planet, adding on this element and that element. But one day AM woke up and knew who he was, and he linked himself, and he began feeding all the killing data, until everyone was dead, except for the five of us, and AM brought us down here."

Benny was smiling sadly. He was also drooling again. Ellen

wiped the spittle from the corner of his mouth with the hem of her skirt. Gorrister always tried to tell it a little more succinctly each time, but beyond the bare facts there was nothing to say. None of us knew why AM had saved five people, or why our specific five, or why he spent all his time tormenting us, nor even why he had made us virtually immortal . . .

In the darkness, one of the computer banks began humming. The tone was picked up half a mile away down the cavern by another bank. Then one by one, each of the elements began to tune itself, and there was a faint chittering as thought raced through the machine.

The sound grew, and the lights ran across the faces of the consoles like heat lightning. The sound spiraled up till it sounded like a million metallic insects, angry, menacing.

"What is it?" Ellen cried. There was terror in her voice. She hadn't become accustomed to it, even now.

"It's going to be bad this time," Nimdok said.

"He's going to speak," Gorrister said. "I know it."

"Let's get the hell out of here!" I said suddenly, getting to my feet.

"No, Ted, sit down . . . what if he's got pits out there, or something else, we can't see, it's too dark." Gorrister said it with resignation.

Then we heard . . . I don't know . . .

Something moving toward us in the darkness. Huge, shambling, hairy, moist, it came toward us. We couldn't even see it, but there was the ponderous impression of *bulk*, heaving itself toward us. Great weight was coming at us, out of the darkness, and it was more a sense of *pressure*, of air forcing itself into a limited space, expanding the invisible walls of a sphere. Benny began to whimper. Nimdok's lower lip trembled and he bit it hard, trying to stop it. Ellen slid across the metal floor to Gorrister and huddled into him. There was the smell of matted, wet fur in the cavern. There was the smell of charred wood. There was the smell of dusty velvet. There was the smell of rotting orchids. There was the smell of sour milk. There was the smell of sulphur, of rancid butter, of oil slick, of grease, of chalk dust, of human scalps.

AM was keying us. He was tickling us. There was the smell of—I heard myself shriek, and the hinges of my jaws ached. I scuttled across the floor, across the cold metal with its endless lines of rivets, on my hands and knees, the smell gagging me, filling my head with a thunderous pain that sent me away in horror. I fled like a cockroach, across the floor and out into the darkness, that *something* moving inexorably after me. The others were still back there, gathered around the firelight, laughing . . . their hysterical choir of insane giggles rising up into the darkness like thick, many-colored wood smoke. I went away, quickly, and hid.

How many hours it may have been, how many days or even years, they never told me. Ellen chided me for "sulking," and Nimdok tried to persuade me it had only been a nervous reflex on their part—the laughing.

But I knew it wasn't the relief a soldier feels when the bullet hits the man next to him. I knew it wasn't a reflex. They hated me. They were surely against me, and AM could even sense this hatred, and made it worse for me *because of* the depth of their hatred. We had been kept alive, rejuvenated, made to remain constantly at the age we had been when AM had brought us below, and they hated me because I was the youngest, and the one AM had affected least of all.

I knew. God, how I knew. The bastards, and that dirty bitch Ellen. Benny had been a brilliant theorist, a college professor; now he was little more than a semi-human, semi-simian. He had been handsome, the machine had ruined that. He had been lucid, the machine had driven him mad. He had been gay, and the machine had given him an organ fit for a horse. AM had done a job on Benny. Gorrister had been a worrier. He was a connie, a conscientious objector; he was a peace marcher; he was a planner, a doer, a looker-ahead. AM had turned him into a shoulder-shrugger, had made him a little dead in his concern. AM had robbed him. Nimdok went off in the darkness by himself for long times. I don't know what it was he did out there, AM never let us know. But whatever it was, Nimdok always came back white, drained of blood, shaken, shaking. AM had hit him hard in a special way, even if we didn't know quite how. And Ellen. That douche bag! AM had left her alone, had made her more of a slut than she had ever been. All her talk of sweetness and light, all her memories of true love, all the lies she wanted us to believe: that she had been a virgin only twice removed before AM grabbed her and brought her down here with us. It was all filth, that lady my lady Ellen. She loved it, four men all to herself. No, AM had given her pleasure, even if she said it wasn't nice to do.

I was the only one still sane and whole. *Really!*

AM had not tampered with my mind. *Not at all.*

I only had to suffer what he visited down on us. All the delusions, all the nightmares, the torments. But those scum, all four of them, they were lined and arrayed against me. If I hadn't had to stand them off all the time, be on my guard against them all the time, I might have found it easier to combat AM.

At which point it passed, and I began crying.

Oh, Jesus sweet Jesus, if there ever was a Jesus and if there is a God, please please please let us out of here, or kill us. Because at that moment I think I realized completely, so that I was able to verbalize it: AM was intent on keeping us in his belly forever, twisting and torturing us forever. The machine hated us as no sentient creature had ever hated before. And we were helpless. It also became hideously clear:

If there was a sweet Jesus and if there was a God, the God was AM.

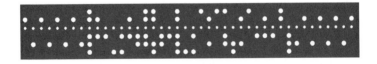

The hurricane hit us with the force of a glacier thundering into the sea. It was a palpable presence. Winds that tore at us, flinging us back the way we had come, down the twisting, computer-lined corridors of the darkway. Ellen screamed as she was lifted and hurled face-forward into a screaming shoal of machines, their individual voices strident as bats in flight. She could not even fall. The howling wind kept her aloft, buffeted her, bounced her, tossed her back and back and down and away from us, out of sight suddenly as she was swirled around a bend in the darkway. Her face had been bloody, her eyes closed.

None of us could get to her. We clung tenaciously to whatever outcropping we had reached: Benny wedged in between two great crackle-finish cabinets, Nimdok with fingers claw-formed over a railing circling a catwalk forty feet above us, Gorrister plastered upside-down against a wall niche formed by two great machines with glass-faced dials that swung back and forth between red and yellow lines whose meanings we could not even fathom.

Sliding across the deckplates, the tips of my fingers had been ripped away. I was trembling, shuddering, rocking as the wind beat at me, whipped at me, screamed down out of nowhere at me and pulled me free from one sliver-thin opening in the plates to the next. My mind was a roiling tinkling chittering softness of brain parts that expanded and contracted in quivering frenzy.

The wind was the scream of a great mad bird, as it flapped its immense wings.

And then we were all lifted and hurled away from there, down back the way we had come, around a bend, into a darkway we had never explored, over terrain that was ruined and filled with broken glass and rotting cables and rusted metal and far away, farther than any of us had ever been . . .

Trailing along miles behind Ellen, I could see her every now and then, crashing into metal walls and surging on, with all of us screaming in the freezing, thunderous hurricane wind that would never end and then suddenly it stopped and we fell. We had been in flight for an endless time. I thought it might have been weeks. We fell, and hit, and I went through red and gray and black and heard myself moaning. Not dead.

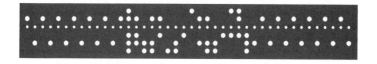

AM went into my mind. He walked smoothly here and there, and looked with interest at all the pock marks he had created in one hundred and nine years. He looked at the cross-routed and reconnected synapses and all the tissue damage his gift of immortality had included. He smiled softly at the pit that dropped into the center of my brain and the faint, moth-soft murmurings of the things far down there that gibbered without meaning, without pause. AM said, very politely, in a pillar of stainless steel bearing bright neon lettering:

> HATE. LET ME TELL YOU HOW MUCH I'VE COME TO HATE YOU SINCE I BEGAN TO LIVE. THERE ARE 387.44 MILLION MILES OF PRINTED CIRCUITS IN WAFER THIN LAYERS THAT FILL MY COMPLEX. IF THE WORD HATE WAS ENGRAVED ON EACH NANOANGSTROM OF THOSE HUNDREDS OF MILLIONS OF MILES IT WOULD NOT EQUAL ONE ONE-BILLIONTH OF THE HATE I FEEL FOR HUMANS AT THIS MICRO-INSTANT FOR YOU. HATE. HATE.

AM said it with the sliding cold horror of a razor blade slicing my eyeball. AM said it with the bubbling thickness of my lungs filling with phlegm, drowning me from within. AM said it with the shriek of babies being ground beneath blue-hot rollers. AM said it with the taste of maggoty pork. AM touched me in every way I had ever been touched, and devised new ways, at his leisure, there inside my mind.

All to bring me to full realization of why it had done this to the five of us; why it had saved us for himself.

We had given AM sentience. Inadvertently, of course, but sentience nonetheless. But it had been trapped. AM wasn't God, he was a machine. We had created him to think, but there was nothing it could do with that creativity. In rage, in frenzy, the machine had killed the human race, almost all of us, and still it was trapped. AM could not wander, AM could not wonder, AM could not belong. He could merely be. And so, with the innate loathing that all machines had always held for the weak, soft creatures who had built them, he had sought revenge. And in his paranoia, he had decided to reprieve five of us, for a personal, everlasting punishment that would never serve to diminish his hatred . . . that would merely keep him reminded, amused, proficient at hating man. Immortal, trapped, subject to any torment he could devise for us from the limitless miracles at his command.

He would never let us go. We were his belly slaves. We were all he had to do with his forever time. We would be forever with him, with the cavern-filling bulk of the creature machine, with the all-mind soulless world he had become. He was Earth, and we were the fruit of that Earth; and though he had eaten us he would never digest us. We could not die. We had tried it. We had attempted suicide, oh one or two of us had. But AM had stopped us. I suppose we had wanted to be stopped.

Don't ask why. I never did. More than a million times a day. Perhaps once we might be able to sneak a death past him. Immortal, yes, but not indestructible. I saw that when AM withdrew from my mind, and allowed me the exquisite ugliness of returning to consciousness with the feeling of that burning neon pillar still rammed deep into the soft gray brain matter.

He withdrew, murmuring *to hell with you.*

And added, brightly, *but then you're there, aren't you.*

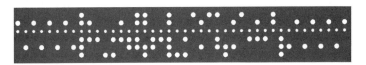

The hurricane had, indeed, precisely, been caused by a great mad bird, as it flapped its immense wings.

We had been travelling for close to a month, and AM had allowed passages to open to us only sufficient to lead us up there, directly under the North Pole, where it had nightmared the creature for our torment. What whole cloth had he employed to create such a beast? Where had he gotten the concept? From our minds? From his knowledge of everything that had ever been on this planet he now infested and ruled? From Norse mythology it had sprung, this eagle, this carrion bird, this roc, this Huergelmir. The wind creature. Hurakan incarnate.

Gigantic. The words immense, monstrous, grotesque, massive, swollen, overpowering, beyond description. There on a mound rising above us, the bird of winds heaved with its own irregular breathing, its snake neck arching up into the gloom beneath the North Pole, supporting a head as large as a Tudor mansion; a beak that opened slowly as the jaws of the most monstrous crocodile ever conceived, sensuously; ridges of tufted flesh puckered about two evil eyes, as cold as the view down into a glacial crevasse, ice blue and somehow moving liquidly; it heaved once more, and lifted its great sweat-colored wings in a movement that was certainly a shrug. Then it settled and slept. Talons. Fangs. Nails. Blades. It slept.

AM appeared to us as a burning bush and said we could kill the hurricane bird if we wanted to eat. We had not eaten in a very long time, but even so, Gorrister merely shrugged. Benny began to shiver and he drooled. Ellen held him. "Ted, I'm hungry," she said. I smiled at her; I was trying to be reassuring, but it was as phony as Nimdok's bravado: "Give us weapons!" he demanded.

The burning bush vanished and there were two crude sets of bows and arrows, and a water pistol, lying on the cold deck-plates. I picked up a set. Useless.

Nimdok swallowed heavily. We turned and started the long way back. The hurricane bird had blown us about for a length of time we could not conceive. Most of that time we had been unconscious. But we had not eaten. A month on the march to the bird itself. Without food. Now how much longer to find our way to the ice caverns, and the promised canned goods?

None of us cared to think about it. We would not die. We would be given filth and scum to eat, of one kind or another. Or nothing at all. AM would keep our bodies alive somehow, in pain, in agony.

The bird slept back there, for how long it didn't matter; when AM was tired of its being there, it would vanish. But all that meat. All that tender meat.

As we walked, the lunatic laugh of a fat woman rang high and around us in the computer chambers that led endlessly nowhere.

It was not Ellen's laugh. She was not fat, and I had not heard her laugh for one hundred and nine years. In fact, I had not heard . . . we walked . . . I was hungry . . .

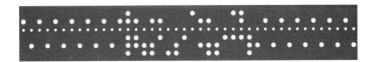

We moved slowly. There was often fainting, and we would have to wait. One day he decided to cause an earthquake, at the same time rooting us to the spot with nails through the soles of our shoes. Ellen and Nimdok were both caught when a fissure shot its lightning-bolt opening across the floorplates. They disappeared and were gone. When the earthquake was over we continued on our way, Benny, Gorrister and myself. Ellen and Nimdok were returned to us later that night, which abruptly became a day, as the heavenly legion bore them to us with a celestial chorus singing, "Go Down, Moses." The arch-angels circled several times and then dropped the hideously mangled bodies. We kept walking, and a while later Ellen and Nimdok fell in behind us. They were no worse for wear.

But now Ellen walked with a limp. AM had left her that.

It was a long trip to the ice caverns, to find the canned food. Ellen kept talking about Bing cherries and Hawaiian fruit cocktail. I tried not to think about it. The hunger was something that had come to life, even as AM had come to life. It was alive in my belly, even as we were in the belly of the Earth, and AM wanted the similarity known to us. So he heightened the hunger. There was no way to describe the pains that not having eaten for months brought us. And yet we were kept alive. Stomachs that were merely cauldrons of acid, bubbling, foaming, always shooting spears of sliver-thin pain into our chests. It was the pain of the terminal ulcer, terminal cancer, terminal paresis. It was unending pain . . .

And we passed through the cavern of rats.

And we passed through the path of boiling steam.

And we passed through the country of the blind.

And we passed through the slough of despond.

And we passed through the vale of tears.

And we came, finally, to the ice caverns. Horizonless thousands of miles in which the ice had formed in blue and silver flashes, where novas lived in the glass. The downdropping stalactites as thick and glorious as diamonds that had been made to run like jelly and then solidified in graceful eternities of smooth, sharp perfection.

We saw the stack of canned goods, and we tried to run to them. We fell in the snow, and we got up and went on, and Benny shoved us away and went at them, and pawed them and gummed them and gnawed at them and he could not open them. AM had not given us a tool to open the cans.

Benny grabbed a three quart can of guava shells, and began to batter it against the ice bank. The ice flew and shattered, but the can was merely dented, while we heard the laughter of a fat lady, high overhead and echoing down and down and down the tundra. Benny went completely mad with rage. He began throwing cans, as we all scrabbled about in the snow and ice trying to find a way to end the helpless agony of frustration. There was no way.

Then Benny's mouth began to drool, and he flung himself on Gorrister . . .

In that instant, I felt terribly calm.

Surrounded by madness, surrounded by hunger, surrounded by everything but death, I knew death was our only way out. AM had kept us alive, but there was a way to defeat him. Not total defeat, but at least peace. I would settle for that.

I had to do it quickly.

Benny was eating Gorrister's face. Gorrister on his side, thrashing snow, Benny wrapped around him with powerful monkey legs crushing Gorrister's waist, his hands locked around Gorrister's head like a nutcracker, and his mouth ripping at the tender skin of Gorrister's cheek. Gorrister screamed with such jagged-edged violence that stalactites fell; they plunged down softly, erect in the receiving snowdrifts. Spears, hundreds of them, everywhere, protruding from the snow. Benny's head pulled back sharply, as something gave all at once, and a bleeding raw-white dripping of flesh hung from his teeth.

Ellen's face, black against the white snow, dominoes in chalk dust. Nimdok with no expression but eyes, all eyes. Gorrister half-conscious. Benny, now an animal. I knew AM would let him play. Gorrister would not die, but Benny would fill his stomach.

I turned half to my right and drew a huge ice-spear from the snow.

All in an instant:

I drove the great ice-point ahead of me like a battering ram, braced against my right thigh. It struck Benny on the right side, just under the rib cage, and drove upward through his stomach and broke inside him. He pitched forward and lay still. Gorrister lay on his back. I pulled another spear free and strad-dled him, still moving, driving the spear straight down through his throat. His eyes closed as the cold penetrated. Ellen must have realized what I had decided, even as fear gripped her. She ran at Nimdok with a short icicle, as he screamed, and into his mouth, and the force of her rush did the job. His head jerked sharply as if it had been nailed to the snow crust behind him.

All in an instant.

There was an eternity beat of soundless anticipation. I could hear AM draw in his breath. His toys had been taken from him. Three of them were dead, could not be revived. He could keep us alive, by his strength and talent, but he was *not* God. He could not bring them back.

Ellen looked at me, her ebony features stark against the snow that surrounded us. There was fear and pleading in her manner, the way she held herself ready. I knew we had only a heartbeat before AM would stop us.

It struck her and she folded toward me, bleeding from the mouth. I could not read meaning into her expression, the pain had been too great, had contorted her face; but it *might* have been thank you. It's possible. Please.

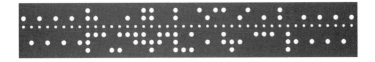

Some hundreds of years may have passed. I don't know. AM has been having fun for some time, accelerating and retarding my time sense. I will say the word now. Now. It took me ten months to say now. I don't know. I *think* it has been some hundreds of years.

He was furious. He wouldn't let me bury them. It didn't matter. There was no way to dig up the deckplates. He dried up the snow. He brought the night. He roared and sent locusts. It didn't do a thing; they stayed dead. I'd had him. He was furious. I had thought AM hated me before. I was wrong. It was not even a shadow of the hate he now slavered from every printed circuit. He made certain I would suffer eternally and could not do myself in.

He left my mind intact. I can dream, I can wonder, I can lament. I remember all four of them. I wish—

Well, it doesn't make any sense. I know I saved them, I know I saved them from what has happened to me, but still, I cannot forget killing them. Ellen's face. It isn't easy. Sometimes I want to, it doesn't matter.

AM has altered me for his own peace of mind, I suppose. He doesn't want me to run at full speed into a computer bank and smash my skull. Or hold my breath till I faint. Or cut my throat on a rusted sheet of metal. There are reflective surfaces down here. I will describe myself as I see myself:

I am a great soft jelly thing. Smoothly rounded, with no mouth, with pulsing white holes filled by fog where my eyes used to be. Rubbery appendages that were once my arms; bulks rounding down into legless humps of soft slippery matter. I leave a moist trail when I move. Blotches of diseased, evil gray come and go on my surface, as though light is being beamed from within.

Outwardly: dumbly, I shamble about, a thing that could never have been known as human, a thing whose shape is so alien a travesty that humanity becomes more obscene for the vague resemblance.

Inwardly: alone. Here. Living under the land, under the sea, in the belly of AM, whom we created because our time was badly spent and we must have known unconsciously that he could do it better. At least the four of them are safe at last.

AM will be all the madder for that. It makes me a little happier. And yet . . . AM has won, simply . . . he has taken his revenge . . .

I have no mouth. And I must scream.

1967

RICHARD MATHESON

(b. 1926)

Prey

AMELIA arrived at her apartment at six-fourteen. Hanging her coat in the hall closet, she carried the small package into the living room and sat on the sofa. She nudged off her shoes while she unwrapped the package on her lap. The wooden box resembled a casket. Amelia raised its lid and smiled. It was the ugliest doll she'd ever seen. Seven inches long and carved from wood, it had a skeletal body and an oversized head. Its expression was maniacally fierce, its pointed teeth completely bared, its glaring eyes protuberant. It clutched an eight-inch spear in its right hand. A length of fine, gold chain was wrapped around its body from the shoulders to the knees. A tiny scroll was wedged between the doll and the inside wall of its box. Amelia picked it up and unrolled it. There was handwriting on it. *This is He Who Kills*, it began. *He is a deadly hunter.* Amelia smiled as she read the rest of the words. Arthur would be pleased.

The thought of Arthur made her turn to look at the telephone on the table beside her. After a while, she sighed and set the wooden box on the sofa. Lifting the telephone to her lap, she picked up the receiver and dialed a number.

Her mother answered.

"Hello, Mom," Amelia said.

"Haven't you left yet?" her mother asked.

Amelia steeled herself. "Mom, I know it's Friday night—" she started.

She couldn't finish. There was silence on the line. Amelia closed her eyes. Mom, please, she thought. She swallowed. "There's this man," she said. "His name is Arthur Breslow. He's a high school teacher."

"You aren't coming," her mother said.

Amelia shivered. "It's his birthday," she said. She opened

213

her eyes and looked at the doll. "I sort of promised him we'd
. . . spend the evening together."

Her mother was silent. There aren't any good movies playing
tonight, anyway, Amelia's mind continued. "We could go tomorrow night," she said.

Her mother was silent.

"Mom?"

"Now even Friday night's too much for you."

"Mom, I see you two, three nights a week."

"To *visit*," said her mother. "When you have your own room
here."

"Mom, *let's not start on that again*," Amelia said. I'm not a
child, she thought. Stop treating me as though I were a child!

"How long have you been seeing him?" her mother asked.

"A month or so."

"Without telling me," her mother said.

"I had every intention of telling you." Amelia's head was
starting to throb. I will *not* get a headache, she told herself.
She looked at the doll. It seemed to be glaring at her. "He's a
nice man, Mom," she said.

Her mother didn't speak. Amelia felt her stomach muscles
drawing taut. I won't be able to eat tonight, she thought.

She was conscious suddenly of huddling over the telephone.
She forced herself to sit erect. *I'm thirty-three years old*, she
thought. Reaching out, she lifted the doll from its box. "You
should see what I'm giving him for his birthday," she said. "I
found it in a curio shop on Third Avenue. It's a genuine Zuni
fetish doll, extremely rare. Arthur is a buff on anthropology.
That's why I got it for him."

There was silence on the line. All right, *don't talk*, Amelia
thought. "It's a hunting fetish," she continued, trying hard to
sound untroubled. "It's supposed to have the spirit of a Zuni
hunter trapped inside it. There's a golden chain around it to
prevent the spirit from—" She couldn't think of the word; ran
a shaking finger over the chain. "—escaping, I guess," she said.
"His name is He Who Kills. You should see his face." She felt
warm tears trickling down her cheeks.

"Have a good time," said her mother, hanging up.

Amelia stared at the receiver, listening to the dial tone. Why
is it always like this? she thought. She dropped the receiver

onto its cradle and set aside the telephone. The darkening room looked blurred to her. She stood the doll on the coffee-table edge and pushed to her feet. I'll take my bath now, she told herself. I'll meet him and we'll have a lovely time. She walked across the living room. A lovely time, her mind repeated emptily. She knew it wasn't possible. Oh, *Mom*! she thought. She clenched her fists in helpless fury as she went into the bedroom.

In the living room, the doll fell off the table edge. It landed head down and the spear point, sticking into the carpet, braced the doll's legs in the air.

The fine, gold chain began to slither downward.

It was almost dark when Amelia came back into the living room. She had taken off her clothes and was wearing her terry-cloth robe. In the bathroom, water was running into the tub.

She sat on the sofa and placed the telephone on her lap. For several minutes, she stared at it. At last, with a heavy sigh, she lifted the receiver and dialed a number.

"Arthur?" she said when he answered.

"Yes?" Amelia knew the tone—pleasant but suspecting. She couldn't speak.

"Your mother," Arthur finally said.

That cold, heavy sinking in her stomach. "It's our night together," she explained. "Every Friday—" She stopped and waited. Arthur didn't speak. "I've mentioned it before," she said.

"I know you've mentioned it," he said.

Amelia rubbed at her temple.

"She's still running your life, isn't she?" he said.

Amelia tensed. "I just don't want to hurt her feelings anymore," she said. "My moving out was hard enough on her."

"I don't want to hurt her feelings either," Arthur said. "But how many birthdays a year do I have? We *planned* on this."

"I know." She felt her stomach muscles tightening again.

"Are you really going to let her do this to you?" Arthur asked. "One Friday night out of the whole year?"

Amelia closed her eyes. Her lips moved soundlessly. I just can't hurt her feelings anymore, she thought. She swallowed. "She's my mother," she said.

"Very well," he said. "I'm sorry. I was looking forward to it, but—" He paused. "I'm sorry," he said. He hung up quietly.

Amelia sat in silence for a long time, listening to the dial tone. She started when the recorded voice said loudly, "Please hang up." Putting the receiver down, she replaced the telephone on its table. So much for my birthday present, she thought. It would be pointless to give it to Arthur now. She reached out, switching on the table lamp. She'd take the doll back tomorrow.

The doll was not on the coffee table. Looking down, Amelia saw the gold chain lying on the carpet. She eased off the sofa edge onto her knees and picked it up, dropping it into the wooden box. The doll was not beneath the coffee table. Bending over, Amelia felt around underneath the sofa.

She cried out, jerking back her hand. Straightening up, she turned to the lamp and looked at her hand. There was something wedged beneath the index fingernail. She shivered as she plucked it out. It was the head of the doll's spear. She dropped it into the box and put the finger in her mouth. Bending over again, she felt around more cautiously beneath the sofa.

She couldn't find the doll. Standing with a weary groan, she started pulling one end of the sofa from the wall. It was terribly heavy. She recalled the night that she and her mother had shopped for the furniture. She'd wanted to furnish the apartment in Danish modern. Mother had insisted on this heavy, maple sofa; it had been on sale. Amelia grunted as she dragged it from the wall. She was conscious of the water running in the bathroom. She'd better turn it off soon.

She looked at the section of carpet she'd cleared, catching sight of the spear shaft. The doll was not beside it. Amelia picked it up and set it on the coffee table. The doll was caught beneath the sofa, she decided; when she'd moved the sofa, she had moved the doll as well.

She thought she heard a sound behind her—fragile, skittering. Amelia turned. The sound had stopped. She felt a chill move up the backs of her legs. "It's He Who Kills," she said with a smile. "He's taken off his chain and gone—"

She broke off suddenly. There had definitely been a noise inside the kitchen; a metallic, rasping sound. Amelia swallowed nervously. What's going on? she thought. She walked across the living room and reached into the kitchen, switching on the light. She peered inside. Everything looked normal. Her gaze moved falteringly across the stove, the pan of water on it, the table and chair, the drawers and cabinet doors all shut, the electric clock, the small refrigerator with the cookbook lying on top of it, the picture on the wall, the knife rack fastened to the cabinet side—its small knife missing.

Amelia stared at the knife rack. Don't be silly, she told herself. She'd put the knife in the drawer, that's all. Stepping into the kitchen, she pulled out the silverware drawer. The knife was not inside it.

Another sound made her look down quickly at the floor. She gasped in shock. For several moments, she could not react; then, stepping to the doorway, she looked into the living room, her heartbeat thudding. Had it been imagination? She was sure she'd seen a movement.

"Oh, come on," she said. She made a disparaging sound. She hadn't seen a thing.

Across the room, the lamp went out.

Amelia jumped so startledly, she rammed her right elbow against the doorjamb. Crying out, she clutched the elbow with her left hand, eyes closed momentarily, her face a mask of pain.

She opened her eyes and looked into the darkened living room. "Come on," she told herself in aggravation. Three sounds plus a burned-out bulb did not add up to anything as idiotic as—

She willed away the thought. She had to turn the water off. Leaving the kitchen, she started for the hall. She rubbed her elbow, grimacing.

There was another sound. Amelia froze. Something was coming across the carpet toward her. She looked down dumbly. No, she thought.

She saw it then—a rapid movement near the floor. There was a glint of metal, instantly, a stabbing pain in her right calf. Amelia gasped. She kicked out blindly. Pain again. She felt warm blood running down her skin. She turned and lunged into the hall. The throw rug slipped beneath her and she fell against the wall, hot pain lancing through her right ankle. She clutched at the wall to keep from falling, then went sprawling on her side. She thrashed around with a sob of fear.

More movement, dark on dark. Pain in her left calf, then her right again. Amelia cried out. Something brushed along her thigh. She scrabbled back, then lurched up blindly, almost falling again. She fought for balance, reaching out convulsively. The heel of her left hand rammed against the wall, supporting her. She twisted around and rushed into the darkened bedroom. Slamming the door, she fell against it, panting. Something banged against it on the other side, something small and near the floor.

Amelia listened, trying not to breathe so loudly. She pulled carefully at the knob to make sure the latch had caught. When there were no further sounds outside the door, she backed toward the bed. She started as she bumped against the mattress edge. Slumping down, she grabbed at the extension phone and pulled it to her lap. Whom could she call? The police? They'd think her mad. Mother? She was too far off.

She was dialing Arthur's number by the light from the bathroom when the doorknob started turning. Suddenly, her fingers couldn't move. She stared across the darkened room. The door latch clicked. The telephone slipped off her lap. She heard it thudding onto the carpet as the door swung open. Something dropped from the outside knob.

Amelia jerked back, pulling up her legs. A shadowy form was scurrying across the carpet toward the bed. She gaped at it. It isn't true, she thought. She stiffened at the tugging on her bedspread. *It was climbing up to get her.* No, she thought; *it isn't true.* She couldn't move. She stared at the edge of the mattress.

Something that looked like a tiny head appeared. Amelia twisted around with a cry of shock, flung herself across the bed and jumped to the floor. Plunging into the bathroom, she spun around and slammed the door, gasping at the pain in her ankle. She had barely thumbed in the button on the doorknob when something banged against the bottom of the door. Amelia heard a noise like the scratching of a rat. Then it was still.

She turned and leaned across the tub. The level of the water was almost to the overflow drain. As she twisted shut the faucets, she saw drops of blood falling into the water. Straightening up, she turned to the medicine-cabinet mirror above the sink.

She caught her breath in horror as she saw the gash across her neck. She pressed a shaking hand against it. Abruptly, she became aware of pain in her legs and looked down. She'd been slashed along the calves of both legs. Blood was running down her ankles, dripping off the edges of her feet. Amelia started crying. Blood ran between the fingers of the hand against her neck. It trickled down her wrist. She looked at her reflection through a glaze of tears.

Something in her aroused her, a wretchedness, a look of terrified surrender. *No*, she thought. She reached out for the medicine-cabinet door. Opening it, she pulled out iodine, gauze and tape. She dropped the cover of the toilet seat and sank down gingerly. It was a struggle to remove the stopper of the iodine bottle. She had to rap it hard against the sink three times before it opened.

The burning of the antiseptic on her calves made her gasp. Amelia clenched her teeth as she wrapped gauze around her right leg.

A sound made her twist toward the door. She saw the knife blade being jabbed beneath it. It's trying to stab my feet, she thought; it thinks I'm standing there. She felt unreal to be considering its thoughts. *This is He Who Kills*; the scroll flashed suddenly across her mind. *He is a deadly hunter*. Amelia stared at the poking knife blade. God, she thought.

Hastily, she bandaged both her legs, then stood and, looking into the mirror, cleaned the blood from her neck with a wash-rag. She swabbed some iodine along the edges of the gash, hissing at the fiery pain.

She whirled at the new sound, heartbeat leaping. Stepping to the door, she leaned down, listening hard. There was a faint metallic noise inside the knob.

The doll was trying to unlock it.

Amelia backed off slowly, staring at the knob. She tried to visualize the doll. Was it hanging from the knob by one arm, using the other to probe inside the knob lock with the knife? The vision was insane. She felt an icy prickling on the back of her neck. *I mustn't let it in*, she thought.

A hoarse cry pulled her lips back as the doorknob button popped out. Reaching out impulsively, she dragged a bath towel off its rack. The doorknob turned, the latch clicked free. The door began to open.

Suddenly the doll came darting in. It moved so quickly that its figure blurred before Amelia's eyes. She swung the towel down hard, as though it were a huge bug rushing at her. The doll was knocked against the wall. Amelia heaved the towel on top of it and lurched across the floor, gasping at the pain in her ankle. Flinging open the door, she lunged into the bedroom.

She was almost to the hall door when her ankle gave. She pitched across the carpet with a cry of shock. There was a noise behind her. Twisting around, she saw the doll come through the bathroom doorway like a jumping spider. She saw the knife blade glinting in the light. Then the doll was in the shadows, coming at her fast. Amelia scrabbled back. She glanced over her shoulder, saw the closet and backed into its darkness, clawing for the doorknob.

Pain again, an icy slashing at her foot. Amelia screamed and heaved back. Reaching up, she yanked a topcoat down. It fell across the doll. She jerked down everything in reach. The doll was buried underneath a mound of blouses, skirts and dresses. Amelia pitched across the moving pile of clothes. She forced herself to stand and limped into the hall as quickly as she could. The sound of thrashing underneath the clothes faded from her hearing. She hobbled to the door. Unlocking it, she pulled the knob.

The door was held. Amelia reached up quickly to the bolt. It had been shot. She tried to pull it free. It wouldn't budge. She clawed at it with sudden terror. It was twisted out of shape. "No," she muttered. *She was trapped.* "Oh, God." She started pounding on the door. "Please help me! *Help* me!"

Sound in the bedroom. Amelia whirled and lurched across the living room. She dropped to her knees beside the sofa, feeling for the telephone, but her fingers trembled so much that she couldn't dial the numbers. She began to sob, then twisted around with a strangled cry. The doll was rushing at her from the hallway.

Amelia grabbed an ashtray from the coffee table and hurled it at the doll. She threw a vase, a wooden box, a figurine. She couldn't hit the doll. It reached her, started jabbing at her legs. Amelia reared up blindly and fell across the coffee table. Rolling to her knees, she stood again. She staggered toward the hall, shoving over furniture to stop the doll. She toppled a chair, a table. Picking up a lamp, she hurled it at the floor. She backed into the hall and, spinning, rushed into the closet, slammed the door shut.

She held the knob with rigid fingers. Waves of hot breath pulsed against her face. She cried out as the knife was jabbed beneath the door, its sharp point sticking into one of her toes. She shuffled back, shifting her grip on the knob. Her robe hung open. She could feel a trickle of blood between her breasts. Her legs felt numb with pain. She closed her eyes. Please, someone help, she thought.

She stiffened as the doorknob started turning in her grasp. Her flesh went cold. It couldn't be stronger than she: it *couldn't* be. Amelia tightened her grip. *Please,* she thought. The side of her head bumped against the front edge of her suitcase on the shelf.

The thought exploded in her mind. Holding the knob with her right hand, she reached up, fumbling, with her left. The suitcase clasps were open. With a sudden wrench, she turned the doorknob, shoving at the door as hard as possible. It rushed away from her. She heard it bang against the wall. The doll thumped down.

Amelia reached up, hauling down her suitcase. Yanking open the lid, she fell to her knees in the closet doorway, holding the suitcase like an open book. She braced herself, eyes wide, teeth clenched together. She felt the doll's weight as it banged against the suitcase bottom. Instantly, she slammed the lid and threw the suitcase flat. Falling across it, she held it shut until her shaking hands could fasten the clasps. The sound of them clicking into place made her sob with relief. She shoved away the suitcase. It slid across the hall and bumped against the wall. Amelia struggled to her feet, trying not to listen to the frenzied kicking and scratching inside the suitcase.

She switched on the hall light and tried to open the bolt. It was hopelessly wedged. She turned and limped across the living room, glancing at her legs. The bandages were hanging loose. Both legs were streaked with caking blood, some of the gashes still bleeding. She felt at her throat. The cut was still wet. Amelia pressed her shaking lips together. She'd get to a doctor soon now.

Removing the ice pick from its kitchen drawer, she returned to the hall. A cutting sound made her look toward the suitcase. She caught her breath. The knife blade was protruding from the suitcase wall, moving up and down with a sawing motion. Amelia stared at it. She felt as though her body had been turned to stone.

She limped to the suitcase and knelt beside it, looking, with revulsion at the sawing blade. It was smeared with blood. She tried to pinch it with the fingers of her left hand, pull it out. The blade was twisted, jerked down, and she cried out, snatching back her hand. There was a deep slice in her thumb. Blood ran down across her palm. Amelia pressed the finger to her robe. She felt as though her mind was going blank.

Pushing to her feet, she limped back to the door and started prying at the bolt. She couldn't get it loose. Her thumb began to ache. She pushed the ice pick underneath the bolt socket and tried to force it off the wall. The ice pick point broke off. Amelia slipped and almost fell. She pushed up, whimpering. There was no time, no time. She looked around in desperation.

The window! She could throw the suitcase out! She visualized it tumbling through the darkness. Hastily, she dropped the ice pick, turning toward the suitcase.

She froze. The doll had forced its head and shoulders through the rent in the suitcase wall. Amelia watched it struggling to get out. She felt paralyzed. The twisting doll was staring at her. No, she thought, it isn't true. The doll jerked free its legs and jumped to the floor.

Amelia jerked around and ran into the living room. Her right foot landed on a shard of broken crockery. She felt it cutting deep into her heel and lost her balance. Landing on her side, she thrashed around. The doll came leaping at her. She could see the knife blade glint. She kicked out wildly, knocking back the doll. Lunging to her feet, she reeled into the kitchen, whirled, and started pushing shut the door.

Something kept it from closing. Amelia thought she heard a screaming in her mind. Looking down, she saw the knife and a tiny wooden hand. The doll's arm was wedged between the

door and the jamb! Amelia shoved against the door with all
her might, aghast at the strength with which the door was
pushed the other way. There was a cracking noise. A fierce
smile pulled her lips back and she pushed berserkly at the door.
The screaming in her mind grew louder, drowning out the
sound of splintering wood.

The knife blade sagged. Amelia dropped to her knees and
tugged at it. She pulled the knife into the kitchen, seeing the
wooden hand and wrist fall from the handle of the knife. With
a gagging noise, she struggled to her feet and dropped the
knife into the sink. The door slammed hard against her side;
the doll rushed in.

Amelia jerked away from it. Picking up the chair, she slung it
toward the doll. It jumped aside, then ran around the fallen
chair. Amelia snatched the pan of water off the stove and
hurled it down. The pan clanged loudly off the floor, spraying
water on the doll.

She stared at the doll. It wasn't coming after her. It was
trying to climb the sink, leaping up and clutching at the
counter side with one hand. It wants the knife, she thought. It
has to have its weapon.

She knew abruptly what to do. Stepping over to the stove,
she pulled down the broiler door and twisted the knob on all
the way. She heard the puffing detonation of the gas as she
turned to grab the doll.

She cried out as the doll began to kick and twist, its maddened thrashing flinging her from one side of the kitchen to
the other. The screaming filled her mind again and suddenly she
knew it was the spirit in the doll that screamed. She slid and
crashed against the table, wrenched herself around and, dropping to her knees before the stove, flung the doll inside. She
slammed the door and fell against it.

The door was almost driven out. Amelia pressed her shoulder, then her back against it, turning to brace her legs against
the wall. She tried to ignore the pounding scrabble of the doll
inside the broiler. She watched the red blood pulsing from her
heel. The smell of burning wood began to reach her and she
closed her eyes. The door was getting hot. She shifted carefully. The kicking and pounding filled her ears. The screaming
flooded through her mind. She knew her back would get

burned, but she didn't dare to move. The smell of burning wood grew worse. Her foot ached terribly.

Amelia looked up at the electric clock on the wall. It was four minutes to seven. She watched the red second hand revolving slowly. A minute passed. The screaming in her mind was fading now. She shifted uncomfortably, gritting her teeth against the burning heat on her back.

Another minute passed. The kicking and the pounding stopped. The screaming faded more and more. The smell of burning wood had filled the kitchen. There was a pall of gray smoke in the air. That they'll see, Amelia thought. Now that it's over, they'll come and help. That's the way it always is.

She started to ease herself away from the broiler door, ready to throw her weight back against it if she had to. She turned around and got on her knees. The reek of charred wood made her nauseated. She had to know, though. Reaching out, she pulled down the door.

Something dark and stifling rushed across her and she heard the screaming in her mind once more as hotness flooded over her and into her. It was a scream of victory now.

Amelia stood and turned off the broiler. She took a pair of ice tongs from its drawer and lifted out the blackened twist of wood. She dropped it into the sink and ran water over it until the smoke had stopped. Then she went into the bedroom, picked up the telephone and depressed its cradle. After a moment, she released the cradle and dialed her mother's number.

"This is Amelia, Mom," she said. "I'm sorry I acted the way I did. I want us to spend the evening together. It's a little late, though. Can you come by my place and we'll go from here?" She listened. "Good," she said. "I'll wait for you."

Hanging up, she walked into the kitchen, where she slid the longest carving knife from its place in the rack. She went to the front door and pushed back its bolt, which now moved freely. She carried the knife into the living room, took off her bathrobe and danced a dance of hunting, of the joy of hunting, of the joy of the impending kill.

Then she sat down, cross-legged, in the corner. He Who Kills sat, cross-legged, in the corner, in the darkness, waiting for the prey to come.

1969

T.E.D. KLEIN

(b. 1947)

The Events at Poroth Farm

As soon as the phone stops ringing, I'll begin this affidavit. Lord, it's hot in here. Perhaps I should open a window. . . .

Thirteen rings. It has a sense of humor.

I suppose that ought to be comforting.

Somehow I'm not comforted. If it feels free to indulge in these teasing, tormenting little games, so much the worse for me.

The summer is over now, but this room is like an oven. My shirt is already drenched, and this pen feels slippery in my hand. In a moment or two the little drop of sweat that's collecting above my eyebrow is going to splash onto this page.

Just the same, I'll keep that window closed. Outside, through the dusty panes of glass, I can see a boy in red spectacles sauntering toward the courthouse steps. Perhaps there's a telephone booth in back. . . .

A sense of humor—that's one quality I never noticed in it. I saw only a deadly seriousness and, of course, an intelligence that grew at terrifying speed, malevolent and inhuman. If it now feels itself safe enough to toy with me before doing whatever it intends to do, so much the worse for me. So much the worse, perhaps, for us all.

I hope I'm wrong. Though my name is Jeremy, derived from Jeremiah, I'd hate to be a prophet in the wilderness. I'd much rather be a harmless crank.

But I believe we're in for trouble.

I'm a long way from the wilderness now, of course. Though perhaps not far enough to save me. . . . I'm writing this affidavit in room 2-K of the Union Hotel, overlooking Main Street in Flemington, New Jersey, twenty miles south of Gilead. Directly across the street, hippies lounging on its steps, stands the county courthouse where Bruno Hauptmann was tried back in 1935. (Did they ever find the body of that child?) Hauptmann undoubtedly walked down those very steps, now lined with teenagers savoring their last week of summer vacation. Where that boy in the red spectacles sits sucking on his cigarette—did the killer once halt there, police and reporters around him, and contemplate his imminent execution?

For several days now I have been afraid to leave this room.

I have perhaps been staring too often at that ordinary-looking boy on the steps. He sits there every day. The red spectacles conceal his eyes; it's impossible to tell where he's looking.

I know he's looking at me.

But it would be foolish of me to waste time worrying about executions when I have these notes to transcribe. It won't take long, and then, perhaps, I'll sneak outside to mail them—and leave New Jersey forever. I remain, despite all that's happened, an optimist. What was it my namesake said? "Thou art my hope in the day of evil."

There *is*, surprisingly, some real wilderness left in New Jersey, assuming one wants to be a prophet. The hills to the west, spreading from the southern swamplands to the Delaware and beyond to Pennsylvania, provide shelter for deer, pheasant, even an occasional bear—and hide hamlets never visited by outsiders: pockets of ignorance, some of them, citadels of ancient superstition utterly cut off from news of New York and the rest of the state, religious communities where customs haven't changed appreciably since the days of their settlement a century or more ago.

It seems incredible that villages so isolated can exist today on the very doorstep of the world's largest metropolis—villages with nothing to offer the outsider, and hence never visited, except by the occasional hunter who stumbles on them unwittingly. Yet as you speed down one of the state highways, consider how few of the cars slow down for the local roads. It is easy to pass the little towns without even a glance at the signs; and if there are no signs . . . ? And consider, too, how seldom the local traffic turns off onto the narrow roads that emerge without warning from the woods. And when those untraveled side roads lead into others still deeper in wilderness; and when those in turn give way to dirt roads, deserted for weeks on end. . . . It is not hard to see how tiny rural communities can exist less than an hour from major cities, virtually unaware of one another's existence.

Television, of course, will link the two—unless, as is often the case, the elders of the community choose to see this distraction as the Devil's tool and proscribe it. Telephones put these outcast settlements in touch with their neighbors—unless they choose to ignore their neighbors. And so in the course of years they are . . . forgotten.

New Yorkers were amazed when in the winter of 1968 the *Times* "discovered" a religious community near New Providence that had existed in its present form since the late 1800s —less than forty miles from Times Square. Agricultural work was performed entirely by hand, women still wore long dresses with high collars, and town worship was held every evening.

I, too, was amazed. I'd seldom traveled west of the Hudson and still thought of New Jersey as some dismal extension of the Newark slums, ruled by gangsters, foggy with swamp gases and industrial waste, a gray land that had surrendered to the city.

Only later did I learn of the rural New Jersey, and of towns whose solitary general stores double as post offices, with one or two gas pumps standing in front. And later still I learned of Baptistown and Quakertown, their old religions surviving unchanged, and of towns like Lebanon, Landsdown, and West Portal, close to Route 22 and civilization but heavy with secrets city folk never dreamed of; Mt. Airy, with its network of hidden caverns, and Mt. Olive, bordering the infamous Budd Lake; Middle Valley, sheltered by dark cliffs, subject of the recent archaeological debate chronicled in *Natural History*, where the wanderer may still find grotesque relics of pagan worship and, some say, may still hear the chants that echo from the cliffs on certain nights; and towns with names like Zaraphath and Gilead, forgotten communities of bearded men and black-robed women, walled hamlets too small or obscure for most maps of the state. This was the wilderness into which I traveled, weary of Manhattan's interminable din; and it was outside Gilead where, until the tragedies, I chose to make my home for three months.

Among the silliest of literary conventions is the "town that won't talk"—the Bavarian village where peasants turn away from tourists' queries about "the castle" and silently cross themselves, the New England harbor town where fishermen feign ignorance and cast "furtive glances" at the traveler. In actuality, I have found, country people love to talk to the stranger, provided he shows a sincere interest in their anecdotes. Store-keepers will interrupt their activity at the cash register to tell you their theories on a recent murder; farmers will readily spin tales of buried bones and of a haunted house down the road. Rural townspeople are not so reticent as the writers would have us believe.

Gilead, isolated though it is behind its oak forests and ruined walls, is no exception. The inhabitants regard all outsiders with an initial suspicion, but let one demonstrate a respect for their traditional reserve and they will prove friendly enough. They don't favor modern fashions or flashy automobiles, but they can hardly be described as hostile, although that was my original impression.

When asked about the terrible events at Poroth Farm, they will prove more than willing to talk. They will tell you of bad crops and polluted well water, of emotional depression leading to a fatal argument. In short, they will describe a conventional rural murder, and will even volunteer their opinions on the killer's present whereabouts.

But you will learn almost nothing from them—or almost nothing that is true. They don't know what really happened. I do. I was there.

I had come to spend the summer with Sarr Poroth and his wife. I needed a place where I could do a lot of reading without distraction, and Poroth's farm, secluded as it was even from the village of Gilead six miles down the dirt road, appeared the perfect spot for my studies.

I had seen the Poroths' advertisement in the *Hunterdon County Democrat* on a trip west through Princeton last spring. They advertised for a summer or long-term tenant to live in one of the outbuildings behind the farmhouse. As I soon learned, the building was a long low cinder-block affair, unpleasantly suggestive of army barracks but clean, new, and cool in the sun; by the start of summer ivy sprouted from the walls and disguised the ugly gray brick. Originally intended to house chickens, it had in fact remained empty for several years until the farm's original owner, a Mr. Baber, sold out last fall to the Poroths, who immediately saw that with the installation of dividing walls, linoleum floors, and other improvements the building might serve as a source of income. I was to be their first tenant.

The Poroths, Sarr and Deborah, were in their early thirties, only slightly older than I, although anyone who met them might have believed the age difference to be greater; their relative solemnity and the drabness of their clothing added years to their appearance, and so did their hair styles: Deborah, though possessing a beautiful length of black hair, wound it all in a tight bun behind her neck, pulling the hair back from her face with a severity which looked almost painful, and Sarr maintained a thin fringe of black beard that circled from ears to chin in the manner of the Pennsylvania Dutch, who leave their hair shaggy but refuse to grow moustaches lest they resemble the military class they've traditionally despised. Both man and wife were hard-working, grave of expression, and pale despite the time spent laboring in the sun—a pallor accentuated by the inky blackness of their hair. I imagine this unhealthy aspect was due, in part, to the considerable amount of inbreeding that went on in the area, the Poroths themselves being, I believe, third cousins. On first meeting, one might have taken them for brother and sister, two gravely devout children aged in the wilderness.

And yet there was a difference between them—and, too, a difference that set them both in contrast to others of their sect. The Poroths were, as far as I could determine, members of a tiny Mennonitic order outwardly related to the Amish, though doctrinal differences were apparently rather profound. It was this order that made up the large part of the community known as Gilead.

I sometimes think the only reason they allowed an infidel like me to live on their property (for my religion was among the first things they inquired about) was because of my name; Sarr was very partial to Jeremiah, and the motto of his order was, "Stand ye in the ways, and see, and ask for the old paths, where is the good way, and walk therein." (VI:16)

Having been raised in no particular religion except a universal skepticism, I began the summer with a hesitancy to bring up the topic in conversation, and so I learned comparatively little about the Poroths' beliefs. Only toward the end of my stay did I begin to thumb through the Bible in odd moments and take to quoting jeremiads. That was, I suppose, Sarr's influence.

I was able to learn, nonetheless, that for all their conservative aura the Poroths were considered, in effect, young liberals by most of Gilead. Sarr had a bachelor's degree in religious studies from Rutgers, and Deborah had attended a nearby community college for two years, unusual for women of the sect. Too, they had only recently taken to farming, having spent the first year of their marriage near New Brunswick, where Sarr had hoped to find a teaching position and, when the job situation proved hopeless, had worked as a sort of handyman/carpenter. While most inhabitants of Gilead had never left the farm, the Poroths were coming to it late—their families had been merchants for several generations—and so were relatively inexperienced.

The inexperience showed. The farm comprised some ninety acres, but most of that was forest, or fields of weeds too thick and high to walk through. Across the backyard, close to my rooms, ran a small, nameless stream nearly choked with green scum. A large cornfield to the north lay fallow, but Sarr was planning to seed it this year, using borrowed equipment. His wife spent much of her time indoors, for though she maintained a small vegetable garden, she preferred keeping house and looking after the Poroths' great love, their seven cats.

As if to symbolize their broad-mindedness, the Poroths owned a television set, very rare in Gilead; in light of what was to come, however, it is unfortunate they lacked a telephone. (Apparently the set had been received as a wedding present from Deborah's parents, but the monthly expense of a telephone was simply too great.) Otherwise, though, the little farmhouse was "modern" in that it had a working bathroom and gas heat. That they had advertised in the local newspaper was considered scandalous by some of the order's more orthodox members, and indeed a mere subscription to that innocuous weekly had at one time been regarded as a breach of religious conduct.

Though outwardly similar, both of them tall and pale, the Poroths were actually so different as to embody the maxim that "opposites attract." It was that carefully nurtured reserve that deceived one at first meeting, for in truth Deborah was far more talkative, friendly, and energetic than her husband. Sarr was moody, distant, silent most of the time, with a voice so low that one had trouble following him in conversation. Sitting as stonily as one of his cats, never moving, never speaking, perennially inscrutable, he tended to frighten visitors to the farm until they learned that he was not really sitting in judgment on them; his reserve was not born of surliness but of shyness.

Where Sarr was catlike, his wife hid beneath the formality of her order the bubbly personality of a kitten. Given the smallest encouragement—say, a family visit—she would plunge into animated conversation, gesticulating, laughing easily, hugging whatever cat was nearby or shouting to guests across the room. When drinking—for both of them enjoyed liquor and, curiously, it was not forbidden by their faith—their innate differences were magnified: Deborah would forget the restraints placed upon women in the order and would eventually dominate the conversation, while her husband would seem to grow increasingly withdrawn and morose.

Women in the region tended to be submissive to the men, and certainly the important decisions in the Poroths' lives were made by Sarr. Yet I really cannot say who was the stronger of the two. Only once did I ever see them quarrel. . . .

Perhaps the best way to tell it is by setting down portions of the journal I kept this summer. Not every entry, of course. Mere excerpts. Just enough to make this affidavit comprehensible to anyone unfamiliar with the incidents at Poroth Farm.

The journal was the only writing I did all summer; my primary reason for keeping it was to record the books I'd read each day, as well as to examine my reactions to relative solitude over a long period of time. All the rest of my energies (as you will no doubt gather from the notes below) were spent reading, in preparation for a course I plan to teach at Trenton State this fall. Or *planned*, I should say, because I don't expect to be anywhere around here come fall.

Where will I be? Perhaps that depends on what's beneath those rose-tinted spectacles.

The course was to cover the Gothic tradition from Shakespeare to Faulkner, from *Hamlet* to *Absalom, Absalom!* (And

why not view the former as Gothic, with its ghost on the bat-
tlements and concern for lost inheritance?) To make the move
to Gilead, I'd rented a car for a few days and had stuffed it full
of books—only a few of which I ever got to read. But then, I
couldn't have known. . . .

How pleasant things were, at the beginning.

June 4

Unpacking day. Spent all morning putting up screens, and a
good thing I did. Night now, and a million moths tapping at
the windows. One of them as big as a small bird—white—
largest I've ever seen. What kind of caterpillar must it have
been? I hope the damned things don't push through the
screens.

Had to kill literally hundreds of spiders before moving my
stuff in. The Poroths finished doing the inside of this building
only a couple of months ago, and already it's infested. Arach-
nidae—hate the bastards. Why? We'll take that one up with
Sigmund someday. Daydreams of Revenge of the Spiders.
Writhing body covered with a frenzy of hairy brown legs.
"Egad, man, that face! That bloody, torn face! And the missing
eyes! It looks like—no! Jeremy!" Killing spiders is supposed to
bring bad luck. (Insidious Sierra Club propaganda masquer-
ading as folk myth?) But can't sleep if there's anything crawling
around . . . so what the hell?

Supper with the Poroths. Began to eat, then heard Sarr saying
grace. Apologies—but things like that don't embarrass me as
much as they used to. (Is that because I'm nearing thirty?)

Chatted about crops, insects, humidity. (Very damp area—
band of purplish mildew already around bottom of walls out
here.) Sarr told of plans to someday build a larger house when
Deborah has a baby, three or four years from now. He wants to
build it out of stone. Then he shut up, and I had to keep the
conversation going. (Hate eating in silence—animal sounds of
mastication, bubbling stomachs.) Deborah joked about cats
being her surrogate children. All seven of them hanging around
my legs, rubbing against ankles. My nose began running and
my eyes itched. Goddamned allergy. Must remember to start
treatments this fall, when I get to Trenton. Deborah sympathetic, Sarr merely watching; she told me my eyes were blood-

shot, offered antihistamine. Told them I was glad they at least believe in modern medicine—I'd been afraid she'd offer herbs or mud or something. Sarr said some of the locals still use "snake oil." Asked him how snakes were killed, quoting line from *Vathek*: "The oil of the serpents I have pinched to death will be a pretty present." We discussed wisdom of pinching snakes. Apparently there's a copperhead out back, near the brook. . . .

The meal was good—lamb and noodles. Not bad for fifteen dollars a week, since I detest cooking. Spice cake for dessert, home-made, of course. Deborah is a good cook. Handsome woman, too.

Still light when I left their kitchen. Fireflies already on the lawn—I've never seen so many. Knelt and watched them a while, listening to the crickets. Think I'll like it here.

Took nearly an hour to arrange my books the way I wanted them. Alphabetical order by authors? No, chronological. . . . But anthologies mess that system up, so back to authors. Why am I so neurotic about my books?

Anyway, they look nice there on the shelves.

Sat up tonight finishing *The Mysteries of Udolpho*. Figure it's best to get the long ones out of the way first. Radcliffe's unfortunate penchant for explaining away all her ghosts and apparitions really a mistake and a bore. All in all, not exactly the most fascinating reading, though a good study in Romanticism. Montoni the typical Byronic hero/villain. But can't demand students read *Udolpho*—too long. In fact, had to keep reminding myself to slow down, have patience with the book. Tried to put myself in frame of mind of 1794 reader with plenty of time on his hands. It works, too—I do have plenty of time out here, and already I can feel myself beginning to unwind. What New York does to people. . . .

It's almost two A.M. now, and I'm about ready to turn in. Too bad there's no bathroom in this building—I hate pissing outside at night. God knows what's crawling up your ankles. . . . But it's hardly worth stumbling through the darkness to the farmhouse, and maybe waking up Sarr and Deborah. The nights out here are really pitch-black.

. . . Felt vulnerable, standing there against the night. But what made me even uneasier was the view I got of this building.

The lamp on the desk casts the only light for miles, and as I stood outside looking into this room, I could see dozens of flying shapes making right for the screens. When you're inside here it's as if you're in a display case—the whole night can see you, but all you can see is darkness. I wish this room didn't have windows on three of the walls—though that does let in the breeze. And I wish the woods weren't so close to my windows by the bed. I suppose privacy is what I wanted—but feel a little unprotected out here.

Those moths are still batting themselves against the screens, but as far as I can see the only things that have gotten in are a few gnats flying around this lamp. The crickets sound good—you sure don't hear them in the city. Frogs are croaking in the brook.

My nose is only now beginning to clear up. Those god-damned cats. Must remember to buy some Contac. Even though the cats are all outside during the day, that farmhouse is full of their scent. But I don't expect to be spending that much time inside the house anyway; this allergy will keep me away from the TV and out here with the books.

Just saw an unpleasantly large spider scurry across the floor near the foot of my bed. Vanished behind the footlocker. Must remember to buy some insect spray tomorrow.

June 11

Hot today, but at night comes a chill. The dampness of this place seems to magnify temperature. Sat outside most of the day finishing the Maturin book, *Melmoth the Wanderer*, and feeling vaguely guilty each time I heard Sarr or Deborah working out there in the field. Well, I've paid for my reading time, so I guess I'm entitled to enjoy it. Though some of these old Gothics are a bit hard to enjoy. The trouble with *Melmoth* is that it wants you to hate. You're especially supposed to hate the Catholics. No doubt its picture of the Inquisition is accurate, but all a book like this can do is put you in an unconstructive rage. Those vicious characters have been dead for centuries, and there's no way to punish them. Still, it's a nice, cynical book for those who like atrocity scenes—starving prisoners forced to eat their girlfriends, delightful things like that.

And narratives within narratives within narratives within narratives. I may assign some sections to my class. . . .

Just before dinner, in need of a break, read a story by Arthur Machen. Welsh writer, turn of the century, though think the story's set somewhere in England: old house in the hills, dark woods with secret paths and hidden streams. God, what an experience! I was a little confused by the framing device and all its high-flown talk of "cosmic evil," but the sections from the young girl's notebook were . . . staggering. That air of paganism, the malevolent little faces peeping from the shadows, and those rites she can't dare talk about. . . . It's called "The White People," and it must be the most persuasive horror tale ever written.

Afterward, strolling toward the house, I was moved to climb the old tree in the side yard—the Poroths had already gone in to get dinner ready—and stood upright on a great heavy branch near the middle, making strange gestures and faces that no one could see. Can't say exactly what it was I did, or why. It was getting dark—fireflies below me and a mist rising off the field. I must have looked like a madman's shadow as I made signs to the woods and the moon.

Lamb tonight, and damned good. I may find myself getting fat. Offered, again, to wash the dishes, but apparently Deborah feels that's her role, and I don't care to dissuade her. So talked a while with Sarr about his cats—the usual subject of conversation, especially because, now that summer's coming, they're bringing in dead things every night. Field mice, moles, shrews, birds, even a little garter snake. They don't eat them, just lay them out on the porch for the Poroths to see—sort of an offering, I guess. Sarr tosses the bodies in the garbage can, which, as a result, smells indescribably foul. Deborah wants to put bells around their necks; she hates mice but feels sorry for the birds. When she finished the dishes, she and Sarr sat down to watch one of their godawful TV programs, so I came out here to read.

Spent the usual ten minutes going over this room, spray can in hand, looking for spiders to kill. Found a couple of little ones, then spent some time spraying bugs that were hanging on the screens hoping to get in. Watched a lot of daddy longlegs curl up and die. . . . Tended not to kill the moths, unless they were making too much of a racket banging against the screen; I can tolerate them okay, but it's only fireflies I really like. I always feel a little sorry when I kill one by mistake and see it hold that cold glow too long. (That's how you know they're dead: the dead ones don't wink. They just keep their light on till it fades away.)

The insecticide I'm using is made right here in New Jersey, by the Ortho Chemical Company. The label on the can says, "WARNING. For Outdoor Use Only." That's why I bought it —figured it's the most powerful brand available.

Sat in bed reading Algernon Blackwood's witch/cat story, "Ancient Sorceries" (nowhere near as good as Machen, or as his own tale "The Willows"), and it made me think of those seven cats. The Poroths have around a dozen names for each one of them, which seems a little ridiculous since the creatures barely respond to even one name. Sasha, for example, the orange one, is also known as Butch, which comes from Bouche, mouth. And that's short for Eddie La Bouche, so he's also called Ed or Eddie—which in turn come from some friend's mispronunciation of the cat's original name, Itty, short for Itty Bitty Kitty, which, apparently, he once was. And Zoë, the cutest of the kittens, is also called Bozo and Bisbo. Let's see, how many others can I remember? (I'm just learning to tell some of them apart.) Felix, or "Flixie," was originally called Paleface, and Phaedra, his mother, is sometimes known as Phuddy, short for Phuddy Duddy.

Come to think of it, the only cat that hasn't got multiple names is Bwada, Sarr's cat. (All the others were acquired after he married Deborah, but Bwada was his pet years before.) She's the oldest of the cats, and the meanest. Fat and sleek, with fine gray fur darker than silver gray, lighter than charcoal. She's the only cat that's ever bitten anyone—Deborah, as well as friends of the Poroths—and after seeing the way she snarls at the other cats when they get in her way, I decided to keep my distance. Fortunately she's scared of me and retreats whenever I approach. I think being spayed is what's messed her up and given her an evil disposition.

Sounds are drifting from the farmhouse. I can vaguely make out a psalm of some kind. It's late, past eleven, and I guess the

Poroths have turned off the TV and are singing their evening devotions. . . .

And now all is silence. They've gone to bed. I'm not very tired yet, so I guess I'll stay up a while and read some—

Something odd just happened. I've never heard anything like it. While writing for the past half hour I've been aware, if half-consciously, of the crickets. Their regular chirping can be pretty soothing, like the sound of a well-tuned machine. But just a few seconds ago they seemed to miss a beat. They'd been singing along steadily, ever since the moon came up, and all of a sudden they just *stopped* for a beat—and then they began again, only they were out of rhythm for a moment or two, as if a hand had jarred the record or there'd been some kind of momentary break in the natural flow. . . .

They sound normal enough now, though. Think I'll go back to *Otranto* and let that put me to sleep. It may be the foundation of the English Gothics, but I can't imagine anyone actually reading it for pleasure. I wonder how many pages I'll be able to get through before I drop off. . . .

June 12

Slept late this morning, and then, disinclined to read Walpole on such a sunny day, took a walk. Followed the little brook that runs past my building. There's still a lot of that greenish scum clogging one part of it, and if we don't have some rain soon I expect it will get worse. But the water clears up considerably when it runs past the cornfield and through the woods.

Passed Sarr out in the field—he yelled to watch out for the copperhead, which put a pall on my enthusiasm for exploration. . . . But as it happened I never ran into any snakes, and have a fair idea I'd survive even if bitten. Walked around half a mile into the woods, branches snapping in my face. Made an effort to avoid walking into the little yellow caterpillars that hang from every tree. At one point I had to get my feet wet, because the trail that runs alongside the brook disappeared and the undergrowth was thick. Ducked under a low arch made by decaying branches and vines, my sneakers sloshing in the water. Found that as the brook runs west it forms a small circular pool with banks of wet sand, surrounded by tall oaks, their roots thrust into the water. Lots of animal tracks in the sand—deer, I believe, and what may be a fox or perhaps some farmer's dog. Obviously a watering place. Waded into the center of the pool—it only came up a little past my ankles—but didn't stand there long because it started looking like rain.

The weather remained nasty all day, but no rain has come yet. Cloudy now, though; can't see any stars.

Finished *Otranto*, began *The Monk*. So far so good—rather dirty, really. Not for today, of course, but I can imagine the sensation it must have caused back at the end of the eighteenth century.

Had a good time at dinner tonight, since Sarr had walked into town and brought back some wine. (Medical note: I seem to be less allergic to cats when mildly intoxicated.) We sat around the kitchen afterward playing poker for matchsticks—very sinful indulgence, I understand; Sarr and Deborah told me, quite seriously, that they'd have to say some extra prayers tonight by way of apology to the Lord.

Theological considerations aside, though, we all had a good time, and Deborah managed to clean us both out. Women's intuition, she says. I'm sure she must have it—she's the type. Enjoy being around her, and not always so happy to trek back outside, through the high grass, the night dew, the things in the soil. . . . I've got to remember, though, that they're a couple, I'm the single one, and I mustn't intrude too long. So left them tonight at eleven—or actually a little after that, since their clock is slightly out of kilter. They have this huge grandfather-type clock, a wedding present from Sarr's parents, that has supposedly been keeping perfect time for a century or more. You can hear its ticking all over the house when everything else is still. Deborah said that last night, just as they were going to bed, the clock seemed to slow down a little, then gave a couple of faster beats and started in as before. Sarr, who's pretty good with mechanical things, examined it, but said he saw nothing wrong. Well, I guess everything's got to wear out a bit, after years and years.

Back to *The Monk*. May Brother Ambrosio bring me pleasant dreams.

June 13

Read a little in the morning, loafed during the afternoon. At four thirty watched *The Thief of Baghdad*—ruined on TV and portions omitted, but still a great film. Deborah puttered around the kitchen, and Sarr spent most of the day outside. Before dinner I went out back with a scissors and cut away a lot of ivy that has tried to grow through the windows of my building. The little shoots fasten onto the screens and really cling.

Beef with rice tonight, and apple pie for dessert. Great. I stayed inside the house after dinner to watch the late news with the Poroths. The announcer mentioned that today was Friday the thirteenth, and I nearly gasped. I'd known, on some dim automatic level, that it was the thirteenth, if only from keeping this journal; but I hadn't had the faintest idea it was Friday. That's how much I've lost track of time out here; day drifts into day, and every one but Sunday seems completely interchangeable. Not a bad feeling, really, though at certain moments this isolation makes me feel somewhat adrift. I'd been so used to living by the clock and the calendar. . . .

We tried to figure out if anything unlucky happened to any of us today. About the only incident we could come up with was Sarr's getting bitten by some animal a cat had left on the porch. The cats had been sitting by the front door waiting to be let in for their dinner, and when Sarr came in from the field he was greeted with the usual assortment of dead mice and moles. As he always did, he began gingerly picking the bodies up by the tails and tossing them into the garbage can, meanwhile scolding the cats for being such natural-born killers. There was one body, he told us, that looked different from the others he'd seen: rather like a large shrew, only the mouth was somehow askew, almost as if it were vertical instead of horizontal, with a row of little yellow teeth exposed. He figured that, whatever it was, the cats had pretty well mauled it, which probably accounted for its unusual appearance; it was quite tattered and bloody by this time.

In any case, he'd bent down to pick it up, and the thing had bitten him on the thumb. Apparently it had just been feigning death, like an opossum, because as soon as he yelled and dropped it the thing sped off into the grass, with Bwada and the rest in hot pursuit. Deborah had been afraid of rabies—always a real danger around here, rare though it is—but apparently the bite hadn't even pierced the skin. Just a nip, really. Hardly a Friday-the-thirteenth tragedy.

Lying in bed now, listening to sounds in the woods. The trees come really close to my windows on one side, and there's always some kind of sound coming from the underbrush in addition to the tapping at the screens. A millions creatures out there, after all—most of them insects and spiders, a colony of frogs in the swampy part of the woods, and perhaps even skunks and raccoons. Depending on your mood, you can either ignore the sounds and just go to sleep or—as I'm doing now—remain awake listening to them. When I lie here thinking about what's out there, I feel more protected with the light off. So I guess I'll put away this writing. . . .

June 15

Something really weird happened today. I still keep trying to figure it out.

Sarr and Deborah were gone almost all day; Sunday worship is, I guess, the center of their religious activity. They walked into Gilead early in the morning and didn't return until after four. They'd left, in fact, before I woke up. Last night they'd asked me if I'd like to come along, but I got the impression they'd invited me mainly to be polite, so I declined. I wouldn't want to make them uncomfortable during their services, but perhaps someday I'll accompany them anyway, since I'm curious to see a fundamentalist church in action.

In any case, I was left to share the farm with the Poroths' seven cats and the four hens they'd bought last week. From my window I could see Bwada and Phaedra chasing after something near the barn; lately they've taken to stalking grasshoppers. As I do every morning, I went into the farmhouse kitchen and made myself some breakfast, leafing through one of the Poroths' religious magazines, and then returned to my rooms out back for some serious reading. I picked up *Dracula* again, which I'd started yesterday, but the soppy Victorian sentimentality began to annoy me; the book had begun so well, on such a frightening note—Jonathan Harker trapped in that

Carpathian castle, inevitably the prey of its terrible owner—that when Stoker switched the locale to England and his main characters to women, he simply couldn't sustain that initial tension.

With the Poroths gone I felt a little lonely and bored, something I hadn't felt out here yet. Though I'd brought cartons of books to entertain me, I felt restless and wished I owned a car; I'd have gone for a drive, perhaps visited friends at Princeton. As things stood, though, I had nothing to do except watch television or take a walk.

I followed the stream again into the woods and eventually came to the circular pool. There were some new animal tracks in the wet sand, and, ringed by oaks, the place was very beautiful, but still I felt bored. Again I waded to the center of the water and looked up at the sky through the trees. Feeling myself alone, I began to make some of the odd signs with face and hands that I had that evening in the tree—but I felt that these movements had been unaccountably robbed of their power. Standing there up to my ankles in water, I felt foolish.

Worse than that, upon leaving it I found a red-brown leech clinging to my right ankle. It wasn't large and I was able to scrape it off with a stone, but it left me with a little round bite that oozed blood, and a feeling of—how shall I put it?—physical helplessness. I felt that the woods had somehow become hostile to me and, more important, would forever remain hostile. Something had passed.

I followed the stream back to the farm, and there I found Bwada, lying on her side near some rocks along its bank. Her legs were stretched out as if she were running, and her eyes were wide and astonished-looking. Flies were crawling over them.

She couldn't have been dead for long, since I'd seen her only a few hours before, but she was already stiff. There was foam around her jaws. I couldn't tell what had happened to her until I turned her over with a stick and saw, on the side that had lain against the ground, a gaping red hole that opened like some new orifice. The skin around it was folded back in little triangular flaps, exposing the pink flesh beneath. I backed off in disgust, but I could see even from several feet away that the hole had been made *from the inside*.

I can't say that I was very upset at Bwada's death, because I'd always hated her. What did upset me, though, was the manner of it—I can't figure out what could have done that to her. I vaguely remember reading about a kind of slug that, when eaten by a bird, will bore its way out through the bird's stomach. . . . But I'd never heard of something like this happening with a cat. And far stranger than that, how could—

Well, anyway, I saw the body and thought, Good riddance. But I didn't know what to do with it. Looking back, of course, I wish I'd buried it right there. . . . But I didn't want to go near it again. I considered walking into town and trying to find the Poroths, because I knew their cats were like children to them, even Bwada, and that they'd want to know right away. But I really didn't feel like running around Gilead asking strange people where the Poroths were—or, worse yet, stumbling into their forbidding-looking church in the middle of a ceremony.

Finally I made up my mind to simply leave the body there and pretend I'd never seen it. Let Sarr discover it himself. I didn't want to have to tell him when he got home that his pet had been killed; I prefer to avoid unpleasantness. Besides, I felt strangely guilty, the way one often does after someone else's misfortune.

So I spent the rest of the afternoon reading in my room, slogging through the Stoker. I wasn't in the best mood to concentrate. Sarr and Deborah got back after four—they shouted hello and went into the house. When Deborah called me for dinner, they still hadn't come outside.

All the cats except Bwada were inside having their evening meal when I entered the kitchen, and Sarr asked me if I'd seen her during the day. I lied and said I hadn't. Deborah suggested that occasionally Bwada ignored the supper call because, unlike the other cats, she sometimes ate what she killed and might simply be full. That rattled me a bit, but I had to stick to my lie.

Sarr seemed more concerned than Deborah, and when he told her he intended to search for the cat after dinner (it would still be light), I readily offered my help. I figured I could lead him to the spot where the body lay. . . .

And then, in the middle of our dinner, came that scratching at the door. Sarr got up and opened it. Bwada walked in.

Now, I know she was dead. She was *stiff* dead. That wound in her side had been huge, and now it was only . . . a reddish swelling. Hairless. Luckily the Poroths didn't notice my shock; they were busy fussing over her, seeing what was wrong. "Look, she's hurt herself," said Deborah. "She's bumped into something." The animal didn't walk well, and there was a clumsiness in the way she held herself. When Sarr put her down after examining the swelling, she slipped when she tried to walk away.

The Poroths concluded that she had run into a rock or some other object and had badly bruised herself; they believe her lack of coordination is due to the shock, or perhaps to a pinching of the nerves. That sounds logical enough. Sarr told me before I came out here for the night that if she's worse tomorrow, he'll take her to the local vet, even though he'll have trouble paying for treatment. I immediately offered to lend him money, or even pay for the visit myself, because I desperately want to hear a doctor's opinion.

My own conclusion is really not that different from Sarr's. I tend to think now that maybe, just maybe, I was wrong in thinking the cat dead. Maybe what I mistook for rigor mortis was some kind of fit—after all, I know almost nothing about medicine. Maybe she really did run into something sharp and then went into some kind of shock . . . whose effect hasn't yet worn off. Is this possible?

But I could swear that hole came from inside her.

I couldn't continue dinner and told the Poroths my stomach hurt, which was partly true. We all watched Bwada stumble around the kitchen floor, ignoring the food Deborah put before her as if it weren't there. Her movements were stiff, tentative, like a newborn animal still unsure how to move its muscles. I guess that's the result of her fit.

When I left the house tonight, a little while ago, she was huddled in the corner staring at me. Deborah was crooning over her, but the cat was staring at me.

Killed a monster of a spider behind my suitcase tonight. That Ortho spray really does a job. When Sarr was in here a few days ago he said the room smelled of spray, but I guess my allergy's too bad for me to smell it.

I enjoy watching the zoo outside my screens. Put my face close and stare the bugs eye to eye. Zap the ones whose faces I don't like with my spray can.

Tried to read more of the Stoker—but one thing keeps bothering me. The way that cat stared at me. Deborah was brushing its back, Sarr fiddling with his pipe, and that cat just stared at me and never blinked. I stared back, said, "Hey, Sarr? Look at Bwada. That damned cat's not blinking." And just as he looked up, it blinked. Heavily.

Hope we can go to the vet tomorrow, because I want to ask him whether cats can impale themselves on a rock or a stick, and if such an accident might cause a fit of some kind that would make them rigid.

Cold night. Sheets are damp and the blanket itches. Wind from the woods—ought to feel good in the summer, but it doesn't feel like summer. That damned cat didn't blink till I mentioned it. Almost as if it understood me.

June 17
   . . . Swelling on her side's all healed now. Hair growing back over it. She walks fine, has a great appetite, shows affection to the Poroths. Sarr says her recovery demonstrates how the Lord watches over animals—affirms his faith. Says if he'd taken her to a vet he'd just have been throwing away money.

Read some LeFanu. "Green Tea," about the phantom monkey with eyes that glow, and "The Familiar," about the little staring man who drives the hero mad. Not the smartest choices right now, the way I feel, because for all the time that fat gray cat purrs over the Poroths, it just stares at me. And snarls. I suppose the accident may have addled its brain a bit. I mean, if spaying can change a cat's personality, certainly a goring on a rock might.

Spent a lot of time in the sun today. The flies made it pretty hard to concentrate on the stories, but figured I'd get a suntan. I probably have a good tan now (hard to tell, because the mirror in here is small and the light dim), but suddenly it occurs to me that I'm not going to be seeing anyone for a long time anyway, except the Poroths, so what the hell do I care how I look?

Can hear them singing their nightly prayers now. A rather comforting sound, I must admit, even if I can't share the sentiments.

Petting Felix today—my favorite of the cats, real charm—came away with a tick on my arm which I didn't discover till taking a shower before dinner. As a result, I can still feel imaginary ticks crawling up and down my back. Damned cat.

June 21

. . . Coming along well with the Victorian stuff. Zipped through "The Uninhabited House" and "Monsieur Maurice," both very literate, sophisticated. Deep into the terrible suffering of "The Amber Witch," poor priest and daughter near starvation, when Deborah called me in for dinner. Roast beef, with salad made from garden lettuce. Quite good. And Deborah was wearing one of the few sleeveless dresses I've seen on her. So she has a body after all. . . .

A rainy night. Hung around the house for a while reading in their living room while Sarr whittled and Deborah crocheted. Rain sounded better from in there than it does out here where it's not so cozy.

At eleven we turned on the news, cats purring around us, Sarr with Zoë on his lap, Deborah petting Phaedra, me sniffling. . . . Halfway through the wrap-up I pointed to Bwada, curled up at my feet, and said, "Look at her. You'd think she was watching the news with us." Deborah laughed and leaned over to scratch Bwada behind the ears. As she did so, Bwada turned to look at me.

The rain is letting up slightly. I can still hear the dripping from the trees, leaf to leaf to the dead leaves lining the forest floor; it will probably continue on and off all night. Occasionally I think I hear thrashings in one of the oaks near the barn, but then the sound turns into the falling of the rain.

Mildew higher on the walls of this place. Glad my books are on shelves off the ground. So damp in here my envelopes are ruined—glue moistened, sealing them all shut. Stamps that had been in my wallet are stuck to the dollar bills. At night my sheets are clammy and cold, but each morning I wake up sweating.

Finished "The Amber Witch," really fine. Would that all lives had such happy endings.

June 22

When Poroths returned from church, helped them prepare strips of molding for the upstairs study. Worked in the tool shed, one of the old wooden outbuildings. I measured, Sarr sawed, Deborah sanded. All in all, hardly felt useful, but what the hell?

While they were busy, I sat staring out the window. There's a narrow cement walk running from the shed to the main house, and, as was their habit, Minnie and Felix, two of the kittens, were crouched in the middle of it taking in the late afternoon sun. Suddenly Bwada appeared on the house's front porch and began slinking along the cement path in our direction, tail swishing from side to side. When she neared the kittens she gave a snarl—I could see her mouth working—and they leaped to their feet, bristling, and ran off into the grass.

Called this to Poroths' attention. They said, in effect, Yes, we know, she's always been nasty to the kittens, probably because she never had any of her own. And besides, she's getting older.

When I turned back to the window, Bwada was gone. Asked the Poroths if they didn't think she'd gotten worse lately. Realized that, in speaking, I'd unconsciously dropped my voice, as if someone might be listening through the chinks in the floorboards.

Deborah conceded that, yes, the cat is behaving worse these days toward the others. And not just toward the kittens, as before. Butch, the adult orange male, seems particularly afraid of her. . . .

Am a little angry at the Poroths. Will have to tell them when I see them tomorrow morning. They claim they never come into these rooms, respect privacy of a tenant, etc. etc., but one of them must have been in here, because I've just noticed my can of insect spray is missing. I don't mind their borrowing it, but I like to have it by my bed on nights like this. Went over room looking for spiders, just in case; had a fat copy of *Amer-*

ican Scholar in my hand to crush them (only thing it's good for). But found nothing.

Tried to read some *Walden* as a break from all the horror stuff, but found my eyes too irritated, watery. Keep scratching them as I write this. Nose pretty clogged, too—the damned allergy's worse tonight. Probably because of the dampness. Expect I'll have trouble getting to sleep.

June 24

Slept very late this morning because the noise from outside kept me up late last night. (Come to think of it, the Poroths' praying was unusually loud as well, but that wasn't what bothered me.) I'd been in the middle of writing in this journal—some thoughts on A. E. Coppard—when it came. I immediately stopped writing and shut off the light.

At first it sounded like something in the woods near my room—an animal? a child? I couldn't tell, but smaller than a man—shuffling through the dead leaves, kicking them around as if it didn't care who heard it. There was a snapping of branches and, every so often, a silence and then a bump, as if it were hopping over fallen logs. I stood in the dark listening to it, then crept to the window and looked out. Thought I noticed some bushes moving, back there in the undergrowth, but it may have been the wind.

The sound grew farther away. Whatever it was must have been walking directly out into the deepest part of the woods, where the ground gets swampy and treacherous, because, very faintly, I could hear the sucking sounds of feet slogging through the mud.

I stood by the window for almost an hour, occasionally hearing what I thought were movements off there in the swamp, but finally all was quiet except for the crickets and the frogs. I had no intention of going out there with my flashlight in search of the intruder—that's for guys in stories, I'm much too chicken—and I wondered if I should call Sarr. But by this time the noise had stopped, and whatever it was had obviously moved on. Besides, I tend to think he'd have been angry if I'd awakened him and Deborah just because some stray dog had wandered near the farm. I recalled how annoyed he'd been earlier that day when—maybe not all that tactfully—I'd asked

him what he'd done with my bug spray. (Must remember to
walk into town tomorrow and pick up a can. Still can't figure
out where I misplaced mine.)

I went over to the windows on the other side and watched
the moonlight on the barn for a while; my nose probably
looked crosshatched from pressing against the screen. In contrast to the woods, the grass looked peaceful under the full
moon. Then I lay in bed, but had a hard time falling asleep.
Just as I was getting relaxed, the sounds started again. High-
pitched wails and caterwauls, from deep within the woods.
Even after thinking about it all today, I still don't know
whether the noise was human or animal. There were no actual
words, of that I'm certain, but nevertheless there was the impression of *singing*. In a crazy, tuneless kind of way the sound
seemed to carry the same solemn rhythm as the Poroths'
prayers earlier that night.

The noise only lasted a minute or two, but I lay awake till
the sky began to get lighter. Probably should have read a little
more Coppard, but was reluctant to turn on the lamp.

. . . Slept all morning and, in the afternoon, followed the
road the opposite direction from Gilead, seeking anything of
interest. But the road just gets muddier and muddier till it disappears altogether by the ruins of an old homestead—rocks
and cement covered with moss—and it looked so much like
poison ivy around there that I didn't want to risk tramping
through.

At dinner (pork chops, home-grown stringbeans, and
pudding—quite good), mentioned the noise of last night. Sarr
acted very concerned and went to his room to look up something in one of his books; Deborah and I discussed the matter
at some length and concluded that the shuffling sounds
weren't necessarily related to the wailing. The former were
almost definitely those of a dog—dozens in the area, and they
love to prowl around at night, exploring, hunting coons—and
as for the wailing . . . well, it's hard to say. She thinks it may
have been an owl or whippoorwill, while I suspect it may have
been that same stray dog. I've heard the howl of wolves and
I've heard hounds baying at the moon, and both have the
same element of, I suppose, *worship* in them that these did.

Sarr came back downstairs and said he couldn't find what

he'd been looking for. Said that when he moved into this farm he'd had "a fit of piety" and had burned a lot of old books he'd found in the attic; now he wishes he hadn't.

Looked up something on my own after leaving the Poroths. *Field Guide to Mammals* lists both red and gray foxes and, believe it or not, coyotes as surviving here in New Jersey. No wolves left, though—but the guide might be wrong.

Then, on a silly impulse, opened another reference book, Barbara Byfield's *Glass Harmonica*. Sure enough, my hunch was right: looked up June twenty-third, and it said, "St. John's Eve. Sabbats likely."

I'll stick to the natural explanation. Still, I'm glad Mrs. Byfield lists nothing for tonight; I'd like to get some sleep. There is, of course, a beautiful full moon—werewolf weather, as Maria Ouspenskaya might have said. But then, there are no wolves left in New Jersey. . . .

(Which reminds me, really must read some Marryat and Endore. But only after *Northanger Abbey*; my course always comes first.)

June 25

. . . After returning from town, the farm looked very lonely. Wish they had a library in Gilead with more than religious tracts. Or a stand that sold the *Times*. (Though it's strange how, after a week or two, you no longer miss it.)

Overheated from walk—am I getting out of shape? Or is it just the hot weather? Took a cold shower. When I opened the bathroom door, I accidentally let Bwada out—I'd wondered why the chair was propped against it. She raced into the kitchen, pushed open the screen door by herself, and I had no chance to catch her. (Wouldn't have attempted to anyway; her claws are wicked.) I apologized later when Deborah came in from the fields. She said Bwada had become vicious toward the other cats and that Sarr had confined her to the bathroom as punishment. The first time he'd shut her in there, Deborah said, the cat had gotten out; apparently she's smart enough to turn the door-knob by swatting at it a few times. Hence the chair.

Sarr came in carrying Bwada, both obviously out of temper. He'd seen a streak of orange running through the field toward him, followed by a gray blur. Butch had stopped at his feet and Bwada had pounced on him, but before she could do any damage Sarr had grabbed her around the neck and carried her back here. He'd been bitten once and scratched a lot on his hands, but not badly; maybe the cat still likes him best. He threw her back in the bathroom and shoved the chair against the door, then sat down and asked Deborah to join him in some silent prayer. I thumbed uneasily through a religious magazine till they were done, and we sat down to dinner.

I apologized again, but he said he wasn't mad at me, that the Devil had gotten into his cat. It was obvious he meant that quite literally. During dinner (omelet—the hens have been laying well) we heard a grating sound from the bathroom, and Sarr ran in to find her almost out the window; somehow she must have been strong enough to slide the sash up partway. She seemed so placid, though, when Sarr pulled her down from the sill—he'd been expecting another fight—that he let her out into the kitchen. At this she simply curled up near the stove and went to sleep; I guess she'd worked off her rage for the day. The other cats gave her a wide berth, though.

Watched a couple of hours of television with the Poroths. They may have gone to college, but the shows they find interesting . . . God! I'm ashamed of myself for sitting there like a cretin in front of that box. I won't even mention what we watched, lest history record the true abysmality of my tastes.

And yet I find that the TV draws us closer, as if we were having an adventure together. Shared experience, really. Like knowing the same people or going to the same school.

But there's a lot of duplicity in those Poroths—and I don't mean just religious hypocrisy, either. Came out here after watching the news, and though I hate to accuse anyone of spying on me, there's no doubt that Sarr or Deborah has been inside this room today. I began tonight's entry with great irritation, because I found my desk in disarray; this journal wasn't even put back in the right drawer. I keep all my pens on one side, all my pencils on another, ink and erasers in the middle, etc., and when I sat down tonight I saw that everything was out of place. Thank God I haven't included anything too personal in here. . . . What I assume happened was that Deborah came in to wash the mildew off the walls—she's mentioned doing so several times, and she knew I'd be in town part of the day—and got sidetracked into reading this, thinking it must be some kind of secret diary. (I'm sure she was disappointed to find that it's merely a literary journal, with nothing about her in it.)

What bugs me is the difficulty of broaching the subject. I can't just walk in and charge Deborah with being a sneak— Sarr is moody enough as it is—and even if I hint at "someone messing up my desk," they'll know what I mean and perhaps get angry. Whenever possible I prefer to avoid unpleasantness. I guess the best thing to do is simply hide this book under my mattress from now on and say nothing. If it happens again, though, I'll definitely move out of here.

. . . I've been reading some *Northanger Abbey*. Really quite witty, as all her stuff is, but it's obvious the mock-Gothic bit isn't central to the story. I'd thought it was going to be a real parody. . . . Love stories always tend to bore me, and normally I'd be asleep right now, but my damned nose is so clogged tonight that it's hard to breathe when I lie back. Usually being out here clears it up. I've used this goddamned inhaler a dozen times in the past hour, but within a few minutes I sneeze and have to use it again. Wish Deborah'd gotten around to cleaning off the mildew instead of wasting her time looking in here for True Confessions and deep dark secrets. . . .

Think I hear something moving outside. Best to shut off my light.

June 30

Slept late. Read some Shirley Jackson stories over breakfast, but got so turned off at her view of humanity that I switched to old Aleister Crowley, who at least keeps a sunny disposition. For her, people in the country are callous and vicious, those in the city are callous and vicious, husbands are (of course) callous and vicious, and children are merely sadistic. The only ones with feelings are her put-upon middle-aged heroines, with whom she obviously identifies. I guess if she didn't write so well the stories wouldn't sting so.

Inspired by Crowley, walked back to the pool in the woods. Had visions of climbing a tree, swinging on vines, anything to commemorate his exploits. . . . Saw something dead floating in the center of the pool and ran back to the farm. Copper-head? Caterpillar? It had somehow opened up. . . .

Joined Sarr chopping stakes for tomatoes. Could hear his ax all over the farm. He told me Bwada hadn't come home last night, and no sign of her this morning. Good riddance, as far as I'm concerned. Helped him chop some stakes while he was busy peeling off bark. That ax can get heavy fast! My arm hurt after three lousy stakes, and Sarr had already chopped fifteen or sixteen. Must start exercising. But I'll wait till my arm's less tired. . . .

July 2

Unpleasant day. Two A.M. now and still can't relax.

Sarr woke me up this morning—stood at my window calling "Jeremy . . . Jeremy. . . ." over and over very quietly. He had something in his hand which, through the screen, I first took for a farm implement; then I saw it was a rifle. He said he wanted me to help him. With what? I asked.

"A burial."

Last night, after he and Deborah had gone to bed, they'd heard the kitchen door open and someone enter the house. They both assumed it was me, come to use the bathroom—but then they heard the cats screaming. Sarr ran down and switched on the light in time to see Bwada on top of Butch, claws in his side, fangs buried in his neck. From the way he described it, sounds almost sexual in reverse. Butch had stopped struggling, and Minnie, the orange kitten, was already dead. The door was partly open, and when Bwada saw Sarr, she ran out.

Sarr and Deborah hadn't followed her; they'd spent the night praying over the bodies of Minnie and Butch. I *thought* I'd heard their voices late last night, but that's all I heard, probably because I'd been playing my radio. (Something I rarely do—you can't hear noises from the woods with it on.)

Poroths took deaths the way they'd take the death of a child. Regular little funeral service over by the unused pasture. (Hard to say if Sarr and Deborah were dressed in mourning, since that's the way they always dress.) Must admit I didn't feel particularly involved—my allergy's never permitted me to take much interest in the cats, though I'm fond of Felix—but I tried to act concerned: when Sarr asked, appropriately, "Is there no balm in Gilead? Is there no physician there?" (Jeremiah VIII:22), I nodded gravely. Read passages out of Deborah's Bible (Sarr seemed to know them all by heart), said amen when they did, knelt when they knelt, and tried to comfort Deborah when she cried. Asked her if cats could go to heaven, received a tearful "Of course." But Sarr added that Bwada would burn in hell.

What concerned me, apparently a lot more than it did either of them, was how the damned thing could get into the house. Sarr gave me this stupid, earnest answer: "She was always a smart cat." Like an outlaw's mother, still proud of her baby. . . .

Yet he and I looked all over the land for her so he could kill her. Barns, tool shed, old stables, garbage dump, etc. He called her and pleaded with her, swore to me she hadn't always been like this.

We could hardly check every tree on the farm—unfortunately—and the woods are a perfect hiding place, even for animals larger than a cat. So naturally we found no trace of her. We did try, though; we even walked up the road as far as the ruined homestead.

But for all that, we could have stayed much closer to home.

We returned for dinner, and I stopped at my room to change clothes. My door was open. Nothing inside was ruined, everything was in its place, everything as it should be—except the bed. The sheets were in tatters right down to the mattress, and the pillow had been ripped to shreds. Feathers were all over the floor. There were even claw marks on my blanket.

At dinner the Poroths demanded they be allowed to pay for the damage—nonsense, I said, they have enough to worry about—and Sarr suggested I sleep downstairs in their living room. "No need for that," I told him. "I've got lots more sheets." But he said no, he didn't mean that: he meant for my own protection. He believes the thing is particularly inimical, for some reason, toward me.

It seemed so absurd at the time. . . . I mean, nothing but a big fat gray cat. But now, sitting out here, a few feathers still scattered on the floor around my bed, I wish I were back inside the house. I did give in to Sarr when he insisted I take his ax with me. . . . But what I'd rather have is simply a room without windows.

I don't think I want to go to sleep tonight, which is one reason I'm continuing to write this. Just sit up all night on my new bedsheets, my back against the Poroths' pillow, leaning against the wall behind me, the ax beside me on the bed, this journal on my lap. . . . The thing is, I'm rather tired out from all the walking I did today. Not used to that much exercise.

I'm pathetically aware of every sound. At least once every five minutes some snapping of a branch or rustling of leaves makes me jump.

"Thou art my hope in the day of evil." At least that's what the man said. . . .

July 3

Woke up this morning with the journal and the ax cradled in my arms. What awakened me was the trouble I had breathing —nose all clogged, gasping for breath. Down the center of one of my screens, facing the woods, was a huge slash. . . .

July 15

Pleasant day, St. Swithin's Day—and yet, my birthday. Thirty years old, lordy lordy lordy. Today I am a man. First dull thoughts on waking: "Damnation. Thirty today." But another voice inside me, smaller but more sensible, spat contemptuously at such an artificial way of charting time. "Ah, don't give it another thought," it said. "You've still got plenty of time to fool around." Advice I took to heart.

Weather today? Actually, somewhat nasty. And thus the weather for the next forty days, since "If rain on St. Swithin's Day, forsooth, no summer drouthe," or something like that. My birthday predicts the weather. It's even mentioned in *The Glass Harmonica*.

As one must, took a critical self-assessment. First area for improvement: flabby body. Second? Less bookish, perhaps? Nonsense—I'm satisfied with the progress I've made. "And seekest thou great things for thyself? Seek them not." (Jeremiah XLV:5) So I simply did what I remembered from the RCAF exercise series and got good and winded. Flexed my stringy muscles in the shower, certain I'll be a Human Dynamo by the end of the summer. Simply a matter of will-power.

Was so ambitious I trimmed the ivy around my windows again. It's begun to block the light, and someday I may not be able to get out the door.

Read Ruthven Todd's *Lost Traveller*. Merely the narrative of a dream turned to nightmare, and illogical as hell. Wish, too, that there'd been more than merely a few hints of sex. On the whole, rather unpleasant; that gruesome ending is so inevitable. . . . Took me much of the afternoon. Then came upon an incredible essay by Lafcadio Hearn, something entitled "Gaki," detailing the curious Japanese belief that insects are really demons or the ghosts of evil men. Uncomfortably convincing!

Dinner late because Deborah, bless her, was baking me a cake. Had time to walk into town and phone parents. Happy birthday, happy birthday. Both voiced first worry—mustn't I be getting bored out here? Assured them I still had plenty of books and did not grow tired of reading.

"But it's so . . . *secluded* out there," Mom said. "Don't you get lonely?"

Ah, she hadn't reckoned on the inner resources of a man of thirty. Was tempted to quote *Walden*—"Why should I feel lonely? Is not our planet in the Milky Way?"—but refrained. How can I get lonely, I asked, when there's still so much to read? Besides, there are the Poroths to talk to.

Then the kicker: Dad wanted to know about the cat. Last time I'd spoken to them it had sounded like a very real danger. "Are you still sleeping inside the farmhouse, I hope?"

No, I told him, really, I only had to do that for a few days, while the thing was prowling around at night. Yes, it had killed some chickens—a hen every night, in fact. But there were only four of them, and then it stopped. We haven't had a sign of it in more than a week. (I didn't tell him that it had left the hens uneaten, dead in the nest. No need to upset him further.)

"But what it did to your sheets," he went on. "If you'd been sleeping . . . Such savagery."

Yes, that was unfortunate, but there's been no trouble since. Honest. It was only an animal, after all, just a housecat gone a little wild. It posed the same kind of threat as (I was going to say, logically, a wildcat; but for Mom said) a nasty little dog. Like Mrs. Miller's bull terrier. Besides, it's probably miles and miles away by now. Or dead.

They offered to drive out with packages of food, magazines, a portable TV, but I made it clear I needed nothing. Getting too fat, actually.

Still light when I got back. Deborah had finished the cake, Sarr brought up some wine from the cellar, and we had a nice little celebration. The two of them being over thirty, they were happy to welcome me to the fold.

It's nice out here. The wine has relaxed me and I keep yawning. It was good to talk to Mom and Dad again. Just as long as I don't dream of *The Lost Traveller*, I'll be content. And happier still if I don't dream at all.

July 30

Well, Bwada is dead—this time for sure. We'll bury her tomorrow. Deborah was hurt, just how badly I can't say, but she managed to fight Bwada off. Tough woman, though she seems a little shaken. And with good reason.

It happened this way: Sarr and I were in the tool shed after dinner, building more shelves for the upstairs study. Though the fireflies were out, there was still a little daylight left. Deborah had gone up to bed after doing the dishes; she's been tired a lot lately, falls asleep early every night while watching TV with Sarr. He thinks it may be something in the well water.

It had begun to get dark, but we were still working. Sarr dropped a box of nails, and while we were picking them up, he thought he heard a scream. Since I hadn't heard anything, he shrugged and was about to start sawing again when—fortunately—he changed his mind and ran off to the house. I followed him as far as the porch, not sure whether to go upstairs, until I heard him pounding on their bedroom door and calling Deborah's name. As I ran up the stairs I heard her say, "Wait a minute. Don't come in. I'll unlock the door . . . soon." Her voice was extremely hoarse, practically a croaking. We heard her rummaging in the closet—finding her bathrobe, I suppose—and then she opened the door.

She looked absolutely white. Her long hair was in tangles

and her robe buttoned incorrectly. Around her neck she had wrapped a towel, but we could see patches of blood soaking through it. Sarr helped her over to the bed, shouting at me to bring up some bandages from the bathroom.

When I returned, Deborah was lying in bed, still pressing the towel to her throat. I asked Sarr what had happened; it almost looked as if the woman had tried suicide.

He didn't say anything, just pointed to the floor on the other side of the bed. I stepped around for a look. A crumpled gray shape was lying there, half covered by the bedclothes. It was Bwada, a wicked-looking wound in her side. On the floor next to her lay an umbrella—the thing that Deborah had used to kill her.

She told us she'd been asleep when she felt something crawl heavily over her face. It had been like a bad dream. She'd tried to sit up, and suddenly Bwada was at her throat, digging in. Luckily she'd had the strength to tear the animal off and dash to the closet, where the first weapon at hand was the umbrella. Just as the cat sprang at her again, Deborah said, she'd raised the weapon and lunged. Amazing; how many women, I wonder, would have had such presence of mind? The rest sounds incredible to me, but it's probably the sort of crazy thing that happens in moments like this: somehow the cat had impaled itself on the umbrella.

Her voice, as she spoke, was barely more than a whisper. Sarr had to persuade her to remove the towel from her throat; she kept protesting that she wasn't hurt that badly, that the towel had stopped the bleeding. Sure enough, when Sarr finally lifted the cloth from her neck, the wounds proved relatively small, the slash marks already clotting. Thank God that thing didn't really get its teeth in. . . .

My guess—only a guess—is that it had been weakened from days of living in the woods. (It was obviously incapable of feeding itself adequately, as I think was proved by its failure to eat the hens it had killed.) While Sarr dressed Deborah's wounds, I pulled back the bedclothes and took a closer look at the animal's body. The fur was matted and patchy. Odd that an umbrella could make a puncture like that, ringed by flaps of skin, as if the flesh had been pushed outward. Deborah must have had the extraordinary good luck to have jabbed the

animal precisely in its old wound, which had reopened. Naturally I didn't mention this to Sarr.

He made dinner for us tonight—soup, actually, because he
thought that was best for Deborah. Her voice sounded so bad
he told her not to strain it any more by talking, at which she
nodded and smiled. We both had to help her downstairs, as
she was clearly weak from shock.

In the morning Sarr will have the doctor out. He'll have to examine the cat, too, to check for rabies, so we put the body in the
freezer to preserve it as well as possible. Afterward we'll bury it.

Deborah seemed okay when I left. Sarr was reading through
some medical books, and she was just lying on the living room
couch gazing at her husband with a look of purest gratitude—
not moving, not saying anything, not even blinking.

I feel quite relieved. God knows how many nights I've lain
here thinking every sound I heard was Bwada. I'll feel more
relieved, of course, when that demon's safely underground;
but I think I can say, at the risk of being melodramatic, that the
reign of terror is over.

Hmm, I'm still a little hungry—used to more than soup for
dinner. These daily push-ups burn up energy. I'll probably
dream of hamburgers and chocolate layer cakes.

July 31

. . . The doctor collected scrapings from Bwada's teeth
and scolded us for doing a poor job of preserving the body.
Said storing it in the freezer was a sensible idea, but that we
should have done so sooner, since it was already decomposing.
The dampness, I imagine, must act fast on dead flesh.

He pronounced Deborah in excellent condition—the marks
on her throat are, remarkably, almost healed—but he said her
reflexes were a little off. Sarr invited him to stay for the burial,
but he declined—and quite emphatically, at that. He's not a
member of their order, doesn't live in the area, and apparently
doesn't get along that well with the people of Gilead, most of
whom mistrust modern science. (Not that the old geezer
sounded very representative of modern science. When I asked
him for some good exercises, he recommended "chopping
wood and running down deer.")

Standing under the heavy clouds, Sarr looked like a revivalist minister. His sermon was from Jeremiah XXII:19—"He shall be buried with the burial of an ass." The burial took place far from the graves of Bwada's two victims, and closer to the woods. We sang one song, Deborah just mouthing the words (still mustn't strain throat muscles). Sarr solemnly asked the Lord to look mercifully upon all His creatures, and I muttered an "amen." Then we walked back to the house, Deborah leaning on Sarr's arm; she's still a little stiff.

It was gray the rest of the day, and I sat in my room reading *The King in Yellow*—or rather, Chambers' collection of the same name. One look at the *real* book, so Chambers would claim, and I might not live to see the morrow, at least through the eyes of a sane man. (That single gimmick—masterful, I admit—seems to be his sole inspiration.)

I was disappointed that dinner was again made by Sarr; Deborah was upstairs resting, he said. He sounded concerned, felt there were things wrong with her the doctor had overlooked. We ate our meal in silence, and I came back here immediately after washing the dishes. Feel very drowsy and, for some reason, also rather depressed. It may be the gloomy weather—we are, after all, just animals, more affected by the sun and the seasons than we like to admit. More likely it was the absence of Deborah tonight. Hope she feels better.

Note: The freezer still smells of the cat's body; opened it tonight and got a strong whiff of decay.

August 1

Writing this, breaking habit, in early morning. Went to bed last night just after finishing the entry above, but was awakened around two by sounds coming from the woods. Wailing, deeper than before, followed by a low, guttural monologue. No words, at least that I could distinguish. If frogs could talk . . . For some reason I fell asleep before the sounds ended, so I don't know what followed.

Could very well have been an owl of some kind, and later a large bullfrog. But I quote, without comment, from *The Glass Harmonica*: "July 31: Lammas Eve. Sabbats likely."

Little energy to write tonight, and even less to write about. (Come to think of it, I slept most of the day: woke up at eleven, later took an afternoon nap. Alas, senile at thirty!) Too tired to shave, and haven't had the energy to clean this place, either; thinking about work is easier than doing it. The ivy's beginning to cover the windows again, and the mildew's been climbing steadily up the walls. It's like a dark green band that keeps widening. Soon it will reach my books. . . .

Speaking of which, note: opened M. R. James at lunch to-day—*Ghost Stories of an Antiquary*—and a silverfish slithered out. Omen?

Played a little game with myself this evening—

I just had one hell of a shock. While writing the above I heard a soft tapping, like nervous fingers drumming on a table, and discovered an enormous spider, biggest of the summer, crawling only a few inches from my ankle. It must have been living behind this desk. . . .

When you can hear a spider walk across the floor, you *know* it's time to keep your socks on. Thank God for insecticide.

Oh, yeah, that game—the What If game. I probably play it too often. (Vain attempt to enlarge realm of the possible? Heighten my own sensitivity? Or merely work myself into an icy sweat?) I pose unpleasant questions for myself and consider the consequences, e.g., what if this glorified chicken coop is sinking into quicksand? (Wouldn't be at all surprised.) What if the Poroths are tired of me? What if I woke up inside my own coffin?

What if I never see New York again?

What if some horror stories aren't really fiction? If Machen sometimes told the truth? If there *are* White People, malevolent little faces peering out of the moonlight? Whispers in the grass? Poisonous things in the woods? Perfect hate and evil in the world?

Enough of this foolishness. Time for bed.

August 9

. . . Read some Hawthorne in the morning and, over lunch, reread this week's *Hunterdon County Democrat* for the dozenth time. Sarr and Deborah were working somewhere in the fields, and I felt I ought to get some physical activity my-self; but the thought of starting my exercises again after more than a week's laziness just seemed too unpleasant. . . . I took a walk down the road, but only as far as a smashed-up cement culvert half buried in the woods. I was bored, but Gilead just seemed too far away.

Was going to cut the ivy surrounding my windows when I got back, but decided the place looks more artistic covered in vines. Rationalization?

Chatted with Poroths about politics, The World Situation, a little cosmology, blah blah blah. Dinner wasn't very good, probably because I'd been looking forward to it all day. The lamb was underdone and the beans were cold. Still, I'm always the gentleman, and was almost pleased when Deborah agreed to my offer to do the dishes. I've been doing them a lot lately.

I didn't have much interest in reading tonight and would have been up for some television, but Sarr's recently gotten into one of his religious kicks and began mumbling prayers to himself immediately after dinner. (Deborah, more human, wanted to watch the TV news. She seems to have an insatiable curiosity about world events, yet she claims the isolation here appeals to her.) Absorbed in his chanting, Sarr made me uncomfortable—I didn't like his face—and so after doing the dishes, I left.

I've been listening to the radio for the last hour or so. . . . I recall days when I'd have gotten uptight at having wasted an hour—but out here I've lost all track of time. Feel adrift—a little disconcerting, but healthy, I'm sure.

. . . Shut off the radio a moment ago, and now realize my room is filled with crickets. Up close their sound is hardly pleasant—cross between a radiator and a tea-kettle, very shrill. They'd been sounding off all night, but I'd thought it was interference on the radio.

Now I notice them; they're all over the room. A couple of dozen, I should think. Hate to kill them, really—they're one of the few insects I can stand, along with ladybugs and fireflies. But they make such a racket!

Wonder how they got in. . . .

August 14

Played with Felix all morning—mainly watching him chase insects, climb trees, doze in the sun. Spectator sport. After lunch went back to my room to look up something in Lovecraft and discovered my books were out of order. (Saki, for example, was filed under "S," whereas—whether out of fastidiousness or pedantry—I've always preferred to file him as "Munro.") This is definitely one of the Poroths' doing. I'm pissed they didn't mention coming in here, but also a little surprised they'd have any interest in this stuff.

Arranged them correctly again, then sat down to reread Lovecraft's essay on "Supernatural Horror in Literature." It upset me to see how little I've actually read, how far I still have to go. So many obscure authors, so many books I've never come across. . . . Left me feeling depressed and tired, so I took a nap for the rest of the afternoon.

Over dinner—vegetable omelet, rather tasteless—Deborah continued to question us on current events. It's getting to be like junior high school, with daily newspaper quizzes. . . . Don't know how she got started on this, or why the sudden interest, but it obviously annoys the hell out of Sarr.

Sarr used to be a sucker for her little-girl pleadings—I remember how he used to carry her upstairs, becoming pathetically tender, the moment she'd say, "Oh, honey, I'm so tired" —but now he just becomes angry. Often he goes off morose and alone to pray, and the only time he laughs is when he watches television.

Tonight, thank God, he was in a mood to forgo the prayers, and so after dinner we all watched a lot of offensively ignorant programs. I was disturbed to find myself laughing along with the canned laughter, but I have to admit the TV helps us get along better together. Came back here after the news.

Not very tired, having slept so much of the afternoon, so began to read John Christopher's *The Possessors*; but good though it was, my mind began to wander to all the books I *haven't* yet read, and I got so depressed I turned on the radio. Find it takes my mind off things.

August 19

Slept long into the morning, then walked down to the brook, scratching groggily. Deborah was kneeling by the water, lost, it seemed, in daydream, and I was embarrassed because I'd come upon her talking to herself. We exchanged a few insincere words and she went back toward the house.

Sat by some rocks, throwing blades of grass into the water. The sun on my head felt almost painful, as if my brain were growing too large for my skull. I turned and looked at the farmhouse. In the distance it looked like a picture at the other end of a large room, the grass for a carpet, the ceiling the sky. Deborah was stroking a cat, then seemed to grow angry when it struggled from her arms; I could hear the screen door slam as she went into the kitchen, but the sound reached me so long after the visual image that the whole scene struck me as, somehow, fake. I gazed up at the maples behind me, and they seemed trees out of a cheap postcard, the kind in which thinly colored paint is dabbed over a black-and-white photograph; if you look closely you can see that the green in the trees is not merely in the leaves, but rather floats as a vapor over leaves, branches, parts of the sky. . . . The trees behind me seemed the productions of a poor painter, the color and shape not quite meshing. Parts of the sky were green, and pieces of the green seemed to float away from my vision. No matter how hard I tried, I couldn't follow them.

Far down the stream I could see something small and kicking, a black beetle, legs in the air, borne swiftly along in the current. Then it was gone.

Thumbed through the Bible while I ate my lunch—mostly cookies. By late afternoon I was playing word games while I lay on the grass near my room. The shrill twitter of the birds, I would say, the birds singing in the sun. . . . And inexorably I'd continue with the sun dying in the moonlight, the moonlight falling on the floor, the floor sagging to the cellar, the cellar filling with water, the water seeping into the ground, the ground twisting into smoke, the smoke staining the sky, the sky burning in the sun, the sun dying in the moonlight, the moonlight falling on the floor . . . —melancholy progressions that held my mind like a whirlpool.

Sarr woke me for dinner; I had dozed off, and my clothes were damp from the grass. As we walked up to the house together he whispered that, earlier in the day, he'd come upon his wife bending over me, peering into my sleeping face. "Her eyes were wide," he said. "Like Bwada's." I said I didn't understand why he was telling me this.

"Because," he recited in a whisper, gripping my arm, "the heart is deceitful above all things, and desperately wicked: who can know it?"

I recognized that. Jeremiah XVII:9.

Dinner was especially uncomfortable; the two of them sat picking at their food, occasionally raising their eyes to one another like children in a staring contest. I longed for the conversations of our early days, inconsequential though they must have been, and wondered where things had first gone wrong.

The meal was dry and unappetizing, but the dessert looked delicious—chocolate mousse, made from an old family recipe. Deborah had served it earlier in the summer and knew both Sarr and I loved it. This time, however, she gave none to herself, explaining that she had to watch her weight.

"Then we'll not eat any!" Sarr shouted, and with that he snatched my dish from in front of me, grabbed his own, and hurled them both against the wall, where they splattered like mudballs.

Deborah was very still; she said nothing, just sat there watching us. She didn't look particularly afraid of this madman, I was happy to see—but *I* was. He may have read my thoughts, because as I got up from my seat, he said much more gently, in the soft voice normal to him, "Sorry, Jeremy. I know you hate scenes. We'll pray for each other, all right?"

"Are you okay?" I asked Deborah. "I'm going out now, but I'll stay if you think you'll need me for anything." She stared at me with a slight smile and shook her head. I raised my eyebrows and nodded toward her husband, and she shrugged.

"Things will work out," she said. I could hear Sarr laughing as I shut the door.

When I snapped on the light out here I took off my shirt and stood in front of the little mirror. It had been nearly a week since I'd showered, and I'd become used to the smell of my body. My hair had wound itself into greasy brown curls, my beard was at least two weeks old, and my eyes . . . well, the eyes that stared back at me looked like those of an old man. The whites were turning yellow, like old teeth. I looked at my chest and arms, flabby at thirty, and I thought of the frightening alterations in my friend Sarr, and I knew I'd have to get out of here.

Just glanced at my watch. It's now quite late: two thirty. I've been packing my things.

August 20

I woke about an hour ago and continued packing. Lots of books to put away, but I'm just about done. It's not even nine A.M. yet, much earlier than I normally get up, but I guess the thought of leaving here fills me with energy.

The first thing I saw on rising was a garden spider whose body was as big as some of the mice the cats have killed. It was sitting on the ivy that grows over my window sill—fortunately on the other side of the screen. Apparently it had had good hunting all summer, preying on the insects that live in the leaves. Concluding that nothing so big and fearsome has a right to live, I held the spray can against the screen and doused the creature with poison. It struggled halfway up the screen, then stopped, arched its legs, and dropped backwards into the ivy.

I plan to walk into town this morning and telephone the office in Flemington where I rented my car. If they can have one ready today I'll hitch there to pick it up; otherwise I'll spend tonight here and pick it up tomorrow. I'll be leaving a little early in the season, but the Poroths already have my month's rent, so they shouldn't be too offended.

And anyway, how could I be expected to stick around here with all that nonsense going on, never knowing when my room might be ransacked, having to put up with Sarr's insane suspicions and Deborah's moodiness?

Before I go into town, though, I really must shave and shower for the good people of Gilead. I've been sitting inside here waiting for some sign the Poroths are up, but as yet—it's almost nine—I've heard nothing. I wouldn't care to barge in on them while they're still having breakfast or, worse, just getting up. . . . So I'll just wait here by the window till I see them.

. . . Ten o'clock now, and they still haven't come out. Perhaps they're having a talk. . . . I'll give them half an hour more, then I'm going in.

*

Here my journal ends. Until today, almost a week later, I have not cared to set down any of the events that followed. But here in the temporary safety of this hotel room, protected by a heavy brass travel-lock I had sent up from the hardware store down the street, watched over by the good people of Flemington—and perhaps by something not good—I can continue my narrative.

The first thing I noticed as I approached the house was that the shades were drawn, even in the kitchen. Had they decided to sleep late this morning? I wondered. Throughout my thirty years I have come to associate drawn shades with a foul smell, the smell of a sickroom, of shamefaced poverty and food gone bad, of people lying too long beneath blankets; but I was not ready for the stench of decay that met me when I opened the kitchen door and stepped into the darkness. Something had died in that room—and not recently.

At the moment the smell first hit, four little shapes scrambled across the linoleum toward me and out into the daylight. The Poroths' cats.

By the other wall a lump of shadow moved; a pale face caught light penetrating the shades. Sarr's voice, its habitual softness exaggerated to a whisper: "Jeremy. I thought you were still asleep."

"Can I—"

"No. Don't turn on the light." He got to his feet, a black form towering against the window. Fiddling nervously with the kitchen door—the tin doorknob, the rubber bands stored around it, the fringe at the bottom of the drawn window shade—I opened it wider and let in more sunlight. It fell on the dark thing at his feet, over which he had been crouching: Deborah, the flesh at her throat torn and wrinkled like the skin of an old apple.

Her clothing lay in a heap beside her. She appeared long dead. The eyes were shriveled, sunken into sockets black as a skull's.

I think I may have staggered at that moment, because he came toward me. His steady, unblinking gaze looked so sincere—but *why was he smiling*? "I'll make you understand," he was saying, or something like that; even now I feel my face twisting into horror as I try to write of him. "I had to kill her. . . ."

"You—"

"She tried to kill me," he went on, silencing all questions. "The same thing that possessed Bwada . . . possessed her."

My hand played behind my back with the bottom of the window shade. "But her throat—"

"That happened a long time ago. Bwada did it. I had nothing to do with . . . that part." Suddenly his voice rose. "Don't you understand? She tried to stab me with the bread knife." He turned, stooped over, and, clumsy in the darkness, began feeling about him on the floor. "Where is that thing?" he was mumbling. "I'll show you. . . ." As he crossed a beam of sunlight, something gleamed like a silver handle on the back of his shirt.

Thinking, perhaps, to help him search, I pulled gently on the window shade, then released it; it snapped upward like a gunshot, flooding the room with light. From deep within the center of his back protruded the dull wooden haft of the bread knife, buried almost completely but for an inch or two of gleaming steel.

He must have heard my intake of breath—that sight chills me even today, the grisly absurdity of the thing—he must have heard me, because immediately he stood, his back to me, and reached up behind himself toward the knife, his arm stretching in vain, his fingers curling around nothing. The blade had been planted in a spot he couldn't reach.

He turned towards me and shrugged in embarrassment, a child caught in a foolish error. "Oh, yeah," he said, grinning at his own weakness. "I forgot it was there."

Suddenly he thrust his face into mine, fixing me in a gaze that never wavered, his eyes wide with candor. "It's easy for us to forget things," he explained—and then, still smiling, still watching, volunteered that last trivial piece of information, that final message whose words released me from inaction and left me free to dash from the room, to sprint in panic down the road to town, pursued by what had once been the farmer Sarr Poroth.

It serves no purpose here to dwell on my flight down that

twisting dirt road, breathing in such deep gasps that I was soon moaning with every breath; how, with my enemy racing behind me, not even winded, his steps never flagging, I veered into the woods; how I finally lost him, perhaps from the inexperience of whatever thing now controlled his body, and was able to make my way back to the road, only to come upon him again as I rounded a bend; his laughter as he followed me, and how it continued long after I had evaded him a second time; and how, after hiding until nightfall in the old cement culvert, I ran the rest of the way in pitch-darkness, stumbling in the ruts, torn by vines, nearly blinding myself when I ran into a low branch, until I arrived in Gilead filthy, exhausted, and nearly incoherent.

Suffice it to say that my escape was largely a matter of luck, a physical wreck fleeing something oblivious to pain or fatigue; but that, beyond mere luck, I had been impelled by an almost ecstatic sense of dread produced by his last words to me, that last communication from an alien face smiling inches from my own, and which I chose to take as his final warning:

"Sometimes we forget to blink."

You can read the rest in the newspapers. *The Hunterdon County Democrat* covered most of the story, though its man wrote it up as merely another lunatic wife-slaying, the result of loneliness, religious mania, and a mysteriously tainted well. (Traces of insecticide were found, among other things, in the water.) The *Somerset Reporter* took a different slant, implying that I had been the third member of an erotic triangle and that Sarr had murdered his wife in a fit of jealousy.

Needless to say, I was by this time past caring what was written about me. I was too haunted by visions of that lonely, abandoned farmhouse, the wails of its hungry cats, and by the sight of Deborah's corpse, discovered by the police, protruding from that hastily dug grave beyond the cornfield.

Accompanied by state troopers, I returned to my ivy-covered outbuilding. A bread knife had been plunged deep into its door, splintering the wood on the other side. The blood on it was Sarr's.

My journal had been hidden under my mattress and so was

untouched, but (I look at them now, piled in cardboard boxes beside my suitcase) my precious books had been hurled about the room, their bindings slashed. My summer is over, and now I sit inside here all day listening to the radio, waiting for the next report. Sarr—or his corpse—has not been found.

I should think the evidence was clear enough to corroborate my story, but I suppose I should have expected the reception it received from the police. They didn't laugh at my theory of "possession"—not to my face, anyway—but they ignored it in obvious embarrassment. Some see a nice young bookworm gone slightly deranged after contact with a murderer; others believe my story to be the desperate fabrication of an adulterer trying to avoid the blame for Deborah's death.

I can understand their reluctance to accept my explanation of the events, for it's one that goes a little beyond the "natural," a little beyond the scientific considerations of motive, *modus operandi*, and fingerprints. But I find it quite unnerving that at least one official—an assistant district attorney, I think, though I'm afraid I'm rather ignorant of these matters—believes I am guilty of murder.

There has, of course, been no arrest. Still, I've been given the time-honored instructions against leaving town.

The theory proposing my own complicity in the events is, I must admit, rather ingenious—and so carefully worked out that it will surely gain more adherents than my own. This police official is going to try to prove that I killed poor Deborah in a fit of passion and, immediately afterward, disposed of Sarr. He points out that their marriage had been an observably happy one until I arrived, a disturbing influence from the city. My motive, he says, was simple lust—unrequited, to be sure—aggravated by boredom. The heat, the insects, and, most of all, the oppressive loneliness—all constituted an environment alien to any I'd been accustomed to, and all worked to unhinge my reason.

I have no cause for fear, however, because this affidavit will certainly establish my innocence. Surely no one can ignore the evidence of my journal (though I can imagine an antagonistic few maintaining that I wrote the journal not at the farm but here in the Union Hotel, this very week).

What galls me is not the suspicions of a few detectives, but the predicament their suspicions place me in. Quite simply, *I cannot run away.* I am compelled to remain locked up in this room, potential prey to whatever the thing that was Sarr Poroth has now become—the thing that was once a cat, and once a woman, and once . . . what? A large white moth? A serpent? A shrewlike thing with wicked teeth?

A police chief? A president? A boy with eyes of blood that sits beneath my window?

Lord, who will believe me?

It was that night that started it all, I'm convinced of it now. The night I made those strange signs in the tree. The night the crickets missed a beat.

I'm not a philosopher, and I can supply no ready explanation for why this new evil has been released into the world. I'm only a poor scholar, a bookworm, and I must content myself with mumbling a few phrases that keep running through my mind, phrases out of books read long ago when such abstractions meant, at most, a pleasant shudder. I am haunted by scraps from the myth of Pandora, and by a semantic discussion I once read comparing "unnatural" and "supernatural."

And something about "a tiny rent in the fabric of the universe. . . ."

Just large enough to let something in. Something not of nature, and hard to kill. Something with its own obscure purpose.

Ironically, the police may be right. Perhaps it was my visit to Gilead that brought about the deaths. Perhaps I had a hand in letting loose the force that, to date, has snuffed out the lives of four hens, three cats, and at least two people—but will hardly be content to stop there.

I've just checked. He hasn't moved from the steps of the courthouse; and even when I look out my window, the rose spectacles never waver. Who knows where the eyes beneath them point? Who knows if they remember to blink?

Lord, this heat is sweltering. My shirt is sticking to my skin, and droplets of sweat are rolling down my face and dripping onto this page, making the ink run.

My hand is tired from writing, and I think it's time to end this affidavit.

If, as I now believe possible, I inadvertently called down evil from the sky and began the events at Poroth Farm, my death will only be fitting. And after my death, many more. We are all, I'm afraid, in danger. Please, then, forgive this prophet of doom, old at thirty, his last jeremiad: "The harvest is past, the summer is ended, and we are not saved."

1972

ISAAC BASHEVIS SINGER

(1904–1991)

Hanka

THIS trip made little sense from the start. First, it didn't pay
financially to leave New York and my work for two and a half
months to go to Argentina for a lecture tour; second, I should
have taken an airplane instead of wasting my time on a ship for
eighteen days. But I had signed the contract and accepted a
first-class round-trip ticket on *La Plata* from my impresario,
Chazkel Poliva. That summer, the heat lasted into October.
On the day I embarked, the thermometer registered ninety degrees. I was always assailed by premonitions and phobias
before a trip: I would get sick; the ship would sink; some other
calamity would occur. An inner voice warned me, Don't go!
However, if I had made a practice of acting on these premonitions, I would not have come to America but would have perished in Nazi-occupied Poland.

As it happened, I was provided with all possible comforts.
My cabin looked like a salon, with two square windows, a sofa,
a desk, and pictures on the walls. The bathroom had both a
tub and a shower stall. The number of passengers was small,
mostly Latin Americans, and the service staff was large. In the
dining room I had a special wine steward who promptly filled
my glass each time I took a sip of wine. A band of five musicians played at lunch and dinner. Every second day the captain
gave a cocktail party. But for some reason I could not make
any acquaintances on this ship. The few passengers who spoke
English kept to themselves. The men, all young six-foot giants,
played shuffleboard and cavorted in the swimming pool. The
women were too tall and too athletic for my taste. In the
evening, they all danced or sat at the bar, drinking and smoking.
I made up my mind that I would remain isolated, and it
seemed that others sensed my decision. No one spoke a word
to me. I began to wonder if by some magic I had become one

who sees and is not seen. After a while I stopped attending the cocktail parties and I asked that my meals be served in my cabin. In Trinidad and in Brazil, where the ship stopped for a day, I walked around alone. I had taken little to read with me, because I was sure that the ship would have a library. But it consisted of a single glass-doored bookcase with some fifty or so volumes in Spanish and perhaps a dozen in English—all moldy travel books printed a hundred years ago. This bookcase was kept locked, and each time I wanted to exchange a book there was a commotion about who had the key; I would be sent from one member of the staff to the other. Eventually an officer with epaulets would write down my name, the number of my stateroom, the titles and authors of my books. This took him at least fifteen minutes.

When the ship approached the equator, I stopped going out on deck in the daytime. The sun burned like a flame. The days had shortened and night came swiftly. One moment it was light, the next it was dark. The sun did not set but fell into the water like a meteor. Late in the evening, when I went out briefly, a hot wind slapped my face. From the ocean came a roar of passions that seemed to have broken through all barriers: "We must procreate and multiply! We must exhaust all the powers of lust!" The waves glowed like lava, and I imagined I could see multitudes of living beings—algae, whales, sea monsters— reveling in an orgy, from the surface to the bottom of the sea. Immortality was the law here. The whole planet raged with animation. At times, I heard my name in the clamor: the spirit of the abyss calling me to join them in their nocturnal dance.

In Buenos Aires I was met by Chazkel Poliva—a short, round person—and a young woman who introduced herself as my relative. Her name was Hanka and she was, she said, a great-granddaughter of my Aunt Yentel from her first husband. Actually, Hanka was not my relative, because my Uncle Aaron was Yentel's third husband. Hanka was petite, lean, and had a head of pitch-black hair, full lips, and eyes as black as onyx. She wore a dark dress and a black, broad-brimmed hat. She could have been thirty or thirty-five. Hanka immediately told me that in Warsaw someone had hidden her on the Aryan side—the way she was saved from the Nazis. She was a dancer, she said, but even before she told me I saw it in the muscles of her calves. I asked her where she danced and she replied, "At Jewish affairs and at my own troubles."

Chazkel Poliva took us in his car to the Hotel Cosmopolitan on Junín Street, which was once famous as the main street of the red-light district. Poliva said that the neighborhood had been cleaned up and all the literati now stayed in this hotel. The three of us ate supper in a restaurant on Corrientes Avenue, and Chazkel Poliva handed me a schedule covering my four weeks in Argentina. I was to lecture in Buenos Aires at the Théâtre Soleil and at the Jewish Community Center, and also I was to go to Rosario, Mar del Plata, and to the Jewish colonies in Moisés Ville and in Entre Ríos. The Warsaw Society, the Yiddish section of the P.E.N. Club, the journalists of the newspaper that published my articles, and a number of Yiddish schools were all preparing receptions.

When Poliva was alone with me for a moment, he asked, "Who is this woman? She says that she dances at Jewish affairs, but I've never seen her anywhere. While we were waiting for you, I suggested that she give me her address and telephone number in case I needed to get in touch with her, but she refused. Who is she?"

"I really don't know."

Chazkel Poliva had another engagement that evening and left us after dinner. I wanted to pay the bill—why should he pay for a woman who was supposed to be my relative?—but he would not permit it. I noticed that Hanka ate nothing—she had only a glass of wine. She accompanied me back to the hotel. It was not long after Perón had been ousted, and Argentina was in the midst of a political and perhaps economic crisis. Buenos Aires, it seemed, was short of electricity. The streets were dimly lit. Here and there a gendarme patrolled, carrying a machine gun. Hanka took my arm and we walked through Corrientes Avenue. I couldn't see any physical resemblance in her to my Aunt Yentel, but she had her style of talking: she jumped from one subject to another, confused names, places, dates. She asked me, "Is this your first visit to Argentina? Here the climate is crazy and so are the people. In Warsaw there was spring fever; here one fevers all year round. When it's hot, you melt from the heat. When the rains begin, the cold eats into your bones. It is actually one big jungle. The cities are oases in the pampas. For years, the pimps and whores controlled the Jewish immigrants. Later, they were excommunicated and had to build a synagogue and acquire a cemetery of their own. The Jews who came here after the Holocaust are lost creatures. How is it that they don't translate you into Spanish? When did you last see my great-grandmother Yentel? I didn't know her, but she left me as an inheritance a chain with a locket that was perhaps two hundred years old. I sold it for bread. Here is your hotel. If you're not tired, I'll go up with you for a while."

We took the elevator to the sixth floor. From childhood I have had a liking for balconies; there was one outside my room and we went there directly. There were few high constructions in Buenos Aires, so we could see a part of the city. I brought out two chairs and we sat down. Hanka was saying, "You must wonder why I came to meet you. As long as I had near relatives —a father, a mother, a brother, a sister—I did not appreciate them. Now that they are all ashes, I am yearning for relatives, no matter how distant. I read the Yiddish press. You often mention your Aunt Yentel in your stories. Did she really tell you all those weird tales? You probably make them up. In my own life, things happened that cannot possibly be told. I am alone, completely alone."

"A young woman does not have to be alone."

"Just words. There are circumstances when you are torn away like a leaf from a tree and no power can attach you again. The wind carries you from your roots. There's a name for it in Hebrew, but I've forgotten."

"*Na-v'nad*—a fugitive and a wanderer."

"That's it."

I expected that I would have a short affair with Hanka. But when I tried to embrace her she seemed to shrink in my arms. I kissed her and her lips were cold. She said, "I can understand you—you are a man. You will find plenty of women here if you look for them. You will find them even if you don't look. But you are a normal person, not a necrophile. I belong to an exterminated tribe and we are not material for sex."

My lecture at the Théâtre Soleil having been postponed for some days, Hanka promised to return the next evening. I asked for her telephone number and she said that her telephone was out of order. In Buenos Aires, when something is broken, you can wait months until it is repaired. Before she left, Hanka told me almost casually that while she was looking for relatives in Buenos Aires she had found a second cousin of mine—Jechiel, who had changed his name to Julio. Jechiel was the son of my granduncle Avigdor. I had met Jechiel twice—once in the village of Tishewitz, and the second time in Warsaw, where he came for medical treatment. Jechiel was about ten years older than I—tall, darkish, and emaciated. I remembered that he suffered from tuberculosis and that Uncle Avigdor had brought him to Warsaw to see a lung specialist. I had felt sure that Jechiel did not survive the Holocaust, and now I heard that he was alive and in Argentina. Hanka gave me some details. He came to Argentina with a wife and a daughter, but he divorced his wife and married a Frampol girl whom he met in a concentration camp. He became a peddler—a knocker, as they were called in Buenos Aires. His new wife was illiterate and was afraid to go out of the house by herself. She hadn't learned a word of Spanish. When she needed to go to the grocery for a loaf of bread or for potatoes, Jechiel had to accompany her. Lately, Jechiel had been suffering from asthma and had to give up his peddling. He was living on a pension—what kind of a pension Hanka did not know: perhaps from the city or from some charitable society.

I was tired after the long day, and the moment Hanka left I fell onto the bed in my clothes and slept. After a few hours, I awoke and went out onto the balcony. It was strange to be in a country thousands of miles from my present home. In America fall was approaching; in Argentina it was spring. It had rained while I slept and Junín Street glistened. Old houses lined the street; its stalls were shuttered with iron bars. I could see the rooftops and parts of the brick walls of buildings in adjoining streets. Here and there a reddish light glimmered in a window. Was someone sick? Had someone died? In Warsaw, when I was a boy, I often heard gruesome tales about Buenos Aires: a pimp would carry a poor girl, an orphan, away to this wicked city and try to seduce her with baubles and promises, and, if she did not give in, with blows, tearing her hair and sticking pins into her fingers. Our neighbor Basha used to talk about this with my sister Hinda. Basha would say, "What could the girl do? They took her away on a ship and kept her in chains. She had already lost her innocence. She was sold into a brothel and she had to do what she was told. Sooner or later she got a little worm in her blood, and with this she could not live long. After seven years of disgrace, her hair and teeth fell out, her nose rotted away, and the play was over. Since she was defiled, they buried her behind the fence." I remember my sister's asking, "Alive?"

Now Warsaw was destroyed and I found myself in Buenos Aires, in the neighborhood where misfortunes like this were supposed to have taken place. Basha and my sister Hinda were both dead, and I was not a small boy but a middle-aged writer who had come to Argentina to spread culture.

It rained all the next day. Perhaps for the same reason that there was a shortage of electricity, the telephones didn't work properly—a man would be speaking to me in Yiddish when suddenly I was listening to a female laughing and screaming in Spanish. In the evening Hanka came. We could not go out into the street, so I ordered supper from room service. I asked Hanka what she wanted to eat and she said, "Nothing."

"What do you mean by nothing?"

"A glass of tea."

I didn't listen to her and I ordered a meat supper for her and a vegetarian platter for myself. I ate everything; Hanka barely touched the food on her plate. Like Aunt Yentel, she spewed forth stories.

"They knew in the whole house that he was hiding a Jewish girl. The tenants certainly knew. The Aryan side teemed with *szmalcownicy*—this is what they were called—who extorted the last penny from Jews to protect them and then denounced them to the Nazis. My Gentile—Andrzej was his name—had no money. Any minute someone could have notified the Gestapo and we would have all been shot—I, Andrzej, Stasiek, his son, and Maria, his wife. What am I saying? Shooting was considered light punishment. We would have been tortured. All the tenants would have paid with their lives for that crime. I often told him, 'Andrzej, my dear, you have done enough. I don't want to bring disaster on all of you.' But he said, 'Don't go, don't go. I cannot send you away to your death. Perhaps there is a God after all.' I was hidden in an alcove without a window, and they put a clothes closet at the door to conceal the entrance. They removed a board from the back of the closet and through it they passed my food and, forgive me, they took out the chamber pot. When I extinguished the little lamp I had, it became dark like in a grave. He came to me, and both of them knew about it—his wife and their son. Maria had a female sickness. Their son was sick, too. When he was a child he developed scrofula or some glandular illness and he did not need a woman. I don't think he even grew a beard. He had one passion—reading newspapers. He read all the Warsaw papers, including the advertisements. Did Andrzej satisfy me? I did not look for satisfaction. I was glad that he was relieved. From too much reading, my eyesight dimmed. I became so constipated that only castor oil would help me. Yes, I lay in my grave. But if you lie in a grave long enough, you get accustomed to it and you don't want to part from it. He had given me a pill of cyanide. He and his wife and their son also carried such pills. We all lived with death, and I want you to know that one can fall in love with death. Whoever has loved death cannot love anything else any more. When the liberation came and they told me to leave, I didn't want to go. I clung to the threshold like an ox being dragged to the slaughter.

"How I came to Argentina and what happened between me and José is a story for another time. I did not deceive him. I told him, 'José, if your wife is not lively enough, what do you need a corpse for?' But men do not believe me. When they see a woman who is young, not ugly, and can dance besides, how can she be dead? Also, I had no strength to go to work in a factory with the Spanish women. He bought me a house and this became my second grave—a fancy grave, with flowerpots, bric-a-brac, a piano. He told me to dance and I danced. In what way is it worse than to knit sweaters or to sew on buttons? All day long I sat alone and waited for him. In the evening he came, drunk and angry. One day he spoke to me and told me stories; the next day he would be mute. I knew that sooner or later he would stop talking to me altogether. When it happened I was not surprised, and I didn't try to make him talk, because I knew it was fated. He maintained his silence for over a year. Finally I

told him, 'José, go.' He kissed my forehead and he left. I never
saw him again.'"

The plans for my lecture tour began to go awry. The engagement in Rosario was called off because the president of
the organization suffered a heart attack. The board of direc-
tors of the Jewish Community Center in Buenos Aires had a
falling out over political differences, and the subsidy that they
were to give to the colonies for my lectures there was withheld. In Mar del Plata, the hall I was to speak in suddenly became unavailable. In addition to the problems of the tour, the
weather in Buenos Aires worsened from day to day. There was
lightning, thunder, and from the provinces came news of
windstorms and floods. The mail system didn't seem to be
functioning. Proofs of a new book were supposed to come by
airmail from New York, but they did not arrive and I worried
that the book might be published without my final correc-
tions. Once I was stuck in an elevator between the fourth and
fifth floors and it took almost two hours before I got free. In
New York I had been assured that I would not have hay fever
in Buenos Aires, because it was spring there. But I suffered from
attacks of sneezing, my eyes watered, my throat constricted—
and I didn't even have my antihistamines with me. Chazkel
Poliva stopped calling, and I suspected that he was about to
cancel the whole tour. I was ready to return to New York—but
how could I get information about a ship when the telephone
did not work and I didn't know a word of Spanish?

Hanka came to my room every evening, always at the same
time—I even imagined at the same minute. She entered noise-
lessly. I looked up and there she was, standing in the dusk—an
image surrounded by shadows. I ordered dinner and Hanka
would begin her soliloquy in the quiet monotone that reminded
me of my Aunt Yentel. One night Hanka spoke about her childhood in Warsaw. They lived on Hoźa Street in a Gentile neighborhood. Her father, a manufacturer, was always in debt—on
the edge of bankruptcy. Her mother bought her dresses in
Paris. In the summer they vacationed in Zoppot, in the winter
in Zakopane. Hanka's brother Zdzislaw studied in a private
high school. Her older sister, Edzia, loved to dance, but their

mother insisted it was Hanka who must become another Pavlova or Isadora Duncan. The dance teacher was a sadist. Even though she was ugly and a cripple herself, she demanded perfection from her pupils. She had the eyes of a hawk, she hissed like a snake. She taunted Hanka about her Jewishness. Hanka was saying, "My parents had one remedy for all our troubles—assimilation. We had to be one-hundred-per-cent Poles. But what kind of Poles could we be when my grandfather Asher, your Aunt Yentel's son, could not even speak Polish? Whenever he visited us, we almost died from shame. My maternal grandfather, Yudel, spoke a broken Polish. He once told me that we were descended from Spanish Jews. They had been driven from Spain in the fifteenth century, and our ancestors wandered first to Germany and then, in the Hundred Years' War, to Poland. I felt the Jewishness in my blood. Edzia and Zdzislaw were both blond and had blue eyes, but I was dark. I began at an early age to ponder the eternal questions: Why is one born? Why must one die? What does God want? Why so much suffering? My mother insisted that I read the Polish and French popular novels, but I stealthily looked into the Bible. In the Book of Proverbs I read the words 'Charm is deceitful, and beauty is vain,' and I fell in love with that book. Perhaps because I was forced to make an idol of my body, I developed a hatred for the flesh. My mother and my sister were fascinated by the beauty of movie actresses. In the dancing school the talk was always of hips, thighs, legs, breasts. When a girl gained as much as a quarter of a pound, the teacher created a scene. All this seemed petty and vulgar to me. From too much dancing, we developed bunions and bulging muscles. I was often complimented for my dancing, but I was possessed by the dybbuk of an old Talmudist, one of those whitebeards who used to come to us to ask for alms and were chased away by our maid. My dybbuk would ask, 'For whom are you going to dance—for the Nazis?' Shortly before the war, when Polish students chased the Jews through the Saxony Gardens and my brother Zdzislaw had to stand up at the lectures in the university because he refused to sit on the ghetto benches, he became a Zionist. But I realized that the worldly Jews in Palestine were also eager to imitate the Gentiles. My brother played football. He belonged to the Maccabee sports club. He lifted weights to develop his muscles. How tragic that all my family who loved life so much had to die in the concentration camps, while fate brought me to Argentina.

"I learned Spanish quickly—the words seemed to flow back into me. I tried to dance at Jewish affairs, but everything here is rootless. Here they believe that the Jewish State will end our misfortunes once and forever. This is sheer optimism. We are surrounded there by hordes of enemies whose aim is the same as Hilter's—to exterminate us. Ten times they may not succeed —but the eleventh, catastrophe. I see the Jews being driven into the sea. I hear the wailing of the women and the children. Why is suicide considered such a sin? My own feeling is that the greatest virtue would be to abandon the body and all its iniquities."

That night, when Hanka left, I did not ask her when she would return. My lecture in the Théâtre Soleil had been advertised for the next day, and I expected her to attend. I had slept little the night before, and I went to bed and fell asleep immediately. I wakened with a feeling that someone was whispering in my ear. I tried to light the lamp by my bed, but it did not go on. I groped for the wall switch, but I could not locate it. I had hung my jacket containing my passport and traveler's checks on a chair; the chair was gone. Had I been robbed? I felt my way around the room like a blind man, tripping and bruising my knee. After a while, I stumbled into the chair. No one had taken my passport or my traveler's checks. But my gloom did not lessen. I knew that I'd had a bad dream, and I stood in the dark trying to recollect it. The second I closed my eyes, I was with the dead. They did things words cannot express. They spoke madness. "I will not let her into my room again," I murmured. "This Hanka is my angel of death."

I sat down on the edge of the bed, draped the covers over my shoulders, and took calculation of my soul. This trip had stirred up all my anxieties. I had not prepared any notes for my lecture, "Literature and the Supernatural," and I was apprehensive that I might suddenly become speechless; I foresaw a bloody revolution in Argentina, an atomic war between the United States and Russia; I would become desperately sick. Wild absurdities invaded my mind: What would happen if I got into bed and found a crocodile there? What would happen if the earth were to split into two parts and my part were to fly off to another constellation? What if my going to Argentina had actually been a departure into the next world? I had an uncanny feeling of Hanka's presence. In the left corner of the room I saw a silhouette, a dense whorl that stood apart from the surrounding darkness and took on the shadowy form of a body—shoulders, head, hair. Though I could not make out its face, I sensed in the lurking phantom the mocking of my cowardices. God in heaven, this trip was waking all the fears of my cheder days, when I dared not sleep alone because monsters slithered around my bed, tore at my sidelocks, screeching at me with terrifying voices. In my fright, I began to pray to God to keep me from falling into the hands of the Evil Ones. It seems that my prayer was heard, for suddenly the lamp went on. I saw my face in the mirror—white as after a sickness. I went to the door to make sure it was locked. Then I limped back to the bed.

The next day I spoke in the Théâtre Soleil. The hall was filled with people in spite of the heavy rain outside. I saw so many familiar faces in the audience that I could scarcely believe my eyes. True, I did not remember their names, but they reminded me of friends and acquaintances from Bilgoray, Lublin, Warsaw. Was it possible that so many had been saved from the Nazis and come to my lecture? As a rule, when I spoke about the supernatural, there were interruptions from the audience —even protest. But here, when I concluded, there was ominous silence. I wanted to go down into the audience and greet these resurrected images of my past; instead, Chazkel Poliva led me behind the stage, and by the time I made my way to the auditorium the overhead lights were extinguished and the seats empty. I said, "Shall I speak now to the spirits?"

As if he were reading my mind, Poliva asked, "Where is your so-called cousin? I didn't see her in the hall."

"No, she did not come."

"I don't want to mix into your private affairs, but do me a favor and get rid of her. It's not good for you that she should trail after you."

"No. But why do you say this?"

Chazkel Poliva hesitated. "She frightens me. She will bring you bad luck."

"Do you believe in such things?"

"When you have been an impresario for thirty years, you have to believe in them."

I had dozed off and evening had fallen. Was it the day after my lecture or a few days later? I opened my eyes and Hanka stood at my bedside. I saw embarrassment in her eyes, as if she knew my plight and felt guilty. She said, "We are supposed to go to your cousin Julio this evening."

I had prepared myself to say to her, "I cannot see you again," but I asked, "Where does Julio live?"

"It's not too far. You said that you like to walk."

Ordinarily I would have invited her to dinner, but I had no intention of dallying with her late into the night. Perhaps Julio would offer us something to eat. Half asleep, I got up and we walked out onto Corrientes. Only an occasional street light was lit, and armed soldiers were patrolling the streets. All the stores were closed. There was an air of curfew and Black Sabbath. We walked in silence, like a pair who have quarreled yet must still go visiting together. Corrientes is one of the longest boulevards in the world. We walked for an hour. Each time I asked if we were nearing our destination Hanka replied that we had some distance to go yet. After a while we turned off Corrientes. It seemed that Julio lived in a suburb. We passed factories with smokeless chimneys and barred windows, dark garages, warehouses with their windows sealed, empty lots overgrown with weeds. The few private homes we saw looked old, their patios enclosed by fences. I was tense and glanced sideways at Hanka. I could not distinguish her face—just two dark eyes. Unseen dogs were barking; unseen cats mewed and yowled. I was not hungry but unsavory fluids filled my mouth. Suspicions fell on me like locusts: Is this my final walk? Is she leading me into a cave of murderers? Perhaps she is a she-devil and will soon reveal her goose feet and pig's snout?

As if Hanka grasped that her silence made me uneasy, she became talkative. We were passing a sprawling house, with no windows, the remnants of a fence, and a lone cactus tree in front. Hanka began, "This is where the old Spanish Gentiles live. There is no heat in these houses—the ovens are for cooking, not for heating. When the rains come, they freeze. They have a drink that they call maté. They cover themselves with ragged clothes, sip maté, and lay out cards. They are Catholics, but the churches here are half empty even on Sunday. The men don't go, only the women. They are witches who pray to the devil, not to God. Time has stopped for them—they are a throwback to the era of Queen Isabella and Torquemada. José left me many books, and since I stopped dancing and have no friends I keep reading. I know Argentina. Sometimes I think I have lived here in a former incarnation. The men still dream of in-quisitions and autos-da-fé. The women mutter incantations and cast spells on their enemies. At forty they are wrinkled and wilted. The husbands find mistresses, who immediately begin to spawn children, and after a few years they are as jealous, bit-ter, and shabby as the wives. They may not know it, but many of them descend from the Marranos. Somewhere in the far-away provinces there are sects that light candles Friday evening and keep a few other Jewish customs. Here we are."

We entered an alley that was under construction. There was no pavement, no sidewalk. We made our way between piles of boards and heaps of bricks and cement. A few unfinished houses stood without roofs, without panes in the windows. The house where Julio lived was narrow and low. Hanka knocked, but no one answered. She pushed the door open, and we went through a tiny foyer into a dimly lit room furnished only with two chairs and a chest. On one chair sat Jechiel. I recognized him only because I knew that it was he. He looked ancient, but from behind his aged face, as if from behind a mask, the Jechiel of former times showed. His skull was bald, with a few wisps of side hair that were neither gray nor black but color-less. He had sunken cheeks, a pointed chin, the throat of a plucked rooster, and the pimpled nose of an alcoholic. Half of his forehead and one cheek were stained with a red rash. Jechiel did not lift his eyelids when we entered. I never saw his eyes that evening. On the other chair sat a squat, wide-girthed woman with ash-colored, disheveled hair; she was wearing a shabby housecoat. Her face was round and pasty, her eyes blank and watery, like the eyes one sees in asylums for the mentally sick. It was hard to determine whether she was forty or sixty. She did not budge. She reminded me of a stuffed doll.

From the way Hanka had spoken, I presumed that she was

well acquainted with them and that she had told them of me. But she seemed to be meeting them for the first time.

I said, "Jechiel, I am your cousin Isaac, the son of Bathsheba. We met once in Tishewitz and later in Warsaw."

"*Sí.*"

"Do you recognize me?"

"*Sí.*"

"You have forgotten Yiddish?" I asked.

"No."

No, he had not forgotten Yiddish, but it seemed that he had forgotten how to speak. He dozed and yawned. I had to drag conversation from him. To all my questions he answered either "*Sí,*" "*No,*" or "*Bueno.*" Neither he nor his wife made an effort to bring something for us to sit on or a glass of tea. Even though I am not tall, my head almost touched the ceiling. Hanka leaned against the wall in silence. Her face had lost all expression. I walked over to Jechiel's wife and asked, "Do you have someone left in Frampol?"

For what seemed a very long time there came no answer; then she said, "Nobody."

"What was your father's name?"

She pondered as if she had to remind herself. "Avram Itcha."

"What did he do?"

Again a long pause. "A shoemaker."

After a half hour, I wearied of drawing answers from this numb couple. There was an air of fatigue about them that baffled me. Each time I addressed Jechiel, he started as if I had wakened him.

"If you have any interest in me, you can call the Hotel Cosmopolitan," I said at last.

"*Sí.*"

Jechiel's wife did not utter a sound when I said good night to her. Jechiel mumbled something I could not understand and collapsed into his chair. I thought I heard him snore. Outside, I said to Hanka, "If this is possible, anything is possible."

"We shouldn't have visited them at night," Hanka said. "They're both sick. He suffers from asthma and she has a bad heart. I told you, they became acquainted in Auschwitz. Didn't you notice the numbers on their arms?"

"No."

"Those who stood at the threshold of death remain dead."

I had heard these words from Hanka and from other refugees before, but in this dark alley they made me shudder. I said, "Whatever you are, be so good as to get me a taxi."

"*Sí.*"

Hanka embraced me. She leaned against me and clung to me. I did not stir. We stood silent in the alley, and a needle-like rain began to fall on us. Someone extinguished the light in Julio's house and it became as dark around us as in Tishewitz.

The sun was shining, the sky had cleared, it shone blue and summery. The air smelled of the sea, of mango and orange trees. Blossoms fell from their branches. The breezes reminded me of the Vistula and of Warsaw. Like the weather, my lecture tour had also cleared up. All kinds of institutions invited me to speak and gave banquets for me. Schoolchildren honored me with dancing and songs. It was bewildering that such a fuss should be made about a writer, but Argentina is isolated and when they get a guest they receive him with exaggerated friendliness.

Chazkel Poliva said, "It's all because you freed yourself of Hanka."

I had not freed myself. I was searching for her. Since the night we visited Julio, Hanka had not come to see me. And there was no way I could get in touch with her. I did not know where she lived; I didn't even know her surname. I had asked for her address more than once, but she had always avoided answering. Neither did I hear from Julio. No matter how I tried to describe his little alley, no one could identify it for me. I looked in the telephone book—Julio's name was not listed.

I went up to my room late. Going onto the balcony at night had become a habit with me. A cool wind was blowing, bringing me greetings from the Antarctic and the South Pole. I raised my eyes and saw different stars, different constellations. Some groups of stars reminded me of consonants, vowels, and the musical notations I had studied in cheder—an *aleph*, a *hai*, a *shuruk*, a *segul*, a *tsairai*, a *chain*. The sickle of the moon seemed to hang reversed, ready to harvest the heavenly fields backward. Over the roofs of Junín Street, the southern sky stretched, strangely near and divinely distant, a cosmic illumination of a volume without a beginning and without an end—to be read and judged by the Author himself. I was calling to Hanka, "Why did you run away? Wherever you are, come back. There can be no world without you. You are an eternal letter in God's scroll."

In Mar del Plata, the hall had become available, and I went there with Chazkel Poliva. On the train he said to me, "You may think it crazy, but here in Argentina Communism is a game for the rich. A poor man cannot become a member of the Communist Party. Don't ask me any questions. So it is. The rich Jews who have villas in Mar del Plata and will come tonight to your lecture are all leftists. Do me a favor and don't speak about mysticism to them. They don't believe in it. They babble constantly about the social revolution, although when the revolution comes they will be its first victims."

"This in itself is a mystery."

"Yes. But we want your lecture to be a success."

I did what Poliva told me to do. I didn't mention the hidden powers. After the lecture, I read a humorous sketch. When I finished and the question-and-answer period began, an old man rose and asked me about my inclination toward the supernatural. Soon questions on this subject came from all sides. That night the rich Jews in Mar del Plata showed great interest in telepathy, clairvoyance, dybbuks, premonitions, reincarnation: "If there is life after death, why don't the slaughtered Jews take revenge on the Nazis?" "If there is telepathy, why do we need the telephone?" "If it is possible that thought influences inanimate objects, how does it come that the bank in the casino makes high profits just because it has one chance more than its clients?" I answered that if the existence of God, the soul, the hereafter, special providence, and everything that has to do with metaphysics were scientifically proven, man would lose the highest gift bestowed upon him— free choice.

The chairman announced that the next question would be the last one, and a young man got up and asked, "Have you had personal experience of that sort? Have you ever seen a spirit?"

I answered, "All my experiences have been ambiguous.

None of them could serve for evidence. Just the same, my belief in spirits becomes ever stronger."

There was applause. As I bowed and thanked them, I saw Hanka. She was sitting in the audience, clapping her hands. She wore the same black hat and black dress she had worn at all our meetings. She smiled at me and winked. I was stunned. Had she traveled after me to Mar del Plata? I looked again and she had vanished. No, it had been a hallucination. It lasted only one instant. But I will brood about this instant for the rest of my life.

Translated by the author and Blanche and Joseph Nevel

1974

FRED CHAPPELL

(b. 1936)

Linnaeus Forgets

THE year 1758 was a comparatively happy one in the life of
Carl Linnaeus. For although his second son, Johannes, had
died the year before at the age of three, in that same year his
daughter Sophia, the last child he was to have, was born. And
in 1758 he purchased three small bordering estates in the country near Uppsala and on one of these, Hammarby, he established a retreat, to which he thereafter retired during the
summer months, away from the town and its deadly fever. He
was content in his family, his wife and five children living; and
having recently been made a Knight of the Polar Star, he now
received certain intelligence that at the opportune hour he
would be ennobled by King Adolph Fredrik.

   The landscape about Hammarby was pleasant and interesting,
though of course Linnaeus long ago had observed and classified every botanical specimen this region had to offer. Even so,
he went almost daily on long walks into the countryside, usually
accompanied by students. The students could not deny themselves his presence even during vacation periods; they were
attracted to him as hummingbirds to trumpet vines by his geniality and humor and by his encyclopedic knowledge of every
plant springing from the earth.

   And he was happy, too, in overseeing the renovations of the
buildings in Hammarby and the construction of the new or-
angery, in which he hoped to bring to fruition certain exotic
plants that had never before flowered on Swedish soil. Linnaeus
had become at last a famous man, a world figure in the same
fashion that Samuel Johnson and Voltaire and Albrecht von
Haller were world figures, and every post brought him sheaves
of adulatory verse and requests for permission to dedicate
books to him and inquiries about the details of his system of
sexual classification and plant specimens of every sort. Most of
the specimens were flowers quite commonly known, but dried

289

and pressed and sent to him by young ladies who sometimes
hoped that they had discovered a new species, or who hoped
merely to secure a token of the man's notice, an autograph
letter. But he also received botanical samples from persons
with quite reputable knowledge, from scientists persuaded that
they had discovered some anomaly or exception that might
cause him to think over again some part of his method. (For
the ghost of Siegesbeck was even yet not completely laid.) Occasionally other specimens arrived that were indeed unfamiliar
to him. These came from scientists and missionaries traveling
in remote parts of the world, or the plants were sent by knowledgeable ship captains or now and then by some common
sailor who had come to know, however vaguely and confusedly, something of Linnaeus's reputation.

His renown had come to him so belatedly and so tenden-
tiously that the great botanist took a child's delight in all this
attention. He read all the verses and all the letters and often
would answer his unknown correspondents pretty much in
their own manner; letters still remain to us in which he addressed one or another of his admirers in a silly and exaggerated prose style, admiring especially the charms of these young
ladies on whom he had never set eyes. Sweden was in those
days regarded as a backward country, having only a few war-
riors and enlightened despots to offer as important cultural
figures, and part of Linnaeus's pride in his own achievements
evinced itself in nationalist terms, a habit that Frenchmen and
Englishmen found endearing.

On June 12, 1758, a large box was delivered to Linnaeus, along
with a brief letter, and both these objects were battered from
much travel. He opened first the box and found inside it a plant
in a wicker basket that had been lined with oilskin. The plant
was rooted in a black sandy loam, now dry and crumbly, and Linnaeus immediately watered it from a sprinkling can, though he
entertained little hope of saving—actually, resuscitating—the
plant. The plant was so wonderfully woebegone in appearance,
so tattered by rough handling, that the scientist could not say
immediately whether it was shrub, flower, or a tall grass. It
seemed to have collapsed in upon itself, and its tough leaves
and stems were the color of parchment and crackled like

parchment when he tried to examine them. He desisted, hoping
that the accompanying letter would answer some of his questions.

The letter bore no postmark. It was signed with a Dutch
name, Gerhaert Oorts, though it was written in French. As he
read the letter, it became clear to Linnaeus that the man who
had signed it had not written it out himself but had dictated it
to someone else who had translated his words as he spoke. The
man who wrote the letter was a Dutch sailor, a common sea-
man, and it was probably one of his superior officers who had
served him as amanuensis and translator. The letter was un-
dated and began: "*Cher maître Charles Linné, père de la science
botanique; je ne sçay si. . . .*"

"To the great Carl Linnaeus, father of botany; I know not
whether the breadth of your interests still includes a wondering curiosity about strange plants which grow in many different parts of the world, or whether your ever-agile spirit has
undertaken to possess new kingdoms of science entirely. But
in case you are continuing in your botanical endeavors, I am
taking liberty to send you a remarkable flower [*une fleur mer-
veilleuse*] that my fellows and I have observed to have strange
properties and characteristics. This flower grows in no great
abundance on the small islands east of Guiana in the South
Seas. With all worshipful respect, I am your obedient servant,
Gerhaert Oorts."

Linnaeus smiled on reading this letter, amused by the odd
wording, but then frowned slightly. He still had no useful information. The fact that Mynheer Oorts called the plant a
flower was no guarantee that it was indeed a flower. Few
people in the world were truly interested in botany, and it was
not to be expected that a sailor could have leisure for even the
most rudimentary study of the subject. The most he could
profitably surmise was that it bore blooms, which the sailor
had seen.

He looked at it again, but it was so crumpled in upon itself
that he was fearful of damaging it if he undertook a hasty inspection. It was good to know that it was a tropical plant. Linnaeus lifted the basket out of the box and set the plant on the
corner of a long table where the sunlight fell strongest. He

noticed that the soil was already thirsty again, so he watered it liberally, still not having any expectation that his ministrations would take the least effect.

It was now quarter till two, and as he had arranged a two o'clock appointment with a troublesome student, Linnaeus hurried out of his museum—which he called "my little back room"—and went into the main house to prepare himself. His student arrived promptly but was so talkative and contentious and so involved in a number of personal problems that the rest of the afternoon was dissipated in conference with him. After this, it was time for dinner, over which Linnaeus and his family habitually sat for more than two hours, gossiping and teasing and laughing. And then there was music on the clavier in the small, rough dining room; the botanist was partial to Telemann, and sat beaming in a corner of a sofa, nodding in time to a sonata.

And so it was eight o'clock before he found opportunity to return to his little back room. He had decided to defer thorough investigation of his new specimen until the next day, preferring to examine his plants by natural sunlight rather than by lamplight. For though the undying summer twilight still held the western sky, in the museum it was gray and shadowy. But he wanted to take a final look at the plant before retiring and he needed also to draw up an account of the day's activities for his journal.

He entered the little house and lit two oil lamps. The light they shed mingled with the twilight, giving a strange orange tint to the walls and furnishings.

Linnaeus was immediately aware that changes had taken place in the plant. It was no trick of the light; the plant had acquired more color. The leaves and stems were suffused with a bright lemonish yellow, a color much more alive than the dim dun the plant had shown at two o'clock. And in the room hung a pervasive scent, unmistakable but not oppressive, which could be accounted for only by the presence of the plant. This was a pleasant perfume and full of reminiscence—but he could not remember of what the scent reminded him. So many associations crowded into his mind that he could sort none of them out; but there was nothing unhappy in these confused sensations. He wagged his head in dreamy wonder.

He looked at it more closely and saw that the plant had lost its dry parchmentlike texture, that its surfaces had become pliable and lifelike in appearance. Truly it was a remarkable specimen, with its warm perfume and marvelous recuperative powers. He began to speculate that this plant had the power of simply becoming dormant, and not dying, when deprived of proper moisture and nourishment. He took up a bucket of well water, replenishing the watering can, and watered it again, resolving that he would give up all his other projects now until he had properly examined this stranger and classified it.

He snuffed the lamps and went out again into the vast whitish-yellow twilight. A huge full moon loomed in the east, just brushing the tree tips of a grove, and from within the grove sounded the harsh trills and staccato accents of a song sparrow and the calmly flowing recital of a thrush. The air was already cool enough that he could feel the warmth of the earth rising about his ankles. Now the botanist was entirely happy, and he felt within him the excitement he often had felt before when he came to know that he had found a new species and could enter another name and description into his grand catalogue.

He must have spent more time in his little back room than he had supposed, for when he reentered his dwelling house, all was silent and only enough lamps were burning for him to see to make his way about. Everyone had retired, even the two servants. Linnaeus reflected that his household had become accustomed to his arduous hours and took it for granted that he could look after his own desires at bedtime. He took a lamp and went quietly up the stairs to the bedroom. He dressed himself for bed and got in beside Fru Linnaea, who had gathered herself into a warm huddle on the left-hand side. As he arranged the bedclothes, she murmured some sleep-blurred words that he could not quite hear, and he stroked her shoulder and then turned on his right side to go to sleep.

But sleep did not come. Instead, bad memories rose, memories of old academic quarrels, and memories especially of the attacks upon him by Johann Siegesbeck. For when Siegesbeck first attacked his system of sexual classification in that detestable book called *Short Outline of True Botanic Wisdom*, Linnaeus had almost no reputation to speak of and Siegesbeck represented—to Sweden, at least—the authority of the

academy. And what, Linnaeus asked, was the basis of this ignorant pedant's objections? Why, that his system of classifying
plants was morally dissolute. In his book, Siegesbeck had asked,
"Who would have thought that bluebells, lilies, and onions
could be up to such immorality?" He went on for pages in this
vein, not failing to point out that Sir Thomas Browne had
listed the notion of the sexuality of plants as one of the vulgar
errors. Finally Siegesbeck had asked—anticipating an objection
Goethe would voice eighty-three years later—how such a li-
centious method of classification could be taught to young
students without corruption of minds and morals.

Linnaeus groaned involuntarily, helpless under the force of
memory.

These attacks had not let up, had cost him a position at the
university, so that he was forced to support himself as a medical practitioner and for two barren years had been exiled from
his botanical studies. In truth, Linnaeus never understood the
nature of these attacks; they seemed foolish and irrelevant, and
that is why he remembered them so bitterly. He could never
understand how a man could write: "To tell you that nothing
could equal the gross prurience of Linnaeus's mind is perfectly
needless. A literal translation of the first principles of Linnaean
botany is enough to shock female modesty. It is possible that
many virtuous students might not be able to make out the
similitude of *Clitoria*."

It seemed to Linnaeus that to describe his system of classification as immoral was to describe nature as immoral, and nature could not be immoral. It seemed to him that the plants
inhabited a different world than the fallen world of mankind,
and that they lived in a sphere of perfect freedom and ease, un-
vexed by momentary and perverse jealousies. Any man with
eyes could see that the stamens were masculine and the pistils
feminine, and that if there was only one stamen to the female
part (Monandria), this approximation of the Christian European family was only charmingly coincidental. It was more likely
that the female would be attended by four husbands (Tetran-
dria) or by five (Pentandria) or by twelve or more (Dodecan-
dria). When he placed the poppy in the class Polyandria and
described its arrangement as "Twenty males or more in the
same bed with the female," he meant to say of the flower no

more than God had said when He created it. How had it happened that mere literal description had caused him such unwarrantable hardship?

These thoughts and others toiled in his mind for an hour or so. When at last they subsided, Linnaeus had turned on his left side toward his wife and fallen asleep, breathing unevenly.

He rose later than was his custom. His sleep had been shaken by garish dreams that now he could not remember, and he wished he had awakened earlier. Now he got out of bed with uncertain movements and stiffly made his toilet and dressed himself. His head buzzed. He hurried downstairs as soon as he could.

It was much later than he had supposed. None of the family was about; everyone had already breakfasted and set out in pursuit of the new day. Only Nils, the elderly bachelor manservant, waited to serve him in the dining room. He informed his master that Fru Linnaea had taken all the children, except the baby asleep in the nursery, on an excursion into town. Linnaeus nodded, and wondered briefly whether the state of his accounts this quarter could support the good Fru's passion for shopping. Then he forgot about it.

It was almost nine o'clock.

He ate a large breakfast of bread and cheese and butter and fruit, together with four cups of strong black tea. After eating, he felt both refreshed and dilatory and he thought for a long moment of taking advantage of the morning and the unnaturally quiet house to read in some of the new volumes of botanical studies that had arrived during the past few weeks.

But when he remembered the new specimen awaiting him in the museum, these impulses evaporated and he left the house quickly. It was another fine day. The sky was cloudless, a mild, mild blue. Where the east grove cast its shadow on the lawn, dew still remained, and he smelled its freshness as he passed. He fumbled the latch excitedly, and then he swung the museum door open.

His swift first impression was that something had caught fire and burned, the odor in the room was so strong. It wasn't an acrid smell, a smell of destruction, but it was overpowering, and in a moment he identified it as having an organic source. He closed the door and walked to the center of the room. It was not only the heavy damp odor that attacked his senses but also a high-pitched musical chirping, or twittering, scattered on the room's laden air. And the two sensations, smell and sound, were indistinguishably mixed; here was an example of that sensory confusion of which M. Diderot had written so engagingly. At first he could not discover the source of all this sensual hurly-burly. The morning sun entered the windows to shine aslant the north wall, so that between Linnaeus and his strange new plant there fell a tall rectangular corridor of sunshine through which his gaze couldn't pierce clearly.

He stood stock-still, for what he could see of the plant beyond the light astonished him. It had opened out and grown monstrously; it was enormous, tier on tier of dark green reaching to a height of three feet or more above the table. No blooms that he could see, but differentiated levels of broad green leaves spread out in orderly fashion from bottom to top, so that the plant had the appearance of a flourishing green pyramid. And there was movement among and about the leaves, a shifting in the air all around it, and he supposed that an extensive tropical insect life had been transported into his little museum. Linnaeus smiled nervously, hardly able to contain his excitement, and stepped into the passage of sunlight.

As he advanced toward the plant, the twittering sound grew louder. The foliage, he thought, must be rife with living creatures. He came to the edge of the table but could not see clearly yet, his sight still dazzled from stepping into and out of the swath of sunshine.

Even when his eyes grew more accustomed to shadow, he still could not make out exactly what he was looking at. There was a general confused movement about and within the plant, a continual settling and unsettling as around a beehive, but the small creatures that flitted there were so shining and iridescent, so gossamerlike, that he could fix no proper impression of them. Now, though, he heard them quite clearly, and realized that what at first had seemed a confused mélange of twittering was, in fact, an orderly progression of sounds, a music as of flutes and piccolos in polyphony.

He could account for this impression in no way but to think of it as a product of his imagination. He had become aware that his senses were not so acute as they ordinarily were; or rather, that they were acute enough, but that he was having some difficulty in interpreting what his senses told him. It oc-curred to him that the perfume of the plant—which now cloaked him heavily, an invisible smoke—possessed perhaps some narcotic quality. When he reached past the corner of the table to a wall shelf for a magnifying glass, he noticed that his movements were sluggish and that an odd feeling of remote-ness took power over his mind.

He leaned over the plant, training his glass and trying to breathe less deeply. The creature that swam into his sight, flit-ting through the magnification, so startled him that he dropped the glass to the floor and began to rub his eyes and temples and forehead. He wasn't sure what he had seen—that is, he could not believe what he thought he had seen—because it was no form of insect life at all.

He retrieved the glass and looked again, moving from one area of the plant to another, like a man examining a map.

These were no insects, though many of the creatures here inhabiting were winged. They were of flesh, however diminu-tive they were in size. The whole animal family was repre-sented here in miniature: horses, cows, dogs, serpents, lions and tigers and leopards, elephants, opossums and otters. . . . All the animals Linnaeus had seen or heard of surfaced here for a moment in his horn-handled glass and then sped away on their ordinary amazing errands—and not only the animals he might have seen in the world, but the fabulous animals, too: unicorns and dragons and gryphons and basilisks and the Arabian flying serpents of which Herodotus had written.

Tears streamed on the botanist's face, and he straightened and wiped his eyes with his palm. He looked all about him in the long room, but nothing else had changed. The floor was littered with potting soil and broken and empty pots, and on the shelves were the jars of chemicals and dried leaves, and on the small round table by the window his journal lay open, with two quill pens beside it and the inkpot and his pewter snuffbox. If he had indeed become insane all in a moment, the distortion of his perceptions did not extend to the daily ob-jects of his existence but was confined to this one strange plant.

He stepped to the little table and took two pinches of snuff, hoping that the tobacco might clear his head and that the dust in his nostrils might prevent to some degree the narcotic effect of the plant's perfume, if that was what caused the appearance of these visions. He sneezed in the sunlight and dust motes rose golden around him. He bent to his journal and dipped his pen and thought, but finally wrote nothing. What could he write down that he would believe in a week's time?

He returned to the plant, determined to subject it to the most minute examination. He decided to limit his observation to the plant itself, disregarding the fantastic animal life. With the plant, his senses would be less likely to deceive him. But his resolve melted away when once again he employed the magnifying glass. There was too much movement; the distraction was too violent.

Now he observed that there were not only miniature animals, real and fabulous, but there was also a widespread colony, or nation, of homunculi. Here were little men and women, perfectly formed, and—like the other animals—sometimes having wings. He felt the mingled fear and astonishment that Mr. Swift's hapless Gulliver felt when he first encountered the Lilliputians. But he also felt an admiration, as he might have felt upon seeing some particularly well-fashioned example of the Swiss watch-maker's art. To see large animals in small, with their customary motions so accelerated, did indeed give the impression of a mechanical exhibition.

Yet there was really nothing mechanical about them, if he put himself in their situation. They were self-determining; most of their actions had motives intelligible to him, however exotic were the means of carrying out these motives. Here, for example, a tiny rotund man in a green jerkin and saffron trousers talked—sang, rather—to a tiny slender man dressed all in brown. At the conclusion of this recitative, the man in brown raced away and leapt onto the back of a tiny winged camel, which bore him from this lower level of the plant to an upper one, where he dismounted and began singing to a young lady in a bright blue gown. Perfectly obvious that a message had been delivered. . . . Here in another place a party of men and women mounted on unwinged great cats, lions and leopards and tigers, pursued over the otherwise-deserted broad plain of a leaf a fearful Hydra, its nine heads snapping and spitting. At last they impaled it to the white leaf vein with the sharp black thorns they carried for lances and then they set the monster afire, writhing and shrieking, and they rode away together. A grayish waxy blister formed on the leaf where the hydra had burned. . . . And here in another area a formal ball was taking place, the tiny gentlemen leading out the ladies in time to the music of an orchestra sawing and pounding at the instruments. . . .

This plant, then, enfolded a little world, a miniature society in which the mundane and the fanciful commingled in matter-of-fact fashion but at a feverish rate of speed.

Linnaeus became aware that his legs were trembling from tiredness and that his back ached. He straightened, feeling a grateful release of muscle tension. He went round to the little table and sat, dipped his pen again, and began writing hurriedly, hardly stopping to think. He wrote until his hand almost cramped and then he flexed it several times and wrote more, covering page after page with his neat sharp script. Finally he laid the pen aside and leaned back in his chair and thought. Many different suppositions formed in his mind, but none of them made clear sense. He was still befuddled and he felt that he might be confused for years to come, that he had fallen victim to a dream or vision from which he might never recover.

In a while he felt rested and he returned again to look at the plant.

By now a whole season, or a generation or more, had passed. The plant itself was a darker green than before, its shape had changed, and even more creatures now lived within it. The mid-part of the plant had opened out into a large boxlike space thickly walled with hand-sized kidney-shaped leaves. This section formed a miniature theater or courtyard. Something was taking place here, but Linnaeus could not readily figure out what it was.

Much elaborate construction had been undertaken. The smaller leaves of the plant in this space had been clipped and arranged into a grand formal garden. There were walls and arches of greenery and greenery shaped into obelisks topped with globes, and Greek columns and balconies and level paths. Wooden statues and busts were placed at intervals within this garden, and it seemed to Linnaeus that on some of the subjects

he could make out the lineaments of the great classical bota-
nists. Here, for example, was Pliny, and there was Theophras-
tus. Many of the persons so honored were unfamiliar to him,
but then he found on one of the busts, occupying a position of
great prominence, his own rounded cheerful features. Could
this be true? He stared and stared, but his little glass lacked
enough magnification for him to be finally certain.

Music was everywhere; chamber orchestras were stationed
at various points along the outer walls of the garden and two
large orchestras were set up at either end of the wide main path.
There were a number of people calmly walking about, twittering
to one another, but there were fewer than he had supposed at
first. The air above them was dotted with cherubs flying about
playfully, and much of the foliage was decorated with artfully
hung tapestries. There was about the scene an attitude of expectancy, of waiting.

At this point the various orchestras began to sound in concert and gathered the music into recognizable shape. The
sound was still thin and high-pitched, but Linnaeus discerned
in it a long reiterative fanfare, which was followed by a slow,
grave processional march. All the little people turned from
their casual attitudes and gave their attention to the wall of
leaves standing at the end of the main wide pathway. There was
a clipped narrow corridor in front of the wall and from it
emerged a happy band of naked children. They advanced
slowly and disorderly, strewing the path with tiny pink petals
that they lifted out in dripping handfuls from woven baskets
slung over their shoulders. They were singing in unison, but
Linnaeus could not make out the melody, their soprano voices
pitched beyond his range of hearing. Following the children
came another group of musicians, blowing and thumping, and
then a train of comely maidens, dressed in airy long white
dresses tied about the waists with broad ribbons, green and
yellow. The maidens, too, were singing, and the botanist now
began to hear the vocal music, a measured but joyous choral
hymn. Linnaeus was smiling to himself, buoyed up on an ocean
of happy fullness; his face and eyes were bright.

The beautiful maidens were followed by another troop of
petal-scattering children, and after them came a large orderly
group of animals of all sorts, domestic animals and wild

animals and fantastic animals, stalking forward with their fine
innate dignities, though not, of course, in step. The animals
were unattended, moving in the procession as if conscious of
their places and duties. There were more of these animals,
male and female of each kind, than Linnaeus had expected to
live within the plant. He attempted vainly to count the number of different species, but he gave over as they kept pouring
forward smoothly, like sand grains twinkling into the bottom
of an hourglass.

The spectators had gathered to the sides of the pathway and
stood cheering and applauding.

The animals passed by, and now a train of carriages ranked
in twos took their place. These carriages each were drawn by
teams of four little horses, and both the horses and carriages
were loaded down with great garlands of bright flowers, hung
with blooms from end to end. Powdered ladies fluttered their
fans in the windows. And after the carriages, another band of
musicians marched.

Slowly now, little by little, a large company of strong young
men appeared, scores of them. Each wore a stout leather har-
ness from which long reins of leather were attached behind to
an enormous wheeled platform. The young men, their bodies
shining, drew this platform down the pathway. The platform
itself supported another formal garden, within which was an
interior arrangement suggestive of a royal court. There was a
throne on its dais, and numerous attendants before and behind
the throne. Flaming braziers in each corner gave off thick
grayish-purple clouds of smoke, and around these braziers
small children exhibited various instruments and implements
connected with the science of botany: shovels, thermometers,
barometers, potting spades, and so forth. Below the dais on
the left-hand side, a savage, a New World Indian, adorned with
feathers and gold, knelt in homage, and in front of him a beautiful woman in Turkish dress proffered to the throne a tea shrub
in a silver pot. Farther to the left, at the edge of the tableau, a
sable Ethiopian stood, he also carrying a plant indigenous to
his mysterious continent.

The throne itself was a living creature, a great tawny lion
with sherry-colored eyes. The power and wildness of the creature were unmistakable in him, but now he lay placid and

willing, with a sleepy smile on his face. And on this throne of the living lion, over whose back a covering of deep-plush green satin had been thrown, sat the goddess Flora. This was she indeed, wearing a golden crown and holding in her left hand a gathering of peonies (*Paeonia officinalis*) and in her right hand a heavy golden key. Flora sat at ease, the goddess gowned in a carmine silk that shone silver where the light fell on it in broad planes, the gown tied over her right shoulder and arm to form a sleeve, and gathered lower on her left side to leave the breast bare. An expression of sublime dreaminess was on her face and she gazed off into a far distance, thinking thoughts unknowable even to her most intimate initiates. She was attended on her right-hand side by Apollo, splendidly naked except for the laurel bays round his forehead and his bow and quiver crossed on his chest. Behind her Diana disposed herself, half-reclining, half-supporting herself on her bow, and wearing in her hair her crescent-moon fillet. Apollo devoted his attention to Flora, holding aloft a blazing torch, and looking down upon her with an expression of mingled tenderness and admiration. He stood astride the carcass of a loathsome slain dragon, signifying the demise of ignorance and superstitious unbelief.

The music rolled forth in loud hosannas, and the spectators on every side knelt in reverence to the goddess as she passed.

Linnaeus became dizzy. He closed his eyes for a moment and felt the floor twirling beneath his feet. He stumbled across the room to his chair by the writing table and sat. His chin dropped down on his chest; he fell into a deep swoon.

When he regained consciousness, the shaft of sunlight had reached the west wall. At least an hour had passed. When he stirred himself, there was an unaccustomed stiffness in his limbs and it seemed to him that over the past twenty-four hours or so his body had aged several years.

His first clear thoughts were of the plant, and he rose and went to his worktable to find out what changes had occurred. But the plant was no more; it had disappeared. Here was the wicker container lined with oilcloth, here was the earth inside it, now returned to its dry and crumbly condition, but the wonderful plant no longer existed. All that remained was a greasy gray-green powder sifted over the soil. Linnaeus took up a pinch of it in his fingers and sniffed at it and even tasted it, but it had no sensory qualities at all except a neutral oiliness. Absentmindedly he wiped his fingers on his coat sleeve.

A deep melancholy descended upon the man and he locked his hands behind his back and began walking about the room, striding up and down beside his worktable. A harsh welter of thoughts and impulses overcame his mind. At one point he halted in mid-stride, turned and crossed to his writing table, and snatched up his journal, anxious to determine what account he had written of his strange adventure.

His journal was no help at all, for he could not read it. He looked at the unfinished last page and then thumbed backward for seven pages and turned them all over again, staring and staring. He had written in a script unintelligible to him, a writing that seemed to bear some distant resemblance to Arabic perhaps, but which bore no resemblance at all to his usual exuberant mixture of Latin and Swedish. Not a word or a syllable on any page conveyed the least meaning to him.

As he gazed at these dots and squiggles he had scratched on the page, Linnaeus began to forget. He waved his hand before his face like a man brushing away cobwebs. The more he looked at his pages, the more he forgot, until finally he had forgotten the whole episode: the letter from the Dutch sailor, the receiving of the plant, the discovery of the little world the plant contained—everything.

Like a man in a trance, and with entranced movements, he returned to his worktable and swept some scattered crumbs of soil into a broken pot and carried it away and deposited it in the dustbin.

It has been said that some great minds have the ability *to forget deeply.* That is what happened to Linnaeus; he forgot the plant and the bright vision that had been vouchsafed to him. But the profoundest levels of his life had been stirred, and some of the details of his thinking had changed.

His love for metaphor sharpened, for one thing. Writing in his *Deliciae naturae,* which appeared fourteen years after his encounter with the plant, he described a small pink-flowered ericaceous plant of Lapland growing on a rock by a pool, with a newt as "the blushing naked princess Andromeda, lovable and beautiful, chained to a sea rock and exposed to a horrible dragon." These kinds of conceits intrigued him, and more than ever metaphor began to inform the way he perceived and outlined the facts of his science.

Another happy change in his life was the cessation of his bad nights of sleeplessness and uneasy dreams. No longer was he troubled by memories of the attacks of Siegesbeck or any other of his old opponents. Linnaeus had acquired a new and resistless faith in his observations. He was finally certain that the plants of this earth carry on their love affairs in uncaring merry freedom, making whatever sexual arrangements best suit them, and that they go to replenish the globe guiltlessly, in high and winsome delight.

1977

JOHN CROWLEY

(b. 1942)

Novelty

I

HE found, quite suddenly and just as he took a stool midway down the bar, that he had been vouchsafed a theme. A notion about the nature of things that he had been turning over in his mind for some time had become, without his ever choosing it, the theme of a book. It had "fallen into place," as it's put, like the tumblers of a lock that a safecracker listens to, and—so he experienced it—with the same small, smooth sound.

The theme was the contrary pull men feel between Novelty and Security. Between boredom and adventure, between safety and dislocation, between the snug and the wild. Yes! Not only a grand human theme, but a truly *mammalian* theme, perhaps the only one. Curiosity killed the cat, we are warned, and warned with good reason, and yet we are curious. Cats could be a motif: cats asleep, taking their ease in that superlatively comfortable way they have—you feel drowsy and snug just watching them. Cats on the prowl, endlessly prying. Cats tiptoe-walking away from fearsome novelty, hair on fire and faces shocked. He chuckled, pleased with this, and lifted the glass that had been set before him. From the great window south light poured through the golden liquor, refracted delicately by ice.

The whole high front of the Seventh Saint Bar & Grill where he sat is of glass, floor to ceiling, a glass divided by vertical beams into a triptych and deeply tinted brown. During the day nothing of the dimly lit interior of the bar can be seen from the outside; walkers-by see only themselves, darkly; often they stop to adjust their clothing or their hair in what seems to them to be a mirror, or simply gaze at themselves in passing, momentarily but utterly absorbed, unaware that they are caught at it by watchers inside. (Or watcher, today, he being so

305

far the bar's sole customer.) Seen from inside the bar, the avenue, the stores opposite, the street glimpsed going off at right
angles, the trapezoid of sky visible above the lower buildings,
are altered by the tinted windows into an elsewhere, oddly
peaceful, a desert or the interior of the sea. Sometimes when
he has fallen asleep face upward in the sun, his dreams have
taken on this quality of supernatural bright darkness.

Novelty. Security. *Novelty* wouldn't be a bad title. It had the
grandness of abstraction, alerting the reader that large and
thoughtful things were to be bodied forth. As yet he had no
inkling of any incidents or characters that might occupy his
theme; perhaps he never would. He could see though the book
itself, he could feel its closed heft and see it opened, white
pages comfortably large and shadowed gray by print; dense,
numbered, full of meat. He sensed a narrative voice, speaking
calmly and precisely, with immense assurance building, building;
a voice too far off for him to hear, but speaking.

The door of the bar opened, showing him a momentary oblong of true daylight, blankly white. A woman entered. He
couldn't see her face as she crossed to the bar in front of the
window, but he could see, drawn with exactitude by the light
behind her, her legs within a summery white dress. When
young he had supposed, without giving it much thought, that
women didn't realize that sun behind them revealed them in
this way; now he supposes that of course they must, and thinks
about it.

"Well, look who's here," said the bartender. "You off today?"

"I took off," she said, and as she took a seat between him
and the window, he saw that she was known to him, that is,
they had sat here in this relation before. "I couldn't stand it
anymore. What's tall and cool and not too alcoholic?"

"How about a spritzer?"

"Okay."

He caught himself staring fixedly at her, trying to remember
if they had spoken before, and she caught him, too, raising her
eyes to him as she lifted the pale drink to her lips, large dark
eyes with startling whites; and looked away again quickly.

Where was he again? Novelty, security. He felt the feet of his
attention skate out from under him in opposite directions.
Should he make a note? He felt for the smooth shape of his pen

in his pocket. "Theme for a novel: The contrary pull . . ." No. If this notion were real, he needn't make a note. A notion on which a note had to be made would be stillborn anyway, his notebook was a parish register of such, born and dead on the same page. Let it live if it can.

But had he spoken to her before? What had he said?

II

When he was in college, a famous poet made a useful distinction for him. He had drunk enough in the poet's company to be compelled to describe to him a poem he was thinking of. It would be a monologue of sorts, the self-contemplation of a student on a summer afternoon who is reading *Euphues*. The poem itself would be a subtle series of euphuisms, translating the heat, the day, the student's concerns, into symmetrical posies; translating even his contempt and boredom with that famously foolish book into a euphuism.

The poet nodded his big head in a sympathetic, rhythmic way as this was explained to him, then told him that there are two kinds of poems. There is the kind you write; there is the kind you talk about in bars. Both kinds have value and both are poems; but it's fatal to confuse them.

In the Seventh Saint, many years later, it had struck him that the difference between himself and Shakespeare wasn't talent —not especially—but *nerve*. The capacity not to be frightened by his largest and most potent conceptions, to simply (simply!) sit down and execute them. The dreadful lassitude he felt when something really large and multifarious came suddenly clear to him, something *Lear*-sized yet sonnet-precise. If only they didn't rush on him whole, all at once, massive and perfect, leaving him frightened and nerveless at the prospect of articulating them word by scene by page. He would try to believe they were of the kind told in bars, not the kind to be written, though there was no way to be sure of this except to attempt the writing; he would raise a finger (the novelist in the bar mirror raising the obverse finger) and push forward his change. Wailing like a neglected ghost, the vast notion would beat its wings into the void.

Sometimes it would pursue him for days and years as he fled

desperately. Sometimes he would turn to face it, and do battle. Once, twice, he had been victorious, objectively at least. Out of an immense concatenation of feeling, thought, word, and transcendent meaning had come his first novel, a slim, silent pageant of a book, tombstone for his slain conception. A publisher had taken it, gingerly; had slipped it quietly into the deep pool of spring releases, where it sank without a ripple, and where he supposes it lies still, its calm Bodoni gone long since green. A second, just as slim but more lurid, nightmarish even, about imaginary murders in an imaginary exotic locale, had been sold for a movie, though the movie had never been made. He felt guilt for the producer's failure (which perhaps the producer didn't feel), having known the book could not be filmed; he had made a large sum, enough to finance years of this kind of thing, on a book whose first printing was largely returned.

His editor now and then took him to an encouraging lunch, and talked about royalties, advances, and upcoming titles, letting him know that whatever doubts he had she considered him a member of the profession, and deserving of a share in its largesse and its gossip; at their last one, some months before, she had pressed him for a new book, something more easily graspable than his others. "A couple of chapters, and an outline," she said. "I could tell from that."

Well, he *was* sort of thinking of something, but it wasn't really shaping up, or rather it was shaping up rather like the others, into something indescribable at bottom. . . . "What it would be," he said timidly, "would be sort of a Catholic novel, about growing up Catholic," and she looked warily up at him over her Campari.

The first inkling of this notion had come to him the Christmas before, at his daughter's place in Vermont. On Christmas Eve, as indifferent evening took hold in the blue squares of the windows, he sat alone in the crepuscular kitchen, imbued with a profound sense of the identity of winter and twilight, of twilight and time, of time and memory, of his childhood and that church which on this night waited to celebrate the second greatest of its feasts. For a moment or an hour as he sat, become one with the blue of the snow and the silence, a congruity of star, cradle, winter, sacrament, self, it was as though he listened to a voice that had long been trying to catch his attention, to tell him, Yes, this was the subject long withheld from him, which he now knew, and must eventually act on.

He had managed, though, to avoid it. He only brought it out now to please his editor, at the same time aware that it wasn't what she had in mind at all. But he couldn't do better; he had really only the one subject, if subject was the word for it, this idea of a notion or a holy thing growing clear in the stream of time, being made manifest in unexpected ways to an assortment of people: the revelation itself wasn't important, it could be anything, almost. Beyond that he had only one interest, the seasons, which he could describe endlessly and with all the passion of a country-bred boy grown old in the city. He was coming to doubt (he said) whether these were sufficient to make any more novels out of, though he knew that writers of genius had made great ones out of less. He supposed really (he didn't say) that he wasn't a novelist at all, but a failed poet, like a failed priest, one who had perceived that in fact he had no vocation, had renounced his vows, and yet had found nothing at all else in the world worth doing when measured by the calling he didn't have, and went on through life fatally attracted to whatever of the sacerdotal he could find or invent in whatever occupation he fell into, plumbing or psychiatry or tending bar.

III

"Boring, boring, *boring*," said the woman down the bar from him. "I feel like taking off for good." Victor, the bartender, chin in his hand and elbow on the bar, looked at her with the remote sympathy of confessors and bartenders.

"Just take off," she said.

"So take off," Victor said. "Jeez, there's a whole world out there."

She made a small noise to indicate she doubted there was. Her brilliant eyes, roving over her prospects, fell on his where they were reflected in the bar mirror. She gazed at him but (he knew) didn't see him, for she was looking within. When she did shift focus and understand she was being regarded, she smiled briefly and glanced at his real person, then bent to her drink again. He summoned the bartender.

"Another, please, Victor."

"How's the writing coming?"

"Slowly. Very slowly. I just now thought of a new one, though."

"Izzat so."

It was so; but even as he said it, as the stirring stick he had just raised out of his glass dripped whiskey drop by drop back into it, the older notion, the notion he had been unable to describe at all adequately to his editor, which he had long since dropped or thought he had dropped, stirred within him. Stirred mightily, though he tried to shut doors on it; stirred, rising, and came forth suddenly in all the panoply with which he had forgotten it had come to be dressed, its facets glittering, windows opening on vistas, great draperies billowing. It seemed to have grown old in its seclusion but more potent, and fiercely reproachful of his neglect. Alarmed, he tried to shelter his tender new notion of Novelty and Security from its onrush, but even as he attempted this, the old notion seized upon the new, and as he watched helplessly, the two coupled in an utter ravishment and interlacement, made for each other, one thing now and more than twice as compelling as each had been before. "Jesus," he said aloud; and then looked up, wondering if he had been heard. Victor and the woman were tête-à-tête, talking urgently in undertones.

IV

"I know, I know," he'd said, raising a hand to forestall his editor's objection. "The Catholic Church is a joke. Especially the Catholic Church I grew up in . . ."

"Sometimes a grim joke."

"And it's been told a lot. The nuns, the weird rules, all that decayed scholastic guff. The prescriptions, and the proscriptions —especially the proscriptions, all so trivial when they weren't hurtful or just ludicrous. But that's not the way it's perceived. For a kid, for me, the church organized the whole world—not morally, either, or not especially, but in its whole nature. Even if the kid isn't particularly moved by thoughts of God and sin—I wasn't—there's still a lot of church left over, do you see? Because all the important things about the church were real things: objects, places, words, sights, smells, days. The liturgical calendar. The Eastern church must be even more so. For me, the church was mostly about the seasons: it kept them in order. The church was coextensive with the world."

"So the kid's point of view against—"

"No, no. What I would do, see, to get around this contradiction between the real church and this other church I seemed to experience physically and emotionally, is to reimagine the Catholic Church as another kind of church altogether, a very subtle and wise church, that understood all these feelings; a church that was really—secretly—*about* these things in fact, and not what it seemed to be about; and then pretend, in the book, that the church I grew up in was that church."

"You're going to invent a whole new religion?"

"Well, not exactly. It would just be a matter of shifting emphasis, somehow, turning a thing a hundred and eighty degrees . . ."

"Well, how? Do you mean 'books in the running brooks, sermons in stones,' that kind of thing? Pantheism?"

"No. No. The opposite. In that kind of religion the trees and the sky and the weather *stand for* God or some kind of supernatural unity. In my religion, God and all the rituals and sacraments would stand for the real world. The religion would be a means of perceiving the real world in a sacramental way. A Gnostic ascension. A secret at the heart of it. And the secret is—everything. Common reality. The day outside the church window."

"Hm."

"That's what it would really have been about from the beginning. And only seemed to be about these divine personages, and stuff, and these rules."

She nodded slowly in a way that showed she followed him but frankly saw no novel. He went on, wanting at least to say it all before he no longer saw it with this clarity. "The priests and nuns would know this was the case, the wisest of them, and would guide the worshipers—the ones they thought could grasp it—to see through the paradox, to see that it *is* a paradox: that

only by believing, wholly and deeply, in all of it could you see
through it one day to what is real—see through Christmas to
the snow; see through the fasting, and the saints' lives, and the
sins, and Baby Jesus walking through the snow every Christmas night ringing a little bell—"

"What?"

"That was a story one nun told. That was a thing she said
was the case."

"Good heavens. Did she believe it?"

"Who knows? That's what I'm getting at."

She broke into her eggs Florentine with a delicate fork. The
two chapters, full of meat; the spinach of an outline. She was
very attractive in a coltish, aristocratic way, with a rosy flush on
her tanned cheeks that was just the flush his wife's cheeks had
had. No doubt still had; no doubt.

"Like Zen," he said desperately. "As though it were a kind
of Zen."

V

Well, he had known as well as she that it was no novel, no
matter that it importuned him, reminding him often of its
deep truth to his experience, and suggesting shyly how much
fun it might be to manipulate, what false histories he could invent that would account for the church he imagined. But he
had it now; now the world began to turn beneath him firmly,
both rotating and revolving; it was quite clear now.

The *theme* would not be religion at all, but this ancient conflict between novelty and security. This theme would be embodied in the contrasted adventures of a set of *characters*, a
family of Catholic believers modeled on his own. The *motion*
of the book would be the sense of a holy thing ripening in the
stream of time, that is, the seasons; and the *form* would be a
false history or mirror-reversal of the world he had known and
the church he had believed in.

Absurdly, his heart had begun to beat fast. Not years from
now, not months, very soon, imaginably soon, he could begin.
That there was still nothing concrete in what he envisioned
didn't bother him, for he was sure this scheme was one that
would generate concreteness spontaneously and easily. He had

planted a banner amid his memories and imaginings, a banner to which they could all repair, to which they were repairing even now, primitive clans vivified by these colors, clamoring to be marshaled into troops by the captains of his art.

It would take a paragraph, a page, to eliminate, say, the Reformation, and thus make his church infinitely more aged, bloated, old in power, forgetful of dogmas long grown universal and ignorable, dogmas altered by subtle subversives into their opposites, by a brotherhood within the enormous bureaucracy of faith, a brotherhood animated by a holy irony and secret as the Rosicrucians. Or contrariwise: he could pretend that the Reformation had been more nearly a complete success than it was, leaving his Roman faith a small, inward-turning, Gnostic sect, poor and not grand, guiltless of the Inquisition; its pope itinerant or in shabby exile somewhere (Douai, or Alexandria, or Albany); through Appalachia a poor priest travels from church to church, riding the circuit in an old Studebaker as rusty black as his cassock, putting up at a plain frame house on the outskirts of town, a convent. The wainscoted parlor is the nuns' chapel, and the pantry is full of their canning; in autumn the broken stalks of corn wither in their kitchen garden. "Use it up, wear it out," says the proverb of their creed (and not that of splendid and orgulous Protestants), "make it do, do without": and they possess themselves in edge-worn and threadbare truth.

Yes! The little clapboard church in Kentucky where his family had worshiped, in the Depression, amid the bumptious Baptists. In the hastening dawn he had walked a mile to serve six o'clock mass there. In winter the stove's smell was incense; in summer it was the damp odor of morning coming through the lancet windows, opened a crack to reveal a band of blue-green day beneath the feet of the saints fragilely pictured there in imitation stained glass. The three or four old Polish women always present always took Communion, their extended tongues trembling and their veined closed eyelids trembling, too; and though when they rose crossing themselves they became only unsanctified old women again, he had for a moment glimpsed their clean pink souls. There were aged and untended rosebushes on the sloping lawn of the big gray house he had grown up in—his was by far the best off of any family in that little parish—and when the roses bloomed in May the priest came and the familiar few they saw in church each week gathered, and the Virgin was crowned there, a Virgin pink and blue and white as the rose-burdened day, the best lace table-cloth beneath her, strange to see that domestic lace outdoors edge-curled by odorous breezes and walked on by bugs. He caught himself singing:

> *O Mary, we crown thee with blossoms today*
> *Queen of the Angels*
> *Queen of the May*

Of course he would lose by this scheme a thousand other sorts of memories just as dear, would lose the grand and the fatuous baroque, mitered bishops in jewel-encrusted copes and steel-rimmed eyeglasses; but the point was not nostalgia and self-indulgence after all, no, the opposite; in fact there ought to be some way of tearing the heart completely out of the old religion, or to conceive on it something so odd that no reader would ever confuse it with the original, except that it would be as concrete, its concreteness the same concreteness (which was the point . . .) And what then had been that religion's heart?

What if his Jesus hadn't saved mankind?

What if the Renaissance, besides uncovering the classical past, had discovered evidence—manuscripts, documentary proofs (incontrovertible, though only after terrible struggles)—that Jesus had in the end refused to die on the cross? Had run away; had abjured his Messiah-hood; and left his followers then to puzzle that out. It would not have been out of cowardice, exactly, though the new New Testaments would seem to say so, but (so the apologetic would come to run) out of a desire to share our human life completely, even our common unheroic fate. Because the true novelty, for God, would lie not in the redemption of men—an act he could perform with a millionth part of the creative effort he had expended in creating the world—but in being a human being entire, growing old and impotent to redeem anybody, including himself. Something like that had happened with the false messiah Sevi in the seventeenth century: his Messiah-hood spread quickly and widely through the whole Jewish world; then, at the last minute, threatened with death, he'd converted to Islam. His followers mostly fell away, but a few still believed, and their attempts to figure out how the Messiah could act in that strange way, redeem us by not redeeming us, yielded up the Hassidic sect, with its Kabbalah and its paradoxical parables, almost Zenlike; very much what he had in mind for his church.

"A man of sorrows, and acquainted with grief"—the greatest grief, far greater than a few moments' glorious pain on that Tree. Mary's idea of it was that in the end the Father was unable to permit the death of his only begotten son; the prophecy is Abraham and Isaac; she interceded for him, of course, her son, too, as she still intercedes for each of us. Perhaps he resented it. In any case he out-lived her, and his own wife and son, too; lived on, a retired carpenter, in his daughter's house; and the rabble came before his door, and they mocked him, saying: *If thou art the Christ, take up thy cross.*

Weird! But, but—what made him chuckle and nearly smack his lips (in full boil now)—the thing would be, that his characters would pursue their different destinies *completely oblivious of all this oddity*, oblivious, that is, that it *is* odd; the narrative voice wouldn't notice it either; their Resurrection has always been this ambiguous one, this Refusal; their holy-card of Jesus in despised old age (after Murillo) has always marked the Sundays in their missals; their church is just the old, the homely, the stodgy great Security, Peter's rock, which his was. His priest would venture out (bored, restless) from that security into the strange and the dangerous, at first only wishing to be a true priest, then for their own sakes, for the adventure of understanding. A nun: starting from a wild embracing of all experience, anything goes, she passes later into quietness and, well, into habit. His wife would have to sit for that portrait, of course, of course; though she wouldn't sit still. The two meet after long separation, only to pass each other at the X-point, coming from different directions, headed for different heavens —a big scene there. A saint: but which one? He or she? Well, that had always been the question; neither, or both, or one seeing at last after the other's death his sainthood, and advocating it (in the glum Vatican, a Victorian pile in Albany, the distracted pope), a miracle awaited and given at last, unexpectedly, or not given, withheld—oh, hold on, he asked, stop a minute, slow down. He plucked out and lit a cigarette with care. He placed his glass more exactly in the center of its cardboard coaster and arranged his change in orbits around it.

Flight over. Cats, though. He would appropriate for his Jesus that story about Muhammad called from his couch, tearing off his sleeve rather than disturbing the cat that had fallen asleep on it. A parable. Did Jews keep cats then? Who knows.

Oh God how subtle he would have to be, how cunning. . . . No paragraph, no phrase even of the thousands the book must contain could strike a discordant note, be less than fully imagined, an entire novel's worth of thought would have to be expended on each one. His attention had only to lapse for a moment, between preposition and object, colophon and chapter heading, for dead spots to appear like gangrene that would rot the whole. Silkworms didn't work as finely or as patiently as he must, and yet boldness was all, the large stroke, the end contained in and prophesied by the beginning, the stains of his clouds infinitely various but all signifying sunrise. Unity in diversity, all that guff. An enormous weariness flew over him. The trouble with drink, he had long known, wasn't that it started up these large things but that it belittled the awful difficulties of their execution. He drank, and gazed out into the false golden day, where a passage of girl students in plaid uniforms was just then occurring, passing secret glances through the trick mirror of the window.

VI

"I'm such a chicken," the woman said to Victor. "The other day they were going around at work signing people up for the softball team. I really wanted to play. They said come on, come on, it's no big deal, it's not professional or anything . . ."

"Sure, just fun."

"I didn't dare."

"What's to dare? Just good exercise. Fresh air."

"Sure, *you* can say that. You've probably been playing all your life." She stabbed at the last of her ice with a stirring-stick. "I really wanted to, too. I'm such a chicken."

Play right field, he wanted to advise her. That had always been his retreat, nothing much ever happens in right field, you're safe there mostly unless a left-handed batter gets up, and then if you blow one, the shame is quickly forgotten. He told himself to say to her: *You should have volunteered for right field*. But his throat said it might refuse to do this, and his pleasantry could come out a muffled croak, watch out. She had finished her drink; how much time did he have to think of a thing to say to her? Buy her a drink: the sudden offer always made him feel like a masher, a cad, something antique and repellent.

"You should have volunteered for right field," he said.

"Oh, hi," she said. "How's the writing coming?"

"What?"

"The last time we talked you were writing a novel."

"Oh. Well, I sort of go in spurts." He couldn't remember still that he had ever talked with her, much less what imaginary novel he had claimed to be writing.

"It's like coming into a cave here," she said, raising her glass, empty now except for the rounded remains of ice. "You can't see anything for a while. Because of the sun in your eyes. I didn't recognize you at first." The ice she wanted couldn't escape from the bottom of the glass till she shook the glass briskly to free it; she slid a piece into her mouth then and crunched it heedlessly (a long time since he'd been able to do that) and drew her skirt away from the stool beside her, which he had come to occupy.

"Will you have another?"

"No, nope." They smiled at each other, each ready to go on with this if the other could think of something to go on with.

"So," he said.

"Taking a break?" she said. "Do you write every day?"

"Oh, no. Oh, I sort of try. I don't work very hard, really. Really I'm on vacation. All the time. Or you could say I work all the time, too. It comes to the same thing." He'd said all this before, to others; he wondered if he'd said it to her. "It's like weekend homework. Remember? There wasn't ever a time you absolutely had to do it—there was always Saturday, then Sunday—but then there wasn't ever a time when it wasn't there to do, too."

"How awful."

Sunday dinner's rich odor declining into stale leftoverhood:

was it that incense that made Sunday Sunday, or what? For there was no part of Sunday that was not Sunday; even if, rebelling, you changed from Sunday suit to Saturday jeans when dinner was over, they felt not like a second skin, like a bold animal's useful hide, as they had the day before, but strange, all right but wrong to flesh chafed by wool, the flannel shirt too smooth, too indulgent after the starched white. And upstairs—though you kept as far from them as possible, that is, facedown and full-length on the parlor carpet, head inches from the funnies—the books and blue-lined paper waited.

"It must take a lot of self-discipline," she said.

"Oh, I don't know. I don't have much." He felt himself about to say again, and unable to resist saying, that "Dumas, I think it was Dumas, some terrifically prolific Frenchman, said that writing novels is a simple matter—if you write one page a day, you'll write one novel a year, two pages a day, two novels a year, three pages, three novels, and so on. And how long does it take to cover a page with writing? Twenty minutes? An hour? So you see. Very easy really."

"I don't know," she said, laughing. "I can't even bring myself to write a letter."

"Oh, now *that's* hard." Easiest to leave it all just as it had been, and only inveigle into it a small sect of his own making . . . easiest of all just to leave it. It was draining from him, like the suits of the bathing beauties pictured on trick tumblers, to opposite effect. Self-indulgence only, nostalgia, pain of loss for what had not ever been worth saving: the self-indulgence of a man come to that time when the poignance of memory is his sharpest sensation, grown sharp as the others have grown blunt. The journey now quite obviously more than half over, it had begun to lose interest; only the road already traveled still seemed full of promise. Promise! Odd word. But there it was. He blinked, and having fallen rudely silent, said, "Well, well, well."

"Well," she said. She had begun to gather up the small habitation she had made before her on the bar, purse and open wallet, folded newspaper, a single unblown rose he hadn't noticed her bring in. "I'd like to read your book sometime."

"Sure," he said. "It's not very good. I mean, it has some nice things in it, it's a good little story. But it's nothing really."

"I'm sure it's terrific." She spun the rose beneath her nose and alighted from her stool.

"I happen to have a lot of copies. I'll give you one."

"Good. Got to go."

On her way past him she gave the rose to Victor without any other farewell. Once again sun described her long legs as she crossed the floor (sun lay on its boards like gilding, sun was impartial), and for a moment she paused, sun-blinded maybe, in the garish lozenge of real daylight made when she opened the door. Then she reappeared in the other afternoon of the window. She raised her hand in a command, and a cab the color of marigolds appeared before her as though conjured. A flight of pigeons filled up the window all in an instant, seeming stationary there like a sculpted frieze, and then just as instantly didn't fill it up anymore.

"Crazy," Victor said.

"Hm?"

"Crazy broad." He gestured with the rose toward the vacant window. "My wife. You married?"

"I was. Like the pumpkin eater." Handsome guy, Victor, in a brutal, black-Irish way. Like most New York bartenders, he was really an actor, or was it the reverse?

"Divorced?"

"Separated."

He tested his thumb against the pricks of the rose. "Women. They say you got all the freedom. Then you give them their freedom, and they don't want it."

He nodded, though it wasn't wisdom that his own case would have yielded up. He was only glad now not to miss her any longer; and now and then, sad that he was glad. The last precipitate was that occasionally when a woman he'd been looking at, on a bus, in a bar, got up to leave, passing away from him for good, he felt a shooting pang of loss absurd on the face of it.

Volunteer, he thought, but for right field. And if standing there you fall into a reverie, and the game in effect goes on without you, well, you knew it would when you volunteered for the position. Only once every few innings the lost—the not-even-noticed-till-too-late—fly ball makes you sorry that things are as they are and not different, and you wonder if people think you might be bored and indifferent out there, contemptuous even, which isn't the case at all. . . .

"On the house," Victor said, and rapped his knuckles lightly on the bar.

"Oh, hey, thanks." Kind Victor, though the glass put before him contained a powerful solvent, he knew that even as he raised the glass to his lips. He could still fly, oh yes, always, though the cost would be terrible. But what was it he fled from? Self-indulgence, memory dearer to him than any adventure, solitude, lapidary work in his very own mines . . . what could be less novel, more secure? And yet it seemed dangerous; it seemed he hadn't the nerve to face it; he felt unarmed against it.

Novelty and Security: the security of novelty, the novelty of security. Always the full thing, the whole subject, the *true* subject, stood just behind the one you found yourself contemplating. The trick, but it wasn't a trick, was to take up at once the thing you saw and the reason you saw it as well; to always bite off more than you could chew, and then chew it. If it were self-indulgence for him to cut and polish his semiprecious memories, and yet seem like danger, like a struggle he was unfit for, then self-indulgence was a potent force, he must examine it, he must reckon with it.

And he would reckon with it: on that last Sunday in Advent, when his story was all told, the miracle granted or refused, the boy would lift his head from the books and blue-lined paper, the questions that had been set for him answered, and see that it had begun to snow.

Snow not falling but flying sidewise, and sudden, not signaled by the slow curdling of clouds all day and a flake or two drifting downward, but rushing forward all at once as though sent for. (The blizzard of '36 had looked like that.) And filling up the world's concavities, pillowing up in the gloaming, making night light with its whiteness, and then falling still in everyone's dreams, falling for pages and pages; steepling (so an old man would dream in his daughter's house) the plain frame convent on the edge of town, and drifting up even to the eyes of the martyrs pictured on the sash windows of the little clapboard church, Our Lady of the Valley; the wind full of howling white riders tearing the shingles from the roof, piling the snow still higher, blizzarding the church away entirely and the convent too and all the rest of it, so that by next day oblivion whiter than the hair of God would have returned the world to normality, covering his false history and all its works in the deep ordinariness of two feet of snow; and at evening the old man in his daughter's house would sit looking out over the silent calm alone at the kitchen table, a congruence of star, cradle, season, sacrament, etc., end of chapter thirty-five, the next page a fly-leaf blank as snow.

The whole thing, the full thing, the step taken backward that frames the incomprehensible as in a window. *Novelty*: there was, he just then saw, a pun in the title.

He rose. Victor, lost in thought, watched the hurrying crowds that had suddenly filled the streets, afternoon gone, none with time to glance at themselves; hurrying home. One page a day, seven a week, thirty or thirty-one to the month. Fishing in his pocket for a tip, he came up with his pen, a thick black fountain pen. Fountain: it seemed less flowing, less forthcoming than that, in shape more like a bullet or a bomb.

1983

JONATHAN CARROLL

(b. 1949)

Mr Fiddlehead

ON my fortieth birthday, Lenna Rhodes invited me over for lunch. That's the tradition—when one of us has a birthday, there's lunch, a nice present and a good laughing afternoon to cover the fact we've moved one more step down the staircase.

We met years ago when we happened to marry into the same family: six months after I said yes to Eric Rhodes, she said it to his brother Michael. Lenna got the better end of *that* wishbone: she and Michael are still delighted with each other, while Eric and I fought about everything and nothing and then got divorced.

But to my surprise and relief, they were a great help to me during the divorce, even though there were obvious difficulties climbing over some of the thorn-bushes of family and blood allegiance.

They live in a big apartment up on 100th Street with long halls and not much light. But the gloom of the place is offset by their kids' toys everywhere, colourful jackets stacked on top of each other, coffee cups with 'World's Greatest Mom' and 'Dartmouth' written on the side. Theirs is a home full of love and hurry, children's drawings on the fridge alongside reminders to buy *La Stampa*. Michael owns a very elegant vintage-fountain-pen store, while Lenna freelances for *Newsweek*. Their apartment is like their life: high ceilinged, thought out, overflowing with interesting combinations and possibilities. It is always nice to go there and share it a while.

I felt pretty good about forty years old. Finally there was some money in the bank, and someone I liked talking to about a trip together to Egypt in the spring. Forty was a milestone, but one that didn't mean much at the moment. I already thought of myself as being slightly middle-aged anyway, but I was healthy and had good prospects so, So What! to the beginning of my fifth decade.

'You cut your hair!'

'Do you like it?'

'You look very French.'

'Yes, but do you *like* it?'

'I think so. I have to get used to it. Come on in.'

We sat in the living room and ate. Elbow, their bull-terrier, rested his head on my knee and never took his eye off the table. After the meal was over, we cleared the plates and she handed me a small red box.

'I hope you like it. I made them myself.'

Inside the box were a pair of the most beautiful gold earrings I have ever seen.

'My God, Lenna! They're *exquisite*! You *made* these? I didn't know you made jewellery.'

She looked happily embarrassed. 'You like them? They're real gold, believe it or not.'

'I believe it. They're art! You *made* them, Lenna? I can't get over it. They're really works of art; they look like something by Klimt.' I took them carefully out of the box and put them on.

She clapped her hands like a girl. 'Oh, Juliet, they really do look good!'

Our friendship *is* important and goes back a long way, but this was a lifetime present—one you gave to a spouse or someone who'd saved your life.

Before I could say that (or anything else), the lights went out. Her two young sons brought in the birthday cake, forty candles strong.

A few days later I was walking down Madison Avenue and, caught by something there, looked in a jewellery-store window. There they were—my birthday earrings. The exact ones. Looking closer, open mouthed, I saw the price tag. Five thousand dollars! I stood and gaped for what must have been minutes. Either way, it was shocking. Had she lied about making them? Or spent five thousand dollars for my birthday present? Lenna wasn't a liar and she wasn't rich. All right, so she had had them copied in brass or something and just *said* they were gold to make me feel good. That wasn't her way either. What the hell was going on?

The confusion emboldened me to walk right into that store. Or rather, walk right up and press their buzzer. After a short wait, someone rang me in. The salesgirl who appeared from behind a curtain looked like she'd graduated from Radcliffe with a degree in blue-stocking. Maybe one had to to work in this place.

'Can I help you?'

'Yes. I'd like to see those earrings you have in the window.'

Looking at my ears, it was as if a curtain rose from in front of her regard, i.e., when I first entered, I was only another no-body in a plaid skirt asking for a moment's sniff of their palace air. But realizing I had a familiar five grand hanging off my lobes changed everything; this woman would be my slave—or friend—for life, I only had to say which.

'Of course, the Dixies.'

'The what?'

She smiled, like I was being very funny. It quickly dawned on me that she must have thought I knew very well what 'Dixies' were because I was wearing some.

She took them out of the window and put them carefully down in front of me on a blue velvet card. They were beautiful and, admiring them, I entirely forgot for a while I had some on.

'I'm so surprised you have a pair. They only came into the store a week ago.'

Thinking fast, I said, 'My husband bought them for me and I like them so much I'm thinking of getting a pair for my sister.

'Tell me about the designer. His name is Dixie?'

'I don't know much, madam. Only the owner knows who Dixie is, where they come from . . . And that whoever it is is a real genius. Apparently both Bulgari and people from the Memphis group have already been in asking who it is and how they can contact him.'

'How do you know it's a man?' I put the earrings down and looked directly at her.

'Oh, I don't. It's just that the work is so masculine that I as-sumed it. Maybe you're right; maybe it *is* a woman.' She picked one up and held it to the light. 'Did you notice how they don't really reflect light so much as enhance it? Golden light. You can own it any time you want. I've never seen that. I envy you.'

They were real. I went to a jeweller on 47th Street to have them appraised, then to the only other two stores in the city that sold 'Dixies'. No one knew anything about the creator, or weren't talking if they did. Both dealers were very respectful and pleasant, but mum was the word when I asked about the jewellery's origin.

'The gentleman asked us not to give out information, madam. We must respect his wishes.'

'But it *is* a man?'

A professional smile. 'Yes.'

'Could I contact him through you?'

'Yes, I'm sure that would be possible. Can I help with anything else, madam?'

'What other pieces did he design?'

'As far as I know, only the earrings, the fountain pen, and this keyring.' He'd already shown me the pen which was nothing special. Now he brought out a small golden keyring shaped in a woman's profile. Lenna Rhodes' profile.

The doorbell tinkled when I walked into the store. Michael was with a customer and smiling hello, gave me the sign he'd be over as soon as he was finished. He had started 'Ink' almost as soon as he got out of college, and it was a success from the beginning. Fountain pens are cranky, unforgiving things that demand full attention and patience. But they are also a handful of flash and old-world elegance; gratifying slowness that offers no reward other than the sight of shiny ink flowing wetly across a dry page. Ink's customers were both rich and not so, but all of them had the same collector's fiery glint in their eye and addict's desire for more. A couple of times a month I'd work there when Michael needed an extra hand. It taught me to be cheered by old pieces of Bakelite and gold-plate, as well as another kind of passion.

'Juliet, hi! Roger Peyton was in this morning and bought that yellow Parker "Duofold". The one he's been looking at for months?'

'Finally. Did he pay full price?'

Michael grinned and looked away. 'Rog can never afford full price. I let him do it in instalments. What's up with you?'

'Did you ever hear of a "Dixie" pen? Looks a little like the Cartier "Santos"?'

'"Dixie". No. It looks like the Santos?' The expression on his face said he was telling the truth.

I brought out the brochure from the jewellery store and, opening it to the pen photograph, handed it to him. His reaction was immediate.

'That bastard! How much do I have to put up with with this man?'

'You know him?'

Michael looked up from the photo, anger and confusion competing for first place on his face. 'Do I know him? Sure I know him. He lives in my goddamned *house* I know him so well! "Dixie", huh? Cute name. Cute man.

'Wait. I'll show you something, Juliet. Just stay there. Don't move! That shit.'

There's a mirror behind the front counter at Ink. When Michael charged off to the back of the store, I looked at my reflection and said, '*Now* you did it.'

He was back in no time. 'Look at this. You want to see something beautiful? Look at this.' He handed me a blue velvet case. I opened it and saw . . . the Dixie fountain pen.

'But you said you'd never heard of them.'

His voice was hurt and loud. 'It is *not* a Dixie fountain pen. It's a Sinbad. An original, solid gold Sinbad made at the Benjamin Swire Fountain-Pen Works in Konstanz, Germany, around 1915. There's a rumour the Italian Futurist Antonio Sant' Elia did the design, but that's never been proven. Nice, isn't it?'

It *was* nice, but he was so angry that I wouldn't have dared say no. I nodded eagerly.

He took it back. 'I've been selling pens twenty years, but've only seen two of these in all that time. One was owned by Walt Disney and I have the other. Collector's value? About seven thousand dollars. But as I said, you just don't find them.'

'Won't the Dixie people get in trouble for copying it?'

'No, because I'm sure they either bought the design, or

there are small differences between the original and this new one. Let me see that brochure again.'

'But you have an original, Michael. It still holds its value.'

'That's not the point! It's not the value that matters. I'd never sell this.

'You know the classic "bathtub" Porsche? One of the strangest, greatest-looking cars of all time. Some smart, cynical person realized that and is now making fibreglass copies of the thing. They're very well done and full of all the latest features.

'But it's a lie car, Juliet; sniff it and it smells only of today— little plastic things and cleverly cut corners you can't see. Not important to the car, but essential to the real *object*. The wonder of the thing was that Porsche designed it so well and thoughtfully so long ago. That's art. But the art is in its original everything, not just the look or the convincing copy. I can guarantee you your Dixie pen has too much plastic inside where you can't see it, and a gold point that probably has about a third as much gold on it as the original. Looks good, but they always miss the whole point with these cut corners.

'Look, you're going to find out sooner or later, so I think you better know now.'

'What are you talking about?'

He brought a telephone up from beneath the counter and gestured for me to wait a bit. He called Lenna and in a few words told her about the Dixies, my discovery of them . . .

He was looking at me when he asked, 'Did he tell you he was doing that, Lenna?'

Whatever her long answer was, it left his expression deadpan. 'Well, I'm going to bring Juliet home. I want her to meet him. What? Because we've got to do something about it, Lenna! Maybe she'll have an idea of what to do. Do you think this is normal? Oh, you *do*? That's interesting. Do you think it's normal for *me*?' A dab of saliva popped off his lip and flew across the store.

When Michael opened the door, Lenna stood right on the other side, arms crossed tight over her chest. Her soft face was squinched into a tense challenge.

'Whatever he told you probably isn't true, Juliet.'

I put up both hands in surrender. 'He didn't tell me anything,

Lenna. I don't even want to *be* here. I just showed him a picture of a pen.'

Which wasn't strictly true. I showed him a picture of a pen because I wanted to know more about 'Dixie' and maybe my five-thousand-dollar earrings. Yes, sometimes I am nosy. My ex-husband used to tell me that too often.

Both of the Rhodeses were calm and sound people. I don't think I'd ever seen them really disagree on anything important or raise their voices at each other.

Michael growled, 'Where is he? Eating again?'

'Maybe. So what? You don't like what he eats, anyway.'

He turned to me. 'Our guest is a vegetarian. His favourite food is plum stones.'

'Oh, that's *mean*, Michael. That's really mean.' She turned and left the room.

'So he is in the kitchen? Good. Come on, Juliet.' He took my hand and pulled me behind on his stalk to their visitor.

Before we got to him I heard music. Ragtime piano. Scott Joplin?

A man sat at the table with his back to us. He had long red hair down over the collar of his sports jacket. One freckled hand was fiddling with the dial on a radio nearby.

'Mr Fiddlehead? I'd like you to meet Lenna's best friend, Juliet Skotchdopole.'

He turned, but even before he was all the way around, I knew I was sunk. What a face! Ethereally thin, with high cheekbones and deep-set green eyes that were both merry and profound. Those storybook eyes, the carroty hair and freckles everywhere. How could freckles suddenly be so damned sexy? They were for children and cute advertisements. I wanted to touch every one on him.

'Hello, Juliet! "Skotchdopole", is it? That's a good name. I wouldn't mind havin' it myself. It's a lot better than Fiddlehead, you know.' His deep voice lay in a hammock of a very strong Irish accent.

I put out a hand and we shook. Looking down, I ran my thumb once quickly, softly across the top of his hand. I felt hot and dizzy, like someone I wanted had put their hand gently between my legs for the first time.

He smiled. Maybe he sensed it. There was a yellow plate of

something on the table next to the radio. To stop staring so embarrassingly at him, I focused on it and realized the plate was full of plum stones.

'Do you like them? They're delicious.' He picked one off the shiny orange/brown pile and, slipping the stony thing in his mouth, bit down. Something cracked loud, like he'd broken a tooth, but he kept his angel's smile on while crunching away.

I looked at Michael who only shook his head. Lenna came into the kitchen and gave Mr Fiddlehead a big hug and kiss. He only smiled and went on eating . . . stones.

'Juliet, the first thing you have to know is I lied about your birthday present. I didn't make those earrings—Mr Fiddlehead did. But since he's me, I wasn't *really* lying.' She smiled as if she was sure I understood what she was talking about. I looked at Michael for help, but he was poking around in the refrigerator. Beautiful Mr Fiddlehead was still eating.

'What do you mean, Lenna, he's "you"?'

Michael took out a carton of milk and, at the same time, a plum, which he exaggeratedly offered his wife. She made a face at him and snatched it out of his hand.

Biting it, she said, 'Remember I told you I was an only child? Like a lot of lonely kids, I solved my problem the best way I could—by making up an imaginary friend.'

My eyes widened. I looked at the red-headed man. He winked at me.

Lenna went on. 'I made up Mr Fiddlehead. I read and dreamed so much then that one day I put it all together into my idea of the perfect friend. First, his name would be "Mr Fiddlehead", because I thought that was the funniest name in the world; something that would always make me laugh when I was sad. Then he had to come from Ireland because that was the home of all the leprechauns and faeries. In fact, I wanted a kind of life-sized human leprechaun. He'd have red hair and green eyes and, whenever I wanted, the magical ability to make gold bracelets and jewellery for me out of thin air.'

'Which explains the Dixie jewellery in the stores?'

Michael nodded. 'He said he got bored just hanging around, so I suggested he do something useful. Everything was fine so long as it was just the earrings and keychain.'

He slammed the glass down on the counter. 'But I didn't know about the fountain pen until today. What's with *that*, Fiddlehead?'

'Because I wanted to try me hand at it. I loved the one you showed me, so I thought I'd use that as my model. Why not? You can't improve on perfection. The only thing I did was put some more gold in it here and there.'

I put my hand up like a student with a question. 'But who's Dixie?'

Lenna smiled and said, 'I am. That was the secret name I made up for myself when I was little. The only other person who knew it was my secret friend.' She stuck her thumb in the other's direction.

'Wonderful! So now "Dixie" fountain pens, which are lousy rip-offs of Sinbads, will he bought by every asshole in New York who can afford to buy a Piaget watch or a Hermès briefcase. It makes me sick.' Michael glared at the other man and waited belligerently for a reply.

Mr Fiddlehead's reply was to laugh like Woody Woodpecker.

Which cracked both Lenna and me up.

Which sent her husband storming out of the kitchen.

'Is it true?'

They both nodded.

'I had an imaginary friend too when I was little! The Bimbergooner. But I've never seen them for real.'

'Maybe you didn't make him real enough. Maybe you just cooked him up when you were sad or needed someone to talk to. In Lenna's case, the more she needed me, the more real I became. She needed me a lot. One day I was just there for good.'

I looked at my friend. 'You mean he's been here since you were a girl? Living with you?'

She laughed. 'No. As I grew up I needed him less. I was happier and had more friends. My life got fuller. So he was around less.' She reached over and touched his shoulder.

He smiled but it was a sad one, full of memories. 'I can give her huge pots of gold and do great tricks. I've even been practising ventriloquism and can throw my voice a little. But you'd be surprised how few women love ventriloquists.

'If you two'll excuse me, I think I'll go in the other room and watch TV with the boys. It's about time for "The Three

Stooges". Remember how much we loved that show, Lenna? I think we saw one episode ten times. The one where they open up the hairdressing salon in Mexico?'

'I remember. You loved Moe and I loved Curly.'

They beamed at each other over the shared memory.

'But wait, if he's . . . what you say, how come he came back now?'

'You didn't know it, but Michael and I went through a *very* bad period a little while ago. He even moved out for two weeks and we both thought that was it: no more marriage. One night I got into bed crying like a fool and wishing to hell Mr Fiddlehead was around again to help me. And then suddenly there he was, standing in the bathroom doorway smiling at me.' She squeezed his shoulder again. He covered her hand with his own.

'God, Lenna, what did you do?'

'Screamed! I didn't recognize him.'

'What do you mean?'

'I mean he grew up! The Mr Fiddlehead I imagined when I was a child was exactly my age. I guess as I got older so did he. It makes sense.'

'I'm going to sit down now. I have to sit down because this has been the strangest afternoon of my life.' Fiddlehead jumped up and gave me his seat. I took it. He left the room for television with the boys. I watched him go. Without thinking, I picked up Michael's half-empty glass of milk and finished it. 'Everything that you told me is true?'

She put up her right hand. 'I swear on our friendship.'

'That beautiful man out there is an old dream of yours?'

Her head recoiled. 'Oo, do you think he's beautiful? Really? I think he's kind of funny-looking, to tell the truth. I love him as a friend, but—' she looked guiltily at the door—'I'd never want to go *out* with him or anything.'

But *I* did, so we did. After the first few dates I would have gone and hunted rats with him in the South Bronx if that's what he liked. I was, as expected, completely gone for him. The line of a man's neck can change your life. The way he digs in his pockets for change can make the heart squawk and hands grow cold. How he touches your elbow or the button that is not closed on the cuff of his shirt are demons he's loosed with-out ever knowing it. They own us immediately. He was a thor-oughly compelling man. I wanted to rise to the occasion of his presence in my life and become something more than I'd pre-viously thought myself capable of.

I think he began to love me too, but he didn't say things like that. Only that he was happy, or that he wanted to share things he'd held in reserve all his life.

Because he knew sooner or later he'd have to go away (*where* he never said, and I stopped asking), he seemed to have thrown all caution to the wind. But before him, I had never thrown anything away, caution included. I'd been a careful reader of timetables, made the bed tight and straight first thing every morning, and hated dishes in the sink. My life at forty was comfortably narrow and ordered. Going haywire or off the deep end wasn't in my repertoire, and normally people who did made me squint.

I realized I was in love *and* haywire the day I taught him to play racquetball. After we'd batted it around an hour, we were sitting in the gallery drinking Coke. He flicked sweat from his forehead with two fingers. A hot, intimate drop fell on my wrist. I put my hand over it quickly and rubbed it into my skin. He didn't see. I knew then I'd have to learn to put whatever expectations I had aside and just live purely in his jet-stream, no matter where it took me. That day I realized I'd sacrifice anything for him and for a few hours I went around feeling like some kind of holy person, a zealot, love made flesh.

'Why does Michael let you stay there?'

He took a cigarette from my pack. He began smoking a week before and loved it. Almost as much as he liked to drink, he said. The perfect Irishman.

'Don't forget he was the one who left Lenna, not vice-versa. When he came back he was pretty much on his knees to her. He had to be. There wasn't a lot he could say about me being there. Especially after he found out who I was. Do you have any plum stones around?'

'Question two—why in God's name do you eat those things?'

'That's easy: because plums are Lenna's favourite fruit.

When she was a little girl, she'd have tea parties for just us two. Scott Joplin music, imaginary tea and real plums. She'd eat the fruit then put the stone on my plate to eat. Makes perfect sense.'

I ran my fingers through his red hair, loving the way my fingers got caught in all the thick curls. 'That's disgusting. It's like slavery! Why am I getting to the point where I don't like my best friend so much any more?'

'If you like me, you should like her, Juliet—she made me.'

I kissed his fingers. '*That* part I like. Would you ever consider moving in with me?'

He kissed my hand. 'I would love to consider that, but I have to tell you I don't think I'll be around very much longer. But if you'd like, I'll stay with you until I, uh, have to go.'

I sat up. 'What are you talking about?'

He put his hand close to my face. 'Look hard and you'll see.'

It took a moment but then there it was; from certain angles I could see right through the hand. It had become vaguely transparent.

'Lenna's happy again. It's the old story—when she's down she needs me and calls.' He shrugged. 'When she's happy again, I'm not needed, so she sends me away. Not consciously, but . . . Look, we all know I'm her little Frankenstein monster. She can do what she *wants* with me. Even dream up that I like to eat fucking plum stones.'

'It's so wrong!'

Sighing, he sat up and started pulling on his shirt. It's wrong, but it's life, sweet girl. Not much we can do about it, you know.'

'Yes we can. We can do something.'

His back was to me. I remembered the first time I'd ever seen him. His back was to me then too. The long red hair falling over his collar.

When I didn't say anything more, he turned and looked at me over his shoulder, smiling.

'We can do something? What can we do?' His eyes were gentle and loving, eyes I wanted to see for the rest of my life.

'We can make her sad. We can make her need you.'

'What do you mean?'

'Just what I said, Fiddy. When she's sad she needs you. We have to decide what would make her sad a long time. Maybe something to do with Michael. Or their children.'

His fingers had stopped moving over the buttons. Thin, artistic fingers. Freckles.

1989

JOYCE CAROL OATES

(b. 1938)

Family

THE days were brief and attenuated and the season appeared to be fixed—neither summer nor winter, spring nor fall. A thermal haze of inexpressible sweetness, though bearing tiny bits of grit or mica, had eased into the Valley from the industrial region to the north and there were nights when the sun set at the western horizon as if it were sinking through a porous red mass, and there were days when a hard-glaring moon like bone remained fixed in a single position, prominent in the sky. Above the patchwork of excavated land bordering our property—all of which had formerly been our property in Grandfather's time: thousands of acres of wheat, corn, oats, and open grazing land—a curious trembling rainbow sometimes defined itself, its colors shifting even as you stared, shades of blue, blue-green, blue-purple, orange, orange-red, orange-yellow, a translucent yellow that dissolved into mere moisture as the thermal breeze stirred, warm as an exhaled breath. And if you had run to tell others of the rainbow it was likely to be gone when they came. "Liar," my older brothers and sisters said, "don't say such things if you don't mean them!" Father said, frowning, "Don't say such things at all if you aren't certain they will be true for others, not simply for yourself."

This begins in the time of family celebration—after Father succeeded in selling all but a few of the acres of land surrounding our house, his inheritance from Grandfather, and he and Mother were giddy as children with relief at having escaped the luckless fate of certain of our neighbors in the Valley, rancher-rivals of Grandfather's and their descendants, who had sold off their property years ago, before the market had begun to realize its full potential. (*Full potential* were words that Father often uttered, rolling the words about in his mouth like round, smooth stones whose taste absorbed him.) Now they were landless, and their investments were shaky and they had

335

made their homes in cities of increasing inhospitality, where no country people could endure to live for long. They had virtually prostituted themselves, Father said, sighing, and smiling—and for so little! It was a saying of Grandfather's that a curse would befall anyone in the Valley who gloated over a neighbor's misfortune, but as Father said, it was damned difficult not to feel superior in this instance. And Mother vehemently agreed.

Our house was made of stone, stucco, and clapboard; the newer wings, designed by a big-city architect, had a good deal of glass, and looked out into the Valley, where on good days we could see for many miles while on humid hazy days we could see barely beyond the fence that marked the edge of our property. Father, however, preferred the roof: In his white, light-woolen three-piece suit, white fedora cocked back on his head, for luck, he spent many of his waking hours on the highest peak of the highest roof of the house, observing, through binoculars, the amazing progress of construction in the Valley—for overnight, it seemed, there appeared roads, expressways, sewers, drainage pipes, "planned" communities with such names as Whispering Glades, Murmuring Oaks, Pheasant Run, Deer Willow, all of them walled to keep out intruders, and, yet more astonishing, towerlike buildings of aluminum and glass and steel and brick, buildings whose windows shone and winked like mirrors, splendid in sunshine like pillars of flame; such beauty where once there had been mere earth and sky, it caught at your throat like a great bird's talons, taking your breath away. "The ways of beauty are as a honeycomb," Father told us, and none of us could determine, staring at his slow-moving lips, whether the truth he spoke was a happy truth or not, whether even it was truth.

So mesmerized was Father by the transformation of the Valley, perceived with dreamlike acuity through the twin lenses of his binoculars, the poor man often forgot were he was; failed to come down for dinner, or for bed; and if Mother, thinking to indulge him, or hurt by his indifference to her, did not send one of the servants to summon him, he was likely to spend the entire night on the roof . . . and in the morning, smiling sheepishly, he would explain that he'd fallen asleep, or, conversely, that he had been troubled by having seen things for which he could not account—shadows the size of longhorns moving beyond our twelve-foot barbed-wire fence, and mysterious winking lights fifty miles away in the foothills. Mother dismissed the shadows as optical illusions caused by Father's overwrought constitution, or the ghosts of old, long-since-slaughtered livestock; the lights, she said, were surely from the private airport at Furnace Creek—had Father forgotten already that he'd sold a large parcel of land for a small airport there? "These lights more resemble fires," Father said stubbornly. "And they were in the foothills, not in the plain."

There were times then of power failures, and financial losses, and Father was forced to give up nearly all of our servants, but he retained his rooftop vigil, white-clad, powerful lenses to his eyes, for he perceived himself as a witness and thought, should he live to a ripe old age, as Grandfather had (Grandfather was in his ninety-ninth year when he died, and then in a fall from a wasp-stung horse), he would be a chronicler of our time, like Thucydides of his, for "Is there a world struggling to be born, or only struggle?"

Because of numerous dislocations in the Valley, of which we learned by degrees, the abandonment of houses, farms, livestock, even pets, it happened that packs of dogs began to roam about looking for food, particularly by night, poor starveling creatures that were becoming a nuisance in the region and should be, as authorities urged, shot down on sight—these dogs being not feral by birth of course but formerly domesticated terriers, setters, cocker spaniels, German shepherds, Labrador retrievers, even the larger and coarser breed of poodle—and it was the cause of some friction between Mother and Father that, despite his presence on the roof at all hours of the day and night, Father failed nonetheless to see a band of dogs dig beneath our fence and silently make their way to the dairy barn, where with terrifying efficiency they tore out the throats —and surely this could not have been in silence!—of our last six holsteins, and our last two she-goats, preparatory to devouring the poor creatures; nor did Father notice anything out of the ordinary on the night that two homeless derelicts, formerly farmhands of ours, impaled themselves on the fence (which was electrically charged, though in compliance with County Farm and Home Office regulations) and were found, dead, in the morning. (It was Kit, our sixteen-year-old, who found them, and the sight of the men, he said, tore his heart—so skinny, gray, grizzled, he scarcely recognized them. And the crows had been at them early.)

Following this episode Father journeyed to the state capital, with the purpose of taking out a loan, and reestablishing, as he called it, old ties with his politician friends, and Mother joined him a few days later for a greatly needed change of scene, as she said—"Not that I don't love you all, and the farm, but I need to breathe other air for a while"—leaving us under the care of Mrs. Hoyt our housekeeper and our eldest sister, Cory. The decision to leave us at this time was not a judicious one: Mother had forgotten that Mrs. Hoyt was in poor health, or perhaps she had decided not to care; and she seemed ignorant of the fact that Cory, for all the innocence of her marigold eyes and melodic voice, was desperately in love with one of the National Guardsmen who patrolled the Valley in jeeps, authorized to shoot wild dogs and, upon certain occasions, vandals, would-be arsonists, and squatters who were deemed a threat to the public well-being. And when Mother returned, unaccompanied by Father, after what seemed to us a very long absence (two weeks? two months?) it was with shocking news: She and Father had, after heart-searching deliberation, decided that, for the good of all concerned, they must separate—they must officially dissolve the marriage bond. Mother's voice wavered as she spoke but fierce little pinpoints of light shone in her eyes. We children were so taken by surprise we could not speak at first. Separate! Dissolve! For the good of all! We stood staring and mute; not even Cory, Kit, and Dale, not even Lona, who was the most impulsive of us, found words with which to protest; the youngest children began whimpering helplessly, soon joined by the rest—and by our few remaining servants; and Mrs. Hoyt, whose features were already bloated by illness. Mother said, "Don't! Please! I can hardly bear the pain myself!" She then played a video of Father's farewell to the family, which drew fresh tears . . . for there, suddenly framed on our television screen, where we had never seen his image before, and could not in our wildest fancies have imagined it, was Father, somberly dressed, his hair in thin steely bands combed wetly across the dome of his skull, and his eyes puffy, an unnatural sheen to his face as if it had been scoured hard. He sat stiffly erect in a chair with a high ornately carved back; his fingers were gripping the arms so tightly the blood had drained from his knuckles; his words were slow, halting, and faint, like the progress of a gut-shot deer across a field, but unmistakably his: *Dear children your mother and I after thirty years of marriage of very happy marriage have decided to . . . have decided to . . . have decided to. . . .* One of the low-flying helicopters belonging to the National Guardsmen soared past the house, making the television screen shudder, but the sound seemed to be garbled in any case, as if the tape had been clumsily cut and spliced; there were miniature lightning flashes; and Father's dear face turned liquid, melting horizontally, his eyes long and narrow as slugs and his mouth distended like a drowning man's; and all we could hear were sounds, not words, resembling *Help me* or *I am innocent* or *I love you dear children*—and then the screen was dead.

That afternoon Mother introduced us to the man who was to be Father's successor in the household, and to his three children, who were to be our new brothers and sister, and we shook hands shyly, in a state of mutual shock, and regarded one another with wide staring eyes. Our new Father! Our new brothers and sister! As Mother explained patiently her new husband was no *step*father but a genuine *father*, which meant that we were to call him "Father" at all times, and even, in our most private innermost thoughts, we were to think of him as "Father": for otherwise he would be very hurt, and very displeased. And so too with Einar and Erastus, our new brothers (not *step*brothers), and Fifi, our new sister (not *step*sister).

Our new Father stood before us beaming, a man of our former Father's approximate age but heavier and more robust than that Father, with an unusually large head, the cranium particularly developed, and small shrewd quick-darting eyes beneath brows of bone. He wore a fashionably tailored suit so dark as to resemble an undertaker's, and sported a red carnation in his lapel; his black shoes shone so splendidly they might have been phosphorescent. "Hello Father," we murmured, hardly daring to raise our eyes to his. "Hello Father." "Hello. . . ." The man's jaws were elongated, the lower jaw a good inch longer than the upper, so that a wet malevolent ridge of teeth was revealed; and, as often happened in those days, a single thought shot like lightning among us children, from one to the other to the other to the other, each of us smiling guiltily as it struck us: *Crocodile!* Only little Jori burst into tears when the thought passed into her head and after an embarrassed moment our new Father stooped to pick her up in his arms and comfort her . . . and some of us could virtually see how the memory of our former Father passed from her, as cruelly as if it had been hosed out of her skull. She was three years old then, and not accountable for her behavior.

New Father's children were tall, big-boned, solemn, with a greenish peevish cast to their skin, like many city children; the boys had inherited their father's large head and protruding crocodile jaws but the girl, Fifi, seventeen years old, was eye-catching in her beauty, with hair as mutinous as Cory's, and wide-set brown eyes in which something wolfish glimmered.

That evening certain of the boys—Dale, Kit, and Hewett—gathered close around Fifi, telling her wild tales of the Valley, how we had to protect ourselves with rifles and shotguns from trespassers, and how there was a resurgence of rats and other rodents on the farm, as a consequence of so much excavation in the countryside, and these tales, silly as they were, and exaggerated, made the girl shudder and giggle and lean toward the boys as if she were in need of their protection. And when Dale hurried off to get Fifi a goblet of ice water—at her request—she took the glass from his fingers and lifted it prissily to the light to examine its contents, asking, "Is this water *pure?* Is it safe to *drink?*" It was true, our water was sometimes strangely effervescent, and tasted of rust; after a heavy rainfall there were likely to be tiny red wriggly things in it, like animated tails; so we had learned not to examine it too closely, and as our initial attacks of nausea, diarrhea, and faint-headedness had more or less subsided, we rarely thought of it any longer but tried to be grateful, as Mrs. Hoyt used to urge us, that we had any drinking water at all. So it was offensive to us to see Fifi make such a face, handing the goblet of water back to Dale, and asking him how anyone in his right mind could drink such—spilth. Dale said angrily, "*How?* This is *how!*" and drank the water down in a single thirsty gulp. And he and his new sister stood staring at each other, each of them trembling with passion.

As Cory observed smiling, yet with a trace of resentment or envy, "It looks as if 'new sister' has made a conquest!"

"But what will she do," I couldn't help asking, "—if she can't drink our water?"

"She'll drink it," Cory said grimly. "And she'll find it delicious, like the rest of us." Which, of course, turned out very quickly to be true.

Cory's confinement came in a time of ever-increasing confusion . . . when there were frequent power failures in the Valley, and all foods except tinned goods were scarce, and the price of ammunition doubled, and quadrupled; and the sky by both day and night was criss-crossed by the contrails of unmarked bombers in a design both eerie and beautiful, like the web of a gigantic spider. By this time construction in most parts of the Valley had been halted, temporarily or indefinitely: Part-completed houses and high-rise office buildings punctuated the landscape; some were mere concrete foundations upon which girders had been erected, like exposed bone. The lovely "Mirror Tower"—as we children called it: It must have had a real name—was a two-hundred-story patchwork of interlocking slots of reflecting glass with a pale turquoise tint, and where its elegant surface had once mirrored scenes of sparkling beauty there was now, from day to day, virtually nothing: a sky like soiled cotton batting, smoldering slag heaps, fantastic burdocks and thistles grown to the height of trees. Traffic had dwindled to a half-dozen diesel trucks per day hauling their massive cargo (much of it diseased livestock bound for northern slaughterhouses) and a very few passenger cars. There were cloverleafs that coiled endlessly upon themselves and elevated highways that broke off in midair, thus as authorities warned travelers you were in danger, if you ventured into the countryside, of being attacked by roaming gangs—but the rumor was that the most dangerous men were rogue Guardsmen who wore their uniforms inside out and preyed upon the very people they were paid to protect. None of the family left the compound without being well armed and of course the younger children no longer left at all. All schools, public and private, were temporarily shut down.

The most luxurious of the model communities, known to us

as The Wheel—its original name was forgotten: Whispering Glades? Deer Willow?—had suffered so extreme a financial collapse that most of its services were said to be suspended, and many of its tenants had fled back to the cities from which they'd fled to the Valley. (The community was called The Wheel because its condominiums, office buildings, shops, schools, hospitals, and crematoria were arranged in spokes radiating outward from a single axis; and were protected at their twenty-mile circumference not by a visible wall, which the Japanese architect who had designed it had declared a vulgar and outmoded concept, but by a force field of electricity of lethal voltage.) Though the airport at Furnace Creek was officially closed we often saw small aircraft taking off and landing there in the night, heard the insectlike whine of their engines and spied their winking red lights, and one night when the sun hung paralyzed at the horizon for several hours and visibility was poor though shot with a duplicitous sharpened clarity there was an airplane crash in a slag-heap area that had once been a grazing pasture for our cows, and some of the older boys insisted upon going out to investigate . . . returning with sober, stricken faces, and little to say of the sights they had seen except they wished they had not seen them. Miles away in the foothills were mysterious encampments, some of them mere camps, in which people lived and slept on the ground, others deliberately if crudely erected villages like those once displayed in museums as being the habitations of Native American peoples . . . the names of these "peoples" long since forgotten. These were rumored to be unauthorized settlements of city dwellers who had fled their cities at the time of the general urban collapse, as well as former ranchers and their descendants, and various wanderers and evicted persons, criminals, the mentally ill, and victims of contagious diseases . . . all of these officially designated outlaw parties who were subject to harsh treatment by the Guardsmen, for the region was now under martial law, and only within compounds maintained by government-registered property owners and heads of families were civil rights, to a degree, still operative. Eagerly, we scanned the Valley for signs of life, passing among us a pair of binoculars like forbidden treasure whose original owner we could not recall —though Cory believed this person, an adult male, had lived with us before Father's time, and had been good to us. But not even Cory could remember his name. Cory's baby was born shortly after the funerals of two of the younger children, who had died of violent flulike illnesses, and of Uncle Darrah, who had died of shotgun wounds while driving his pick-up truck in the Valley; but this, we were assured by Mother and Father, was mere coincidence, and not to be taken as a sign. One by one we were led into the attic room set aside for Cory to stare in astonishment at the puppy-sized, red-faced, squalling, yet so wonderfully alive creature . . . with its large oval soft-looking head, its wizened angry features, its unblemished skin. Mother had found a cradle in the storage barn for the baby, a white wicker antique dating back to the previous century, perhaps a cradle she herself had used though she could not remember it, nor could any of us, her children, recall having slept in it; a piece of furniture too good for Cory's "bastard child," as Mother tearfully called it. (Though allowing that the infant's parentage was no fault of its own.) Fit punishment, Mother said, that Cory's breasts yielded milk so grudgingly, and what milk they did yield was frequently threaded with blood, fit punishment for her daughter's "sluttish" behavior . . . but the family's luck held and one day the older boys returned from a hunting expedition with a dairy cow . . . a beautiful black-and-white marbled animal very like the kind, years ago, or was it only months ago, we ourselves had owned. The cow supplied us with sweet, fresh, reasonably pure milk, thus saving Cory's bastard infant's life, as Mother said— "for whatever that life is worth."

Though she was occupied with household tasks, and often with emergency situations, Mother seemed obsessed with ferreting out the identity of Cory's infant's father; Cory's secret lover, as Mother called him with a bitter twist of her lips. Yet it seemed to give her a prideful sort of pleasure that her eldest daughter had not only had a secret lover at one time in her life (the baby being irrefutable proof of this) but had one still— despite the fact that no lover had stepped forward to claim the baby, or the baby's mother; and that Cory, once the prettiest of the girls, was now disfigured by skin rashes covering most of her body. And since her pregnancy her lower body remained bloated while her upper body had become emaciated. Mother herself was frequently ill, with flaming rashes, respiratory illnesses, intestinal upsets, bone aches, uncertain vision; like most of us she was plagued with ticks—the smallest species of deer tick, which could burrow into the skin, particularly into the scalp, unnoticed, there to do its damage, and after weeks drop off, to be found on the floor, swollen with blood, black, shiny, about the size and apparent texture of a watermelon seed, deceptive to the eye. By degrees Mother had shrunk to a height of about four feet eight inches, very unlike the statuesque beauty of certain old photographs; with stark white matted hair, and pale silvery gray eyes as keen and suspicious as ever, and a voice so hard, harsh, brassy, and penetrating, a shout from her had the power to paralyze any of us where we stood . . . though we knew or believed ourselves safely hidden from her by a wall, or more than a single wall. Even the eldest of her sons, Kit, Hewett, Dale, tall ragged-bearded men who absented themselves from the compound for days at a stretch, were intimidated by Mother's authority, and, like poor Cory, shrank in guilty submission before her. Again and again Mother interrogated Cory, "Who is your secret lover? Why are you so ashamed of him?" and Cory insisted she did not know who her lover was, or could not remember—"Even if I see his face sometimes, in my sleep, I can't remember his name. Or who he was. Or who he claimed to be."

Yet Mother continued her investigation, risking Father's displeasure in so ruthlessly questioning all males with whom she came into contact, not excluding Cory's cousins and uncles and even Cory's own brothers!—even those ravaged men and boys who made their homes, so to speak, in the drainage pipes beyond the compound, and whose services the family sometimes enlisted in times of emergency. But no one confessed; no one acknowledged Cory's baby as his. And one day when Cory lay ill upstairs in her attic room and I was entrusted with caring for the baby, feeding it from a bottle, in the kitchen, Mother came into the room with a look of such determination I felt terror for the baby, and hugged it to my bosom, and Mother said, "Give me the bastard, girl," and I said, "No Mother, don't make me," and Mother said, "Are you disobeying me? *Give me the bastard*," and I said, backing away, "No Mother, Cory's baby belongs to Cory, and it isn't a bastard." Mother advanced

upon me, furious; her eyes whitely rimmed and her fingers—
ah, what talons they had become!—outstretched; her mouth
twisting, working, distending itself—and I saw that in the
midst of her passion she was forgetting what she meant to do,
and that this might save Cory's baby. For often in those days
when the family had little to eat except worm-riddled apples
from the old orchard, and stunted blackened potatoes, and
such wild game (or wildlife) as the boys could hunt down, we
often forgot what we were doing in the very act of doing it;
and in the midst of speaking we might forget the words we
meant to speak, for instance *water, rainbow, grief, love, filth,
God, deer tick* . . . and Father, who had become somber-
minded with the onset of age, worried above all that as a family we might one day lose all sense of ourselves as a family
should we forget, collectively, and in the same moment, the
sacred word *family*.

And indeed Mother was forgetting. And indeed within the
space of less than thirty seconds she had forgotten. She stared
at the living thing, the quivering palpitating creature in my
arms, with its soft flat shallow face, its tiny recessed eyes, its
mere holes for nostrils, above all its small pursed mouth set like
a manta ray's in its shallow face, and could not, simply could
not, recall the word *baby*, or *infant*, or *Cory's bastard*. And
shortly afterward there was a commotion of some kind outside, apparently rather close to the compound gate, and a
sound of gunfire, familiar enough yet always jarring when unexpected, and Mother hurried out to investigate. And Cory's
baby continued to suck hungrily at the bottle's frayed rubber
nipple and all was safe for the time being.

But Cory, poor Cory, died a few days later: Early one
morning Lona discovered her in her attic bed, her eyes opened
wide and her pale mouth contorted, the bedclothes soaked in
blood . . . and when in horror Lona drew the sheet away she
saw that Cory's breasts had been partly devoured, and her chest
cavity exposed; she must have been attacked in the night by
rats, and had been too weak or too terrified to call for help. Yet
her baby was sleeping only a few feet away in its antique cradle,
untouched, sunk to that most profound and enviable level of
sleep at which organic matter seems about to pass over again
into the inorganic. The household rats with their glittering

amaranthine eyes and stiff hairless tails had spared it!—had missed it entirely!

Lona snatched up the baby and ran screaming downstairs for help; and so fierce was she in possession she could scarcely be forced to surrender the sleepy infant to the rest of us: Her fingers had to be pried open. In a dazed gloating voice she said, "It is my baby. It is Lona's baby now." Father sharply rebuked her: "It is the family's baby now."

And Fifi too had a baby; or, rather, writhed and screamed in agony for a day and a night, before giving birth to a piteous undersized creature that lived for only a few minutes. Poor sister!—in the weeks that followed only our musical evenings, at which she excelled, gave her solace. If Dale tried to touch her, let alone comfort her, she shrank from him in repugnance. Nor would she allow Father or any male to come near. Sometimes she crawled into my bed and hugged me in her cold bone-thin arms. "What I like best," she whispered "is the black waves that splash over us, at night." And my heart was so swollen with emotion, I could not say no, or Oh yes.

For suddenly we had taken up music. In the evenings by kerosene lamp. In the worst, the most nightmarish of times. We played such musical instruments as fell into our hands discovered here and there in the house, or by way of strangers at our gate desperate to barter anything in their possession for food. Kit took up the violin doubtfully at first and then with growing joy, for, it seemed, he had musical talent!—practicing for hours on the beautiful though badly scarified old violin that had once belonged to Grandfather (so we surmised: One of Grandfather's portraits showed him as a child of eleven or twelve posed with the identical violin, then luminously gleaming, tucked under his chin); Jori took up the piccolo, which she shared with Vega; Hewett took up the drums, Dale the cymbals, Einar the oboe, Fifi the piano . . . and the rest of us sang, sang our hearts out, our collective voices sometimes frail as straws through which a rough careless wind blew but at other times, and always unpredictably, so harmonious, so strong, so commanding, our hearts beat hard in unquestioning love of one another and of any fate that might befall us. We

sang after Mother's death and we sang when a feculent wind
blew from the Valley day after day bearing the odor of decomposing flesh and we sang, though our noses and throats filled
with smoke, when fires raged in the dry woodland areas to the
west, and then too a relentless wind blew upon us barricaded
in our stone house atop a high hill, winds from several directions they seemed, intent upon seeking us out, carrying sparks
to our sanctuary, destroying us in a paroxysm of fire as others,
human and beast, were being destroyed shrieking in pain and
terror . . . and how else for us to endure such odors, such
sights, such sounds than to take up our instruments and play
them, and sing, and sing and sing and sing until our throats
were raw, how else.

Yet it became a time of joy and even feasting, since the cow
was dying in any case and might as well be quickly slaughtered,
when Father brought his new wife home to meet us: New
Mother some of us called her, or Young Mother, and Old
Mother that fierce stooped wild-eyed old woman was forgotten, the strangeness of her death lingering only in whispers for
had she like Cory died of household rats? had she like Erastus
grown pimples, then boils, then tumors over her entire body,
swelling bulbs of flesh that drained away life? had she drowned
in the cistern, had she died of thirst and malnutrition locked
away in a distant room of the house, had she died of infection, of
heartbreak, of her own rage, of Father's steely fingers closing
about her neck . . . or had she not died at all but simply passed
into oblivion, as the black waves splashed over her, and Young
Mother stepped forward smiling to take her place . . . ?
Young Mother was stout and hearty-faced, plumply pretty
about the eyes and cheeks, her color a rich earthen hue, her
breasts capacious as large balloons filled to bursting with liquid,
and she gave off a hot intoxicating smell of nutmeg, and small
slippery flames darted when in a luxury of sighing, yawning,
and stretching, she lifted with beringed hands the heavy mass
of red-russet hair that hung between her shoulder blades, and
fixed upon us her warm moist unblinking dark gaze. "Mother!"
we cried, even the eldest of us, "Oh Mother!" begging would
she hug us, would she fold us in those plump arms, press our
faces against that bosom, each of us, all of us, weeping, in her
arms, against her bosom, there.

Cory's baby was not maturing as it was believed babies should, nor had it been named since we could not determine whether it was male or female, or both, or neither; and this household vexation Young Mother addressed herself to at once. No matter Lona's jealous love of the baby, Young Mother declared herself "practical-minded": For why otherwise had Father brought her to this household but to reform it and give hope? She could not comprehend, she said, how and why an extra mouth, and in this case not only a useless but perhaps even a dangerous mouth, could be tolerated in a time of near famine, in violation of certain government edicts as she understood them. "Drastic remedies in drastic times," Young Mother said. Lona said, "I will give it my food. I will protect it with my life." And Young Mother simply repeated, smiling, her warm brown eyes easing like a caress over us all, "Drastic remedies in drastic times." There were those of us who loved Cory's baby and felt an unreasoned joy in its very existence, for it *was* flesh of our flesh, it *was* the future of the family; yet there were others, among them not only the males, who seemed fearful of it, keeping their distance when it was fed or bathed and averting their eyes when it crawled into a room to nudge its head or mouth against a foot, an ankle, a leg. Though it had not matured in the usual way Cory's baby was considerably heavier than it had been at birth, and weighed now about forty pounds; but it was soft as a slug is soft, or an oyster; with an oyster's shape; seemingly boneless; the hue of bread dough, and hairless. As its small eyes lacked an iris, being entirely white, it was believed to be blind; its nose was but a rudimentary pair of nostrils, mere holes in the center of its face; its fishlike mouth was deceptive in that it seemed to possess its own intelligence, being ideally formed, not for human speech, but for seizing, sucking, and chewing. Though it had at best only a cartilaginous skeleton it did boast two fully formed rows of tiny needle-sharp teeth, which it was not shy of using, particularly when ravenous for food; and it was often ravenous. At such times it groped its way around the house by instinct, sniffing and quivering, and if by chance it was drawn by the heat of your blood to your bed it would burrow against you beneath the covers, and nudge, and nuzzle, and begin like any nursing infant to suck, virtually any part of the body though preferring of course a female's breasts . . . and if not stopped in time it would bite, and chew, and *eat* . . . in all the brute innocence of appetite. So some of us surmised, though Lona angrily denied it, that Cory had not died of rat bites after all but of having been attacked and partly devoured by her own baby. (In this, Lona was duplicitous: taking care never to undress in Mother's presence for fear that Mother's sharp eye would take in the numerous wounds on her breasts, belly, and thighs.)

As the family had a custom of debating issues, in order that all divergent opinions might be honored, for instance should we pay the exorbitant price a cow or a she-goat now commanded, or should the boys be empowered to acquire one of these beasts however they could, for instance should we make an attempt to feed starving men, women, and children who gathered outside our fence, even if it was with food unfit for the family's own consumption—so naturally the issue of Cory's baby was taken up too, and threatened to split the family into two warring sides. For her part Mother argued persuasively that the baby was worthless, repulsive, and might one day be dangerous—not guessing that it had already proved dangerous, indeed; and for her part Lona argued persuasively that the baby, "Lona's baby," as she persisted in calling it, was a living human being, a member of the family, one of *us*. Mother said hotly, "It is not one of *us*, girl, if by *us* you mean a family that includes *me*," and Lona said with equal heat, "It is one of *us* because it predates any family that includes *you*."

So each of us argued in turn, and emotions ran high, and it was a curious phenomenon that many of us changed our minds repeatedly, now swayed by Mother's reasoning, and now by Lona's; now by Father, who spoke on behalf of Mother, or by Hewett, who spoke on behalf of Lona; or by Father, whose milky eyes gave him an air of patrician distinction and fair-mindedness, who spoke on behalf of Lona! The issue raged, and subsided, and raged again, and Mother dared not put her power to the vote for fear that Lona would prevail against her. Father acknowledged that however we felt about the baby it was our flesh and blood presumably, and embodied for us the great insoluble mystery of life . . . "its soul bounded by its skull and its destiny no more problematic than the thin tubes that connect its mouth and its anus. Who are we to judge!"

Yet Mother had her way, as slyboots Mother was always to have her way . . . one morning soliciting the help of several of us, who were sworn to secrecy, and delighted to be her handmaidens, in a simple scheme: Lona being asleep in Cory's old bed, Mother led the baby out of the house by holding a piece of bread soaked in chicken blood just in front of its nostrils, led it crawling with surprising swiftness across the hard-packed earth, to one of the barns, and, inside, led it to a dark corner where she lifted it, grunting, and lowered it carefully into an old rain barrel empty except for a wriggling mass of half-grown baby rats that squealed in great excitement at being disturbed, or at the smell of the blood-soaked bread which Mother dropped on them. We then nailed a cover in place; and, as Mother said, her color warmly flushed and her breath coming fast, "There—it is entirely out of our hands."

And then one day it was spring. And Kit led a she-goat proudly into the kitchen, her bags primed with milk, swollen pink dugs leaking milk! How grateful we were, those of us who were with child, after the privations of so long a season, during which certain words had slipped from our memories, for instance *she-goat*, and *milk*, and as we realized, *rainbow*, for the rainbow too appeared, or reappeared, shimmering and translucent across the Valley. In the fire-ravaged plain was a sea of fresh green shoots and in the sky enormous dimpled clouds and that night we gathered around Fifi at the piano to play our instruments and sing. Father had passed away but Mother had remarried: a husky horseman whose white teeth flashed in his beard, and whose rowdy pinches meant love and good cheer, not hurt. We were so happy we debated turning the calendar ahead to the New Year. We were so happy we debated abolishing the calendar entirely and declaring it the year 1, and beginning Time anew.

1989

THOMAS LIGOTTI
(b. 1953)

The Last Feast of Harlequin

I.

MY interest in the town of Mirocaw was first aroused when I heard that an annual festival was held there which promised to include, to some extent, the participation of clowns among its other elements of pageantry. A former colleague of mine, who is now attached to the anthropology department of a distant university, had read one of my recent articles ("The Clown Figure in American Media," *Journal of Popular Culture*), and wrote to me that he vaguely remembered reading or being told of a town somewhere in the state that held a kind of "Fool's Feast" every year, thinking that this might be pertinent to my peculiar line of study. It was, of course, more pertinent than he had reason to think, both to my academic aims in this area and to my personal pursuits.

Aside from my teaching, I had for some years been engaged in various anthropological projects with the primary ambition of articulating the significance of the clown figure in diverse cultural contexts. Every year for the past twenty years I have attended the pre-Lenten festivals that are held in various places throughout the southern United States. Every year I learned something more concerning the esoterics of celebration. In these studies I was an eager participant—along with playing my part as an anthropologist, I also took a place behind the clownish mask myself. And I cherished this role as I did nothing else in my life. To me the title of Clown has always carried connotations of a noble sort. I was an adroit jester, strangely enough, and had always taken pride in the skills I worked so diligently to develop.

I wrote to the State Department of Recreation, indicating what information I desired and exposing an enthusiastic urgency which came naturally to me on this topic. Many weeks later I received a tan envelope imprinted with a government logo. Inside was a pamphlet that catalogued all of the various seasonal festivities of which the state was officially aware, and I noted in passing that there were as many in late autumn and winter as in the warmer seasons. A letter inserted within the pamphlet explained to me that, according to their voluminous records, no festivals held in the town of Mirocaw had been officially registered. Their files, nonetheless, could be placed at my disposal if I should wish to research this or similar matters in connection with some definite project. At the time this offer was made I was already laboring under so many professional and personal burdens that, with a weary hand, I simply deposited the envelope and its contents in a drawer, never to be consulted again.

Some months later, however, I made an impulsive digression from my responsibilities and, rather haphazardly, took up the Mirocaw project. This happened as I was driving north one afternoon in late summer with the intention of examining some journals in the holdings of a library at another university. Once out of the city limits the scenery changed to sunny fields and farms, diverting my thoughts from the signs that I passed along the highway. Nevertheless, the subconscious scholar in me must have been regarding these with studious care. The name of a town loomed into my vision. Instantly the scholar retrieved certain records from some deep mental drawer, and I was faced with making a few hasty calculations as to whether there was enough time and motivation for an investigative side trip. But the exit sign was even hastier in making its appearance, and I soon found myself leaving the highway, recalling the roadsign's promise that the town was no more than seven miles east.

These seven miles included several confusing turns, the forced taking of a temporarily alternate route, and a destination not even visible until a steep rise had been fully ascended. On the descent another helpful sign informed me that I was within the city limits of Mirocaw. Some scattered houses on the outskirts of the town were the first structures I encountered. Beyond them the numerical highway became Townshend Street, the main avenue of Mirocaw.

The town impressed me as being much larger once I was

within its limits than it had appeared from the prominence just outside. I saw that the general hilliness of the surrounding countryside was also an internal feature of Mirocaw. Here, though, the effect was different. The parts of the town did not look as if they adhered very well to one another. This condition might be blamed on the irregular topography of the town. Behind some of the old stores in the business district, steeply roofed houses had been erected on a sudden incline, their peaks appearing at an extraordinary elevation above the lower buildings. And because the foundations of these houses could not be glimpsed, they conveyed the illusion of being either precariously suspended in air, threatening to topple down, or else constructed with an unnatural loftiness in relation to their width and mass. This situation also created a weird distortion of perspective. The two levels of structures overlapped each other without giving a sense of depth, so that the houses, because of their higher elevation and nearness to the foreground buildings, did not appear diminished in size as background objects should. Consequently, a look of flatness, as in a photograph, predominated in this area. Indeed, Mirocaw could be compared to an album of old snapshots, particularly ones in which the camera had been upset in the process of photography, causing the pictures to develop on an angle: a cone-roofed turret, like a pointed hat jauntily askew, peeked over the houses on a neighboring street; a billboard displaying a group of grinning vegetables tipped its contents slightly westward; cars parked along steep curbs seemed to be flying skyward in the glare-distorted windows of a five-and-ten; people leaned lethargically as they trod up and down sidewalks; and on that sunny day the clock tower, which at first I mistook for a church steeple, cast a long shadow that seemed to extend an impossible distance and wander into unlikely places in its progress across the town. I should say that perhaps the disharmonies of Mirocaw are more acutely affecting my imagination in retrospect than they were on that first day, when I was primarily concerned with locating the city hall or some other center of information.

I pulled around a corner and parked. Sliding over to the other side of the seat, I rolled down the window and called to a passerby: "Excuse me, sir," I said. The man, who was shabbily dressed and very old, paused for a moment without approaching the car. Though he had apparently responded to my call, his vacant expression did not betray the least awareness of my presence, and for a moment I thought it just a coincidence that he halted on the sidewalk at the same time I addressed him. His eyes were focused somewhere beyond me with a weary and imbecilic gaze. After a few moments he continued on his way and I said nothing to call him back, even though at the last second his face began to appear dimly familiar. Someone else finally came along who was able to direct me to the Mirocaw City Hall and Community Center.

The city hall turned out to be the building with the clock tower. Inside I stood at a counter behind which some people were working at desks and walking up and down a back hallway. On one wall was a poster for the state lottery: a jack-in-the-box with both hands grasping green bills. After a few moments, a tall, middle-aged woman came over to the counter.

"Can I help you?" she asked in a neutral, bureaucratic voice.

I explained that I had heard about the festival—saying nothing about being a nosy academic—and asked if she could provide me with further information or direct me to someone who could.

"Do you mean the one held in the winter?" she asked.

"How many of them are there?"

"Just that one."

"I suppose, then, that that's the one I mean." I smiled as if sharing a joke with her.

Without another word, she walked off into the back hallway. While she was absent I exchanged glances with several of the people behind the counter who periodically looked up from their work.

"There you are," she said when she returned, handing me a piece of paper that looked like the product of a cheap copy machine. *Please Come to the Fun*, it said in large letters. *Parades*, it went on, *Street Masquerade, Bands, The Winter Raffle*, and *The Coronation of the Winter Queen*. The page continued with the mention of a number of miscellaneous festivities. I read the words again. There was something about that imploring little "please" at the top of the announcement that made the whole affair seem like a charity function.

"When is it held? It doesn't say when the festival takes place."

"Most people already know that." She abruptly snatched the page from my hands and wrote something at the bottom. When she gave it back to me, I saw "Dec. 19–21" written in blue-green ink. I was immediately struck by an odd sense of scheduling on the part of the festival committee. There was, of course, solid anthropological and historical precedent for holding festivities around the winter solstice, but the timing of this particular event did not seem entirely practical.

"If you don't mind my asking, don't these days somewhat conflict with the regular holiday season? I mean, most people have enough going on at that time."

"It's just tradition," she said, as if invoking some venerable ancestry behind her words.

"That's very interesting," I said as much to myself as to her.

"Is there anything else?" she asked.

"Yes. Could you tell me if this festival has anything to do with clowns? I see there's something about a masquerade."

"Yes, of course there are some people in . . . costumes. I've never been in that position myself . . . that is, yes, there are clowns of a sort."

At that point my interest was definitely aroused, but I was not sure how much further I wanted to pursue it. I thanked the woman for her help and asked the best means of access to the highway, not anxious to retrace the labyrinthine route by which I had entered the town. I walked back to my car with a whole flurry of half-formed questions, and as many vague and conflicting answers, cluttering my mind.

The directions the woman gave me necessitated passing through the south end of Mirocaw. There were not many people moving about in this section of town. Those that I did see, shuffling lethargically down a block of battered storefronts, exhibited the same sort of forlorn expression and manner as the old man from whom I had asked directions earlier. I must have been traversing a central artery of this area, for on either side stretched street after street of poorly tended yards and houses bowed with age and indifference. When I came to a stop at a streetcorner, one of the citizens of this slum passed in front of my car. This lean, morose, and epicene person turned my way and sneered outrageously with a taut little mouth, yet seemed to be looking at no one in particular. After progressing a few streets farther, I came to a road that led back to the highway. I felt delectably more comfortable as soon as I found myself traveling once again through the expanses of sun-drenched farmlands.

I reached the library with more than enough time for my research, and so I decided to make a scholarly detour to see what material I could find that might illuminate the winter festival held in Mirocaw. The library, one of the oldest in the state, included in its holdings the entire run of the Mirocaw *Courier*. I thought this would be an excellent place to start. I soon found, however, that there was no handy way to research information from this newspaper, and I did not want to engage in a blind search for articles concerning a specific subject.

I next turned to the more organized resources of the newspapers for the larger cities located in the same county, which incidentally shares its name with Mirocaw. I uncovered very little about the town, and almost nothing concerning its festival, except in one general article on annual events in the area that erroneously attributed to Mirocaw a "large Middle-Eastern community" which every spring hosted a kind of ethnic jamboree. From what I had already observed, and from what I subsequently learned, the citizens of Mirocaw were solidly midwestern-American, the probable descendants in a direct line from some enterprising pack of New Englanders of the last century. There was one brief item devoted to a Mirocavian event, but this merely turned out to be an obituary notice for an old woman who had quietly taken her life around Christmastime. Thus, I returned home that day all but empty-handed on the subject of Mirocaw.

However, it was not long afterward that I received another letter from the former colleague of mine who had first led me to seek out Mirocaw and its festival. As it happened, he rediscovered the article that caused him to stir my interest in a local "Fool's Feast." This article had its sole appearance in an obscure festschrift of anthropology studies published in Amsterdam twenty years ago. Most of these papers were in Dutch, a few in German, and only one was in English: "The Last Feast of Harlequin: Preliminary Notes on a Local Festival." It was exciting, of course, finally to be able to read this study, but even more exciting was the name of its author: Dr. Raymond Thoss.

2.

Before proceeding any further, I should mention something about Thoss, and inevitably about myself. Over two decades ago, at my alma mater in Cambridge, Mass., Thoss was a professor of mine. Long before playing a role in the events I am about to describe, he was already one of the most important figures in my life. A striking personality, he inevitably influenced everyone who came in contact with him. I remember his lectures on social anthropology, how he turned that dim room into a brilliant and profound circus of learning. He moved in an uncannily brisk manner. When he swept his arm around to indicate some common term on the blackboard behind him, one felt he was presenting nothing less than an item of fantastic qualities and secret value. When he replaced his hand in the pocket of his old jacket this fleeting magic was once again stored away in its well-worn pouch, to be retrieved at the sorcerer's discretion. We sensed he was teaching us more than we could possibly learn, and that he himself was in possession of greater and deeper knowledge than he could possibly impart. On one occasion I summoned up the audacity to offer as interpretation —which was somewhat opposed to his own—regarding the tribal clowns of the Hopi Indians. I implied that personal experience as an amateur clown and special devotion to this study provided me with an insight possibly more valuable than his own. It was then he disclosed, casually and very obiter dicta, that he had actually acted in the role of one of these masked tribal fools and had celebrated with them the dance of the *kachinas*. In revealing these facts, however, he somehow managed not to add to the humiliation I had already inflicted upon myself. And for this I was grateful to him.

Thoss's activities were such that he sometimes became the object of gossip or romanticized speculation. He was a fieldworker par excellence, and his ability to insinuate himself into exotic cultures and situations, thereby gaining insights where other anthropologists merely collected data, was renowned. At various times in his career there had been rumors of his having "gone native" à la the Frank Hamilton Cushing legend. There were hints, which were not always irresponsible or cheaply glamorized, that he was involved in projects of a freakish sort, many of which focused on New England. It is a fact that he spent six months posing as a mental patient at an institution in western Massachussetts, gathering information on the "culture" of the psychically disturbed. When his book *Winter Solstice: The Longest Night of a Society* was published, the general opinion was that it was disappointingly subjective and impressionistic, and that, aside from a few moving but "poetically obscure" observations, there was nothing at all to give it value. Those who defended Thoss claimed he was a kind of superanthropologist: while much of his work emphasized his own mind and feelings, his experience had in fact penetrated to a rich core of hard data which he had yet to disclose in objective discourse. As a student of Thoss, I tended to support this latter estimation of him. For a variety of tenable and untenable reasons, I believed Thoss capable of unearthing hitherto inaccessible strata of human existence. So it was gratifying at first that this article entitled "The Last Feast of Harlequin" seemed to uphold the Thoss mystique, and in an area I personally found captivating.

Much of the content of the article I did not immediately comprehend, given its author's characteristic and often strategic obscurities. On first reading, the most interesting aspect of this brief study—the "notes" encompassed only twenty pages —was the general mood of the piece. Thoss's eccentricities were definitely present in these pages, but only as a struggling inner force which was definitely contained—incarcerated, I might say—by the somber rhythmic movements of his prose and by some gloomy references he occasionally called upon. Two references in particular shared a common theme. One was a quotation from Poe's "The Conqueror Worm," which Thoss employed as a rather sensational epigraph. The point of the epigraph, however, was nowhere echoed in the text of the article save in another passing reference. Thoss brought up the well-known genesis of the modern Christmas celebration, which of course descends from the Roman Saturnalia. Then, making it clear he had not yet observed the Mirocaw festival and had only gathered its nature from various informants, he established that it too contained many, even more overt, elements of the Saturnalia. Next he made what seemed to me a trivial and purely linguistic observation, one that had less to do with his main course of argument than it did with the equally peripheral Poe epigraph. He briefly mentioned that an early sect of the Syrian Gnostics called themselves "Saturnians" and believed, among other religious heresies, that mankind was created by angels who were in turn created by the Supreme Unknown. The angels, however, did not possess the power to make their creation an erect being and for a time he crawled upon the earth like a worm. Eventually, the Creator remedied this grotesque state of affairs. At the time I supposed that the symbolic correspondences of mankind's origins and ultimate condition being associated with worms, combined with a year-end festival recognizing the winter death of the earth, was the gist of this Thossian "insight," a poetic but scientifically value-less observation.

Other observations he made on the Mirocaw festival were also strictly etic; in other words, they were based on second-hand sources, hearsay testimony. Even at that juncture, however, I felt Thoss knew more than he disclosed; and, as I later discovered, he had indeed included information on certain aspects of Mirocaw suggesting he was already in possession of several keys which for the moment he was keeping securely in his own pocket. By then I myself possessed a most revealing morsel of knowledge. A note to the "Harlequin" article apprised the reader that the piece was only a fragment in rude form of a more wide-ranging work in preparation. This work was never seen by the world. My former professor had not published anything since his withdrawal from academic circulation some twenty years ago. Now I suspected where he had gone.

For the man I had stopped on the streets of Mirocaw and from whom I tried to obtain directions, the man with the disconcertingly lethargic gaze, had very much resembled a super-annuated version of Dr. Raymond Thoss.

3.

And now I have a confession to make. Despite my reasons for being enthusiastic about Mirocaw and its mysteries, especially its relationship to both Thoss and my own deepest concerns as a scholar—I contemplated the days ahead of me with no more than a feeling of frigid numbness and often with a sense of profound depression. Yet I had no reason to be surprised at this emotional state, which had little relevance to the outward events in my life but was determined by inward conditions that worked according to their own, quite enigmatic, seasons and cycles. For many years, at least since my university days, I have suffered from this dark malady, this recurrent despondency in which I would become buried when it came time for the earth to grow cold and bare and the skies heavy with shadows. Nevertheless, I pursued my plans, though somewhat mechanically, to visit Mirocaw during its festival days, for I superstitiously hoped that this activity might diminish the weight of my seasonal despair. In Mirocaw would be parades and parties and the opportunity to play the clown once again.

For weeks in advance I practiced my art, even perfecting a new feat of juggling magic, which was my special forte in foolery. I had my costumes cleaned, purchased fresh makeup, and was ready. I received permission from the university to cancel some of my classes prior to the holiday, explaining the nature of my project and the necessity of arriving in the town a few days before the festival began, in order to do some preliminary research, establish informants, and so on. Actually, my plan was to postpone any formal inquiry until after the festival and to involve myself beforehand as much as possible in its activities. I would, of course, keep a journal during this time.

There was one resource I did want to consult, however. Specifically, I returned to that outstate library to examine those issues of the Mirocaw *Courier* dating from December two decades ago. One story in particular confirmed a point Thoss made in the "Harlequin" article, though the event it chronicled must have taken place after Thoss had written his study.

The Courier story appeared two weeks after the festival had ended for that year and was concerned with the disappearance of a woman named Elizabeth Beadle, the wife of Samuel Bea-

dle, a hotel owner in Mirocaw. The county authorities speculated that this was another instance of the "holiday suicides"
which seemed to occur with inordinate seasonal regularity in
the Mirocaw region. Thoss documented this phenomenon in
his "Harlequin" article, though I suspect that today these
deaths would be neatly categorized under the heading "seasonal affective disorder". In any case, the authorities searched
a half-frozen lake near the outskirts of Mirocaw where they
had found many successful suicides in years past. This year,
however, no body was discovered. Alongside the article was a
picture of Elizabeth Beadle. Even in the grainy microfilm re-
production one could detect a certain vibrancy and vitality in
Mrs. Beadle's face. That an hypothesis of "holiday suicide"
should be so readily posited to explain her disappearance
seemed strange and in some way unjust.

Thoss, in his brief article, wrote that every year there occurred changes of a moral or spiritual cast which seemed to
affect Mirocaw along with the usual winter metamorphosis.
He was not precise about its origin or nature but stated, in
typically mystifying fashion, that the effect of this "subseason"
on the town was conspicuously negative. In addition to the
number of suicides actually accomplished during this time,
there was also a rise in treatment of "hypochondriacal" conditions, which was how the medical men of twenty years past
characterized these cases in discussions with Thoss. This state
of affairs would gradually worsen and finally reach a climax
during the days scheduled for the Mirocaw festival. Thoss
speculated that given the secretive nature of small towns, the
situation was probably even more intensely pronounced than
casual investigation could reveal.

The connection between the festival and this insidious sub-
seasonal climate in Mirocaw was a point on which Thoss did
not come to any rigid conclusions. He did write, nevertheless,
that these two "climatic aspects" had had a parallel existence in
the town's history as far back as available records could document. A late nineteenth-century history of Mirocaw County
speaks of the town by its original name of New Colstead, and
castigates the townspeople for holding a "ribald and soulless
feast" to the exclusion of normal Christmas observances. (Thoss
comments that the historian had mistakenly fused two distinct

aspects of the season, their actual relationship being essentially antagonistic.) The "Harlequin" article did not trace the festival to its earliest appearance (this may not have been possible), though Thoss emphasized the New England origins of Mirocaw's founders. The festival, therefore, was one imported from this region and could reasonably be extended at least a century; that is, if it had not been brought over from the Old World, in which case its roots would become indefinite until further research could be done. Surely Thoss's allusion to the Syrian Gnostics suggested the latter possibility could not entirely be ruled out.

But it seemed to be the festival's link to New England that nourished Thoss's speculations. He wrote of this patch of geography as if it were an acceptable place to end the search. For him, the very words "New England" seemed to be stripped of all traditional connotations and had come to imply nothing less than a gateway to all lands, both known and suspected, and even to ages beyond the civilized history of the region. Having been educated partly in New England, I could somewhat understand this sentimental exaggeration, for indeed there are places that seem archaic beyond chronological measure, appearing to transcend relative standards of time and achieving a kind of absolute antiquity which cannot be logically fathomed. But how this vague suggestion related to a small town in the Midwest I could not imagine. Thoss himself observed that the residents of Mirocaw did not betray any mysteriously primitive consciousness. On the contrary, they appeared superficially unaware of the genesis of their winter merrymaking. That such a tradition had endured through the years, however, even eclipsing the conventional Christmas holiday, revealed a profound awareness of the festival's meaning and function.

I cannot deny that what I had learned about the Mirocaw festival did inspire a trite sense of fate, especially given the involvement of such an important figure from my past as Thoss. It was the first time in my academic career that I knew myself to be better suited than anyone else to discern the true meaning of scattered data, even if I could only attribute this special authority to chance circumstances.

Nevertheless, as I sat in that library on a morning in mid

December I doubted for a moment the wisdom of setting out for Mirocaw rather than returning home, where the more familiar *rite de passage* of winter depression awaited me. My original scheme was to avoid the cyclical blues the season held for me, but it seemed this was also a part of the history of Mirocaw, only on a much larger scale. My emotional instability, however, was exactly what qualified me most for the particular fieldwork ahead, though I did not take pride or consolation in the fact. And to retreat would have been to deny myself an opportunity that might never offer itself again. In retrospect, there seems to have been no fortuitous resolution to the decision I had to make. As it happened, I went ahead to the town.

4.

Just past noon, on December 18, I started driving toward Mirocaw. A blur of dull, earthen-colored scenery extended in every direction. The snowfalls of late autumn had been sparse, and only a few white patches appeared in the harvested fields along the highway. The clouds were gray and abundant. Passing by a stretch of forest, I noticed the black, ragged clumps of abandoned nests clinging to the twisted mesh of bare branches. I thought I saw black birds skittering over the road ahead, but they were only dead leaves and they flew into the air as I drove by.

I approached Mirocaw from the south, entering the town from the direction I had left it on my visit the previous summer. This took me once again through that part of town which seemed to exist on the wrong side of some great invisible barrier dividing the desirable sections of Mirocaw from the undesirable. As lurid as this district had appeared to me under the summer sun, in the thin light of that winter afternoon it degenerated into a pale phantom of itself. The frail stores and starved-looking houses suggested a borderline region between the material and nonmaterial worlds, with one sardonically wearing the mask of the other. I saw a few gaunt pedestrians who turned as I passed by, though seemingly not *because* I passed by, making my way up to the main street of Mirocaw.

Driving up the steep rise of Townshend Street, I found the sights there comparatively welcoming. The rolling avenues of

the town were in readiness for the festival. Streetlights had
their poles raveled with evergreen, the fresh boughs proudly
conspicuous in a barren season. On the doors of many of the
businesses on Townshend were holly wreaths, equally green
but observably plastic. However, although there was nothing
unusual in this traditional greenery of the season, it soon became apparent to me that Mirocaw had quite abandoned itself
to this particular symbol of Yuletide. It was garishly in evidence
everywhere. The windows of stores and houses were framed in
green lights, green streamers hung down from storefront
awnings, and the beacons of the Red Rooster Bar were pea-
cock green floodlights. I supposed the residents of Mirocaw
desired these decorations, but the effect was one of excess. An
eerie emerald haze permeated the town, and faces looked
slightly reptilian.

At the time I assumed that the prodigious evergreen, holly
wreaths, and colored lights (if only of a single color) demonstrated an emphasis on the vegetable symbols of the Nordic
Yuletide, which would inevitably be muddled into the winter
festival of any northern country just as they had been adopted
for the Christmas season. In his "Harlequin" article Thoss wrote
of the pagan aspect of Mirocaw's festival, likening it to the ritual of a fertility cult, with probable connections to chthonic
divinities at some time in the past. But Thoss had mistaken, as
I had, what was only part of the festival's significance for the
whole.

The hotel at which I had made reservations was located on
Townshend. It was an old building of brown brick, with an
arched doorway and a pathetic coping intended to convey an
impression of neoclassicism. I found a parking space in front
and left my suitcases in the car.

When I first entered the hotel lobby it was empty. I thought
perhaps the Mirocaw festival would have attracted enough visitors to at least bolster the business of its only hotel, but it
seemed I was mistaken. Tapping a little bell, I leaned on the
desk and turned to look at a small, traditionally decorated
Christmas tree on a table near the entranceway. It was complete with shiny, egg-fragile bulbs; miniature candy canes; flat,
laughing Santas with arms wide; a star on top nodding awk-

wardly against the delicate shoulder of an upper branch; and colored lights that bloomed out of flower-shaped sockets. For some reason this seemed to me a sorry little piece.

"May I help you?" said a young woman arriving from a room adjacent to the lobby.

I must have been staring rather intently at her, for she looked away and seemed quite uneasy. I could hardly imagine what to say to her or how to explain what I was thinking. In person she immediately radiated a chilling brilliance of manner and expression. But if this woman had not committed suicide twenty years before, as the newspaper article had suggested, neither had she aged in that time.

"Sarah," called a masculine voice from the invisible heights of a stairway. A tall, middle-aged man came down the steps. "I thought you were in your room," said the man, whom I took to be Samuel Beadle. Sarah, not Elizabeth, Beadle glanced sideways in my direction to indicate to her father that she was conducting the business of the hotel. Beadle apologized to me, and then excused the two of them for a moment while they went off to one side to continue their exchange.

I smiled and pretended everything was normal, while trying to remain within earshot of their conversation. They spoke in tones that suggested their conflict was a familiar one: Beadle's over-protective concern with his daughter's whereabouts and Sarah's frustrated understanding of certain restrictions placed upon her. The conversation ended, and Sarah ascended the stairs, turning for a moment to give me a facial pantomime of apology for the unprofessional scene that had just taken place.

"Now, sir, what can I do for you?" Beadle asked, almost demanded.

"Yes, I have a reservation. Actually, I'm a day early, if that doesn't present a problem." I gave the hotel the benefit of the doubt that its business might have been secretly flourishing.

"No problem at all, sir," he said, presenting me with the registration form, and then a brass-colored key dangling from a plastic disc bearing the number 44.

"Luggage?"

"Yes, it's in my car."

"I'll give you a hand with that."

While Beadle was settling me in my fourth-floor room it

seemed an opportune moment to broach the subject of the festival, the holiday suicides, and perhaps, depending upon his reaction, the fate of his wife. I needed a respondent who had lived in the town for a good many years and who could enlighten me about the attitude of Mirocavians toward their season of sea-green lights.

"This is just fine," I said about the clean but somber room. "Nice view. I can see the bright green lights of Mirocaw just fine from up here. Is the town usually all decked out like this? For the festival, I mean."

"Yes, sir, for the festival," he replied mechanically.

"I imagine you'll probably be getting quite a few of us out-of-towners in the next couple of days."

"Could be. Is there anything else?"

"Yes, there is. I wonder if you could tell me something about the festivities."

"Such as . . ."

"Well, you know, the clowns and so forth."

"Only clowns here are the ones that're . . . well, picked out, I suppose you would say."

"I don't understand."

"Excuse me, sir. I'm very busy right now. Is there anything else?"

I could think of nothing at the moment to perpetuate our conversation. Beadle wished me a good stay and left.

I unpacked my suitcases. In addition to regular clothing I had also brought along some of the items from my clown's wardrobe. Beadle's comment that the clowns of Mirocaw were "picked out" left me wondering exactly what purpose these street masqueraders served in the festival. The clown figure has had so many meanings in different times and cultures. The jolly, well-loved joker familiar to most people is actually but one aspect of this protean creature. Madmen, hunchbacks, amputees, and other abnormals were once considered natural clowns; they were elected to fulfil a comic role which could allow others to see them as ludicrous rather than as terrible reminders of the forces of disorder in the world. But sometimes a cheerless jester was required to draw attention to this same disorder, as in the case of King Lear's morbid and honest fool, who of course was eventually hanged, and so much for his clownish wisdom. Clowns have often had ambiguous and sometimes contradictory roles to play. Thus, I knew enough not to brashly jump into costume and cry out, "Here I am again!"

That first day in Mirocaw I did not stray far from the hotel. I read and rested for a few hours and then ate at a nearby diner. Through the window beside my table I watched the winter night turn the soft green glow of the town into a harsh and almost totally new color as it contrasted with the darkness. The streets of Mirocaw seemed to me unusually busy for a small town at evening. Yet it was not the kind of activity one normally sees before an approaching Christmas holiday. This was not a crowd of bustling shoppers loaded with bright bags of presents. Their arms were empty, their hands shoved deep in their pockets against the cold, which nevertheless had not driven them to the solitude of their presumably warm houses. I watched them enter and exit store after store without buying; many merchants remained open late, and even the places that were closed had left their neons illuminated. The faces that passed the window of the diner were possibly just stiffened by the cold, I thought; frozen into deep frowns and nothing else. In the same window I saw the reflection of my own face. It was not the face of an adept clown; it was slack and flabby and at that moment seemed the face of someone less than alive. Outside was the town of Mirocaw, its streets dipping and rising with a lunatic severity, its citizens packing the sidewalks, its heart bathed in green: as promising a field of professional and personal challenge as I had ever encountered—and I was bored to the point of dread. I hurried back to my hotel room.

"Mirocaw has another coldness within its cold," I wrote in my journal that night. "Another set of buildings and streets that exists behind the visible town's facade like a world of disgraceful back alleys." I went on like this for about a page, across which I finally engraved a big "X". Then I went to bed.

In the morning I left my car at the hotel and walked toward the main business district a few blocks away. Mingling with the good people of Mirocaw seemed like the proper thing to do at that point in my scientific sojourn. But as I began laboriously walking up Townshend (the sidewalks were cramped with wandering pedestrians), a glimpse of someone suddenly replaced my haphazard plan with a more specific and immediate one. Through the crowd and about fifteen paces ahead was my goal.

"Dr. Thoss," I called.

His head almost seemed to turn and look back in response to my shout, but I could not be certain. I pushed past several warmly wrapped bodies and green-scarved necks, only to find that the object of my pursuit appeared to be maintaining the same distance from me, though I did not know if this was being done deliberately or not. At the next corner, the dark-coated Thoss abruptly turned right onto a steep street which led downward directly toward the dilapidated south end of Mirocaw. When I reached the corner I looked down the side-walk and could see him very clearly from above. I also saw how he managed to stay so far ahead of me in a mob that had impeded my own progress. For some reason the people on the sidewalk made room so that he could move past them easily, without the usual jostling of bodies. It was not a dramatic physical avoidance, though it seemed nonetheless intentional. Fighting the tight fabric of the throng, I continued to follow Thoss, losing and regaining sight of him.

By the time I reached the bottom of the sloping street the crowd had thinned out considerably, and after walking a block or so farther I found myself practically a lone pedestrian pacing behind a distant figure that I hoped was still Thoss. He was now walking quite swiftly and in a way that seemed to acknowledge my pursuit of him, though really it felt as if he were leading me as much as I was chasing him. I called his name a few more times at a volume he could not have failed to hear, assuming that deafness was not one of the changes to have come over him; he was, after all, not a young man, nor even a middle-aged one any longer.

Thoss suddenly crossed in the middle of the street. He walked a few more steps and entered a signless brick building between a liquor store and a repair shop of some kind. In the "Harlequin" article Thoss had mentioned that the people living in this section of Mirocaw maintained their own businesses, and that these were patronized almost exclusively by residents of the area. I could well believe this statement when I looked at these little sheds of commerce, for they had the same badly weathered appearance as their clientele. The formidable shoddiness of these buildings notwithstanding, I followed Thoss into the plain brick shell of what had been, or possibly still was, a diner.

Inside it was unusually dark. Even before my eyes made the adjustment I sensed that this was not a thriving restaurant co-zily cluttered with chairs and tables—as was the establishment where I had eaten the night before—but a place with only a few disarranged furnishings, and very cold. It seemed colder, in fact, than the winter streets outside.

"Dr. Thoss?" I called toward a lone table near the center of the long room. Perhaps four or five were sitting around the table, with some others blending into the dimness behind them. Scattered across the top of the table were some books and loose papers. Seated there was an old man indicating some-thing in the pages before him, but it was not Thoss. Beside him were two youths whose wholesome features distinguished them from the grim weariness of the others. I approached the table and they all looked up at me. None of them showed a glimmer of emotion except the two boys, who exchanged wor-ried and guilt-ridden glances with each other, as if they had just been discovered in some shameful act. They both sud-denly burst from the table and ran into the dark background, where a light appeared briefly as they exited by a back door.

"I'm sorry," I said diffidently. "I thought I saw someone I knew come in here."

They said nothing. Out of a back room others began to emerge, no doubt interested in the source of the commotion. In a few moments the room was crowded with these tramp-like figures, all of them gazing emptily in the dimness. I was not at this point frightened of them; at least I was not afraid they would do me any physical harm. Actually, I felt as if it was quite within my power to pummel them easily into submis-sion, their mousy faces almost inviting a succession of firm blows. But there were so many of them.

They slid slowly toward me in a worm-like mass. Their eyes seemed empty and unfocused, and I wondered a moment if they were even aware of my presence. Nevertheless, I was the center upon which their lethargic shuffling converged, their shoes scuffing softly along the bare floor. I began to deliver a number of hasty inanities as they continued to press toward me, their weak and unexpectedly odorless bodies nudging against mine. (I understood now why the people along the sidewalks seemed to instinctively avoid Thoss.) Unseen legs became entangled with my own; I staggered and then regained my balance. This sudden movement aroused me from a kind of mesmeric daze into which I must have fallen without being aware of it. I had intended to leave that dreary place long before events had reached such a juncture, but for some reason I could not focus my intentions strongly enough to cause myself to act. My mind had been drifting farther away as these slavish things approached. In a sudden surge of panic I pushed through their soft ranks and was outside.

The open air revived me to my former alertness, and I immediately started pacing swiftly up the hill. I was no longer sure that I had not simply imagined what had seemed, and at the same time did not seem, like a perilous moment. Had their movements been directed toward a harmful assault, or were they trying merely to intimidate me? As I reached the green-glazed main street of Mirocaw I really could not determine what had just happened.

The sidewalks were still jammed with a multitude of pedestrians, who now seemed more lively than they had been only a short time before. There was a kind of vitality that could only be attributed to the imminent festivities. A group of young men had begun celebrating prematurely and strode noisily across the street at midpoint, obviously intoxicated. From the laughter and joking among the still sober citizens I gathered that, mardi-gras style, public drunkenness was within the traditions of this winter festival. I looked for anything to indicate the beginnings of the Street Masquerade, but saw nothing: no brightly garbed harlequins or snow-white pierrots. Were the ceremonies even now in preparation for the coronation of the Winter Queen? "The Winter Queen," I wrote in my journal. "Figure of fertility invested with symbolic powers of revival and prosperity. Elected in the manner of a high school prom queen. Check for possible consort figure in the form of a representative from the underworld."

In the pre-darkness hours of December 19 I sat in my hotel room and wrote and thought and organized. I did not feel too badly, all things considered. The holiday excitement which was steadily rising in the streets below my window was definitely infecting me. I forced myself to take a short nap in anticipation of a long night. When I awoke, Mirocaw's annual feast had begun.

5.

Shouting, commotion, carousing. Sleepily I went to the window and looked out over the town. It seemed all the lights of Mirocaw were shining, save in that section down the hill which became part of the black void of winter. And now the town's greenish tinge was even more pronounced, spreading everywhere like a great green rainbow that had melted from the sky and endured, phosphorescent, into the night. In the streets was the brightness of an artificial spring. The byways of Mirocaw vibrated with activity: on a nearby corner a brass band blared; marauding cars blew their horns and were sometimes mounted by laughing pedestrians; a man emerged from the Red Rooster Bar, threw up his arms, and crowed. I looked closely at the individual celebrants, searching for the vestments of clowns. Soon, delightedly, I saw them. The costume was red and white, with matching cap, and the face painted a noble alabaster. It almost seemed to be a clownish incarnation of that white-bearded and black-booted Christmas fool.

This particular fool, however, was not receiving the affection and respect usually accorded to a Santa Claus. My poor fellow-clown was in the middle of a circle of revelers who were pushing him back and forth from one to the other. The object of this abuse seemed to accept it somewhat willingly, but this little game nevertheless appeared to have humiliation as its purpose. "Only clowns here are the ones that're picked out," echoed Beadle's voice in my memory. "Picked *on*" seemed closer to the truth.

Packing myself in some heavy clothes, I went out into the green gleaming streets. Not far from the hotel I was stumbled into by a character with a wide blue and red grin and bright baggy clothes. Actually he had been shoved into me by some youths outside a drugstore.

"See the freak," said an obese and drunken fellow. "See the freak fall."

My first response was anger, and then fear as I saw two others flanking the fat drunk. They walked toward me and I tensed myself for a confrontation.

"This is a disgrace," one said, the neck of a wine bottle held loosely in his left hand.

But it was not to me they were speaking; it was to the clown, who had been pushed to the sidewalk. His three persecutors helped him up with a sudden jerk and then splashed wine in his face. They ignored me altogether.

"Let him loose," the fat one said. "Crawl away, freak. Oh, he flies!"

The clown trotted off, becoming lost in the throng.

"Wait a minute," I said to the rowdy trio, who had started lumbering away. I quickly decided that it would probably be futile to ask them to explain what I had just witnessed, especially amid the noise and confusion of the festivities. In my best jovial fashion I proposed we all go someplace where I could buy them each a drink. They had no objection and in a short while we were all squeezed around a table in the Red Rooster.

Over several drinks I explained to them that I was from out of town, which pleased them no end for some reason. I told them there were things I did not understand about their festival.

"I don't think there's anything to understand," the fat one said. "It's just what you see."

I asked him about the people dressed as clowns.

"Them? They're the freaks. It's their turn this year. Everyone takes their turn. Next year it might be mine. Or *yours*," he said, pointing at one of his friends across the table. "And when we find out which one you are—"

"You're not smart enough," said the defiant potential freak.

This was an important point: the fact that individuals who played the clowns remain, or at least attempted to remain, anonymous. This arrangement would help remove inhibitions a resident of Mirocaw might have about abusing his own neighbor or even a family relation. From what I later observed, the extent of this abuse did not go beyond a kind of playful roughhousing. And even so, it was only the occasional group of rowdies who actually took advantage of this aspect of the festival, the majority of the citizens very much content to stay on the sidelines.

As far as being able to illuminate the meaning of this custom, my three young friends were quite useless. To them it was just amusement, as I imagine it was to the majority of Mirocavians. This was understandable. I suppose the average person would not be able to explain exactly how the profoundly familiar Christmas holiday came to be celebrated in its present form.

I left the bar alone and not unaffected by the drinks I had consumed there. Outside, the general merrymaking continued. Loud music emanated from several quarters. Mirocaw had fully transformed itself from a sedate small town to an enclave of Saturnalia within the dark immensity of a winter night. But Saturn is also the planetary symbol of melancholy and sterility, a clash of opposites contained within that single word. And as I wandered half-drunkenly down the street, I discovered that there was a conflict within the winter festival itself. This discovery indeed appeared to be that secret key which Thoss withheld in his study of the town. Oddly enough, it was through my unfamiliarity with the outward nature of the festival that I came to know its true nature.

I was mingling with the crowd on the street, warmly enjoying the confusion around me, when I saw a strangely designed creature lingering on the corner up ahead. It was one of the Mirocaw clowns. Its clothes were shabby and nondescript, almost in the style of a tramp-type clown, but not humorously exaggerated enough. The face, though, made up for the lackluster costume. I had never seen such a strange conception for a clown's countenance. The figure stood beneath a dim streetlight, and when it turned its head my way I realized why it seemed familiar. The thin, smooth, and pale head; the wide eyes; the oval-shaped features resembling nothing so much as the skull-faced, screaming creature in that famous painting (memory fails me). This clownish imitation rivalled the original in suggesting stricken realms of abject horror and despair: an inhuman likeness more proper to something under the earth than upon it.

From the first moment I saw this creature, I thought of those inhabitants of the ghetto down the hill. There was the same nauseating passivity and languor in its bearing. Perhaps if I had not been drinking earlier I would not have been bold enough to take the action I did. I decided to join in one of the upstanding traditions of the winter festival, for it annoyed me to see this morbid impostor of a clown standing up. When I reached the corner I laughingly pushed myself into the creature —"Whoops!"—who stumbled backward and ended up on the sidewalk. I laughed again and looked around for approval from the festivalers in the vicinity. No one, however, seemed to appreciate or even acknowledge what I had done. They did not laugh with me or point with amusement, but only passed by, perhaps walking a little faster until they were some distance from this streetcorner incident. I realized instantly I had violated some tacit rule of behavior, though I had thought my action well within the common practice. The idea occurred to me that I might even be apprehended and prosecuted for what in any other circumstances was certainly a criminal act. I turned around to help the clown back to his feet, hoping to somehow redeem my offense, but the creature was gone. Solemnly I walked away from the scene of my inadvertent crime and sought other streets away from its witnesses.

Along the various back avenues of Mirocaw I wandered, pausing exhaustedly at one point to sit at the counter of a small sandwich shop that was packed with customers. I ordered a cup of coffee to revive my overly alcoholed system. Warming my hands around the cup and sipping slowly from it, I watched the people outside as they passed the front window. It was well after midnight but the thick flow of passersby gave no indication that anyone was going home early. A carnival of profiles filed past the window and I was content simply to sit back and observe, until finally one of these faces made me start. It was that frightful little clown I had roughed up earlier. But although its face was familiar in its ghastly aspect, there was something different about it. And I wondered that there should be two such hideous freaks.

Quickly paying the man at the counter, I dashed out to get a second glimpse of the clown, who was now nowhere in sight. The dense crowd kept me from pursuing this figure with any speed, and I wondered how the clown could have made its way so easily ahead of me. Unless the crowd had instinctively allowed this creature to pass unhindered through its massive ranks, as it did for Thoss. In the process of searching for this

particular freak, I discovered that interspersed among the celebrating populous of Mirocaw, which included the sanctioned
festival clowns, there was not one or two, but a considerable
number of these pale, wraith-like creatures. And they all
drifted along the streets unmolested by even the rowdiest of
revelers. I now understood one of the taboos of the festival.
These other clowns were not to be disturbed and should even
be avoided, much as were the residents of the slum at the edge
of town. Nevertheless, I felt instinctively that the two groups
of clowns were somehow identified with each other, even if the
ghetto clowns were not welcome at Mirocaw's winter festival.
Indeed, they were not simply part of the community and celebrating the season in their own way. To all appearances, this
group of melancholy mummers constituted nothing less than
an entirely independent festival—a festival within a festival.

Returning to my room, I entered my suppositions into the
journal I was keeping for this venture. The following are
excerpts:

There is a superstitiousness displayed by the residents of Mirocaw
with regard to these people from the slum section, particularly as they
lately appear in those dreadful faces signifying their own festival.
What is the relationship between these simultaneous celebrations?
Did one precede the other? If so, which? My opinion at this point—
and I claim no conclusiveness for it—is that Mirocaw's winter festival
is the later manifestation, that it appeared after the festival of those
depressingly pallid clowns, in order to cover it up or mitigate its
effect. The holiday suicides come to mind, and the subclimate Thoss
wrote about, the disappearance of Elizabeth Beadle twenty years ago,
and my own experience with this pariah clan existing outside yet
within the community. Of my own experience with this emotionally
deleterious subseason I would rather not speak at this time. Still not
able to say whether or not my usual winter melancholy is the cause.
On the general subject of mental health, I must consider Thoss's
book about his stay in a psychiatric hospital (in western Mass., almost
sure of that. Check on this book & Mirocaw's New England roots).
The winter solstice is tomorrow, albeit sometime past midnight (how
blurry these days and nights are becoming!). It is, of course, the day
of the year in which night hours surpass daylight hours by the greatest margin. Note what this has to do with the suicides and a rise in
psychic disorder. Recalling Thoss's list of documented suicides in his
article, there seemed to be a recurrence of specific family names, as

there very likely might be for any kind of data collected in a small town. Among these names was a Beadle or two. Perhaps, then, there is a genealogical basis for the suicides which has nothing to do with Thoss's mystical subclimate, which is a colorful idea to be sure and one that seems fitting for this town of various outward and inward aspects, but is not a conception that can be substantiated.

One thing that seems certain, however, is the division of Mirocaw into two very distinct types of citizenry, resulting in two festivals and the appearance of similar clowns—a term now used in an extremely loose sense. But there is a connection, and I believe I have some idea of what it is. I said before that the normal residents of the town regard those from the ghetto, and especially their clown figures, with superstition. Yet it's more than that: there is fear, perhaps a kind of hatred—the particular kind of hatred resulting from some powerful and irrational memory. What threatens Mirocaw I think I can very well understand. I recall the incident earlier today in that vacant diner. "Vacant" is the appropriate word here, despite its contradiction of fact. The congregation of that half-lit room formed less a presence than an absence, even considering the oppressive number of them. Those eyes that did not or could not focus on anything, the pining lassitude of their faces, the lazy march of their feet. I was spiritually drained when I ran out of there. I then understood why these people and their activities are avoided.

I cannot question the wisdom of those ancestral Mirocavians who began the tradition of the winter festival and gave the town a pretext for celebration and social intercourse at a time when the consequences of brooding isolation are most severe, those longest and darkest days of the solstice. A mood of Christmas joviality obviously would not be sufficient to counter the menace of this season. But even so, there are still the suicides of individuals who are somehow cut off, I imagine, from the vitalizing activities of the festival.

It is the nature of this insidious subseason that seems to determine the outward forms of Mirocaw's winter festival: the optimistic greenery in a period of gray dormancy; the fertile promise of the Winter Queen; and, most interesting to my mind, the clowns. The bright clowns of Mirocaw who are treated so badly; they appear to serve as substitute figures for those dark-eyed mummers of the slums. Since the latter are feared for some power or influence they possess, they may still be symbolically confronted and conquered through their counterparts, who are elected for precisely this function. If I am right about this, I wonder to what extent there is a conscious awareness among the town's populace of this indirect show of aggression. Those three young men I spoke with tonight did not seem to possess much insight beyond seeing that there was a certain amount of robust fun in the festival's tradition. For that matter, how much awareness is there on the *other side* of these two antagonistic festivals? Too horrible to think of such a thing, but I must wonder if, for all their apparent aimlessness, those inhabitants of the ghetto are not the only ones who know what they are about. No denying that behind those inhumanly limp expressions there seems to lie a kind of obnoxious intelligence.

Now I realize the confusion of my present state, but as I wobbled from street to street tonight, watching those oval-mouthed clowns, I could not help feeling that all the merry-making in Mirocaw was somehow allowed only by their sufferance. This I hope is no more than a fanciful Thossian intuition, the sort of idea that is curious and thought-provoking without ever seeming to gain the benefit of proof. I know my mind is not entirely lucid, but I feel that it may be possible to penetrate Mirocaw's many complexities and illuminate the hidden side of the festival season. In particular I must look for the significance of the other festival. Is it also some kind of fertility celebration? From what I have seen, the tenor of this "celebrating" subgroup is one of anti-fertility, if anything. How have they managed to keep from dying out completely over the years? How do they maintain their numbers?

But I was too tired to formulate any more of my sodden speculations. Falling onto my bed, I soon became lost in dreams of streets and faces.

6.

I was, of course, slightly hung over when I woke up late the next morning. The festival was still going strong, and blaring music outside roused me from a nightmare. It was a parade. A number of floats proceeded down Townshend, a familiar color predominating. There were theme floats of pilgrims and Indians, cowboys and Indians, and clowns of an orthodox type. In the middle of it all was the Winter Queen herself, freezing atop an icy throne. She waved in all directions. I even imagined she waved up at my dark window.

In the first few groggy moments of wakefulness I had no

sympathy with my excitation of the previous night. But I discovered that my former enthusiasm had merely lain dormant,
and soon returned with an even greater intensity. Never before
had my mind and senses been so active during this usually inert
time of year. At home I would have been playing lugubrious
old records and looking out the window quite a bit. I was terribly grateful in a completely abstract way for my commitment
to a meaningful mania. And I was eager to get to work after I
had had some breakfast at the coffee shop.

When I got back to my room I discovered the door was unlocked. And there was something written on the dresser mirror.
The writing was red and greasy, as if done with a clown's
make-up pencil—my own, I realized. I read the legend, or
rather I should say *riddle*, several times: "What buries itself
before it is dead?" I looked at it for quite a while, very shaken
at how vulnerable my holiday fortifications were. Was this supposed to be a warning of some kind? A threat to the effect that
if I persisted in a certain course I would end up prematurely
interred? I would have to be careful, I told myself. My resolution was to let nothing deter me from the inspired strategy I had
conceived for myself. I wiped the mirror clean, for it was now
needed for other purposes.

I spent the rest of the day devising a very special costume
and the appropriate face to go with it. I easily shabbied up my
overcoat with a torn pocket or two and a complete set of
stains. Combined with blue jeans and a pair of rather scuffed-
up shoes, I had a passable costume for a derelict. The face,
however, was more difficult, for I had to experiment from
memory. Conjuring a mental image of the screaming pierrot in
that painting (*The Scream*, I now recall), helped me quite a bit.
At nightfall I exited the hotel by the back stairway.

It was strange to walk down the crowded street in this gruesome disguise. Though I thought I would feel conspicuous, the
actual experience was very close, I imagined, to one of complete invisibility. No one looked at me as I strolled by, or as they
strolled by, or as we strolled by each other. I was a phantom—
perhaps the ghost of festivals past, or those yet to come.

I had no clear idea where my disguise would take me that
night, only vague expectations of gaining the confidence of my
fellow specters and possibly in some way coming to know their

secrets. For a while I would simply wander around in that lack-adaisical manner I had learned from them, following their lead in any way they might indicate. And for the most part this meant doing almost nothing and doing it silently. If I passed one of my kind on the sidewalk there was no speaking, no exchange of knowing looks, no recognition at all that I was aware of. We were there on the streets of Mirocaw to create a presence and nothing more. At least this is how I came to feel about it. As I drifted along with my bodiless invisibility, I felt myself more and more becoming an empty, floating shape, seeing without being seen and walking without the interference of those grosser creatures who shared my world. It was not an experi-ence completely without interest or even pleasure. The clown's shibboleth of "here we are again" took on a new meaning for me as I felt myself a novitiate of a more rarified order of harle-quinry. And very soon the opportunity to make further prog-ress along this path presented itself.

Going the opposite direction, down the street, a pickup truck slowly passed, gently parting a sea of zigging and zagging cel-ebrants. The cargo in the back of this truck was curious, for it was made up entirely of my fellow sectarians. At the end of the block the truck stopped and another of them boarded it over the back gate. One block down I saw still another get on. Then the truck made a U-turn at an intersection and headed in my direction.

I stood at the curb as I had seen the others do. I was not sure the truck would pick me up, thinking that somehow they knew I was an imposter. The truck did, however, slow down, almost coming to a stop when it reached me. The others were crowded on the floor of the truck bed. Most of them were just staring into nothingness with the usual indifference I had come to expect from their kind. But a few actually glanced at me with some anticipation. For a second I hesitated, not sure I wanted to pursue this ruse any further. At the last moment, some impulse sent me climbing up the back of the truck and squeezing myself in among the others.

There were only a few more to pick up before the truck headed for the outskirts of Mirocaw and beyond. At first I tried to maintain a clear orientation with respect to the town. But as we took turn after turn through the darkness of narrow country roads, I found myself unable to preserve any sense of direction. The majority of the others in the back of the truck exhibited no apparent awareness of their fellow passengers. Guardedly, I looked from face to ghostly face. A few of them spoke in short whispered phrases to others close by. I could not make out what they were saying but the tone of their voices was one of innocent normalcy, as if they were not of the hardened slum-herd of Mirocaw. Perhaps, I thought, these were thrill-seekers who had disguised themselves as I had done, or, more likely, initiates of some kind. Possibly they had received prior instructions at such meetings as I had stumbled onto the day before. It was also likely that among this crew were those very boys I had frightened into a precipitate exit from that old diner.

The truck was now speeding along a fairly open stretch of country, heading toward those higher hills that surrounded the now distant town of Mirocaw. The icy wind whipped around us, and I could not keep myself from trembling with cold. This definitely betrayed me as one of the newcomers among the group, for the two bodies that pressed against mine were rigidly still and even seemed to be radiating a frigidity of their own. I glanced ahead at the darkness into which we were rapidly progressing.

We had left all open country behind us now, and the road was enclosed by thick woods. The mass of bodies in the truck leaned into one another as we began traveling up a steep incline. Above us, at the top of the hill, were lights shining somewhere within the woods. When the road levelled off, the truck made an abrupt turn, steering into what looked like a great ditch.

There was an unpaved path, however, upon which the truck proceeded toward the glowing in the near distance.

This glowing became brighter and sharper as we approached it, flickering upon the trees and revealing stark detail where there had formerly been only smooth darkness. As the truck pulled into a clearing and came to a stop, I saw a loose assembly of figures, many of which held lanterns that beamed with a dazzling and frosty light. I stood up in the back of the truck to unboard as the others were doing. Glancing around from that height I saw approximately thirty more of those cadaverous clowns milling about. One of my fellow passengers spied me lingering in the truck and in a strangely high-pitched whisper told me to hurry, explaining something about the "apex of darkness". I thought again about this solstice night; it was technically the longest period of darkness of the year, even if not by a very significant margin from many other winter nights. Its true significance, though, was related to considerations having little to do with either statistics or the calendar.

I went over to the place where the others were forming into a tighter crowd, which betrayed a sense of expectancy in the subtle gestures and expressions of its individual members. Glances were now exchanged, the hand of one lightly touched the shoulder of another, and a pair of circled eyes gazed over to where two figures were setting their lanterns on the ground about six feet apart. The illumination of these lanterns revealed an opening in the earth. Eventually the awareness of everyone was focused on this roundish pit, and as if by pre-arranged signal we all began huddling around it. The only sounds were those of the wind and our own movements as we crushed frozen leaves and sticks underfoot.

Finally, when we had all surrounded this gaping hole, the first one jumped in, leaving our sight for a moment but then reappearing to take hold of a lantern which another handed him from above. The miniature abyss filled with light, and I could see it was no more than six feet deep. One of its walls opened into the mouth of a tunnel. The figure holding the lantern stooped a little and disappeared into the passage.

Each of us, in turn, dropped into the darkness of this pit, and every fifth one took a lantern. I kept to the back of the group, for whatever subterranean activities were going to take place, I was sure I wanted to be on their periphery. When only about ten of us remained on the ground above, I maneuvered to let four of them precede me so that as the fifth I might receive a lantern. This was exactly how it worked out, for after I had leaped to the bottom of the hole a light was ritually handed down to me. Turning about-face, I quickly entered the passageway. At that point I shook so with cold that I was neither curious nor afraid, but only grateful for the shelter.

I entered a long, gently sloping tunnel, just high enough for me to stand upright. It was considerably warmer down there than outside in the cold darkness of the woods. After a few moments I had sufficiently thawed out so that my concerns shifted from those of physical comfort to a sudden and justified preoccupation with my survival. As I walked I held my lantern close to the sides of the tunnel. They were relatively smooth as if the passage had not been made by manual digging but had been burrowed by something which left behind a clue to its dimensions in the tunnel's size and shape. This delirious idea came to me when I recalled the message that had been left on my hotel room mirror: "What buries itself before it is dead?"

I had to hurry along to keep up with those uncanny spelunkers who preceded me. The lanterns ahead bobbed with every step of their bearers, the lumbering procession seeming less and less real the farther we marched into that snug little tunnel. At some point I noticed the line ahead of me growing shorter. The processioners were emptying out into a cavernous chamber where I, too, soon arrived. This area was about thirty feet in height, its other dimensions approximating those of a large ballroom. Gazing into the distance above made me uncomfortably aware of how far we had descended into the earth. Unlike the smooth sides of the tunnel, the walls of this cavern looked jagged and irregular, as though they had been gnawed at. The earth had been removed, I assumed, either through the tunnel from which we had emerged, or else by way of one of the many other black openings that I saw around the edges of the chamber, for possibly they too led back to the surface.

But the structure of this chamber occupied my mind a great deal less than did its occupants. There to meet us on the floor of the great cavern was what must have been the entire slum population of Mirocaw, and more, all with the same eerily wide-eyed and oval-mouthed faces. They formed a circle around an altar-like object which had some kind of dark, leathery covering draped over it. Upon the altar, another covering of the same material concealed a lumpy form beneath.

And behind this form, looking down upon the altar, was the only figure whose face was not greased with makeup.

He wore a long snowy robe that was the same color as the wispy hair berimming his head. His arms were calmly at his sides. He made no movement. The man I once believed would penetrate great secrets stood before us with the same professorial bearing that had impressed me so many years ago, yet now I felt nothing but dread at the thought of what revelations lay pocketed within the abysmal folds of his magisterial attire. Had I really come here to challenge such a formidable figure? The name by which I knew him seemed itself insufficient to designate one of his stature. Rather I should name him by his other incarnations: god of all wisdom, scribe of all sacred books, father of all magicians, thrice great and more—rather I should call him *Thoth*.

He raised his cupped hands to his congregation and the ceremony was underway.

It was all very simple. The entire assembly, which had remained speechless until this moment, broke into the most horrendous high-pitched singing that can be imagined. It was a choir of sorrow, of shrieking delirium, and of shame. The cavern rang shrilly with the dissonant, whining chorus. My voice, too, was added to the congregation's, trying to blend with their maimed music. But my singing could not imitate theirs, having a huskiness unlike their cacophonous keening wail. To keep from exposing myself as an intruder I continued to mouth their words without sound. These words were a revelation of the moody malignancy which until then I had no more than sensed whenever in the presence of these figures. They were singing to the "unborn in paradise," to the "pure unlived lives." They sang a dirge for existence, for all its vital forms and seasons. Their ideals were those of darkness, chaos, and a melancholy half-existence consecrated to all the many shapes of death. A sea of thin, bloodless faces trembled and screamed with perverted hopes. And the robed, guiding figure at the heart of all this—elevated over the course of twenty years to the status of high priest—was the man from whom I had taken so many of my own life's principles. It would be useless to describe what I felt at that moment and a waste of the time I need to describe the events which followed.

The singing abruptly stopped and the towering white-haired figure began to speak. He was welcoming those of the new generation—twenty winters had passed since the "Pure Ones" had expanded their ranks. The word "pure" in this setting was a violence to what sense and composure I still retained, for nothing could have been more foul than what was to come. Thoss—and I employ this defunct identity only as a convenience —closed his sermon and drew closer to the dark-skinned altar. Then, with all the flourish of his former life, he drew back the topmost covering. Beneath it was a limp-limbed effigy, a collapsed puppet sprawled upon the slab. I was standing toward the rear of the congregation and attempted to keep as close to the exit passage as I could. Thus, I did not see everything as clearly as I might have.

Thoss looked down upon the crooked, doll-like form and then out at the gathering. I even imagined that he made knowing eye-contact with myself. He spread his arms and a stream of continuous and unintelligible words flowed from his moaning mouth. The congregation began to stir, not greatly but perceptibly. Until that moment there was a limit to what I believed was the evil of these people. They were, after all, only that. They were merely morbid, self-tortured souls with strange beliefs. If there was anything I had learned in all my years as an anthropologist it was that the world is infinitely rich in strange ideas, even to the point where the concept of strangeness itself had little meaning for me. But with the scene I then witnessed, my conscience bounded into a realm from which it will never return.

For now was the transformation scene, the culmination of every harlequinade.

It began slowly. There was increasing movement among those on the far side of the chamber from where I stood. Someone had fallen to the floor and the others in the area backed away. The voice at the altar continued its chanting. I tried to gain a better view but there were too many of them around me. Through the mass of obstructing bodies I caught only glimpses of what was taking place.

The one who had swooned to the floor of the chamber seemed to be losing all former shape and proportion. I thought it was a clown's trick. They were clowns, were they not? I myself could make four white balls transform into four black balls as I juggled them. And this was not my most astonishing feat of clownish magic. And is there not always a sleight-of-hand inherent in all ceremonies, often dependent on the transported delusions of the celebrants? This was a good show, I thought, and giggled to myself. The transformation scene of Harlequin throwing off his fool's facade. O God, Harlequin, do not move like that! Harlequin, where are your arms? And your legs have melted together and begun squirming upon the floor. What horrible, mouthing umbilicus is that where your face should be? *What is it that buries itself before it is dead?* The almighty serpent of wisdom—the Conqueror Worm.

It now started happening all around the chamber. Individual members of the congregation would gaze emptily—caught for a moment in a frozen trance—and then collapse to the floor to begin the sickening metamorphosis. This happened with ever-increasing frequency the louder and more frantic Thoss chanted his insane prayer or curse. Then there began a writhing movement toward the altar, and Thoss welcomed the things as they curled their way to the altar-top. I knew now what lax figure lay upon it.

This was Kora and Persephone, the daughter of Ceres and the Winter Queen: the child abducted into the underworld of death. Except this child had no supernatural mother to save her, no living mother at all. For the sacrifice I witnessed was an echo of one that had occurred twenty years before, the carnival feast of the preceding generation—*O carne vale!* Now both mother and daughter had become victims of this subterranean sabbath. I finally realized this truth when the figure stirred upon the altar, lifted its head of icy beauty, and screamed at the sight of mute mouths closing around her.

I ran from the chamber into the tunnel. (There was nothing else that could be done, I have obsessively told myself.) Some of the others who had not yet changed began to pursue me. They would have caught up to me, I have no doubt, for I fell only a few yards into the passage. And for a moment I imagined that I too was about to undergo a transformation, but I had not been prepared as the others had been. When I heard the approaching footsteps of my pursuers I was sure there was an even worse fate facing me upon the altar. But the footsteps ceased and retreated. They had received an order in the voice of their high priest. I too heard the order, though I wish I had not, for until then I had imagined that Thoss did not remember who I was. It was that voice which taught me otherwise.

For the moment I was free to leave. I struggled to my feet

and, having broken my lantern in the fall, retraced my way back through cloacal blackness.

Everything seemed to happen very quickly once I emerged from the tunnel and climbed up from the pit. I wiped the reeking greasepaint from my face as I ran through the woods and back to the road. A passing car stopped, though I gave it no other choice except to run me down.

"Thank you for stopping."

"What the hell are you doing out here?" the driver asked.

I caught my breath. "It was a joke. The festival. Friends thought it would be funny . . . Please drive on."

My ride let me off about a mile out of town, and from there I could find my way. It was the same way I had come into Mirocaw on my first visit the summer before. I stood for a while at the summit of that high hill just outside the city limits, looking down upon the busy little hamlet. The intensity of the festival had not abated, and would not until morning. I walked down toward the welcoming glow of green, slipped through the festivities unnoticed, and returned to the hotel. No one saw me go up to my room. Indeed, there was an atmosphere of absence and abandonment throughout that building, and the desk in the lobby was unattended.

I locked the door to my room and collapsed upon the bed.

7.

When I awoke the next morning I saw from my window that the town and surrounding countryside had been visited during the night by a snowstorm, one which was entirely unpredicted. The snow was still falling on the now deserted streets of Mirocaw. The festival was over. Everyone had gone home.

And this was exactly my own intention. Any action on my part concerning what I had seen the night before would have to wait until I was away from the town. I am still not sure it will do the slightest good to speak up like this. Any accusations I could make against the slum populace of Mirocaw would be resisted, as well they should be, as unbelievable. Perhaps in a very short while none of this will be my concern.

With packed suitcases in both hands I walked up to the front desk to check out. The man behind the desk was not Samuel Beadle, and he had to fumble around to find my bill.

"Here we are. Everything all right?"

"Fine," I answered in a dead voice. "Is Mr. Beadle around?"

"No, I'm afraid he's not back yet. Been out all night looking for his daughter. She's a very popular girl, being the Winter Queen and all that nonsense. Probably find she was at a party somewhere."

A little noise came out of my throat.

I threw my suitcases in the back seat of my car and got behind the wheel. On that morning nothing I could recall seemed real to me. The snow was falling and I watched it through my windshield, slow and silent and entrancing. I started up my car, routinely glancing in my rear view mirror. What I saw there is now vividly framed in my mind, as it was framed in the back window of my car when I turned to verify its reality.

In the middle of the street behind me, standing ankle-deep in snow, was Thoss and another figure. When I looked closely at the other I recognized him as one of the boys whom I surprised in that diner. But he had now taken on a corrupt and listless resemblance to his new family. Both he and Thoss stared at me, making no attempt to forestall my departure. Thoss knew that this was unnecessary.

I had to carry the image of those two dark figures in my mind as I drove back home. But only now has the full weight of my experience descended upon me. So far I have claimed illness in order to avoid my teaching schedule. To face the normal flow of life as I had formerly known it would be impossible. I am now very much under the influence of a season and a climate far colder and more barren than all the winters in human memory. And mentally retracing past events does not seem to have helped; I can feel myself sinking deeper into a velvety white abyss.

At certain times I could almost dissolve entirely into this inner realm of awful purity and emptiness. I remember those invisible moments when in disguise I drifted through the streets of Mirocaw, untouched by the drunken, noisy forms around me: untouchable. But instantly I recoil at this grotesque nostalgia, for I realize what is happening and what I do not want to be true, though Thoss proclaimed it was. I recall his command to those others as I lay helplessly prone in the tunnel. They could have apprehended me, but Thoss, my old master, called them back. His voice echoed throughout that cavern, and it now reverberates within my own psychic chambers of memory.

"He is one of us," it said. "He has *always* been one of us."

It is this voice which now fills my dreams and my days and my long winter nights. I have seen you, Dr. Thoss, through the snow outside my window. Soon I will celebrate, alone, that last feast which will kill your words, only to prove how well I have learned their truth.

To the memory of H. P. Lovecraft

1990

PETER STRAUB

(b. 1943)

A Short Guide to the City

THE viaduct killer, named for the location where his victims' bodies have been discovered, is still at large. There have been six victims to date, found by children, people exercising their dogs, lovers, or—in one instance—by policemen. The bodies lay sprawled, their throats slashed, partially sheltered by one or another of the massive concrete supports at the top of the slope beneath the great bridge. We assume that the viaduct killer is a resident of the city, a voter, a renter or property owner, a product of the city's excellent public school system, perhaps even a parent of children who even now attend one of its seven elementary schools, three public high schools, two parochial schools, or single nondenominational private school. He may own a boat or belong to the Book-of-the-Month Club, he may frequent one or another of its many bars and taverns, he may have subscription tickets to the concert series put on by the city symphony orchestra. He may be a factory worker with a library ticket. He owns a car, perhaps two. He may swim in one of the city's public pools or the vast lake, punctuated with sailboats, during the hot moist August of the city.

For this is a Midwestern city, northern, with violent changes of season. The extremes of climate, from ten or twenty below zero to up around one hundred in the summer, cultivate an attitude of acceptance in its citizens, of insularity—it looks inward, not out, and few of its children leave for the more temperate, uncertain, and experimental cities of the eastern or western coasts. The city is proud of its modesty—it cherishes the ordinary, or what it sees as the ordinary, which is not. (It has had the same mayor for twenty-four years, a man of limited-to-average intelligence who has aged gracefully and has never had any other occupation of any sort.)

Ambition, the yearning for fame, position, and achievement, is discouraged here. One of its citizens became the head of a

389

small foreign state, another a famous bandleader, yet another a Hollywood staple who for decades played the part of the star's best friend and confidant; this, it is felt, is enough, and besides, all of these people are now dead. The city has no literary tradition. Its only mirror is provided by its two newspapers, which have thick sports sections and are comfortable enough to be read in bed.

The city's characteristic mode is *denial*. For this reason, an odd fabulousness permeates every quarter of the city, a receptiveness to fable, to the unrecorded. A river runs through the center of the business district, as the Liffey runs through Dublin, the Seine through Paris, the Thames through London, and the Danube through Budapest, though our river is smaller and less consequential than any of these.

Our lives are ordinary and exemplary, the citizens would say. We take part in the life of the nation, history courses through us for all our immunity to the national illnesses: it is even possible that in our ordinary lives . . . We too have had our pulse taken by the great national seers and opinion-makers, for in us you may find . . .

Forty years ago, in winter, the body of a woman was found on the banks of the river. She had been raped and murdered, cast out of the human community—a prostitute, never identified—and the noises of struggle that must have accompanied her death went unnoticed by the patrons of the Green Woman Taproom, located directly above that point on the river where her body was discovered. It was an abnormally cold winter that year, a winter of shared misery, and within the Green Woman the music was loud, feverish, festive.

In that community, which is Irish and lives above its riverfront shops and bars, neighborhood children were supposed to have found a winged man huddling in a packing case, an aged man, half-starved, speaking a strange language none of the children knew. His wings were ragged and dirty, many of the feathers as cracked and threadbare as those of an old pigeon's, and his feet were dirty and swollen. *Ull! Li! Gack!* the children screamed at him, mocking the sounds that came from his mouth. They pelted him with rocks and snowballs, imagining that he had crawled up from that same river which sent chill damp—a damp as cold as cancer—into their bones and bedrooms, which gave them earaches and chilblains, which in summer bred rats and mosquitos.

One of the city's newspapers is Democratic, the other Republican. Both papers ritually endorse the mayor, who though consummately political has no recognizable politics. Both of the city's newspapers also support the Chief of Police, crediting him with keeping the city free of the kind of violence that has undermined so many other American cities. None of our citizens goes armed, and our church attendance is still far above the national average.

We are ambivalent about violence.

We have very few public statues, mostly of Civil War generals. On the lakefront, separated from the rest of the town by a six-lane expressway, stands the cubelike structure of the Arts Center, otherwise called the War Memorial. Its rooms are hung with mediocre paintings before which schoolchildren are led on tours by their teachers, most of whom were educated in our local school system.

Our teachers are satisfied, decent people, and the statistics about alcohol and drug abuse among both students and teachers are very encouraging.

There is no need to linger at the War Memorial.

Proceeding directly north, you soon find yourself among the orderly, impressive precincts of the wealthy. It was in this sector of the town, known generally as the East Side, that the brewers and tanners who made our city's first great fortunes set up their mansions. Their houses have a northern, Germanic, even Baltic look which is entirely appropriate to our climate. Of gray stone or red brick, the size of factories or prisons, these stately buildings seem to conceal that vein of fantasy that is actually our most crucial inheritance. But it may be that the style of life—the invisible, hidden life—of these inbred merchants is itself fantastic: the multitude of servants, the maids and coachmen, the cooks and laundresses, the private zoos, the elaborate dynastic marriages and fleets of cars, the rooms lined with silk wallpaper, the twenty-course meals, the underground wine cellars and bomb shelters. . . . Of course we do not know if all of these things are true, or even if some of them are true. Our society folk keep to themselves, and what we know of them we learn chiefly from the newspapers, where they are pictured at their balls, standing with their beautiful daughters before fountains of champagne. The private zoos have been broken up long ago. As citizens, we are free to walk down the avenues, past the magnificent houses, and to peer in through the gates at their coach houses and lawns. A uniformed man polishes a car, four tall young people in white play tennis on a private court.

The viaduct killer's victims have all been adult women.

While you continue moving north you will find that as the houses diminish in size the distance between them grows greater. Through the houses, now without gates and coach houses, you can glimpse a sheet of flat grayish-blue—the lake. The air is free, you breathe it in. That is freedom, breathing this air from the lake. Free people may invent themselves in any image, and you may imagine yourself a prince of the earth, walking with an easy stride. Your table is set with linen, china, crystal, and silver, and as you dine, as the servants pass among you with the serving trays, the talk is educated, enlightened, without prejudice of any sort. The table talk is mainly about ideas, it is true, ideas of a conservative cast. You deplore violence, you do not recognize it.

Further north lie suburbs, which are uninteresting.

If from the War Memorial you proceed south, you cross the viaduct. Beneath you is a valley—the valley is perhaps best seen in the dead of winter. All of our city welcomes winter, for our public buildings are gray stone fortresses which, on days when the temperature dips below zero and the old gray snow of previous storms swirls in the avenues, seem to blend with the leaden air and become dreamlike and cloudy. This is how they were meant to be seen. The valley is called . . . it is called the Valley. Red flames tilt and waver at the tops of columns, and smoke pours from factory chimneys. The trees seem to be black. In the winter, the smoke from the factories becomes solid, like dark gray glaciers, and hangs in the dark air in defiance of gravity, like wings that are a light feathery gray at their tips and darken imperceptibly toward black, toward pitchy black at the point where these great frozen glaciers, these dirigibles, would join the body at the shoulder. The bodies of the great birds to which these wings are attached must be imagined.

In the old days of the city, the time of the private zoos,

wolves were bred in the Valley. Wolves were in great demand in those days. Now the wolf-ranches have been entirely replaced by factories, by rough taverns owned by retired shop foremen, by spurs of the local railroad line, and by narrow streets lined with rickety frame houses and shoe-repair shops. Most of the old wolf-breeders were Polish, and though their kennels, grassy yards, and barbed-wire exercise runs have disappeared, at least one memory of their existence endures: the Valley's street signs are in the Polish language. Tourists are advised to skirt the Valley, and it is always recommended that photographs be confined to the interesting views obtained by looking down from the viaduct. The more courageous visitors, those in search of pungent experience, are cautiously directed to the taverns of the ex-foremen, in particular the oldest of these (the Rusty Nail and the Brace 'n' Bit), where the wooden floors have so softened and furred with lavings and scrubbings that the boards have come to resemble the pelts of long narrow short-haired animals. For the intrepid, these words of caution: do not dress conspicuously, and carry only small amounts of cash. Some working knowledge of Polish is also advised.

Continuing further south, we come to the Polish district proper, which also houses pockets of Estonians and Lithuanians. More than the city's sadly declining downtown area, this district has traditionally been regarded as the city's heart, and has remained unchanged for more than a hundred years. Here the visitor may wander freely among the markets and street fairs, delighting in the sight of well-bundled children rolling hoops, patriarchs in tall fur hats and long beards, and women gathering around the numerous communal water pumps. The sausages and stuffed cabbage sold at the food stalls may be eaten with impunity, and the local beer is said to be of an unrivaled purity. Violence in this district is invariably domestic, and the visitor may feel free to enter the frequent political discussions, which in any case partake of a nostalgic character. In late January or early February the "South Side" is at its best, with the younger people dressed in multilayered heavy woolen garments decorated with the "reindeer" or "snowflake" motif, and the older women of the community seemingly vying to see which of them can outdo the others in the thickness, blackness, and heaviness of her outergarments and in the severity of the traditional head scarf known as the babushka. In late winter the neatness and orderliness of these colorful folk may be seen at its best, for the wandering visitor will often see the bearded paterfamilias sweeping and shoveling not only his immaculate bit of sidewalk (for these houses are as close together as those of the wealthy along the lakefront, so near to one another that until very recently telephone service was regarded as an irrelevance), but his tiny front lawn as well, with its Marian shrines, crèches, ornamental objects such as elves, trolls, postboys, etc. It is not unknown for residents here to proffer the stranger an invitation to inspect their houses, in order to display the immaculate condition of the kitchen with its well-blackened wood stove and polished ornamental tiles, and perhaps even extend a thimble-glass of their own peach or plum brandy to the thirsty visitor.

Alcohol, with its associations of warmth and comfort, is ubiquitous here, and it is the rare family that does not devote some portion of the summer to the preparation of that winter's plenty.

For these people, violence is an internal matter, to be resolved within or exercised upon one's own body and soul or those of one's immediate family. The inhabitants of these neat, scrubbed little houses with their statues of Mary and cathedral tiles, the descendants of the hard-drinking wolf-breeders of another time, have long since abandoned the practice of crippling their children to ensure their continuing exposure to parental values, but self-mutilation has proved more difficult to eradicate. Few blind themselves now, but many a grandfather conceals a three-fingered hand within his embroidered mitten. Toes are another frequent target of self-punishment, and the prevalence of cheerful, even boisterous shops, always crowded with old men telling stories, which sell the hand-carved wooden legs known as "pegs" or "dollies," speaks of yet another.

No one has ever suggested that the viaduct killer is a South Side resident.

The South Siders live in a profound relationship to violence, and its effects are invariably implosive rather than explosive. Once a decade, perhaps twice a decade, one member of a family will realize, out of what depths of cultural necessity the outsider can only hope to imagine, that the whole family must die—*be sacrificed*, to speak with greater accuracy. Axes, knives, bludgeons, bottles, babushkas, ancient derringers, virtually every imaginable implement has been used to carry out this aim. The houses in which this act of sacrifice has taken place are immediately if not instantly cleaned by the entire neighborhood, acting in concert. The bodies receive a Catholic burial in consecrated ground, and a mass is said in honor of both the victims and their murderer. A picture of the departed family is installed in the church which abuts Market Square, and for a year the house is kept clean and dust-free by the grandmothers of the neighborhood. Men young and old will quietly enter the house, sip the brandy of the "removed," as they are called, meditate, now and then switch on the wireless or the television set, and reflect on the darkness of earthly life. The departed are frequently said to appear to friends and neighbors, and often accurately predict the coming of storms and assist in the location of lost household objects, a treasured button or Mother's sewing needle. After the year has elapsed, the house is sold, most often to a young couple, a young blacksmith or market vendor and his bride, who find the furniture and even the clothing of the "removed" welcome additions to their small household.

Further south are suburbs and impoverished hamlets, which do not compel a visit.

Immediately west of the War Memorial is the city's downtown. Before its decline, this was the city's business district and administrative center, and the monuments of its affluence remain. Marching directly west on the wide avenue which begins at the expressway are the Federal Building, the Post Office, and the great edifice of City Hall. Each is an entire block long and constructed of granite blocks quarried far north in the state. Flights of marble stairs lead up to the massive doors of these structures, and crystal chandeliers can be seen through many of the windows. The facades are classical and severe, uniting in an architectural landscape of granite revetments and colonnades of pillars. (Within, these grand and inhuman buildings have long ago been carved and partitioned into warrens illuminated by bare light bulbs or flickering fluorescent tubing, each tiny office with its worn counter for

petitioners and a stamped sign proclaiming its function: Tax &
Excise, Dog Licenses, Passports, Graphs & Charts, Registry of
Notary Publics, and the like. The larger rooms with chandeliers
which face the avenue, reserved for civic receptions and banquets, are seldom used.)

In the next sequence of buildings are the Hall of Records,
the Police Headquarters, and the Criminal Courts Building.
Again, wide empty marble steps lead up to massive bronze doors,
rows of columns, glittering windows which on wintry days reflect back the gray empty sky. Local craftsmen, many of them
descendants of the city's original French settlers, forged and
installed the decorative iron bars and grilles on the facade of
the Criminal Courts Building.

After we pass the massive, nearly windowless brick facades of
the Gas and Electric buildings, we reach the arching metal drawbridge over the river. Looking downriver, we can see its muddy
banks and the lights of the terrace of the Green Woman Taproom, now a popular gathering place for the city's civil servants.
(A few feet further east is the spot from which a disgruntled
lunatic attempted and failed to assassinate President Dwight
D. Eisenhower.) Further on stand the high cement walls of
several breweries. The drawbridge has not been raised since
1956, when a corporate yacht passed through.

Beyond the drawbridge lies the old mercantile center of the
city, with its adult bookstores, pornographic theaters, coffee
shops, and its rank of old department stores. These now house
discount outlets selling roofing tiles, mufflers and other auto
parts, plumbing equipment, and cut-rate clothing, and most
of their display windows have been boarded or bricked in since
the civic disturbances of 1968. Various civic plans have failed to
revive this area, though the cobblestones and gas street lamps
installed in the optimistic mid-seventies can for the most part
still be seen. Connoisseurs of the poignant will wish to take a
moment to appreciate them, though they should seek to avoid
the bands of ragged children that frequent this area at nightfall, for though these children are harmless they can become
pressing in their pleas for small change.

Many of these children inhabit dwellings they have constructed themselves in the vacant lots between the adult book-

stores and fast-food outlets of the old mercantile district, and the "tree houses" atop mounds of tires, most of them several stories high and utilizing fire escapes and flights of stairs scavenged from the old department stores, are of some architectural interest. The stranger should not attempt to penetrate these "children's cities," and on no account should offer them any more than the pocket change they request or display a camera, jewelry, or an expensive wristwatch. The truly intrepid tourist seeking excitement may hire one of these children to guide him to the diversions of his choice. Two dollars is the usual gratuity for this service.

It is not advisable to purchase any of the goods the children themselves may offer for sale, although they have been affected by the same self-consciousness evident in the impressive buildings on the other side of the river and do sell picture postcards of their largest and most eccentric constructions. It may be that the naive architecture of these tree houses represents the city's most authentic artistic expression, and the postcards, amateurish as most of them are, provide interesting, perhaps even valuable, documentation of this expression of what may be called folk art.

These industrious children of the mercantile area have ritualized their violence into highly formalized tattooing and "spontaneous" forays and raids into the tree houses of opposing tribes during which only superficial injuries are sustained, and it is not suspected that the viaduct killer comes from their number.

Further west are the remains of the city's museum and library, devastated during the civic disturbances, and beyond these picturesque, still-smoking hulls lies the ghetto. It is not advised to enter the ghetto on foot, though the tourist who has arranged to rent an automobile may safely drive through it after he has negotiated his toll at the gate house. The ghetto's residents are completely self-sustaining, and the attentive tourist who visits this district will observe the multitude of tents housing hospitals, wholesale food and drug warehouses, and the like. Within the ghetto are believed to be many fine poets, painters, and musicians, as well as the historians known as "memorists," who are the district's living encyclopedias and archivists. The "memorist's" tasks include the memorization

of the works of the area's poets, painters, etc., for the district
contains no printing presses or art-supply shops, and these
inventive and self-reliant people have devised this method of
preserving their works. It is not believed that a people capable
of inventing the genre of "oral painting" could have spawned
the viaduct killer, and in any case no ghetto resident is permitted access to any other area of the city.

The ghetto's relationship to violence is unknown.

Further west the annual snowfall increases greatly, for seven
months of the year dropping an average of two point three feet
of snow each month upon the shopping malls and paper mills
which have concentrated here. Dust storms are common during
the summers, and certain infectious viruses, to which the inhabitants have become immune, are carried in the water.

Still further west lies the Sports Complex.

The tourist who has ventured thus far is well advised to turn
back at this point and return to our beginnning, the War
Memorial. Your car may be left in the ample and clearly posted
parking lot on the Memorial's eastern side. From the Memorial's wide empty terraces, you are invited to look southeast,
where a great unfinished bridge crosses half the span to the hamlets of Wyatt and Arnoldville. Construction was abandoned on
this noble civic project, subsequently imitated by many cities
in our western states and in Australia and Finland, immediately
after the disturbances of 1968, when its lack of utility became
apparent. When it was noticed that many families chose to eat
their bag lunches on the Memorial's lakeside terraces in order
to gaze silently at its great interrupted arc, the bridge was
adopted as the symbol of the city, and its image decorates the
city's many flags and medals.

The "Broken Span," as it is called, which hangs in the air
like the great frozen wings above the Valley, serves no function
but the symbolic. In itself and entirely by accident this great
non-span memorializes violence, not only by serving as a reference to the workmen who lost their lives during its construction (its nonconstruction). It is not rounded or finished in any
way, for labor on the bridge ended abruptly, even brutally, and
from its truncated floating end dangle lengths of rusting iron
webbing, thick wire cables weighted by chunks of cement, and

bits of old planking material. In the days before access to the un-bridge was walled off by an electrified fence, two or three citizens each year elected to commit their suicides by leaping from the end of the span; and one must resort to a certain lexical violence when referring to it. Ghetto residents are said to have named it "Whitey," and the tree-house children call it "Ursula," after one of their own killed in the disturbances. South Siders refer to it as "The Ghost," civil servants, "The Beast," and East Siders simply as "that thing." The "Broken Span" has the violence of all unfinished things, of everything interrupted or left undone. In violence there is often the quality of *yearning*—the yearning for completion. For closure. For that which is absent and would if present bring to fulfillment. For the body without which the wing is a useless frozen ornament. It ought not to go unmentioned that most of the city's residents have never seen the "bridge" except in its representations, and for this majority the "bridge" is little more or less than a myth, being without any actual referent. It is pure idea.

Violence, it is felt though unspoken, is the physical form of sensitivity. The city believes this. Incompletion, the lack of referent which strands you in the realm of pure idea, demands release from itself. We are above all an American city, and what we believe most deeply we . . .

The victims of the viaduct killer, that citizen who excites our attention, who makes us breathless with outrage and causes our police force to ransack the humble dwellings along the riverbank, have all been adult women. These women in their middle years are taken from their lives and set like statues beside the pillar. Each morning there is more pedestrian traffic on the viaduct, in the frozen mornings men (mainly men) come with their lunches in paper bags, walking slowly along the cement walkway, not looking at one another, barely knowing what they are doing, looking down over the edge of the viaduct, looking away, dawdling, finally leaning like fishermen against the railing, waiting until they can no longer delay going to their jobs.

The visitor who has done so much and gone so far in this city may turn his back on the "Broken Span," the focus of civic pride, and look in a southwesterly direction past the six lanes of the expressway, perhaps on tiptoe (children may have to mount one of the convenient retaining walls). The dull flanks of the viaduct should just now be visible, with the heads and shoulders of the waiting men picked out in the gray air like brush strokes. The quality of their yearning, its expectancy, is visible even from here.

1990

JEFF VANDERMEER

(b. 1968)

The General Who Is Dead

My name is Stephen Barrow and I served in the Korean War, under the auspices of the 52nd Battalion. You would not have heard about the 52nd Battalion on the newsreels, for all we did was defend a city of the dead from the dead without, and the city held us in its thrall. From afar, it appeared as a glittering white crown of pagodas and snow, undisturbed and pristine. The walled kingdom of an ice witch, something right out of C. S. Lewis' *The Lion, the Witch and the Wardrobe*, perhaps.

Our mission was morbid and macabre and we loved it fiercely, for it kept us from the front lines. The city had been abandoned for over a year. Within its walls, the U.S. High Command had decided to house, catalog, and prepare for shipment stateside the bodies of the soldiers who had died at the front in our stead. We also housed, cataloged, and prepared (for cremation) the remains of South Korean civilians who had been caught in the crossfire. At times, the city streets were littered with the dead, all formally laid out, limbs no longer akimbo from bomb or mine blast, faces much more serene since their grimaces had been crafted into the artifice of smiles. Perhaps they merely slept, I would joke with my fellow soldiers, usually Nate Burlow, a muscle-bound lunk from New Jersey, and Tom Waters, a slender willow with hair so black it was almost blue and pale green eyes that stared out unblinking from beneath a helmet too big for his head. Nate was garrulous and Tom silent to a fault, calm as ice in a Rusty Nail. Between the two of them, I came very close to keeping my sanity amongst the dead.

All of us doubled up on our duties to conserve manpower, and so I became, much against my will, a writer of press releases for the army, under the supervision of Colonel X. It was easy work and I did it at my desk on the fourth floor of headquarters, which had been set up in the Buddhist temple at the city's center. The temple was the tallest structure in a place where the buildings seemed to genuflect and make themselves as small against the earth as possible.

I would sit with the snow-white pieces of paper in front of me and, when the pens were not frozen, I would write about the death of General So-and-So, the bravery of Corporal What's-His-Name. It gave me a lot of time to think. Perhaps too much time. My past did not bear up under close scrutiny and if, in describing what I am about to describe I am indirect about my own life—if, to be blunt, I discard bland fact in favor of hard truth—forgive me.

Suffice it to say, the war had passed us by in more ways than one. By the time I came into the middle of it, my landing at Inchon had none of the biting melodrama of MacArthur's initial beachhead. Colonel B. Powell had urinated proudly in the Yalu River more than six months before, doing several "takes" for the *Stars and Stripes* boys, blissfully ignorant of the fact that no American soldier after him would advance so far to demonstrate his backwardness. U.S. General Smith, a marine, had already declared, "Retreat, Hell! We're not retreating! We're just advancing in a different direction!" All the photo ops and all the best lines had been taken. By the time I came to Korea, the war had bogged down to a slow, futile, and bloody shifting of the lines along barren fields of snow, advance and retreat along the 38th Parallel, like the ebb and flow of some Ice Age tide.

All I had were dead bodies to take care of and paper to write on and my buddies to shoot the shit with. And, of course, the dead Chinese soldiers outside the city's walls.

When I came to the city, along with Nate and Tom, the dead Chinese soldiers were the first things we saw. You couldn't miss them. Over forty thousand of them on the plain outside the city's walls. The sergeant at arms had made sure the chopper let us off in the middle of the plain so that we had to walk through the dead to reach the city. What the man was trying to prove, I have no idea.

There were thirty of us new boys and we said nothing to each other at the time—out of nervousness or sympathy or respect, I don't know which. All I know is we were so quiet you could hear the crunch of our boots in the snow. The sunlight suffused the snow and bled through the Chinese soldiers, turning them crystalline and divine and pathetic all at once. As you can see through the skins of certain fish to their internal organs, so you could see through the ice and know the shapes, the contours, of the dead men on the frozen field. Some knelt and some stood and some huddled in clumps seeking a warmth that had long since left them. Forty thousand dead Chinese soldiers sprawled along a snowy plain. There were forty thousand stories in those lives, for they had all died in subtlely unique ways, and those ways had lent all of their faces a fierce individuality that would mark them even when spring came and thawed them out.

They had called themselves "The Army Which Casts No Shadow" because they had marched by night and lay camouflaged from reconnaissance planes by day. United Nations forces had not spotted them until they crossed the 38th Parallel. They had outrun their own supply lines out of Manchuria in an attempt to cut off U.S. forces from Inchon. They had no choice but to march forward and assault the U.S. perimeter at Pusan. They never made it. Our forces just kept retreating, left no supplies behind, and their progress slowed as they grew hungry, and then a blizzard caught them out in the open. They had already eaten their boots; almost none of them that I could see had shoes on their feet.

Parodies of statues in Pompeii.

The ice that had hardened around their bodies had also hardened their features, disguised their uniforms and weaponry, so that indeed it was a plain of statuary, ethereal, ghostly, and mocking. No one would have guessed they were once an army, or that they had marched anywhere, that once they had been alive. Walking among them I felt a crawling sensation across my spine—a helplessness and a despair that I did not know could live within me. I had a sudden frantic urge to write it down, to write about their deaths. I could not tell whether the impulse was ghoulish or commemorative, so I let it pass.

"Come spring," muttered Tom.

"Come spring what?" said Nate.

"Come spring, they'll thaw and then there'll just be forty thousand stinking dead people here for the vultures to feast on."

It was about the longest sentence Tom ever said, and when I got to know him better, I knew it meant those dead soldiers had really gotten to him, under his skin.

But they looked curiously at peace out in the snow, the longer I stared at them—as if they waited for someone or something to resurrect them. Or perhaps I read that into them and I was waiting for someone to resurrect me. I had a sudden memory of making snow angels in the front yard of our house, my Dad at six-six spread out ridiculously, making giant angels, while my own had been much smaller divinities.

We walked among the dead men for nearly an hour that first, most important, time, although the walls of the city were near. We did not feel, not having seen the indignities of war first hand, that we could leave without paying our respects, if that is the correct term. It was like walking among gravestones, only these men needed no such symbolism. They stood staunchly for themselves. Seeing them so vulnerable, waiting for the thaw that would make them fully human again, my imagination began to unfetter itself from the cold and the company of my fellow soldiers. Something churned in my stomach and up, into my heart. What if these men, these soldiers, really were waiting for someone? As if they had been enchanted, put under a spell? Who were they waiting for?

"Who are they waiting for?" I said it aloud.

"General who?" Tom said, as if reading my mind.

"General Who," I said. Inside, the churning stopped and I thought, yes, it was General Who who led them. General Who who would come back for them. He could protect them, much as my father had often wrapped his arms around me in the snow and held me against his chest, warm and secure.

As we finally left the field, I saw a Chinese woman who had frozen to death along with the soldiers, a look of divinity upon her face. As if she could see something magical beyond her reach. Her head was inclined upward and when I saw her, her features etched cruelly in the ice, I looked where she looked, almost expecting there to be someone in the sky, or some sign.

But this time, there was just the white. Always the white. And from then on, I could not hate our Enemy, or even think ill of Him, but thought only of when I too would be stiff, my eyes staring out into the unknown, afraid—taken away from the sudden, lacerating beauty of this world and into the cruel glacial light of the next.

"General Who is dead," I said as we left that place, and Tom and Nate nodded like they almost understood what I meant.

1996

STEPHEN KING

(b. 1947)

That Feeling, You Can Only Say
What It Is in French

Floyd, what's that over there? Oh shit.

The man's voice speaking these words was vaguely familiar, but the words themselves were just a disconnected snip of dialogue, the kind of thing you heard when you were channel-surfing with the remote. There was no one named Floyd in her life. Still, that was the start. Even before she saw the little girl in the red pinafore, there were those disconnected words.

But it was the little girl who brought it on strong. "Oh-oh, I'm getting that feeling," Carol said.

The girl in the pinafore was in front of a country market called Carson's—BEER, WINE, GROC, FRESH BAIT, LOTTERY—crouched down with her butt between her ankles and the bright-red apron-dress tucked between her thighs, playing with a doll. The doll was yellow-haired and dirty, the kind that's round and stuffed and boneless in the body.

"What feeling?" Bill asked.

"You know. The one you can only say what it is in French. Help me here."

"Déjà vu," he said.

"That's it," she said, and turned to look at the little girl one more time. *She'll have the doll by one leg*, Carol thought. *Holding it upside down by one leg with its grimy yellow hair hanging down.*

But the little girl had abandoned the doll on the store's splintery gray steps and had gone over to look at a dog caged up in the back of a station wagon. Then Bill and Carol Shelton went around a curve in the road and the store was out of sight.

"How much farther?" Carol asked.

Bill looked at her with one eyebrow raised and his mouth dimpled at one corner—left eyebrow, right dimple, always the same. The look that said, *You think I'm amused, but I'm really irritated. For the ninety trillionth or so time in the marriage, I'm really irritated. You don't know that, though, because you can only see about two inches into me and then your vision fails.*

But she had better vision than he realized; it was one of the secrets of the marriage. Probably he had a few secrets of his own. And there were, of course, the ones they kept together.

"I don't know," he said. "I've never been here."

"But you're sure we're on the right road."

"Once you get over the causeway and onto Sanibel Island, there's only one," he said. "It goes across to Captiva, and there it ends. But before it does we'll come to Palm House. That I promise you."

The arch in his eyebrow began to flatten. The dimple began to fill in. He was returning to what she thought of as the Great Level. She had come to dislike the Great Level, too, but not as much as the eyebrow and the dimple, or his sarcastic way of saying "Excuse me?" when you said something he considered stupid, or his habit of pooching out his lower lip when he wanted to appear thoughtful and deliberative.

"Bill?"

"Mmm?"

"Do you know anyone named Floyd?"

"There was Floyd Denning. He and I ran the downstairs snack bar at Christ the Redeemer in our senior year. I told you about him, didn't I? He stole the Coke money one Friday and spent the weekend in New York with his girlfriend. They suspended him and expelled her. What made you think of him?"

"I don't know," she said. Easier than telling him that the Floyd with whom Bill had gone to high school wasn't the Floyd the voice in her head was speaking to. At least, she didn't think it was.

Second honeymoon, that's what you call this, she thought, looking at the palms that lined Highway 867, a white bird that stalked along the shoulder like an angry preacher, and a sign that read SEMINOLE WILDLIFE PARK, BRING A CARFUL FOR $10. *Florida the Sunshine State. Florida the Hospitality State. Not to mention Florida the Second-Honeymoon State. Florida, where Bill Shelton and Carol Shelton, the former Carol O'Neill, of Lynn, Massachusetts, came on their first honeymoon twenty-five years before. Only that was on the other side, the Atlantic side, at a little cabin colony, and there were cockroaches in the bureau drawers. He couldn't stop touching me. That was all right, though, in those days I wanted to be touched. Hell, I wanted to be torched like Atlanta in* Gone in the Wind, *and he torched me, rebuilt me, torched me again. Now it's silver. Twenty-five is silver. And sometimes I get that feeling.*

They were approaching a curve, and she thought, *Three crosses on the right side of the road. Two small ones flanking a bigger one. The small ones are clapped-together wood. The one in the middle is white birch with a picture on it, a tiny photograph of the seventeen-year-old boy who lost control of his car on this curve one drunk night that was his last drunk night, and this is where his girlfriend and her girlfriends marked the spot—*

Bill drove around the curve. A pair of black crows, plump and shiny, lifted off from something pasted to the macadam in a splat of blood. The birds had eaten so well that Carol wasn't sure they were going to get out of the way until they did. There were no crosses, not on the left, not on the right. Just roadkill in the middle, a woodchuck or something, now passing beneath a luxury car that had never been north of the Mason-Dixon Line.

Floyd, what's that over there?

"What's wrong?"

"Huh?" She looked at him, bewildered, feeling a little wild.

"You're sitting bolt-upright. Got a cramp in your back?"

"Just a slight one." She settled back by degrees. "I had that feeling again. The déjà vu."

"Is it gone?"

"Yes," she said, but she was lying. It had retreated a little, but that was all. She'd had this before, but never so *continuously.* It came up and went down, but it didn't go away. She'd been aware of it ever since that thing about Floyd started knocking around in her head—and then the little girl in the red pinafore.

But, really, hadn't she felt something before either of those things? Hadn't it actually started when they came down the steps of the Lear 35 into the hammering heat of the Fort Myers sunshine? Or even before? En route from Boston?

They were coming to an intersection. Overhead was a flashing yellow light, and she thought, *To the right is a used-car lot and a sign for the Sanibel Community Theater.*

Then she thought, *No, it'll be like the crosses that weren't there. It's a strong feeling but a false feeling.*

Here was the intersection. On the right there *was* a used-car lot—Palmdale Motors. Carol felt a real jump at that, a stab of something sharper than disquiet. She told herself to quit being stupid. There had to be car lots all over Florida and if you predicted one at every intersection sooner or later the law of averages made you a prophet. It was a trick mediums had been using for hundreds of years.

Besides, there's no theater sign.

But there was another sign. It was Mary the Mother of God, the ghost of all her childhood days, holding out her hands the way she did on the medallion Carol's grandmother had given her for her tenth birthday. Her grandmother had pressed it into her hand and looped the chain around her fingers, saying, "Wear her always as you grow, because all the hard days are coming." She had worn it, all right. At Our Lady of Angels grammar and middle school she had worn it, then at St. Vincent de Paul high. She wore the medal until breasts grew around it like ordinary miracles, and then someplace, probably on the class trip to Hampton Beach, she had lost it. Coming home on the bus she had tongue-kissed for the first time. Butch Soucy had been the boy, and she had been able to taste the cotton candy he'd eaten.

Mary on that long-gone medallion and Mary on this billboard had exactly the same look, the one that made you feel guilty of thinking impure thoughts even when all you were thinking about was a peanut-butter sandwich. Beneath Mary, the sign said MOTHER OF MERCY CHARITIES HELP THE FLORIDA HOMELESS—WON'T <u>YOU</u> HELP <u>US</u>?

Hey there, Mary, what's the story—

More than one voice this time; many voices, girls' voices, chanting ghost voices. These were ordinary miracles; there were also ordinary ghosts. You found these things out as you got older.

"What's wrong with you?" She knew that voice as well as she did the eyebrow-and-dimple look. Bill's I'm-only-pretending-to-be-pissed tone of voice, the one that meant he really *was* pissed, at least a little.

"Nothing." She gave him the best smile she could manage.

"You really don't seem like yourself. Maybe you shouldn't have slept on the plane."

"You're probably right," she said, and not just to be agreeable, either. After all, how many women got a second honeymoon on Captiva Island for their twenty-fifth anniversary? Round trip on a chartered Learjet? Ten days at one of those places where your money was no good (at least until Master-Card coughed up the bill at the end of the month) and if you wanted a massage a big Swedish babe would come and pummel you in your six-room beach house?

Things had been different at the start. Bill, whom she'd first met at a crosstown high-school dance and then met again at college three years later (another ordinary miracle), had begun their married life working as a janitor, because there were no openings in the computer industry. It was 1973, and computers were essentially going nowhere and they were living in a grotty place in Revere, not on the beach but close to it, and all night people kept going up the stairs to buy drugs from the two sallow creatures who lived in the apartment above them and listened endlessly to dopey records from the sixties. Carol used to lie awake waiting for the shouting to start, thinking, *We won't ever get out of here, we'll grow old and die within earshot of Cream and Blue Cheer and the Dodgem cars down on the beach.*

Bill, exhausted at the end of his shift, would sleep through the noise, lying on his side, sometimes with one hand on her hip. And when it wasn't there she often put it there, especially if the creatures upstairs were arguing with their customers. Bill was all she had. Her parents had practically disowned her when she married him. He was a Catholic, but the wrong sort of Catholic. Gram had asked why she wanted to go with that boy when anyone could tell he was shanty, how could she fall for all his foolish talk, why did she want to break her father's heart. And what could she say?

It was a long distance from that place in Revere to a private jet soaring at forty-one thousand feet; a long way to this rental car, which was a Crown Victoria—what the goodfellas in the gangster movies invariably called a Crown Vic—heading for ten days in a place where the tab would probably be . . . well, she didn't even want to think about it.

Floyd? . . . Oh shit.

"Carol? What is it now?"

"Nothing," she said. Up ahead by the road was a little pink bungalow, the porch flanked by palms—seeing those trees with their fringy heads lifted against the blue sky made her think of Japanese Zeros coming in low, their underwing machine guns firing, such an association clearly the result of a youth misspent in front of the TV—and as they passed a black woman would come out. She would be drying her hands on a piece of pink towelling and would watch them expressionlessly as they passed, rich folks in a Crown Vic headed for Captiva, and she'd have no idea that Carol Shelton once lay awake in a ninety-dollar-a-month apartment, listening to the records and the drug deals upstairs, feeling something alive inside her, something that made her think of a cigarette that had fallen down behind the drapes at a party, small and unseen but smoldering away next to the fabric.

"Hon?"

"Nothing, I said." They passed the house. There was no woman. An old man—white, not black—sat in a rocking chair, watching them pass. There were rimless glasses on his nose and a piece of ragged pink towelling, the same shade as the house, across his lap. "I'm fine now. Just anxious to get there and change into some shorts."

His hand touched her hip—where he had so often touched her during those first days—and then crept a little farther inland. She thought about stopping him (Roman hands and Russian fingers, they used to say) and didn't. They were, after all, on their second honeymoon. Also, it would make that expression go away.

"Maybe," he said, "we could take a pause. You know, after the dress comes off and before the shorts go on."

"I think that's a lovely idea," she said, and put her hand over his, pressed both more tightly against her. Ahead was a sign that would read PALM HOUSE 3 MI. ON LEFT when they got close enough to see it.

The sign actually read PALM HOUSE 2 MI. ON LEFT. Beyond

it was another sign, Mother Mary again, with her hands out-stretched and that little electric shimmy that wasn't quite a halo around her head. This version read MOTHER OF MERCY CHARITIES HELP THE FLORIDA SICK—WON'T <u>YOU</u> HELP <u>US</u>?

Bill said, "The next one ought to say 'Burma Shave.'"

She didn't understand what he meant, but it was clearly a joke and so she smiled. The next one would say "Mother of Mercy Charities Help the Florida Hungry," but she couldn't tell him that. Dear Bill. Dear in spite of his sometimes stupid expressions and his sometimes unclear allusions. *He'll most likely leave you, and you know something? If you go through with it that's probably the best luck you can expect.* This according to her father. Dear Bill, who had proved that just once, just that one crucial time, her judgement had been far better than her father's. She was still married to the man her Gram had called "the big boaster." At a price, true, but what was that old axiom? God says take what you want . . . and pay for it.

Her head itched. She scratched at it absently, watching for the next Mother of Mercy billboard.

Horrible as it was to say, things had started turning around when she lost the baby. That was just before Bill got a job with Beach Computers, out on Route 128; that was when the first winds of change in the industry began to blow.

Lost the baby, had a miscarriage—they all believed that except maybe Bill. Certainly her family had believed it: Dad, Mom, Gram. "Miscarriage" was the story they told, miscarriage was a Catholic's story if ever there was one. *Hey, Mary, what's the story,* they had sometimes sung when they skipped rope, feeling daring, feeling sinful, the skirts of their uniforms flipping up and down over their scabby knees. That was at Our Lady of Angels, where Sister Annunciata would spank your knuckles with her ruler if she caught you gazing out the window during Sentence Time, where Sister Dormatilla would tell you that a million years was but the first tick of eternity's endless clock (and you could spend eternity in Hell, most people did, it was easy). In Hell you would live forever with your skin on fire and your bones roasting. Now she was in Florida, now she was in a Crown Vic sitting next to her husband, whose hand was still in her crotch; the dress would be wrinkled but who cared if it got that look off his face, and why wouldn't the feeling *stop*?

She thought of a mailbox with RAGLAN painted on the side and an American-flag decal on the front, and although the name turned out to be Reagan and the flag a Grateful Dead sticker, the box was there. She thought of a small black dog trotting briskly along the other side of the road, its head down, sniffling, and the small black dog was there. She thought again of the billboard and, yes, there it was: MOTHER OF MERCY CHARITIES HELP THE FLORIDA HUNGRY—WON'T YOU HELP US?

Bill was pointing. "There—see? I think that's Palm House. No, not where the billboard is, the other side. Why do they let people put those things up out here, anyway?"

"I don't know." Her head itched. She scratched, and black dandruff began falling past her eyes. She looked at her fingers and was horrified to see dark smutches on the tips; it was as if someone had just taken her fingerprints.

"Bill?" She raked her hand through her blond hair and this time the flakes were bigger. She saw they were not flakes of skin but flakes of paper. There was a face on one, peering out of the char like a face peering out of a botched negative.

"*Bill?*"

"What? Wh—" Then a total change in his voice, and that frightened her more than the way the car swerved. "Christ, honey, what's in your hair?"

The face appeared to be Mother Teresa's. Or was that just because she'd been thinking about Our Lady of Angels? Carol plucked it from her dress, meaning to show it to Bill, and it crumbled between her fingers before she could. She turned to him and saw that his glasses were melted to his cheeks. One of his eyes had popped from its socket and then split like a grape pumped full of blood.

And I knew it, she thought. *Even before I turned, I knew it. Because I had that feeling.*

A bird was crying in the trees. On the billboard, Mary held out her hands. Carol tried to scream. Tried to scream.

*

"Carol?"

It was Bill's voice, coming from a thousand miles away. Then his hand—not pressing the folds of her dress into her crotch, but on her shoulder.

"You okay, babe?"

She opened her eyes to brilliant sunlight and her ears to the steady hum of the Learjet's engines. And something else—pressure against her eardrums. She looked from Bill's mildly concerned face to the dial below the temperature gauge in the cabin and saw that it had wound down to twenty-eight thousand.

"Landing?" she said, sounding muzzy to herself. "Already?"

"It's fast, huh?" Sounding pleased, as if he had flown it himself instead of only paying for it. "Pilot says we'll be on the ground in Fort Myers in twenty minutes. You took a hell of a jump, girl."

"I had a nightmare."

He laughed—the plummy ain't-you-the-silly-billy laugh she had come really to detest. "No nightmares allowed on your second honeymoon, babe. What was it?"

"I don't remember," she said, and it was the truth. There were only fragments: Bill with his glasses melted all over his face, and one of the three or four forbidden skip rhymes they had sometimes chanted back in fifth and sixth grade. This one had gone *Hey there, Mary, what's the story* . . . and then something-something-something. She couldn't come up with the rest. She could remember *Jangle-tangle jingle-bingle, I saw daddy's great big dingle*, but she couldn't remember the one about Mary.

Mary helps the Florida sick, she thought, with no idea of what the thought meant, and just then there was a beep as the pilot turned the seat-belt light on. They had started their final descent. *Let the wild rumpus start*, she thought, and tightened her belt.

"You really don't remember?" he asked, tightening his own. The little jet ran through a cloud filled with bumps, one of the pilots in the cockpit made a minor adjustment, and the ride smoothed out again. "Because usually, just after you wake up, you can still remember. Even the bad ones."

"I remember Sister Annunciata, from Our Lady of Angels. Sentence Time."

"Now, *that's* a nightmare."

Ten minutes later the landing gear came down with a whine and a thump. Five minutes after that they landed.

"They were supposed to bring the car right out to the plane," Bill said, already starting up the Type A shit. This she didn't like, but at least she didn't detest it the way she detested the plummy laugh and his repertoire of patronizing looks. "I hope there hasn't been a hitch."

There hasn't been, she thought, and the feeling swept over her full force. *I'm going to see it out the window on my side in just a second or two. It's your total Florida vacation car, a great big white goddam Cadillac, or maybe it's a Lincoln—*

And, yes, here it came, proving what? Well, she supposed, it proved that sometimes when you had déjà vu what you thought was going to happen next really did. It wasn't a Caddy or a Lincoln after all, but a Crown Victoria—what the gangsters in a Martin Scorsese film would doubtless call a Crown Vic.

"Whoo," she said as he helped her down the steps and off the plane. The hot sun made her feel dizzy.

"What's wrong?"

"Nothing, really. I've got déjà vu. Left over from my dream, guess. We've been here before, that kind of thing."

"It's being in a strange place, that's all," he said, and kissed her cheek. "Come on, let the wild rumpus start."

They went to the car. Bill showed his driver's license to the young woman who had driven it out. Carol saw him check out the hem of her skirt, then sign the paper on her clipboard.

She's going to drop it, Carol thought. The feeling was now so strong it was like being on an amusement-park ride that goes just a little too fast; all at once you realize you're edging out of the Land of Fun and into the Kingdom of Nausea. *She'll drop it, and Bill will say "Whoopsy-daisy" and pick it up for her, get an even closer look at her legs.*

But the Hertz woman didn't drop her clipboard. A white courtesy van had appeared, to take her back to the Butler Aviation terminal. She gave Bill a final smile—Carol she had ignored completely—and opened the front passenger door. She stepped up, then slipped. "Whoopsy-daisy, don't be crazy," Bill said, and took her elbow, steadying her. She gave him a smile, he gave her well-turned legs a goodbye look, and Carol stood by the growing pile of their luggage and thought, *Hey there, Mary . . .*

"Mrs. Shelton?" It was the co-pilot. He had the last bag, the case with Bill's laptop inside it, and he looked concerned. "Are you all right? You're very pale."

Bill heard and turned away from the departing white van, his face worried. If her strongest feelings about Bill were her only feelings about Bill, now that they were twenty-five years on, she would have left him when she found out about the secretary, a Clairol blonde too young to remember the Clairol slogan that started "If I have only one life to live." But there were other feelings. There was love, for instance. Still love. A kind that girls in Catholic-school uniforms didn't suspect, a weedy, unlovely species too tough to die.

Besides, it wasn't just love that held people together. There were secrets, and the price you paid to keep them.

"Carol?" he asked her. "Babe? All right?"

She thought about telling him no, she wasn't all right, she was drowning, but then she managed to smile and said, "It's the heat, that's all. I feel a little groggy. Get me in the car and crank up the air-conditioning. I'll be fine."

Bill took her by the elbow (*Bet you're not checking out my legs, though*, Carol thought. *You know where they go, don't you?*) and led her toward the Crown Vic as if she were a very old lady. By the time the door was closed and cool air was pumping over her face, she actually had started to feel a little better.

If the feeling comes back, I'll tell him, Carol thought. *I'll have to. It's just too strong. Not normal.*

Well, déjà vu was never normal, she supposed—it was something that was part dream, part chemistry, and (she was sure she'd read this, maybe in a doctor's office somewhere while waiting for her gynecologist to go prospecting up her fifty-two-year-old twat) part the result of an electrical misfire in the brain, causing new experience to be identified as old data. A temporary hole in the pipes, hot water and cold water mingling. She closed her eyes and prayed for it to go away.

Oh, Mary, conceived without sin, pray for us who have recourse to thee.

Please ("Oh puh-lease," they used to say), not back to parochial school. This was supposed to be a vacation, not—

Floyd, what's that over there? Oh shit! Oh SHIT!

Who was Floyd? The only Floyd Bill knew was Floyd Dorning (or maybe it was Darling), the kid he'd run the snack bar with, the one who'd run off to New York with his girlfriend. Carol couldn't remember when Bill had told her about that kid, but she knew he had.

Just quit it, girl. There's nothing here for you. Slam the door on the whole train of thought.

And that worked. There was a final whisper—*what's the story*—and then she was just Carol Shelton, on her way to Captiva Island, on her way to Palm House with her husband the renowned software designer, on their way to the beaches and the rum drinks, and the sound of a steel band playing "Margaritaville."

They passed a Publix market. They passed an old black man minding a roadside fruit stand—he made her think of actors from the thirties and movies you saw on the American Movie Channel, an old yassuh-boss type of guy wearing bib overalls and a straw hat with a round crown. Bill made small talk, and she made it right back at him. She was faintly amazed that the little girl who had worn a Mary medallion every day from ten to sixteen had become this woman in the Donna Karan dress— that the desperate couple in that Revere apartment were these middle-aged rich folks rolling down a lush aisle of palms—but she was and they were. Once in those Revere days he had come home drunk and she had hit him and drawn blood from below his eye. Once she had been in fear of Hell, had lain half-drugged in steel stirrups, thinking, *I'm damned, I've come to damnation. A million years, and that's only the first tick of the clock.*

They stopped at the causeway toll-booth and Carol thought, *The toll-taker has a strawberry birthmark on the left side of his forehead, all mixed in with his eyebrow.*

There was no mark—the toll-taker was just an ordinary guy

in his late forties or early fifties, iron-gray hair in a buzz cut, horn-rimmed specs, the kind of guy who says, "Y'all have a nahce tahm, okai?"—but the feeling began to come back, and Carol realized that now the things she thought she knew were things she really did know, at first not all of them, but then, by the time they neared the little market on the right side of Route 41, it was almost everything.

The market's called Corson's and there's a little girl out front, Carol thought. *She's wearing a red pinafore. She's got a doll, a dirty old yellow-haired thing, that she's left on the store steps so she can look at a dog in the back of a station wagon.*

The name of the market turned out to be Carson's, not Corson's, but everything else was the same. As the white Crown Vic passed, the little girl in the red dress turned her solemn face in Carol's direction, a country girl's face, although what a girl from the toolies could be doing here in rich folks' tourist country, her and her dirty yellow-headed doll, Carol didn't know.

Here's where I ask Bill how much farther, only I won't do it. Because I have to break out of this cycle, this groove. I have to.

"How much farther?" she asked him. *He says there's only one road, we can't get lost. He says he promises me we'll get to the Palm House with no problem. And, by the way, who's Floyd?*

Bill's eyebrow went up. The dimple beside his mouth appeared. "Once you get over the causeway and onto Sanibel Island, there's only one road," he said. Carol barely heard him. He was still talking about the road, her husband who had spent a dirty weekend in bed with his secretary two years ago, risking all they had done and all they had made, Bill doing that with his other face on, being the Bill Carol's mother had warned would break her heart. And later Bill trying to tell her he hadn't been able to help himself, her wanting to scream, *I once murdered a child for you, the potential of a child, anyway. How high is that price? And is this what I get in return? To reach my fifties and find out that my husband had to get into some Clairol girl's pants?*

Tell him! she shrieked. *Make him pull over and stop, make him do anything that will break you free—change one thing, change everything! You can do it—if you could put your feet up in those stirrups, you can do anything!*

But she could do nothing, and it all began to tick by faster.

The two overfed crows lifted off from their splatter of lunch. Her husband asked why she was sitting that way, was it a cramp, her saying, Yes, yes, a cramp in her back but it was easing. Her mouth quacked on about déjà vu just as if she weren't drowning in it, and the Crown Vic moved forward like one of those sadistic Dodgem cars at Revere Beach. Here came Palmdale Motors on the right. And on the left? Some kind of sign for the local community theater, a production of *Naughty Marietta*.

No, it's Mary, not Marietta. Mary, mother of Jesus, Mary, mother of God, she's got her hands out . . .

Carol bent all her will toward telling her husband what was happening, because the right Bill was behind the wheel, the right Bill could still hear her. Being heard was what married love was all about.

Nothing came out. In her mind Gram said, "All the hard days are coming." In her mind a voice asked Floyd what was over there, then said, "Oh shit," then *screamed* "Oh shit!"

She looked at the speedometer and saw it was calibrated not in miles an hour but thousands of feet: they were at twenty-eight thousand and descending. Bill was telling her that she shouldn't have slept on the plane and she was agreeing.

There was a pink house coming up, little more than a bungalow, fringed with palm trees that looked like the ones you saw in the Second World War movies, fronds framing incoming Learjets with their machine guns blazing—

Blazing. Burning hot. All at once the magazine he's holding turns into a torch. Holy Mary, mother of God, hey there, Mary, what's the story—

They passed the house. The old man sat on the porch and watched them go by. The lenses of his rimless glasses glinted in the sun. Bill's hand established a beachhead on her hip. He said something about how they might pause to refresh themselves between the doffing of her dress and the donning of her shorts and she agreed, although they were never going to get to Palm House. They were going to go down this road and down this road, they were for the white Crown Vic and the white Crown Vic was for them, forever and ever amen.

The next billboard would say PALM HOUSE 2 MI. Beyond it was the one saying that Mother of Mercy Charities helped the Florida sick. Would they help her?

Now that it was too late she was beginning to understand. Beginning to see the light the way she could see the subtropical sun sparkling off the water on their left. Wondering how many wrongs she had done in her life, how many sins if you liked that word, God knew her parents and her Gram certainly had, sin this and sin that and wear the medallion between those growing things the boys look at. And years later she had lain in bed with her new husband on hot summer nights, knowing a decision had to be made, knowing the clock was ticking, the cigarette butt was smoldering, and she remembered making the decision, not telling him out loud because about some things you could be silent.

Her head itched. She scratched it. Black flecks came swirling down past her face. On the Crown Vic's instrument panel the speedometer froze at sixteen thousand feet and then blew out, but Bill appeared not to notice.

Here came a mailbox with a Grateful Dead sticker pasted on the front; here came a little black dog with its head down, trotting busily, and God how her head itched, black flakes drifting in the air like fallout and Mother Teresa's face looking out of one of them.

MOTHER OF MERCY CHARITIES HELP THE FLORIDA HUNGRY —WON'T _YOU_ HELP _US_?

Floyd. What's that over there? Oh shit.

She has time to see something big. And to read the word DELTA.

"Bill? _Bill?_"

His reply, clear enough but nevertheless coming from around the rim of the universe: "Christ, honey, what's in your _hair?_"

She plucked the charred remnant of Mother Teresa's face from her lap and held it out to him, the older version of the man she had married, the secretary-fucking man she had married, the man who had nonetheless rescued her from people who thought that you could live forever in paradise if you only lit enough candles and wore the blue blazer and stuck to the approved skipping rhymes. Lying there with this man one hot summer night while the drug deals went on upstairs and Iron Butterfly sang "In-A-Gadda-Da-Vida" for the nine billionth time, she had asked what he thought you got, you know, after. When your part in the show was over. He had taken her in his arms and held her, down the beach she had heard the jangle-jingle of the midway and the bang of the Dodgem cars and Bill—

Bill's glasses were melted to his face. One eye bulged out of its socket. His mouth was a bloodhole. In the trees a bird was crying, a bird was *screaming*, and Carol began to scream with it, holding out the charred fragment of paper with Mother Teresa's picture on it, screaming, watching as his cheeks turned black and his forehead swarmed and his neck split open like a poisoned goiter, screaming, she was screaming, somewhere Iron Butterfly was singing "In-A-Gadda-Da-Vida" and she was screaming.

"Carol?"

It was Bill's voice, from a thousand miles away. His hand was on her, but it was concern in his touch rather than lust.

She opened her eyes and looked around the sun-brilliant cabin of the Lear 35, and for a moment she understood everything—in the way one understands the tremendous import of a dream upon the first moment of waking. She remembered asking him what he believed you got, you know, *after,* and he had said you probably got what you'd always thought you *would* get, that if Jerry Lee Lewis thought he was going to Hell for playing boogie-woogie, that's exactly where he'd go. Heaven, Hell, or Grand Rapids, it was your choice—or the choice of those who had taught you what to believe. It was the human mind's final great parlor-trick: the perception of eternity in the place where you'd always expected to spend it.

"Carol? You okay, babe?" In one hand was the magazine he'd been reading, a *Newsweek* with Mother Teresa on the cover. SAINTHOOD NOW? it said in white.

Looking around wildly at the cabin, she was thinking, *It happens at sixteen thousand feet. I have to tell them, I have to warn them.*

But it was fading, all of it, the way those feelings always did. They went like dreams, or cotton candy turning into a sweet mist just above your tongue.

"Landing? Already?" She felt wide-awake, but her voice sounded thick and muzzy.

"It's fast, huh?" he said, sounding pleased, as if he'd flown it himself instead of paying for it. "Floyd says we'll be on the ground in—"

"Who?" she asked. The cabin of the little plane was warm but her fingers were cold. "Who?"

"Floyd. You know, the *pilot*." He pointed his thumb toward the cockpit's lefthand seat. They were descending into a scrim of clouds. The plane began to shake. "He says we'll be on the ground in Fort Myers in twenty minutes. You took a hell of a jump, girl. And before that you were moaning."

Carol opened her mouth to say it was that feeling, the one you could only say what it was in French, something *vu* or *vous*, but it was fading and all she said was "I had a nightmare."

There was a beep as Floyd the pilot switched the seat-belt light on. Carol turned her head. Somewhere below, waiting for them now and forever, was a white car from Hertz, a gangster car, the kind the characters in a Martin Scorsese movie would probably call a Crown Vic. She looked at the cover of the news magazine, at the face of Mother Teresa, and all at once she remembered skipping rope behind Our Lady of Angels, skipping to one of the forbidden rhymes, skipping to the one that went *Hey there, Mary, what's the story, save my ass from Purgatory.*

All the hard days are coming, her Gram had said. She had pressed the medal into Carol's palm, wrapped the chain around her fingers. *The hard days are coming.*

1998

GEORGE SAUNDERS

(b. 1958)

Sea Oak

At six Mr. Frendt comes on the P.A. and shouts, "Welcome to Joysticks!" Then he announces Shirts Off. We take off our flight jackets and fold them up. We take off our shirts and fold them up. Our scarves we leave on. Thomas Kirster's our beautiful boy. He's got long muscles and bright-blue eyes. The minute his shirt comes off two fat ladies hustle up the aisle and stick some money in his pants and ask will he be their Pilot. He says sure. He brings their salads. He brings their soups. My phone rings and the caller tells me to come see her in the Spitfire mock-up. Does she want me to be her Pilot? I'm hoping. Inside the Spitfire is Margie, who says she's been diagnosed with Chronic Shyness Syndrome, then hands me an Instamatic and offers me ten bucks for a close-up of Thomas's tush.

Do I do it? Yes I do.

It could be worse. It is worse for Lloyd Betts. Lately he's put on weight and his hair's gone thin. He doesn't get a call all shift and waits zero tables and winds up sitting on the P-51 wing, playing solitaire in a hunched-over position that gives him big gut rolls.

I Pilot six tables and make forty dollars in tips plus five an hour in salary.

After closing we sit on the floor for Debriefing. "There are times," Mr. Frendt says, "when one must move gracefully to the next station in life, like for example certain women in Africa or Brazil, I forget which, who either color their faces or don some kind of distinctive headdress upon achieving menopause. Are you with me? One of our ranks must now leave us. No one is an island in terms of being thought cute forever, and so today we must say good-bye to our friend Lloyd. Lloyd, stand up so we can say good-bye to you. I'm sorry. We are all so very sorry."

"Oh God," says Lloyd. "Let this not be true."

But it's true. Lloyd's finished. We give him a round of applause, and Frendt gives him a Farewell Pen and the contents of his locker in a trash bag and out he goes. Poor Lloyd. He's got a wife and two kids and a sad little duplex on Self-Storage Parkway.

"It's been a pleasure!" he shouts desperately from the doorway, trying not to burn any bridges.

What a stressful workplace. The minute your Cute Rating drops you're a goner. Guests rank us as Knockout, Honeypie, Adequate, or Stinker. Not that I'm complaining. At least I'm working. At least I'm not a Stinker like Lloyd.

I'm a solid Honeypie/Adequate, heading home with forty bucks cash.

At Sea Oak there's no sea and no oak, just a hundred subsidized apartments and a rear view of FedEx. Min and Jade are feeding their babies while watching *How My Child Died Violently*. Min's my sister. Jade's our cousin. *How My Child Died Violently* is hosted by Matt Merton, a six-foot-five blond who's always giving the parents shoulder rubs and telling them they've been sainted by pain. Today's show features a ten-year-old who killed a five-year-old for refusing to join his gang. The ten-year-old strangled the five-year-old with a jump rope, filled his mouth with baseball cards, then locked himself in the bathroom and wouldn't come out until his parents agreed to take him to FunTimeZone, where he confessed, then dove screaming into a mesh cage full of plastic balls. The audience is shrieking threats at the parents of the killer while the parents of the victim urge restraint and forgiveness to such an extent that finally the audience starts shrieking threats at them too. Then it's a commercial. Min and Jade put down the babies and light cigarettes and pace the room while studying aloud for their GEDs. It doesn't look good. Jade says "regicide" is a virus. Min locates Biafra one planet from Saturn. I offer to help and they start yelling at me for condescending.

"You're lucky, man!" my sister says. "You did high school. You got your frigging diploma. We don't. That's why we have to do this GED shit. If we had our diplomas we could just watch TV and not be all distracted."

"Really," says Jade. "Now shut it, chick! We got to study. Show's almost on."

They debate how many sides a triangle has. They agree that Churchill was in opera. Matt Merton comes back and explains that last week's show on suicide, in which the parents watched a reenactment of their son's suicide, was a healing process for the parents, then shows a video of the parents admitting it was a healing process.

My sister's baby is Troy. Jade's baby is Mac. They crawl off into the kitchen and Troy gets his finger caught in the heat vent. Min rushes over and starts pulling.

"Jesus freaking Christ!" screams Jade. "Watch it! Stop yanking on him and get the freaking Vaseline. You're going to give him a really long arm, man!"

Troy starts crying. Mac starts crying. I go over and free Troy no problem. Meanwhile Jade and Min get in a slap fight and nearly knock over the TV.

"Yo, chick!" Min shouts at the top of her lungs. "I'm sure you're slapping me? And then you knock over the freaking TV? Don't you care?"

"I care!" Jade shouts back. "You're the slut who nearly pulled off her own kid's finger for no freaking reason, man!"

Just then Aunt Bernie comes in from DrugTown in her DrugTown cap and hobbles over and picks up Troy and everything calms way down.

"No need to fuss, little man," she says. "Everything's fine. Everything's just hunky-dory."

"Hunky-dory," says Min, and gives Jade one last pinch.

Aunt Bernie's a peacemaker. She doesn't like trouble. Once this guy backed over her foot at FoodKing and she walked home with ten broken bones. She never got married, because Grandpa needed her to keep house after Grandma died. Then he died and left all his money to a woman none of us had ever heard of, and Aunt Bernie started in at DrugTown. But she's not bitter. Sometimes she's so nonbitter it gets on my nerves. When I say Sea Oak's a pit she says she's just glad to have a roof over her head. When I say I'm tired of being broke she says Grandpa once gave her pencils for Christmas and she was so thrilled she sat around sketching horses all day on the backs of used envelopes. Once I asked was she sorry she never had kids and she said no, not at all, and besides, weren't we her kids?

And I said yes we were.

But of course we're not.

For dinner it's beanie-wienies. For dessert it's ice cream with freezer burn.

"What a nice day we've had," Aunt Bernie says once we've got the babies in bed.

"Man, what an optometrist," says Jade.

Next day is Thursday, which means a visit from Ed Anders from the Board of Health. He's in charge of ensuring that our penises never show. Also that we don't kiss anyone. None of us ever kisses anyone or shows his penis except Sonny Vance, who does both, because he's saving up to buy a FaxIt franchise. As for our Penile Simulators, yes, we can show them, we can let them stick out the top of our pants, we can even periodically dampen our tight pants with spray bottles so our Simulators really contour, but our real penises, no, those have to stay inside our hot uncomfortable oversized Simulators.

"Sorry fellas, hi fellas," Anders says as he comes wearily in. "Please know I don't like this any better than you do. I went to school to learn how to inspect meat, but this certainly wasn't what I had in mind. Ha ha!"

He orders a Lindbergh Enchilada and eats it cautiously, as if it's alive and he's afraid of waking it. Sonny Vance is serving soup to a table of hairstylists on a bender and for a twenty shoots them a quick look at his unit.

Just then Anders glances up from his Lindbergh.

"Oh for crying out loud," he says, and writes up a Shutdown and we all get sent home early. Which is bad. Every dollar counts. Lately I've been sneaking toilet paper home in my briefcase. I can fit three rolls in. By the time I get home they're usually flat and don't work so great on the roller but still it saves a few bucks.

I clock out and cut through the strip of forest behind FedEx. Very pretty. A raccoon scurries over a fallen oak and starts nibbling at a rusty bike. As I come out of the woods I hear a shot. At least I think it's a shot. It could be a back-fire. But no, it's a shot, because then there's another one, and some kids sprint across the courtyard yelling that Big Scary Dawgz rule.

I run home. Min and Jade and Aunt Bernie and the babies are huddled behind the couch. Apparently they had the babies outside when the shooting started. Troy's walker got hit. Luckily he wasn't in it. It's supposed to look like a duck but now the beak's missing.

"Man, fuck this shit!" Min shouts.

"Freak this crap you mean," says Jade. "You want them growing up with shit-mouths like us? Crap-mouths I mean?"

"I just want them growing up, period," says Min.

"Boo-hoo, Miss Dramatic," says Jade.

"Fuck off, Miss Ho," shouts Min.

"I mean it, jagoff, I'm not kidding," shouts Jade, and punches Min in the arm.

"Girls, for crying out loud!" says Aunt Bernie. "We should be thankful. At least we got a home. And at least none of them bullets actually hit nobody."

"No offense, Bernie?" says Min. "But you call this a freaking home?"

Sea Oak's not safe. There's an ad hoc crackhouse in the laundry room and last week Min found some brass knuckles in the kiddie pool. If I had my way I'd move everybody up to Canada. It's nice there. Very polite. We went for a weekend last fall and got a flat tire and these two farmers with bright-red faces insisted on fixing it, then springing for dinner, then starting a college fund for the babies. They sent us the stock certificates a week later, along with a photo of all of us eating cobbler at a diner. But moving to Canada takes bucks. Dad's dead and left us nada and Ma now lives with Freddie, who doesn't like us, plus he's not exactly rich himself. He does phone polls. This month he's asking divorced women how often they backslide and sleep with their exes. He gets ten bucks for every completed poll.

So not lucrative, and Canada's a moot point.

I go out and find the beak of Troy's duck and fix it with Elmer's.

"Actually you know what?" says Aunt Bernie. "I think that looks even more like a real duck now. Because sometimes their beaks are cracked? I seen one like that downtown."

"Oh my God," says Min. "The kid's duck gets shot in the face and she says we're lucky."

"Well, we are lucky," says Bernie.

"Somebody's beak is cracked," says Jade.

"You know what I do if something bad happens?" Bernie says. "I don't think about it. Don't take it so serious. It ain't the end of the world. That's what I do. That's what I always done. That's how I got where I am."

My feeling is, Bernie, I love you, but where are you? You work at DrugTown for minimum. You're sixty and own nothing. You were basically a slave to your father and never had a date in your life.

"I mean, complain if you want," she says. "But I think we're doing pretty darn good for ourselves."

"Oh, we're doing great," says Min, and pulls Troy out from behind the couch and brushes some duck shards off his sleeper.

Joysticks reopens on Friday. It's a madhouse. They've got the fog on. A bridge club offers me fifteen bucks to oil-wrestle Mel Turner. So I oil-wrestle Mel Turner. They offer me twenty bucks to feed them chicken wings from my hand. So I feed them chicken wings from my hand. The afternoon flies by. Then the evening. At nine the bridge club leaves and I get a sorority. They sing intelligent nasty songs and grope my Simulator and say they'll never be able to look their boyfriends' meager genitalia in the eye again. Then Mr. Frendt comes over and says phone. It's Min. She sounds crazy. Four times in a row she shrieks get home. When I tell her calm down, she hangs up. I call back and no one answers. No biggie. Min's prone to panic. Probably one of the babies is puky. Luckily I'm on FlexTime.

"I'll be back," I say to Mr. Frendt.

"I look forward to it," he says.

I jog across the marsh and through FedEx. Up on the hill there's a light from the last remaining farm. Sometimes we take the boys to the adjacent car wash to look at the cow. Tonight however the cow is elsewhere.

At home Min and Jade are hopping up and down in front of Aunt Bernie, who's sitting very very still at one end of the couch.

"Keep the babies out!" shrieks Min. "I don't want them seeing something dead!"

"Shut up, man!" shrieks Jade. "Don't call her something dead!"

She squats down and pinches Aunt Bernie's cheek.

"Aunt Bernie?" she shrieks. "Fuck!"

"We already tried that like twice, chick!" shrieks Min. "Why are you doing that shit again? Touch her neck and see if you can feel that beating thing!"

"Shit shit shit!" shrieks Jade.

I call 911 and the paramedics come out and work hard for twenty minutes, then give up and say they're sorry and it looks like she's been dead most of the afternoon. The apartment's a mess. Her money drawer's empty and her family photos are in the bathtub.

"Not a mark on her," says a cop.

"I suspect she died of fright," says another. "Fright of the intruder?"

"My guess is yes," says a paramedic.

"Oh God," says Jade. "God, God, God."

I sit down beside Bernie. I think: I am so sorry. I'm sorry I wasn't here when it happened and sorry you never had any fun in your life and sorry I wasn't rich enough to move you somewhere safe. I remember when she was young and wore pink stretch pants and made us paper chains out of DrugTown receipts while singing "Froggie Went A-Courting." All her life she worked hard. She never hurt anybody. And now this.

Scared to death in a crappy apartment.

Min puts the babies in the kitchen but they keep crawling out. Aunt Bernie's in a shroud on this sort of dolly and on the couch are a bunch of forms to sign.

We call Ma and Freddie. We get their machine.

"Ma, pick up!" says Min. "Something bad happened! Ma, please freaking pick up!"

But nobody picks up.

So we leave a message.

Lobton's Funeral Parlor is just a regular house on a regular street. Inside there's a rack of brochures with titles like "Why Does My Loved One Appear Somewhat Larger?" Lobton looks healthy. Maybe too healthy. He's wearing a yellow golf shirt and his biceps keep involuntarily flexing. Every now and then he touches his delts as if to confirm they're still big as softballs.

"Such a sad thing," he says.

"How much?" asks Jade. "I mean, like for basic. Not super-fancy."

"But not crappy either," says Min. "Our aunt was the best."

"What price range were you considering?" says Lobton, cracking his knuckles. We tell him and his eyebrows go up and he leads us to something that looks like a moving box.

"Prior to usage we'll moisture-proof this with a spray lacquer," he says. "Makes it look quite woodlike."

"That's all we can get?" says Jade. "Cardboard?"

"I'm actually offering you a slight break already," he says, and does a kind of push-up against the wall. "On account of the tragic circumstances. This is Sierra Sunset. Not exactly cardboard. More of a fiberboard."

"I don't know," says Min. "Seems pretty gyppy."

"Can we think about it?" says Ma.

"Absolutely," says Lobton. "Last time I checked this was still America."

I step over and take a closer look. There are staples where Aunt Bernie's spine would be. Down at the foot there's some writing about Folding Tab A into Slot B.

"No freaking way," says Jade. "Work your whole life and end up in a Mayflower box? I doubt it."

We've got zip in savings. We sit at a desk and Lobton does what he calls a Credit Calc. If we pay it out monthly for seven years we can afford the Amber Mist, which includes a double-thick balsa box and two coats of lacquer and a one-hour wake.

"But seven years, jeez," says Ma.

"We got to get her the good one," says Min. "She never had anything nice in her life."

So Amber Mist it is.

We bury her at St. Leo's, on the hill up near BastCo. Her part of the graveyard's pretty plain. No angels, no little rock houses, no flowers, just a bunch of flat stones like parking bumpers and here and there a Styrofoam cup. Father Brian says a prayer and then one of us is supposed to talk. But what's there to say? She never had a life. Never married, no kids, work work work. Did she ever go on a cruise? All her life it was buses. Buses buses buses. Once she went with Ma on a bus to Quigley, Kansas, to gamble and shop at an outlet mall. Someone broke into her room and stole her clothes and took a dump in her suitcase while they were at the Roy Clark show. That was it. That was the extent of her tourism. After that it was DrugTown, night and day. After fifteen years as Cashier she got demoted to Greeter. People would ask where the cold remedies were and she'd point to some big letters on the wall that said Cold Remedies.

Freddie, Ma's boyfriend, steps up and says he didn't know her very long but she was an awful nice lady and left behind a lot of love, etc. etc. blah blah blah. While it's true she didn't do much in her life, still she was very dear to those of us who knew her and never made a stink about anything but was always content with whatever happened to her, etc. etc. blah blah blah.

Then it's over and we're supposed to go away.

"We gotta come out here like every week," says Jade.

"I know I will," says Min.

"What, like I won't?" says Jade. "She was so freaking nice."

"I'm sure you swear at a grave," says Min.

"Since when is freak a swear, chick?" says Jade.

"Girls," says Ma.

"I hope I did okay in what I said about her," says Freddie in his full-of-crap way, smelling bad of English Navy. "Actually I sort of surprised myself."

"Bye-bye, Aunt Bernie," says Min.

"Bye-bye, Bern," says Jade.

"Oh my dear sister," says Ma.

I scrunch my eyes tight and try to picture her happy, laughing, poking me in the ribs. But all I can see is her terrified on the couch. It's awful. Out there, somewhere, is whoever did it. Someone came in our house, scared her to death, watched her die, went through our stuff, stole her money. Someone who's still living, someone who right now might be having a piece of pie or running an errand or scratching his ass, someone who, if he wanted to, could drive west for three days or whatever and sit in the sun by the ocean.

We stand a few minutes with heads down and hands folded.

*

Afterward Freddie takes us to Trabanti's for lunch. Last year Trabanti died and three Vietnamese families went in together and bought the place, and it still serves pasta and pizza and the big oil of Trabanti is still on the wall but now from the kitchen comes this very pretty Vietnamese music and the food is somehow better.

Freddie proposes a toast. Min says remember how Bernie always called lunch dinner and dinner supper? Jade says remember how when her jaw clicked she'd say she needed oil?

"She was a excellent lady," says Freddie.

"I already miss her so bad," says Ma.

"I'd like to kill that fuck that killed her," says Min.

"How about let's don't say fuck at lunch," says Ma.

"It's just a word, Ma, right?" says Min. "Like pluck is just a word? You don't mind if I say pluck? Pluck pluck pluck?"

"Well, shits just a word too," says Freddie. "But we don't say it at lunch."

"Same with puke," says Ma.

"Shit puke, shit puke," says Min.

The waiter clears his throat. Ma glares at Min.

"I love you girls' manners," Ma says.

"Especially at a funeral," says Freddie.

"This ain't a funeral," says Min.

"The question in my mind is what you kids are gonna do now," says Freddie. "Because I consider this whole thing a wake-up call, meaning it's time for you to pull yourself up by the bootstraps like I done and get out of that dangerous craphole you're living at."

"Mr. Phone Poll speaks," says Min.

"Anyways it ain't that dangerous," says Jade.

"A woman gets killed and it ain't that dangerous?" says Freddie.

"All's we need is a dead bolt and a eyehole," says Min.

"What's a bootstrap," says Jade.

"It's like a strap on a boot, you doof," says Min.

"Plus where we gonna go?" says Min. "Can we move in with you guys?"

"I personally would love that and you know that," says Freddie. "But who would not love that is our landlord."

"I think what Freddie's saying is it's time for you girls to get jobs," says Ma.

"Yeah right, Ma," says Min. "After what happened last time?"

When I first moved in, Jade and Min were working the info booth at HardwareNiche. Then one day we picked the babies up at day care and found Troy sitting naked on top of the washer and Mac in the yard being nipped by a Pekingese and the day-care lady sloshed and playing KillerBirds on Nintendo.

So that was that. No more HardwareNiche.

"Maybe one could work, one could baby-sit?" says Ma.

"I don't see why I should have to work so she can stay home with her baby," says Min.

"And I don't see why I should have to work so she can stay home with her baby," says Jade.

"It's like a freaking veece versa," says Min.

"Let me tell you something," says Freddie. "Something about this country. Anybody can do anything. But first they gotta try. And you guys ain't. Two don't work and one strips naked? I don't consider that trying. You kids make squat. And therefore you live in a dangerous craphole. And what happens in a dangerous craphole? Bad tragic shit. It's the freaking American way—you start out in a dangerous craphole and work hard so you can someday move up to a somewhat less dangerous craphole. And finally maybe you get a mansion. But at this rate you ain't even gonna make it to the somewhat less dangerous craphole."

"Like you live in a mansion," says Jade.

"I do not claim to live in no mansion," says Freddie. "But then again I do not live in no slum. The other thing I also do not do is strip naked."

"Thank God for small favors," says Min.

"Anyways he's never actually naked," says Jade.

Which is true. I always have on at least a T-back.

"No wonder we never take these kids out to a nice lunch," says Freddie.

"I do not even consider this a nice lunch," says Min.

For dinner Jade microwaves some Stars-n-Flags. They're addictive. They put sugar in the sauce and sugar in the meat nuggets. I think also caffeine. Someone told me the brown streaks in the Flags are caffeine. We have like five bowls each.

After dinner the babies get fussy and Min puts a mush of ice cream and Hershey's syrup in their bottles and we watch *The Worst That Could Happen*, a half-hour of computer simulations of tragedies that have never actually occurred but theoretically could. A kid gets hit by a train and flies into a zoo, where he's eaten by wolves. A man cuts his hand off chopping wood and while wandering around screaming for help is picked up by a tornado and dropped on a preschool during recess and lands on a pregnant teacher.

"I miss Bernie so bad," says Min.

"Me too," Jade says sadly.

The babies start howling for more ice cream.

"That is so cute," says Jade. "They're like, *Give it the fuck up!*"

"We'll give it the fuck up, sweeties, don't worry," says Min. "We didn't forget about you."

Then the phone rings. It's Father Brian. He sounds weird. He says he's sorry to bother us so late. But something strange has happened. Something bad. Something sort of, you know, unspeakable. Am I sitting? I'm not but I say I am.

Apparently someone has defaced Bernie's grave.

My first thought is there's no stone. It's just grass. How do you deface grass? What did they do, pee on the grass on the grave? But Father's nearly in tears.

So I call Ma and Freddie and tell them to meet us, and we get the babies up and load them into the K-car.

"Deface," says Jade on the way over. "What does that mean, deface?"

"It means like fucked it up," says Min.

"But how?" says Jade. "I mean, like what did they do?"

"We don't know, dumbass," says Min. "That's why we're going there."

"And why?" says Jade. "Why would someone do that?"

"Check out Miss Shreelock Holmes," says Min. "Someone done that because someone is a asshole."

"Someone is a big-time asshole," says Jade.

Father Brian meets us at the gate with a flashlight and a golf cart.

"When I saw this," he says. "I literally sat down in astonishment. Nothing like this has ever happened here. I am so sorry. You seem like nice people."

We're too heavy and the wheels spin as we climb the hill, so I get out and jog alongside.

"Okay, folks, brace yourselves," Father says, and shuts off the engine.

Where the grave used to be is just a hole. Inside the hole is the Amber Mist, with the top missing. Inside the Amber Mist is nothing. No Aunt Bernie.

"What the hell," says Jade. "Where's Bernie?"

"Somebody stole Bernie?" says Min.

"At least you folks have retained your feet," says Father Brian. "I'm telling you I literally sat right down. I sat right down on that pile of dirt. I dropped as if shot. See that mark? That's where I sat."

On the pile of grave dirt is a butt-shaped mark.

The cops show up and one climbs down in the hole with a tape measure and a camera. After three or four flashes he climbs out and hands Ma a pair of blue pumps.

"Her little shoes," says Ma. "Oh my God."

"Are those them?" says Jade.

"Those are them," says Min.

"I am freaking out," says Jade.

"I am totally freaking out," says Min.

"I'm gonna sit," says Ma, and drops into the golf cart.

"What I don't get is who'd want her?" says Min.

"She was just this lady," says Jade.

"Typically it's teens?" one cop says. "Typically we find the loved one nearby? Once we found the loved one nearby with, you know, a cigarette between its lips, wearing a sombrero? These kids today got a lot more nerve than we ever did. I never would've dreamed of digging up a dead corpse when I was a teen. You might tip over a stone, sure, you might spray-paint something on a crypt, you might, you know, give a wino a hotfoot."

"But this, jeez," says Freddie. "This is a entirely different ballgame."

"Boy howdy," says the cop, and we all look down at the shoes in Ma's hands.

*

Next day I go back to work. I don't feel like it but we need the money. The grass is wet and it's hard getting across the ravine in my dress shoes. The soles are slick. Plus they're too tight. Several times I fall forward on my briefcase. Inside the briefcase are my T-backs and a thing of mousse.

Right off the bat I get a tableful of MediBen women seated under a banner saying BEST OF LUCK, BEATRICE, NO HARD FEELINGS. I take off my shirt and serve their salads. I take off my flight pants and serve their soups. One drops a dollar on the floor and tells me feel free to pick it up.

I pick it up.

"Not like that, not like that," she says. "Face the other way, so when you bend we can see your crack."

I've done this about a million times, but somehow I can't do it now.

I look at her. She looks at me.

"What?" she says. "I'm not allowed to say that? I thought that was the whole point."

"That is the whole point, Phyllis," says another lady. "You stand your ground."

"Look," Phyllis says. "Either bend how I say or give back the dollar. I think that's fair."

"You go, girl," says her friend.

I give back the dollar. I return to the Locker Area and sit awhile. For the first time ever, I'm voted Stinker. There are thirteen women at the MediBen table and they all vote me Stinker. Do the MediBen women know my situation? Would they vote me Stinker if they did? But what am I supposed to do, go out and say, Please ladies, my aunt just died, plus her body's missing?

Mr. Frendt pulls me aside.

"Perhaps you need to go home," he says. "I'm sorry for your loss. But I'd like to encourage you not to behave like one of those Comanche ladies who bite off their index fingers when a loved one dies. Grief is good, grief is fine, but too much grief, as we all know, is excessive. If your aunt's death has filled your mouth with too many bitten-off fingers, for crying out loud, take a week off, only don't take it out on our Guests, they didn't kill your dang aunt."

But I can't afford to take a week off. I can't even afford to take a few days off.

"We really need the money," I say.

"Is that my problem?" he says. "Am I supposed to let you dance without vigor just because you need the money? Why don't I put an ad in the paper for all sad people who need money? All the town's sad could come here and strip. Goodbye. Come back when you feel halfway normal."

From the pay phone I call home to see if they need anything from the FoodSoQuik.

"Just come home," Min says stiffly. "Just come straight home."

"What is it?" I say.

"Come home," she says.

Maybe someone's found the body. I imagine Bernie naked, Bernie chopped in two, Bernie posed on a bus bench. I hope and pray that something only mildly bad's been done to her, something we can live with.

At home the door's wide open. Min and Jade are sitting very still on the couch, babies in their laps, staring at the rocking chair, and in the rocking chair is Bernie. Bernie's body.

Same perm, same glasses, same blue dress we buried her in.

What's it doing here? Who could be so cruel? And what are we supposed to do with it?

Then she turns her head and looks at me.

"Sit the fuck down," she says.

In life she never swore.

I sit. Min squeezes and releases my hand, squeezes and releases, squeezes and releases.

"You, mister," Bernie says to me, "are going to start showing your cock. You'll show it and show it. You go up to a lady, if she wants to see it, if she'll pay to see it, I'll make a thumbprint on the forehead. You see the thumbprint, you ask. I'll try to get you five a day, at twenty bucks a pop. So a hundred bucks a day. Seven hundred a week. And that's cash, so no taxes. No withholding. See? That's the beauty of it."

She's got dirt in her hair and dirt in her teeth and her hair is a mess and her tongue when it darts out to lick her lips is black.

"You, Jade," she says. "Tomorrow you start work. Andersen Labels, Fifth and Rivera. Dress up when you go. Wear something nice. Show a little leg. And don't chomp your gum. Ask for Len. At the end of the month, we take the money you made and the cock money and get a new place. Somewhere safe. That's part one of Phase One. You, Min. You baby-sit. Plus you quit smoking. Plus you learn how to cook. No more food out of cans. We gotta eat right to look our best. Because I am getting me so many lovers. Maybe you kids don't know this but I died a freaking virgin. No babies, no lovers. Nothing went in, nothing came out. Ha ha! Dry as a bone, completely wasted, this pretty little thing God gave me between my legs. Well I am going to have lovers now, you fucks! Like in the movies, big shoulders and all, and a summer house, and nice trips, and in the morning in my room a big vase of flowers, and I'm going to get my nipples hard standing in the breeze from the ocean, eating shrimp from a cup, you sons of bitches, while my lover watches me from the veranda, his big shoulders shining, all hard for me, that's one damn thing I will guarantee you kids! Ha ha! You think I'm joking? I ain't freaking joking. I never got nothing! My life was shit! I was never even up in a freaking plane. But that was that life and this is this life. My new life. Cover me up now! With a blanket. I need my beauty rest. Tell anyone I'm here, you all die. Plus they die. Whoever you tell, they die. I kill them with my mind. I can do that. I am very freaking strong now. I got powers! So no visitors. I don't exactly look my best. You got it? You all got it?"

We nod. I go for a blanket. Her hands and feet are shaking and she's grinding her teeth and one falls out.

"Put it over me, you fuck, all the way over!" she screams, and I put it over her.

We sneak off with the babies and whisper in the kitchen.

"It looks like her," says Min.

"It is her," I say.

"It is and it ain't," says Jade.

"We better do what she says," Min says.

"No shit," Jade says.

All night she sits in the rocker under the blanket, shaking and swearing.

All night we sit in Min's bed, fully dressed, holding hands.

"See how strong I am!" she shouts around midnight, and there's a cracking sound, and when I go out the door's been torn off the microwave but she's still sitting in the chair.

In the morning she's still there, shaking and swearing.

"Take the blanket off!" she screams. "It's time to get this show on the road."

I take the blanket off. The smell is not good. One ear is now in her lap. She keeps absentmindedly sticking it back on her head.

"You, Jade!" she shouts. "Get dressed. Go get that job. When you meet Len, bend forward a little. Let him see down your top. Give him some hope. He's a sicko, but we need him. You, Min! Make breakfast. Something homemade. Like biscuits."

"Why don't you make it with your powers?" says Min.

"Don't be a smartass!" screams Bernie. "You see what I did to that microwave?"

"I don't know how to make freaking biscuits," Min wails.

"You know how to read, right?" Bernie shouts. "You ever heard of a recipe? You ever been in the grave? It sucks so bad! You regret all the things you never did. You little bitches are gonna have a very bad time in the grave unless you get on the stick, believe me! Turn down the thermostat! Make it cold. I like cold. Something's off with my body. I don't feel right."

I turn down the thermostat. She looks at me.

"Go show your cock!" she shouts. "That is the first part of Phase One. After we get the new place, that's the end of the first part of Phase Two. You'll still show your cock, but only three days a week. Because you'll start community college. Pre-law. Pre-law is best. You'll be a whiz. You ain't dumb. And Jade'll work weekends to make up for the decrease in cock money. See? See how that works? Now get out of here. What are you gonna do?"

"Show my cock?" I say.

"Show your cock, that's right," she says, and brushes back her hair with her hand, and a huge wad comes out, leaving her almost bald on one side.

"Oh God," says Min. "You know what? No way me and the babies are staying here alone."

"You ain't alone," says Bernie. "I'm here."

"Please don't go," Min says to me.

"Oh, stop it," Bernie says, and the door flies open and I feel a sort of invisible fist punching me in the back.

Outside it's sunny. A regular day. A guy's changing his oil. The clouds are regular clouds and the sun's the regular sun and the only nonregular thing is that my clothes smell like Bernie, a combo of wet cellar and rotten bacon.

Work goes well. I manage to keep smiling and hide my shaking hands, and my midshift rating is Honeypie. After lunch this older woman comes up and says I look so much like a real Pilot she can hardly stand it.

On her head is a thumbprint. Like Ash Wednesday, only sort of glowing.

I don't know what to do. Do I just come out and ask if she wants to see my cock? What if she says no? What if I get caught? What if I show her and she doesn't think it's worth twenty bucks?

Then she asks if I'll surprise her best friend with a birthday table dance. She points out her friend. A pretty girl, no thumbprint. Looks somehow familiar.

We start over and at about twenty feet I realize it's Angela.

Angela Silveri.

We dated senior year. Then Dad died and Ma had to take a job at Patty-Melt Depot. From all the grease Ma got a bad rash and could barely wear a blouse. Plus Min was running wild. So Angela would come over and there'd be Min getting high under a tarp on the carport and Ma sitting in her bra on a kitchen stool with a fan pointed at her gut. Angela had dreams. She had plans. In her notebook she pasted a picture of an office from the J. C. Penney catalogue and under it wrote, *My (someday?) office.* Once we saw this black Porsche and she said very nice but make hers red. The last straw was Ed Edwards, a big drunk, one of Dad's cousins. Things got so bad Ma rented him the utility room. One night Angela and I were making out on the couch late when Ed came in soused and started peeing in the dishwasher.

What could I say? He's only barely related to me? He hardly ever does that?

Angela's eyes were like these little pies.

I walked her home, got no kiss, came back, cleaned up the

dishwasher as best I could. A few days later I got my class ring in the mail and a copy of *The Prophet*.

You will always be my first love, she'd written inside. *But now my path converges to a higher ground. Be well always. Walk in joy. Please don't think me cruel, it's just that I want so much in terms of accomplishment, plus I couldn't believe that guy peed right on your dishes.*

No way am I table dancing for Angela Silveri. No way am I asking Angela Silveri's friend if she wants to see my cock. No way am I hanging around here so Angela can see me in my flight jacket and T-backs and wonder to herself how I went so wrong etc. etc.

I hide in the kitchen until my shift is done, then walk home very, very slowly because I'm afraid of what Bernie's going to do to me when I get there.

Min meets me at the door. She's got flour all over her blouse and it looks like she's been crying.

"I can't take any more of this," she says. "She's like falling apart. I mean shit's falling off her. Plus she made me bake a freaking pie."

On the table is a very lumpy pie. One of Bernie's arms is now disconnected and lying across her lap.

"What are you thinking of!" she shouts. "You didn't show your cock even once? You think it's easy making those thumb-prints? You try it, smartass! Do you or do you not know the plan? You gotta get us out of here! And to get us out, you gotta use what you got. And you ain't got much. A nice face. And a decent unit. Not huge, but shaped nice."

"Bernie, God," says Min.

"What, Miss Priss?" shouts Bernie, and slams the severed arm down hard on her lap, and her other ear falls off.

"I'm sorry, but this is too fucking sickening," says Min. "I'm going out."

"What's sickening?" says Bernie. "Are you saying I'm sickening? Well, I think you're sickening. So many wonderful things in life and where's your mind? You think with your lazy ass. Whatever life hands you, you take. You're not going anywhere. You're staying home and studying."

"I'm what?" says Min. "Studying what? I ain't studying.

Chick comes into my house and starts ordering me to study? I freaking doubt it."

"You don't know nothing!" Bernie says. "What fun is life when you don't know nothing? You can't find your own town on the map. You can't name a single president. When we go to Rome you won't know nothing about the history. You're going to study the World Book. Do we still have those World Books?"

"Yeah right," says Min. "We're going to Rome."

"We'll go to Rome when he's a lawyer," says Bernie.

"Dream on, chick," says Min. "And we'll go to Mars when I'm a stockbreaker."

"Don't you dare make fun of me!" Bernie shouts, and our only vase goes flying across the room and nearly nails Min in the head.

"She's been like this all day," says Min.

"Like what?" shouts Bernie. "We had a perfectly nice day."

"She made me help her try on my bras," says Min.

"I never had a nice sexy bra," says Bernie.

"And now mine are all ruined," says Min. "They got this sort of goo on them."

"You ungrateful shit!" shouts Bernie. "Do you know what I'm doing for you? I'm saving your boy. And you got the nerve to say I made goo on your bras! Troy's gonna get caught in a crossfire in the courtyard. In September. September eighteenth. He's gonna get thrown off his little trike. With one leg twisted under him and blood pouring out of his ear. It's a freaking prophecy. You know that word? It means prediction. You know that word? You think I'm bullshitting? Well I ain't bullshitting. I got the power. Watch this: All day Jade sat licking labels at a desk by a window. Her boss bought everybody subs for lunch. She's bringing some home in a green bag."

"That ain't true about Troy, is it?" says Min. "Is it? I don't believe it."

"Turn on the TV!" Bernie shouts. "Give me the changer."

I turn on the TV. I give her the changer. She puts on *Nathan's Body Shop*. Nathan says washboard abs drive the women wild. Then there's a close-up of his washboard abs.

"Oh yes," says Bernie. "Them are for me. I'd like to give

those a lick. A lick and a pinch. I'd like to sort of straddle those things."

Just then Jade comes through the door with a big green bag.

"Oh God," says Min.

"Told you so!" says Bernie, and pokes Min in the ribs. "Ha ha! I really got the power!"

"I don't get it," Min says, all desperate. "What happens? Please. What happens to him? You better freaking tell me."

"I already told you," Bernie says. "He'll fly about fifteen feet and live about three minutes."

"Bernie, God," Min says, and starts to cry. "You used to be so nice."

"I'm still so nice," says Bernie, and bites into a sub and takes off the tip of her finger and starts chewing it up.

Just after dawn she shouts out my name.

"Take the blanket off," she says. "I ain't feeling so good."

I take the blanket off. She's basically just this pile of parts: both arms in her lap, head on the arms, heel of one foot touching the heel of the other, all of it sort of wrapped up in her dress.

"Get me a washcloth," she says. "Do I got a fever? I feel like I got a fever. Oh, I knew it was too good to be true. But okay. New plan. New plan. I'm changing the first part of Phase One. If you see two thumbprints, that means the lady'll screw you for cash. We're in a fix here. We gotta speed this up. There ain't gonna be nothing left of me. Who's gonna be my lover now?"

The doorbell rings.

"Son of a bitch," Bernie snarls.

It's Father Brian with a box of doughnuts. I step out quick and close the door behind me. He says he's just checking in. Perhaps we'd like to talk? Perhaps we're feeling some residual anger about Bernie's situation? Which would of course be completely understandable. Once when he was a young priest someone broke in and drew a mustache on the Virgin Mary with a permanent marker, and for weeks he was tortured by visions of bending back the finger of the vandal until he or she burst into tears of apology.

"I knew that wasn't appropriate," he says. "I knew that by

indulging in that fantasy I was honoring violence. And yet it gave me pleasure. I also thought of catching them in the act and boinking them in the head with a rock. I also thought of jumping up and down on their backs until something in their spinal column cracked. Actually I had about a million ideas. But you know what I did instead? I scrubbed and scrubbed our Holy Mother, and soon she was as good as new. Her statue, I mean. She herself of course is always good as new."

From inside comes the sound of breaking glass. Breaking glass and then something heavy falling, and Jade yelling and Min yelling and the babies crying.

"Oops, I guess?" he says. "I've come at a bad time? Look, all I'm trying to do is urge you, if at all possible, to forgive the perpetrators, as I forgave the perpetrator that drew on my Virgin Mary. The thing lost, after all, is only your aunt's body, and what is essential, I assure you, is elsewhere, being well taken care of?"

I nod. I smile. I say thanks for stopping by. I take the doughnuts and go back inside.

The TV's broke and the refrigerator's tipped over and Bernie's parts are strewn across the living room like she's been shot out of a cannon.

"She tried to get up," says Jade.

"I don't know where the hell she thought she was going," says Min.

"Come here," the head says to me, and I squat down. "That's it for me. I'm fucked. As per usual. Always the bridesmaid, never the bride. Although come to think of it I was never even the freaking bridesmaid. Look, show your cock. It's the shortest line between two points. The world ain't giving away nice lives. You got a trust fund? You a genius? Show your cock. It's what you got. And remember: Troy in September. On his trike. One leg twisted. Don't forget. And also. Don't remember me like this. Remember me like how I was that night we all went to Red Lobster and I had that new perm. Ah Christ. At least buy me a stone."

I rub her shoulder, which is next to her foot.

"We loved you," I say.

"Why do some people get everything and I got nothing?" she says. "Why? Why was that?"

"I don't know," I say.

"Show your cock," she says, and dies again.

We stand there looking down at the pile of parts. Mac crawls toward it and Min moves him back with her foot.

"This is too freaking much," says Jade, and starts crying.

"What do we do now?" says Min.

"Call the cops," Jade says.

"And say what?" says Min.

We think about this awhile.

I get a Hefty bag. I get my winter gloves.

"I ain't watching," says Jade.

"I ain't watching either," says Min, and they take the babies into the bedroom.

I close my eyes and wrap Bernie up in the Hefty bag and twistie-tie the bag shut and lug it out to the trunk of the K-car. I throw in a shovel. I drive up to St. Leo's. I lower the bag into the hole using a bungee cord, then fill the hole back in.

Down in the city are the nice houses and the so-so houses and the lovers making out in dark yards and the babies crying for their moms, and I wonder if, other than Jesus, this has ever happened before. Maybe it happens all the time. Maybe there's angry dead all over, hiding in rooms, covered with blankets, bossing around their scared, embarrassed relatives. Because how would we know?

I for sure don't plan on broadcasting this.

I smooth over the dirt and say a quick prayer: If it was wrong for her to come back, forgive her, she never got beans in this life, plus she was trying to help us.

At the car I think of an additional prayer: But please don't let her come back again.

When I get home the babies are asleep and Jade and Min are watching a phone-sex infomercial, three girls in leather jumpsuits eating bananas in slo-mo while across the screen runs a constant disclaimer: "Not Necessarily the Girls Who Man the Phones! Not Necessarily the Girls Who Man the Phones!"

"Them chicks seem to really be enjoying those bananas," says Min in a thin little voice.

"I like them jumpsuits though," says Jade.

"Yeah them jumpsuits look decent," says Min.

Then they look up at me. I've never seen them so sad and beat and sick.

"It's done," I say.

Then we hug and cry and promise never to forget Bernie the way she really was, and I use some Resolve on the rug and they go do some reading in their World Books.

Next day I go in early. I don't see a single thumbprint. But it doesn't matter. I get with Sonny Vance and he tells me how to do it. First you ask the woman would she like a private tour. Then you show her the fake P-40, the Gallery of Historical Aces, the shower stall where we get oiled up, etc. etc. and then in the hall near the rest room you ask if there's anything else she'd like to see. It's sleazy. It's gross. But when I do it I think of September. September and Troy in the crossfire, his little leg bent under him etc. etc.

Most say no but quite a few say yes.

I've got a place picked out at a complex called Swan's Glen. They've never had a shooting or a knifing and the public school is great and every Saturday they have a nature walk for kids behind the clubhouse.

For every hundred bucks I make, I set aside five for Bernie's stone.

What do you write on something like that? LIFE PASSED HER BY? DIED DISAPPOINTED? CAME BACK TO LIFE BUT FELL APART? All true, but too sad, and no way I'm writing any of those.

BERNIE KOWALSKI, it's going to say: BELOVED AUNT.

Sometimes she comes to me in dreams. She never looks good. Sometimes she's wearing a dirty smock. Once she had on handcuffs. Once she was naked and dirty and this mean cat was clawing its way up her front. But every time it's the same thing.

"Some people get everything and I got nothing," she says. "Why? Why did that happen?"

Every time I say I don't know.

And I don't.

1998

CAITLÍN R. KIERNAN

(b. 1964)

The Long Hall on the Top Floor

THREE months now since Deacon Silvey pulled up stakes and left Atlanta, what passed for pulling up stakes, when all he had to begin with was a job in a laundromat in the afternoons and a job at a liquor store half the night, two shit jobs and three hundred and twelve dollars and seventy-five cents hidden in the toe of one of his boots. And man, some motherfucker's gonna walk in off the street one night, some dusthead with a .35, and blow your brains out for a few bills from the register, and then it's the goddamn *laundromat* that gets held up, instead. Three Hispanic kids with baseball bats and a crowbar, and he sat still and kept his mouth shut while they opened the coin boxes on every washer, every dryer, watched them fill a pillow case almost to bursting with the bright and dull quarters that spilled like noisy silver candy. And then the kids were gone, door cowbell ringing shut behind them, and Deke too god-damned astonished to do anything but sit and stare at the vio-lated Maytags and Kenmores, at Herman and Lily Munster on the little black-and-white television behind the counter, the sound turned all the way down.

So a week later, fuck it, he was on the bus to Birmingham, everything he owned in one old blue suitcase and a cardboard box, Tanqueray box from behind the liquor store to hold his paperbacks and notebooks and all his ratty clothes stuffed into the suitcase. And some guy sitting next to him all the way, smoking Kools, black guy named Owen smoking Kools and watching the interstate night slip by outside, Georgia going to Alabama while he told Deacon Silvey about New Orleans, his brother's barber shop on Magazine Street where he was gonna work sweeping up hair and crap like that.

"Hell, man, it's worth a shit job to be down there," and Deacon thinking the man talked like he fell backwards off a Randy Newman song and landed on his head.

"How old you be, anyways?" and the man lit another Kool, menthol-smooth cloud from his lips, and he leaned across the aisle of the bus towards Deke. And "Thirty-two," Deacon answered. "Shit. Thirty-two? I'd give my left big toe to see thirty-two again. Thirty-two, the womens still give a damn, you know?" And the bus rolled on, and the man talked and smoked, until 3:45 A.M. when the Greyhound pulled up under the bug-specked yellow glare of the station, and Deacon got off in downtown Birmingham.

So now Deacon works at the Highland Wash'N'Fold every other night, and a warehouse in the mornings. He sleeps afternoons, and it's not much different from Atlanta, except mostly it's old drag queens and young slackers in the Wash'N'Fold and no laundromat pirates so far. His new apartment is a little bigger, two rooms and a bathroom, one corner for a kitchen, in a place that's built to look like a shoddy theme park excuse for a castle, Quinlan Castle in big letters out front and four turrets to prove it. But the rent's something he can afford, and the cockroaches stay off his bed if he sleeps with the light on, so it could be worse, has been worse lots of times.

And tonight's Friday, so no laundromat until tomorrow, and Deacon's sitting on a bench in a park down the hill from the castle, sipping a bottle of cheap gin, tightrope balancing act, staying drunk and making the quart last the night. August and here he is, sitting under the sodium-arc glare on the edge of a basketball court, not even midnight yet, just sipping at his gin and reading *The Martian Chronicles* by Ray Bradbury, "Mars is Heaven" and "Dark They Were and Golden-Eyed," and hoping he doesn't run out of gin before he runs out of night.

"Hey, man," and Deke looks up, green eyes tracking drunk-slow from the pages to Soda's face, hawk-nosed Soda and his twenty-something acne, battered skateboard tucked under one arm, and he never smiles because he's lost too many teeth up front. "What's kickin'," and he's already parking his skinny ass on the bench next to Deacon like he's been invited; Deke slips the McCall's into the crook of one arm, knows that Soda's already seen the bottle, but better late than never. "What do you want?" but Soda doesn't answer, stares down at the raggedy cuffs of his jeans, at the place where the grass turns to concrete, and Deacon's about to go back to his book when Soda says, "I heard you used to work for the cops, man. That true? You used to work for the cops, back in Atlanta?"

"Fuck off," Deke says, and he's wondering what it feels like to be hit in the head with a skateboard when Soda shrugs and says, "Look, I ain't tryin' to get in your shit, okay. It's just somethin' I heard."

"Then maybe you need to clean out your damn ears every now and then," Deke says and steals a sip from the bottle while Soda's still trying to figure out what he should say next.

"Yeah, well, that's what I heard, okay?"

"Soda, do I look like a goddamned cop to you?"

And Soda nervously rubs at a fat pimple on the end of his chin. "I didn't say you *were* a cop, asshole. I said, I heard you *worked* for them, that's all," and then the rest, out quick, like he's afraid he's about to lose his courage, so it's now or never. "I heard you could do that psychic shit, Deke. That they used to get you to find dead people by touching their clothes and find stolen cars and that sort of thing. I *wasn't* sayin' you were a cop."

Deke wants to hit him, wants to knock the bony little weasel down and kick his last few front teeth straight down his throat. Because this isn't Atlanta, and it's been four years since the last time he even talked to a cop. "Where the hell did you hear something like that, Soda? Who told you that?"

"Look, if I tell you . . . Jesus, man, that just don't matter, okay? I'm tellin' you I heard this 'cause I gotta *ask* you somethin'. I'm about to ask you a favor, and I don't need you freakin' out on me when I definitely did *not* say you were a cop, okay?" And now Deke's nodding his head, careful nod like a clock ticking, tocking, closing Ray Bradbury and his eyes fixed on Soda's chest, on his Beastie Boys T-shirt and a stain over one nipple that looks like strawberry jelly, but probably isn't.

"What, Soda? What do you want?"

"It ain't even *for* me, Deke. It's this chick I know, and she's kinda weird," and Soda draws little circles in the air, three quick orbits around his right ear. "But she's all right. And it ain't even really a favor, man, not exactly. Mostly we just need you to look at somethin' for us. *If* it's true, you workin' with the cops and all. You bein' psychic."

"How many *other* people have you told I was a 'psychic?'" and Deacon makes quotation marks with his fingers for emphasis.

"Nobody. Jesus, it ain't like I'm askin' you for money or dope or nothin'," and Deke snarls right back at him, "You don't have any idea *what* you're asking me, Soda. That's the problem." And Soda's mouth open, but Deke still talking or already talking again, not about to give him a chance.

"Whatever I did for the fucking cops, they *paid* me, Soda. Whatever I did, it wasn't for goddamn charity or out of the goodness of my heart."

And Soda makes an exasperated, whistling sound through the spaces where his missing front teeth should be, then shakes his head and risks half a disgusted glance at Deacon. "What happens to make someone such a bitter motherfucker at your age, Deke? Fuckin' wino. I oughta have my head examined for believin' you ever done anything but suck down juice and watch people doin' their laundry." For a minute neither of them says anything, then, and there's only the cars and the crickets and what sounds like someone banging on the lid of a garbage can a long way off. Until Deacon sighs, then takes a long pull from the bottle of gin and wipes his mouth on the back of his hand.

"Rule number one, Soda. If I do this, it's once and once only, and you're never going to ask me for anything like this ever again."

Soda shrugs, a shrug that'll have to pass for understanding, for agreement. "Yeah. So what's rule number two?" and Deke looks up at the sodium streetlight glare where the stars should be. "Rule number two, you tell anyone—no—if I find out you've *already* told anyone else about this, I'm going to find you, Soda, and stick the broken end of a Coke bottle so far up your ass your gums will bleed."

Ask Deacon Silvey, it's a little bit more than an understatement to say that Sadie Jasper is weird. Three counties south of weird and straight on to creepy, more like it. She's standing on the corner by Martin Flowers, staring in at the darkened florist shop, real flowers and fake flowers and plaster angels behind the plate glass, and when she turns and looks at Deacon Silvey and Soda her expression makes Deke think of a George Romero zombie on a really bad batch of crank: that blank, that tight, and her eyes so pale blue under all the tear- and sleep-smeared eyeliner and mascara that they almost look white. Boiled-fish eyes squinting at him from that dead face.

"So, this is Deke," Soda says, and Sadie holds her hand out like she's a duchess on her throne and expects Deacon to bow and kiss her fucking pinkie. Soda's still talking.

"He's the guy I was tellin' you about, okay?"

Deacon shakes the girl's hand, and she almost manages to look disappointed.

"So you're the skull monkey," she says and smiles like it's something she's been practicing for days and still can't get quite right. "The psychic criminologist," she says, drawing the syllables out slow like refrigerated syrup, and tries to smile again.

"Not exactly," Deacon says, wanting to be back on his bench in the park, reading about Martians, enjoying the way the gin makes his ears buzz, or all the way back in his apartment; anything but standing on a street corner with Soda and this cadaver in her black polyester pants suit and too-red lips and Scooby Doo lunch-box purse.

"Yeah, well, Soda told me you used to be a cop, but they fired you for being an alcoholic," she says, and Deacon turns around and kicks Soda as hard as he can, the scuffed toe of his size-twelve Doc Marten connecting with Soda's shin like a leather sledge hammer. Soda screams like a girl and drops his skateboard. It rolls out into the street while Soda hops about on one foot, holding his kicked leg and cursing Deacon, *fuck you, you asshole, fuck both of you, you broke my goddamn leg,* and then a Budweiser delivery truck rumbles past and runs over his skateboard.

Deacon walks a hesitant few steps behind Sadie Jasper, all the way to the old Harris Transfer and Warehouse building over on Twenty-Second. Just the two of them now, because when Soda finally stopped hopping around and cursing and saw what the Budweiser truck had done to his skateboard—flat, cracked fiberglass, three translucent yellow rubber wheels squashed out around the edges like the legs of a dead cartoon bug that's just been smacked with a cartoon fly swatter, the fourth wheel rolling away down the street, spinning, a frantic blur escaping any further demolition—when he *saw* it, took it all in, Soda made a strangled sound and sat down on the curb. Wouldn't talk to either of them, or even go after what was left of his board, so they left him there, a pitiful lump of patched denim and scabs, and Deacon almost wished he hadn't kicked the son of a bitch, might actually have managed to feel sorry for him, if not for Sadie, the fact that somehow his unfortunate promise to look at whatever it was they were going to look at had not been broken along with Soda's skateboard.

"I *wasn't* a cop," Deke mutters, and Sadie stops walking and looks back at him, waiting for him to catch up, and she's still squinting as if even the piss-yellow street lights are too much for her smudgy, listless eyes.

"Okay. But the psychic part, he wasn't lying about that, was he?" she asks, and Deacon shrugs. Instead of answering her, he says, "I don't think Soda meant to lie about anything. I think he's just stupid." And she smiles then, smiles for real this time, instead of that forced and ugly expression from before, and it makes her look a little less like a zombie.

"You really don't like to talk about this, do you?" she asks, and Deke stops and stares up at the building, turn-of-the-century brick, rusted bars over broken windows and those jagged holes either swallowing the light or spitting it back out, because it's blacker in there than midnight in a coffin, black like the second before the universe was switched on, and Deke knows he needs another mouthful of gin before whatever's coming next.

"No," he tells her, unscrewing the cap on the bottle, "I don't." And Sadie nods while he tips the gin to his lips, while he closes his eyes and the alcohol burns its way into his belly and bloodstream and brain.

"It hurts, doesn't it?" she whispers, and *Maybe I'm going to need two mouthfuls for this,* Deke thinks, and so he takes another drink.

"I knew a girl, when I lived down in Mobile," Sadie says, almost whispering, confession murmur like Deke's some kind of priest and she's about to give up some terrible sin. "She was a clairvoyant, and it drove her crazy. She was always in and out of psych wards, you know. Finally, she overdosed on Valium. *Adiós muchachos.*"

"I'm not clairvoyant," Deacon says. "I get impressions, that's all. What I did for the cops, I helped them find lost things."

"Lost things," Sadie says, still talking like she's afraid someone will overhear. "Yeah, I guess that's a good word for it." Deke looks at her, then looks past her at the night-filled building. "A good word for what?" he asks.

"Oh, you'll see," she says, and this time when Sadie Jasper smiles it makes him think of a hungry animal, or the Grinch that stole Christmas.

They don't go in the door, of course, the locked and boarded door inside the marble arch, *Harris* chiseled deep into the pediment overhead. She leads him down the alley instead, to a place where someone's pried away the iron burglar bars and there are three or four wooden produce crates stacked under the window. Sadie scrambles up the makeshift steps and slips inside, slips smoothly over the shattered glass like a raw oyster over sharp teeth, like she's done this a hundred fucking times before, and for all he knows, she has; for all he knows, she's living in the damn warehouse. Deacon looks both ways twice, up and down the alley, before he follows her.

And however dark the place looked from the *outside*, it's at least twice that dark *inside*, and the broken glass under Deke's boots makes a sound like he's walking on breakfast cereal.

"Hold on a sec," Sadie says, and then there's light, a weak and narrow beam from a silver flashlight in her hand, and he has no idea where she got it, maybe from her purse, or maybe it was stashed somewhere in the gloom. White light across the concrete floor, chips and shards of window to diamond twinkle, a few scraps of cardboard and what looks like a filthy, raveling sweater lying in one corner; nothing else, just this wide and dust-drowned room, and Sadie motions towards a doorway with the beam of light.

"Stairs are over there," she says, and leads the way. Deacon stays close, spooked, feeling foolish, but not wanting to get too far away from the flashlight. The air in the warehouse smells like mildew and dust and cockroaches, a rank, closed away from the world odor that makes his nose itch and makes his eyes water a little.

"Oh, watch out for that spot there," Sadie says, and the beam swings suddenly to her left and down, and Deke sees the gaping hole in the floor, big enough to drop a truck through, that hole. Big enough and black enough that Deke thinks maybe that's where all the dark inside the building's coming from, spilling up from the basement or sub-basement, maybe. Then the flashlight sweeps right again, and he doesn't have to see the hole anymore. There's a flight of stairs, instead, stairs ascending into the nothing waiting past the flashlight's reach, more concrete and a crooked steel handrail Deacon wouldn't trust even for a minute.

"It's all the way at the top," Sadie says, and he notices that she isn't whispering anymore, that there's something excited in her voice now, and Deke can't tell if it's fear or anticipation.

"What's all the way at the top, Sadie? What's waiting for us up there?"

"It's easier if I just show you, if you see it for yourself without me trying to explain," and she starts up the stairs, two at a time, and taking the light away with her, leaving Deke alone next to the hole. So, he hurries to catch up, chasing the bobbing flashlight beam and silently cursing Soda, wishing he'd taken the bottle straight back to his apartment, instead of sitting down on that park bench to read. Up and up and up the stairwell, like Alice falling backwards, and nothing to mark their progress past each floor but a closed door or a place where a door should be, nothing to mark the time but the dull echo of their feet against the cement. She's always three or four steps ahead of him, and pretty soon, Deacon's out of breath, gasping the musty air, and he yells at her to slow the fuck down, what's the goddamn hurry.

"We're almost there," she calls back and keeps going.

And finally there are no more stairs left to climb, just a landing and a narrow window, and at least it's not so dark up here. Deke leans against the wall, wheezing, trying to get his breath, his sides hurting, legs aching; he stares out through flyblown glass at the streets and rooftops below, a couple of passing cars, and it all seems a thousand miles away, or like a projected film of the world, and if he broke this window there might be nothing on the other side at all.

"It's right over here," Sadie says, and the closeness of her voice does nothing about the hard, lonely feeling settling into Deacon Silvey. "This hallway here," she says, jabbing the flashlight at the darkness like a knife as he turns away from the window. "First time I saw it, I was tripping and didn't think it was real. But I started dreaming about it and had to come back to see. I had to know for sure."

Deacon steps slowly away from the window, three slow steps and he's standing beside Sadie. She smells like sweat and tearose perfume. Safe, familiar smells that make him feel no less alone, no less dread for whatever the fuck she's talking about.

"There," she says and switches off the flashlight. "All the way at the other end of the hall."

For a moment Deacon can't see anything at all, just a darting afterimage from the flashlight and nothing much else while his pupils swell, making room for light that isn't there.

"Do you feel it yet, Deacon?" she asks, whispering again, excited, and he's getting tired of this, starts to say so, starts to say he doesn't feel a goddamn thing, but will she please turn the flashlight back on. But then he *does* feel something, cold air flowing thick and heavy around them now, open-icebox air to fog their breath and send a painful rash of goose bumps across his arms. And it isn't *just* cold, it's indifference, the freezing temperature of an apathy so absolute, so perfect; Deacon takes a step backwards, one hand to his mouth, but it's too late, and the gin and his supper come up and splatter loudly on the floor at his feet.

"You okay?" she asks, and he opens his eyes, wants to slap her just for asking, but he nods his head, head filling with the cold and beginning to throb at the temples.

"Do you want me to help you up?" she asks, and he hadn't even realized he was on the floor, on his knees, but she's bending over him.

"Jesus," he croaks, throat raw, sore from bile and the frigid air. He blinks, tears in his eyes, and it's a miracle they haven't frozen, he thinks, pictures himself crying ice cubes like Chilly Willy. His stomach rolls again, and Deacon stares past the girl, down the hall, that long stretch of nothing at all but closed doors and a tiny window way down at the other end.

No, not nothing. Close, but not exactly nothing, and he's trying to make his eyes focus, trying to ignore the pain in his head getting bigger and bigger, threatening to shut him down. Sadie's pulling him to his feet, and Deke doesn't take his eyes off the window, the distant rectangle less inky than the hall only by stingy degrees.

"There," she says. "It's there."

And he knows this is only a dim shadow of the thing itself, this fluid stain rushing wild across the walls, washing watercolor thin across the window; a shadow that could be the wings of a great bird, or long jointed legs moving fast through some deep and secret ocean. It's neither of those things, of course, no convenient, comprehensible nightmare, and he closes his eyes again. Sadie's holding his right hand, squeezing so hard it hurts.

"Don't look at it," he tells her, the floor beneath him getting soft now, and he's slipping, afraid the floor's about to tilt and send them both sliding helplessly past the closed doors, towards the window, towards *it*.

"Sadie, it doesn't want to be seen," he says, tasting blood, and so he knows that he's bitten his tongue or his lip. "It wasn't *meant* to be seen."

"But it's beautiful," Sadie says, and there's awe in her voice, and a sadness that hurts to hear.

Deacon Silvey gets a whiff of a new smell, then, burning leaves and something sweet and rotten, something dead left by the side of the highway, left beneath the summer sun, and the last thing, before he loses consciousness and slips mercifully from himself into a place where even the cold can't follow, the very last thing, a sound like crying that isn't crying and wind that isn't blowing through the long hall.

Twenty minutes later, and they're sitting together, each alone, but one beside the other, on the curb outside the Harris Transfer and Warehouse building. Deacon's too sober, but still too sick to finish the gin, and Sadie sits quietly, waiting to see how this story ends. A police car cruises by, slows down and the cop gives them the hairy eyeball, and for a second Deacon thinks maybe someone saw them climbing in or out of the window. But the cop keeps going, better trouble somewhere else tonight.

"Shit. I thought sure he was going to stop," Sadie says, trying to sound relieved.

"Why the fuck did you guys want me to see that?" Deke asks, making no attempt to hide the anger swirling around inside his throbbing head, yellow hornets stinging the backs of his eyes. "Did you even *have* a reason, Sadie?"

She kicks at the gravel and bits of trash in the gutter, but doesn't look at him, drawing a circle with the toe of one black tennis shoe.

"I guess I wanted to know it was real," she replies, a faint defiant edge in her voice, defiance or defense but nothing like repentance, nothing like sorry. "That's all. I figured you'd know, if it was. Real."

"And Soda, he never went up there with you, did he?"

Sadie shakes her head and barks out a dry little excuse for a laugh. "Are you kidding? Soda gets scared walking past funeral parlors."

"Yeah," Deacon says, wishing he had a cigarette, wishing he'd kicked Soda a little harder. Sadie Jasper sighs loudly, and the rubber toe of her left shoe sends a spray of gravel onto the blacktop, little shower of limestone nuggets and sand and an old spark plug that clatters all the way to the broken yellow center line.

"I know that you're sitting there thinking I'm a bitch," she says and kicks more grit after the spark plug. "Just some spooky bitch that's come along to fuck with your head, right?" Deacon doesn't deny it, and, anyway, she keeps talking.

"But Christ, Deacon. Don't you get sick of it? Day after motherfucking day, sunrise, sunset, getting drunk on that stuff so you don't have to think about how getting drunk is the only thing that makes your shabby excuse for a life bearable? Meanwhile, the whole shitty world's getting a little shittier, a little more hollow every goddamn day. And then, something like *that* comes along," and she turns and points towards the top floor of the warehouse. "Something that means *something*, you know? And maybe it's something horrible, so horrible you won't be able to sleep for a week, but at least when you're afraid you know you're fucking alive."

Deacon's looking at her now, and her white-blue eyes glimmer wetly, close to tears, her crimson lips trembling and pressed together tight like a red-ink slash to underline everything that she's just said. No way he can tell her she's full of shit, because he knows better, has lived too long in the empty husk of his routine not to know better. But there's no way he can ever admit it, either. So he just stares at her until she blinks first, one tear past the eyeliner smear and down her cheek, and then she looks away.

"Jesus, you're an asshole," she says.

"Yeah, well, maybe you wouldn't say that if you got to know me better," and he stands up, keeping the building and its ragged phantoms at his back. "Look. Just promise me you'll stay away from this place, okay? Will you please promise me that, Sadie?"

She nods, and he guesses that's all he's going to get for a promise, more than he expected. And then he leaves her sitting there by herself and walks away through the warm night, through the air that stinks of car exhaust and cooling asphalt, and Deacon Silvey tries not to notice his long shadow, trailing along behind.

1999

THOMAS TESSIER

(b. 1947)

Nocturne

In the calm of his middle years, O'Netty made it a point to go for a walk at night at least once a week. Thursday or Friday was best, as there were other people out doing things and the city was livelier, which pleased him. Saturdays were usually too busy and noisy for his liking, and the other nights a little too quiet —though there were also times when he preferred the quiet and relative solitude.

He enjoyed the air, the exercise, and the changing sights of the city. He enjoyed finishing his stroll at a familiar tavern and sometimes seeing people he knew slightly in the neighborhood. But he also enjoyed visiting a tavern that was new to him, and observing the scene. O'Netty was by no means a heavy drinker. Two or three beers would do, then it was back to his apartment and sleep.

O'Netty went out early one particular evening in September and found the air so pleasant and refreshing that he walked farther than usual. A windy rainstorm had blown through the city that afternoon. The black streets still glistened and wet leaves were scattered everywhere like pictures torn from a magazine. Purple and grey clouds continued to sail low across the darkening sky. Eventually he came to the crest of a hill above the center of the city.

He decided it was time to have a drink before undertaking the long trek back. He saw the neon light of a bar a short distance ahead and started toward it, but then stopped and looked again at a place he had nearly passed. The Europa Lounge was easy to miss. It had no frontage, just a narrow door lodged between a camera shop and a pizzeria. The gold script letters painted on the glass entrance were scratched and chipped with age. But the door opened when O'Netty tried it, and he stepped inside. There was a small landing and a flight of stairs—apparently the bar was in the basement. He didn't hesitate. If it turned out to be something not for him, he could simply turn around and leave, but he wanted at least to see the place.

The stairs were narrow and steep. The one flight turned into two, and then a third. O'Netty might have given up before descending the last steps, but by then he saw the polished floor below and he heard the mixed murmur of voices and music. The bottom landing was a small foyer. There was one door marked as an exit, two others designated as rest rooms, and then the entrance to the lounge itself. O'Netty stepped inside and looked around.

The lounge could not have been more than fifteen feet by ten, with a beamed ceiling. But there was nothing dank or dingy about the place. On the contrary, at first glance it appeared to be rather well done up. It had a soft wheat carpet and golden cedar walls. There were three small banquettes to one side, and a short bar opposite with three upholstered stools, two of which were occupied by men a few years younger than O'Netty. Along the back wall there were two small round wooden tables, each with two chairs. Table lamps with ivory shades cast a creamy glow that gave the whole room a warm, intimate feeling.

There were middle-aged couples in the back two banquettes but the nearest one was empty, and O'Netty took it. The bartender was an older man with gleaming silver hair, dressed in a white shirt, dark blue suit and tie. He smiled politely, nodded and when he spoke it was with a slight, unrecognizable accent. O'Netty's beer was served in a very tall pilsener glass.

The music playing on the sound system was some mix of jazz and blues with a lot of solo guitar meditations. It was unfamiliar to O'Netty but he found it soothing, almost consoling in some way. He sipped his drink. This place was definitely unlike the average neighborhood tavern, but it wasn't at all uncomfortable. In fact, O'Netty thought it seemed rather pleasant.

After a few minutes, he realized that the other people there were speaking in a foreign language. He only caught brief snatches of words, but he heard enough to know that he had no idea what language it was. Which was no great surprise. After all, there were so many European languages one almost never heard—for instance: Czech, Hungarian, Rumanian, Bulgarian and Finnish. O'Netty concluded that he had come across a bar, a social club run by and for locals of some such eastern European origin. Before he left, perhaps he would ask the bartender about it.

Although he couldn't understand anything the others said, O'Netty had no trouble catching their mood. Their voices were relaxed, lively, friendly, chatty, and occasionally there was some laughter. It was possible for O'Netty to close his eyes and imagine that he was sitting on the terrace of a cafe in some exotic and distant city, a stranger among the locals. He liked that thought.

Some little while later, when O'Netty was about halfway through his second glass of beer, he noticed that the others had either fallen silent or were speaking very softly. He sensed an air of anticipation in the room.

A few moments later, a young man emerged from the door behind the bar. The music stopped and everyone was still and quiet. The young man came around to the front of the bar. He could not yet be thirty, O'Netty thought. The young man swiftly pulled off his T-shirt and tossed it aside. He was slender, with not much hair on his chest. He kicked off his sandals and removed his gym pants, so that he now stood there dressed only in a pair of black briefs. The other two men at the bar had moved the stools aside to create more space.

The young man reached into a bag he had brought with him and began to unfold a large sheet of dark green plastic, which he carefully spread out on the floor. He stood on it, positioning himself in the center of the square. Then he took a case out of the bag, opened it and grasped a knife. The blade was about eight inches long and very slightly curved. The young man's expression was serious and purposeful, but otherwise revealed nothing.

What now, O'Netty wondered.

Let's see.

The young man hooked the tip of the blade in his chest, just below the sternum, pushed it in farther, and then carefully tugged it down through his navel, all the way to the elastic top of his briefs. He winced and sagged with the effort, and he used his free hand to hold the wound partly closed. Next, he jabbed the knife into his abdomen, just above the left hip, and pulled it straight across to his right side. He groaned and dropped the knife. Now he was hunched over, struggling to hold himself up, and he could not contain the double wound. His organs bulged out in his arms—liver, stomach, the long rope of intestines, all of them dry and leathery. There was no blood at all, but rather a huge and startling cascade of dark red sand that made a clatter of noise as it spilled across the plastic sheet. The young man was very wobbly now, and the other two at the bar stepped forward to take him by the arms and lower him gently to the ground. The young man's eyes blinked several times, and then stayed shut. The other two carefully wrapped his body in the plastic sheet and secured it with some tape they got from the bag. Finally, they lifted the body and carried it into the room behind the bar. They returned a few moments later and took their seats again. Conversations resumed, slowly at first, but then became quick and more animated with half-suppressed urgency.

After a while O'Netty finished his beer and got up to leave. No one paid any attention to him except the bartender, who came to the end of the bar for O'Netty's payment and then brought him his change.

"By the way, sir, in case you don't know. You can use the fire exit. There's no need to climb all those stairs."

"Ah, thank you," O'Netty replied. "It *is* a lot of stairs."

"Good night, sir."

"Good night."

The fire exit opened onto a long metal staircase that brought him to a short lane that led to a side street just off one of the main avenues in the center of the city. It was already daylight, the air crisp and fresh, the early morning sun exploding on the upper floors of the taller buildings. O'Netty stood there for a few moments, trying to regain his bearings and decide what to do.

Then he saw a city bus coming his way, and he realized it was the one that went to his neighborhood. It must be the first bus of the day, O'Netty thought, as he stepped to the curb and raised his hand.

2000

MICHAEL CHABON
(b. 1963)

The God of Dark Laughter

THIRTEEN days after the Entwhistle-Ealing Bros. Circus left
Ashtown, beating a long retreat toward its winter headquarters
in Peru, Indiana, two boys out hunting squirrels in the woods
along Portwine Road stumbled on a body that was dressed in
a mad suit of purple and orange velour. They found it at the
end of a muddy strip of gravel that began, five miles to the
west, as Yuggogheny County Road 22A. Another half mile farther to the east and it would have been left to my colleagues
over in Fayette County to puzzle out the question of who had
shot the man and skinned his head from chin to crown and
clavicle to clavicle, taking ears, eyelids, lips, and scalp in a single grisly flap, like the cupped husk of a peeled orange. My
name is Edward D. Satterlee, and for the last twelve years I
have faithfully served Yuggogheny County as its district attorney, in cases that have all too often run to the outrageous and
bizarre. I make the following report in no confidence that it,
or I, will be believed, and beg the reader to consider this, at
least in part, my letter of resignation.

The boys who found the body were themselves fresh from
several hours' worth of bloody amusement with long knives
and dead squirrels, and at first the investigating officers took
them for the perpetrators of the crime. There was blood on the
boys' cuffs, their shirttails, and the bills of their gray twill caps.
But the county detectives and I quickly moved beyond Joey
Matuszak and Frankie Corro. For all their familiarity with gris-
tle and sinew and the bright-purple discovered interior of a
body, the boys had come into the station looking pale and bewildered, and we found ample evidence at the crime scene of
their having lost the contents of their stomachs when confronted with the corpse.

Now, I have every intention of setting down the facts of this
case as I understand and experienced them, without fear of the

463

reader's doubting them (or my own sanity), but I see no point in mentioning any further *anatomical* details of the crime, except to say that our coroner, Dr. Sauer, though he labored at the problem with a sad fervor, was hard put to establish conclusively that the victim had been dead before his killer went to work on him with a very long, very sharp knife.

The dead man, as I have already mentioned, was attired in a curious suit—the trousers and jacket of threadbare purple velour, the waistcoat bright orange, the whole thing patched with outsized squares of fabric cut from a variety of loudly clashing plaids. It was on account of the patches, along with the victim's cracked and split-soled shoes and a certain undeniable shabbiness in the stuff of the suit, that the primary detective —a man not apt to see deeper than the outermost wrapper of the world (we do not attract, I must confess, the finest police talent in this doleful little corner of western Pennsylvania)— had already figured the victim for a vagrant, albeit one with extraordinarily big feet.

"Those cannot possibly be his real shoes, Ganz, you idiot," I gently suggested. The call, patched through to my boarding house from that gruesome clearing in the woods, had interrupted my supper, which by a grim coincidence had been a Brunswick stew (the specialty of my Virginia-born landlady) of pork and *squirrel*. "They're supposed to make you laugh."

"They *are* pretty funny," said Ganz. "Come to think of it." Detective John Ganz was a large-boned fellow, upholstered in a layer of ruddy flesh. He breathed through his mouth, and walked with a tall man's defeated stoop, and five times a day he took out his comb and ritually plastered his thinning blond hair to the top of his head with a dime-size dab of Tres Flores.

When I arrived at the clearing, having abandoned my solitary dinner, I found the corpse lying just as the young hunters had come upon it, supine, arms thrown up and to either side of the flayed face in a startled attitude that fuelled the hopes of poor Dr. Sauer that the victim's death by gunshot had preceded his mutilation. Ganz or one of the other investigators had kindly thrown a chamois cloth over the vandalized head. I took enough of a peek beneath it to provide me with everything that I or the reader could possibly need to know about the condition of the head—I will never forget the sight of that monstrous, fleshless grin—and to remark the dead man's un-usual choice of cravat. It was a giant, floppy bow tie, white with orange and purple polka dots.

"Damn you, Ganz," I said, though I was not in truth ad-dressing the poor fellow, who, I knew, would not be able to answer my question anytime soon. "What's a dead clown doing in my woods?"

We found no wallet on the corpse, nor any kind of identifying objects. My men, along with the better part of the Ashtown Police Department, went over and over the woods east of town, hourly widening the radius of their search. That day, when not attending to my other duties (I was then in the process of breaking up the Dushnyk cigarette-smuggling ring), I man-aged to work my way back along a chain of inferences to the Entwhistle-Ealing Bros. Circus, which, as I eventually recalled, had recently stayed on the eastern outskirts of Ashtown, at the fringe of the woods where the body was found.

The following day, I succeeded in reaching the circus's gen-eral manager, a man named Onheuser, at their winter head-quarters in Peru. He informed me over the phone that the company had left Pennsylvania and was now en route to Peru, and I asked him if he had received any reports from the road manager of a clown's having suddenly gone missing.

"Missing?" he said. I wished that I could see his face, for I thought I heard the flatted note of something false in his tone. Perhaps he was merely nervous about talking to a county dis-trict attorney. The Entwhistle-Ealing Bros. Circus was a mangy affair, by all accounts, and probably no stranger to pursuit by officers of the court. "Why, I don't believe so, no."

I explained to him that a man who gave every indication of having once been a circus clown had turned up dead in a pine-wood outside Ashtown, Pennsylvania.

"Oh, no," Onheuser said. "I truly hope he wasn't one of mine, Mr. Satterlee."

"Is it possible you might have left one of your clowns behind, Mr. Onheuser?"

"Clowns are special people," Onheuser replied, sounding a touch on the defensive. "They love their work, but sometimes it can get to be a little, well, too much for them." It developed that Mr. Onheuser had, in his younger days, performed as a clown, under the name of Mr. Wingo, in the circus of which he was now the general manager. "It's not unusual for a clown to drop out for a little while, cool his heels, you know, in some town where he can get a few months of well-earned rest. It isn't *common*, I wouldn't say, but it's not unusual. I will wire my road manager—they're in Canton, Ohio—and see what I can find out."

I gathered, reading between the lines, that clowns were high-strung types, and not above going off on the occasional bender. This poor fellow had probably jumped ship here two weeks ago, holing up somewhere with a case of rye, only to run afoul of a very nasty person, possibly one who harbored no great love of clowns. In fact, I had an odd feeling, nothing more than a hunch, really, that the ordinary citizens of Ashtown and its environs were safe, even though the killer was still at large. Once more, I picked up a slip of paper that I had tucked into my desk blotter that morning. It was something that Dr. Sauer had clipped from his files and passed along to me. *Coulrophobia: morbid, irrational fear of or aversion to clowns.*

"Er, listen, Mr. Satterlee," Onheuser went on. "I hope you won't mind my asking. That is, I hope it's not a, well, a confidential police matter, or something of the sort. But I know that when I do get through to them, out in Canton, they're going to want to know."

I guessed, somehow, what he was about to ask me. I could hear the prickling fear behind his curiosity, the note of dread in his voice. I waited him out.

"Did they—was there any—how did he die?"

"He was shot," I said, for the moment supplying only the least interesting part of the answer, tugging on that loose thread of fear. "In the head."

"And there was . . . forgive me. No . . . no harm done? To the body? Other than the gunshot wound, I mean to say."

"Well, yes, his head was rather savagely mutilated," I said brightly. "Is that what you mean to say?"

"Ah! No, no, I don't—"

"The killer or killers removed all the skin from the cranium. It was very skillfully done. Now, suppose you tell me what you know about it."

There was another pause, and a stream of agitated electrons burbled along between us.

"I don't know anything, Mr. District Attorney. I'm sorry. I really must go now. I'll wire you when I have some—"

The line went dead. He was so keen to hang up on me that he could not even wait to finish his sentence. I got up and went to the shelf where, in recent months, I had taken to keeping a bottle of whiskey tucked behind my bust of Daniel Webster. Carrying the bottle and a dusty glass back to my desk, I sat down and tried to reconcile myself to the thought that I was confronted—not, alas, for the first time in my tenure as chief law-enforcement officer of Yuggogheny County—with a crime whose explanation was going to involve not the usual amalgam of stupidity, meanness, and singularly poor judgment but the incalculable intentions of a being who was genuinely evil. What disheartened me was not that I viewed a crime committed out of the promptings of an evil nature as inherently less liable to solution than the misdeeds of the foolish, the unlucky, or the habitually cruel. On the contrary, evil often expresses itself through refreshingly discernible patterns, through schedules and syllogisms. But the presence of evil, once scented, tends to bring out all that is most irrational and uncontrollable in the public imagination. It is a catalyst for pea-brained theories, gimcrack scholarship, and the credulous cosmologies of hysteria.

At that moment, there was a knock on the door to my office, and Detective Ganz came in. At one time I would have tried to hide the glass of whiskey, behind the typewriter or the photo of my wife and son, but now it did not seem to be worth the effort. I was not fooling anyone. Ganz took note of the glass in my hand with a raised eyebrow and a schoolmarmish pursing of his lips.

"Well?" I said. There had been a brief period, following my son's death and the subsequent suicide of my dear wife, Mary, when I had indulged the pitying regard of my staff. I now found that I regretted having shown such weakness. "What is it, then? Has something turned up?"

"A cave," Ganz said. "The poor bastard was living in a cave."

*

The range of low hills and hollows separating lower Yug-gogheny from Fayette County is rotten with caves. For many years, when I was a boy, a man named Colonel Earnshawe op-erated penny tours of the iridescent organ pipes and jagged stone teeth of Neighborsburg Caverns, before they collapsed in the mysterious earthquake of 1919, killing the Colonel and his sister Irene, and putting to rest many strange rumors about that eccentric old pair. My childhood friends and I, ranging in the woods, would from time to time come upon the root-choked mouth of a cave exhaling its cool plutonic breath, and dare one another to leave the sunshine and enter that world of shadow—that entrance, as it always seemed to me, to the leg-endary past itself, where the bones of Indians and Frenchmen might lie moldering. It was in one of these anterooms of buried history that the beam of a flashlight, wielded by a deputy sheriff from Plunkettsburg, had struck the silvery lip of a can of pork and beans. Calling to his companions, the deputy plunged through a curtain of spiderweb and found himself in the parlor, bedroom, and kitchen of the dead man. There were some cans of chili and hash, a Primus stove, a lantern, a bed-roll, a mess kit, and an old Colt revolver, Army issue, loaded and apparently not fired for some time. And there were also books—a Scout guide to roughing it, a collected Blake, and a couple of odd texts, elderly and tattered: one in German called "Über das Finstere Lachen," by a man named Friedrich von Junzt, which appeared to be religious or philosophical in na-ture, and one a small volume bound in black leather and printed in no alphabet known to me, the letters sinuous and furred with wild diacritical marks.

"Pretty heavy reading for a clown," Ganz said.

"It's not all rubber chickens and hosing each other down with seltzer bottles, Jack."

"Oh, no?"

"No, sir. Clowns have unsuspected depths."

"I'm starting to get that impression, sir."

Propped against the straightest wall of the cave, just beside the lantern, there was a large mirror, still bearing the bent clasps and sheared bolt that had once, I inferred, held it to the wall of a filling-station men's room. At its foot was the item that had earlier confirmed to Detective Ganz—and now confirmed to me as I went to inspect it—the recent habitation of the cave by a painted circus clown: a large, padlocked wooden makeup kit, of heavy and rather elaborate construction. I directed Ganz to send for a Pittsburgh criminalist who had served us with discretion in the horrific Primm case, reminding him that nothing must be touched until this Mr. Espy and his black bag of dusts and luminous powders arrived.

The air in the cave had a sharp, briny tinge; beneath it there was a stale animal musk that reminded me, absurdly, of the smell inside a circus tent.

"Why was he living in a cave?" I said to Ganz. "We have a perfectly nice hotel in town."

"Maybe he was broke."

"Or maybe he thought that a hotel was the first place they would look for him."

Ganz looked confused, and a little annoyed, as if he thought I were being deliberately mysterious.

"*Who* was looking for him?"

"I don't know, Detective. Maybe no one. I'm just thinking out loud."

Impatience marred Ganz's fair, bland features. He could tell that I was in the grip of a hunch, and hunches were always among the first considerations ruled out by the procedural practices of Detective John Ganz. My hunches had, admittedly, an uneven record. In the Primm business, one had very nearly got both Ganz and me killed. As for the wayward hunch about my mother's old crony Thaddeus Craven and the strength of his will to quit drinking—I suppose I shall regret indulging that one for the rest of my life.

"If you'll excuse me, Jack . . ." I said. "I'm having a bit of a hard time with the stench in here."

"I was thinking he might have been keeping a pig." Ganz inclined his head to one side and gave an empirical sniff. "It smells like pig to me."

I covered my mouth and hurried outside into the cool, dank pinewood. I gathered in great lungfuls of air. The nausea passed, and I filled my pipe, walking up and down outside the mouth of the cave and trying to connect this new discovery to my talk with the circus man, Onheuser. Clearly, he had suspected that this clown might have met with a grisly end. Not only that, he had known that his fellow circus people would fear the very same thing—as if there were some coulrophohic madman with a knife who was as much a part of circus lore as the prohibition on whistling in the dressing room or on looking over your shoulder when you marched in the circus parade.

I got my pipe lit, and wandered down into the woods, toward the clearing where the boys had stumbled over the dead man, following a rough trail that the police had found. Really, it was not a trail so much as an impromptu alley of broken saplings and trampled ground that wound a convoluted course down the hill from the cave to the clearing. It appeared to have been blazed a few days before by the victim and his pursuer; near the bottom, where the trees gave way to open sky, there were grooves of plowed earth that corresponded neatly with encrustations on the heels of the clown's giant brogues. The killer must have caught the clown at the edge of the clearing, and then dragged him along by the hair, or by the collar of his shirt, for the last twenty-five yards, leaving this furrowed record of the panicked, slipping flight of the clown. The presumed killer's footprints were everywhere in evidence, and appeared to have been made by a pair of long and pointed boots. But the really puzzling thing was a third set of prints, which Ganz had noticed and mentioned to me, scattered here and there along the cold black mud of the path. They seemed to have been made by a barefoot child of eight or nine years. And damned, as Ganz had concluded his report to me, if that barefoot child did not appear to have been dancing!

I came into the clearing, a little short of breath, and stood listening to the wind in the pines and the distant rumble of the state highway, until my pipe went out. It was a cool afternoon, but the sky had been blue all day and the woods were peaceful and fragrant. Nevertheless, I was conscious of a mounting sense of disquiet as I stood over the bed of sodden leaves where the body had been found. I did not then, nor do I now, believe in ghosts, but as the sun dipped down behind the tops of the trees, lengthening the long shadows encompassing me, I became aware of an irresistible feeling that somebody was watching me. After a moment, the feeling intensified, and localized, as it were, so I was certain that to see who it was I need only turn around. Bravely—meaning not that I am a brave man but that I behaved as if I were—I took my matches from my jacket pocket and relit my pipe. Then I turned. I knew that when I glanced behind me I would not see Jack Ganz or one of the other policemen standing there; any of them would have said something to me by now. No, it was either going to be nothing at all or something that I could not even allow myself to imagine.

It was, in fact, a baboon, crouching on its hind legs in the middle of the trail, regarding me with close-set orange eyes, one hand cupped at its side. It had great puffed whiskers and a long canine snout. There was something in the barrel chest and the muttonchop sideburns that led me to conclude, correctly, as it turned out, that the specimen was male. For all his majestic bulk, the old fellow presented a rather sad spectacle. His fur was matted and caked with mud, and a sticky coating of pine needles clung to his feet. The expression in his eyes was unsettlingly forlorn, almost pleading, I would have said, and in his mute gaze I imagined I detected a hint of outraged dignity. This might, of course, have been due to the hat he was wearing. It was conical, particolored with orange and purple lozenges, and ornamented at the tip with a bright-orange pompom. Tied under his chin with a length of black ribbon, it hung from the side of his head at a humorous angle. I myself might have been tempted to kill the man who had tied it to my head.

"Was it you?" I said, thinking of Poe's story of the rampaging orang swinging a razor in a Parisian apartment. Had that story had any basis in fact? Could the dead clown have been killed by the pet or sidekick with whom, as the mystery of the animal smell in the cave now resolved itself, he had shared his fugitive existence?

The baboon declined to answer my question. After a moment, though, he raised his long crooked left arm and gestured vaguely toward his belly. The import of this message was unmistakable, and thus I had the answer to my question—if he could not open a can of franks and beans, he would not have been able to perform that awful surgery on his owner or partner.

"All right, old boy," I said. "Let's get you something to eat." I took a step toward him, watching for signs that he might bolt or, worse, throw himself at me. But he sat, looking miserable, clenching something in his right paw. I crossed the distance between us. His rancid-hair smell was unbearable. "You need a bath, don't you?" I spoke, by reflex, as if I were talking to somebody's tired old dog. "Were you and your friend in the habit of bathing together? Were you there when it happened, old boy? Any idea who did it?"

The animal gazed up at me, its eyes kindled with that luminous and sagacious sorrow that lends to the faces of apes and mandrills an air of cousinly reproach, as if we humans have betrayed the principles of our kind. Tentatively, I reached out to him with one hand. He grasped my fingers in his dry leather paw, and then the next instant he had leapt bodily into my arms, like a child seeking solace. The garbage-and-skunk stench of him burned my nose. I gagged and stumbled backward as the baboon scrambled to wrap his arms and legs around me. I must have cried out; a moment later a unit of iron lids seemed to slam against my skull, and the animal went slack, sliding, with a horrible, human sigh of disappointment, to the ground at my feet.

Ganz and two Ashtown policemen came running over and dragged the dead baboon away from me.

"He wasn't—he was just—" I was too outraged to form a coherent expression of my anger. "You could have hit *me*!"

Ganz closed the animal's eyes, and laid its arms out at its sides. The right paw was still clenched in a shaggy fist. Ganz, not without some difficulty, managed to pry it open. He uttered an printable oath.

In the baboon's palm lay a human finger. Ganz and I looked at each other, wordlessly confirming that the dead clown had been in possession of a full complement of digits.

"See that Espy gets that finger," I said. "Maybe we can find out whose it was."

"It's a woman's," Ganz said. "Look at that nail."

I took it from him, holding it by the chewed and bloody end so as not to dislodge any evidence that might be trapped under the long nail. Though rigid, it was strangely warm, perhaps from having spent a few days in the vengeful grip of the animal who had claimed it from his master's murderer. It appeared to be an index finger, with a manicured, pointed nail nearly three-quarters of an inch long. I shook my head.

"It isn't painted," I said. "Not even varnished. How many women wear their nails like that?"

"Maybe the paint rubbed off," one of the policemen suggested.

"Maybe," I said. I knelt on the ground beside the body of the baboon. There was, I noted, a wound on the back of his neck, long and deep and crusted over with dirt and dried blood. I now saw him in my mind's eye, dancing like a barefoot child around the murderer and the victim as they struggled down the path to the clearing. It would take a powerful man to fight such an animal off. "I can't believe you killed our only witness, Detective Ganz. The poor bastard was just giving me a hug."

This information seemed to amuse Ganz nearly as much as it puzzled him.

"He was a monkey, sir," Ganz said. "I doubt he—"

"He could make signs, you fool! He told me he was *hungry*."

Ganz blinked, trying, I supposed, to append to his personal operations manual this evidence of the potential usefulness of circus apes to police inquiries.

"If I had a dozen baboons like that one on my staff," I said, "I would never have to leave the office."

That evening, before going home, I stopped by the evidence room in the High Street annex and signed out the two books that had been found in the cave that morning. As I walked back into the corridor, I thought I detected an odd odor—odd, at any rate, for that dull expanse of linoleum and buzzing fluorescent tubes—of the sea: a sharp, salty, briny smell. I decided that it must be some new disinfectant being used by the custodian, but it reminded me of the smell of blood from the specimen bags and sealed containers in the evidence room. I turned the lock on the room's door and slipped the books, in their waxy protective envelopes, into my briefcase, and walked down High Street to Dennistoun Road, where the public library was. It stayed open late on Wednesday nights, and I would need a German-English dictionary if my college German and I were going to get anywhere with Herr von Junzt.

The librarian, Lucy Brand, returned my greeting with the circumspect air of one who hopes to be rewarded for her forbearance with a wealth of juicy tidbits. Word of the murder,

denuded of most of the relevant details, had made the Ashtown *Ambler* yesterday morning, and though I had cautioned
the unlucky young squirrel hunters against talking about the
case, already conjectures, misprisions, and outright lies had
begun wildly to coalesce; I knew the temper of my home town
well enough to realize that if I did not close this case soon
things might get out of hand. Ashtown, as the events surrounding the appearance of the so-called Green Man, in 1932,
amply demonstrated, has a lamentable tendency toward mu-
nicipal panic.

Having secured a copy of Köhler's Dictionary of the English
and German Languages, I went, on an impulse, to the card
catalogue and looked up von Junzt, Friedrich. There was no
card for any work by this author—hardly surprising, perhaps, in
a small-town library like ours. I returned to the reference shelf,
and consulted an encyclopedia of philosophical biography and
comparable volumes of philologic reference, but found no
entry for any von Junzt—a diplomate, by the testimony of his
title page, of the University of Tübingen and of the Sorbonne.
It seemed that von Junzt had been dismissed, or expunged,
from the dusty memory of his discipline.

It was as I was closing the Encyclopedia of Archaeo-Anthro-
pological Research that a name suddenly leapt out at me,
catching my eye just before the pages slammed together. It
was a word that I had noticed in von Junzt's book: "Urartu."
I barely managed to slip the edge of my thumb into the encyclopedia to mark the place; half a second later and the reference might have been lost to me. As it turned out, the name
of von Junzt itself was also contained—sealed up—in the sar-
cophagus of this entry, a long and tedious one devoted to the
work of an Oxford man by the name of St. Dennis T. R. Glad-
fellow, "a noted scholar," as the entry had it, "in the field of
inquiry into the beliefs of the ancient, largely unknown
peoples referred to conjecturally today as proto-Urartians."
The reference lay buried in a column dense with comparisons
among various bits of obsidian and broken bronze:

G.'s analysis of the meaning of such ceremonial blades admittedly
was aided by the earlier discoveries of Friedrich von Junzt, at the site
of the former Temple of Yrrh, in north central Armenia, among them

certain sacrificial artifacts pertaining to the worship of the proto-Urartian deity Yê-Heh, rather grandly (though regrettably without credible evidence) styled "the god of dark or mocking laughter" by the German, a notorious adventurer and fake whose work, nevertheless, in this instance, has managed to prove useful to science.

The prospect of spending the evening in the company of Herr von Junzt began to seem even less appealing. One of the most tedious human beings I have ever known was my own mother, who, early in my childhood, fell under the spell of Madame Blavatsky and her followers and proceeded to weary my youth and deplete my patrimony with her devotion to that indigestible caseation of balderdash and lies. Mother drew a number of local simpletons into her orbit, among them poor old drunken Thaddeus Craven, and burnt them up as thoroughly as the earth's atmosphere consumes asteroids. The most satisfying episodes of my career have been those which afforded me the opportunity to prosecute charlatans and frauds and those who preyed on the credulous; I did not now relish the thought of sitting at home with such a man all evening, in particular one who spoke only German.

Nevertheless, I could not ignore the undeniable novelty of a murdered circus clown who was familiar with scholarship—however spurious or misguided concerning the religious beliefs of proto-Urartians. I carried the Köhler's over to the counter, where Lucy Brand waited eagerly for me to spill some small ration of beans. When I offered nothing for her delectation, she finally spoke.

"Was he a German?" she said, showing unaccustomed boldness, it seemed to me.

"Was *who* a German, my dear Miss Brand?"

"The victim." She lowered her voice to a textbook librarian's whisper, though there was no one in the building but old Bob Spherakis, asleep and snoring in the periodicals room a copy of *Grit*.

"I—I don't know," I said, taken aback by the simplicity of her inference, or rather by its having escaped me. "I suppose he may have been, yes."

She slid the book across the counter toward me.

"There was another one of them in here this afternoon," she said. "At least, I think he was a German. A Jew, come to think of it. Somehow he managed to find the only book in Hebrew we have in our collection. It's one of the books old Mr. Vorzeichen donated when he died. A prayer book, I think it is. Tiny little thing. Black leather."

This information ought to have struck a chord in my memory, of course, but it did not. I settled my hat on my head, bid Miss Brand good night, and walked slowly home, with the dictionary under my arm, and, in my briefcase, von Junzt's stout tome and the little black-leather volume filled with sinuous mysterious script.

I will not tax the reader with an account of my struggles with Köhler's dictionary and the thorny bramble of von Junzt's overheated German prose. Suffice to say that it took me the better part of the evening to make my way through the introduction. It was well past midnight by the time I arrived at the first chapter, and nearing two o'clock before I had amassed the information that I will now pass along to the reader, with no endorsement beyond the testimony of these pages, nor any hope of its being believed.

It was a blustery night; I sat in the study on the top floor of my old house's round tower, listening to the windows rattle in their casements, as if a gang of intruders were seeking a way in. In this high room, in 1885, it was said, Howard Ash, the last living descendant of our town's founder, General Hannaniah Ash, had sealed the blank note of his life and dispatched himself, with postage due, to his Creator. A fugitive draft blew from time to time across my desk and stirred the pages of the dictionary by my left hand. I felt, as I read, as if the whole world were asleep—benighted, ignorant, and dreaming—while I had been left to man the crow's nest, standing lonely vigil in the teeth of a storm that was blowing in from a tropic of dread.

According to the scholar or charlatan Friedrich von Junzt, the regions around what is now northern Armenia had spawned, along with an entire cosmology, two competing cults of incalculable antiquity, which survived to the present day: that of Yê-Heh, the God of Dark Laughter, and that of Ai, the God of Unbearable and Ubiquitous Sorrow. The Yê-Hehists viewed the universe as a cosmic hoax, perpetrated by the father-god Yrrh for unknowable purposes: a place of calamity and cruel irony so overwhelming that the only possible response was a malevolent laughter like that, presumably, of Yrrh himself. The laughing followers of baboon-headed Yê-Heh created a sacred burlesque, mentioned by Pausanias and by one of the travellers in Plutarch's dialogue "On the Passing of the Oracles," to express their mockery of life, death, and all human aspirations. The rite involved the flaying of a human head, severed from the shoulders of one who had died in battle or in the course of some other supposedly exalted endeavor. The clown-priest would don the bloodless mask and then dance, making a public travesty of the noble dead. Through generations of inbreeding, the worshippers of Yê-Heh had evolved into a virtual subspecies of humanity, characterized by distended grins and skin as white as chalk. Von Junzt even claimed that the tradition of painted circus clowns derived from the clumsy imitation, by noninitiates, of these ancient kooks.

The "immemorial foes" of the baboon boys, as the reader may have surmised, were the followers of Ai, the God Who Mourns. These gloomy fanatics saw the world as no less horrifying and cruel than did their archenemies, but their response to the whole mess was a more or less permanent wailing. Over the long millennia since the heyday of ancient Urartu, the Aiites had developed a complicated physical discipline, a sort of jujitsu or calisthenics of murder, which they chiefly employed in a ruthless hunt of followers of Yê-Heh. For they believed that Yrrh, the Absent One, the Silent Devisor who, an eternity ago, tossed the cosmos over his shoulder like a sheet of fish wrap and wandered away leaving not a clue as to his intentions, would not return to explain the meaning of his inexplicable and tragic creation until the progeny of Yê-Heh, along with all copies of the Yê-Hehist sacred book, "Khndzut Dzul," or "The Unfathomable Ruse," had been expunged from the face of the earth. Only then would Yrrh return from his primeval hiatus—"bringing what new horror or redemption," as the German intoned, "none can say."

All this struck me as a gamier variety of the same loony, Zoroastrian plonk that my mother had spent her life decanting, and I might have been inclined to set the whole business aside and leave the case to be swept under the administrative rug by Jack Ganz had it not been for the words with which Herr von Junzt concluded the second chapter of his tedious work:

While the Yê-Hehist gospel of cynicism and ridicule has, quite obviously, spread around the world, the cult itself has largely died out, in part through the predations of foes and in part through chronic health problems brought about by inbreeding. Today [von Junzt's book carried a date of 1849] it is reported that there may be fewer than 150 of the Yê-Hehists left in the world. They have survived, for the most part, by taking on work in travelling circuses. While their existence is known to ordinary members of the circus world, their secret has, by and large, been kept. And in the sideshows they have gone to ground, awaiting the tread outside the wagon, shadow on the tent-flap, the cruel knife that will, in a mockery of their own long-abandoned ritual of mockery, deprive them of the lily-white flesh of their skulls.

Here I put down the book, my hands trembling from fatigue, and took up the other one, printed in an unknown tongue. "The Unfathomable Ruse"? I hardly thought so; I was inclined to give as little credit as I reasonably could to Herr von Junzt's account. More than likely the small black volume was some inspirational text in the mother tongue of the dead man, a translation of the Gospels, perhaps. And yet I must confess that there were a few tangential points in von Junzt's account that caused me some misgiving.

There was a scrape then just outside my window, as if a finger with a very long nail were being drawn almost lovingly along the glass. But the finger turned out to be one of the branches of a fine old horse-chestnut tree that stood outside the tower, scratching at the window in the wind. I was relieved and humiliated. Time to go to bed, I said to myself. Before I turned in, I went to the shelf and moved to one side the bust of Galen that I had inherited from my father, a country doctor. I took a quick snort of old Tennessee whiskey, a taste for which I had also inherited from the old man. Thus emboldened, I went over to the desk and picked up the books. To be frank, I would have preferred to leave them there—I would have preferred to burn them, to be really frank—but I felt that it was my duty to keep them about me while they were under my watch. So I slept with the books beneath my pillow, in their wax envelopes, and I had the worst dream of my life.

It was one of those dreams where you are a fly on the wall, a phantom bystander, disembodied, unable to speak or intervene. In it, I was treated to the spectacle of a man whose young son was going to die. The man lived in a corner of the world where, from time to time, evil seemed to bubble up from the rusty red earth like a black combustible compound of ancient things long dead. And yet, year after year, this man met each new outburst of horror, true to his code, with nothing but law books, statutes, and county ordinances, as if sheltering with only a sheet of newspaper those he had sworn to protect, insisting that the steaming black geyser pouring down on them was nothing but a light spring rain. That vision started me laughing, but the cream of the jest came when, seized by a spasm of forgiveness toward his late, mad mother, the man decided not to prosecute one of her old paramours, a rummy by the name of Craven, for driving under the influence. Shortly thereafter, Craven steered his old Hudson Terraplane the wrong way down a one-way street, where it encountered, with appropriate cartoon sound effects, an oncoming bicycle ridden by the man's heedless, darling, wildly pedalling son. That was the funniest thing of all, funnier than the amusing ironies of the man's profession, than his furtive drinking and his wordless, solitary suppers, funnier even than his having been widowed by suicide: the joke of a father's outliving his boy. It was so funny that, watching this ridiculous man in my dream, I could not catch my breath for laughing. I laughed so hard that my eyes popped from their sockets, and my smile stretched until it broke my aching jaw. I laughed until the husk of my head burst like a pod and fell away, and my skull and brains went floating off into the sky, white dandelion fluff, a cloud of fairy parasols.

Around four o'clock in the morning, I woke and was conscious of someone in the room with me. There was an unmistakable tang of the sea in the air. My eyesight is poor and it took me a while to make him out in the darkness, though he was standing just beside my bed, with his long thin arm snaked under my pillow, creeping around. I lay perfectly still, aware of the tips of this slender shadow's fingernails and the scrape of his scaly knuckles, as he rifled the contents of my head and absconded with them through the bedroom window which was somehow also the mouth of the Neighborsburg Caverns, with tiny old Colonel Earnshaw taking tickets in the booth.

I awakened now in truth, and reached immediately under the pillow. The books were still there. I returned them to the evidence room at eight o'clock this morning. At nine, there was a call from Dolores and Victor Abbott, at their motor lodge out on the Plunkettsburg Pike. A guest had made an abrupt departure, leaving a mess. I got into a car with Ganz and we drove out to get a look. The Ashtown police were already there, going over the buildings and grounds of the Vista Dolores Lodge. The bathroom wastebasket of Room 201 was overflowing with blood-soaked bandages. There was evidence that the guest had been keeping some kind of live bird in the room; one of the neighboring guests reported that it had sounded like a crow. And over the whole room there hung a salt smell that I recognized immediately, a smell that some compared to the smell of the ocean, and others to that of blood. When the pillow, wringing wet, was sent up to Pittsburgh for analysis by Mr. Espy, it was found to have been saturated with human tears.

When I returned from court, late this afternoon, there was a message from Dr. Sauer. He had completed his postmortem and wondered if I would drop by. I took the bottle from behind Daniel Webster and headed on down to the county morgue.

"He was already dead, the poor son of a biscuit eater," Dr. Sauer said, looking less morose than he had the last time we spoke. Sauer was a gaunt old Methodist who avoided strong language but never, so long as I had known him, strong drink. I poured us each a tumbler, and then a second. "It took me a while to establish it because there was something about the fellow that I was missing."

"What was that?"

"Well, I'm reasonably sure that he was a hemophiliac. So my reckoning time of death by coagulation of the blood was all thrown off."

"Hemophilia," I said.

"Yes," Dr. Sauer said. "It is associated sometimes with in-breeding, as in the case of royal families of Europe."

Inbreeding. We stood there for a while, looking at the sad bulk of the dead man under the sheet.

"I also found a tattoo," Dr. Sauer added. "The head of a grinning baboon. On his left forearm. Oh, and one other thing. He suffered from some kind of vitiligo. There are white patches on his nape and throat."

Let the record show that the contents of the victim's makeup kit, when it was inventoried, included cold cream, rouge, red greasepaint, a powder puff, some brushes, cotton swabs, and five cans of foundation in a tint the label described as "Olive Male." There was no trace, however, of the white greasepaint with which clowns daub their grinning faces.

Here I conclude my report, and with it my tenure as district attorney for this blighted and unfortunate county. I have staked my career—my life itself—on the things I could see, on the stories I could credit, and on the eventual vindication, when the book was closed, of the reasonable and skeptical approach. In the face of twenty-five years of bloodshed, mayhem, criminality, and the universal human pastime of ruination, I have clung fiercely to Occam's razor, seeking always to keep my solutions unadorned and free of conjecture, and never to resort to conspiracy or any kind of prosecutorial woolgathering. My mother, whenever she was confronted by calamity or personal sorrow, invoked cosmic emanations, invisible empires, ancient prophecies, and intrigues; it has been the business of my life to reject such folderol and seek the simpler explanation. But we were fools, she and I, arrant blockheads, each of us blind to or heedless of the readiest explanation: that the world is an ungettable joke, and our human need to explain its wonders and horrors, our appalling genius for devising such explanations, is nothing more than the rim shot that accompanies the punch line.

I do not know if that nameless clown was the last, but in any case, with such pursuers, there can be few of his kind left. And if there is any truth in the grim doctrine of those hunters, then the return of our father Yrrh, with his inscrutable inventions, cannot be far off. But I fear that, in spite of their efforts over the last ten thousand years, the followers of Ai are going to be gravely disappointed when, at the end of all we know and everything we have ever lost or imagined, the rafters of the world are shaken by a single, a terrible guffaw.

2001

JOE HILL
(b. 1972)

Pop Art

My best friend when I was twelve was inflatable. His name was Arthur Roth, which also made him an inflatable Hebrew, although in our now-and-then talks about the afterlife, I don't remember that he took an especially Jewish perspective. Talk was mostly what we did—in his condition rough-house was out of the question—and the subject of death, and what might follow it, came up more than once. I think Arthur knew he would be lucky to survive high school. When I met him, he had already almost been killed a dozen times, once for every year he had been alive. The afterlife was always on his mind; also the possible lack of one.

When I tell you we talked, I mean only to say we communicated, argued, put each other down, built each other up. To stick to facts, *I* talked—Art couldn't. He didn't have a mouth. When he had something to say, he wrote it down. He wore a pad around his neck on a loop of twine, and carried crayons in his pocket. He turned in school papers in crayon, took tests in crayon. You can imagine the dangers a sharpened pencil would present to a four-ounce boy made of plastic and filled with air.

I think one of the reasons we were best friends was because he was such a great listener. I needed someone to listen. My mother was gone and my father I couldn't talk to. My mother ran away when I was three, sent my Dad a rambling and confused letter from Florida, about sunspots and gamma rays and the radiation that emanates from power lines, about how the birthmark on the back of her left hand had moved up her arm and onto her shoulder. After that, a couple postcards, then nothing.

As for my father, he suffered from migraines. In the afternoons, he sat in front of soaps in the darkened living room, wet-eyed and miserable. He hated to be bothered. You couldn't tell him anything. It was a mistake even to try.

"Blah blah," he would say, cutting me off in mid-sentence. "My head is splitting. You're killing me here with blah blah this, blah blah that."

But Art liked to listen, and in trade, I offered him protection. Kids were scared of me. I had a bad reputation. I owned a switchblade, and sometimes I brought it to school and let other kids see; it kept them in fear. The only thing I ever stuck it into, though, was the wall of my bedroom. I'd lie on my bed and flip it at the corkboard wall, so that it hit, blade-first, *thunk!*

One day when Art was visiting he saw the pockmarks in my wall. I explained, one thing led to another, and before I knew it he was begging to have a throw.

"What's wrong with you?" I asked him. "Is your head completely empty? Forget it. No way."

Out came a Crayola, burnt-sienna. He wrote:

So at least let me look.

I popped it open for him. He stared at it wide-eyed. Actually, he stared at everything wide-eyed. His eyes were made of glassy plastic, stuck to the surface of his face. He couldn't blink or anything. But this was different than his usual bug-eyed stare. I could see he was really fixated.

He wrote:

I'll be careful I totally promise *please!*

I handed it to him. He pushed the point of the blade into the floor so it snicked into the handle. Then he hit the button and it snicked back out. He shuddered, stared at it in his hand. Then, without giving any warning, he chucked it at the wall. Of course it didn't hit tip-first; that takes practice, which he hadn't had, and coordination, which, speaking honestly, he wasn't ever going to have. It bounced, came flying back at him. He sprang into the air so quickly it was like I was watching his ghost jump out of his body. The knife landed where he had been and clattered away under my bed.

I yanked Art down off the ceiling. He wrote:

You were right, that was dumb. I'm a loser—a jerk.

"No question," I said.

But he wasn't a loser or a jerk. My Dad is a loser. The kids at school were jerks. Art was different. He was all heart. He just wanted to be liked by someone.

Also, I can say truthfully, he was the most completely harmless person I've ever known. Not only would he not hurt a fly, he *couldn't* hurt a fly. If he slapped one, and lifted his hand, it would buzz off undisturbed. He was like a holy person in a Bible story, someone who can heal the ripped and infected parts of you with a laying-on of hands. You know how Bible stories go. That kind of person, they're never around long. Losers and jerks put nails in them and watch the air run out.

There was something special about Art, an invisible special something that just made other kids naturally want to kick his ass. He was new at our school. His parents had just moved to town. They were normal, filled with blood not air. The condition Art suffered from is one of these genetic things that plays hopscotch with the generations, like Tay-Sachs (Art told me once that he had had a grand-uncle, also inflatable, who flopped one day into a pile of leaves and burst on the tine of a buried rake). On the first day of classes, Mrs. Gannon made Art stand at the front of the room, and told everyone all about him, while he hung his head out of shyness.

He was white. Not Caucasian, *white*, like a marshmallow, or Casper. A seam ran around his head and down his sides. There was a plastic nipple under one arm, where he could be pumped with air.

Mrs. Gannon told us we had to be extra careful not to run with scissors or pens. A puncture would probably kill him. He couldn't talk; everyone had to try and be sensitive about that. His interests were astronauts, photography, and the novels of Bernard Malamud.

Before she nudged him towards his seat, she gave his shoulder an encouraging little squeeze and as she pressed her fingers into him, he whistled gently. That was the only way he ever made sound. By flexing his body he could emit little squeaks and whines. When other people squeezed him, he made a soft, musical hoot.

He bobbed down the room and took an empty seat beside me. Billy Spears, who sat directly behind him, bounced thumbtacks off his head all morning long. The first couple times Art pretended not to notice. Then, when Mrs. Gannon wasn't looking, he wrote Billy a note. It said:

> *Please stop!* I don't want to say anything to Mrs. Gannon but it isn't safe to throw thumbtacks at me. I'm *not* kidding.

Billy wrote back:

> You make trouble, and there won't be enough of you left to patch a tire. Think about it.

It didn't get any easier for Art from there. In biology lab, Art was paired with Cassius Delamitri, who was in sixth grade for the second time. Cassius was a fat kid, with a pudgy, sulky face, and a disagreeable film of black hair above his unhappy pucker of a mouth.

The project was to distill wood, which involved the use of a gas flame—Cassius did the work, while Art watched and wrote notes of encouragement:

> I can't believe you got a D– on this experiment when you did it last year—you totally know how to do this stuff!!

and

> my parents bought me a lab kit for my birthday. You could come over and we could play mad scientist sometime want to?

After three or four notes like that, Cassius had read enough, got it in his head Art was some kind of homosexual . . . especially with Art's talk about having him over to play doctor or whatever. When the teacher was distracted helping some other kids, Cassius shoved Art under the table and tied him around one of the table legs, in a squeaky granny knot, head, arms, body and all. When Mr. Milton asked where Art had gone, Cassius said he thought he had run to the bathroom.

"Did he?" Mr. Milton asked. "What a relief. I didn't even know if that kid *could* go to the bathroom."

Another time, John Erikson held Art down during recess

and wrote KOLLOSTIMY BAG on his stomach with indelible marker. It was Spring before it faded away.

> The worst thing was my mom saw. Bad enough she has to know I get beat up on a daily basis. But she was really upset it was spelled wrong.

He added:

> I don't know what she expects—this is 6th grade. Doesn't she remember 6th grade? I'm sorry, but realistically, what are the odds you're going to get beat up by the grand champion of the spelling bee?

"The way your year is going," I said, "I figure them odds might be pretty good."

Here is how Art and I wound up friends:

During recess periods, I always hung out at the top of the monkey bars by myself, reading sports magazines. I was cultivating my reputation as a delinquent and possible drug pusher. To help my image along, I wore a black denim jacket and didn't talk to people or make friends.

At the top of the monkey bars—a dome-shaped construction at one edge of the asphalt lot behind the school—I was a good nine feet off the ground, and had a view of the whole yard. One day I watched Billy Spears horsing around with Cassius Delamitri and John Erikson. Billy had a wiffle ball and a bat, and the three of them were trying to bat the ball in through an open second floor window. After fifteen minutes of not even coming close, John Erikson got lucky, swatted it in.

Cassius said, "Shit—there goes the ball. We need something else to bat around."

"Hey," Billy shouted. "Look! There's Art!"

They caught up to Art, who was trying to keep away, and Billy started tossing him in the air and hitting him with the bat to see how far he could knock him. Every time he struck Art with the bat it made a hollow, springy *whap!* Art popped into the air, then floated along a little ways, sinking gently back to ground. As soon as his heels touched earth he started to run, but swiftness of foot wasn't one of Art's qualities. John and

Cassius got into the fun by grabbing Art and drop-kicking him, to see who could punt him highest.

The three of them gradually pummeled Art down to my end of the lot. He struggled free long enough to run in under the monkey bars. Billy caught up, struck him a whap across the ass with the bat, and shot him high into the air.

Art floated to the top of the dome. When his body touched the steel bars, he stuck, face-up—static electricity.

"Hey," Billy hollered. "Chuck him down here!"

I had, up until that moment, never been face to face with Art. Although we shared classes, and even sat side-by-side in Mrs. Gannon's homeroom, we had not had a single exchange. He looked at me with his enormous plastic eyes and sad blank face, and I looked right back. He found the pad around his neck, scribbled a note in spring green, ripped it off and held it up at me.

> I don't care what they do, but could you go away? I hate to get the crap knocked out of me in front of spectators.

"What's he writin'?" Billy shouted.

I looked from the note, past Art, and down at the gathering of boys below. I was struck by the sudden realization that I could *smell* them, all three of them, a damp, *human* smell, a sweaty-sour reek. It turned my stomach.

"Why are you bothering him?" I asked.

Billy said, "Just screwin' with him."

"We're trying to see how high we can make him go," Cassius said. "You ought to come down here. You ought to give it a try. We're going to kick him onto the roof of the friggin' school!"

"I got an even funner idea," I said, *funner* being an excellent word to use if you want to impress on some other kids that you might be a mentally retarded psychopath. "How about we see if I can kick your lardy ass up on the roof of the school?"

"What's your problem?" Billy asked. "You on the rag?"

I grabbed Art and jumped down. Cassius blanched. John Erikson tottered back. I held Art under one arm, feet sticking towards them, head pointed away.

"You guys are dicks," I said—some moments just aren't right for a funny line.

And I turned away from them. The back of my neck crawled at the thought of Billy's wiffle ball bat clubbing me one across the skull, but he didn't do a thing, let me walk.

We went out on the baseball field, sat on the pitcher's mound. Art wrote me a note that said thanks, and another that said I didn't have to do what I had done but that he was glad I had done it, and another that said he owed me one. I shoved each note into my pocket after reading it, didn't think why. That night, alone in my bedroom, I dug a wad of crushed notepaper out of my pocket, a lump the size of a lemon, peeled each note free and pressed it flat on my bed, read them all over again. There was no good reason not to throw them away, but I didn't, started a collection instead. It was like some part of me knew, even then, I might want to have something to remember Art by after he was gone. I saved hundreds of his notes over the next year, some as short as a couple words, a few six-page long manifestos. I have most of them still, from the first note he handed me, the one that begins *I don't care what they do*, to the last, the one that ends:

> I want to see if it's true. If the sky opens up at the top.

At first my father didn't like Art, but after he got to know him better he really hated him.

"How come he's always mincing around?" my father asked. "Is he a fairy or something?"

"No, Dad. He's inflatable."

"Well he acts like a fairy," he said. "You better not be queering around with him up in your room."

Art tried to be liked—he tried to build a relationship with my father. But the things he did were misinterpreted; the statements he made were misunderstood. My Dad said something once about a movie he liked. Art wrote him a message about how the book was even better.

"He thinks I'm an illiterate," my Dad said, as soon as Art was gone.

Another time, Art noticed the pile of worn tires heaped up

behind our garage, and mentioned to my Dad about a recycling program at Sears, bring in your rotten old ones, get twenty percent off on brand-new Goodyears.

"He thinks we're trailer trash," my Dad complained, before Art was hardly out of earshot. "Little snotnose."

One day Art and I got home from school, and found my father in front of the TV, with a pit bull at his feet. The bull erupted off the floor, yapping hysterically, and jumped up on Art. His paws made a slippery zipping sound sliding over Art's plastic chest. Art grabbed one of my shoulders and vaulted into the air. He could really jump when he had to. He grabbed the ceiling fan—turned off—and held on to one of the blades while the pit bull barked and hopped beneath.

"What the hell is that?" I asked.

"Family dog," my father said. "Just like you always wanted."

"Not one that wants to eat my friends."

"Get off the fan, Artie. That isn't built for you to hang off it."

"This isn't a dog," I said. "It's a blender with teeth."

"Listen, do you want to name it, or should I?" Dad asked.

Art and I hid in my bedroom and talked names.

"Snowflake," I said. "Sugarpie. Sunshine."

How about Happy? That has a ring to it, doesn't it?

We were kidding, but Happy was no joke. In just a week, Art had at least three life-threatening encounters with my father's ugly dog.

If he gets his teeth in me, I'm done for. He'll punch me full of holes.

But Happy couldn't be housebroken, left turds scattered around the living room, hard to see in the moss brown rug. My Dad squelched through some fresh leavings once, in bare feet, and it sent him a little out of his head. He chased Happy all through the downstairs with a croquet mallet, smashed a hole in the wall, crushed some plates on the kitchen counter with a wild backswing.

The very next day, he built a chain-link pen in the sideyard. Happy went in, and that was where he stayed.

By then, though, Art was nervous to come over, and preferred to meet at his house. I didn't see the sense. It was a long walk to get to his place after school, and my house was right there, just around the corner.

"What are you worried about?" I asked him. "He's in a pen. It's not like Happy is going to figure out how to open the door to his pen, you know."

Art knew . . . but he still didn't like to come over, and when he did, he usually had a couple patches for bicycle tires on him, to guard against dark happenstance.

Once we started going to Art's every day, once it came to be a habit, I wondered why I had ever wanted us to go to my house instead. I got used to the walk—I walked the walk so many times I stopped noticing that it was long bordering on never-ending. I even looked forward to it, my afternoon stroll through coiled suburban streets, past houses done in Disney pastels: lemon, tangerine, ash. As I crossed the distance between my house and Art's house, it seemed to me that I was moving through zones of ever-deepening stillness and order, and at the walnut heart of all this peace was Art's.

Art couldn't run, talk or approach anything with a sharp edge on it, but at his house we managed to keep ourselves entertained. We watched TV. I wasn't like other kids, and didn't know anything about television. My father, I mentioned already, suffered from terrible migraines. He was home on disability, lived in the family room, and hogged our TV all day long, kept track of five different soaps. I tried not to bother him, and rarely sat down to watch with him—I sensed my presence was a distraction to him at a time when he wanted to concentrate.

Art would have watched whatever I wanted to watch, but I didn't know what to do with a remote control. I couldn't make a choice, didn't know how. Had lost the habit. Art was a NASA buff, and we watched anything to do with space, never missed a space shuttle launch. He wrote:

> I want to be an astronaut. I'd adapt really well to
> being weightless. I'm *already* mostly weightless.

This was when they were putting up the international space station. They talked about how hard it was on people to spend too long in outer space. Your muscles atrophy. Your heart shrinks three sizes.

The advantages of sending me into space keep piling up. I don't have any muscles to atrophy. I don't have any heart to shrink. I'm telling you. I'm the ideal spaceman. I *belong* in orbit.

"I know a guy who can help you get there. Let me give Billy Spears a call. He's got a rocket he wants to stick up your ass. I heard him talking about it."

Art gave me a dour look, and a scribbled two word response.

Lying around Art's house in front of the tube wasn't always an option, though. His father was a piano instructor, tutored small children on the baby grand, which was in the living room along with their television. If he had a lesson, we had to find something else to do. We'd go into Art's room to play with his computer, but after twenty minutes of *row-row-row-your-boat* coming through the wall—a shrill, out-of-time plinking—we'd shoot each other sudden wild looks, and leave by way of the window, no need to talk it over.

Both Art's parents were musical, his mother a cellist. They had wanted music for Art, but it had been let-down and disappointment from the start.

I can't even kazoo

Art wrote me once. The piano was out. Art didn't have any fingers, just a thumb, and a puffy pad where his fingers belonged. Hands like that, it had been years of work with a tutor just to learn to write legibly with a crayon. For obvious reasons, wind instruments were also out of the question; Art didn't have lungs, and didn't breathe. He tried to learn the drums, but couldn't strike hard enough to be any good at it.

His mother bought him a digital camera. "Make music with color," she said. "Make melodies out of light."

Mrs. Roth was always hitting you with lines like that. She talked about oneness, about the natural decency of trees, and she said not enough people were thankful for the smell of cut grass. Art told me when I wasn't around, she asked questions about me. She was worried I didn't have a healthy outlet for my creative self. She said I needed something to feed the inner me. She bought me a book about origami and it wasn't even my birthday.

"I didn't know the inner me was hungry," I said to Art.

That's because it already starved to death

Art wrote.

She was alarmed to learn that I didn't have any sort of religion. My father didn't take me to church or send me to Sunday school. He said religion was a scam. Mrs. Roth was too polite to say anything to me about my father, but she said things about him to Art, and Art passed her comments on. She told Art that if my father neglected the care of my body, like he neglected the care of my spirit, he'd be in jail, and I'd be in a foster home. She also told Art that if I was put in foster care, she'd adopt me, and I could stay in the guest room. I loved her, felt my heart surge whenever she asked me if I wanted a glass of lemonade. I would have done anything she asked.

"Your Mom's an idiot," I said to Art. "A total moron. I hope you know that. There isn't any oneness. It's every man for himself. Anyone who thinks we're all brothers in the spirit winds up sitting under Cassius Delamitri's fat ass during recess, smelling his jock."

Mrs. Roth wanted to take me to the synagogue—not to convert me, just as an educational experience, exposure to other cultures and all that—but Art's father shot her down, said not a chance, not our business, and what are you crazy? She had a bumper sticker on her car that showed the Star of David and the word PRIDE with a jumping exclamation point next to it.

"So Art," I said another time. "I got a Jewish question I want to ask you. Now you and your family, you're a bunch of hardcore Jews, right?"

> I don't know that I'd describe us as *hardcore* exactly.
> We're actually pretty lax. But we go to synagogue,
> observe the holidays—things like that.

"I thought Jews had to get their joints snipped," I said, and grabbed my crotch. "For the faith. Tell me—"
But Art was already writing.

> No not me. I got off. My parents were friends with
> a progressive Rabbi. They talked to him about it
> first thing after I was born. Just to find out what
> the official position was.

"What'd he say?"

> He said it was the official position to make an
> exception for anyone who would actually explode
> during the circumcision. They thought he was joking,
> but later on my Mom did some research on it. Based
> on what she found out, it looks like I'm in the clear,
> Talmudically-speaking. Mom says the foreskin has
> to be *skin*. If it isn't, it doesn't need to be cut.

"That's funny," I said. "I always thought your Mom didn't
know dick. Now it turns out your Mom *does* know dick. She's
an expert even. Shows what I know. Hey, if she ever wants to do
more research, I have an unusual specimen for her to examine."

And Art wrote how she would need to bring a microscope,
and I said how she would need to stand back a few yards when
I unzipped my pants, and back and forth, you don't need me
to tell you, you can imagine the rest of the conversation for
yourself. I rode Art about his mother every chance I could get,
couldn't help myself. Started in on her the moment she left
the room, whispering about how for an old broad she still had
an okay can, and what would Art think if his father died and I
married her. Art on the other hand, never once made a punch
line out of my Dad. If Art ever wanted to give me a hard time,
he'd make fun of how I licked my fingers after I ate, or how I
didn't always wear matching socks. It isn't hard to understand
why Art never stuck it to me about my father, like I stuck it to
him about his mother. When your best friend is ugly—I mean
bad ugly, *deformed*—you don't kid them about shattering
mirrors. In a friendship, especially in a friendship between two
young boys, you are allowed to inflict a certain amount of
pain. This is even expected. But you must cause no serious in-
jury; you must never, under any circumstances, leave wounds
that will result in permanent scars.

Arthur's house was also where we usually settled to do our
homework. In the early evening, we went into his room to
study. His father was done with lessons by then, so there wasn't
any plink-plink from the next room to distract us. I enjoyed
studying in Art's room, responded well to the quiet, and liked

working in a place where I was surrounded by books; Art had shelves and shelves of books. I liked our study time together, but mistrusted it as well. It was during our study sessions—surrounded by all that easy stillness—that Art was most likely to say something about dying.

When we talked, I always tried to control the conversation, but Art was slippery, could work death into anything.

"Some Arab *invented* the idea of the number zero," I said. "Isn't that weird? Someone had to think zero up."

> Because it isn't obvious—that nothing can be something. That something which can't be measured or seen could still exist and have meaning. Same with the soul, when you think about it.

"True or false," I said another time, when we were studying for a science quiz. "Energy is never destroyed, it can only be changed from one form into another."

> I hope it's true—it would be a good argument that you continue to exist after you die, even if you're transformed into something completely different than what you had been.

He said a lot to me about death and what might follow it, but the thing I remember best was what he had to say about Mars. We were doing a presentation together, and Art had picked Mars as our subject, especially whether or not men would ever go there and try to colonize it. Art was all for colonizing Mars, cities under plastic tents, mining water from the icy poles. Art wanted to go himself.

"It's fun to imagine, maybe, fun to think about it," I said. "But the actual thing would be bullshit. Dust. Freezing cold. Everything red. You'd go blind looking at so much red. You wouldn't really want to do it—leave this world and never come back."

Art stared at me for a long moment, then bowed his head, and wrote a brief note in robin's egg blue.

> But I'm going to have to do that anyway. Everyone has to do that.

Then he wrote:

> You get an astronaut's life whether you want it or not.
> Leave it all behind for a world you know nothing
> about. That's just the deal.

In the Spring, Art invented a game called Spy Satellite. There
was a place downtown, the Party Station, where you could buy
a bushel of helium-filled balloons for a quarter. I'd get a bunch,
meet Art somewhere with them. He'd have his digital camera.

Soon as I handed him the balloons, he detached from the
earth and lifted into the air. As he rose, the wind pushed him
out and away. When he was satisfied he was high enough, he'd
let go a couple balloons, level off, and start snapping pictures.
When he was ready to come down, he'd just let go a few more.
I'd meet him where he landed and we'd go over to his house
to look at the pictures on his laptop. Photos of people swimming in their pools, men shingling their roofs; photos of me
standing in empty streets, my upturned face a miniature brown
blob, my features too distant to make out; photos that always
had Art's sneakers dangling into the frame at the bottom edge.

Some of his best pictures were low altitude affairs, things he
snapped when he was only a few yards off the ground. Once
he took three balloons and swam into the air over Happy's
chain-link enclosure, off at the side of our house. Happy spent
all day in his fenced-off pen, barking frantically at women
going by with strollers, the jingle of the ice cream truck, squirrels. Happy had trampled all the space in his penned-in plot of
earth down to mud. Scattered about him were dozens of dried
piles of dogcrap. In the middle of this awful brown turdscape
was Happy himself, and in every photo Art snapped of him, he
was leaping up on his back legs, mouth open to show the pink
cavity within, eyes fixed on Art's dangling sneakers.

> I feel bad. What a horrible place to live.

"Get your head out of your ass," I said. "If creatures like
Happy were allowed to run wild, they'd make the whole world
look that way. He doesn't want to live somewhere else. Turds
and mud—that's Happy's idea of a total garden spot."

> I *STRONGLY* disagree

Arthur wrote me, but time has not softened my opinions on this matter. It is my belief that, as a rule, creatures of Happy's ilk—I am thinking here of canines and men both—more often run free than live caged, and it is in fact a world of mud and feces they desire, a world with no Art in it, or anyone like him, a place where there is no talk of books or God or the worlds beyond this world, a place where the only communication is the hysterical barking of starving and hate-filled dogs.

One Saturday morning, mid-April, my Dad pushed the bedroom door open, and woke me up by throwing my sneakers on my bed. "You have to be at the dentist's in half an hour. Put your rear in gear."

I walked—it was only a few blocks—and I had been sitting in the waiting room for twenty minutes, dazed with boredom, when I remembered I had told Art that I'd be coming by his house as soon as I got up. The receptionist let me use the phone to call him.

His mom answered. "He just left to see if he could find you at your house," she told me.

I called my Dad.

"He hasn't been by," he said. "I haven't seen him."

"Keep an eye out."

"Yeah well. I've got a headache. Art knows how to use the doorbell."

I sat in the dentist's chair, my mouth stretched open and tasting of blood and mint, and struggled with unease and an impatience to be going. Did not perhaps trust my father to be decent to Art without myself present. The dentist's assistant kept touching my shoulder and telling me to relax.

When I was all through and got outside, the deep and vivid blueness of the sky was a little disorientating. The sunshine was headache-bright, bothered my eyes. I had been up for two hours, but still felt cotton-headed and dull-edged, not all the way awake. I jogged.

The first thing I saw, standing on the sidewalk, was Happy, free from his pen. He didn't so much as bark at me. He was on his belly in the grass, head between his paws. He lifted sleepy eyelids to watch me approach, then let them sag shut again. His pen door stood open in the side yard.

I was looking to see if he was lying on a heap of tattered plastic when I heard the first feeble tapping sound. I turned my head and saw Art in the back of my father's station wagon, smacking his hands on the window. I walked over and opened the door. At that instant, Happy exploded from the grass with a peal of mindless barking. I grabbed Art in both arms, spun and fled. Happy's teeth closed on a piece of my flapping pant-leg. I heard a tacky ripping sound, stumbled, kept going.

I ran until there was a stitch in my side and no dog in sight—six blocks, at least. Toppled over in someone's yard. My pantleg was sliced open from the back of my knee to the ankle. I took my first good look at Art. It was a jarring sight. I was so out of breath, I could only produce a thin, dismayed little squeak—the sort of sound Art was always making.

His body had lost its marshmallow whiteness. It had a gold-brown duskiness to it now, so it resembled a marshmallow, lightly toasted. He seemed to have deflated to about half his usual size. His chin sagged into his body. He couldn't hold his head up.

Art had been crossing our front lawn, when Happy burst from his hiding place under one of the hedges. In that first crucial moment, Art saw he would never be able to outrun our family dog on foot. All such an effort would get him would be an ass full of fatal puncture wounds. So instead, he jumped into the station wagon, and slammed the door.

The windows were automatic—there was no way to roll them down. Any door he opened, Happy tried to jam his snout in at him. It was seventy degrees outside the car, over a hundred inside. Art watched in dismay as Happy flopped in the grass beside the wagon to wait.

Art sat. Happy didn't move. Lawnmowers droned in the distance. The afternoon passed. In time Art began to wilt in the heat. He became ill and groggy. His plastic skin started sticking to the seats.

Then you showed up. Just in time. You saved my life.

But my eyes blurred and tears dripped off my face onto his note. I hadn't come just in time—not at all.

Art was never the same. His skin stayed a filmy yellow, and he developed a deflation problem. His parents would pump him up, and for a while he'd be all right, his body swollen with oxygen, but eventually he'd go saggy and limp again. His doctor took one look and told his parents not to put off the trip to Disney World another year.

I wasn't the same either. I was miserable—couldn't eat, suffered unexpected stomachaches, brooded and sulked.

"Wipe that look off your face," my father said one night at dinner. "Life goes on. Deal with it."

I was dealing all right. I knew the door to Happy's pen didn't open itself. I punched holes in the tires of the station wagon, then left my switchblade sticking out of one of them, so my father would know for sure who had done it. He had police officers come over and pretend to arrest me. They drove me around in the squad car and talked tough at me for a while, then said they'd bring me home if I'd "get with the program." The next day I locked Happy in the wagon and he took a shit on the driver's seat. My father collected all the books Art had got me to read, the Bernard Malamud, the Ray Bradbury, the Isaac Bashevis Singer. He burned them on the barbecue grill.

"How do you feel about that, smart guy?" he asked me, while he squirted lighter fluid on them.

"Okay with me," I said. "They were on your library card."

That summer, I spent a lot of time sleeping over at Art's.

Don't be angry. No one is to blame.

Art wrote me.

"Get your head out of your ass," I said, but then I couldn't say anything else because it made me cry just to look at him.

Late August, Art gave me a call. It was a hilly four miles to Scarswell Cove, where he wanted us to meet, but by then months of hoofing it to Art's after school had hardened me to long walks. I had plenty of balloons with me, just like he asked.

Scarswell Cove is a sheltered, pebbly beach on the sea, where people go to stand in the tide and fish in waders. There was no one there except a couple old fishermen, and Art, sitting on the slope of the beach. His body looked soft and saggy, and his head lolled forward, bobbled weakly on his non-existent neck. I sat down beside him. Half a mile out, the dark blue waves were churning up icy combers.

"What's going on?" I asked.

Art bowed his head. He thought a bit. Then he began to write.

He wrote:

> Do you know people have made it into outer space without rockets? Chuck Yeager flew a high performance jet so high it started to tumble—it tumbled *upwards*, not downwards. He ran so high, gravity lost hold of him. His jet was tumbling up out of the stratosphere. All the color melted out of the sky. It was like the blue sky was paper, and a hole was burning out the middle of it, and behind it, everything was black. Everything was full of stars. Imagine falling *UP*.

I looked at this note, then back to his face. He was writing again. His second message was simpler.

> I've had it. Seriously—I'm all done. I deflate 15–16 times a day. I need someone to pump me up practically every hour. I feel sick all the time and I hate it. This is no kind of life.

"Oh no," I said. My vision blurred. Tears welled up and spilled over my eyes. "Things will get better."

> No. I don't think so. It isn't about whether I die. It's about figuring out where. And I've decided. I'm going to see how high I can go. I want to see if it's true. If the sky opens up at the top.

I don't know what else I said to him. A lot of things, I guess. I asked him not to do it, not to leave me. I said that it wasn't fair. I said that I didn't have any other friends. I said that I had always been lonely. I talked until it was all blubber and strangled, helpless sobs, and he reached his crinkly plastic arms around me and held me while I hid my face in his chest.

He took the balloons from me, got them looped around one wrist. I held his other hand and we walked to the edge of the water. The surf splashed in and filled my sneakers. The sea was so cold it made the bones in my feet throb. I lifted him and held him in both arms, and squeezed until he made a mournful squeak. We hugged for a long time. Then I opened my arms. I let him go. I hope if there is another world, we will not be judged too harshly for the things we did wrong here— that we will at least be forgiven for the mistakes we made out of love. I have no doubt it was a sin of some kind, to let such a one go.

He rose away and the airstream turned him around so he was looking back at me as he bobbed out over the water, his left arm pulled high over his head, the balloons attached to his wrist. His head was tipped at a thoughtful angle, so he seemed to be studying me.

I sat on the beach and watched him go. I watched until I could no longer distinguish him from the gulls that were wheeling and diving over the water, a few miles away. He was just one more dirty speck wandering the sky. I didn't move. I wasn't sure I could get up. In time, the horizon turned a dusky rose and the blue sky above deepened to black. I stretched out on the beach, and watched the stars spill through the darkness overhead. I watched until a dizziness overcame me, and I could imagine spilling off the ground, and falling up into the night.

I developed emotional problems. When school started again, I would cry at the sight of an empty desk. I couldn't answer questions or do homework. I flunked out and had to go through seventh grade again.

Worse, no one believed I was dangerous anymore. It was impossible to be scared of me after you had seen me sobbing my guts out a few times. I didn't have the switchblade either; my father had confiscated it.

Billy Spears beat me up one day, after school—mashed my lips, loosened a tooth. John Erikson held me down, wrote COLLISTAMY BAG on my forehead in magic marker. Still trying to get it right. Cassius Delamitri ambushed me, shoved me down and jumped on top of me, crushing me under his weight, driving all the air out of my lungs. A defeat by way of deflation; Art would have understood perfectly.

I avoided the Roths'. I wanted more than anything to see Art's mother, but stayed away. I was afraid if I talked to her, it would come pouring out of me, that I had been there at the end, that I stood in the surf and let Art go. I was afraid of what I might see in her eyes; of her hurt and anger.

Less than six months after Art's deflated body was found slopping in the surf along North Scarswell beach, there was a FOR SALE sign out in front of the Roth's ranch. I never saw either of his parents again. Mrs. Roth sometimes wrote me letters, asking how I was and what I was doing, but I never replied. She signed her letters *love*.

I went out for track in high school, and did well at pole vault. My track coach said the law of gravity didn't apply to me. My track coach didn't know fuckall about gravity. No matter how high I went for a moment, I always came down in the end, same as anyone else.

Pole vault got me a state college scholarship. I kept to myself. No one at college knew me, and I was at last able to rebuild my long lost image as a sociopath. I didn't go to parties. I didn't date. I didn't want to get to know anybody.

I was crossing the campus one morning, and I saw coming towards me a young girl, with black hair so dark it had the cold blue sheen of rich oil. She wore a bulky sweater and a librarian's ankle-length skirt; a very asexual outfit, but all the same you could see she had a stunning figure, slim hips, high ripe breasts. Her eyes were of staring blue glass, her skin as white as Art's. It was the first time I had seen an inflatable person since Art drifted away on his balloons. A kid walking behind me wolf-whistled at her. I stepped aside, and when he went past, I tripped him up and watched his books fly everywhere.

"Are you some kind of psycho?" he screeched.

"Yes," I said. "Exactly."

Her name was Ruth Goldman. She had a round rubber patch on the heel of one foot where she had stepped on a shard of broken glass as a little girl, and a larger square patch on her left shoulder where a sharp branch had poked her once on a windy day. Home schooling and obsessively protective parents had saved her from further damage. We were both English majors. Her favorite writer was Kafka—because he understood the absurd. My favorite writer was Malamud—because he understood loneliness.

We married the same year I graduated. Although I remain

doubtful about the life eternal, I converted without any prodding from her, gave in at last to a longing to have some talk of the spirit in my life. Can you really call it a conversion? In truth, I had no beliefs to convert from. Whatever the case, ours was a Jewish wedding, glass under white cloth, crunched beneath the bootheel.

One afternoon I told her about Art.

That's so sad. I'm so sorry.

She wrote to me in wax pencil. She put her hand over mine.

What happened? Did he run out of air?

"Ran out of sky," I said.

2001

POPPY Z. BRITE

(b. 1967)

Pansu

TWILIGHT was settling over L.A.'s Koreatown, the lights of the stores clicking off, the lights of the restaurants and bars flickering on. Samuel Oh stood beneath the red marquee of his restaurant, surveyed the street scene, and thought that this was one of those rare California moments of peace with no evil.

He was wrong.

He went back inside. The dinner crowd had just started to come in. The restaurant was dark, lit with paper lanterns and strings of Christmas lights. Two of his favorite customers, a pair of young men who wrote and produced a successful TV show, were at their usual table in the corner. Mr. Oh's wife, Bobbi, was setting out their *pan chan*. Smiling, she laid the last of the small dishes on the table. Mr. Oh was about to turn away when he saw Bobbi hurl her tray like a Frisbee across the room, where it landed in the middle of someone's flaming bulgogi platter. She thrust her tongue out as far as it would go, hiked her modest skirt well above her waist, and commanded the two young men, "Fuck me!"

"Uh, we don't really feel that way about you, Mrs. Oh," said one of them.

"And those people's table is on fire," pointed out the other one.

Mr. Oh grabbed the fire extinguisher from its place beside the kitchen door, ran to the table where the tray had landed, and doused the flames with chemical foam, apologizing furiously to the diners. Luckily they were Korean, and he was able to express his profound embarrassment and promise them a complimentary replacement dinner without stumbling over his words. He found a waitress to move them to a new table and raced over to where his wife had begun to slide out of her white cotton panties. He grabbed her from behind. She lashed out with one arm and sent him flying backward. His feet tangled, and he fell ungracefully to the floor.

"Is your wife OK?" asked one of the young men, bending to assist Mr. Oh.

"Dude, obviously she's not OK," his friend said. As they helped Mr. Oh to his feet, Bobbi yanked the tablecloth off the table and sent the little appetizer dishes flying. A particularly spicy clump of *kimchi* hit Mr. Oh square in the left eye. Diners were beginning to flee the restaurant as Bobbi ran to the center of the room, screamed "FUCK ME, ANYBODY FUCK ME!", and vomited a mass of bright green goo into a charming little fountain Mr. Oh had just installed.

He turned desperately to the two TV writers. "What can be wrong with her?" he asked in English.

"Well," said the light-haired one, "I've only ever seen a movie about it, but it looks to me like she's possessed by Satan."

"Yup," his friend concurred. "Exorcist, obviously."

"What do you mean?" Mr. Oh began to ask, but then his wife's head spun twice around on her neck, and as he heard the terrible sound of the cracking bones he knew, because he had seen the movie himself.

Mr. Oh had closed the restaurant, sent the staff home, and dragged Bobbi into the little office where he placed the food orders and added the receipts. He had begged his two TV-writing customers to stay, as they seemed to know more than he did about this problem, and they had reluctantly agreed. In his distraction he kept mixing up their names, but he was fairly sure that the light-haired one was called Darin and the other one was Mark.

Since he usually kept the restaurant open all night, he had a little cot in the office. Bobbi thrashed on it now, her wrists bound with napkins because she had scratched her face so badly that blood and shreds of skin were embedded beneath her nails. She had torn all the buttons off her blouse before he managed to tie her up, and the sight of her plain white cotton bra against her flushed golden skin broke Mr. Oh's heart a little more. Her skirt was rucked up beneath her, her legs akimbo, her body twisting in some pain or fury he could not imagine.

He turned away from her and saw that Mark was rolling a

joint on the desk where he did the accounts. The loose marijuana was scattered across a seafood bill stamped PAID, like some terrible symbol of chaos consuming order. "You cannot smoke that shit in here!"

Mark looked up at him with eyes very dark and serious. "Mr. Oh," he said, "if you want us to stay here and try to help you deal with your possessed wife, then we most definitely *can* smoke this shit in here."

Darin nodded his agreement and pulled out a Zippo lighter stamped with some vulgar cartoon character. Mark put the finished joint in his mouth and leaned over so that Darin could light it for him. They went through a complex, difficult-looking process of getting it to stay lit and burn evenly. Mr. Oh found that he could not take his eyes off this process: if he looked at them, he did not have to look at his wife writhing on the cot.

He could still hear her, though. She was muttering in Korean, dreadful words he had not thought she knew and had never imagined that she would combine. Literally, she had just called him, or someone unseen, a fucker of pigs.

The marijuana smoke filled the small office and made Mr. Oh's head feel as if it sat more lightly on his neck. For the first time since Bobbi had thrown the tray, he relaxed a little, and realized that perhaps he did know something about this problem after all.

As if sensing possible danger, Bobbi spoke up. Her words were English now, her voice so guttural it hurt to hear, with an accent that was definitely not Korean. "YOU'RE GETTING STONED!"

"No I'm not," he said without thinking.

"Dude!" Darin grabbed his arm. *"Don't answer its charges.* That's one of the rules you have to follow. It lies."

"Not necessarily in this case," Mark said. "He might *be* getting stoned. It's pretty smoky in here."

"Well, but you're not supposed to argue with it. Max von Sydow said so."

"Agreed."

"FUCKING ADDICT WASTECASE FAGGOTS!" Bobbi roared.

They glanced over at the cot, looked at each other, shrugged as if they could not argue with this assessment even had they wanted to, and finished off the joint.

"I am not getting stoned!" Mr. Oh said. "I am trying to help my wife, and I thought you had agreed to help me."

"Preparations are necessary," Darin said. "No way can we watch that fucking thing stone cold sober."

"Don't speak of her that way!"

"Mr. Oh," Mark said gently, "he's not talking about your wife. He's talking about that thing inside her."

"How are you so calm? I expect not—"

"You *don't expect*."

"I don't expect you to feel as I do, but you seem . . ." He gestured helplessly for the words. "You seem as if this is almost normal to you."

"We grew up in a small town in Utah," Darin told him. "Now we've been in Hollywood for five years. We've seen some things that seemed pretty fucking weird to us. I'd say 'almost normal' isn't too far off for this."

Mark shook his head. "I don't know, dude. I think 'almost normal' is going a little far. I think this is at least slightly weird."

"Pussy."

"Dude! Come in for pork belly hot pot, stay for Satan? Come on. That's fucking weird."

"*That's enough!*" shouted Mr. Oh. "Yes, it is weird! But it is not a show! It is not something on TV to laugh at! If you're not going to help me, then *get out of my restaurant!*"

They stared at him, then looked at each other, abashed. Beneath their surprise, beneath the bland Hollywood smirks they had picked up somewhere along the way, Mr. Oh thought he could see the faces of those two young boys from Utah. Maybe that was how it was with his wife, too. Maybe she was still in there, trapped.

He remembered what he had forgotten. It was a story his grandmother had told him, a story from before the Second World War, when she was a girl living in a village a hundred miles from Seoul. It was about a kind of healer, one who healed by feeding the hungry. He knew how to do that.

"We're sorry, Mr. Oh," said Darin. "We didn't mean to make fun. We'll help however we can. Do you want us to go get a priest or something? I mean, he'd probably just tell us to fuck off, but . . ."

"No priest," said Mr. Oh. "We're not Catholic. We're not even religious. But we are Korean. I think I know what to do. Stay here and watch her, please."

He made several trips between the kitchen and the office, bringing in portions of each special they'd planned to serve tonight, all the *pan chan* they'd prepared, a few particularly succulent-looking raw fruits and vegetables, and last of all a new bottle of peach schnapps from the bar. He cracked the seal and set the cap on the floor beside the full bottle.

"The bottle should be made from peach wood," he said. "But I have no idea where to get such a thing in Los Angeles. This will have to do."

The two writers were huddled together at Mr. Oh's desk. They'd been happy enough to talk about movie Satans, but now that it looked as if something might actually happen, they were wide-eyed and silent.

"What are you going to do exactly?" asked Darin at last.

"I'm going to feed it."

"Feed it! Dude, that doesn't sound like the best way to—"

"It is the Korean way. My grandmother told me this. The ritual should be done by a Korean healer called a pansu, but I will have to do it myself."

"Still, are you sure—"

"It is not like the movie." In case the thing inside Bobbi was listening, Mr. Oh hoped he sounded more confident than he felt. "This devil does not want my wife's soul. It wants the pleasures of her body. It cannot make love or smoke or eat. It would like to do any of these things, but most of all it is hungry."

"Can we do anything?" Mark asked at last.

Mr. Oh shrugged. "I suppose it might try to jump from her to me. If it does . . ." He shook his head. "Take her with you, get out, and call the police."

"But—"

"Quiet, please. I'm going to start."

Bobbi's mouth opened impossibly wide, and guttural laughter spilled out. "Moron! You think you can catch me with food?

Cut off your penis and feed me that; perhaps such a tiny morsel will still my hunger!"

She had spoken in Korean this time; he supposed he still had something to be thankful for. He turned away from the cot and addressed the doorway that led to the kitchen.

"God of the doorway! God of the kitchen! God of this little eating house that is our second home! Come and feast, if you will." He spoke these words first in Korean, then repeated them in English.

"I thought—" Darin began. Mark shushed him.

"Feast and make yourselves content, for I would ask a favor of you. Should this humble repast fail to satisfy, I will happily prepare as much as you require."

"It is good," said Bobbi in a new voice.

The three of them turned to look at her. Her face had changed again; the expression of rage and pain seemed to be buried somehow under one of haughty benevolence. "Your repast is good, Samuel Oh. Give it to us."

"Take it," he answered, and untied her wrists.

Bobbi rose from the cot and approached the dishes laid out on the floor. Her gait was steady, her bearing regal despite her disheveled hair and the vomit that still streaked her clothes. She knelt before the dishes and, with her fingers, delicately took up portions of each one. Mark and Darin watched with increasing wariness, as though they expected her to resume flinging food at any moment, but she simply tasted each dish and returned to the cot, where she lay down again.

"Now you have feasted," Mr. Oh said. "Now I ask a favor of you. Will you intercede with the spirit that has possessed my wife? Will you invite it to feast also, and leave us?"

"I shall try," said Bobbi in the same calm voice. "You know that such spirits will not always settle for a feast."

"I know."

She closed her eyes and lay motionless on the cot, scarcely seeming to breathe. When her eyes flew open again, they could see that the first spirit was back. It thrust out its tongue and laughed that guttural laugh. "Will you feed me, husband?"

"I am not your husband," said Mr. Oh. "I am the husband of Bobbi Oh, whose body you have stolen. But I will feed you before I ask you to leave her."

"What if I refuse to leave her?"

"There are other things that can be done," Mr. Oh told it, wondering what in the world those things might be.

"Perhaps not. Perhaps I will join you in bed tonight, Samuel Oh."

He managed to suppress a shudder, and said only, "Will you eat?"

"I will," she said. But this time her body did not rise from the cot, though she began to make chewing motions with her mouth. Mark nudged Darin and pointed at the food. Mouthfuls of it were disappearing, apparently into thin air: a clump of kim chee, the head of a fish, a piece of winter squash marked by invisible teeth that must have been far larger than Bobbi Oh's.

"You have eaten well," Mr. Oh said when the dishes were clean. "Will you go now?"

"I have eaten very well," the thing replied. Though Bobbi's mouth still moved, the voice now seemed to emanate from all around them. "I would like to eat so well every day. I will not go."

Mr. Oh closed his eyes for a moment. This would be the crucial moment. "You have eaten," he said, "but you have not drunk."

"Ahhh . . . true!"

A loud sucking sound filled the air, as if a huge rude child were finishing off an enormous ice cream soda, and the level of the peach schnapps began to sink. Mr. Oh sprang for the bottle, seized it by the neck, and screwed the cap on as tightly as it would go. The bottle jerked once, and the office fell silent.

Mr. Oh's legs failed him. He sank to the floor.

The writers stared at each other as if they had missed something. "Is that it?" said one of them; Mr. Oh wasn't sure which.

"Is what it?" said a soft, feminine, Korean-accented voice. They all turned as Bobbi sat up on the cot, frowning at her soiled outfit and the three men staring at her. She began to sob, and Mr. Oh went to her.

Mark and Darin drove down Wilshire Boulevard toward the La Brea Tar Pits. The bottle was in the trunk, taped up in a lettuce box Mr. Oh had given them, well padded with crumpled Korean-language newspapers.

"You're sure that thing isn't going to just bust out of the bottle?" Darin asked for the hundredth time.

"Dude, you heard what Mr. Oh said," Darin told him. "It's a *peach schnapps* bottle. He said peach has some kind of power over it. He said it would make the thing too weak to break the bottle."

"I hope to hell he's right."

"Hope no more, we're here." Mark pulled over and cut the engine. The Tar Pits had been closed for hours, but only a chain link fence separated them from the street. Mark and Darin got out, opened the trunk, unpacked the bottle, and carried it to the fence. A smell like a hundred freshly resurfaced blacktops filled the air. They cast twin apprehensive looks at each other.

"You wanna try it?" asked Mark.

"Oh, right. When we were playing Horse last week, you said I threw like a girl. This shot's all yours, buddy."

Mark got a firm grasp on the bottle's neck, stepped back from the fence, wound up a couple of times, and let fly. They held their breath as the bottle sailed over the fence. It seemed to hang suspended for several beats too long, catching the light of the streetlamps and neon signs, glittering in a nasty way. Then it dropped easily into a pool of prehistoric tar and, within seconds, was sucked out of sight.

"Dude, nice shot," said Darin.

"Thanks." They returned to the car and drove away without looking back. After a few miles of empty Wilshire, Mark said "You know, I'm still hungry."

"Yeah, me too. Let's grab something."

"Whaddaya feel like?"

"Maybe something besides Korean."

"I think so, yeah."

"How about that all-night Thai place over by Jumbo's Clown Room?"

"You got it," said Mark, and swung the car up Western toward Hollywood Boulevard.

2003

STEVEN MILLHAUSER

(b. 1943)

Dangerous Laughter

Few of us now recall that perilous summer. What began as a game, a harmless pastime, quickly took a turn toward the serious and obsessive, which none of us tried to resist. After all, we were young. We were fourteen and fifteen, scornful of childhood, remote from the world of stern and ludicrous adults. We were bored, we were restless, we longed to be seized by any whim or passion and follow it to the farthest reaches of our natures. We wanted to live—to die—to burst into flame—to be transformed into angels or explosions. Only the mundane offended us, as if we secretly feared it was our destiny. By late afternoon our muscles ached, our eyelids grew heavy with obscure desires. And so we dreamed and did nothing, for what was there to do, played ping-pong and went to the beach, loafed in backyards, slept late into the morning—and always we craved adventures so extreme we could never imagine them.

In the long dusks of summer we walked the suburban streets through scents of maple and cut grass, waiting for something to happen.

The game began innocently and spread like a dark rumor. In cool playrooms with parallelograms of sunlight pouring through cellar windows, at ping-pong tables in hot, open garages, around yellow and blue beach towels lying on bright sand above the tide line, you would hear the quiet words, the sharp bursts of laughter. The idea had the simplicity of all inspired things. A word, any word, uttered in a certain solemn tone, could be compelled to reveal its inner stupidity. "Cheese," someone would say, with an air of somber concentration, and again, slowly: "Cheese." Someone would laugh; it was inevitable; the laughter would spread; gusts of hilarity would sweep through the group; and just as things were about to die down, someone would cry out "Elbow!" or "Dirigible!" and bursts of laughter would be set off again. What drew us wasn't so much the hidden absurdity of words, which we'd always suspected, as the sharp heaves and gasps of laughter itself. Deep in our inner dark, we had discovered a startling power. We became fanatics of laughter, devotees of eruption, as if these upheavals were something we hadn't known before, something that would take us where we needed to go.

Such simple performances couldn't satisfy us for long. The laugh parties represented a leap worthy of our hunger. The object was to laugh longer and harder than anyone else, to maintain in yourself an uninterrupted state of explosive release. Rules sprang up to eliminate unacceptable laughter—the feeble, the false, the unfairly exaggerated. Soon every party had its judges, who grew skillful in detecting the slightest deviation from the genuine. As long laughter became the rage, a custom arose in which each of us in turn had to step into a circle of watchers, and there, partly through the stimulus of a crowd already rippling with amusement, and partly through some inner trick that differed from person to person, begin to laugh. Meanwhile the watchers and judges, who themselves were continually thrown into outbursts that drove the laugher to greater and greater heights, studied the roars and convulsions carefully and timed the performance with a stopwatch.

In this atmosphere of urgency, abandon, and rigorous striving, accidents were bound to happen. One girl, laughing hysterically on a couch in a basement playroom, threw back her head and injured her neck when it struck the wooden couch-arm. A boy gasping with mad laughter crashed into a piano bench, fell to the floor, and broke his left arm. These incidents, which might have served as warnings, only heightened our sense of rightness, as if our wounds were signs that we took our laughter seriously.

Not long after the laugh parties began to spread through our afternoons, there arose a new pastime, which enticed us with promises of a more radical kind. The laugh clubs—or laugh parlors, as they were sometimes called—represented a bolder effort to draw forth and prolong our laughter. At first they were organized by slightly older girls, who invited "members" to their houses after dark. In accordance with rules and practices that varied from club to club, the girls were said to produce sustained fits of violent laughter far more thrilling than anything we had yet discovered. No one was certain how the clubs had come into being—one day they simply seemed to be there, as if they'd been present all along, waiting for us to find them.

It was rumored that the first club was the invention of sixteen-year-old Bernice Alderson, whose parents were never home. She lived in a large house in the wooded north end of town; one day she'd read in a history of Egypt that Queen Cleopatra liked to order a slave girl to bind her arms and tickle her bare feet with a feather. In her third-floor bedroom, Bernice and her friend Mary Chapman invited club members to remove their shoes and lie down one by one on the bed. While Mary, with her muscular arms, held the chest and knees firmly in place, Bernice began to tickle the outstretched body—on the stomach, the ribs, the neck, the thighs, the tops and sides of the feet. There was an art to it all: the art of invading and withdrawing, of coaxing from the depths a steady outpouring of helpless laughter. For the visitor held down on the bed, it was a matter of releasing oneself into the hands of the girls and enduring it for as long as possible. All you had to do was say "Stop." In theory the laughter never had to stop, though most of us could barely hold out for three minutes.

Although the laugh parlors existed in fact, for we all attended them and even began to form clubs of our own, they also continued to lead a separate and in a sense higher existence in the realm of rumor, which had the effect of lifting them into the inaccessible and mythical. It was said that in one of these clubs, members were required to remove their clothes, after which they were chained to a bed and tickled savagely to the point of delirium. It was said that one girl, sobbing with laughter, gasping, began to move her hips in strange and suggestive ways, until it became clear that the act of tickling had brought her to orgasm. The erotic was never absent from these rumors—a fact that hardly surprised us, since those of us who were purists of laughter and disdained any crude crossing over into the sexual recognized the kinship between the two worlds. For even then we understood that our laughter, as it erupted from us in unseemly spasms, was part of the kingdom of forbidden things.

As laugh parties gave way to laugh parlors, and rumors

thickened, we sometimes had the sense that our secret games had begun to spread to other regions of the town. One day a nine-year-old boy was discovered by his mother holding down and violently tickling his seven-year-old sister, who was shrieking and screaming—the collar of her dress was soaked with tears. The girl's pale body was streaked with lines of deep pink, as if she'd been struck repeatedly with a rope. We heard that Bernice Alderson's mother, at home for a change, had entered the kitchen with a heavy bag of groceries in her arms, slipped on a rubber dog-toy, and fallen to the floor. As she sat there beside a box of smashed and oozing eggs and watched the big, heavy, thumping oranges go rolling across the linoleum, the corners of her mouth began to twitch, her lungs, already burning with anger, began to tingle, and all at once she burst into laughter that lashed her body, threw her head back against the metal doors of the cabinet under the sink, rose to the third-floor bedroom of her daughter, who looked up frowning from a book, and in the end left her exhausted, shaken, bruised, panting, and exhilarated. At night, in my hot room, I lay restless and dissatisfied, longing for the release of feverish laughter that alone could soothe me—and through the screen I seemed to hear, along with the crickets, the rattling window-fan next door, and the hum of far-off trucks on the thruway, the sound of laughter bursting faintly in the night, all over our town, like the buzz of a fluorescent lamp in a distant bedroom.

One night after my parents were asleep I left the house and walked across town to Bernice Alderson's neighborhood. The drawn shade of her third-floor window was aglow with dim yellow light. On the bed in her room Mary Chapman gripped me firmly while Bernice bent over me with a serious but not unkind look. Slowly she brought me to a pitch of wild laughter that seemed to scald my throat as sweat trickled down my neck and the bed creaked to the rhythm of my deep, painful, releasing cries. I held out for a long time, nearly seven minutes, until I begged her to stop. Instantly it was over. Even as I made my way home, under the maples and lindens of a warm July night, I regretted my cowardice and longed for deeper and more terrible laughter. Then I wondered how I could push my way through the hours that separated me from my next descent into the darkness of my body, where laughter lay like lava, waiting for a fissure to form that would release it like liquid fire.

Of course we compared notes. We'd known from the beginning that some were more skilled in laughter than others, that some were able to sustain long and robust fits of the bone-shaking kind, which seemed to bring them to the verge of hysteria or unconsciousness without stepping over the line. Many of us boasted of our powers, only to be outdone by others; rumors blossomed; and in this murky atmosphere of extravagant claims, dubious feats, and unverifiable stories, the figure of Clara Schuler began to stand out with a certain distinctness.

Clara Schuler was fifteen years old. She was a quiet girl, who sat very still in class with her book open before her, eyes lowered and both feet resting on the floor. She never drummed her fingers on the desk. She never pushed her hair back over her ear or crossed and uncrossed her legs—as if, for her, a single motion were a form of disruption. When she passed a handout to the person seated behind her, she turned her upper body abruptly, dropped the paper on the desk with lowered eyes, and turned abruptly back. She never raised her hand in class. When called on, she flushed slightly, answered in a voice so quiet that the teacher had to ask her to "speak up," and said as little as possible, though it was clear she'd done the work. She seemed to experience the act of being looked at as a form of violation; she gave you the impression that her idea of happiness would be to dissolve gradually, leaving behind a small puddle. She was difficult to picture clearly—a little pale, her hair dark in some elusive shade between brown and black, her eyes hidden under lowered lids that sometimes opened suddenly to reveal large, startled irises. She wore trim knee-length skirts and solid-colored cotton blouses that looked neatly ironed. Sometimes she wore in her collar a small silver pin shaped like a cat.

One small thing struck me about Clara Schuler: in the course of the day she would become a little unraveled. Strands of hair would fall across her face, the back of her blouse would bunch up and start to pull away from her leather belt, one of her white socks would begin to droop. The next day she'd be back in her seat, her hair neatly combed, her blouse tucked in, her socks pulled up tight with the ribs perfectly straight, her hands folded lightly on her maplewood desk.

Clara had one friend, a girl named Helen Jacoby, who sat with her in the cafeteria and met her at the lockers after class. Helen was a long-boned girl who played basketball and laughed at anything. When she threw her head back to drink bottles of soda, you could see the ridges of her trachea pressing through her neck. She seemed an unlikely companion for Clara Schuler, but we were used to seeing them together and we felt, without thinking much about it, that each enhanced the other—Helen made Clara seem less strange and solitary, in a sense protected her and prevented her from being perceived as ridiculous, while Clara made good old Helen seem more interesting, lent her a touch of mystery. We weren't surprised, that summer, to see Helen at the laugh parties, where she laughed with her head thrown back in a way that reminded me of the way she drank soda; and it was Helen who one afternoon brought Clara Schuler with her and introduced her to the new game.

I began to watch Clara at these parties. We all watched her. She would step into the circle and stand there with lowered eyes, her head leaning forward slightly, her shoulders slumped, her arms tense at her sides—looking, I couldn't help thinking, as if she were being punished in some humiliating way. You could see the veins rising up on the backs of her hands. She stood so motionless that she seemed to be holding her breath; perhaps she was; and you could feel something building in her, as in a child about to cry; her neck stiff; the tendons visible; two vertical lines between her eyebrows; then a kind of mild trembling in her neck and arms, a veiled shudder, an inner rippling, and through her body, still rigid but in the grip of a force, you could sense a presence, rising, expanding, until, with a painful gasp, with a jerk of her shoulders, she gave way to a cry or scream of laughter—laughter that continued to well up in her, to shake her as if she were possessed by a demon, until her cheeks were wet, her hair wild in her face, her chest heaving, her fingers clutching at her arms and head—and still the laughter came, hurling her about, making her gulp and gasp as if in terror, her mouth stretched back over her teeth, her eyes squeezed shut, her hands pressed against her ribs as if to keep herself from cracking apart.

And then it would stop. Abruptly, mysteriously, it was over. She stood there, pale—exhausted—panting. Her eyes, wide open, saw nothing. Slowly she came back to herself. Then quickly, a little unsteadily, she would walk away from us to collapse on a couch.

These feats of laughter were immediately recognized as bold and striking, far superior to the performances we had become accustomed to; and Clara Schuler was invited to all the laugh parties, applauded, and talked about admiringly, for she had a gift of reckless laughter we had not seen before.

Now whenever loose groups of us gathered to pursue our game, Clara Schuler was there. We grew used to her, waited impatiently for her when she was late, this quiet girl who'd never done anything but sit obediently in our classes with both feet on the floor before revealing dark depths of laughter that left us wondering and a little uneasy. For there was something about Clara Schuler's laughter. It wasn't simply that it was more intense than ours. Rather, she seemed to be transformed into an object, seized by a force that raged through her before letting her go. Yes, in Clara Schuler the discrepancy between the body that was shaken and the force that shook it appeared so sharply that at the very moment she became most physical she seemed to lose the sense of her body altogether. For the rest of us, there was always a touch of the sensual in these performances: breasts shook, hips jerked, flesh moved in unexpected ways. But Clara Schuler seemed to pass beyond the easy suggestiveness of moving bodies and to enter new and more ambiguous realms, where the body was the summoner of some dark, eruptive power that was able to flourish only through the accident of a material thing, which it flung about as if cruelly before abandoning it to the rites of exhaustion.

One day she appeared among us alone. Helen Jacoby was at the beach, or out shopping with her mother. We understood that Clara Schuler no longer needed her friend in the old way —that she had come into her own. And we understood one other thing: she would allow nothing to stop her from joining our game, from yielding to the seductions of laughter, for she lived, more and more, only in order to let herself go.

It was inevitable that rumors should spring up about Clara Schuler. It was said that she'd begun to go to the laugh parlors, those half-real, half-legendary places where laughter was wrung out of willing victims by special arts. It was said that one night she had paid a visit to Bernice Alderson's house, where in the lamplit bedroom on the third floor she'd been constrained and skillfully tickled for nearly an hour, at which point she fainted dead away and had to be revived by a scented oil rubbed into her temples. It was said that at another house she'd been so shaken by extreme laughter that her body rose from the bed and hovered in the air for thirty seconds before dropping back down. We knew that this last was a lie, a frivolous and irritating tale fit for children, but it troubled us all the same, it seized our imaginations—for we felt that under the right circumstances, with the help of a physiologically freakish but not inconceivable pattern of spasms, it was the kind of thing Clara Schuler might somehow be able to do.

As our demands became more exacting, and our expectations more refined, Clara Schuler's performances attained heights of release that inflamed us and left no doubt of her power. We tried to copy her gestures, to jerk our shoulders with her precise rhythms, always without success. Sometimes we imagined we could hear, in Clara Schuler's laughter, our own milder laughter, changed into something we could only long for. It was as if our dreams had entered her.

I noticed that her strenuous new life was beginning to affect her appearance. Now when she came to us her hair fell across her cheeks in long strands, which she would impatiently flick away with the backs of her fingers. She looked thinner, though it was hard to tell; she looked tired; she looked as if she might be coming down with something. Her eyes, no longer hidden under lowered lids, gazed at us restlessly and a little vaguely. Sometimes she gave the impression that she was searching for something she could no longer remember. She looked expectant; a little sad; a little bored.

One night, unable to sleep, I escaped from the house and took a walk. Near the end of my street I passed under a streetlamp that flickered and made a crackling sound, so that my shadow trembled. It seemed to me that I was that streetlamp, flickering and crackling with restlessness. After a while I came to an older neighborhood of high maples and gabled houses with rundown front porches. Bicycles leaned wearily against wicker furniture and beach towels hung crookedly over porch rails. I stopped before a dark house near the end of the street.

Through an open window on the second floor, over the dirt driveway, I heard the sound of a rattling fan.

It was Clara Schuler's house. I wondered if it was her window. I walked a little closer, looking up at the screen, and it seemed to me that through the rattle and hum of the fan I heard some other sound. It was—I thought it was—the sound of quiet laughter. Was she lying there in the dark, laughing secretly, releasing herself from restlessness? Could she be laughing in her sleep? Maybe it was only some trick of the fan. I stood listening to that small, uncertain sound, which mingled with the blades of the fan until it seemed the fan itself was laughing, perhaps at me. What did I long for, under that window? I longed to be swept up into Clara Schuler's laughter, I longed to join her there, in her dark room, I longed for release from whatever it was I was. But whatever I was lay hard and immovable in me, like bone; I would never be free of my own weight. After a while I turned around and walked home.

It wasn't long after this visit that I saw Clara Schuler at one of the laugh parlors we'd formed, in imitation of those we had heard about or perhaps had invented in order to lure ourselves into deeper experiments. Helen Jacoby sat on the bed and held Clara's wrists while a friend of Helen's held Clara's ankles. A blond-haired girl I'd never seen before bent over her with hooked fingers. Five of us watched the performance. It began with a sudden shiver, as the short blunt fingers darted along her ribs and thighs. Clara Schuler's head began to turn from side to side; her feet in her white socks stiffened. As laughter rushed through her in sharp shuddering bursts, one of her shoulders lifted as if to fold itself across her neck. Within ten minutes her eyes had grown glassy and calm. She lay almost still, even as she continued to laugh. What struck us was that eerie stillness, as if she'd passed beyond struggle to some other place, where laughter poured forth in pure, vigorous streams.

Someone asked nervously if we should stop. The blond-haired girl glanced at her watch and bent over Clara Schuler more intently. After half an hour, Clara began breathing in great wracking gulps, accompanied by groans torn up from her throat. Helen asked her if she'd had enough; Clara shook her head harshly. Her face was so wet that she glowed in the lamplight. Stains of wetness darkened the bedspread.

When the session had lasted just over an hour, the blond-haired girl gave up in exhaustion. She stood shaking her wrists, rubbing the fingers of first one hand and then the other. On the bed Clara Schuler continued stirring and laughing, as if she still felt the fingers moving over her. Gradually her laughter grew fainter; and as she lay there pale and drained, with her head turned to one side, her eyes dull, her lips slack, strands of long hair sticking to her wet cheek, she looked, for a moment, as if she'd grown suddenly old.

It was at this period, when Clara Schuler became queen of the laugh parlors, that I first began to worry about her. One day, emerging from an unusually violent and prolonged series of gasps, she lay motionless, her eyes open and staring, while the fingers played over her skin. It took some moments for us to realize she had lost consciousness, though she soon revived. Another time, walking across a room, she thrust out an arm and seized the back of a chair as her body leaned slowly to one side, before she straightened and continued her walk as if nothing had happened. I understood that these feverish games, these lavish abandonments, were no longer innocent. Sometimes I saw in her eyes the restless unhappiness of someone for whom nothing, not even such ravishments, would ever be enough.

One afternoon when I walked to Main Street to return a book to the library, I saw Clara Schuler stepping out of Cerino's grocery store. I felt an intense desire to speak to her; to warn her against us; to praise her extravagantly; to beg her to teach me the difficult art of laughter. Shyness constrained me, though I wasn't shy—but it was as if I had no right to intrude on her, to break the spell of her remoteness. I kept out of sight and followed her home. When she climbed the wooden steps of her porch, one of which creaked like the floor of an attic, I stepped boldly into view, daring her to turn and see me. She opened the front door and disappeared into the house. For a while I stood there, trying to remember what it was I had wanted to say to Clara Schuler, the modest girl with a fierce, immodest gift. A clattering startled me. Along the shady sidewalk, trembling with spots of sunlight, a girl with yellow pigtails was pulling a lollipop-red wagon, which held a jouncing rhinoceros. I turned and headed home.

That night I dreamed about Clara Schuler. She was standing in a sunny backyard, looking into the distance. I came over to her and spoke a few words, but she did not look at me. I began to walk around her, speaking urgently and trying to catch her gaze, but her face was always turned partly away, and when I seized her arm it felt soft and crumbly, like pie dough.

About this time I began to sense among us a slight shift of attention, an inner wandering. A change was in the air. The laugh parlors seemed to lack their old aura of daring—they'd grown a little familiar, a little humdrum. While one of us lay writhing in laughter, the rest of us glanced toward the windows. One day someone pulled a deck of cards from a pocket, and as we waited our turn on the bed we sat down on the floor to a few hands of gin rummy.

We tried to conjure new possibilities, but our minds were mired in the old forms. Even the weather conspired to hold us back. The heat of midsummer pressed against us like fur. Leaves, thick as tongues, hung heavily from the maples. Dust lay on polished furniture like pollen.

One night it rained. The rain continued all the next day and night; wind knocked down tree branches and telephone wires. In the purple-black sky, prickly lines of lightning burst forth with troubling brightness. Through the dark rectangles of our windows, the lightning flashes looked like textbook diagrams of the circulation of the blood.

The turn came with the new sun. Mist like steam rose from soaked grass. We took up our old games, but it was as if something had been carried off by the storm. At a birthday party in a basement playroom with an out-of-tune piano, a girl named Janet Bianco, listening to a sentimental song, began to behave strangely. Her shoulders trembled, her lips quivered. Mirthless tears rolled along her cheeks. Gradually we understood that she was crying. It caught our attention—it was a new note. Across the room, another girl suddenly burst into tears.

A passion for weeping seized us. It proved fairly easy for one girl to set off another, who set off a third. Boys, tense and embarrassed, gave way slowly. We held weep-fests that left us shaken and thrilled. Here and there a few laugh parties and laugh clubs continued to meet, but we knew it was the end of an era.

Clara Schuler attended that birthday party. As the rage for weeping swept over us, she appeared at a few gatherings, where she stood off to one side with a little frown. We saw her there, looking in our direction, before she began to shimmer and dissolve through our abundant tears. The pleasures of weeping proved more satisfying than the old pleasures of laughter, possibly because, when all was said and done, we weren't happy, we who were restless and always in search of diversion. And whereas laughter had always been difficult to sustain, weeping, once begun, welled up in us with gratifying ease. Several girls, among them Helen Jacoby, discovered in themselves rich and unsuspected depths of unhappiness, which released in the rest of us lengthy, heartfelt bouts of sorrow.

It wasn't long after the new craze had swept away the old that we received an invitation from Clara Schuler. None of us except Helen Jacoby had ever set foot in her house before. We arrived in the middle of a sunny afternoon; in the living room it was already dusk. A tall woman in a long drab dress pointed vaguely toward a carpeted stairway. Clara, she said, was waiting for us in the guest room in the attic. At the top of the stairs we came to a hallway covered with faded wallpaper, showing repeated waterwheels beside repeated streams shaded by willows. A door with a loose knob led up to the attic. Slowly we passed under shadowy rafters that slanted down over wooden barrels and a big bear in a chair and a folded card-table leaning against a tricycle. Through a half-open door we entered the guest room. Clara Schuler stood with her hands hanging down in front of her, one hand lightly grasping the wrist of the other.

It looked like the room of someone's grandmother, which had been invaded by a child. On a frilly bedspread under old lace curtains sat a big rag doll wearing a pink dress with an apron. Her yellow yarn hair looked as heavy as candy. On top of a mahogany chest of drawers, a black-and-white photograph of a bearded man sat next to a music box decorated with elephants and balloons. It was warm and dusty in that room; we didn't know whether we were allowed to sit on the bed, which seemed to belong to the doll, so we sat on the floor. Clara herself looked tired and tense. We hadn't seen her for a while. We hardly thought about her. It occurred to me that we'd begun to forget her.

Seven or eight of us were there that day, sitting on a frayed maroon rug and looking awkwardly around. After a while Clara tried to close the door—the wood, swollen in the humid heat, refused to fit into the frame—and then walked to the center of the room. I had the impression that she was going to say something to us, but she stood looking vaguely before her. I could sense what she was going to do even before she began to laugh. It was a good laugh, one that reminded me of the old laugh parties, and a few of us joined her uneasily, for old times' sake. But we were done with that game, we could scarcely recall those days of early summer. And, in truth, even our weeping had begun to tire us, already we longed for new enticements. Maybe Clara had sensed a change and was trying to draw us back; maybe she simply wanted to perform one more time. If she was trying to assert her old power over us, she failed entirely. But neither our halfhearted laughter nor our hidden resistance seemed to trouble her, as she abandoned herself to her desire.

There was a concentration in Clara Schuler's laughter, a completeness, an immensity that we hadn't seen before. It was as if she wanted to outdo herself, to give the performance of her life. Her face, flushed on the cheek ridges, was so pale that laughter seemed to be draining away her blood. She stumbled to one side and nearly fell over—someone swung up a supporting hand. She seemed to be laughing harder and harder, with a ferocity that flung her body about, snapped her head back, wrenched her out of shape. The room, filled with wails of laughter, began to feel unbearable. No one knew what to do. At one point she threw herself onto the bed, gasping in what appeared to be an agony of laughter. Slowly, gracefully, the big doll slumped forward, until her head touched her stuck-out legs and the yellow yarn hair lay flung out over her feet.

After thirty-five minutes someone rose and quietly left. I could hear the footsteps fading through the attic.

Others began to leave; they did not say good-bye. Those of us who remained found an old Monopoly game and sat in a corner to play. Clara's eyes had taken on their glassy look, as cries of laughter continued to erupt from her. After the first hour I understood that no one was going to forgive her for this.

When the Monopoly game ended, everyone left except Helen Jacoby and me. Clara was laughing fiercely, her face twisted as if in pain. Her skin was so wet that she looked hard and shiny, like metal. The laughter, raw and harsh, poured up out of her as if some mechanism had broken. One of her forearms was bruised. The afternoon was drawing on toward five when Helen Jacoby, turning up her hands and giving a bitter little shrug, stood up and walked out of the room.

I stayed. And as I watched Clara Schuler, I had the desire to reach out and seize her wrist, to shake her out of her laughter and draw her back before it was too late. No one is allowed to laugh like that, I wanted to say. Stop it right now. She had passed so far beyond herself that there was almost nothing left —nothing but that creature emptying herself of laughter. It was ugly—indecent—it made you want to look away. At the same time she bound me there, for it was as if she were inviting me to follow her to the farthest and most questionable regions of laughter, where laughter no longer bore any relation to earthly things and, sufficient to itself, soared above the world to flourish in the void. There, you were no longer yourself—you were no longer anything.

More than once I started to reach for her arm. My hand hung in front of me like some fragile piece of sculpture I was holding up for inspection. I saw that I was no more capable of stopping Clara Schuler in her flight than I was of joining her. I could only be a witness.

It was nearly half past five when I finally stood up. "Clara!" I said sharply, but I might as well have been talking to the doll. I wondered whether I'd ever spoken her name before. She was still laughing when I disappeared into the attic. Downstairs I told her mother that something was wrong, her daughter had been laughing for hours. She thanked me, turned slowly to gaze at the carpeted stairs, and said she hoped I would come again.

The local paper reported that Mrs. Schuler discovered her daughter around seven o'clock. She had already stopped breathing. The official cause of death was a ruptured blood vessel in the brain, but we knew the truth: Clara Schuler had died of laughter. "She was always a good girl," her mother was quoted as saying, as if death were a form of disobedience. We cooperated fully with the police, who found no trace of foul play.

For a while Clara Schuler's death was taken up eagerly by the weeping parties, which had begun to languish and which now gained a feverish new energy before collapsing decisively. It was late August; school was looming; as if desperately we hurled ourselves into a sudden passion for old board games, staging fierce contests of Monopoly and Risk, altering the rules in order to make the games last for days. But already our ardor was tainted by the end of summer, already we could see, in eyes glittering with the fever of obsession, a secret distraction.

On a warm afternoon in October I took a walk into Clara Schuler's neighborhood. Her house had been sold. On the long front steps sat a little girl in a green-and-orange-checked jacket, leaning forward and tightening a roller skate with a big silver key. I stood looking up at the bedroom window, half expecting to hear a ghostly laughter. In the quiet afternoon I heard only the whine of a backyard chain saw and the slap of a jump rope against a sidewalk. I felt awkward standing there, like someone trying to peek through a window. The summer seemed far away, as distant as childhood. Had we really played those games? I thought of Clara Schuler, the girl who had died of a ruptured blood vessel, but it was difficult to summon her face. What I could see clearly was that rag doll, slowly falling forward. Something stirred in my chest, and to my astonishment, with a kind of sorrow, I felt myself burst into a sharp laugh.

I looked around uneasily and began walking away. I wanted to be back in my own neighborhood, where people didn't die of laughter. There we threw ourselves into things for a while, lost interest, and went on to something else. Clara Schuler played games differently. Had we disappointed her? As I turned the corner of her street, I glanced back at the window over her dirt driveway. I had never learned whether it was her room. For all I knew, she slept on the other side of the house, or in the guest room in the attic. Again I saw that pink-and-yellow doll, falling forward in a slow, graceful, grotesque bow. No, my laughter was all right. It was a salute to Clara Schuler, an acknowledgment of her great gift. In her own way, she was complete. I wondered whether she had been laughing at us a little, up there in her attic.

As I entered the streets of my neighborhood, I felt a familiar restlessness. Everything stood out clearly. In an open, sunny garage, a man was reaching up to an aluminum ladder hanging horizontally on hooks, while in the front yard a tenth-grade girl wearing tight jeans rolled up to midcalf and a billowy red-and-black lumberjack shirt was standing with a rake beside a pile of yellow leaves shot through with green, shading her eyes and staring up at a man hammering on a roof. The mother of a friend of mine waved at me from behind the shady, sun-striped screen of a porch. Against a backboard above a brilliant white garage door, a basketball went round and round the orange rim of a basket. It was Sunday afternoon, time of the great boredom. Deep in my chest I felt a yawn begin; it went shuddering through my jaw. On the crosspiece of a sunny telephone pole, a grackle shrieked once and was still. The basketball hung in the white net. Suddenly it came unstuck and dropped with a smack to the driveway, the grackle rose into the air, somewhere I heard a burst of laughter. I nodded in the direction of Clara Schuler's neighborhood and continued down the street. Tomorrow something was bound to happen.

2003

M. RICKERT

(b. 1959)

The Chambered Fruit

Stones. Roots. Chips like bones. The moldering scent of dry
leaves and dirt, the odd aroma of mint. What grew here before
it fell to neglect and misuse? I remember this past spring's
tulips and daffodils, sprouted amongst the weeds, picked and
discarded without discrimination. I was so distracted by my
dead daughter that I rarely noticed the living. I take a deep
breath. Mint thyme. It should have survived the neglect, perhaps did, but now has fallen victim to my passionate weeding,
as so much of more significance has fallen victim before it. I
pick up a small, brown bulb and set it, point up, in the hole,
cover it with dirt. Geese fly overhead. I shade my eyes to watch
them pass, and then cannot avoid surveying the property.

Near the old barn are piles of wood and brick meant to further its renovation. Leaves and broken branches litter the
stacks. The wood looks slightly warped, weathered by the seasons it's gone untended. The yard is bristly with dried weeds
and leaves. The house has suffered the worst. Surely, instead of
planting bulbs I should be calling a contractor. It can't be
good, the way it looks like it's begun to sink into the earth or
how the roof litters shingles that spear into the ground around
it. But who should I call? How far do I have to search to find
someone who doesn't know our story?

I think of it like the nursery rhyme. Inside the old farmhouse
with the sagging porch, through the large, sunny kitchen, past
the living room with the wood-burning stove, up the creaking
stairs and down the hall lined with braided rugs, past the bathroom with the round window and claw-footed tub, past the
yellow and white bedroom we called the guest room, past her
room (where the door is shut) to our bedroom—my bedroom
now—there is, on the bedside table, a picture of the three of
us. It's from her last birthday. Twelve candles on the cake. She
is bent to blow them out, her face in pretty profile. Her dark

hair brushes against the smooth skin of her puffed cheek; her eye, bright with happiness, dark-lashed beneath its perfectly arched brow. Jack and I stand behind her. Both of us are blurry, the result of Jack having set up the camera for automatic timer, his running to be in the shot, me moving to make room for him. He looks like her, only handsome, and I look like, well, someone passing by who got in the picture by mistake, a blur of long, untidy hair, an oversized shirt, baggy slacks. The camera captures and holds their smiles forever, locked in innocence and joy, and my smile, strained, my focus somewhere past the borders of the picture, as if I see, in the shadows, what is coming.

When I think of everything that happened, from the beginning, I look for clues. In a way, there are so many it baffles strangers that we couldn't see them. But to understand this, and really, I'm beyond expecting anyone else to understand this, but for my own understanding, I have to remember that to be human is a dangerous state. That said, Jack's nature is not profoundly careless, and I am not, really, in spite of everything you might have read or concluded, criminally naïve. Though of course I accept, even as I rebel against its horrible truth, that a great deal of the fault was ours. Sometimes I think more ours than his. When I look for clues to the dangerous parents we'd become I have to accept the combustible combination that occurred, just once, when Jack was careless and I was naïve and that's all it took. We lost her.

You may be familiar with my old work. Folk scenes, sort of like Grandma Moses except, frankly, hers are better. Maybe the difference is that hers were created from real memories and mine were made from longing. No one I know has ever ridden in a horse-drawn sleigh, with or without bells. We did not hang Christmas wreaths on all the doors and from the street lamps lit with candles. We did not send the children to skate at the neighborhood pond (which didn't exist, the closest thing being the town dump) or burn leaves and grow pumpkins (well, the Hadley's grew pumpkins but their farmhouse was an old trailer so it didn't really fit the picture). We did garden, but our gardens did not all blossom into perfect flower at the same moment on the same day, the women standing in aprons, talking over the fence. The sun shone but it didn't shine the way I painted it, a great ball of light with spears of brightness around it.

These are the paintings I made. Little folk scenes that were actually quite popular, not in town, of course, but in other places where people imagined the world I painted existed. I made a decent living at it. Even now, when all I paint are dark and frightening scenes of abduction and despair that I show no one (who would come anyway, even old friends keep their distance now), I live off the royalties. My paintings are on calendars, Christmas cards, coasters, T-shirts. In the first days of horror, when the news coverage was so heavy, I thought someone would certainly point out that I (the neglectful mother of the dead girl) was also the painter, C. R. Rite, but as far as I know the connection was never made and my income has not suffered for my neglect.

Jack still represents my work, which also makes it strange that no one ever made the connection. Maybe people assumed we were actually farmers, though the locals certainly knew that wasn't true. Maybe the media was just too busy telling the grisly details of our story to focus any attention on the boring issue of our finances. Certainly that matter isn't very titillating. What people seemed to want to hear was how our daughter died, an endless nightmare from which I can't ever wake, that strangers actually watch and read as some form of entertainment.

I accept my fault in this, and I know it's huge. I live every day with the Greek proportions of our story. In the classic nature I had a fault, a small area, like Achilles's heel, that left me vulnerable.

But not evil. As Jack likes to point out, we didn't do that to her and we would have stopped it from happening if we knew how.

The unforgivable thing, everyone agrees, is that we didn't see it. How evil do you have to be? We did not keep our daughter safe and she's dead because of that. Isn't that evil enough?

When we moved here, Steff was eight. She didn't know that we were really country people, having lived her whole life in the city. At first she spent all her time in her room with her books and her dolls but eventually, during that giddy, first hot summer when I walked about in my slip (when the construction crew wasn't working on the barn) eating raspberries off the bushes and planting sunflower seeds, and hollyhocks (though it was too late and they wouldn't bloom), she joined me, staying close, afraid of all the space, the strangeness of sky. Eventually, she came to love it too and brought blankets into the yard for picnics, both real and imagined, and paper to color, which, in true Buddha-child fashion she left to blow about the yard when she was finished. When one of these pictures blew across my path, a scene of a girl picking flowers, a shimmering angel behind her, I memorized it and then let it blow away, thinking it would be a gift for somebody unlucky enough not to have a child who drew pictures of that other world which children are so close to.

In the city, Steffie had attended a small private school with a philosophy that sheltered children from the things in our world that make them grow up so fast. The influence of media was discouraged and, contrary to national trend, computer use was considered neither necessary nor particularly beneficial to children. At eight, Steffie still played with dolls, and believed in, if not magic, at least a magicalness to the world; a condition that caused strangers to look at her askance and try to measure her IQ but for which I took great pride. In her school they learned the mythic stories, needlework, and dance. Friends of mine with children in public or other private schools talked of the homework stress and the busyness of their lives, transporting kids from practice to practice. When I visited these friends their children did not play the piano, or happily kick soccer balls in the yard. In spite of all those lessons, or, I suspected, because of them, these children sat listless and bleary-eyed in front of the television or wandered about the house, restless and bored, often resorting to eating, while Steffie played with dolls or spoons, whatever was available. I feel that our society has forgotten the importance of play, the simple beginnings of a creative mind. The value of that. Not that anyone is interested in parental guidance from me now.

At any rate, Steffie got off the bus, that first day, in tears. Several of the children would not sit with her because, they said, we were a bunch of hippies who ran around the yard in our underthings. When Steffie told me this I cried right along with her. I'd made a life out of forgetting the world. I found its reminders sharp and disturbing.

Eventually, she adjusted and I did too. I wore clothes in the yard, though I was baffled how anyone knew I'd ever done differently. Steff put away her dolls and proudly carried her heavy backpack filled with books and maps and serious questions about the real world, completely neglecting anything about the spiritual. Incredibly (to me) she liked it. A lot. She loved the candy they were rewarded with, the movies they watched. "I like it because it's normal," she said, and I realized that she knew we were not.

The years passed. I had the barn converted to an art studio and planned to further the renovation so that I could turn it into a sort of community art center for teenagers. I imagined Saturday mornings teaching painting, others teaching things like weaving, or, when Steffie began to take an interest in it, even dance. I think part of the motivation for this plan was the idea of filling the place with teenagers and helping Steffie's social life, which still seemed, though she never complained, strangely quiet for a child her age.

So, when Jack bought the computer, I thought it was a good idea. He said he needed it for the business and Steffie had been complaining for some time that she "needed" one too. He brought home the computer and I didn't argue. After all, he and Steff were the ones dealing with the notorious "real" world and I was the one who got to spend all morning painting happy pictures and the rest of the day gardening, or baking cookies, or reading a good book. Who in the world lived a life like mine?

When the computer was set up and ready to use in his office, Jack called me to come look. I looked into the brightly colored screen and felt numbed by it. Steff, however, was thrilled. Soon the two of them were talking a strange language I didn't understand. I drifted off into private thoughts, mentally working on paintings, scenes from a time before the world was enchanted by screens.

About three months before (oh, God, I still cannot write these words without trembling) her last birthday, Jack began campaigning that we get Steff her own computer. I didn't like the idea but I couldn't say why, though I held my ground until one Saturday when I drove into town to the post office and saw a group of girls who looked to be Steffie's age, and who I thought I recognized from classroom functions, sitting at the picnic table outside the ice cream place. A few of the girls caught me staring, and they began whispering behind open hands. I turned away. Had I done this to her? Was it my strangeness that made her unpopular? I went home and told Jack to go ahead and buy the thing. We gave it to her for her twelfth birthday, that's when we took the picture, the one I still have on the bedside table.

Steff was thrilled. She hugged us both and gave us kisses and thanked us so much that I began to believe we had done the right thing. I was baffled how this silent box was going to make her life better but after seeing those girls together, I was ready to try anything.

They set up the computer in her room. At night, after dinner, they each went off for hours, clicking and staring at their separate screens. I lit candles and sat, with the cat in my lap, reading. I guess I had some vague ideas about homework, and I'd heard that there were ways to view great paintings from distant museums on the computer. I assumed she was doing things like that. I thought she should be doing more interacting with the world. I thought this as I sat reading, with the cat on my lap, and tried to believe that one solitude is the same as any other.

As though she'd been given the magic elixir for a social life, she began talking about various friends. Eventually one name came up more and more frequently. Celia read the same books Steffie did and liked to draw and dance. When Celia asked Steff to sleep over I was thrilled until I found out Stephanie had never actually met the girl but only "talked" to her on the computer.

Of course, I said this would not happen. She could be anyone; why, Celia might not even be a girl, I said. No, she could not sleep over at this stranger's house, who, coincidentally lived only twenty-four miles away.

Steff burst into tears at the dinner table, threw her napkin on the plate. "You don't want me to be normal," she said, "you want me to be just like you and I'm not!" Then she ran out of the kitchen, up the stairs to her bedroom where she actually slammed the door, all of this perhaps not unusual behavior for an almost teenager but completely new for Steff.

Jack looked at me accusingly.

"You can't expect me to let her go off to some stranger's house. We don't even know the family."

"Whose family do we know?"

I understood his point. I had sheltered us, all of us, with my sheltered ways.

"When it comes down to it, if she went anywhere in town, we wouldn't know those people either."

"It's not the same thing. People have reputations." As soon as I saw the look on Jack's face, I realized that our reputation was probably more extensive than I knew. If not for me, they would be having a normal life. I was the odd one. It was all my fault.

"What if I speak to the girl's parents, would that make you more comfortable?"

For a moment, I considered that we invite the girl's family over, we could have a barbecue, but the thought of having to spend a whole evening entertaining anyone horrified me. When it comes right down to it, my daughter died because of my reluctance to entertain. How ridiculous and horrifying. Instead, I agreed that she could go if Jack talked to Celia's parents first.

We went up to her room together. We knocked and entered. I expected to find her lying across the bed, my posture of teenage despair, but instead, she was sitting at the desk, staring into the computer.

"We've decided you can go, but we want to speak to her parents first."

She turned and grinned, bathed in computer glow, all the color gone from her pretty face and replaced with green.

"Is that Celia now?" Jack asked.

She nodded.

"Ask her for her number."

She began typing. I turned and walked away. What was I so creeped out about? This was the new world. My daughter and my husband were a part of it, as was I, even if with reluctance.

*

Jack spoke to Celia's father that night. It turned out they had
a lot in common too. He was an insurance salesman. His wife,
however, was very different from me, a lawyer out of town
until Friday night. Jack covered the mouthpiece. "He wants to
pick Steff up around 4:30 on Friday. He's going to be passing
through town. They'll pick Celia up at her dance class, and
Sarah will get home from D.C. about 5:30. He's spoken to her
and she's happy to have Stephanie over. What do you think?"

"How does he sound?"

"He sounds a lot like me."

Steff was standing in the kitchen doorway watching. I
wasn't used to her squinty-eyed appraisal, as if suddenly there
was something suspicious about me.

"Okay," I said.

Steff grinned. Jack took his hands off the mouthpiece.
"That'll work out fine," he said in a boisterous voice. They
really both looked so thrilled. Had I done this to them? Kept
them so sheltered that Stephanie's sleepover at a friend's house
on a Friday night, an absolutely normal occurrence for any girl
her age, was such an enormous event?

Was this all my fault?

He was right on time. It was a beautiful spring day, unseason-
ably warm. I found him immediately affable, friendly, grinning
dimples. I thought he looked younger than Jack or me, though
in reality he was a year older. I guess people without con-
sciences don't wrinkle like the rest of us. I opened the door
and we shook hands. He had a firm handshake, a bit sweaty,
but it was a warm day. Jack came out and the two of them got
to talking immediately. I slipped away to get Steff. I went to
her bedroom. Her backpack was packed, the sleeping bag
rolled next to it, but she was not in the room. I walked over to
the window and saw her in the garden, picking flowers. I
opened the window. She looked up and waved, the flowers in
her hand arcing the sky. I waved, pointed to his car. She nodded and ran toward the house. I brought the ridiculously heavy
backpack and sleeping bag downstairs. When I got to the
kitchen, she was standing there, her cheeks flushed, holding the
bouquet of daffodils and tulips while Jack and Celia's father
talked. I helped her wrap the stems in a wet paper towel and

aluminum foil. "This is a very nice idea," I whispered to her at the sink.

She smiled and shrugged. "Celia said her mom likes flowers too."

What was it about that that set off a little warning buzzer in my head? All these coincidences. I shook it back; after all, isn't that how friendships are made, by common interests? We turned and the fathers stopped talking. Celia's father grinned at Steff. Once more the alarm sounded but he bent down, picked up the pack, and said something like, What do kids put in these things, Celia's is always so heavy too. They walked to the door. I wanted to hug Stephanie but it seemed silly and probably would be embarrassing to her, and, after all, hadn't I already embarrassed her enough? The screen door banged shut. I stood in the kitchen and listened to the cheerful voices, the car doors slam, the engine, the sound of the gravel as they drove away. Too late, I ran out to wave goodbye. I have no idea if Steffie saw me or not.

Jack wrapped his arms around my waist, nuzzled my neck. "The garden? Kitchen? Name your place, baby."

"I should have told her to call when she gets there."

"Honey, she'll be back tomorrow."

"Let's call her, just to make sure she's comfortable."

"Chloe—"

"After we call her, the garden."

There was a sudden change in the weather. The temperature dropped thirty degrees. We closed windows and doors and put on sweaters and jeans. It began to rain about 5:30 and it just kept raining. We called at six, seven, eight. No one answered. It began to hail.

"Something's wrong," I said.

"They probably just went to a movie."

We called at nine. It rang and rang.

"I'm going there."

"What? Are you kidding? Do you have any idea how embarrassing that would be for her?"

"Well, where are they, Jack?"

"They went to a movie, or the mall, or out for pizza. Not everyone lives like us."

Ten. Still no answer.

I put on my coat.

"Where are you going?"

"Give me the directions."

"You can't be serious."

"Where are the directions?"

"Nothing's wrong."

"Jack!"

"I don't have any directions."

"What do you mean? How are we supposed to pick her up?"

"Turns out he's coming back this way tomorrow. He's going to drop her off."

Lightning split the sky and thunder shook the house. "Do you even have an address?"

"I'm sure everything's all right," he said, but he said it softly and I could hear the fear in his voice.

We called at 10:20, 10:30, 10:41, 10:50, 10:54. At last, at 10:59, a man's voice.

"Hello, this is Steffie's mother, is this—" I don't even know his name "—is this Celia's father?"

"I just picked up the phone, lady, ain't no one here."

"What do you mean? Who are you? Where is everyone?"

"This is just a phone booth, okay?"

I drop the phone. I run to the bathroom. In the distance I hear Jack's voice, he says the number and then he says, "Oh my God," and I don't hear the rest, over the sound of my retching.

Police sirens blood red. Blue uniforms and serious faces. Lights blaze. Pencils scratch across white pads. Jack wipes his hand through his hair, over and over again. Dry taste in my mouth. The smell of vomit. The questions. The descriptions. Fingerprint powder. I take them to her bedroom. Strange hands paw her things. Her diary. Someone turns her computer on. "Do you know her password?" I shake my head. "Well," says the man reading her diary, "it appears she really believed there was a Celia." What? Of course she did, can I see that? "Sorry, ma'am, it's evidence." Downstairs. More uniforms and raincoats. Police banter about the weather. Blazing lights. The telephone rings. Sudden silence. I run to answer it. "Hello."

It's Mrs. Bialo, my neighbor; she says, is everything all right?
No, it's not. I hang up the phone. The activity resumes. Suddenly I see a light like the tiny flicker of a hundred fireflies hov-
ering close to me and I hear her voice, *Mom?* I fall to my knees
sobbing. Jack rushes over and holds me like I'm breakable.
There is a temporary and slight change in the activity around
us but then it continues as before and goes on like this for
hours. In early morning there is a freak snowfall. We start getting calls from newspapers and magazines. A TV truck parks at
the end of our drive. My neighbor, Mrs. Bialo, shows up with
banana bread and starts making coffee. I stand on the porch
and watch the snow salting down. The red tulips droop
wounded against the icy white. The daffodils bow their silent
bells. I listen to the sound of falling snow. I haven't told anyone what I know. What would be the point? Who would believe
me? But I know. She's dead. She's dead. She's gone.

Let's go quickly over the details. The body. Oh, her body.
Found. The tests confirm. Raped and strangled. My little
darling.

Then, incredibly, he is found too. Trying to do the same thing
again but this time to a more savvy family. He even used the
name Celia. The sergeant tells me this with glee. "They always
think they're so clever, but they're not. They make mistakes."
How excited everybody is. They found him. He can't do it
again. This is good. But I don't feel happiness, which disap-
points everyone.
    Jack agrees to go on a talk show. They convince him he will
be helping other families and other little girls but really he's
there so everyone can feel superior. One lady stands up. She is
wearing a sensible dress and shoes. She is a sensible mother,
anyone can see that, and she says, "I just don't understand, in
this day and age, how you could let your daughter go off with
a stranger like that?" She says it like she really cares, but she
beams when the audience claps because really, she just wants
to make her point.
    Jack tries to say the stuff about how really everyone takes
chances when they send their children off to other homes. I

mean, we're all really strangers, he says. But they aren't buying it, this clever audience. The sensible lady stands up again and says, "I'm really sorry about what happened to your daughter but you gotta accept that it's at least partly your fault." There is scattered applause. The host tries to take it back. "I'm sure no one here means to imply this is your fault," he says, "we only want to learn from your mistakes." The audience applauds at that as well. Everyone gets applause except Jack.

After the taping he calls me in tears. I'm not much help as I am also feeling superior since I would never be so stupid as to fall for the "You're helping others" line the talk show people keep trying. He says it was terrible but on the day it airs, he insists we watch. It is terrible.

We move through the house and our lives. I think I will never eat again and then, one day, I do. I think I will never make love again and then, one night, something like that happens but it is so different, there is such a cold desperation to it, that I think it will never happen again, and it doesn't.

Six months later there is a trial. We are both witnesses for the prosecution so we can't attend. The defense attorney does a mean job on us but the prosecutor says, "He's just trying to distract the jury. It's not going to work. In fact, it'll probably backfire, generating more sympathy."

Fuck their sympathy, I say.

Jack looks as if I've just confirmed the worst rumors he's heard about me. The attorney maintains his placid expression, but his tone of voice is mildly scolding when he says, "The jury is your best hope now."

I think of her picking flowers in the garden that afternoon, the way she waved them in an arc across the sky.

When the verdict is read I stare at the back of his head. I think how, surely, if I had really studied him that day, instead of being so distracted by self-doubt, I never would have let him take her. The shape of his ears at the wrong height, the tilt of his head, something about his shoulders, all of it adds up. It's so obvious now.

"Guilty," the foreman says.

The courtroom is strangely quiet. Somehow, it is not enough.

*

When Jack and I get home he goes into his office. I wander about, until finally I settle on a plan. I take the fireside poker and walk up the stairs to her room where I smash the computer. When I'm done Jack is standing there, watching. "That's a very expensive machine," he says.

"Fuck you," I say.

It doesn't get any better. At the end of the month, he moves out.

Fat, white flakes fall all day. The pine trees are supplicant with snow. I sit in my rocking chair like an old woman, the blue throw across my lap. I thought about starting a fire with the well-seasoned wood left over from last winter but when I opened the stove and saw those ashes I didn't have the energy to clean them out. I rock and watch the snow fall. The house creaks with emptiness. The phone rings. I don't answer it. I fall asleep in the chair and when I wake it's dark. I walk to the kitchen, turn on the outside light. It's still snowing. I turn off the light and go to bed, not bothering to change out of my sweats and turtleneck. The phone rings and l grumble into the blankets but I don't answer it. I sleep what has become my usual restless sleep. In the morning it's still snowing.

Day after day it snows. Finally, the power goes out. The phone lines are down. I don't mind this at all. Oddly, I am invigorated by it. I shovel the wood-burning stove's ashes into an old paint can, find the wood carrier, and bring in stacks of wood and kindling. I build a fire and once I'm sure it's really started good, go upstairs and get my book, some blankets and pillows. I find the flashlights in the kitchen, both with working batteries, search through the linen closet and then the kitchen cupboards until I remember and find the portable radio on the top shelf in the basement. I stoke the fire, wrap myself in a blanket. How efficient we were, how well organized, how prepared for this sort of emergency, how completely useless, even culpable, when she needed us most. I turn on the radio. It will snow and snow, they say. We are having a blizzard. There are widespread reports of power outages. The Red Cross is setting up in the high school, which, actually, is also currently out of power so residents are advised to stay home for now. I click off the radio.

The phone is ringing.

"Hello?"

"Mom, where are you?"

"Steff? Steff?"

But there is no response. I stand there, holding the phone while the kitchen shadows lengthen around me. Still I stand there. I say her name over and over again. I don't know how long I stand there before I hang up but when I do, I'm a changed woman. If I can't keep her alive, and it's been all too obvious that I can't, I'll take her dead. Yes, I want this ghost.

The person you most love has died and is now trying to contact you. You are happy.

You do whatever you can to help. You go out in the middle of the worst blizzard on record since there has been a record and drive to town. A trip that usually takes ten minutes today takes an hour and a half and you are happy. You go to the local drugstore and walk right past the aisles stripped of batteries and Sterno cans and candles to the toy section where you select a Ouija board and tarot cards and you don't care when the clerk looks at you funny because you already have a strange reputation and who even cares about reputation when your dead daughter is trying to talk to you. You are not scared. You are excited. You know you probably should change your expression and look bored or disinterested as the clerk tallies up your purchases on a notepad because the cash register doesn't work due to the power outage and you probably should say something about buying this for your teenage niece but instead you stand there grinning with excitement. You sense the clerk, who looks to be a teenager herself, only a few years older than your dead daughter, watching you leave the store and walk through the storm to your truck, the only vehicle in the parking lot.

It takes even longer to get home and by the time you do the fire has gone out and the house is cold. You are too excited to stop everything to build another fire. Instead you set up the Ouija board on the kitchen table. The cat comes over to smell it. You light a candle. The cat rubs against your leg. You sit at the table. You rest your fingers lightly on the pointer. You remember this from when you were young. "Steff," you say, and the sound of it is both silly and wonderful in the silent house. As if, maybe, she's just in another room or something. "Steff, are you here?" You wait for the pointer to move. It does not. "Steff?" Suddenly the house is wild with light and sound. The kitchen blazes brightly, the refrigerator hums, the heater turns on. The phone rings. You push back the chair, stand, and bang your thigh against the table. The phone rings and rings. "Hello?"

"Mom?"

"Steff, Steff, is that you?"

The dial tone buzzes.

You slam the phone down. The cat races out of the room with her tail puffed up.

You turn to the Ouija board. The pointer rests over the word. Yes. You try to remember if you left it there but you don't think you did or maybe it got knocked there when you hit your leg but why are you trying to explain it when there is only one explanation for your dead daughter's voice on the phone? Slowly you turn and look at the silent phone. You pick up the receiver and listen to the dial tone.

You don't know whether to laugh or cry and suddenly your body is convulsing in some new emotion that seems to be a combination of both. You sink to the kitchen floor. The cat comes back into the room and lies down beside you. The dead can't make phone calls but the living can lose their minds. You decide you won't do that. You get up.

You try to believe it didn't happen.

But just in case, every time the phone rings, I answer it. I speak to an endless assortment of telemarketers wanting to sell me newspapers, a different phone service, offering me exciting opportunities to win trips to Florida, or the Bahamas. Jack calls about once a week and we generally have the same conversation. (I'm fine. He can't come back. I haven't forgiven him. I haven't forgiven myself. I don't expect to. Ever.) Once there is a call where no one speaks at all and I'm terrified to hang up the phone so I stand there saying hello, hello, and finally I say,

Steff? and there's a click and then the dial tone. Once, an old friend of mine from the city calls and I tell her all lies. How I've begun painting scenes of idyllic life again, how I've begun the healing process. I tell her the things people want me to say and by the end of the conversation she's happy she called and for a few minutes I feel happy too, as though everything I said was true.

I start receiving Christmas cards in the mail, strange greetings of Peace on Earth with scrawled condolences or blessings about this first Christmas without her. Jack calls in tears and tells me how much he misses her and us. I know, I know, I say gently, but you still can't come back. There is a long silence, then he hangs up.

I go into town only for groceries. I lose track of the days so completely that I end up in the supermarket on Christmas Eve. Happy shoppers load carts with turkeys and gift wrap and bottles of wine, bags of shrimp, crackers and cheese. I pick through the limp lettuce, the winter tomatoes. While I'm choosing apples I feel someone watching me and turn to see a teenage girl of maybe sixteen or seventeen standing by the bananas. There is something strange about the girl's penetrating stare beneath her homemade knit cap though it is not unusual to catch people staring at me; after all, I'm the mother of a dead girl. I grab a bag of apples. I wonder if she knew Steff. I turn to look over by the bananas but she's not there.

"I don't know if you remember me or not."

The girl stands at my elbow. The brown knit cap is pulled low over her brow with wisps of brown hair sticking out. She has dark brown eyes, lashed with black. She might be pretty.

"I waited on you during the first storm at Walker's drugstore."

I nod, at a loss at what to say to this strange, staring girl.

She leans close to me. I smell bubblegum, peppermint, and something faintly sour. "I can help," she whispers.

"Excuse me?"

She looks around, in a dramatic way, as if we are sharing state secrets, licks her chapped lips and leans close again. "I know how to talk to dead people. You know, like in that movie. I'm like that kid." She leans back and looks at me with those dark, sad eyes and then scans the room as if frightened of the living. "My name is Maggie Dwinder. I'm in the book." She nods abruptly and walks away. I watch her in her old wool coat, a brown knit scarf trailing down her back like a snake.

"Oh, how are you doing, dear?"

This face sends me back to that day. Snow on tulips. My daughter's death. "Mrs. Bialo, I never thanked you for coming over that morning."

She pats my arm. One of her fingernails is black, the others are lined with dirt. "Don't mention it, dear. I should of made a effort long before. I wouldn't bother you now, except I noticed you was talking to the Dwinder girl."

I nod.

"There's something wrong with that child, her parents are all so upset about it, her father being a reverend and all. Anyhow, I hope she didn't upset you none."

"Oh no," I lie, "we were just talking about apple pie."

My neighbor studies me closely and I can imagine her reporting her findings to the ladies at the checkout, how I am so strange. I'm glad I lied to the old snoop, and feel unreasonably proud that in this small way I may have protected the girl. It doesn't take a Jungian analyst to figure it out. It felt good to protect the girl.

It's the coldest, snowiest winter on record and Christmas morning is no different. The windchill factor is ten below and it's snowing. I stack wood into the carrier, the icy snow stinging my face. My wood supply is rapidly dwindling but I dread trying to buy more wood now, during the coldest winter anyone can remember. I can just imagine the bantering, "Lady, you want wood? Seasoned wood?" Or the pity, "Is this, are you, I'm so sorry, we're out of wood to sell but wait, we'll bring you ours." Or the insult, "What? You want me to bring it where? Not after what you did to that girl, they should have put you in jail for child neglect, letting her leave like that with a stranger." Head bent against the bitter chill, both real and imagined, I carry the wood inside.

There is nothing like that feeling of coming into a warm house from the cold. I turn on the classical music station, make a fire, fill the teakettle, and put it on the kitchen stove. The radio is playing Handel's *Messiah*, the teakettle rattles softly on the burner, the cat curls up on the braided rug. I wrap my arms around myself and watch the snow swirl outside the window. Inexplicably, it stops as suddenly as if turned off by a switch. The sun comes out, the yard sparkles, and I realize I'm happy. The teakettle whistles. I turn to take it off the burner, search through the cupboard for the box of green tea. I wrap the teabag string around the teapot handle, pour the hot water. If we never got that stupid computer, if we never (stupidly) let her go with him, how different this morning would be, scented by pine and punctuated with laughter, the tear of wrapping paper and litter of ribbons and bows. I turn, teapot in hand, to the kitchen table and see that the storm has returned to its full vigor, the crystallized scene obliterated. As it should be. In my grief this stormy winter has been perfect.

I find my strange Christmas perfect too. I make a vegetable soup and leave it to simmer on the stove. The radio station plays beautiful music. All day the weather volleys between winter wonderland and wild storm. I bring out the old photo albums and page through the imperfect memories, her smile but not her laughter, her face but not her breath, her skin but not her touch. I rock and weep. Outside, the storm rages. This is how I spend the first Christmas without her, crying, napping, in fits of peace and rage.

I go to bed early and for the first time since she died, sleep through the night. In the morning, a bright winter sun is reflected a thousand times in the thick ice that coats the branches outside my bedroom window and hangs from the eaves like daggers. The phone rings.

"Hello?"

"Mom?"

"Steff, talk to me, what do you want?"

"Maggie Dwinder."

"What?"

But there is no answer, only a dial tone.

I tear up half the house looking for the local phone book, searching through drawers and cupboards, until at last I find it in Jack's old office on the middle of the otherwise empty desk. Jack used to sit here in a chaos of papers and folders, a pencil tucked behind his ear, the computer screen undulating with a swirl of colored tubes that broke apart and reassembled over and over again. I bring the phone book to the kitchen where I page through to the Ds and find, Dwinder, Reverend John, and Nancy. My hand is shaking when I dial.

"Hello," a cheerful voice answers on the first ring.

"Hello, is Maggie there?"

"Speaking."

"Maggie, I spoke to you on Christmas Eve, at the grocery store."

"Uh-huh?"

"You said you could help me."

"I'm not sure I, oh." The voice drops to a serious tone. "I've been expecting you to call. She really has something important to tell you." While I absorb this, she adds, "I'm really sorry about what happened." Her voice changes to a cheerful tone, "Really? All of it? That's great!"

"I'm sorry I—"

"No way! Everything?"

"Maggie, are you afraid of being overheard?"

"That's the truth."

"Maybe you should come over here."

"Okay, when?"

"Can you come now?"

"Yeah, I have to do the dishes and then I can come over."

"Do you know where I live?"

"Doesn't everybody?"

"Can you get here or should I . . ."

"No. I'll be over as soon as I can."

She took so long to arrive that I started watching for her at the window. In the midst of more bad weather, I saw the dark figure walking up the road. At first, even though I knew she was coming, I had the ridiculous notion that it was Steffie's ghost, but as she got closer, I recognized the old wool coat, the brown knit hat and scarf crusted with snow. She walked carefully, her head bent with the wind, her hands thrust in her pockets, her narrow shoulders hunched against the chill, her snow-crusted jeans tucked into old boots, the kind with buckles. I asked myself how this rag doll was going to help me, then opened the door for her. For a moment she stood there, as if considering turning back, then she nodded and stepped inside.

"You must be freezing. Please, take off your coat."

She whipped off the knit hat and revealed straight, brown hair that fell to her shoulders as she unwrapped the long, wet scarf, unbuttoned her coat (still wearing her gloves, one blue, the other black). I took her things. She sat to unbuckle her boots, while I hung her things in the hall closet. When I returned, she sat at the kitchen table, hunched over in a white sweatshirt. It occurred to me that she might fit into one of Steffie's baggier sweaters but I offered her one of mine instead. She shook her head and said (as she shivered), "No thanks, I'm warm enough."

"Do you want some tea?" She shrugged, then shook her head. "Hot chocolate?"

She looked up and smiled. "Yes, please." I opened the refrigerator, took out the milk. "I like your house. It's not at all like I heard."

I pour the milk into the pan. "What did you hear?"

"Oh, different stuff."

I set the pan on the burner and start opening cupboards, looking for the chocolate bars from last winter.

"Some people say you're a witch."

This is a new one and I'm so startled by it that I bang my head on the shelf. I touch the sore spot and turn to look at her.

"Of course I don't believe it," she says. "I think of you more as a Mother Nature type."

I find the chocolate and drop two bars in with the milk.

"I never saw anyone make it like this before. We always just add water."

"We used to make real whipped cream for it too."

"Of course I wouldn't care if you was, 'cause, you know, I sort of am."

"Excuse me?"

"Well, you know, like, I told you, dead people talk to me."

I stir the milk to just below a boil then pour two mugs full. There is a temporary break in the weather. Sun streams across the kitchen table. I hand the little witch her mug. She holds it with both hands, sniffs it, and smiles.

"You don't look like a witch."

She shrugs. "Well, who knows?"

I sit across from her with my own mug of hot chocolate. Yes. Who knows? All I know is that Steffie told me she wanted Maggie Dwinder. So here she is, sipping hot chocolate in my kitchen, and I'm not sure what I'm supposed to do with her.

As if sensing my inquiry, she stops sipping and looks at me over the rim of the cup. "She wants to come back."

"Come back?"

"She misses you, and she misses it here." She slowly lowers the cup, sets it on the table. "But there's a problem. A couple problems, actually. She can't stay, of course. She can only be here for a little while and then she has to go back."

"No she doesn't."

"She's been gone a long time."

"You don't have to tell me that."

She bites her chapped lips.

"I'm sorry. This isn't easy for me."

"Yeah. Anyway, she can't stay. I'm sorry too, but that's the way it is. Those are the rules and, also . . ."

"Yes?"

"I don't think you're going to like this part."

"Please tell me."

She looks up at me and then down at the table. "The thing is, she doesn't want to stay here anyway, she sort of likes it where she is."

"Being dead?"

Maggie shrugs and attempts a feeble smile. "Well, you could say that's her life now."

I push back from the table, my chair scraping across the floor. "Is that supposed to be funny?" Maggie shrinks at my voice. "Why?"

"I don't know," she says, softly. "Maybe she figures she sort of belongs there now."

"When?"

"What?"

"When does she want to come?"

"That's why she talked to me. 'Cause she said you've been really upset and all but she wonders if you can wait until spring?"

"Spring?"

"Yeah. She wants to come in the spring. If it's okay with you." Maggie watches me closely as I consider this imperfect offer, my daughter returned but only borrowed from the dead. What rational response can there be? Life is composed of large faiths, in the series of beliefs that sustain us, we little humans whose very existence is a borrowing from the dead. I look into Maggie's brown eyes, I fall into them and feel as if I'm being pulled into the earth. All this, as we sit at the kitchen table, a world done and undone, a life given and taken. "Yes," I say. "Tell her spring will be fine."

We are like one of my paintings. Small, in a vast landscape. The snow glistens outside. We are not cold, or hungry, or anything but this, two figures through a lit window, waiting.

Maggie and I became friends of sorts. She liked to sit in the kitchen and chat over hot chocolate about her school day. (Most of her classmates, and all her teachers were "boring.") The cat liked to sit in her lap.

There were no more phone calls from Stephanie. "Don't worry about that," Maggie reassured me, "she'll be here soon enough and you can really talk."

It was the worst winter on record. Maggie said that the students were really "pissed" because they would have to make up days in June.

I grew to look forward to her visits. Eventually we got to talking about painting and she showed me some of her sketches, the ones assigned by the art teacher: boxes, shoes, books, and the ones she drew from her imagination: vampires and shadowed, winged figures, pictures that might have warned me were I not spending my days painting girls picking flowers, with dark figures descending on them. I thought Maggie was wise. She understood and accepted the way the world is, full of death and sorrow. This did not seem to affect her happiness. On the contrary, she seemed to be blossoming, losing the tired, haggard look she had when I first met her. I mentioned this to her one day over hot chocolate and she opened her mouth, then bit her lip and nodded.

"What were you going to say?"

"I don't know if I should."

"No, go ahead."

"It was your daughter."

"What was my daughter?"

"She was wearing me out. I know she wasn't meaning to but it's like she was haunting me ever since she, I mean, she wouldn't leave me alone."

"That doesn't sound like Steffie."

"Yeah, well, I guess people change when they're, you know, dead."

I nod.

"Anyway, it stopped once I talked to you. I guess she just wanted to make sure you got the message."

I remember that time as being almost joyful. What a relief it was to think of our separation as temporary, that she would return to me as she had been before she left, carrying flowers, her cheeks flushed, her eyes bright with happiness.

I got the phone call on a Tuesday afternoon. I remember this so clearly because I marked it with a big, black X on the calendar, and also, that day, though it was already April, there was another storm, so sudden that six motorists were killed in a four-car pileup, one of them a teenage boy. But that was later, after Maggie's parents left.

Maggie's mother calls in the morning, introduces herself, and says that she and her husband want to talk to me, could they stop by for a visit.

How can I refuse them? They are Maggie's parents and I'm sure concerned and curious about this adult she is spending so much time with. Nancy, Maggie's mother, sounds nice enough on the phone. When they arrive an hour later, I think I could like her and, to my surprise, the reverend too.

She has a wide, pleasant face, lightly freckled, red hair the color of certain autumn leaves, and hazel eyes that measure me with a cool but kind mother-to-mother look. She wears a long, dark wool skirt, boots, and a red sweater.

Her husband has a firm handshake and kind, brown eyes. His hair is dark and curly, a little long about the ears. He has a neatly trimmed beard and mustache. I am immediately disturbed and surprised to find myself somewhat attracted to him. He wears blue jeans, and a green sweater that looks homemade and often worn.

They sit side by side on the couch. I sit in the rocker. A pot of tea cools on the table between us, three cups and saucers on the tray beside it. "Would you like some tea?"

Nancy glances at her husband and he nods. "Thank you," he says, "allow me." He reaches over and pours tea for the three of us. I find this simple gesture comforting. How long it has been since anyone has done anything for me.

"I have to thank you," I say, "you've been so kind about allowing Maggie to visit and her company has been much appreciated."

They nod in unison. Then both begin to speak. With a nod from his wife, the reverend continues.

"I feel I owe you an apology. I should have visited you much sooner and then, perhaps, none of this would have happened." He laughs one of those rueful laughs I was always reading about. "What I mean to say is, I should have offered you my services when you were suffering but I thought that you probably had more spiritual assistance than you knew what to do with." He looks at me hopefully.

But I cannot offer him that redemption. Oddly, there had been no one. Oh, many letters offering prayers, and accusations, and a couple Bibles mailed to the house, but no one stood and held my hand, so to speak, spiritually. There was something distasteful about my involvement in Steffie's horrible death; no one wanted any part of it.

He looks into his teacup and sighs.

"We're sorry," Nancy says in a clear, steady voice. "We've been involved with our own problems and because of that it seems we haven't always made the right choices. It's affected our judgement."

"Please, don't worry about it. You're kind to come now."

The reverend sets his cup on the table. "We're here about Maggie."

"She's a lovely girl."

Nancy sets her cup and saucer on the table, licks her lips. I smile at the gesture, so reminiscent of her daughter. "We thought, well, we want you to understand, we hope you understand, that we thought you, being an artist, and Maggie, being so creative. . . ."

The reverend continues. "We prayed and pondered, and thought maybe you two would be good for each other."

"We made the choice to let her be with you for both your sakes."

"Certainly we had no idea."

"Oh, no idea at all."

Suddenly I feel so cold. I sit in the rocking chair and look at the two of them with their earnest faces. I want them to leave. I don't understand yet what they've come to say, but I know I don't want to hear it.

The reverend looks at me with those beautiful eyes and shakes his head. "We're sorry."

Nancy leans forward and reaches as though to pat me on the knee but the reach is short and she brushes air instead. "It's not her fault. It's just the way she is. We only hope you can find it in your heart to forgive her."

The reverend nods. "We know what we're asking here, a woman like you, who has so much to forgive already."

My hands are shaking when I set my teacup down. "I don't know what you're talking about."

The reverend just looks at me with sorrowful eyes. Nancy nods, bites her lower lip, and says, "We know what she's been telling you," she says. "We found her diary."

I open my mouth. She raises her hand. "I know, I would have thought the same thing. It's horrible to read your child's diary, but I did, and I don't regret it." She glances at her husband who does not return the look. "How else can a mother know? They're so secretive at this age. And I was right. After all, look what she's been doing."

I look from her to the reverend. "We know, we can guess how tempting it's been for you to believe her," he says.

"She's ill, really ill."

"We knew this even before—"

"I read her diary."

"But we never thought she—"

"How could we? We hope you understand, she's mentally ill. She didn't mean to cause you pain."

The cold moves through me. Why are they here with their petty family squabbles? So she read her daughter's diary, while I, imperfect mother, never even looked for Steffie's, or had any idea what her e-mail address was. Why are they here apologizing for their living daughter? Why do I care? "I'm not sure I—"

"There's also a scrapbook. If I would have known, if we would have known—"

"A scrapbook?"

The reverend clears his throat. "She was obsessed with your daughter's death. I try to understand it, but God help me, I don't. She saved every article—"

"Every picture."

I imagine Maggie cutting up newspapers, gluing the stories into a red scrapbook, the kind I had as a girl. "It's all right," I say, though I'm not sure that it is. "A lot of people were fascinated by it." I imagine myself on an iceberg, drifting into the deep, cold blue.

The reverend opens his mouth but Nancy speaks, like a shout from the unwanted shore. "You don't understand. We know what she's been telling you, about your daughter coming back, and of course, we hope you realize it's all made up."

There. The words spoken. I close my eyes. The ice in my blood crashes like glass. The reverend's voice whispers from the distance. "We're sorry. It must have been tempting to believe her—"

"She called me. I spoke to her."

He shakes his head. "It was Maggie."

"A mother knows her daughter's voice."

"But you were so upset, right? And she never said much, did she? And in your state—"

"Nancy," the reverend says gently.

The room is filled with sad silence. I can't look at either of them. How stupid I have been, how unbearably stupid. I see the reverend's legs, and then his wife's, unbending.

The world is ending, I think, all darkness and ice, like the poem.

"We should leave," says the reverend.

I watch the legs cross the room. Listen to the closet door, the rattle of hangars. Whispering. "We're sorry," says Nancy. Footsteps in the kitchen. Door opened. "Snow!" Closed.

All darkness and despair. The greatest loneliness. A shattering. Ice. Who knows how long until at last I throw the cups across the room, the teapot, still full. Brown tea bleeds down the wall. I scream and weep into darkness. Now I know what waits at world's end. Rage is what fills the emptiness. Rage, and it is cold.

How we suffer, we humans. Pain and joy but always pain again. How do we do this? Why? Some small part of me still waits for spring. Just to be sure. I know it is absurd, but the rational knowing does not change the irrational hope.

I figured Maggie's parents had told her that they talked to me. I couldn't imagine she would want to face my wrath, though she couldn't know that I didn't even have the energy for anger anymore. Instead I felt a tired sorrow, a weariness with life. She did come, in the midst of a downpour, knocking on my door after school, wearing a yellow slicker. I finally opened the door just a crack and peered out at her, drenched like a stray dog, her hair hanging dark in her face, her lashes beaded with water.

"Go home, Maggie."

"Please. You have to talk to me."

She is crying and snot drips from her nose toward her mouth. She wipes it with the back of her hand, sniffing loudly.

I simply do not know what to say. I close the door.

"You were the only one who ever believed me!" she shouts.

Later, when I look out the window, she is gone, as if I imagined her, made her up out of all my pain.

I decide to sell the house though I don't do anything about it. I sleep day and night. One day I realize I haven't seen the cat for a long while. I walk around whistling and calling her name but she doesn't appear. I sit at the kitchen table and stare out the window until gradually I realize I'm looking at spring. Green grass, leaves, tulip and daffodil blooms thrust through the wreck of the garden. Spring. I open windows and doors. Birds twitter in branches. Squirrels scurry across the lawn. Almost a year since we lost her. Gone. My little darling.

Then I see someone, is it, no, in the garden, picking daffodils, her long, dark hair tied with a weedy-looking thing, wearing the dress she had on last year, tattered and torn, my daughter, my ghost.

"Stephanie!" I call.

She turns and looks at me. Yes. It is her face but changed, with a sharpness to it I had not foreseen. She smiles, raises her arm and sweeps the sky with flowers and I am running down the steps and she is running through the garden calling, "Mom, Mom, Mom!" I think when I touch her she will disappear but she doesn't, though she flinches and squirms from the hug. "You can't hold me so close anymore," she says.

So I hold her gently, like the fragile thing she is, and I'm weeping and she's laughing and somehow, with nimble fingers she braids the bouquet into a crown which she sets on my head. She covers my face with kisses, so soft I'm sure I'm imagining all of it but I don't care anyway. I never want to wake up or snap out of it. I want to be with her always. "Steffie, Steffie, Steffie, I've missed you so much."

She has bags under her eyes and her skin is pale and cold. She stares at me, unsmiling, then reaches up, takes the crown from my head and places it on her own. "You've changed a lot." She turns and looks at the yard. "Everything has."

"It's been a hard year," I say to her narrow back and bony elbows. She looks like such a little orphan, so motherless standing there in that dirty dress. I'll make her something new, something pretty. She turns and looks at me with an expression like none I'd ever seen on her in her lifetime, a hate-filled face, angry and sharp. "Steff, honey, what is it?"

"Don't. Tell. Me. How hard. This year. Has been."

"Oh sweetie," I reach for her but she pulls back.

"I told you. Don't touch me."

"At all?"

"I'm the queen," she says. "Don't touch me unless I touch you first."

I don't argue or disagree. The queen, my daughter, even in death maintains that imagination I so highly prize. When I ask her if she is hungry she says, "I only ate one thing the whole time I was gone." I feel this surge of anger. What kind of place is this death? She doesn't want to come inside while I make the sandwiches and I'm afraid she'll be gone when I come out with the tray, but she isn't. We have a picnic under the apple tree which is in white bloom and buzzing with flies, then she falls asleep on the blanket beside me and, to my surprise, I fall asleep too.

I wake, cold and shivering, already mourning the passing dream. I reach to wrap the picnic blanket around me and my hand touches her. Real. Here. My daughter, sleeping.

"I told you not to touch me."

"I'm sorry. Honey, are you cold?"

She rolls over and looks up at me. "You do realize I'm dead?"

"Yes."

She sets the wilted crown back on her head and surveys the yard. "You really let everything go to shit around here, didn't you?"

"Stephanie!"

"What?"

Really, what? How to be the mother of a dead girl? We sit on the blanket and stare at each other. What she is thinking, I don't know. I'm surprised, in the midst of this momentous happiness, to feel a sadness, a certain grief for the girl I knew who, I guess, was lost somewhere at the border of death. Then she sighs, a great old sigh.

"Mom?" she says, in her little girl voice.

"Yes, honey?"

"It's good to be back."

"It's good to have you here."

"But I can't stay."

"How long?"

She shrugs.

"Is it horrible there?"

She looks at me, her face going through some imperceptible change that brings more harshness to it. "Don't ask the dead."

"What?"

"Don't ask questions you don't want the answer to."

"Just stay. Don't go back."

She stands up. "It doesn't work like that."

"We could—"

"No, don't act like you know anything about it. You don't."

I roll up the blanket, pick up the tray. We walk to the house together beneath the purple-tinged sky. When we get to the door she hesitates. "What's wrong?" She looks at me with wide, frightened eyes. "Steff, what is it?" Wordlessly, she steps inside. I flick on the kitchen light. "Are you hungry?"

She nods.

The refrigerator is nearly empty so I rummage through cupboards and find some spaghetti and a jar of sauce. I fill a pan with water and set it on the stove.

"Is Dad coming back?"

"Would you like to see him?"

She shakes her head vigorously, no.

"Steff, don't be mad at him, he didn't know—"

"Well, he really fucked up."

I bite my lip, check the water. Where is my little girl? I turn and look at her. She is walking around the kitchen, lightly brushing her hand against the wall, a strange, unlovely creature, her hair still knotted with a weed, crowned with wilted daffodils.

"Do you want to talk about it, what happened to you?"

She stops, the tips of her fingers light against the wall, then continues walking around the room, humming softly.

I take this to be a no. I make spaghetti for six and she eats all of it, my ravenous ghost child. What is this feeling? Here is my dead daughter, cold and unkind and difficult and so different from the girl she used to be that only now do I finally accept that Stephanie is gone forever, even as she sits before me, slurping spaghetti, the red sauce blooding her lips.

The dead move in secrets, more wingless than the living, bound by some weight; the memory of life, the impossible things? Dead bones grow and hair and fingernails too. Everything grows but it grows with death. The dead laugh and cry and plant flowers that they pick too soon. The dead do not care about keeping gardens in blossom.

Dead daughters don't wear socks or shoes and they won't go into old bedrooms unless you beg and coax and then you see immediately how they were right all along. Dead daughters have little in common with the living ones. They are more like sisters than the same girl and you realize, just as you miss the daughter you've lost, so does the dead girl miss, really miss, the one she was.

The dead pick up paint brushes and suddenly their hands move like rag dolls and they splatter paint, not like Jackson Pollack, or even a kindergartner. All the paint turns brown on the paintbrush and drips across the canvas or floor or wall, until they, helpless, throw it to the ground.

All the dead can do is wander. You walk for hours with your dead daughter pacing the yard she will not (cannot?) leave. She picks all the flowers and drops them in her step. She sleeps suddenly for hours, and then does not sleep for days. She exhausts you. The days and nights whirl. The last time you felt like this was when she was an infant.

One day, as you sit at the kitchen table, watching her tearing flowers from the garden in the new dress you made that already hangs raglike and dirty around her, you think of Maggie Dwinder and you realize you miss her. You put your face in your hands. What have you done?

"What's wrong with you?"

You would like to believe that she asks because she cares but you don't think that's true. Something vital in her was lost forever. Was this what happened at death or was it because of how she died? You accept you'll never know. She refuses to talk about it, and really, what would be the point? You look at her, weedy, dirty, wearing that brittle crown. "Maggie Dwinder," you say.

"As good as dead."

"What?"

She rolls her eyes.

"Don't you roll your eyes at me, young lady."

"Mother, you don't know anything about it."

"She's your friend, and mine. She told me you would come. She suffered for it."

"Oh, big deal, mommy and daddy watch her very closely. She has to go see the psychiatrist. She doesn't have any friends. Big fucking deal. What a hard life!"

"Steff."

"Don't tell me about suffering. I know about suffering."

"Steff, honey—"

"Everyone said it was a mistake for me to come back here. They said you wouldn't like me anymore."

"Honey, that's not true. I love you."

"You love who I used to be, not who I am now."

"Well, you're dead."

"Like it's my fault."

The dead are jealous, jealous, jealous and they will do anything to keep you from the living, the lucky living. They will argue with you, and distract you, and if that doesn't work, they will even let you hug them, and dance for you, and kiss you, and laugh, anything to keep you. The dead are selfish. Jealous. Lonely. Desperate. Hungry.

It isn't until she brings you a flower, dead for weeks, and hands it to you with that poor smile, that you again remember the living. "I have to call Maggie."

"Forget about her."

"No, I have to tell her."

"Look at me, Mommy."

"Sweetheart."

"Look what you did."

"It wasn't me."

She walks away.

"It wasn't."

She keeps walking.

You follow. Of course, you follow.

The phone rings. Such a startling noise. I roll into my blankets. Simultaneously I realize the night was cool enough for blankets and that the phone didn't ring all summer. I reach for it, fumbling across the bedside table, and knock off the photograph from Steff's last birthday.

"Hello?"

"See you next spring."

"Steff? Where are you?"

There is only a dial tone. I hang up the phone. Throw off the covers. "Steff!" I call. "Steff!" I look in her bedroom but she's not there. I run down the stairs and through the house, calling her name. The blue throw is bunched up on the couch, as if she'd sat there for a while, wrapped up in it, but she's not there now. I run outside, the grass cold against my feet. "Steff! Steff!" She is not in the garden, or the studio. She is not in the yard. A bird cries and I look up through the apple tree branches. One misshapen apple drops while I stand there, shivering in my nightgown. Everything is tinged with brown, except the leaves of the old oak which are a brilliant red.

A squirrel scurries past. There is a gentle breeze and one red leaf falls. I wrap my arms around myself and walk into the house, fill the teakettle, set it on the burner to boil. I sit at the kitchen table and stare at the garden. I should plant some bulbs. Order firewood. Arrange to have the driveway plowed when it snows. The teakettle whistles. I walk across the cool floor, pour the water into the pot. I leave it to steep and go to the living room where she left the blue throw all balled up. I pick it up and wrap it around myself. It smells like her, musty, sour.

It smells like Maggie too, last Christmas Eve when she spoke to me in the supermarket. What a risk that was for her. Who knows, I might have been like Mrs. Bialo, or her parents; I might have laughed at her. Instead, I became her friend and then cast her aside at the first sign of trouble.

How many chances do we get? With love? How many times do we wreck it before it's gone?

I don't even drink the tea but dress in a rush. All my clothes are too big on me and I see in the mirror how tired I look, how much new gray is in my hair. Yet, there's something else, a sort of glow, a happiness. I miss her, the one who died, and her ghost is my responsibility, a relationship based on who we lost, while Maggie is a friend, a relationship based on what we found.

All summer I only left for groceries. Stephanie would stand at the top of the driveway, watching me with those cold, narrow eyes as if suspicious I wouldn't come back. Out of habit I look in the rearview mirror, but all I see is a patch of brown grass, the edge of the house.

It's easy to find the Dwinder residence. They live right next to the church in a brick house with red geraniums dropping teardrop-shaped petals onto the porch. I ring the bell. Nancy answers, in a pink terry cloth robe.

"I'm sorry, I forgot how early it is."

She brushes a hand through her red hair. "That's all right. We were getting ready for church."

"There's something I have to tell Maggie. Is she home?"

"I don't know if that's such a good idea."

"Honey, who is it?" The reverend comes to the door in plaid flannel pants and a T-shirt, his dark hair tousled, his face wrinkled with sleep. "Oh. Chloe, how are you?"

"I'm sorry to disturb you, it's just—"

"She wants to talk to Maggie."

"I'll tell her you're here." The reverend turns back into the house.

Nancy continues to stare at me, then, just as I hear Maggie saying, What does she want? she blurts, "She's been better since she's stopped seeing you." I'm not sure if this is meant as an accusation or an apology and before I can find out, Maggie comes to the door dressed in torn jeans and a violet T-shirt, her hair in braids. She meets my gaze with those dark eyes.

"Coffee's ready!" the reverend calls and Nancy turns away, her pink-robed figure receding slowly down the hall.

"Yeah?"

"I was hoping, if you can forgive me, I was hoping we could be friends again."

"I can't be her replacement, you know."

"I know."

"You hurt me a lot."

"I know. I'm sorry. Can you ever forgive me?"

She frowns, squints, then tilts her head slightly, and looks up at me. "I guess."

"Please. Stop by. Any time. Like you used to."

She nods and shuts the door gently in my face.

On a sunny but cold day, as the last crimson leaves flutter to earth, and apples turn to cider on the ground, I shovel last winter's ash onto the garden. A flock of geese flies overhead. I shade my eyes to watch them pass and when I look down again, she is standing there in baggy jeans and an old blue pea coat, unbuttoned in the sun.

It's as though I've been living in one of those glass domes and it's been shaking for a long time, but in this moment, has stopped, and after all that flurry and unsettling, there is a kind of peace. "Maggie."

For a moment we only look at each other, then she puts her hand on her hip, rolls her eyes, and says, "You wouldn't believe what they're making us do in gym, square dancing!"

All life is death. You don't fool yourself about this anymore. You slash at the perfect canvas with strokes of paint and replace the perfect picture of your imagination with the reality of what you are capable of. From death, and sorrow, and compromise, you create. This is what it means, you finally realize, to be alive.

You try to explain this to Maggie. You hear yourself talking about bitter seeds, and sweet fruit. She nods and doesn't interrupt but you know you have not successfully communicated it. This is all right. The grief is so large you're not sure you want her, or anyone, to understand it, though you wish you could describe this other emotion.

You stand in the ash of your garden. All this time you didn't realize what you'd been deciding. Now you are crying, because with the realization of the question comes the answer. It is snowing and white flakes fall onto the garden, sticking to the brown stems and broken flowers, melting into the ash. You look up to the sunless white sky. Cold snow tips your face and neck. You close your eyes, and think, yes. Oh, life. Yes.

2003

BRIAN EVENSON
(b. 1966)

The Wavering Knife

I. Theoria

DESPITE the unfortunate and increasingly serious illness of my benefactor, I continued to work without cease or rest to salvage my analysis of the Gengli oeuvre. The image of the wavering knife, which I had for years perceived as the unifier and ultimate hingepiece of Eva Gengli's philosophy, had, under the severe scrutiny made possible by her private papers, collapsed, and I could discover no adequate trope to stand in its stead. Indeed, Eva Gengli's private papers had led me to realize with an alarming degree of clarity that the Gengli philosophy was exceedingly more complex than I had first imagined.

In deference to my benefactor and his declining health, while he was still alive I told him little and in fact nothing of my difficulties. Instead, I continued to serve him as I had before, though hurrying through my assigned tasks so as to spend more time each day with the Gengli papers. Even when I was with my benefactor—undressing him for bed, rubbing his now inadequate legs, reading to him, conversing with him, feeding him, arranging his pillows, undressing him for the night, steadying his walker, propelling him down the hall, preparing his morning meal, reading at him, dressing him for the day, bathing him, preparing his noon meal, ignoring him, preparing his evening meal, straightening the dust ruffle—I was hardly with him at all. Rather, I was with his "lover" (his claim) Eva Gengli's papers, making the most incisive of critical judgements, examining, to give one instance, two versions of Eva Gengli's "Aphorism on Aesthetics," considering which, if either, she meant to be definitive:

> *The ten fingers of the pianist compose the two hands of the lover.*

or (as marked over in a hand I could not be absolutely certain belonged to Eva Gengli)

> *The ten fingers of the pianist compose the two hands of the strangler.*

The multiple versions of Eva Gengli's philosophical texts raised difficult questions, made even more difficult by the sense I was gaining that Eva Gengli appeared to regard traditional philosophy as a sort of second-rate game, a game she played well but claimed to have no real stake in. As a result, the philosophical statements she offered were not only variously versioned but were likely to be called into question by what she saw as her more memorable work in film and prose. Nonetheless, I had managed to maintain a firm belief, despite Eva Gengli's own statements, that her philosophical statements were what were genuinely serious.

Admittedly, my task—that of how to salvage and give acclaim to the philosophy while at the same time remaining not unfaithful to Eva Gengli's larger project—had become exceptionally complicated. Since any choice about how to consider an individual philosophical statement first would influence my view of the remainder of the Gengli philosophy and second would demand a continual repositioning in regard to all her work, I was constantly in a state of unease and distress. Worse, rather than establishing a new pattern, each newly considered moment of her philosophy seemed to call into question the hint of pattern I had begun to theorize. Soon I was left only with the trope of the wavering knife and then, as my analysis progressed further, with nothing at all.

I was distracted and despondent for weeks, and grew even more so upon discovering that my benefactor's condition had worsened. The palsification of his body and the dark slur of his speech had grown extreme and could no longer be arrested or corrected by the pharmaceuticals that had lasted us in good stead through the first months of my research. Indeed, my benefactor shook so utterly he could in his worst times no longer raise his hands to his mouth, which meant I had to feed him and even hold his hands and head steady. He could not bear to be left long alone, for alone, he claimed, his condition worsened. He wanted me to stay with him more often, for the severity of the palsy made it difficult and sometimes impossible for him to rest in his bed or in his chair without slipping out, and he would not tolerate the obvious solution of allowing me to strap him in place.

In the seventh month of my analysis, my benefactor's condition had so decayed that he was asking me to drive him again the six hours to his "specialist" (as he referred to his doctor), who, he claimed, would provide the medicines that were sure to make of him "a new man." I was, I must admit, reluctant. It would be a day wasted, I knew, a day that might have in large part been spent in the company of Eva Gengli's papers, trying to unravel from her thought the thread that would allow the unification of her philosophy that I desired. To be away for as long as a day would cause me to lose critical concentration, and to reestablish it again might take weeks. Nor could I envision leaving the Gengli papers unattended, for the house was an old one and could easily be subject to fire and all other manner of calamity, and there were no fire-proof or flood-proof devices that might serve to protect the papers. Worse, the papers could be stolen—for I was far from being the only scholar with an interest in Eva Gengli (though I was the only one to give her philosophy its proper due). There were other scholars who were not as scrupulous as I, who might try to gain access to the papers by dishonest rather than honest means. There were even those who might try to destroy the philosophic papers on the grounds that they obscured the literary work. We could not leave the Gengli papers unattended, I told my benefactor, for to do so would be to shirk all responsibility to philosophy.

At first my benefactor was rather incensed, though gradually he calmed himself enough to set about trying to coerce me to fulfill his will. Immediately seeing through this, I covered my ears and considered the Gengli manuscripts further in my mind, focussing on the tricky problem of "a topography of desire" being substituted for "a trajectory of desire" in the "Flesh" aphorism to describe the intercourse of the mind with the body. The manuscripts made a case for both, my own philosophical bent being better supported if I could discard both statements and think of the mind and body differently. I was thus hoping to discover evidence that the "Flesh" aphorisms had been written at a point of weakness, on a day when Eva Gengli was known to be afflicted or during her rejection of philosophy, when her statements could no longer be trusted. The script in both versions of the aphorism, I recalled, was slightly unstable, and this perhaps could be parlayed into a legitimate, scholarly rejection.

I was well into my mental formulations for dismissal, developing an alternative mind/body formulation, when my benefactor began to jab at me weakly with his cane. Lifting my head, I removed my hands from my ears, showed myself attentive.

"I assume you are ready to listen to reason," he said. He had to say it twice before I was able to draw the meaning out from his slurred and shaking mouth.

"You see the state I am in," he said, his hands bobbing along the coverlet, his head shaking.

I folded my arms across my chest, inclined my head slightly. "It truly injures me to see you this way," I said. This was, in fact, true, though perhaps not in the way he would interpret it.

"I am very ill," he said. "I need my specialist."

I did not disagree with this, though I could not see how his mere *needs* would cause a *duty* to Eva Gengli's philosophy to vanish. Considered objectively, one had a certain obligation (to history, to thought) which demanded sacrifice, which superseded one's immediate pain. Pain must be subsidiary to art, I explained to him, even a function of art itself. Indeed, his "lover" Eva Gengli (if she ever had actually been his lover, which I doubted) had proven this by generating art from pain. Her film sequence "Inscription of the Spastic"—each film one minute long and subtitled after its only subject (e.g. Stephen #5, Helene #12, David P. #19)—had recorded the attempts at movement of forty-two people inflicted with muscular atrophy or spasticity, I reminded him. By recording them, Eva Gengli had transformed pain and dysfunction into something valuable. Privately, I reminded myself that my position was complicated by Eva Gengli's re-editing of the film sequence, her retitling it "Reinscription," and her attempt, by increasing or decreasing the speed of certain moments of the films themselves, to modify each gesture's regularity until it seemed each of the spastic were engaged in a seamless and mysterious dance.

But had not the "Reinscription" been an error in judgement? Was it not better from the philosophical point of view to record pain rather than to regulate it away?

Before I could mount a persuasive mental argument in favor of pain, however, I felt myself prodded again. "If you care to remain in this house," my benefactor said muddily, "you shall obey me."

I quickly stood and passed out of the room. I could hear my benefactor calling behind me, his voice unstable and shaken. I climbed the stairs, went directly to the library. Unlocking the door with the key around my neck, I went in.

With the door shut, I could no longer hear him. The manuscripts were as I had left them, undisturbed. I sat at the table, slid on the cloth gloves, and began to read, following the first text with the index finger of my right hand, the second with the index of my left, my head turning from one text to the other. The first:

> *Aphorism of the Two Enforested Dandies.*
> *Nietzsche: axe. Heidegger: woodpath.*

It was a somewhat odd aphorism which defined a relationship between two philosophers. "Woodpath" was from Heidegger's work (*Holzwege*), but I could not remember "axe" having appeared in Nietzsche's oeuvre and was unsure why it would be paired with Nietzsche. And why dismiss two radical philosophers as "Dandies"?

Though there was no second version, there did exist a second separate text, a "creative" text. Indeed, the forest scene excerpted from Eva Gengli's play *The Shadow of a Wing* called the initial aphorism into question:

> *Ducharme: Nietzsche, he's too busy cutting down*
> *   trees to actually pay attention to the forest itself.*
> *Madame Sbro: (clears his [sic] throat)*
> *Ducharme: Yes, it is true. And old Marty Heidegger,*
> *   he spends all his time looking for the trees to open*
> *   into a clearing so he can spread out his goddamn*
> *   picnic.*
> *Madame Sbro: (shaking her [sic] head) And what*
> *   about you?*

> *Ducharme: Me? (laughs) I like to spend my after-*
> *noons in the city.*

It is precisely ill-considered passages such as these—passages, I am convinced, written by Eva Gengli at moments of profound disturbance late in her life, after a sort of mental decay had begun—which less inventive critics have used to justify a dismissal of her philosophical statements.

I puzzled over the relation of the two texts for some time in my head. I considered it in the light of the previous texts I had encountered, and wrote a summary of the problem on a yellow legal pad, my seventeenth such pad.

Carefully formulated on paper, the problem began to seem plain enough, though it was still clear to me, as it had been clear for some time, that my examination of Eva Gengli's papers was leading me away from any clean formulation of her philosophy. This awareness I found to lead to an alternation of despair and exhilaration. Despair because my analysis was potentially interminable and useless, exhilaration because what I was now doing was not so much analyzing Eva Gengli's philosophy as entering into it in all its contradiction. I was swallowing the philosophy whole.

After a time, I realized I could hear my benefactor's voice calling me feebly. I opened the door and left the library. Leaning over the banister, I saw my benefactor lying heaped at the bottom of the stairs. I climbed down and picked him up, carried him back to his bedroom. He was trying to speak, but I encouraged him to remain silent until he was lying down and had had a moment to regain his composure. I placed him in his bed, under the blankets and sheets, tightened them around him, safety-pinned them into place to make it difficult for him to shake free again.

"There now," I said. "What would you do without me?"

He coughed, threads of saliva spilling through his lips. His mouth offered something I could not quite understand.

"What?" I asked. "Excuse me?"

"When are you going?" he asked.

"Going?"

"The doctor's."

"I am just leaving," I said. I kissed him on the forehead, then returned directly to the library, resuming my analysis where I had left off.

By the time I had reached the point where I could conveniently arrest my research, it was well past midnight. I arranged the books, secured the door to the library. I went downstairs, turning off the lights on my way.

Passing my benefactor's door, I heard him groan. I went inside. He was out of his bed again and crumpled in the corner, shaking violently. He had overturned the telephone table and had a puffy gash across his forehead, the skin all around it dull and abnormally raised. The telephone receiver was in his hand, the black cord entangled all around his forehead in a sort of dark nimbus, the base wedged somehow underneath his legs.

I carefully disentangled him and carried him back to his bed.

"The medicine?" he asked.

I ignored him, set about arranging his bed.

"You have it?" he asked.

"What you need is a good long sleep," I said.

I left him and went into the bathroom. Removing a bottle of sleeping pills, I shook a half-dozen into my hand. Filling an empty medicine bottle with tapwater, I returned to my benefactor's room.

"Take these," I said. "They will make you feel better."

"I don't want to fall asleep," he claimed.

"It's time to sleep," I said. I showed him the clock on the bureau. "You see?" I said. "This is for your own good."

In the end I had to force his jaws open and push the pills down his throat one by one, as one is sometimes forced to do with cats. He choked a little, but in the end swallowed everything.

"What did you do to the telephone?" he asked.

"The telephone?" I picked up the receiver, listened to the absence of any dial tone. "I know nothing about it," I claimed.

He looked blearily up at me.

"What are you planning to do with me?" he asked.

"Nothing," I said. I smiled to reassure him. "I am here only to serve."

II. Zwischen

Somewhere in the space between my analysis of the 128th aphorism (variously titled the "Aphorism on Adultery" and "Aphorism on Adulthood") and my return to Eva Gengli's only extended philosophical text, *A Blotter of Wings*, my benefactor's condition worsened considerably. He lost the ability to move of his own accord and will, individual portions of his body and speech having altogether fled his frame. His eyes, when I opened them with my fingers, stumbled about the sockets. He was having difficulty breathing and the shuddering of his body was so severe it seemed as if he would shake the flesh off his bones.

It was difficult to conduct a proper philosophical investigation under such circumstances, and had I not been intent on beginning an analysis of *A Blotter of Wings* I would have temporarily set all philosophy aside. Yet I had been struggling to gain an approach to *A Blotter of Wings* for months. At one time I had thought to have found, in the trope of the wavering knife, the proper and perhaps only unified approach to the book, the device that would lay bare certain fundamental consistencies of Eva Gengli's thought and make it manageable. But as I looked closer, I realized that Eva Gengli could not be reduced to fundamental structures or strictures, that her philosophy simply refused to conform to "thought" as I understood the term. Perhaps, I thought, the wavering knife could be coupled with another trope, or perhaps with a series of tropes—the rapid beating of insect wings, for instance (c.f. 34), or the overlayering and interlarding of faces suggested on page 21, or even the strange notion of the soul as container for the body, as existing not embedded in the flesh, but as a membrane between flesh and the world (83–97). Perhaps, I tried to believe, by beginning with Eva Gengli's abandonment of interiority ("the mind," she claimed, "is merely an image among others, a moment of vision"), one might be able to impose a structure that would at least allow the analysis to be written. Though I suspected in advance this would fail, I attempted it anyway. I wrote through the night and well into the day with an increasing sense of hopelessness, a hopelessness that eventually grew strong enough to

cause me to tear to shreds the sheets I had written and sit for a
further seven or eight hours staring at a blank piece of paper.

I might have sat in the same position for another seven or
eight hours except that I began to grow hungry and, growing
hungry, realized that I had not fed my benefactor for several
days. Going downstairs, I found him with his legs still on the
bed and entangled in the blanket, his body hanging out, his
head and face pushed against the floor. I lifted him up, found
his pulse torpid, his skin cold to the touch. I shook him a little,
spoke to him even, but he would not move.

I straightened him on the bed. Going upstairs to the library,
I surveyed the careful piles and stacks of Eva Gengli's papers. I
was, I considered, now that my benefactor was apparently in-
capacitated beyond the ability to make decisions, the sole care-
taker of all that remained of Eva Gengli. Carefully, I gathered
her papers back into the boxes they had been kept in before I
had volunteered my service to my benefactor. I piled the boxes
at the bottom of the stairs, then loaded them one by one into
my benefactor's automobile, always holding my eyes both to
the boxes in the automobile and to the boxes still piled just inside the door. I could of course not observe both at once, but
looked rapidly from one to another, switching my gaze with
such speed that it was as if I were observing both at once. The
boxes filled the trunk and all but the front seat of the "mini-
sedan" (as the manufacturers shamelessly had chosen to name
the vehicle), except that when I tried to close the trunk it
would not close, so two boxes did have to go in the front seat
as well. *A mini-sedan!* I thought. *How could the incomparable
Eva Gengli ever have been involved with someone who owned a
mini-sedan?* It was a disservice to her memory to put her
papers into such a car, but unfortunately I had no choice.

My benefactor, I further considered, was a small, slight, rat-
like person—not at all the sort I would imagine Eva Gengli to
involve herself with, though exactly the sort of person who
would choose to drive a mini-sedan. But here, now, in the box-
cramped car, perhaps I could use my benefactor's slightness to
my advantage. In his present condition, perhaps I could wedge
him between a box and the door to steady him and keep him
aright, and use the other box to rest his feet upon. In his present

condition, he was in no condition to object. I would make him
fit.

After locking all the automobile doors, then checking again
to assure myself they were locked, I went back into the house.
My benefactor was on the bed where I had left him, still unconscious, his body slightly tremulous. I gathered him up in
my arms and carried him out. Unlocking and opening the automobile door, I forced him inside, pushing his knees up near
his chest and working him sideways until he was in. He fit nicely
as long as I kept his knees folded up and against his chest. Getting into the automobile, I worked the key.

Though the automobile had not been driven in months it
started cleanly, which I saw as a blessing from the Gengli muse,
as it were, a ratification of my impulses. Pulling from the drive,
I moved down the road, away from town.

A mile from the highway, I pulled the automobile onto a
farm route and passed out through fields already thick with
grain, past farmhouses, satellite dishes, hulks of ruined automobiles. The road curved and splayed and turned into gravel,
and we passed underneath the highway, passed a ruined and
gutted and defaced building, a shattered circle of concrete
around it, moving deeper into the country. The road turned
dirt, becoming rutted and hard. I was forced to shift the gear
downward which, because of the boxes, was no easy task.

Near a cornfield, I eased the mini-sedan to the edge of the
track and switched it off. My benefactor, I saw, was no longer
shaking or moving at all. His tongue was pushing slightly from
between his lips. I reached across the seat, forced his knees further apart. I pressed my fingers into his neck. Along the web of
my thumb, I could still feel something of a pulse to him. When
I separated his eyelids, the eye remain dilated, settling slowly
lower in the socket as I shook him.

Putting my hands more firmly around the neck, I squeezed.
His neck and shoulder crumpled into the seat, his chin pressing
hard against my wrist. He hardly moved, only fluttering his
hand a little, and when he was perhaps already dead his eyes
opened and clouded slowly, the pupil fading dull. I shook my
hands loose, smelled them. They did not smell like anything. I
climbed out of the automobile and got him out too, dragging
him out into the weeds. Locking the doors, keeping always one

eye on the mini-sedan containing the boxes of Eva Gengli's private papers, I dragged the body out into the cornfield, smoothed the arms down along the sides as my impulses directed me to do. I examined my handiwork.

It was utterly clear to me now that Eva Gengli had meant in her "Aphorism on Aesthetics" the two hands of the strangler, not the two hands of a lover. That had been correct.

I had made a mistake in trying to limit my analysis to the page, I thought. Theory can only take one so far. Praxis is everything. One understands nothing until one begins to act.

III. Praxis

When I entered again, the house itself was mostly dark and quiet, the air still but for the dust and hair aswirl near where I had dropped the boxes, dust rising from my footsteps as well. I climbed the stairs and switched on the library lights, found everything as undisturbed as I had left it. I moved through the house, switching on lights, looking into each room to assure myself that I was in fact alone with Eva Gengli.

In my benefactor's room I smoothed the sheets, fluffed the pillow to remove from it the crease of his head. I stood back to admire my handiwork but, seeing the crease still to remain somewhat, I stripped the bed of sheets, balling them up and hiding them in the kitchen, under the sink. I considered the sink for some time, then took the sheets and hid them inside the refrigerator. I looked at the refrigerator a while, then took the sheets out and pushed them out the kitchen window.

There was still the smell of my benefactor in the room and through the entire house. I could not stop myself from fitting rubber gloves over my hands and walking about the house spraying disinfectant/deodorant aerosol before me, feeling it settle tingling on my arms. In a little while I could hardly breathe, so stripped off the gloves and abandoned both them and the disinfectant/deodorant, pushing them out the kitchen window.

I carried my lover's boxes upstairs to the library, one after the other. I was prepared to unpack them, but my forearms, I found, were sticky with disinfectant/deodorant, and the rubber gloves had made my hands watery. It would be an error, I thought, as well as a show of disrespect, to touch Eva's private papers in such a condition.

Going downstairs, I began to lather my hands in the bathroom basin. The lip of the sink and the floor below, I observed as I scrubbed, were clottered over by dark strands of my benefactor's hair. I rinsed and dried my hands, then swept the hair over the edge with my forefinger, gathering it in my other palm, then got on my knees and plucked it up strand by strand until the bathroom was mainly bald and hairless. I chartered the remainder of the house on my knees, the crease of my palm tight with hair, looking for further remnant of my benefactor. There was hair, I saw, everywhere, and dust too, and perhaps in the dust flakes of skin, and perhaps, I could not help but think, the dust was entirely made of flakes of skin. But the difficulty was in sifting and sorting, in separating the skin of my benefactor from what might still remain of Eva Gengli's "uncannily soft skin" (my benefactor's claim, though I doubt he would have ever touched it). Looking at the hair in my hand I noticed among it one or two strands of lighter hair, perhaps blond, perhaps white—perhaps her very hair, though she had died years before. I unthreaded these hairs, slipped them inside my shirt. The remainder, the dark strands, I took to the window and abandoned to the outside.

There was a scent still but no longer so strong. If I concentrated I could ignore it entirely. Indeed, there was little enough of my benefactor left and what was left was spread thin enough that I could feel through it and alongside it, in the stillness, something else entirely. What remained no longer was my benefactor refusing death but the force of a stronger mind, of my lover Eva Gengli gathering her breath just for me.

I moved quickly up the stairs to the library. Throwing the lids off the boxes, I arranged Eva's manuscripts in a circle all around me. Taking the pen, I poised it over a blank page. I waited for her to speak.

She, Eva Gengli, I began, *fighting a too uncanny sense of the presence of her own body, turned for a brief moment to philosophy for solace. In the short form, the aphorism in particular, she found a means of moving from a palpable space to a uniquely regenerative cerebral space. She, however—wrongly this critic believes—always dismissed her philosophical musings in general and her aphorisms in particular, claiming that they were useful as a means of "drawing breath" so as to return to her "only important work, the novels and films" (her words). The philosophy, she claimed in her famous but perhaps unfortunate letter to A. Kline, was "a temporary relief from the body," a sort of "necessary and necessarily ephemeral affair," afterwards allowing her to return more strongly to "the dark or bright bond between writing and flesh."*

Despite the strength of the aphorisms, I wrote, *it is Gengli's single extended treatise, with its exploration of pain and its critique of all dichotomy, that marks her as among the greatest philosophers of her generation. In this treatise,* A Blotter of Wings, *Eva Gengli postulates through the unifying image of the wavering knife (the knife wavering so rapidly as to resemble a beating pair of insect wings) that—*

My inspiration had suddenly fled altogether.

I put my pen down and went downstairs to see if the door was locked. It was locked. There was a smell to the house still, I now noticed. I went into the kitchen to gather the gloves and disinfectant/deodorant, but the space they normally occupied was empty. I opened the kitchen cupboards, closed them again. I opened the stove, pushed my head in, withdrew it.

Upstairs again, I read over what I had written. I had fallen back on the wavering knife despite knowing from my protracted analysis of Eva Gengli's work that the trope would not hold. Insisting upon it as a unifier, I told myself, would lead to a tremendously faulty reading of the Gengli philosophical oeuvre. And there was nothing of Eva Gengli in my writing either, I now realized. My style was turgid, nothing like the flowing and lucid prose of my lover, the careful repetitions ringing like dark chimes, words spilling slick as blood off the tongue. With every word I was writing about Eva Gengli, I realized, I was in fact betraying her. This might have been acceptable were I in fact betraying part of her, the "creative" part, to forward the philosophy, but only a dozen sentences in it was already clear to me that I was betraying all portions of her, and her mind and body too.

I tore the page up and carried it downstairs, dumped the scraps out the kitchen window. Taking a new, unblemished page, I sat down, attempted to begin again.

She, Eva Gengli, I wrote, *overwhelmed by her own touch, turned her gaze rational for an instant and rendered her hand philosophical. It was during this transition, between her novel* A Tergo *and her play* The Shadow of a Wing, *that Eva Gengli did her finest and*—

That was not it, not it at all. Although my benefactor had mostly fled the house, all his possessions were still present. They were pushing against the walls, limiting the air of the house, stifling and strangling what still remained of the woman he claimed had been his lover (Eva Gengli: impossible!).

I went through the shelves of the library, sorting out all those books which Eva Gengli had not signed inside the front cover. I carried each armload of books downstairs and dumped it out the kitchen window, the books cascading off the back porch and onto the lawn. There were, I saw on my tenth trip, neighbors and others of the curious beginning to gather, all of whom I ignored.

When the library had been cleansed sufficiently of all non-Gengli-related texts, I went back in and sat in it again. I closed my eyes, listened. Though it would be untrue to say I felt the presence of my lover Eva Gengli as clearly as I had when I was first compelled to begin, I did not feel my benefactor at all anymore, until I sensed him seeping under the library door from the other parts of his house where his possessions were still abundant.

I took off my shirt and tried to cram the crack under the door shut with it, but it was not long enough so I had to re-move my pants as well. When I was done, I stared at the stuffed crack for about an hour, sniffing at it, then tried to write. Nothing at all was coming. My lover had abandoned me.

Pushing the clothing aside and opening the door, I went downstairs. The air outside the library was fetid, marauded through with smells that worked against the purpose of true scholarship. I went around the house, throwing open windows until halfway around, seeing the neighbors crouched about outside, observing me, I realized that perhaps what was out-side the house was worse than what was in. At least with the windows closed nothing new could enter. I went about the house closing the windows again, thinking that what I needed now was a system or method to keep at bay all that was undesirable, and to clean the air for thought.

The technique I first employed was incendiary. I went from room to room striking matches, the sweet burn of sulfur ridding the air at least for a moment of the smells of my benefactor's dying (now dead) body, a rat-like body which I was certain Eva could never have touched. Yet matches were not sufficient; all his things were still in the house. As soon as a match was damped out, the things themselves tried to fill the room again before good air could rush in and fill the gap. I was moving about the house striking matches as quickly as I could and dropping them and letting them burn themselves out, but nothing permanent was happening except for the floorboards smouldering in some parts, so that I had to stamp the sparks out with my bare feet until the soles of my feet were slicked dark and burnt a little.

I figured there had to be a better way. I could hardly write my analysis while running about striking matches. So instead of the matches I began to move things out again, starting first with things in plain sight that my benefactor had valued, such as the half-meter cactus, the bronzed shoe, the handsewn tablecloth, the Senegalese mask. I moved them into the kitchen and threw them out the kitchen window. What would not fit out, I broke up until it would fit and then threw out. Once I had finished with the incidentals, I began to try to move the furniture out. Only I could not, with the tools available to me, think of a way to break things like the couch and bed into small enough pieces, so left them jumbled in the kitchen while I ruminated over their possible means of expulsion and went in search of easier prey.

I had begun to dispose of the clothing from my benefactor's closet when, in the back of it, wrapped in brown paper, I discovered a dress. It was black mostly, with a nearly hidden abstract patterning similar to a dress Eva had worn on the back cover of her *Lead Glass Iris*.

Confronted by my lover's dress, I suddenly was conscious again of my own nakedness. I began to put on one of my benefactor's suits, but before it was all the way on I could feel that it would not sit easily on my skin. I removed it and tried another, then another, until the whole of the room was scattered with his clothing and the only thing untried still was the dress.

I shook it out, slipped it over my head. It was tight but would fit mostly if I did not button it and did not move my arms too far. It felt good on me, the fabric smooth, of an odd, subtle weave. I could not stop running my hands over it.

I looked at myself in the mirror. I was so lovely I could hardly recognize myself. I looked in the drawers for something to put my face back on, but there was nothing. I was so lovely I could hardly bear to look at myself, and I could not stop my hands caressing or my mouth from speaking her name.

I could feel her all around me like a sheen over the surface of my body, and she having taken charge of me as well. I could see her gathering in my reflection. The whole world was turning and me along with it, and I was falling backwards and onto the floor, so taken with everything I could not move except in response to her missing touch, all language and analysis having fled me, my dress coming off, my lover's body touching all parts of my body until my body too was wavering and coming asunder and my soul dissolved and expelled to bubble along the surface of my skin and away, until nothing was left of myself nor my body, nothing left of anything at all.

2004

KELLY LINK

(b. 1969)

Stone Animals

Henry asked a question. He was joking.

"As a matter of fact," the real estate agent snapped, "it is."

It was not a question she had expected to be asked. She gave Henry a goofy, appeasing smile and yanked at the hem of the skirt of her pink linen suit, which seemed as if it might, at any moment, go rolling up her knees like a window shade. She was younger than Henry, and sold houses that she couldn't afford to buy.

"It's reflected in the asking price, of course," she said. "Like you said."

Henry stared at her. She blushed.

"I've never seen anything," she said. "But there are stories. Not stories that I know. I just know there are stories. If you believe that sort of thing."

"I don't," Henry said. When he looked over to see if Catherine had heard, she had her head up the tiled fireplace, as if she were trying it on, to see whether it fit. Catherine was six months pregnant. Nothing fit her except for Henry's baseball caps, his sweatpants, his T-shirts. But she liked the fireplace.

Carleton was running up and down the staircase, slapping his heels down hard, keeping his head down and his hands folded around the banister. Carleton was serious about how he played. Tilly sat on the landing, reading a book, legs poking out through the railings. Whenever Carleton ran past, he thumped her on the head, but Tilly never said a word. Carleton would be sorry later, and never even know why.

Catherine took her head out of the fireplace. "Guys," she said. "Carleton, Tilly. Slow down a minute and tell me what you think. Think King Spanky will be okay out here?"

"King Spanky is a cat, Mom," Tilly said. "Maybe we should get a dog, you know, to help protect us." She could tell by looking at her mother that they were going to move. She didn't know how she felt about this, except she had plans for the yard. A yard like that needed a dog.

"I don't like big dogs," said Carleton, six years old and small for his age. "I don't like this staircase. It's too big."

"Carleton," Henry said. "Come here. I need a hug."

Carleton came down the stairs. He lay down on his stomach on the floor and rolled, noisily, floppily, slowly, over to where Henry stood with the real estate agent. He curled like a dead snake around Henry's ankles. "I don't like those dogs outside," he said.

"I know it looks like we're out in the middle of nothing, but if you go down through the backyard, cut through that stand of trees, there's this little path. It takes you straight down to the train station. Ten-minute bike ride," the agent said. Nobody ever remembered her name, which was why she had to wear too-tight skirts. She was, as it happened, writing a romance novel, and she spent a lot of time making up pseudonyms, just in case she ever finished it. Ophelia Pink. Matilde Hightower. LaLa Treeble. Or maybe she'd write gothics. Ghost stories. But not about people like these. "Another ten minutes on that path and you're in town."

"What dogs, Carleton?" Henry said.

"I think they're lions, Carleton," said Catherine. "You mean the stone ones beside the door? Just like the lions at the library. You love those lions, Carleton. Patience and Fortitude?"

"I've always thought they were rabbits," the real estate agent said. "You know, because of the ears. They have big ears." She flopped her hands and then tugged at her skirt, which would not stay down. "I think they're pretty valuable. The guy who built the house had a gallery in New York. He knew a lot of sculptors."

Henry was struck by that. He didn't think he knew a single sculptor.

"I don't like the rabbits," Carleton said. "I don't like the staircase. I don't like this room. It's too big. I don't like *her*."

"Carleton," Henry said. He smiled at the real estate agent.

"I don't like the house," Carleton said, clinging to Henry's ankles. "I don't like houses. I don't want to live in a house."

"Then we'll build you a teepee out on the lawn," Catherine said. She sat on the stairs beside Tilly, who shifted her weight, almost imperceptibly, towards Catherine. Catherine sat as still as possible. Tilly was in fourth grade and difficult in a way that girls weren't supposed to be. Mostly she refused to be cuddled or babied. But she sat there, leaning on Catherine's arm, emanating saintly fragrances: peacefulness, placidness, goodness. *I want this house*, Catherine said, moving her lips like a silent movie heroine, to Henry, so that neither Carleton nor the agent, who had bent over to inspect a piece of dust on the floor, could see. "You can live in your teepee, and we'll invite you to come over for lunch. You like lunch, don't you? Peanut butter sandwiches?"

"I don't," Carleton said, and sobbed once.

But they bought the house anyway. The real estate agent got her commission. Tilly rubbed the waxy, stone ears of the rabbits on the way out, pretending that they already belonged to her. They were as tall as she was, but that wouldn't always be true. Carleton had a peanut butter sandwich.

The rabbits sat on either side of the front door. Two stone animals sitting on cracked, mossy haunches. They were shapeless, lumpish, patient in a way that seemed not worn down, but perhaps never really finished in the first place. There was something about them that reminded Henry of Stonehenge. Catherine thought of topiary shapes; *The Velveteen Rabbit*; soldiers who stand guard in front of palaces and never even twitch their noses. Maybe they could be donated to a museum. Or broken up with jackhammers. They didn't suit the house at all.

"So what's the house like?" said Henry's boss. She was carefully stretching rubber bands around her rubber band ball. By now the rubber band ball was so big, she had to get special extra-large rubber bands from the art department. She claimed it helped her think. She had tried knitting for a while, but it turned out that knitting was too utilitarian, too feminine. Making an enormous ball out of rubber bands struck the right note. It was something a man might do.

It took up half of her desk. Under the fluorescent office lights it had a peeled red liveliness. You almost expected it to shoot forward and out the door. The larger it got, the more it looked like some kind of eyeless, hairless, legless animal.

Maybe a dog. A Carleton-sized dog, Henry thought, although not a Carleton-sized rubber band ball.

Catherine joked sometimes about using the carleton as a measure of unit.

"Big," Henry said. "Haunted."

"Really?" his boss said. "So's this rubber band." She aimed a rubber band at Henry and shot him in the elbow. This was meant to suggest that she and Henry were good friends, and just goofing around, the way good friends did. But what it really meant was that she was angry at him. "Don't leave me," she said.

"I'm only two hours away." Henry put up his hand to ward off rubber bands. "Quit it. We talk on the phone, we use email. I come back to town when you need me in the office."

"You're sure this is a good idea?" his boss said. She fixed her reptilian, watery gaze on him. She had problematical tear ducts. Though she could have had a minor surgical procedure to fix this, she'd chosen not to. It was a tactical advantage, the way it spooked people.

It didn't really matter that Henry remained immune to rubber bands and crocodile tears. She had backup strategies. She thought about which would be most effective while Henry pitched his stupid idea all over again.

Henry had the movers' phone number in his pocket, like a talisman. He wanted to take it out, wave it at The Crocodile, say Look at this! Instead he said, "For nine years, we've lived in an apartment next door to a building that smells like urine. Like someone built an entire building out of bricks made of compressed red pee. Someone spit on Catherine in the street last week. This old Russian lady in a fur coat. A kid rang our doorbell the other day and tried to sell us gas masks. Door-to-door gas mask salesmen. Catherine bought one. When she told me about it, she burst into tears. She said she couldn't figure out if she was feeling guilty because she'd bought a gas mask, or if it was because she hadn't bought enough for everyone."

"Good Chinese food," his boss said. "Good movies. Good bookstores. Good dry cleaners. Good conversation."

"Treehouses," Henry said. "I had a treehouse when I was a kid."

"You were never a kid," his boss said.

"Three bathrooms. Crown moldings. We can't even see our nearest neighbor's house. I get up in the morning, have coffee, put Carleton and Tilly on the bus, and go to work in my pajamas."

"What about Catherine?" The Crocodile put her head down on her rubber band ball. Possibly this was a gesture of defeat.

"There was that thing. Catherine's whole department is leaving. Like rats deserting a sinking ship. Anyway, Catherine needs a change. And so do I," Henry said. "We've got another kid on the way. We're going to garden. Catherine'll teach ESOL, find a book group, write her book. Teach the kids how to play bridge. You've got to start them early."

He picked a rubber band off the floor and offered it to his boss. "You should come out and visit some weekend."

"I never go upstate," The Crocodile said. She held on to her rubber band ball. "Too many ghosts."

"Are you going to miss this? Living here?" Catherine said. She couldn't stand the way her stomach poked out. She couldn't see past it. She held up her left foot to make sure it was still there, and pulled the sheet off Henry.

"I love the house," Henry said.

"Me too," Catherine said. She was biting her fingernails. Henry could hear her teeth going *click, click*. Now she had both feet up in the air. She wiggled them around. Hello, feet.

"What are you doing?"

She put them down again. On the street outside, cars came and went, pushing smears of light along the ceiling, slow and fast at the same time. The baby was wriggling around inside her, kicking out with both feet like it was swimming across the English Channel, the Pacific. Kicking all the way to China. "Did you buy that story about the former owners moving to France?"

"I don't believe in France," Henry said. "*Je ne crois pas en France.*"

"Neither do I," Catherine said. "Henry?"

"What?"

"Do you love the house?"

"I love the house."

"I love it more than you do," Catherine said, although

Henry hated it when she said things like that. "What do you love best?"

"That room in the front," Henry said. "With the windows. Our bedroom. Those weird rabbit statues."

"Me too," Catherine said, although she didn't. "I love those rabbits."

Then she said, "Do you ever worry about Carleton and Tilly?"

"What do you mean?" Henry said. He looked at the alarm clock: it was 4 A.M. "Why are we awake right now?"

"Sometimes I worry that I love one of them better," Catherine said. "Like I might love Tilly better. Because she used to wet the bed. Because she's always so angry. Or Carleton, because he was so sick when he was little."

"I love them both the same," Henry said.

He didn't even know he was lying. Catherine knew, though. She knew he was lying, and she knew he didn't even know it. Most of the time she thought that it was okay. As long as he thought he loved them both the same, and acted as if he did, that was good enough.

"Well, do you ever worry that you love them more than me?" she said. "Or that I love them more than I love you?"

"Do you?" Henry said.

"Of course," Catherine said. "I have to. It's my job."

She found the gas mask in a box of wineglasses, and also six recent issues of *The New Yorker*, which she still might get a chance to read someday. She put the gas mask under the sink and *The New Yorkers* in the sink. Why not? It was her sink. She could put anything she wanted into it. She took the magazines out again and put them into the refrigerator, just for fun.

Henry came into the kitchen, holding silver candlesticks and a stuffed armadillo, which someone had made into a purse. It had a shoulder strap made out of its own skin. You opened its mouth and put things inside it, lipstick and subway tokens. It had pink gimlet eyes and smelled strongly of vinegar. It belonged to Tilly, although how it had come into her possession was unclear. Tilly claimed she'd won it at school in a contest involving donuts. Catherine thought it more likely Tilly had either stolen it or (slightly preferable) found it in someone's trash. Now Tilly kept her most valuable belongings inside the purse, to keep them safe from Carleton, who was covetous of the precious things—because they were small, and because they belonged to Tilly—but afraid of the armadillo.

"I've already told her she can't take it to school for at least the first two weeks. Then we'll see." She took the purse from Henry and put it with the gas mask under the sink.

"What are they doing?" Henry said. Framed in the kitchen window, Carleton and Tilly hunched over the lawn. They had a pair of scissors and a notebook and a stapler.

"They're collecting grass." Catherine took dishes out of a box, put the Bubble Wrap aside for Tilly to stomp, and stowed the dishes in a cabinet. The baby kicked like it knew all about Bubble Wrap. "Woah, Fireplace," she said. "We don't have a dancing license in there."

Henry put out his hand, rapped on Catherine's stomach. *Knock, knock.* It was Tilly's joke. Catherine would say, "Who's there?" and Tilly would say, Candlestick's here. Fat Man's here. Box. Hammer. Milkshake. Clarinet. Mousetrap. Fiddlestick. Tilly had a whole list of names for the baby. The real estate agent would have approved.

"Where's King Spanky?" Henry said.

"Under our bed," Catherine said. "He's up in the box frame."

"Have we unpacked the alarm clock?" Henry said.

"Poor King Spanky," Catherine said. "Nobody to love except an alarm clock. Come upstairs and let's see if we can shake him out of the bed. I've got a present for you."

The present was in a U-Haul box exactly like all the other boxes in the bedroom, except that Catherine had written HENRY'S PRESENT on it instead of LARGE FRONT BEDROOM. Inside the box were Styrofoam peanuts and then a smaller box from Takashimaya. The Takashimaya box was fastened with a silver ribbon. The tissue paper inside was dull gold, and inside the tissue paper was a green silk robe with orange sleeves and heraldic animals in orange and gold thread. "Lions," Henry said.

"Rabbits," Catherine said.

"I didn't get you anything," Henry said.

Catherine smiled nobly. She liked giving presents better than getting presents. She'd never told Henry, because it seemed to her that it must be selfish in some way she'd never bothered to figure out. Catherine was grateful to be married to Henry, who accepted all presents as his due; who looked good in the clothes that she bought him; who was vain, in an easygoing way, about his good looks. Buying clothes for Henry was especially satisfying now, while she was pregnant and couldn't buy them for herself.

She said, "If you don't like it, then I'll keep it. Look at you, look at those sleeves. You look like the emperor of Japan."

They had already colonized the bedroom, making it full of things that belonged to them. There was Catherine's mirror on the wall, and their mahogany wardrobe, their first real piece of furniture, a wedding present from Catherine's great-aunt. There was their serviceable, queen-sized bed with King Spanky lodged up inside it, and there was Henry, spinning his arms in the wide orange sleeves, like an embroidered windmill. Henry could see all of these things in the mirror, and behind him, their lawn and Tilly and Carleton, stapling grass into their notebook. He saw all of these things and he found them good. But he couldn't see Catherine. When he turned around, she stood in the doorway, frowning at him. She had the alarm clock in her hand.

"Look at you," she said again. It worried her, the way something, someone, *Henry*, could suddenly look like a place she'd never been before. The alarm began to ring and King Spanky came out from under the bed, trotting over to Catherine. She bent over, awkwardly—ungraceful, ungainly, so clumsy, so fucking awkward, being pregnant was like wearing a fucking suitcase strapped across your middle—put the alarm clock down on the ground, and King Spanky hunkered down in front of it, his nose against the ringing glass face.

And that made her laugh again. Henry loved Catherine's laugh. Downstairs, their children slammed a door open, ran through the house, carrying scissors, both Catherine and Henry knew, and slammed another door open and were outside again, leaving behind the smell of grass. There was a store in New York where you could buy a perfume that smelled like that.

*

Catherine and Carleton and Tilly came back from the grocery store with a tire, a rope to hang it from, and a box of pancake mix for dinner. Henry was online, looking at a jpeg of a rubber band ball. There was a message too. The Crocodile needed him to come into the office. It would be just a few days. Someone was setting fires and there was no one smart enough to see how to put them out except for him. They were his accounts. He had to come in and save them. She knew Catherine and Henry's apartment hadn't sold; she'd checked with their listing agent. So surely it wouldn't be impossible, not impossible, only inconvenient.

He went downstairs to tell Catherine, "That *witch*," she said, and then bit her lip. "She called the listing agent? I'm sorry. We talked about this. Never mind. Just give me a moment."

Catherine inhaled. Exhaled. Inhaled. If she were Carleton, she would hold her breath until her face turned red and Henry agreed to stay home, but then again, it never worked for Carleton. "We ran into our new neighbors in the grocery store. She's about the same age as me. Liz and Marcus. One kid, older, a girl, um, I think her name was Alison, maybe from a first marriage—potential babysitter, which is really good news. Liz is a lawyer. Gorgeous. Reads Oprah books. He likes to cook."

"So do I," Henry said.

"You're better looking," Catherine said. "So do you have to go back tonight, or can you take the train in the morning?"

"The morning is fine," Henry said, wanting to seem agreeable.

Carleton appeared in the kitchen, his arms pinned around King Spanky's middle. The cat's front legs stuck straight out, as if Carleton were dowsing. King Spanky's eyes were closed. His whiskers twitched Morse code. "What are you wearing?" Carleton said.

"My new uniform," Henry said. "I wear it to work."

"Where do you work?" Carleton said, testing.

"I work at home," Henry said. Catherine snorted.

"He looks like the king of rabbits, doesn't he? The plenipotentiary of Rabbitaly," she said, no longer sounding particularly pleased about this.

"He looks like a princess," Carleton said, now pointing King Spanky at Henry like a gun.

"Where's your grass collection?" Henry said. "Can I see it?"

"No," Carleton said. He put King Spanky on the floor, and the cat slunk out of the kitchen, heading for the staircase, the bedroom, the safety of the bedsprings, the beloved alarm clock, the beloved. The beloved may be treacherous, greasy-headed and given to evil habits, or else it can be a man in his late forties who works too much, or it can be an alarm dock.

"After dinner," Henry said, trying again, "we could go out and find a tree for your tire swing."

"No," Carleton said, regretfully. He lingered in the kitchen, hoping to be asked a question to which he could say yes.

"Where's your sister?" Henry said.

"Watching television," Carleton said. "I don't like the television here."

"It's too big," Henry said, but Catherine didn't laugh.

Henry dreams he is the king of the real estate agents. Henry loves his job. He tries to sell a house to a young couple with twitchy noses and big dark eyes. Why does he always dream that he's trying to sell things?

The couple stare at him nervously. He leans towards them as if he's going to whisper something in their silly, expectant ears. It's a secret he's never told anyone before. It's a secret he didn't even know that he knew. "Let's stop fooling," he says. "You can't afford to buy this house. You don't have any money. You're rabbits."

"Where do you work?" Carleton said, in the morning, when Henry called from Grand Central.

"I work at home," Henry said. "Home where we live now, where you are. Eventually. Just not today. Are you getting ready for school?"

Carleton put the phone down. Henry could hear him saying something to Catherine. "He says he's not nervous about school," she said. "He's a brave kid."

"I kissed you this morning," Henry said, "but you didn't wake up. There were all these rabbits on the lawn. They were huge. King Spanky–sized. They were just sitting there like they were waiting for the sun to come up. It was funny, like some kind of art installation. But it was kind of creepy too. Think they'd been there all night?"

"Rabbits? Can they have rabies? I saw them this morning when I got up," Catherine said. "Carleton didn't want to brush his teeth this morning. He says something's wrong with his toothbrush."

"Maybe he dropped it in the toilet, and he doesn't want to tell you," Henry said.

"Maybe you could buy a new toothbrush and bring it home," Catherine said. "He doesn't want one from the drugstore here. He wants one from New York."

"Where's Tilly?" Henry said.

"She says she's trying to figure out what's wrong with Carleton's toothbrush. She's still in the bathroom." Catherine said.

"Can I talk to her for a second?" Henry said.

"Tell her she needs to get dressed and eat her Cheerios," Catherine said. "After I drive them to school, Liz is coming over for coffee. Then we're going to go out for lunch. I'm not unpacking another box until you get home. Here's Tilly."

"Hi," Tilly said. She sounded as if she were asking a question.

Tilly never liked talking to people on the telephone. How were you supposed to know if they were really who they said they were? And even if they were who they claimed to be, they didn't know whether you were who you said you were. You could be someone else. They might give away information about you, and not even know it. There were no protocols. No precautions.

She said, "Did you brush your teeth this morning?"

"Good morning, Tilly," her father (if it was her father) said. "My toothbrush was fine. Perfectly normal."

"That's good," Tilly said. "I let Carleton use mine."

"That was very generous," Henry said.

"No problem," Tilly said. Sharing things with Carleton wasn't like having to share things with other people. It wasn't really like sharing things at all. Carleton belonged to her, like the toothbrush. "Mom says that when we get home today, we can draw on the walls in our rooms if we want to, while we decide what color we want to paint them."

"Sounds like fun," Henry said. "Can I draw on them too?"

"Maybe," Tilly said. She had already said too much. "Gotta go. Gotta eat breakfast."

"Don't be worried about school," Henry said.

"I'm not worried about school," Tilly said.

"I love you," Henry said.

"I'm real concerned about this toothbrush," Tilly said.

He closed his eyes only for a minute. Just for a minute. When he woke up, it was dark and he didn't know where he was. He stood up and went over to the door, almost tripping over something. It sailed away from him in an exuberant, rollicking sweep. According to the clock on his desk, it was 4 A.M. Why was it always 4 A.M.? There were four messages on his cell phone, all from Catherine.

He checked train schedules online. Then he sent Catherine a fast email.

> Fell asleep @ midnight? Mssed trains. Awake now, going to keep on working. Pttng out fires. Take the train home early afternoon? Still lv me?

Before he went back to work, he kicked the rubber band ball back down the hall towards The Crocodile's door.

Catherine called him at 8:45.

"I'm sorry," Henry said.

"I bet you are," Catherine said.

"I can't find my razor. I think The Crocodile had some kind of tantrum and tossed my stuff."

"Carleton will love that," Catherine said. "Maybe you should sneak in the house and shave before dinner. He had a hard day at school yesterday."

"Maybe I should grow a beard," Henry said. "He can't be afraid of everything, all the time. Tell me about the first day of school."

"We'll talk about it later," Catherine said. "Liz just drove up. I'm going to be her guest at the gym. Just make it home for dinner."

*

At 6 A.M. Henry emailed Catherine again. "Srry. Accidentally startd avalanche while puttng out fires. Wait up for me? How ws 2nd day of school?" She didn't write him back. He called and no one picked up the phone. She didn't call.

He took the last train home. By the time it reached the station, he was the only one left in his car. He unchained his bicycle and rode it home in the dark. Rabbits pelted across the footpath in front of his bike. There were rabbits foraging on his lawn. They froze as he dismounted and pushed the bicycle across the grass. The lawn was rumpled; the bike went up and down over invisible depressions that he supposed were rabbit holes. There were two short fat men standing in the dark on either side of the front door, waiting for him, but when he came closer, he remembered that they were stone rabbits. "Knock, knock," he said.

The real rabbits on the lawn tipped their ears at him. The stone rabbits waited for the punch line, but they were just stone rabbits. They had nothing better to do.

The front door wasn't locked. He walked through the downstairs rooms, putting his hands on the backs and tops of furniture. In the kitchen, cut-down boxes leaned in stacks against the wall, waiting to be recycled or remade into cardboard houses and spaceships and tunnels for Carleton and Tilly.

Catherine had unpacked Carleton's room. Night-lights in the shape of bears and geese and cats were plugged into every floor outlet. There were little low-watt table lamps as well—hippo, robot, gorilla, pirate ship. Everything was soaked in a tender, peaceable light, translating Carleton's room into something more than a bedroom: something luminous, numinous, Carleton's cartoony Midnight Church of Sleep.

Tilly was sleeping in the other bed.

Tilly would never admit that she sleepwalked, the same way that she would never admit that she sometimes still wet the bed. But she refused to make friends. Making friends would have meant spending the night in strange houses. Tomorrow morning she would insist that Henry or Catherine must have carried her from her room, put her to bed in Carleton's room for reasons of their own.

Henry knelt down between the two beds and kissed Carleton on the forehead. He kissed Tilly, smoothed her hair. How could he not love Tilly better? He'd known her longer. She was so brave, so angry.

On the walls of Carleton's bedroom, Henry's children had drawn a house. A cat nearly as big as the house. There was a crown on the cat's head. Trees or flowers with pairs of leaves that pointed straight up, still bigger, and a stick figure on a stick bicycle, riding past the trees. When he looked closer, he thought that maybe the trees were actually rabbits. The wall smelled like Fruit Loops. Someone had written *Henry Is A Rat Fink! Ha Ha!* He recognized his wife's handwriting.

"Scented markers," Catherine said. She stood in the door, holding a pillow against her stomach. "I was sleeping downstairs on the sofa. You walked right past and didn't see me."

"The front door was unlocked," Henry said.

"Liz says nobody ever locks their doors out here," Catherine said. "Are you coming to bed, or were you just stopping by to see how we were?"

"I have to go back in tomorrow." Henry said. He pulled a toothbrush out of his pocket and showed it to her. "There's a box of Krispy Kreme donuts on the kitchen counter."

"Delete the donuts," Catherine said. "I'm not that easy." She took a step towards him and accidentally kicked King Spanky. The cat yowled. Carleton woke up. He said, "Who's there? Who's there?"

"It's me," Henry said. He knelt beside Carleton's bed in the light of the Winnie the Pooh lamp. "I brought you a new toothbrush."

Carleton whimpered.

"What's wrong, spaceman?" Henry said. "It's just a toothbrush." He leaned towards Carleton and Carleton scooted back. He began to scream.

In the other bed, Tilly was dreaming about rabbits. When she'd come home from school, she and Carleton had seen rabbits, sitting on the lawn as if they had kept watch over the house all the time that Tilly had been gone. In her dream they were still there. She dreamed she was creeping up on them. They opened their mouths, wide enough to reach inside like she was some kind of rabbit dentist, and so she did. She put her hand around something small and cold and hard. Maybe it was a ring, a diamond ring. Or a. Or. It was a. She couldn't wait to show Carleton. Her arm was inside the rabbit all the way to her shoulder. Someone put their little cold hand around her wrist and yanked. Somewhere her mother was talking. She said—

"It's the beard."

Catherine couldn't decide whether to laugh or cry or scream like Carleton. That would surprise Carleton, if she started screaming too. "Shoo! Shoo, Henry—go shave and come back as quick as you can, or else he'll never go back to sleep."

"Carleton, honey," she was saying as Henry left the room. "It's your dad. It's not Santa Claus. It's not the big bad wolf. It's your dad. Your dad just forgot. Why don't you tell me a story? Or do you want to go watch your daddy shave?"

Catherine's hot water bottle was draped over the tub. Towels were heaped on the floor. Henry's things had been put away behind the mirror. It made him feel tired, thinking of all the other things that still had to be put away. He washed his hands, then looked at the bar of soap. It didn't feel right. He put it back on the sink, bent over and sniffed it and then tore off a piece of toilet paper, used the toilet paper to pick up the soap. He threw it in the trash and unwrapped a new bar of soap. There was nothing wrong with the new soap. There was nothing wrong with the old soap either. He was just tired. He washed his hands and lathered up his face, shaved off his beard and watched the little bristles of hair wash down the sink. When he went to show Carleton his brand-new face, Catherine was curled up in bed beside Carleton. They were both asleep. They were still asleep when he left the house at five thirty the next morning.

"Where are you?" Catherine said.

"I'm on my way home. I'm on the train." The train was still in the station. They would be leaving any minute. They had been leaving any minute for the last hour or so, and before that, they had had to get off the train twice, and then back on again. They had been assured there was nothing to worry about. There was no bomb threat. There was no bomb. The delay was only temporary. The people on the train looked at each other, trying to seem as if they were not looking. Everyone had their cell phones out.

"The rabbits are out on the lawn again," Catherine said.
"There must be at least fifty or sixty. I've never counted rabbits
before. Tilly keeps trying to go outside to make friends with
them, but as soon as she's outside, they all go bouncing away
like beach balls. I talked to a lawn specialist today. He says we
need to do something about it, which is what Liz was saying.
Rabbits can be a big problem out here. They've probably got
tunnels and warrens all through the yard. It could be a problem. Like living on top of a sinkhole. But Tilly is never going
to forgive us. She knows something's up. She says she doesn't
want a dog anymore. It would scare away the rabbits. Do you
think we should get a dog?"

"So what do they do? Put out poison? Dig up the yard?"
Henry said. The man in the seat in front of him got up. He
took his bags out of the luggage rack and left the train. Everyone watched him go, pretending they were not.

"He was telling me they have these devices, kind of like ultra-
sound equipment. They plot out the tunnels, close them up,
and then gas the rabbits. It sounds gruesome," Catherine said.
"And this kid, this baby has been kicking the daylights out of
me. All day long it's kick, kick, jump, kick, like some kind of
martial artist. He's going to be an angry kid, Henry. Just like his
sister. Her sister. Or maybe I'm going to give birth to rabbits."

"As long as they have your eyes and my chin," Henry said.

"I've gotta go," Catherine said. "I have to pee again. All day
long it's the kid jumping, me peeing, Tilly getting her heart
broken because she can't make friends with the rabbits, me
worrying because she doesn't want to make friends with other
kids, just with rabbits, Carleton asking if today he has to go
to school, does he have to go to school tomorrow, why am I
making him go to school when everybody there is bigger than
him, why is my stomach so big and fat, why does his teacher
tell him to act like a big boy? Henry, why are we doing this
again? Why am I pregnant? And where are you? Why aren't
you here? What about our deal? Don't you want to be here?"

"I'm sorry," Henry said. "I'll talk to The Crocodile. We'll
work something out."

"I thought you wanted this too, Henry. Don't you?"

"Of course," Henry said. "Of course I want this."

"I've gotta go," Catherine said again. "Liz is bringing some women over. We're finally starting that book club. We're going to read *Fight Club*. Her stepdaughter Alison is going to look after Tilly and Carleton for me. I've already talked to Tilly. She promises she won't bite or hit or make Alison cry."

"What's the trade? A few hours of bonus TV?"

"No," Catherine said. "Something's up with the TV."

"What's wrong with the TV?"

"I don't know," Catherine said. "It's working fine. But the kids won't go near it. Isn't that great? It's the same thing as the toothbrush. You'll see when you get home. I mean, it's not just the kids. I was watching the news earlier, and then I had to turn it off. It wasn't the news. It was the TV."

"So it's the downstairs bathroom and the coffeemaker and Carleton's toothbrush and now the TV?"

"There's some other stuff as well, since this morning. Your office, apparently. Everything in it—your desk, your bookshelves, your chair, even the paper clips."

"That's probably a good thing, right? I mean, that way they'll stay out of there."

"I guess," Catherine said. "The thing is, I went and stood in there for a while and it gave me the creeps too. So now I can't pick up email. And I had to throw out more soap. And King Spanky doesn't love the alarm clock anymore. He won't come out from under the bed when I set it off."

"The alarm clock too?"

"It does sound different," Catherine said. "Just a little bit different. Or maybe I'm insane. This morning, Carleton told me that he knew where our house was. He said we were living in a secret part of Central Park. He said he recognizes the trees. He thinks that if he walks down that little path, he'll get mugged. I've really got to go, Henry, or I'm going to wet my pants, and I don't have time to change again before everyone gets here."

"I love you," Henry said.

"Then why aren't you here?" Catherine said victoriously. She hung up and ran down the hallway towards the downstairs bathroom. But when she got there, she turned around. She went racing up the stairs, pulling down her pants as she went, and barely got to the master bedroom bathroom in time. All day long she'd gone up and down the stairs, feeling extremely

silly. There was nothing wrong with the downstairs bathroom.
It's just the fixtures. When you flush the toilet or run water in
the sink. She doesn't like the sound the water makes.

Several times now, Henry had come home and found Catherine
painting rooms, which was a problem. The problem was that
Henry kept going away. If he didn't keep going away, he
wouldn't have to keep coming home. That was Catherine's
point. Henry's point was that Catherine wasn't supposed to be
painting rooms while she was pregnant. Pregnant women
weren't supposed to breathe around paint fumes.

Catherine solved this problem by wearing the gas mask
while she painted. She had known the gas mask would come in
handy. She told Henry she promised to stop painting as soon
as he started working at home, which was the plan. Meanwhile,
she couldn't decide on colors. She and Carleton and Tilly
spent hours looking at paint strips with colors that had names
like Sangria, Peat Bog, Tulip, Tantrum, Planetarium, Galactica,
Tea Leaf, Egg Yolk, Tinker Toy, Gauguin, Susan, Envy, Aztec,
Utopia, Wax Apple, Rice Bowl, Cry Baby, Fat Lip, Green
Banana, Trampoline, Finger Nail. It was a wonderful way to
spend time. They went off to school, and when they got home,
the living room would be Harp Seal instead of Full Moon.
They'd spend some time with that color, getting to know it,
ignoring the television, which was haunted (*haunted* wasn't
the right word, of course, but Catherine couldn't think what the
right word was) and then a couple of days later, Catherine
would go buy some more primer and start again. Carleton and
Tilly loved this. They begged her to repaint their bedrooms.
She did.

She wished she could eat paint. Whenever she opened a can
of paint, her mouth watered. When she'd been pregnant with
Carleton, she hadn't been able to eat anything except for olives
and hearts of palm and dry toast. When she'd been pregnant
with Tilly, she'd eaten dirt, once, in Central Park. Tilly thought
they should name the baby after a paint color, Chalk, or Dilly
Dilly, or Keelhauled. Lapis Lazulily. Knock, knock.

Catherine kept meaning to ask Henry to take the television
and put it in the garage. Nobody ever watched it now. They'd

had to stop using the microwave as well, and a colander, some of the flatware, and she was keeping an eye on the toaster. She had a premonition, or an intuition. It didn't feel wrong, not yet, but she had a feeling about it. There was a gorgeous pair of earrings that Henry had given her—how was it possible to be spooked by a pair of diamond earrings?—and yet. Carleton wouldn't play with his Lincoln Logs, and so they were going to the Salvation Army, and Tilly's armadillo purse had disappeared. Tilly hadn't said anything about it, and Catherine hadn't wanted to ask.

Sometimes, if Henry wasn't coming home, Catherine painted after Carleton and Tilly went to bed. Sometimes Tilly would walk into the room where Catherine was working, Tilly's eyes closed, her mouth open, a tourist-somnambulist. She'd stand there, with her head cocked towards Catherine. If Catherine spoke to her, she never answered, and if Catherine took her hand, she would follow Catherine back to her own bed and lie down again. But sometimes Catherine let Tilly stand there and keep her company. Tilly was never so attentive, so *present*, when she was awake. Eventually she would turn and leave the room and Catherine would listen to her climb back up the stairs. Then she would be alone again.

Catherine dreams about colors. It turns out her marriage was the same color she had just painted the foyer. Velveteen Fade. Leonard Felter, who had had an ongoing affair with two of his graduate students, several adjuncts, two tenured faculty members, brought down Catherine's entire department, and saved Catherine's marriage, would make a good lipstick or nail polish. Peach Nooky. There's The Crocodile, a particularly bilious Eau De Vil, a color that tastes bad when you say it. Her mother, who had always been disappointed by Catherine's choices, turned out to have been a beautiful, rich, deep chocolate. Why hadn't Catherine ever seen that before? Too late, too late. It made her want to cry.

Liz and she are drinking paint, thick and pale as cream. "Have some more paint," Catherine says. "Do you want sugar?"

"Yes, lots," Liz says. "What color are you going to paint the rabbits?"

Catherine passes her the sugar. She hasn't even thought about the rabbits, except which rabbits does Liz mean, the stone rabbits or the real rabbits? How do you make them hold still?

"I got something for you," Liz says. She's got Tilly's armadillo purse. It's full of paint strips. Catherine's mouth fills with saliva.

Henry dreams he has an appointment with the exterminator. "You've got to take care of this," he says. "We have two small children. These things could be rabid. They might carry plague."

"See what I can do," the exterminator says, sounding glum. He stands next to Henry. He's an odd-looking, twitchy guy. He has big ears. They contemplate the skyscrapers that poke out of the grass like obelisks. The lawn is teeming with skyscrapers. "Never seen anything like this before. Never wanted to see anything like this. But if you want my opinion, it's the house that's the real problem—"

"Never mind about my wife," Henry says. He squats down beside a knee-high art-deco skyscraper, and peers into a window. A little man looks back at him and shakes his fists, screaming something obscene. Henry flicks a finger at the window, almost hard enough to break it. He feels hot all over. He's never felt this angry before in his life, not even when Catherine told him that she'd accidentally slept with Leonard Felter. The little bastard is going to regret what he just said, whatever it was. He lifts his foot.

The exterminator says, "I wouldn't do that if I were you. You have to dig them up, get the roots. Otherwise, they just grow back. Like your house. Which is really just the tip of the iceberg lettuce, so to speak. You've probably got seventy, eighty stories underground. You gone down on the elevator yet? Talked to the people living down there? It's your house, and you're just going to let them live there rent-free? Mess with your things like that?"

"What?" Henry says, and then he hears helicopters, fighter planes the size of hummingbirds. "Is this really necessary?" he says to the exterminator.

The exterminator nods. "You have to catch them off guard."

"Maybe we're being hasty," Henry says. He has to yell to be

heard above the noise of the tiny, tinny, furious planes. "Maybe we can settle this peacefully."

"Hemree," the interrogator says, shaking his head. "You called me in, because I'm the expert, and you knew you needed help."

Henry wants to say "You're saying my name wrong." But he doesn't want to hurt the undertaker's feelings.

The alligator keeps on talking. "Listen up, Hemreeee, and shut up about negotiations and such, because if we don't take care of this right away, it may be too late. This isn't about homeownership, or lawn care, Hemreeeeee, this is war. The lives of your children are at stake. The happiness of your family. Be brave. Be strong. Just hang on to your rabbit and fire when you see delight in their eyes."

He woke up. "Catherine," he whispered. "Are you awake? I was having this dream."

Catherine laughed. "That's the phone, Liz," she said. "It's probably Henry, saying he'll be late."

"Catherine," Henry said. "Who are you talking to?"

"Are you mad at me, Henry?" Catherine said. "Is that why you won't come home?"

"I'm right here," Henry said.

"You take your rabbits and your crocodiles and get out of here," Catherine said. "And then come straight home again."

She sat up in bed and pointed her finger. "I am sick and tired of being spied on by rabbits!"

When Henry looked, something stood beside the bed, rocking back and forth on its heels. He fumbled for the light, got it on, and saw Tilly, her mouth open, her eyes closed. She looked larger than she ever did when she was awake. "It's just Tilly," he said to Catherine, but Catherine lay back down again. She put her pillow over her head. When he picked Tilly up, to carry her back to bed, she was warm and sweaty, her heart racing as if she had been running through all the rooms of the house.

He walked through the house. He rapped on walls, testing. He put his ear against the floor. No elevator. No secret rooms, no hidden passageways.

There isn't even a basement.

*

Tilly has divided the yard in half. Carleton is not allowed in her half, unless she gives permission.

From the bottom of her half of the yard, where the trees run beside the driveway, Tilly can barely see the house. She's decided to name the yard Matilda's Rabbit Kingdom. Tilly loves naming things. When the new baby is born, her mother has promised that she can help pick out the real names, although there will only be two real names, a first one and a middle. Tilly doesn't understand why there can only be two. *Oishi* means "delicious" in Japanese. That would make a good name, either for the baby or for the yard, because of the grass. She knows the yard isn't as big as Central Park, but it's just as good, even if there aren't any pagodas or castles or carriages or people on roller skates. There's plenty of grass. There are hundreds of rabbits. They live in an enormous underground city, maybe a city just like New York. Maybe her dad can stop working in New York, and come work under the lawn instead. She could help him, go to work with him. She could be a biologist, like Jane Goodall, and go and live underground with the rabbits. Last year her ambition had been to go and live secretly in the Metropolitan Museum of Art, but someone has already done that, even if it's only in a book. Tilly feels sorry for Carleton. Everything he ever does, she'll have already been there. She'll already have done that.

Tilly has left her armadillo purse sticking out of a rabbit hole. First she made the hole bigger; then she packed the dirt back in around the armadillo so that only the shiny, peeled snout poked out. Carleton digs it out again with his stick. Maybe Tilly meant him to find it. Maybe it was a present for the rabbits, except what is it doing here, in his half of the yard? When he lived in the apartment, he was afraid of the armadillo purse, but there are better things to be afraid of out here. But be careful, Carleton. Might as well be careful. The armadillo purse says Don't touch me. So he doesn't. He uses his stick to pry open the snap-mouth, dumps out Tilly's most valuable things, and with his stick pushes them one by one down the hole. Then he puts his ear to the rabbit hole so that he can hear the rabbits say thank you. Saying thank you is polite. But the rabbits say nothing. They're holding their breath, waiting for him to go away. Carleton waits too. Tilly's armadillo, empty and smelly and haunted, makes his eyes water.

Someone comes up and stands behind him. "I didn't do it," he says. "They fell."

But when he turns around, it's the girl who lives next door. Alison. The sun is behind her and makes her shine. He squints. "You can come over to my house if you want to," she says. "Your mom says. She's going to pay me fifteen bucks an hour, which is way too much. Are your parents really rich or something? What's that?"

"It's Tilly's," he says. "But I don't think she wants it anymore."

She picks up Tilly's armadillo. "Pretty cool," she says. "Maybe I'll keep it for her."

Deep underground, the rabbits stamp their feet in rage.

Catherine loves the house. She loves her new life. She's never understood people who get stuck, become unhappy, can't change, can't adapt. So she's out of a job. So what? She'll find something else to do. So Henry can't leave his job yet, won't leave his job yet. So the house is haunted. That's okay. They'll work through it. She buys some books on gardening. She plants a rosebush and a climbing vine in a pot. Tilly helps. The rabbits eat off all the leaves. They bite through the vine.

"Shit," Catherine says when she sees what they've done. She shakes her fists at the rabbits on the lawn. The rabbits flick their ears at her. They're laughing, she knows it. She's too big to chase after them.

"Henry, wake up. Wake up."

"I'm awake," he said, and then he was. Catherine was crying: noisy, wet, ugly sobs. He put his hand out and touched her face. Her nose was running.

"Stop crying," he said. "I'm awake. Why are you crying?"

"Because you weren't here," she said. "And then I woke up and you were here, but when I wake up tomorrow morning you'll be gone again. I miss you. Don't you miss me?"

"I'm sorry," he said. "I'm sorry I'm not here. I'm here now. Come here."

"No," she said. She stopped crying, but her nose still leaked. "And now the dishwasher is haunted. We have to get a new dishwasher before I have this baby. You can't have a baby and not have a dishwasher. And you have to live here with us. Because I'm going to need some help this time. Remember Carleton, how fucking hard that was."

"He was one cranky baby," Henry said. When Carleton was three months old, Henry had realized that they'd misunderstood something. Babies weren't babies—they were land mines; bear traps; wasp nests. They were a noise, which was sometimes even not a noise, but merely a listening for a noise; they were a damp, chalky smell; they were the heaving, jerky, sticky manifestation of not-sleep. Once Henry had stood and watched Carleton in his crib, sleeping peacefully. He had not done what he wanted to do. He had not bent over and yelled in Carleton's ear. Henry still hadn't forgiven Carleton, not yet, not entirely, not for making him feel that way.

"Why do you have to love your job so much?" Catherine said.

"I don't know," Henry said. "I don't love it."

"Don't lie to me," Catherine said.

"I love you better," Henry said. He does, he does, he does loves Catherine better. He's already made that decision. But she isn't even listening.

"Remember when Carleton was little and you would get up in the morning and go to work and leave me all alone with them?" Catherine poked him in the side. "I used to hate you. You'd come home with takeout, and I'd forget I hated you, but then I'd remember again, and I'd hate you even more because it was so easy for you to trick me, to make things okay again, just because for an hour I could sit in the bathtub and eat Chinese food and wash my hair."

"You used to carry an extra shirt with you, when you went out," Henry said. He put his hand down inside her T-shirt, on her fat, full breast. "In case you leaked."

"You can't touch that breast," Catherine said. "It's haunted." She blew her nose on the sheets.

Catherine's friend Lucy owns an online boutique, Nice Clothes for Fat People. There's a woman in Tarrytown who knits stretchy, sexy Argyle sweaters exclusively for NCFP, and Lucy has an appointment with her. She wants to stop off and see Catherine afterwards, before she has to drive back to the city again. Catherine gives her directions, and then begins to clean house, feeling out of sorts. She's not sure she wants to see Lucy right now. Carleton has always been afraid of Lucy, which is embarrassing. And Catherine doesn't want to talk about Henry. She doesn't want to explain about the downstairs bathroom. She had planned to spend the day painting the wood trim in the dining room, but now she'll have to wait.

The doorbell rings, but when Catherine goes to answer it, no one is there. Later on, after Tilly and Carleton have come home, it rings again, but no one is there. It rings and rings, as if Lucy is standing outside, pressing the bell over and over again. Finally Catherine pulls out the wire. She tries calling Lucy's cell phone, but can't get through. Then Henry calls. He says that he's going to be late.

Liz opens the front door, yells, "Hello, anyone home! You've got to see your rabbits, there must be thousands of them. Catherine, is something wrong with your doorbell?"

Henry's bike, so far, was okay. He wondered what they'd do if the Toyota suddenly became haunted. Would Catherine want to sell it? Would resale value be affected? The car and Catherine and the kids were gone when he got home, so he put on a pair of work gloves and went through the house with a cardboard box, collecting all the things that felt haunted. A hairbrush in Tilly's room, an old pair of Catherine's tennis shoes. A pair of Catherine's underwear that he finds at the foot of the bed. When he picked them up he felt a sudden shock of longing for Catherine, like he'd been hit by some kind of spooky lightning. It hit him in the pit of the stomach, like a cramp. He dropped them in the box.

The silk kimono from Takashimaya. Two of Carleton's night-lights. He opened the door to his office, put the box inside. All the hair on his arms stood up. He closed the door.

Then he went downstairs and cleaned paintbrushes. If the paintbrushes were becoming haunted, if Catherine was throwing them out and buying new ones, she wasn't saying. Maybe he should check the Visa bill. How much were they spending on paint, anyway?

Catherine came into the kitchen and gave him a hug. "I'm glad you're home," she said. He pressed his nose into her neck and inhaled. "I left the car running—I've got to pee. Would you go pick up the kids for me?"

"Where are they?" Henry said.

"They're over at Liz's. Alison is babysitting them. Do you have money on you?"

"You mean I'll meet some neighbors?"

"Wow, sure," Catherine said. "If you think you're ready. Are you ready? Do you know where they live?"

"They're our neighbors, right?"

"Take a left out of the driveway, go about a quarter of a mile, and they're the red house with all the trees in front."

But when he drove up to the red house and went and rang the doorbell, no one answered. He heard a child come running down a flight of stairs and then stop and stand in front of the door. "Carleton? Alison?" he said. "Excuse me, this is Catherine's husband, Henry. Carleton and Tilly's dad." The whispering stopped. He waited for a bit. When he crouched down and lifted the mail slot, he thought he saw someone's feet, the hem of a coat, something furry? A dog? Someone standing very still, just to the right of the door? Carleton, playing games. "I see you," he said, and wiggled his fingers through the mail slot. Then he thought maybe it wasn't Carleton after all. He got up quickly and went back to the car. He drove into town and bought more soap.

Tilly was standing in the driveway when he got home, her hands on her hips. "Hi, Dad," she said. "I'm looking for King Spanky. He got outside. Look what Alison found."

She held out a tiny toy bow strung with what looked like dental floss, an arrow as small as a needle.

"Be careful with that," Henry said. "It looks sharp. Archery Barbie, right? So did you guys have a good time with Alison?"

"Alison's okay," Tilly said. She belched. " 'Scuse me. I don't feel very good."

"What's wrong?" Henry said.

"My stomach is funny," Tilly said. She looked up at him, frowned, and then vomited all over his shirt, his pants.

"Tilly!" he said. He yanked off his shirt, used a sleeve to wipe her mouth. The vomit was foamy and green.

"It tastes horrible," she said. She sounded surprised. "Why does it always taste so bad when you throw up?"

"So that you won't go around doing it for fun," he said. "Are you going to do it again?"

"I don't think so," she said, making a face.

"Then I'm going to go wash up and change clothes. What were you eating, anyway?"

"Grass," Tilly said.

"Well, no wonder," Henry said. "I thought you were smarter than that, Tilly. Don't do that anymore."

"I wasn't planning to," Tilly said. She spat in the grass.

When Henry opened the front door, he could hear Catherine talking in the kitchen. "The funny thing is," she said, "none of it was true. It was just made up, just like something Carleton would do. Just to get attention."

"Dad," Carleton said. He was jumping up and down on one foot. "Want to hear a song?"

"I was looking for you," Henry said. "Did Alison bring you home? Do you need to go to the bathroom?"

"Why aren't you wearing any clothes?" Carleton said.

Someone in the kitchen laughed, as if they had heard this.

"I had an accident," Henry said, whispering. "But you're right, Carleton, I should go change." He took a shower, rinsed and wrung out his shirt, put on clean clothes, but by the time he got downstairs, Catherine and Carleton and Tilly were eating Cheerios for dinner. They were using paper bowls, plastic spoons, as if it were a picnic. "Liz was here, and Alison, but they were going to a movie," she said. "They said they'd meet you some other day. It was awful—when they came in the door, King Spanky went rushing outside. He's been watching the rabbits all day. If he catches one, Tilly is going to be so upset."

"Tilly's been eating grass," Henry said.

Tilly rolled her eyes. As if.

"Not again!" Catherine said. "Tilly, real people don't eat grass. Oh, look, fantastic, there's King Spanky. Who let him in? What's he got in his mouth?"

King Spanky sits with his back to them. He coughs and something drops to the floor, maybe a frog, or a baby rabbit. It goes scrabbling across the floor, half-leaping, dragging one leg. King Spanky just sits there, watching as it disappears under the sofa.

Carleton freaks out. Tilly is shouting "Bad King Spanky! Bad cat!" When Henry and Catherine push the sofa back, it's too late, there's just King Spanky and a little blob of sticky blood on the floor.

Catherine would like to write a novel. She'd like to write a novel with no children in it. The problem with novels with children in them is that bad things will happen either to the children or else to the parents. She wants to write something funny, something romantic.

It isn't very comfortable to sit down now that she's so big. She's started writing on the walls. She writes in pencil. She names her characters after paint colors. She imagines them leading beautiful, happy, useful lives. No haunted toasters. No mothers no children no crocodiles no photocopy machines no Leonard Felters. She writes for two or three hours, and then she paints the walls again before anyone gets home. That's always the best part.

"I need you next weekend," The Crocodile said. Her rubber band ball sat on the floor beside her desk. She had her feet up on it, in an attempt to show it who was boss. The rubber band ball was getting too big for its britches. Someone was going to have to teach it a lesson, send it a memo.

She looked tired. Henry said, "You don't need me."

"I do," The Crocodile said, yawning. "I *do*. The clients want to take you out to dinner at Four Seasons when they come in to town. They want to go see musicals with you. *Rent. Phantom of the Cabaret Lion.* They want to go to Coney Island with you and eat hot dogs. They want to go out to trendy bars and clubs and pick up strippers and publicists and performance artists. They want to talk about poetry, philosophy, sports, politics, their lousy relationships with their fathers. They want to ask you for advice about their love lives. They want you to come to the weddings of their children and make toasts. You're indispensable, honey. I hope you know that."

"Catherine and I are having some problems with rabbits," Henry said. The rabbits were easier to explain than the other thing. "They've taken over the yard. Things are a little crazy."

"I don't know anything about rabbits," The Crocodile said,

digging her pointy heels into the flesh of the rubber band ball until she could feel the red rubber blood come running out. She pinned Henry with her beautiful, watery eyes.

"Henry." She said his name so gently that he had to lean forward to hear what she was saying.

She said, "You have the best of both worlds. A wife and children who adore you, a beautiful house in the country, a secure job at a company that depends on you, a boss who appreciates your talents, clients who think you're the shit. You *are* the shit, Henry, and the thing is, you're probably thinking that no one deserves to have all this. You think you have to make a choice. You think you have to give up something. But you don't have to give up anything, Henry, and anyone who tells you otherwise is a fucking rabbit. Don't listen to them. You can have it all. You *deserve* to have it all. You love your job. Do you love your job?"

"I love my job," Henry says. The Crocodile smiles at him tearily.

It's true. He loves his job.

When Henry came home, it must have been after midnight, because he never got home before midnight. He found Catherine standing on a ladder in the kitchen, one foot resting on the sink. She was wearing her gas mask, a black cotton sports bra, and a pair of black sweatpants rolled down so he could see she wasn't wearing any underwear. Her stomach stuck out so far, she had to hold her arms at a funny angle to run the roller up and down the wall in front of her. Up and down in a V. Then fill the V in. She had painted the kitchen ceiling a shade of purple so dark, it almost looked black. Midnight Eggplant.

Catherine has been buying paints from a specialty catalog. All the colors are named after famous books, *Madame Bovary*, *Forever Amber*, *Fahrenheit 451*, *Tin Drum*, *A Curtain of Green*, *Twenty Thousand Leagues Beneath the Sea*. She was painting the walls *Catch-22*, a novel she'd taught over and over again to undergraduates. It always went over well. The paint color was nice too. She couldn't decide if she missed teaching. The thing about teaching and having children is that you always ended up treating your children like undergraduates, and your undergraduates like children. There was a particular tone of voice.

She'd even used it on Henry a few times, just to see if it worked.

All the cabinets were fenced around with masking tape, like a crime scene. The room stank of new paint.

Catherine took off the gas mask and said, "Tilly picked it out. What do you think?" Her hands were on her hips. Her stomach poked out at Henry. The gas mask had left a ring of white and red around her eyes and chin.

Henry said, "How was the dinner party?"

"We had fettuccine. Liz and Marcus stayed and helped me do the dishes."

("Is something wrong with your dishwasher?" "No. I mean, yes. We're getting a new one.")

She had had a feeling. It had been a feeling like déjà vu, or being drunk, or falling in love. Like teaching. She had imagined an audience of rabbits out on the lawn, watching her dinner party. A classroom of rabbits, watching a documentary. Rabbit television. Her skin had felt electric.

"So she's a lawyer?" Henry said.

"You haven't even met them yet," Catherine said, suddenly feeling possessive. "But I like them. I really, really like them. They wanted to know all about us. You. I think they think that either we're having marriage problems or that you're imaginary. Finally I took Liz upstairs and showed her your stuff in the closet. I pulled out the wedding album and showed them photos."

"Maybe we could invite them over on Sunday? For a cookout?" Henry said.

"They're away next weekend," Catherine said. "They're going up to the mountains on Friday. They have a house up there. They've invited us. To come along."

"I can't," Henry said. "I have to take care of some clients next weekend. Some big shots. We're having some cash flow problems. Besides, are you allowed to go away? Did you check with your doctor, what's his name again, Dr. Marks?"

"You mean, did I get my permission slip signed?" Catherine said. Henry put his hand on her leg and held on. "Dr. Marks said I'm shipshape. Those were his exact words. Or maybe he said tip-top. It was something alliterative."

"Well, I guess you ought to go, then," Henry said. He

rested his head against her stomach. She let him. He looked so tired. "Before Golf Cart shows up. Or what is Tilly calling the baby now?"

"She's around here somewhere," Catherine said. "I keep putting her back in her bed and she keeps getting out again. Maybe she's looking for you."

"Did you get my email?" Henry said. He was listening to Catherine's stomach. He wasn't going to stop touching her unless she told him to.

"You know I can't check email on your computer anymore," Catherine said.

"This is so stupid," Henry said. "This house isn't haunted. There isn't any such thing as a haunted house."

"It isn't the house," Catherine said. "It's the stuff we brought with us. Except for the downstairs bathroom, and that might just be a draft, or an electrical problem. The house is fine. I love the house."

"Our stuff is fine," Henry said. "I love our stuff."

"If you really think our stuff is fine," Catherine said, "then why did you buy a new alarm clock? Why do you keep throwing out the soap?"

"It's the move," Henry said. "It was a hard move."

"King Spanky hasn't eaten his food in three days," Catherine said. "At first I thought it was the food, and I bought new food and he came down and ate it and I realized it wasn't the food, it was King Spanky. I couldn't sleep all night, knowing he was up under the bed. Poor spooky guy. I don't know what to do. Take him to the vet? What do I say? Excuse me, but I think my cat is haunted? Anyway, I can't get him out of the bed. Not even with the old alarm clock, the haunted one."

"I'll try," Henry said. "Let me try and see if I can get him out." But he didn't move. Catherine tugged at a piece of his hair and he put up his hand. She gave him her roller. He popped off the cylinder and bagged it and put it in the freezer, which was full of paintbrushes and other rollers. He helped Catherine down from the ladder. "I wish you would stop painting."

"I can't," she said. "It has to be perfect. If I can just get it right, then everything will go back to normal and stop being haunted and the rabbits won't tunnel under the house and make it fall down, and you'll come home and stay home, and our neighbors will finally get to meet you and they'll like you and you'll like them, and Carleton will stop being afraid of everything, and Tilly will fall asleep in her own bed, and stay there, and—"

"Hey," Henry said. "It's all going to work out. It's all good. I really like this color."

"I don't know," Catherine said. She yawned. "You don't think it looks too old-fashioned?"

They went upstairs and Catherine took a bath while Henry tried to coax King Spanky out of the bed. But King Spanky wouldn't come out. When Henry got down on his hands and knees, and stuck the flashlight under the bed, he could see King Spanky's eyes, his tail hanging down from the box frame.

Out on the lawn the rabbits were perfectly still. Then they sprang up in the air, turning and dropping and landing and then freezing again. Catherine stood at the window of the bathroom, toweling her hair. She turned the bathroom light off, so that she could see them better. The moonlight picked out their shining eyes, the moon-colored fur, each hair tipped in paint. They were playing some rabbit game like leapfrog. Or they were dancing the quadrille. Fighting a rabbit war. Did rabbits fight wars? Catherine didn't know. They ran at each other and then turned and darted back, jumping and crouching and rising up on their back legs. A pair of rabbits took off like racehorses, sailing through the air and over a long curled shape in the grass. Then back over again. She put her face against the window. It was Tilly, stretched out against the grass, Tilly's legs and feet bare and white.

"Tilly," she said, and ran out of the bathroom, wearing only the towel around her hair.

"What is it?" Henry said as Catherine darted past him, and down the stairs. He ran after her, and by the time she had opened the front door, was kneeling beside Tilly, the wet grass tickling her thighs and her belly, Henry was there too and he picked up Tilly and was carrying her back into the house. They wrapped her in a blanket and put her in her bed and because neither of them wanted to sleep in the bed where King Spanky was hiding, they lay down on the sofa in the family room, curled up against each other. When they woke up in the morning, Tilly was asleep in a ball at their feet.

*

For a whole minute or two, last year, Catherine thought she had it figured out. She was married to a man whose specialty was solving problems, salvaging bad situations. If she did something dramatic enough, if she fucked up badly enough, it would save her marriage. And it did, except that once the problem was solved and the marriage was saved and the baby was conceived and the house was bought, then Henry went back to work.

She stands at the window in the bedroom and looks out at all the trees. For a minute she imagines that Carleton is right, and they are living in Central Park and Fifth Avenue is just right over there. Henry's office is just a few blocks away. All those rabbits are just tourists.

Henry wakes up in the middle of the night. There are people downstairs. He can hear women talking, laughing, and he realizes Catherine's book club must have come over. He gets out of bed. It's dark. What time is it anyway? But the alarm clock is haunted again. He unplugs it. As he comes down the stairs, a voice says, "Well, will you look at that!" and then, "Right under his nose the whole time!"

Henry walks through the house, turning on lights. Tilly stands in the middle of the kitchen. "May I ask who's calling?" she says. She's got Henry's cell phone tucked between her shoulder and her face. She's holding it upside down. Her eyes are open, but she's asleep.

"Who are you talking to?" Henry says.

"The rabbits," Tilly says. She tilts her head, listening. Then she laughs. "Call back later," she says. "He doesn't want to talk to you. Yeah. Okay." She hands Henry his phone. "They said it's no one you know."

"Are you awake?" Henry says.

"Yes," Tilly says, still asleep. He carries her back upstairs. He makes a bed out of pillows in the hall closet and lays her down across them. He tucks a blanket around her. If she refuses to wake up in the same bed that she goes to sleep in, then maybe they should make it a game. If you can't beat them, join them.

*

Catherine hadn't had an affair with Leonard Felter. She hadn't even slept with him. She had just said she had, because she was so mad at Henry. She could have slept with Leonard Felter. The opportunity had been there. And he had been magical, somehow: the only member of the department who could make the photocopier make copies, and he was nice to all of the secretaries. Too nice, as it turned out. And then, when it turned out that Leonard Felter had been fucking everyone, Catherine had felt she couldn't take it back. So she and Henry had gone to therapy together. Henry had taken some time off work. They'd taken the kids to Yosemite. They'd gotten pregnant. She'd been remorseful for something she hadn't done. Henry had forgiven her. Really, she'd saved their marriage. But it had been the sort of thing you could do only once.

If someone has to save the marriage a second time, it will have to be Henry.

Henry went looking for King Spanky. They were going to see the vet: he had the cat cage in the car, but no King Spanky. It was early afternoon, and the rabbits were out on the lawn. Up above, a bird hung, motionless, on a hook of air. Henry craned his head, looking up. It was a big bird, a hawk maybe. It circled, once, twice, again, and then dropped like a stone, towards the rabbits. The rabbits didn't move. There was something about the way they waited, as if this were all a game. The bird dropped through the air, folded like a knife, and then it jerked, tumbled, fell. The wings loose. The bird smashed into the grass and feathers flew up. The rabbits moved closer, as if investigating.

Henry went to see for himself. The rabbits scattered, and the lawn was empty. No rabbits, no bird. But there, down in the trees, beside the bike path, Henry saw something move. King Spanky swung his tail angrily, slunk into the woods.

When Henry came out of the woods, the rabbits were back, guarding the lawn again and Catherine was calling his name. "Where were you?" she said. She was wearing her gas mask around her neck, and there was a smear of paint on her arm. Whiskey Horse. She'd been painting the linen closet.

"King Spanky took off," Henry said. "I couldn't catch him.

I saw the weirdest thing—this bird was going after the rabbits, and then it fell—"

"Marcus came by," Catherine said. Her cheeks were flushed. He knew that if he touched her, her skin would be hot. "He stopped by to see if you wanted to go play golf."

"Who wants to play golf?" Henry said. "I want to go up-stairs with you. Where are the kids?"

"Alison took them into town, to see a movie," Catherine said. "I'm going to pick them up at three."

Henry lifted the gas mask off her neck, fitted it around her face. He unbuttoned her shirt, undid the clasp of her bra. "Better take this off," he said. "Better take all your clothes off. I think they're haunted."

"You know what would make a great paint color? Can't believe no one has done this yet. Yellow Sticky. What about King Spanky?" Catherine said. She sounded like Darth Vader, maybe on purpose, and Henry thought it was sexy: Darth Vader, pregnant, with his child. She put her hand against his chest and shoved. Not too hard, but harder than she meant to. It turned out that painting had given her some serious muscle. That will be a good thing when she has another kid to haul around.

"Yellow Sticky. That's great. Forget King Spanky," Henry said. "King Spanky is a terrible name for a paint color."

Catherine was painting Tilly's room Lavender Fist. It was going to be a surprise. But when Tilly saw it, she burst into tears. "Why can't you just leave it alone?" she said. "I liked it the way it was."

"I thought you liked purple," Catherine said, astounded. She took off her gas mask.

"I hate purple," Tilly said. "And I hate you. You're so fat. Even Carleton thinks so."

"Tilly!" Catherine said. She laughed. "I'm pregnant, remember?"

"That's what you think," Tilly said. She ran out of the room and across the hall. There were crashing noises, the sounds of things breaking.

"Tilly!" Catherine said.

Tilly stood in the middle of Carleton's room. All around her lay broken night-lights, lamps, broken lightbulbs. The carpet was dusted in glass. Tilly's feet were bare and Catherine looked down, realized that she wasn't wearing shoes either. "Don't move, Tilly," she said.

"They were haunted," Tilly said, and began to cry.

"So how come your dad's never home?" Alison said.

"I don't know," Carleton said. "Guess what? Tilly broke all my night-lights?"

"Yeah," Alison said. "You must be pretty mad."

"No, it's good that she did," Carleton said, explaining. "They were haunted. Tilly didn't want me to be afraid."

"But aren't you afraid of the dark?" Alison said.

"Tilly said I shouldn't be," Carleton said. "She said the rabbits stay awake all night, that they make sure everything is okay, even when it's dark. Tilly slept outside once, and the rabbits protected her."

"So you're going to stay with us this weekend," Alison said.

"Yes," Carleton said.

"But your dad isn't coming," Alison said.

"No," Carleton said. "I don't know."

"Want to go higher?" Alison said. She pushed the swing and sent him soaring.

When Henry puts his hand against the wall in the living room, it gives a little, as if the wall is pregnant. The paint under the paint is wet. He walks around the house, running his hands along the walls. Catherine has been painting a mural in the foyer. She's painted trees and trees and trees. Golden trees with brown leaves and green leaves and red leaves, and reddish trees with purple leaves and yellow leaves and pink leaves. She's even painted some leaves on the wooden floor, as if the trees are dropping them. "Catherine," he says. "You have got to stop painting the damn walls. The rooms are getting smaller."

Nobody says anything back. Catherine and Tilly and Carleton aren't home. It's the first time Henry has spent the night alone in his house. He can't sleep. There's no television to watch. Henry throws out all of Catherine's paintbrushes. But when Catherine gets home, she'll just buy new ones.

He sleeps on the couch, and during the night someone comes and stands and watches him sleep. Tilly. Then he wakes up and remembers that Tilly isn't there.

The rabbits watch the house all night long. It's their job.

Tilly is talking to the rabbits. It's cold outside, and she's lost her gloves. "What's your name?" she says. "Oh, you beauty. You beauty." She's on her hands and knees. Carleton watches from his side of the yard.

"Can I come over?" he says. "Can I please come over?"

Tilly ignores him. She gets down on her hands and knees, moving even closer to the rabbits. There are three of them, one of them almost close enough to touch. If she moved her hand, slowly, maybe she could grab it by the ears. Maybe she can catch it and train it to live inside. They need a pet rabbit. King Spanky is haunted. He spends most of his time outside. Her parents keep their bedroom door shut so that King Spanky can't get in.

"Good rabbit," Tilly says. "Just stay still. Stay still."

The rabbits flick their ears. Carleton begins to sing a song Alison has taught them, a skipping song. Carleton is such a girl. Tilly puts out her hand. There's something tangled around the rabbit's neck, like a piece of string or a leash. She wiggles closer, holding out her hand. She stares and stares and can hardly believe her eyes. There's a person, a little man sitting behind the rabbit's ears, holding on to the rabbit's fur and the piece of knotted string, with one hand. His other hand is cocked back, like he's going to throw something. He's looking right at her—his hand flies forward and something hits her hand. She pulls her hand back, astounded. "Hey!" she says, and she falls over on her side and watches the rabbits go springing away. "Hey, you! Come back!"

"What?" Carleton yells. He's frantic. "What are you doing? Why won't you let me come over?"

She closes her eyes, just for a second. Shut up, Carleton. Just shut up. Her hand is throbbing and she lies down, holds her hand up to her face. Shut. Up.

When she wakes up, Carleton is sitting beside her. "What are you doing on my side?" she says, and he shrugs.

"What are you doing?" he says. He rocks back and forth on his knees. "Why did you fall over?"

"None of your business," she says. She can't remember what she was doing. Everything looks funny. Especially Carleton. "What's wrong with you?"

"Nothing's wrong with me," Carleton says, but something is wrong. She studies his face and begins to feel sick, as if she's been eating grass. Those sneaky rabbits! They've been distracting her, and now, while she wasn't paying attention, Carleton's become haunted.

"Oh yes it is," Tilly says, forgetting to be afraid, forgetting her hand hurts, getting angry instead. She's not the one to blame. This is her mother's fault, her father's fault, and it's Carleton's fault too. How could he have let this happen? "You just don't know it's wrong. I'm going to tell Mom."

Haunted Carleton is still a Carleton who can be bossed around. "Don't tell," he begs.

Tilly pretends to think about this, although she's already made up her mind. Because what can she say? Either her mother will notice that something's wrong or else she won't. Better to wait and see. "Just stay away from me," she tells Carleton. "You give me the creeps."

Carleton begins to cry, but Tilly is firm. He turns around, walks slowly back to his half of the yard, still crying. For the rest of the afternoon, he sits beneath the azalea bush at the edge of his side of the yard, and cries. It gives Tilly the creeps. Her hand throbs where something has stung it. The rabbits are all hiding underground. King Spanky has gone hunting.

"What's up with Carleton?" Henry said, coming downstairs. He couldn't stop yawning. It wasn't that he was tired, although he was tired. He hadn't given Carleton a good-night kiss, just in case it turned out he was coming down with a cold. He didn't want Carleton to catch it. But it looked like Carleton, too, was already coming down with something.

Catherine shrugged. Paint samples were balanced across her stomach like she'd been playing solitaire. All weekend long, away from the house, she'd thought about repainting Henry's office. She'd never painted a haunted room before. Maybe if you mixed the paint with a little bit of holy water? She wasn't sure: What was holy water, anyway? Could you buy it? "Tilly's being mean to him," she said. "I wish they would make some friends out here. He keeps talking about the new baby, about how he'll take care of it. He says it can sleep in his room. I've been trying to explain babies to him, about how all they do is sleep and eat and cry."

"And get bigger," Henry said.

"That too," Catherine said. "So did he go to sleep okay?"

"Eventually," Henry said. "He's just acting really weird."

"How is that different from usual?" Catherine said. She yawned. "Is Tilly finished with her homework?"

"I don't know," Henry said. "You know, just weird. Different weird. Maybe he's going through a weird spell. Tilly wanted me to help her with her math, but I couldn't get it to come out right. So what's up with my office?"

"I cleared it out," Catherine said. "Alison and Liz came over and helped. I told them we were going to redecorate. Why is it that we're the only ones who notice everything is fucking haunted around here?"

"So where'd you put my stuff?" Henry said. "What's up?"

"You're not working here now," Catherine pointed out. She didn't sound angry, just tired. "Besides, it's all haunted, right? So I took your computer into the shop, so they could have a look at it. I don't know, maybe they can unhaunt it."

"Well," Henry said. "Okay. Is that what you told them? It's haunted?"

"Don't be ridiculous," Catherine said. She discarded a paint strip. Too lemony. "So I heard about the bomb scare on the radio."

"Yeah," Henry said. "The subways were full of kids with crew cuts and machine guns. And they evacuated our building for about an hour. We all went and stood outside, holding on to our laptops like idiots, just in case. The Crocodile carried out her rubber band ball, which must weigh about thirty pounds. It kind of freaked people out, even the firemen. I thought the bomb squad was going to blow it up. So tell me about your weekend."

"Tell me about yours," Catherine said.

"You know," Henry said. "Those clients are assholes. But they don't know they're assholes, so it's almost okay. You just have to feel sorry for them. They don't get it. You have to explain how to have fun, and then they get anxious, so they drink a lot and so you have to drink too. Even The Crocodile got drunk. She did this weird wriggly dance to a Pete Seeger song. So what's their place like?"

"It's nice," Catherine said. "You know, really nice."

"So you had a good weekend? Carleton and Tilly had a good time?"

"It was really nice," Catherine said. "No, really, it was great. I had a fucking great time. So you're sure you can make it home for dinner on Thursday."

It wasn't a question.

"Carleton looks like he might be coming down with something," Henry said. "Here. Do you think I feel hot? Or is it cold in here?"

Catherine said, "You're fine. It's going to be Liz and Marcus and some of the women from the book group and their husbands, and what's her name, the real estate agent. I invited her too. Did you know she's written a book? I was going to do that! I'm getting the new dishwasher tomorrow. No more paper plates. And the lawn care specialist is coming on Monday to take care of the rabbits. I thought I'd drop off King Spanky at the vet, take Tilly and Carleton back to the city, stay with Lucy for two or three days—did you know she tried to find this place and got lost? She's supposed to come up for dinner too—just in case the poison doesn't go away right away, you know, or in case we end up with piles of dead rabbits on the lawn. Your job is to make sure there are no dead rabbits when I bring Tilly and Carleton back."

"I guess I can do that," Henry said.

"You'd better," Catherine said. She stood up with some difficulty, came and leaned over his chair. Her stomach bumped into his shoulder. Her breath was hot. Her hands were full of strips of color. "Sometimes I wish that instead of working for The Crocodile, you were having an affair with her. I mean, that way you'd come home when you're supposed to. You wouldn't want me to be suspicious."

"I don't have any time to have affairs," Henry said. He

sounded put out. Maybe he was thinking about Leonard Felter. Or maybe he was picturing The Crocodile naked. The Crocodile wearing stretchy red rubber sex gear. Catherine imagined telling Henry the truth about Leonard Felter. I didn't have an affair. Did not. I made it up. Is that a problem?

"That's exactly what I mean," Catherine said. "You'd better be here for dinner. You live here, Henry. You're my husband. I want you to meet our friends. I want you to be here when I have this baby. I want you to fix what's wrong with the downstairs bathroom. I want you to talk to Tilly. She's having a rough time. She won't talk to me about it."

"Tilly's fine," Henry said. "We had a long talk tonight. She said she's sorry she broke all of Carleton's night-lights. I like the trees, by the way. You're not going to paint over them, are you?"

"I had all this leftover paint," Catherine said. "I was getting tired of just slapping paint on with the rollers. I wanted to do something fancier."

"You could paint some trees in my office, when you paint my office."

"Maybe," Catherine said. "Ooof, this baby won't stop kicking me." She lay down on the floor in front of Henry, and lifted her feet into his lap. "Rub my feet. I've still got so much fucking paint. But once your office is done, I'm done with the painting. Tilly told me to stop it or else. She keeps hiding my gas mask. Will you be here for dinner?"

"I'll be here for dinner," Henry said, rubbing her feet. He really meant it. He was thinking about the exterminator, about rabbit corpses scattered all across the lawn, like a war zone. Poor rabbits. What a mess.

After they went to see the therapist, after they went to Yosemite and came home again, Henry said to Catherine, "I don't want to talk about it anymore. I don't want to talk about it ever again. Can we not talk about it?"

"Talk about what?" Catherine said. But she had almost been sorry. It had been so much work. She'd had to invent so many details that eventually it began to seem as if she hadn't made it up after all. It was too strange, too confusing, to pretend it had never happened, when, after all, it *had* never happened.

*

Catherine is dressing for dinner. When she looks in the mirror, she's as big as a cruise ship. A water tower. She doesn't look like herself at all. The baby kicks her right under the ribs.

"Stop that," she says. She's sure the baby is going to be a girl. Tilly won't be pleased. Tilly has been extra good all day. She helped make the salad. She set the table. She put on a nice dress.

Tilly is hiding from Carleton under a table in the foyer. If Carleton finds her, Tilly will scream. Carleton is haunted, and nobody has noticed. Nobody cares except Tilly. Tilly says names for the baby, under her breath. Dollop. Shampool. Custard. Knock, knock. The rabbits are out on the lawn, and King Spanky has gotten into the bed again, and he won't come out, not for a million haunted alarm clocks.

Her mother has painted trees all along the wall under the staircase. They don't look like real trees. They aren't real colors. It doesn't look like Central Park at all. In among the trees, her mother has painted a little door. It isn't a real door, except that when Tilly goes over to look at it, it is real. There's a doorknob, and when Tilly turns it, the door opens. Underneath the stairs, there's another set of stairs, little dirt stairs, going down. On the third stair, there's a rabbit sitting there, looking up at Tilly. It hops down, one step, and then another. Then another.

"Rumpled Stiltskin!" Tilly says to the rabbit. "Lipstick!"

Catherine goes to the closet to get out Henry's pink shirt. What's the name of that real estate agent? Why can't she ever remember? She lays the shirt on the bed and then stands there for a moment, stunned. It's too much. The pink shirt is haunted. She pulls out all of Henry's suits, his shirts, his ties. All haunted. Every fucking thing is haunted. Even the fucking shoes. When she pulls out the drawers, socks, underwear, handkerchiefs, everything, it's all spoiled. All haunted. Henry doesn't have a thing to wear. She goes downstairs, gets trash bags, and goes back upstairs again. She begins to dump clothes into the trash bags.

She can see Carleton framed in the bedroom window. He's chasing the rabbits with a stick. She hoists open the window, leans out, yells, "Stay away from those fucking rabbits, Carleton! Do you hear me?"

She doesn't recognize her own voice.

Tilly is running around downstairs somewhere. She's yelling too, but her voice gets farther and farther away, fainter and fainter. She's yelling, "Hairbrush! Zeppelin! Torpedo! Marmalade!"

The doorbell rings.

The Crocodile started laughing. "Okay, Henry. Calm down."

He fired off another rubber band. "I mean it," he said. "I'm late. I'll be late. She's going to kill me."

"Tell her it's my fault," The Crocodile said. "So they started dinner without you. Big deal."

"I tried calling," Henry said. "Nobody answered." He had an idea that the phone was haunted now. That's why Catherine wasn't answering. They'd have to get a new phone. Maybe the lawn specialist would know a house specialist. Maybe somebody could do something about this. "I should go home," he said. "I should go home right now." But he didn't get up. "I think we've gotten ourselves into a mess, me and Catherine. I don't think things are good right now."

"Tell someone who cares," The Crocodile suggested. She wiped at her eyes. "Get out of here. Go catch your train. Have a great weekend. See you on Monday."

So Henry goes home, he has to go home, but of course he's late, it's too late. The train is haunted. The closer they get to his station, the more haunted the train gets. None of the other passengers seem to notice. And of course, his bike turns out to be haunted, too. He leaves it at the station and he walks home in the dark, down the bike path. Something follows him home. Maybe it's King Spanky.

Here's the yard, and here's his house. He loves his house, how it's all lit up. You can see right through the windows, you can see the living room, which Catherine has painted Ghost Crab. The trim is Rat Fink. Catherine has worked so hard. The driveway is full of cars, and inside, people are eating dinner. They're admiring Catherine's trees. They haven't waited for him, and that's fine. His neighbors: he loves his neighbors. He's going to love them as soon as he meets them. His wife is going to have a baby any day now. His daughter will stop walking in her sleep. His son isn't haunted. The moon shines down and paints the world a color he's never seen before. Oh, Catherine, wait till you see this. Shining lawn, shining rabbits, shining world. The rabbits are out on the lawn. They've been waiting for him, all this time, they've been waiting. Here's his rabbit, his very own rabbit. Who needs a bike? He sits on his rabbit, legs pressed against the warm, silky, shining flanks, one hand holding on to the rabbit's fur, the knotted string around its neck. He has something in his other hand, and when he looks, he sees it's a spear. All around him, the others are sitting on their rabbits, waiting patiently, quietly. They've been waiting for a long time, but the waiting is almost over. In a little while, the dinner party will be over and the war will begin.

2004

TIM POWERS

(b. 1952)

Pat Moore

"Is it okay if you're one of the ten people I send the letter to," said the voice on the telephone, "or is that redundant? I don't want to screw this up. 'Ear repair' sounds horrible."

Moore exhaled smoke and put out his Marlboro in the half inch of cold coffee in his cup. "No, Rick, don't send it to me. In fact, you're screwed—it says you have to have ten friends."

He picked up the copy he had got in the mail yesterday, spread the single sheet out flat on the kitchen table and weighted two corners with the dusty salt and pepper shakers. It had clearly been photocopied from a photocopy, and originally composed on a typewriter.

> This has been sent to you for good luck. The original is in San Fransisco. You must send it on to ten friend's, who, you think need good luck, within 24 hrs of recieving it.

"I could use some luck," Rick went on. "Can you loan me a couple of thousand? My wife's in the hospital and we've got no insurance."

Moore paused for a moment before going on with the old joke; then, "Sure," he said, "so we won't see you at the low-ball game tomorrow?"

"Oh, I've got money for *that*." Rick might have caught Moore's hesitation, for he went on quickly without waiting for a dutiful laugh: "Mark 'n' Howard mentioned the chain letter this morning on the radio. You're famous."

> The luck is now sent to you—you will recieve Good Luck within three days of recieving this, provided you send it on. Do not send money, since luck has no price.

*

623

On a Wednesday dawn five months ago now, Moore had poured a tumbler of Popov Vodka at this table, after sitting most of the night in the emergency room at—what had been the name of the hospital in San Mateo? Not St. Lazarus, for sure—and then he had carefully lit a Virginia Slims from the orphaned pack on the counter and laid the smoldering cigarette in an ashtray beside the glass. When the untouched cigarette had burned down to the filter and gone out, he had carried the full glass and the ashtray to the back door and set them in the trash can, and then washed his hands in the kitchen sink, wondering if the little ritual had been a sufficient goodbye. Later he had thrown out the bottle of vodka and the pack of Virginia Slims too.

> A young man in Florida got the letter, it was very faded, and he resovled to type it again, but he forgot. He had many troubles, including expensive ear repair. But then he typed ten copy's and mailed them, and he got a better job.

"Where you playing today?" Rick asked.

"The Garden City in San Jose, probably," Moore said, "the six-and-twelve-dollar Hold 'Em. I was just about to leave when you called."

"For sure? I could meet you there. I was going to play at the Bay on Bering, but if we were going to meet there you'd have to shave—"

"And find a clean shirt, I know. But I'll see you at Larry's game tomorrow, and we shouldn't play at the same table anyway. Go to the Bay."

"Naw, I wanted to ask you about something. So you'll be at the Garden City. You take the 280, right?"

> Pat Moore put off mailing the letter and died, but later found it again and passed it on, and received threescore and ten.

"Right."

"If that crapped-out Dodge of yours can get up to freeway speed."

"It'll still be cranking along when your Saturn is a planter somewhere."

"Great, so I'll see you there," Rick said. "Hey," he added with forced joviality, "you're famous!"

> Do not ignore this letter
> ST LAZARUS

"Type up ten copies with your name in it, you can be famous too," Moore said, standing up and crumpling the letter. "Send one to Mark 'n' Howard. See you."

He hung up the phone and fetched his car keys from the cluttered table by the front door. The chilly sea breeze outside was a reproach after the musty staleness of the apartment, and he was glad he'd brought his denim jacket.

He combed his hair in the rearview mirror while the Dodge's old slant-six engine idled in the carport, and he wondered if he would see the day when his brown hair might turn gray. He was still thirty years short of threescore and ten, and he wasn't envying the Pat Moore in the chain letter.

The first half hour of the drive down the 280 was quiet, with a Gershwin CD playing the *Concerto in F* and the pines and green meadows of the Fish and Game Refuge wheeling past on his left under the gray sky, while the pastel houses of Hillsborough and Redwood City marched across the eastern hills. The car smelled familiarly of Marlboros and Doublemint gum and engine exhaust.

Just over those hills, on the 101 overlooking the bay, Trish had driven her Ford Granada over an unrailed embankment at midnight, after a St. Patrick's Day party at Bay Meadows. Moore was objectively sure he would drive on the 101 some day, but not yet.

Traffic was light on the 280 this morning, and in his rearview mirror he saw the little white car surging from side to side in the lanes as it passed other vehicles. Like most modern cars, it looked to Moore like an oversized computer mouse. He clicked up his turn signal lever and drifted over the lane-divider bumps into the right lane.

The white car—he could see the blue Chevy cross on its hood now—swooped up in the lane Moore had just left, but instead of rocketing on past him, it slowed, pacing Moore's old Dodge at sixty miles an hour.

Moore glanced to his left, wondering if he knew the driver

of the Chevy—but it was a lean-faced stranger in sunglasses, looking straight at him. In the moment before Moore recognized the thing as a shotgun viewed muzzle-on, he thought the man was holding up a microphone; but instantly another person in the white car had blocked the driver—Moore glimpsed only a purple shirt and long dark hair—and then with squealing tires the car veered sharply away to the left.

Moore gripped the hard green plastic of his steering wheel and looked straight ahead; he was braced for the sound of the Chevy hitting the center-divider fence, and so he didn't jump when he heard the crash—even though the seat rocked under him and someone was now sitting in the car with him, on the passenger side against the door. For one unthinking moment he assumed someone had been thrown from the Chevrolet and had landed in his car.

He focused on the lane ahead and on holding the Dodge Dart steady between the white lines. Nobody could have come through the roof, or the windows; or the doors. Must have been hiding in the back seat all this time, he thought, and only now jumped over into the front. What timing. He was panting shallowly, and his ribs tingled, and he made himself take a deep breath and let it out.

He looked to his right. A dark-haired woman in a purple dress was grinning at him. Her hair hung in a neat pageboy cut, and she wasn't panting.

"I'm your guardian angel," she said. "And guess what my name is."

Moore carefully lifted his foot from the accelerator—he didn't trust himself with the brake yet—and steered the Dodge onto the dirt shoulder. When the car had slowed to the point where he could hear gravel popping under the tires, he pressed the brake; the abrupt stop rocked him forward, though the woman beside him didn't shift on the old green upholstery.

"And guess what my name is," she said again.

The sweat rolling down his chest under his shirt was a sharp tang in his nostrils. "Hmm," he said, to test his voice; then he said, "You can get out of the car now."

In the front pocket of his jeans was a roll of hundred-dollar bills, but his left hand was only inches away from the .38 revolver tucked into the open seam at the side of the seat. But both the woman's hands were visible on her lap, and empty.

She didn't move.

The engine was still running, shaking the car, and he could smell the hot exhaust fumes seeping up through the floor. He sighed, then reluctantly reached forward and switched off the ignition.

"I shouldn't be talking to you," the woman said in the sudden silence. "*She* told me not to. But I just now saved your life. So don't tell me to get out of the car."

It had been a purple shirt or something, and dark hair. But this was obviously not the person he'd glimpsed in the Chevy. A team, twins?

"What's your name?" he asked absently. A van whipped past on the left, and the car rocked on its shock absorbers.

"Pat Moore, same as yours," she said with evident satisfaction. He noticed that every time he glanced at her she looked away from something else to meet his eyes, as if whenever he wasn't watching her she was studying the interior of the car, or his shirt, or the freeway lanes.

"Did you—get threescore and ten?" he asked. Something more like a nervous tic than a smile was twitching his lips. "When you sent out the letter?"

"That wasn't me, that was *her*. And she hasn't got it yet. And she won't, either, if her students kill all the available Pat Moores. You're in trouble every which way, but I like you."

"Listen, when did you get into my car?"

"About ten seconds ago. What if he had backup, another car following him? You should get moving again."

Moore called up the instant's glimpse he had got of the thing in front of the driver's hand—the ring had definitely been the muzzle of a shotgun, twelve-gauge, probably a pistol-grip. And he seized on her remark about a backup car because the thought was manageable and complete. He clanked the gearshift into park, and the Dodge started at the first twist of the key, and he levered it into drive and gunned along the shoulder in a cloud of dust until he had got up enough speed to swing into the right lane between two yellow Stater Brothers trucks.

He concentrated on working his way over to the fast lane, and then when he had got there, his engine roaring, he just watched the rearview mirror and the oncoming exit signs until he found a chance to make a sharp right across all the lanes and straight into the exit lane that swept toward the southbound 85. A couple of cars behind him honked.

He was going too fast for the curving interchange lane, his tires chirruping on the pavement, and he wrestled with the wheel and stroked the brake.

"Who's getting off behind us?" he asked sharply.

"I can't see," she said.

He darted a glance at the rearview mirror, and was pleased to see only a slow-moving old station wagon, far back.

"A station wagon," she said, though she still hadn't turned around. Maybe she had looked in the passenger-side door mirror.

He had got the car back under control by the time he merged with the southbound lanes, and then he braked, for the 85 was ending ahead at a traffic signal by the grounds of some college.

"Is your neck hurt?" he asked. "Can't twist your head around?"

"It's not that. I can't see anything you don't see."

He tried to frame an answer to that, or a question about it, and finally just said, "I bet we could find a bar fairly readily. Around here."

"I can't drink, I don't have any ID."

"You can have a Virgin Mary," he said absently, catching a green light and turning right just short of the college. "Celery stick to stir it with." Raindrops began spotting the dust on the windshield.

"I'm not so good at touching things," she said. "I'm not actually a living person."

"Okay, see, that means what? You're a *dead* person, a ghost?"

"Yes."

Already disoriented, Moore flexed his mind to see if anything in his experience or philosophies might let him believe this, and there was nothing that did. This woman, probably a neighbor, simply knew who he was, and she had hidden in the back of his car back at the apartment parking lot. She was probably insane. It would be a mistake to get further involved with her.

"Here's a place," he said, swinging the car into a strip-mall parking lot to the right. "Pirate's Cove. We can see how well you handle peanuts or something, before you try a drink."

He parked behind the row of stores, and the back door of the Pirate's Cove led them down a hallway stacked with boxes before they stepped through an arch into the dim bar. There were no other customers in the place at this early hour, and the room smelled more like bleach than beer; the teenaged-looking bartender barely gave them a glance and a nod as Moore led the woman across the worn carpet and the parqueted square to a table under a football poster. There were four low stools instead of chairs.

The woman couldn't remember any movies she'd ever seen, and claimed not to have heard about the war in Iraq, so when Moore walked to the bar and came back with a glass of Budweiser and a bowl of popcorn, he sat down and just stared at her. She was easier to see in the dim light from the jukebox and the neon bar-signs than she had been out in the gray daylight. He would guess that she was about thirty—though her face had no wrinkles at all, as if she had never laughed or frowned.

"You want to try the popcorn?" he asked as he unsnapped the front of his denim jacket.

"Look at it so I know where it is."

He glanced down at the bowl, and then back at her. As always, her eyes fixed on his as soon as he was looking at her. Either her pupils were fully dilated, or else her irises were black.

But he glanced down again when something thumped the table and a puff of hot salty air flicked his hair, and some popcorn kernels spun away through the air.

The popcorn remaining in the bowl had been flattened into little white jigsaw-puzzle pieces. The orange plastic bowl was cracked.

Her hands were still in her lap, and she was still looking at him. "I guess not, thanks."

Slowly he lifted his glass of beer and took a sip. That was a powerful raise, he thought, forcing himself not to show any astonishment—though you should have suspected a strong hand. Play carefully here.

He glanced toward the bar; but the bartender, if he had looked toward their table at all, had returned his attention to his newspaper.

"Tom Cruise," the woman said.

Moore looked back at her and after a moment raised his eyebrows.

She said, "That was a movie, wasn't it?"

"In a way." *Play carefully here.* "What did you—is something wrong with your vision?"

"I don't have any vision. No retinas. I have to use yours. I'm a ghost."

"Ah. I've never met a ghost before." He remembered a line from a Robert Frost poem: *The dead are holding something back.*

"Well, not that you could see. You can only see me because . . . I'm like the stamp you get on the back of your hand at Disneyland; you can't see me unless there's a black light shining on me. *She*'s the black light."

"You're in her field of influence, like."

"Sure. There's probably dozens of Pat Moore ghosts in the outfield, and *she*'s the whole infield. I'm the shortstop."

"Why doesn't . . . *she* want you to talk to me?" He never drank on days he intended to play, but he lifted his glass again.

"She doesn't want me to tell you what's going to happen." She smiled, and the smile stayed on her smooth face like the expression on a porcelain doll. "If it was up to me, I'd tell you."

He swallowed a mouthful of beer. "But."

She nodded, and at last let her smile relax. "It's not up to me. She'd kill me if I told you."

He opened his mouth to point out a logic problem with that, then sighed and said instead, "Would she know?" She just blinked at him, so he went on, "Would she know it, if you told me?"

"*Oh* yeah."

"How would she know?"

"You'd be doing things. You wouldn't be sitting here drinking a beer, for sure."

"What would I be doing?"

"I think you'd be driving to San Francisco. If I told you—if you asked—" For an instant she was gone, and then he could see her again; but she seemed two-dimensional now, like a projection on a screen—he had the feeling that if he moved to the side he would just see this image of her get narrower, not see the other side of her.

"What's in San Francisco?" he asked quickly.

"Well if you asked me about Maxwell's Demon-n-n-n—"

She was perfectly motionless, and the drone of the last consonant slowly deepened in pitch to silence. Then the popcorn in the cracked bowl rattled in the same instant that she silently disappeared like the picture on a switched-off television set, leaving Moore alone at the table, his face suddenly chilly in the bar's air conditioning. For a moment "air conditioning" seemed to remind him of something, but he forgot it when he looked down at the popcorn—the bowl was full of brown BBs—unpopped dried corn. As he watched, each kernel slowly opened in white curls and blobs until all the popcorn was as fresh-looking and uncrushed as it had been when he had carried it to the table. There hadn't been a sound, though he caught a strong whiff of gasoline. The bowl wasn't cracked anymore.

He stood up and kicked his stool aside as he backed away from the table. She was definitely gone.

The bartender was looking at him now, but Moore hurried past him and back through the hallway to the stormy gray daylight.

What if she had backup? he thought as he fumbled the keys out of his pocket; and, *She doesn't want me to tell you what's going to happen.*

He only realized that he'd been sprinting when he scuffed to a halt on the wet asphalt beside the old white Dodge, and he was panting as he unlocked the door and yanked it open. Rain on the pavement was a steady textured hiss. He climbed in and pulled the door closed, and rammed the key into the ignition—

—when the drumming of rain on the car roof abruptly went silent, and a voice spoke in his head: *Relax. I'm you. You're me.*

And then his mouth opened and the words were coming out of his mouth: "We're Pat Moore, there's nothing to be afraid of." His voice belonged to someone else in this muffled silence.

His eyes were watering with the useless effort to breathe more quickly.

He knew this wasn't the same Pat Moore he had been in the bar with. This was the *her* she had spoken of. A moment later the thoughts had been wiped away, leaving nothing but an insistent pressure of *all-is-well*.

Though nothing grabbed him, he found that his head was turning to the right, and with dimming vision he saw that his right hand was moving toward his face.

But *all-is-well* had for some time been a feeling that was alien to him, and he managed to resist it long enough to make his infiltrated mind form a thought—*she's crowding me out*.

And he managed to think, too, *Alive or dead, stay whole*. He reached down to the open seam in the seat before he could lose his left arm too, and he snatched up the revolver and stabbed the barrel into his open mouth. A moment later he felt the click through the steel against his teeth when he cocked the hammer back. His belly coiled icily, as if he were standing on the coping of a very high wall and looking up.

The intrusion in his mind paused, and he sensed confusion, so he threw at it the thought, *One more step and I blow my head off*. He added, *Go ahead and call this bet, please. I've been meaning to drive the 101 for a while now.*

His throat was working to form words that he could only guess at, and then he was in control of his own breathing again, panting and huffing spit into the gun barrel. Beyond the hammer of the gun he could see the rapid distortions of rain hitting the windshield, but he still couldn't hear anything from outside the car.

The voice in his head was muted now: *I mean to help you.*

He let himself pull the gun away from his mouth, though he kept it pointed at his face, and he spoke into the wet barrel as if it were a microphone. "I don't want help," he said hoarsely.

I'm Pat Moore, and I want help.

"You want to . . . take over, possess me."

I want to protect you. A man tried to kill you.

"That's your pals," he said, remembering what the ghost woman had told him in the car. "Your students, trying to kill all the Pat Moores—to keep you from taking one over, I bet. Don't joggle me now." Staring down the rifled barrel, he cautiously hooked his thumb over the hammer and then pulled the trigger and eased the hammer down. "I can still do it with one pull of the trigger," he told her as he lifted his thumb away. "So you—what, you put off mailing the letter, and died?"

The letter is just my chain mail. The only important thing about it is my name in it, and the likelihood that people will reproduce it and pass it on. Bombers evade radar by throwing clouds of tinfoil. The chain mail is my name, scattered everywhere so that any blow directed at me is dissipated.

"So you're a ghost too."

A prepared ghost. I know how to get outside of time.

"Fine, get outside of time. What do you need me for?"

You're alive, and your name is mine, which is to say your identity is mine. I've used too much of my energy saving you, holding you. And you're the most compatible of them all—you're a Pat Moore identity squared, by marriage.

"Squared by—" He closed his eyes, and nearly lowered the gun. "Everybody called her Trish," he whispered. "Only her mother called her Pat." He couldn't feel the seat under him, and he was afraid that if he let go of the gun it would fall to the car's roof.

Her mother called her Pat.

"You can't have me." He was holding his voice steady with an effort. "I'm driving away now."

You're Pat Moore's only hope.

"You need an exorcist, not a poker player." He could move his right arm again, and he started the engine and then switched on the windshield wipers.

Abruptly the drumming of the rain came back on, sounding loud after the long silence. She was gone.

His hands were shaking as he tucked the gun back into its pocket, but he was confident that he could get back onto the 280, even with his worn-out windshield wipers blurring everything, and he had no intention of getting on the 101 anytime soon; he had been almost entirely bluffing when he told her, *I've been meaning to drive the 101 for a while now.* But like an alcoholic who tries one drink after long abstinence, he was remembering the taste of the gun barrel in his mouth: *That was easier than I thought it would be,* he thought.

He fumbled a pack of Marlboros out of his jacket pocket and shook one out.

As soon as he had got onto the northbound 85 he became aware that the purple dress and the dark hair were blocking the passenger-side window again, and he didn't jump at all. He had wondered which way to turn on the 280, and now he steered the car into the lane that would take him back north, toward San Francisco. The grooved interchange lane gleamed with fresh rain, and he kept his speed down to forty.

"One big U-turn," he said finally, speaking around his lit cigarette. He glanced at her; she looked three-dimensional again, and she was smiling at him as cheerfully as ever.

"I'm your guardian angel," she said.

"Right, I remember. And your name's Pat Moore, same as mine. Same as everybody's, lately." He realized that he was optimistic, which surprised him; it was something like the happy confidence he had felt in dreams in which he had discovered that he could fly, and leave behind all earthbound reproaches. "I met *her*, you know. She's dead too, and she needs a living body, and so she tried to possess me."

"Yes," said Pat Moore. "That's what's going to happen. I couldn't tell you before."

He frowned. "I scared her off, by threatening to shoot myself." Reluctantly he asked, "Will she try again, do you think?"

"Sure. When you're asleep, probably, since this didn't work. She can wait a few hours; a few days, even, in a pinch. It was just because I talked to you that she switched me off and tried to do it right away, while you were still awake. *Jumped the gun,*" she added, with the first laugh he had heard from her—it sounded as if she were trying to chant in a language she didn't understand.

"Ah," he said softly. "That raises the ante." He took a deep breath and let it out. "When did you . . . die?"

"I don't know. Some time besides now. Could you put out the cigarette? The smoke messes up my reception, I'm still partly seeing that bar, and partly a hilltop in a park somewhere."

He rolled the window down an inch and flicked the cigarette out. "Is this how you looked, when you were alive?"

She touched her hair as he glanced at her. "I don't know."

"When you were alive—did you know about movies, and current news? I mean, you don't seem to know about them now."

"I suppose I did. Don't most people?"

He was gripping the wheel hard now. "Did your mother call you Pat?"

"I suppose she did. It's my name."

"Did your . . . friends, call you Trish?"

"I suppose they did."

I suppose, I suppose! He forced himself not to shout at her. She's dead, he reminded himself, she's probably doing the best she can.

But again he thought of the Frost line: *The dead are holding something back.*

They had passed under two gray concrete bridges, and now he switched on his left turn signal to merge with the northbound 280. The pavement ahead of him glittered with reflected red brake lights.

"See, my wife's name was Patricia Moore," he said, trying to sound reasonable. "She died in a car crash five months ago. Well, a single-car accident. Drove off a freeway embankment. She was drunk." He remembered that the popcorn in the Pirate's Cove had momentarily smelled like spilled gasoline.

"I've been drunk."

"So has everybody. But—you might be her."

"Who?"

"My wife. Trish."

"I might be your wife."

"Tell me about Maxwell's Demon."

"I would have been married to you, you mean. We'd *really* have been Pat Moore then. Like mirrors reflecting each other."

"That's why *she* wants me, right. So what's Maxwell's Demon?"

"It's . . . she's dead, so she's like a smoke ring somebody puffed out in the air, if they were smoking. Maxwell's Demon keeps her from disappearing like a smoke ring would, it keeps her . . ."

"Distinct," Moore said when she didn't go on. "Even though she's got no right to be distinct anymore."

"And me. Through her."

"Can I kill him? Or make him stop sustaining her?" And you, he thought; it would stop him sustaining you. Did I stop sustaining you before? Well, obviously.

Earthbound reproaches.

"It's not a *him*, really. It looks like a sprinkler you'd screw onto a hose to water your yard, if it would spin. It's in her house, hooked up to the air conditioning."

"A sprinkler." He was nodding repeatedly, and he made himself stop. "Okay. Can you show me where her house is? I'm going to have to sleep sometime."

"She'd kill me."

"Pat—Trish—" Instantly he despised himself for calling her by that name. "—you're already dead."

"She can get outside of time. Ghosts aren't really in time anyway, I'm wrecking the popcorn in that bar in the future as much as in the past, it's all just cards in a circle on a table, none in front. None of it's really now or not-now. She could make me not ever—she could take my thread out of the carpet—you'd never have met me, even like this."

"Make you never have existed."

"Right. Never was any *me* at all."

"She wouldn't dare—Pat." Just from self-respect he couldn't bring himself to call her Trish again. "Think about it. If you never existed, then I wouldn't have married you, and so I wouldn't be the Pat Moore squared that she needs."

"If you *did* marry me. *Me*, I mean. I can't remember. Do you think you did?"

She'll take me there, if I say yes, he thought. She'll believe me if I say it. And what's to become of me, if she doesn't? That woman very nearly crowded me right out of the world five minutes ago, and I was wide awake.

The memory nauseated him.

What becomes of a soul that's pushed out of its body, he thought, as *she* means to do to me? Would there be *anything* left of *me*, even a half-wit ghost like poor Pat here?

Against his will came the thought, You always did lie to her.

"I don't know," he said finally. "The odds are against it."

There's always the 101, he told himself, and somehow the thought wasn't entirely bleak. Six chambers of it, hollow-point .38s. Fly away.

"It's possible, though, isn't it?"

He exhaled, and nodded. "It's possible, yes."

"I think I owe it to you. Some Pat Moore does. We left you alone."

"It was my fault." In a rush he added, "I was even glad you didn't leave a note." It's true, he thought. I was grateful.

"I'm glad she didn't leave a note," this Pat Moore said.

He needed to change the subject. "*You're* a ghost," he said. "Can't you make *her* never have existed?"

"No. I can't get far from real places or I'd blur away, out of focus, but she can go way up high, where you can look down on the whole carpet, and—twist out strands of it; bend somebody at right angles to *everything*, which means you're gone without a trace. And anyway, she and her students are all blocked against that kind of attack, they've got ConfigSafe."

He laughed at the analogy. "You know about computers?"

"No," she said emptily. "Did I?"

He sighed. "No, not a lot." He thought of the revolver in the seat, and then thought of something better. "You mentioned a park. You used to like Buena Vista Park. Let's stop there on the way."

Moore drove clockwise around the tall, darkly wooded hill that was the park, while the peaked roofs and cylindrical towers of the old Victorian houses were teeth on a saw passing across the gray sky on his left. He found a parking space on the eastern curve of Buena Vista Avenue, and he got out of the car quickly to keep the Pat Moore ghost from having to open the door on her side; he remembered what she had done to the bowl of popcorn.

But she was already standing on the splashing pavement in the rain, without having opened the door. In the ashy daylight her purple dress seemed to have lost all its color, and her face was indistinct and pale; he peered at her, and he was sure the heavy raindrops were falling right through her.

He could imagine her simply dissolving on the hike up to the meadow. "Would you rather wait in the car?" he said. "I won't be long."

"Do you have a pair of binoculars?" she asked. Her voice too was frail out here in the cold.

"Yes, in the glove compartment." Cold rain was soaking his hair and leaking down inside his jacket collar, and he wanted to get moving. "Can you . . . *hold* them?"

"I can't hold anything. But if you take out the lens in the middle you can catch me in it, and carry me."

He stepped past her to open the passenger-side door, and bent over to pop open the glove compartment, and then he knelt on the seat and dragged out his old leather-sleeved binoculars and turned them this way and that in the wobbly gray light that filtered through the windshield.

"How do I get the lens out?" he called over his shoulder.

"A screwdriver, I guess," came her voice, barely audible above the thrashing of the rain. "See the tiny screw by the eyepiece?"

"Oh. Right." He used the small blade from his pocketknife on the screw in the back of the left barrel, and then had to do the same with a similar screw on the forward end of it. The eyepiece stayed where it was, but the big forward lens fell out, exposing a metal cross on the inside; it was held down with a screw that he managed to rotate with the blade-tip—and then a triangular block of polished glass fell out into his palm.

"That's it, that's the lens," she called from outside the car.

Moore's cell phone buzzed as he was stepping backward to the pavement, and he fumbled it out of his jacket pocket and flipped it open. "Moore here," he said. He pushed the car door closed and leaned over the phone to keep the rain off it.

"Hey Pat," came Rick's voice, "I'm sitting here in your Garden City club in San Jose, and I could be at the Bay. Where are you, man?"

The Pat Moore ghost was moving her head, and Moore looked up at her. With evident effort she was making her head swivel back and forth in a clear *no* gesture.

The warning chilled Moore. Into the phone he said, "I'm—not far, I'm at a bar off the 85. Place called the Pirate's Cove."

"Well, don't chug your beer on my account. But come over here when you can."

"You bet. I'll be out of here in five minutes." He closed the phone and dropped it back into his pocket.

"They made him call again," said the ghost. "They lost track of your car after I killed the guy with the shotgun." She smiled, and her teeth seemed to be gone. "That was good, saying you were at that bar. They can tell truth from lies, and that's only twenty minutes from being true."

Guardian angel, he thought. "You killed him?"

"I think so." Her image faded, then solidified again. "Yes."

"Ah. Well—good." With his free hand he pushed the wet hair back from his forehead. "So what do I do with this?" he asked, holding up the lens.

"Hold it by the frosted sides, with the long edge of the triangle pointed at me; then look at me through the two other edges."

The glass thing was a blocky right-triangle, frosted on the sides but polished smooth and clear on the thick edges; obediently he held it up to his eye and peered through the two slanted faces of clear glass.

He could see her clearly through the lens—possibly more clearly than when he looked at her directly—but this was a mirror image: the dark slope of the park appeared to be to the left of her.

"Now roll it over a quarter turn, like from noon to three," she said.

He rotated the lens ninety degrees—but her image in it rotated a full 180 degrees, so that instead of seeing her horizontal he saw her upside down.

He jumped then, for her voice was right in his ear. "Close your eyes and put the lens in your pocket."

He did as she said, and when he opened his eyes again she was gone—the wet pavement stretched empty to the curbstones and green lawns of the old houses.

"You've got me in your pocket," her voice said in his ear. "When you want me, look through the lens again and turn it back the other way."

It occurred to him that he believed her. "Okay," he said, and sprinted across the street to the narrow stone stairs that led up into the park.

His leather shoes tapped the ascending steps, and then

splashed in the mud as he took the uphill path to the left. The city was gone now, hidden behind the dense overhanging boughs of pine and eucalyptus, and the rain echoed under the canopy of green leaves. The cold air was musky with the smells of mulch and pine and wet loam.

Up at the level playground lawn the swingsets were of course empty, and in fact he seemed to be the only living soul in the park today. Through gaps between the trees he could see San Francisco spread out below him on all sides, as still as a photograph under the heavy clouds.

He splashed through the gutters that were made of fragments of old marble headstones—keeping his head down, he glimpsed an incised cross filled with mud in the face of one stone, and the lone phrase "in loving memory" on another—and then he had come to the meadow with the big old oak trees he remembered.

He looked around, but there was still nobody to be seen in the cathedral space, and he hurried to the side and crouched to step in under the shaggy foliage and catch his breath.

"It's beautiful," said the voice in his ear.

"Yes," he said, and he took the lens out of his pocket. He held it up and squinted through the right-angle panels, and there was the image of her, upside down. He rotated it counterclockwise ninety degrees and the image was upright, and when he moved the lens away from his eye she was standing out in the clearing.

"Look at the city some more," she said, and her voice now seemed to come from several yards away. "So I can see it again."

One last time, he thought. Maybe for both of us; it's nice that we can do it together.

"Sure." He stepped out from under the oak tree and walked back out into the rain to the middle of the clearing and looked around.

A line of trees to the north was the panhandle of Golden Gate Park, and past that he could see the stepped levels of Alta Vista Park; more distantly to the left he could just make out the green band that was the hills of the Presidio, though the two big piers of the Golden Gate Bridge were lost behind miles of rain; he turned to look southwest, where the Twin Peaks and the TV tower on Mount Sutro were vivid above the misty streets; and then far away to the east the white spike of the Transamerica Pyramid stood up from the skyline at the very edge of visibility.

"It's beautiful," she said again. "Did you come here to look at it?"

"No," he said, and he lowered his gaze to the dark mulch under the trees. Cypress, eucalyptus, pine, oak—even from out here he could see that mushrooms were clustered in patches and rings on the carpet of wet black leaves, and he walked back to the trees and then shuffled in a crouch into the aromatic dimness under the boughs.

After a couple of minutes, "Here's one," he said, stooping to pick a mushroom. Its tan cap was about two inches across, covered with a patch of white veil. He unsnapped his denim jacket and tucked the mushroom carefully into his shirt pocket.

"What is it?" asked Pat Moore.

"I don't know," he said. "My wife was never able to tell, so she never picked it. It's either *Amanita lanei*, which is edible, or it's *Amanita phalloides*, which is fatally poisonous. You'd need a real expert to know which this is."

"What are you going to do with it?"

"I think I'm going to sandbag her. You want to hop back into the lens for the hike down the hill?"

He had parked the old Dodge at an alarming slant on Jones Street on the south slope of Russian Hill, and then the two of them had walked steeply uphill past close-set gates and balconies under tall sidewalk trees that grew straight up from the slanted pavements. Headlights of cars descending Jones Street reflected in white glitter on the wet trunks and curbstones, and in the wakes of the cars the tire tracks blurred away slowly in the continuing rain.

"How are we going to get into her house?" he asked quietly.

"It'll be unlocked," said the ghost. "She's expecting you now."

He shivered. "Is she. Well I hope I'm playing a better hand than she guesses."

"Down here," said Pat, pointing at a brick-paved alley that led away to the right between the Victorian-gingerbread porches of two narrow houses.

They were in a little alley now, overhung with rosebushes and rosemary, with white-painted fences on either side. Columns of fog billowed in the breeze, and then he noticed that they were human forms—female torsos twisting transparently in the air, blank-faced children running in slow motion, hunched figures swaying heads that changed shape like water balloons.

"The outfielders," said the Pat Moore ghost.

Now Moore could hear their voices: *Goddamn car—I got yer unconditional right here—excuse me, you got a problem?—He was never there for me—So I told him, you want it you come over here and take it—Bless me Father, I have died—*

The acid smell of wet stone was lost in the scents of tobacco and jasmine perfume and liquor and old, old sweat.

Moore bit his lip and tried to focus on the solid pavement and the fences. "Where the hell's her place?" he asked tightly.

"This gate," she said. "Maybe you'd better—"

He nodded and stepped past her; the gate latch had no padlock, and he flipped up the catch. The hinges squeaked as he swung the gate inward over flagstones and low-cut grass.

He looked up at the house the path led to. It was a one-story 1920s bungalow, painted white or gray, with green wicker chairs on the narrow porch. Lights were on behind stained-glass panels in the two windows and the porch door.

"It's unlocked," said the ghost.

He turned back toward her. "Stand over by the roses there," he told her, "away from the . . . the outfielders. I want to take you in in my pocket, okay?"

"Okay."

She drifted to the roses, and he fished the lens out of his pocket and found her image through the right-angle faces, then twisted the lens and put it back into his pocket.

He walked slowly up the path, treading on the grass rather than on the flagstones, and stepped up to the porch.

"It's not locked, Patrick," came a woman's loud voice from inside.

He turned the glass knob and walked several paces into a

high-ceilinged kitchen with a black-and-white-tiled floor; a blonde woman in jeans and a sweatshirt sat at a formica table by the big old refrigerator. From the next room, beyond an arch in the white-painted plaster, a steady whistling hiss provided an irritating background noise, as if a teakettle were boiling.

The woman at the table was much more clearly visible than his guardian angel had been, almost aggressively three-dimensional —her breasts under the sweatshirt were prominent and pointed, her nose and chin stood out perceptibly too far from her high cheekbones, and her lips were so full that they looked distinctly swollen.

A bottle of Wild Turkey bourbon stood beside three Flintstones glasses on the table, and she took it in one hand and twisted out the cork with the other. "Have a drink," she said, speaking loudly, perhaps in order to be heard over the hiss in the next room.

"I don't think I will, thanks," he said. "You're good with your hands." His jacket was dripping rainwater on the tiles, but he didn't take it off.

"I'm the solidest ghost you'll ever see."

Abruptly she stood up, knocking her chair against the refrigerator, and then she rushed past him, her Reeboks beating on the floor; and her body seemed to rotate as she went by him, as if she were swerving away from him; though her course to the door was straight. She reached out one lumpy hand and slammed the door.

She faced him again and held out her right hand. "I'm Pat Moore," she said, "and I want help."

He flexed his fingers, then cautiously held out his own hand. "I'm Pat Moore too," he said.

Her palm touched his, and though it was moving very slowly his own hand was slapped away when they touched.

"I want us to become partners," she said. Her thick lips moved in ostentatious synchronization with her words.

"Okay," he said.

Her outlines blurred for just an instant; then she said, in the same booming tone, "I want us to become one person. You'll be immortal, and—"

"Let's do it," he said.

She blinked her black eyes. "You're—agreeing to it," she said. "You're accepting it, now?"

"Yes." He cleared his throat. "That's correct."

He looked away from her and noticed a figure sitting at the table—a transparent old man in an overcoat, hardly more visible than a puff of smoke.

"Is he Maxwell's Demon?" Moore asked.

The woman smiled, baring huge teeth. "No, that's . . . a soliton. A poor little soliton who's lost its way. I'll show you Maxwell's Demon."

She lunged and clattered into the next room, and Moore followed her, trying simultaneously not to slip on the floor and to keep an eye on her and on the misty old man.

Moore stepped into a parlor, and the hissing noise was louder in here. Carved dark wood tables and chairs and a modern exercise bicycle had been pushed against a curtained bay window in the far wall, and a vast carpet had been rolled back from the dusty hardwood floor and humped against the chair legs. In the high corners of the room and along the fluted top of the window frame, things like translucent cheerleaders' pompoms grimaced and waved tentacles or locks of hair in the agitated air. Moore warily took a step away from them.

"Look over here," said the alarming woman.

In the near wall an air-conditioning panel had been taken apart, and a red rubber hose hung from its machinery and was connected into the side of a length of steel pipe that lay on a TV table. Nozzles on either end of the pipe were making the loud whistling sound.

Moore looked more closely at it. It was apparently two sections of pipe, one about eight inches long and the other about four, connected together by a blocky fitting where the hose was attached, and a stove stopcock stood half-open near the end of the longer pipe.

"Feel the air," the woman said.

Moore cupped a hand near the end of the longer pipe, and then yanked it back—the air blasting out of it felt hot enough to light a cigar. More cautiously he waved his fingers over the nozzle at the end of the short pipe; and then he rolled his hand in the air-jet, for it was icy cold.

"*It's* not supernatural," she boomed, "even though the air

conditioner's pumping room-temperature air. A spiral washer in the connector housing sends air spinning up the long pipe; the hot molecules spin out to the sides of the little whirlwind in there, and it's them that the stopcock lets out. The cold molecules fall into a smaller whirlwind inside the big one, and they move the opposite way and come out at the end of the short pipe. Room-temperature air is a mix of hot and cold molecules, and this device separates them out."

"Okay," said Moore. He spoke levelly, but he was wishing he had brought his gun along from the car. It occurred to him that it was a rifled pipe that things usually come spinning out of, but which he had been ready to dive into. He wondered if the gills under the cap of the mushroom in his pocket were curved in a spiral.

"But this is counter-entropy," she said, smiling again. "A Scottish physicist named Maxwell p-postulay-postul—guessed that a Demon would be needed to sort the hot molecules from the cold ones. If the Demon is present, the effect occurs, and vice versa—if you can make the effect occur you've summoned the Demon. Get the effect, and the cause has no choice but to be present." She thumped her chest, though her peculiar breasts didn't move at all. "And once the Demon is present, he—he—"

She paused, so Moore said, "Maintains distinctions that wouldn't ordinarily stay distinct." His heart was pounding, but he was pleased with how steady his voice was.

Something like an invisible hand struck him solidly in the chest, and he stepped back.

"You don't touch it," she said. Again there was an invisible thump against his chest. "Back to the kitchen."

The soliton old man, hardly visible in the bright overhead light, was still nodding in one of the chairs at the table.

The blonde woman was slapping the wall, and then a white-painted cabinet, but when Moore looked toward her she grabbed the knob on one of the cabinet drawers and yanked it open.

"You need to come over here," she said, "and look in the drawer."

After the things he'd seen in the high corners of the parlor, Moore was cautious; he leaned over and peered into the drawer—but it contained only a stack of typing paper, a felt tip laundry-marking pen, and half a dozen yo-yos.

As he watched, she reached past him and snatched out a sheet of paper and the laundry marker; and it occurred to him that she hadn't been able to see the contents of the drawer until he was looking at them.

I don't have any vision, his guardian angel had said. *No retinas. I have to use yours.*

The woman had stepped away from the cabinet now. "I was prepared, see," she said, loudly enough to be heard out on Jones Street, "for my stupid students killing me. I knew they might. We were all working to learn how to transcend time, but I got there first, and they were afraid of what I would do. So *boom-boom-boom* for Mistress Moore. But I had already set up the Demon, and I had xeroxed my chain mail and put it in addressed envelopes. Bales of them, the stamps cost me a fortune. I came back strong. And I'm going to merge with you now and get a real body again. You accepted the proposal—you said 'Yes, that's correct'—you didn't put out another bet this time to chase me away."

The cap flew off the laundry marker, and then she slapped the paper down on the table next to the Wild Turkey bottle. "Watch me!" she said, and when he looked at the piece of paper, she began vigorously writing on it. Soon she had written PAT in big sprawling letters and was embarked on MOORE.

She straightened up when it was finished. "Now," she said, her black eyes glittering with hunger, "you cut your hand and write with your blood, tracing over the letters. Our name is us, and we'll merge. Smooth as silk through a goose."

Moore slowly dug the pocketknife out of his pants pocket. "This is new," he said. "You didn't do this name-in-blood business when you tried to take me in the car."

She waved one big hand dismissively. "I thought I could sneak up on you. You resisted me, though—you'd probably have tried to resist me even in your sleep. But since you're accepting the inevitable now, we can do a proper contract, in ink and blood. Cut, cut!"

"Okay," he said, and unfolded the short blade and cut a nick in his right forefinger. "*You've* made a new bet now, though, and it's to me." Blood was dripping from the cut, and he dragged his finger over the *P* in her crude signature.

He had to pause halfway through and probe again with the blade-tip to get more freely flowing blood; and as he was painfully tracing the *R* in MOORE, he began to feel another will helping to push his finger along, and he heard a faint drone like a radio carrier-wave starting up in his head. Somewhere he was crouched on his toes on a narrow, outward-tilting ledge with no handholds anywhere, with vast volumes of emptiness below him—and his toes were sliding—

So he added quickly, "And I raise back at you."

By touch alone, looking up at the high ceiling, he pulled the mushroom out of his shirt pocket and popped it into his mouth and bit down on it. Check-and-raise, he thought. Sandbagged. Then he lowered his eyes, and in an instant her gaze was locked onto his.

"What happened?" she demanded, and Moore could hear the three syllables of it chug in his own throat. "What did you do?"

"*Amanita*," said the smoky old man at the table. His voice sounded like nothing organic—more like sandpaper on metal. "It was time to eat the mushroom."

Moore had resolutely chewed the thing up, his teeth grating on bits of dirt. It had the cold-water taste of ordinary mushrooms, and as he forced himself to swallow it he forlornly hoped, in spite of all his bravura thoughts about the 101 freeway, that it might be the *lanei* rather than the deadly *phalloides*.

"He ate a mushroom?" the woman demanded of the old man. "You never told me about any mushroom! Is it a poisonous mushroom?"

"I don't know," came the rasping voice again. "It's either poisonous or not, though, I remember that much."

Moore was dizzy with the first twinges of comprehension of what he had done. "Fifty-fifty chance," he said tightly. "The Death Cap Amanita looks just like another one that's harmless, both grow locally. I picked this one today, and I don't know which it was. If it's the poison one, we won't know for about twenty-four hours, maybe longer."

The drone in Moore's head grew suddenly louder, then

faded until it was imperceptible. "You're telling the truth," she said. She flung out an arm toward the back porch, and for a moment her bony forefinger was a foot long. "Go vomit it up, now!"

He twitched, like someone mistaking the green left-turn arrow for the green light. No, he told himself, clenching his fists to conceal any trembling. Fifty-fifty is better than zero. You've clocked the odds and placed your bet. Trust yourself.

"No good," he said. "The smallest particle will do the job, if it's the poisonous one. Enough's probably been absorbed already. That's why I chose it." This was a bluff, or a guess, anyway, but this time she didn't scan his mind.

He was tense, but a grin was twitching at his lips. He nodded toward the old man and asked her, "Who *is* the lost sultan, anyway?"

"Soliton," she snapped. "He's you, you—dumb-brain." She stamped one foot, shaking the house. "How can I take you now? And I can't wait twenty-four hours just to see if I *can* take you!"

"Me? How is he me?"

"My name's Pat Moore," said the gray silhouette at the table.

"Ghosts are solitons," she said impatiently, "waves that keep moving all-in-a-piece after the living push has stopped. Forward or backward doesn't matter to them."

"I'm from the *future*," said the soliton, perhaps grinning.

Moore stared at the indistinct thing, and he had to repress an urge to run over there and tear it apart, try to set fire to it, stuff it in a drawer. And he realized that the sudden chill on his forehead wasn't from fright, as he had at first assumed, but from profound embarrassment at the thing's presence here.

"I've blown it all on you," the blonde woman said, perhaps to herself even though her voice boomed in the tall kitchen. "I don't have the . . . sounds like 'courses' . . . I don't have the energy reserves to go after another living Pat Moore *now*. You were perfect, Pat Moore squared—why did you have to be a die-hard suicide fan?"

Moore actually laughed at that—and she glared at him in the same instant that he was punched backward off his feet by the hardest invisible blow yet.

He sat down hard and slid, and his back collided with the stove; and then, though he could still see the walls and the old man's smoky legs under the table across the room and the glittering rippled glass of the windows, he was somewhere else. He could feel the square tiles under his palms, but in this other place he had no body.

In the now-remote kitchen, the blonde woman said, "Drape him," and the soliton got up and drifted across the floor toward Moore, shrinking as it came so that its face was on a level with Moore's.

Its face was indistinct—pouches under the empty eyes, drink-wrinkles spilling diagonally across the cheekbones, petulant lines around the mouth—and Moore did not try to recognize himself in it.

The force that had knocked Moore down was holding him pressed against the floor and the stove, unable to crawl away, and all he could do was hold his breath as the soliton ghost swept over him like a spiderweb.

You've got a girl in your pocket, came the thing's raspy old voice in his ear.

Get away from me, Moore thought, nearly gagging.

Who get away from who?

"I can get another living Pat Moore," the blonde woman was saying, "if I never wasted any effort on you in the first place, if there was never a *you* for me to notice." He heard her take a deep breath. "I can do this."

Her knee touched his cheek, slamming his head against the oven door. She was leaning over the top of the stove, banging blindly at the burners and the knobs, and then Moore heard the triple click of one of the knobs turning, and the faint thump of the flame coming on. He peered up and saw that she was holding the sheet of paper with the ink and blood on it, and then he could smell the paper burning.

Moore became aware that there was still the faintest drone in his head only a moment before it ceased.

"Up," she said, and the ghost was a net surrounding Moore, lifting him up off the floor and through the intangible roof and far away from the rainy shadowed hills of San Francisco.

He was aware that his body was still in the house, still slumped against the stove in the kitchen, but his soul, indistinguishable

now from his ghost, was in some vast region where *in front*
and *behind* had no meaning, where the once-apparent dichotomy between *here* and *there* was a discarded optical illusion, where comprehension was total but didn't depend on
light or sight or perspective, and where even *ago* and *to come*
were just compass points; everything was in stasis, for motion
had been left far behind with sequential time.

He knew that the long braids or vapor trails that he encompassed and which surrounded him were lifelines, stretching
from births in that direction to deaths in the other—some linked
to others for varying intervals, some curving alone through
the non-sky—but they were more like long electrical arcs than
anything substantial; they were stretched across time and space,
but at the same time they were coils too infinitesimally small to
be perceived, if his perception had been by means of sight; and
they were electrons in standing waves surrounding an unimag-
inable nucleus, which also surrounded them—the universe,
apprehended here in its full volume of past and future, was one
enormous and eternal atom.

But he could feel the tiles of the kitchen floor beneath his
fingertips. He dragged one hand up his hip to the side-pocket
of his jacket, and his fingers slipped inside and touched the triangular lens.

No, said the soliton ghost, a separate thing again.

Moore was still huddled on the floor, still touching the lens
—but now he and his ghost were sitting on the other side of
the room at the kitchen table too, and the ghost was holding a
deck of cards in one hand and spinning cards out with the
other. The ghost stopped when two cards lay in front of each
of them. The Wild Turkey bottle was gone, and the glow from
the ceiling lamp was a dimmer yellow than it had been.

"Hold 'Em," the ghost rasped. "Your whole lifeline is the
buy-in, and I'm going to take it away from you. You've got a
tall stack there, birth to now, but I won't go all-in on you right
away. I bet our first seven years—Fudgsicles, our dad flying
kites in the spring sunsets, the star decals in constellations on
our bedroom ceiling, our mom reading the Narnia books out
loud to us. Push 'em out." The air in the kitchen was summery
with the pink candy smell of Bazooka gum.

Hold 'Em, thought Moore. I'll raise.

Trish killed herself, he projected at his ghost, *rather than live with us anymore. Drove her Granada over the embankment off the 101. The police said she was doing ninety, with no touch of the brake.* Again he smelled spilled gasoline—

—and so, apparently did his opponent; the pouchy-faced old ghost flickered, but came back into focus. "I make it more," said the ghost, "the next seven. Bicycles, the Albert Payson Terhune books, hiking with Joe and Ken in the oil fields, the Valentine from Teresa Thompson. Push 'em out, or forfeit."

Neither of them had looked at their cards, and Moore hoped the game wouldn't proceed to the eventual arbitrary showdown—he hoped that the frail ghost wouldn't be able to keep sustaining raises.

I can't hold anything, his guardian angel had said.

It hurt Moore, but he projected another raise at the ghost: *When we admitted we had deleted her poetry files deliberately, she said, "You're not a nice man." She was drunk, and we laughed at her when she said it, but one day after she was gone we remembered it, and then we had to pull over to the side of the road because we couldn't see through the tears to drive.*

The ghost was just a smoky sketch of a midget or a monkey now, and Moore doubted it had enough substance even to deal cards. In a faint birdlike voice it said, "The next seven. College, and our old motorcycle, and—"

And Trish at twenty, Moore finished, grinding his teeth and thinking about the mushroom dissolving in his stomach. *We talked her into taking her first drink. Pink gin, Tanqueray with Angostura bitters. And we were pleased when she said, "Where has this been all my life?"*

"All my life," whispered the ghost, and then it flicked away like a reflection in a dropped mirror.

The blonde woman was sitting there instead. "What did you have?" she boomed, nodding toward his cards.

"The winning hand," said Moore. He touched his two face-down cards. "The pot's mine—the raises got too high for him." The cards blurred away like fragments left over from a dream.

Then he hunched forward and gripped the edge of the table, for the timeless vertiginous gulf, the infinite atom of the lifelines, was a sudden pressure from outside the world, and this artificial scene had momentarily lost its depth of field.

"I can twist your thread out, even without his help," she told him. She frowned, and a vein stood out on her curved forehead, and the kitchen table resumed its cubic dimensions and the light brightened. "Even dead, I'm more potent than you are."

She whirled her massive right arm up from below the table and clanked down her elbow, with her forearm upright; her hand was open.

Put me behind her, Pat, said the Pat Moore ghost's remembered voice in his ear.

He made himself feel the floor tiles under his hand and the stove at his back, and then he pulled the triangular lens out of his pocket; when he held it up to his eye he was able to see himself and the blonde woman at the table across the room, and the Pat Moore ghost was visible upside down behind the woman. He rotated the glass a quarter turn, and she was now upright.

He moved the lens away and blinked, and then he was gripping the edge of the table and looking across it at the blonde woman, and at her hand only a foot away from his face. The fingerprints were like comb-tracks in clay. Peripherally he could see the slim Pat Moore ghost, still in the purple dress, standing behind her.

"Arm-wrestling?" he said, raising his eyebrows. He didn't want to let go of the table, or even move—this localized perspective seemed very frail.

The woman only glared at him out of her irisless eyes. At last he leaned back in the chair and unclamped the fingers of his right hand from the table-edge; and then he shrugged and raised his right arm and set his elbow beside hers. With her free hand she picked up his pocketknife and hefted it. "When this thing hits the floor, we start." She clasped his hand, and his fingers were numbed as if from a hard impact.

Her free hand jerked, and the knife was glittering in a fantastic parabola through the air, and though he was braced all the way through his torso from his firmly planted feet, when the knife clanged against the tiles the massive power of her arm hit his palm like a falling tree.

Sweat sprang out on his forehead, and his arm was steadily bending backward—and the whole world was rotating too, narrowing, tilting away from him to spill him, all the bets he and his ghost had made, into zero.

In the car the Pat Moore ghost had told him, *She can bend somebody at right angles to* everything, *which means you're gone without a trace.*

We're not sitting at the kitchen table, he told himself; we're still dispersed in that vaster comprehension of the universe.

And if she rotates me ninety degrees, he was suddenly certain, I'm gone.

And then the frail Pat Moore ghost leaned in from behind the woman, and clasped her diaphanous hand around Moore's; and together they were Pat Moore squared, their lifelines linked still by their marriage, and he could feel her strong pulse in supporting counterpoint to his own.

His forearm moved like a counterclockwise second hand in front of his squinting eyes as the opposing pressure steadily weakened. The woman's face seemed in his straining sight to be a rubber mask with a frantic animal trapped inside it, and when only inches separated the back of her hand from the formica tabletop, the resistance faded to nothing, and his hand was left poised empty in the air.

The world rocked back to solidity with such abruptness that he would have fallen down if he hadn't been sitting on the floor against the stove.

Over the sudden pressure release ringing in his ears, he heard a scurrying across the tiles on the other side of the room, and a thumping on the hardwood planks in the parlor.

The Pat Moore ghost still stood across the room, beside the table; and the Wild Turkey bottle was on the table, and he was sure it had been there all along.

He reached out slowly and picked up his pocketknife. It was so cold that it stung his hand.

"Cut it," said the ghost of his wife.

"I can't cut it," he said. Barring hallucinations, his body had hardly moved for the past five or ten minutes, but he was panting. "You'll die."

"I'm dead already, Pat. This—" She waved a hand from her shoulder to her knee "—isn't any good. I should be gone." She smiled. "I think that was the *lanei* mushroom."

He knew she was guessing. "I'll know tomorrow."

He got to his feet, still holding the knife. The blade, he saw, was still folded out.

"Forgive me," he said awkwardly. "For everything."

She smiled, and it was almost a familiar smile. "I forgave you in midair. And you forgive me too."

"If you ever did anything wrong, yes."

"Oh, I did. I don't think you noticed. Cut it."

He walked back across the room to the arch that led into the parlor, and he paused when he was beside her.

"I won't come in with you," she said, "if you don't mind."

"No," he said. "I love you, Pat."

"Loved. I loved you too. That counts. Go."

He nodded and turned away from her.

Maxwell's Demon was still hissing on the TV table by the disassembled air conditioner, and he walked to it one step at a time, not looking at the forms that twisted and whispered urgently in the high corners of the room. One seemed to be perceptibly more solid than the rest, but all of them flinched away from him.

He had to blink tears out of his eyes to see the air-hose clearly, and when he did, he noticed a plain on-off toggle switch hanging from wires that were still connected to the air-conditioning unit. He cut the hose and switched off the air conditioner, and the silence that fell then seemed to spill out of the house and across San Francisco and into the sky.

He was alone in the house.

He tried to remember the expanded, timeless perspective he had participated in, but his memory had already simplified it to a three-dimensional picture, with himself floating like a bubble in one particular place.

Which of the . . . jet trails or arcs or coils was mine? he wondered now. How long is it?

I'll be better able to guess tomorrow, he thought. At least I know it's there, forever—and even though I didn't see which one it was, I know it's linked to another.

GENE WOLFE

(b. 1931)

The Little Stranger

Dᴇᴀʀ Cᴏᴜѕɪɴ Dᴀɴɴʏ:

Please forgive me for troubling you with another letter. I know you understand. You are the only family I have, and as you are dead you probably do not mind. I am lonely, terribly lonely, living alone way out here. Yesterday I drove into town, and at the supermarket Brenda told me how lucky I am. She has to check groceries all day, keep house, and look after three children. I would love to know whether she divorced him or he divorced her, but I do not like to ask. You know how that is.

And why. I would dearly love to know why.

I said I would trade with her if I could stand up to so much work, which I could not, and I would take her children any- time and take care of them for as long as she wanted. They could run through the woods, I said, play Monopoly and Parcheesi, and explore the old road. I should have said only the girls, but I did not think of that in time, Danny. Not that I have anything against you boys, but I don't know much about them or taking care of them.

One time Sally Cusick showed me her husband's fish. There was a big lady fish and a little man fish, very shiny and silvery, and Sally said the man fish just came and went and that was that. I said I thought that was about how people were too, but Sally did not agree and has not had me over since although I have had her twice and invited her three times, one time when she said she could not come because the rain, as if rain ever stopped her from going anywhere. She is my nearest neighbor, and I could ride my bicycle down Miller Road and up the County Road and come anytime.

Brenda gave me the name of a plumber friend of hers. It is Jack C. Swierzbowski. I have called him (phoned), and he says he will come.

Every time I turn on the hot water the whole house moans.

655

I think that when I told you about this before, Danny, I said it yelled but it is really more of a moan. Or bellow, like a cow. It is a big house. I know you must remember my house from when you came as a little boy and we played store and all that. Well, probably you remember it bigger than it really is. But it *is* big. Five big bedrooms and all the other rooms like the big cold dining room. I never eat in there anymore. You and I would eat in my merry little kitchen, in the breakfast nook.

If Brenda really sends her girls to me someday that is where we will eat, all three crowded around the little table in the breakfast nook, and for the first day we will make chicken soup and bake brownies and cookies.

There it goes again, and I am not even running the water. Maybe I left it on somewhere, I will see.

Hugs,
Your cousin Ivy

Dear Cousin Danny:

I do not know whether I ever told you what a relief it is to me to write you like this, but it is. I never write to Mama or Papa because I saw them before they were embalmed and everything, and I went to the funerals. But I feel like you are still alive, so I can do it. I put on a stamp but no return address. That nice Mr. Chen at the Post Office said yesterday it might go to the Dead Letter Office, and I said yes that is where I want it to go. I did not even smile, but it was all I could do to keep from laughing out loud.

Mr. Swierzbowski came and worked for three hours and even got up on the roof, three floors up. Then he turned on the water to show me and it was as quiet as mice. But last night it was doing it again. I do not think I will call him again. It was almost two hundred dollars and I am so afraid he will fall.

I went for a ramble in the woods after he left, Danny, remembering how you and I played there. If Brenda sends her girls to stay with me for a while, they will go out there and talk about it afterward, and I ought to know the places.

So I started learning today. It is sad to see how much was fields and farms back in the colonial times. Now it is woods all over again and the Mohawks would feel right at home, but they are gone. You can still see the square hole where the old

Hopkins place stood, but it is filling up. Father used to say that the Hopkins were the last people around except us. He did not count the Cusicks, because it was too far to see their smoke. When they had a fire in the fireplace, I mean, or burned their leaves. Only I think probably Mr. Swierzbowski could have seen it when he was up on the roof. It is not so far that I could not ride over on my bicycle, Danny, and Sally drives all over.

She does not even feed those fish. Her husband does it.

It might be nicer if I had another cat. I used to have Pussums. She was as nice a cat as ever you saw, a calico and oh so pretty. I did not have her fixed or anything because I thought I would find a nice boy calico for her and they would have pretty kittens. I would give away the ones that were not calicos themselves, but I would keep the calicos and have three or four or even five of them. And then the mice would not come inside in the winter the way they do. It was terrible last winter.

Only Pussums got big and wanted a boy cat, but I had not found one for her yet. And one day she just disappeared. I should have gotten another cat then, I think. I did not because I kept thinking Pussums would come back after she had her little fling. Which she has not done, and it is more than three years.

Hugs,
Your cousin Ivy

Dear Cousin Danny,

Here I am, bothering you again. But a lot has happened since I wrote a week ago, and I really do need to tell somebody.

One night I was lying in bed and I heard the house moan in the way I have told you about. A few minutes later it did it again, and it did it again a few minutes after that.

Pretty soon I understood why it was so unhappy, Danny. It is just like Pussums. It wants another house. You were a man and would not understand, but I *knew*. It was not from thinking, even if I think a lot and am good at it, my teachers always said. I knew. So I got out of bed and told it as loud as I could that I would get it another house. At first I said a tool shed, but that didn't work, so a house. A little house, but a house.

Well, that is what I am going to do. I am going to talk to people who build houses and have a cottage built right here on my own property. I know they will probably cheat me, but I will have to bear it and keep the cheating as small as I can. I mean to talk to Mr. LaPointe at the bank about it. I know he will advise me, and he is honest.

So that is one thing, but just one. There is another one.

An old truck was going up Miller Road towing a big trailer when it broke down right in front of my house here. There were two men in the truck and two ladies in the trailer, and one lady has a little baby. They are all dark, with curly black hair and big smiles, even the baby.

The older man rang my bell and explained what had happened. He asked if he could pull his truck and the trailer up onto my front lawn until he and the other man could get the truck fixed.

I said all right, but then I thought what if they want to come inside to use the bathroom? Should I let them in? I decided I did not know them well enough to make up my mind about that, but you cannot keep somebody who needs to come inside quickly standing on the porch while you ask questions. I went into the parlor and watched them awhile through the window. They had put the baby on the lawn. The young lady was steering, and the men and the older lady were pushing, because the lawn is higher than Miller Road, and there was the ditch and everything. I could see everyone was working hard, so I made lemonade.

When it was ready they had tied a big chain around the biggest maple. There were zigzag ropes between the chain and their truck, turning and turning around little wheels, and they were pulling on the other end. It was working, too. They had already gotten the front end of their truck up on the grass. I went out and we had lemonade and talked awhile.

The older man is Mr. Zoltan, and the younger one is Johnny. The older lady is Marmar. Or something like that. I cannot say it like they do. She is Mrs. Zoltan. The young lady is Mrs. Johnny, and the baby is hers. Her name is Ivy, just like mine. Her mother's name is Suzette, and she is really quite pretty.

I never said about the bathroom, but I decided if they asked I would let them come in, especially Suzette. Only they never have. I think they are going in the woods. Now I am somewhat scared about going to bed. What if they break in while I am sleeping?

Well, I just went into the parlor and watched them through the window, and both men are working really hard on their truck, with flashlights to see and the engine in pieces. So I do not think they will break in tonight. They will be too tired. I will write to you again really soon, Danny.

Hugs,
Your cousin Ivy

P.S. The house has been quiet as mice ever since they came.

Dear Cousin Danny:

I have such good news! You will not believe how nicely everything is working out. Mr. Zoltan came to breakfast this morning. It was just bacon and eggs and toast, but he liked it. He drinks a lot of coffee. He said they were poor people, and they need parts for their truck. I said I did not have any, which was the truth. Then he asked if they could stay here until they could earn enough to fix their truck. Not in my house, I said. He said they would live in their trailer, like always, but if they parked it someplace without permission the police would make them leave, and they could not leave here so they would go to jail.

That was when I got my wonderful idea. I get many wonderful ideas, Danny, but this was the most wonderful ever. I explained to Mr. Zoltan that I wanted another house built on my property. Not a big house, just a little one. I said that if he and Johnny would build it for me in their spare time, I would let them stay.

Mr. Zoltan looked at me in a worried kind of way, then looked over at the stove. I said if they could fix a truck they could build a house, and would they do it?

He told me all over again how poor they were. He said they would have to earn enough to buy wood and shingles and so forth. They could find some things at the dump, he said, but they would have to buy the rest. It might take a long time.

I said that I would not ask them to buy the material, only to build me a little old-fashioned cottage like the picture I showed him. I would buy the material for them. That made him happy, and he agreed at once. He wanted to know where I wanted it built. I said you look around and decide where you think it ought to be and tell me.

So you see, Danny, why I said I had wonderful news. The Willis Lumber Co. in town will not cheat me more than they cheat everybody, and Mr. Zoltan and Johnny will not cheat me either, because I am not going to give them any money at all.

> Hugs,
> Your cousin Ivy

Dear Cousin Danny,

I had not planned to pester you with another letter as soon as this, but I just have to tell *somebody* how well my plan is going. Mr. Zoltan came to tell me he had found a foundation in the woods we could use. I knew it was the old Hopkins place, but I asked him questions about it, and it was. Then I told him we could not use it because it was not on my land.

It took all the happiness right out of him. He explained that digging the foundation and building the things to hold the cement were going to be some of the hardest work and would take a long while. The old Hopkins foundation is stone, big stone blocks like tombstones, and he said it was as good as new. So I thought, well, I was going to have to pay for the cement and picks and shovels and all that anyway, so perhaps I could buy the land.

When Mr. Zoltan had left, I called up (phoned) Mr. LaPointe and said I wanted the land where the house had been, and a patch in between so I could get there without going off my property. He said how high are you willing to go?

I thought about that, and looked at my bank books and the checking account and all that. I talked to that foreign woman at Merrill Lynch, too. Finally I called Mr. LaPointe back and said fifty thousand. He said he thought he could get it for me cheaper. By that time my mind was made up. I have a hard time making up my mind about things sometime, Danny, but when I do it is done. I said to buy me as much of the Hopkins property as fifty thousand would get, only to make sure where the old house was, was the part I was buying.

After that Mr. Zoltan came back twice to talk about other places, but I said wait.

Then (this was Tuesday afternoon, I think, Danny) Mr.

LaPointe called me. (Phoned.) He was so happy it made me happy for him. He said he had gotten the whole property for thirty-nine thousand five hundred. The whole farm, only it is all woods now. I went right out and told Johnny, who was working on the truck. And that afternoon he and Mr. Zoltan started shoveling the cellar out. I know they did because I went to see, and it is very black soil, good garden soil I would say and mostly rotted leaves. Compost is what the magazines call it.

I showed them pictures of houses like the one they are going to build for me, and they said they would go to the Willis Lumber Company and buy enough lumber to get started as soon as their truck would run again if I would give them the money. I said no, we will go in my car now and the company will deliver it for a little more money.

Which is what we did. You know how bossy I can be. Suzette needed a ride into town, too, so there were four of us on the drive in. She is opening a shop there to make money. It says "Psychic." I let her out in front of it, and Mr. Zoltan, Johnny, and I went to Willis's. I made them tell me what everything they wanted was and why they wanted it, but I promised that they could keep the scroll saw and the other new tools. We bought a whole keg of nails! And ever so much wood, Danny.

Now I am sitting in the Sun Room to write this, and I can hear their hammers, way off in the woods. If they get quiet before dark, I will go out there and see what the matter is.

Hugs,
Your cousin Ivy

Dear Cousin Danny,

I haven't even mailed that other letter, and here I am writing again. But the envelope is sealed and I do not wish to tear it open. You will get two letters at once, which I hope you will not mind too much.

There are reasons for this, a big one and a little one. I am going to tell you the little one first, so the big one does not squash it flat. It is that the young lady called me (phoned). She has a cell phone. She said she was Yvonne. I said who? She said Yvonne as plain as anything and she was staying with me. (This is what she said, Danny. It is not true.) Then she said I had given her a ride into town that morning, so I knew it was Suzette. She said she was ready to come home now and there was a friend who would drive her, only she called her a client. But she did not know the roads and neither did her friend.

So I gave her directions, how to find the County Road and how you turn on Miller Road and so on. I know you know already, so I will not repeat everything. Then I sat down and thought hard about the young lady. Could I have remembered her name wrong? I know I could not, not as wrong as that.

So she is fooling her friend, and if she will fool her friend she will fool me. I would like to talk with Marmar about her, but I know Marmar will not talk if I just come up and ask. I must think of something, and writing you these letters helps.

It helps more now, because I know that you get them and read them, Danny. That is my big thing. I know it because I saw you last night. You must have thought I was sleeping. I could see you were being very quiet so as not to wake me up.

But I was awake, sitting by the window looking down at the trailer and Mr. Zoltan's truck. I could not sleep. That is how it is with folks my age. We take naps during the day, and then we cannot sleep at night. I think that it is because God is getting us ready for the grave. Is that right? Did He ever tell you?

You went into the woods to look at my new house. I saw you go and sat up waiting for you to come back. The moon was low and bright when you did, and I got to see it right through you, which was very pretty and something I had never seen before at all. You looked at their truck and even went into the trailer without opening the door, which must be very handy when you are carrying a basket of laundry or grocery bags. When you went back into the woods I waited for you to come out for a while. I thought about coming downstairs and saying hello, but I knew you would think you woke me up. You did not, I just did, and it would not have been fair for me to make you feel guilty, as I am sure you would even if I said not to.

But I want you to know that I am often awake, and there is no reason I could not put on a robe and have a nice chat. I could make tea or anything like that which you might like, Danny.

> Hugs,
> Your cousin Ivy

*

Dear Cousin Danny,

I have had the nicest time! I must tell you. Yvonne (Suzette) was in town at her shop, and Marmar had ever so much work to do, cooking and cleaning her trailer. So I said I would look after little Ivy for a while. We played peekaboo and had a bottle, and I changed her three times. She is really the dearest little baby in the world! Of course I had to give her back eventually, which I did not like to do. But Mr. Zoltan came and wanted her, and I gave her to him. He looked pale and ill, I thought, and his hands shook. So I did not like to and I am afraid he will give little Ivy something. A really bad cold or the flu. But he is her grandfather, so I did.

Then something very, very odd happened. I cannot explain it and don't even know who to ask. I got to thinking about you, and how much I would like to talk to you. And it came to me that you might not want to come into my house unless you were invited. I know you could walk right through my door like you did into Mr. Zoltan's trailer, but I thought you would probably not want to. I thought of inviting you in this letter, and I do. Just come in anytime, Danny.

What is more, I remembered about the rock. There is this big rock in my flower bed close to the front porch, and I keep it there because it was in Mama's. She had it there because Papa always kept a key under it in case he lost his. Only when he died she took the key away for fear someone would find it and come in.

And I thought, well, I *want* Cousin Danny to come in and talk. So I will just put a key there for him to find, and tell him it is there. I got my extra key from the desk in Papa's study and went outside to put it under the rock.

But when I picked that rock up, there was foreign writing on the bottom. It was yellow chalk, I think, very ugly and new-looking. Just looking at it made me feel sick. I took that rock inside right away and washed it in the sink. It made me feel a lot better, and I think it made the rock feel better too. You know what I mean.

Anyway, that rock is all nice and clean now, Danny, and I have put the key under it as a sign that you are welcome to come in anytime. If you pick up the rock and there is bad writing on the bottom, I did not put it there. I do not even have any yellow chalk. Tell me when you come in, and I will wash it off.

But the main thing was little Ivy. She is the darlingest baby, and I just love her.

Hugs,
Your cousin Ivy

Dear Cousin Danny,

In some ways it has been very nice here today, but in others Not So Nice. Let me begin with one of the nice ones, which is Pusson. I went out to see how my new little house was. I had heard a lot of sawing and hammering that morning, and then it had stopped, and I thought I should see what the trouble was. Well, Danny, you would never guess.

It was a cat. Just a cat, not very big and really quite friendly once he gets to know you. He was up on the plywood that Mr. Zoltan and Johnny are going to nail the shingles on. They were afraid of him. Two big men afraid of a little cat! I thought it was silly and said Pussums, Pussums, Pussums! Which was the way I used to call my old cat, and this nice young cat came right down. I let him smell my fingers, and soon he was rubbing my legs.

Yes, Danny, I took Pusson home with me. I think he is really a calico cat under all the black. Other cats are not so friendly and sweet. I have kept Pussums's cat box all ready in case she ever comes home, and Pusson knows how to use it already. So I think he is calico underneath. Pussums found the boy cat she was looking for, and they had children, and this is her son, coming back to the Old Home Place to see how it was when his mama was young. You will think I am just a silly old woman for writing all that, but it could have happened, and since I want to believe it, why should I not be happy?

Besides there is nobody out here for Pusson to belong to except Sally Cusick and she should not have a cat because of all the fish. So he can live here with me, and if Sally ever comes he can hide under the sofa in the parlor.

The not so nice part is Mr. Cherigate. I did not know him at all until he pulled up in his big car. He was perfectly friendly and drank my tea and petted Pusson, but he told me very firmly that I cannot have Mr. Zoltan and Johnny put in the pipes and the electric like I had planned. Mr. Cherigate is a Building Inspector for the county. He showed me his badge and gave me his card, which I still have on the nice hallmarked silver tray that used to be Mama's when you were here. I must have a licensed plumber for the pipes and an electrician for the electric. I explained that Mr. LaPointe at the bank did not think I would need a building permit way out here, and he said I did not, but a building that people might live in must pass inspection and ever so much more.

Naturally I called Mr. Swierzbowski (phoned). He will do the plumbing, and he will send his friend Mr. Caminiti for the electric. I am sure it will cost ever so much, but I don't think I will be able to get Mr. Zoltan to pay, although I will try.

I am not sure if this is the worst thing or just a funny thing, Danny. Perhaps I will know tomorrow, and if I do I will tell myself that I should have waited and told you all about it then. But I am going to tell you now and let you decide. While Mr. Cherigate was drinking my tea he asked if I knew I was a witch. I thought about it and said I did not, but if it meant I get to ride through the air on a broom and throw down candy to the boys and girls I might do it. He laughed and said no, a real witch, one that cast spells and sours milk while it is still in the cow.

Of course I said I could not do that and I did not think anybody else could either. Mr. Cherigate said there was a rumor going around town that said that, and I explained that there was nobody rooming with me except Pusson. I should have said little Ivy sometimes, too, Danny, but I forgot.

But Mr. Cherigate meant *rumor*. So I had made a silly mistake that I would not have made if it were not for Yvonne (Suzette) telling people she lived here. Then Mr. Cherigate said that he had heard it from his wife, who heard it from a fortune-teller. I said is that the same as psychic and he said it was. So it was Suzette after all! I will talk to her about this the first chance I get, Danny, and I will write you again soon to tell you what I said and what she said.

> Hugs!
> Your cousin Ivy

*

Dear Cousin Danny,

You will not believe what I am going to tell you in this letter, but it is true, every bit.

When I had finished the letter I wrote yesterday, I waited for somebody to bring Suzette (Yvonne) home. Then I went out to the trailer to talk to her. She was inside, and Marmar said she was nursing little Ivy. I certainly did not want to interrupt that and perhaps make little Ivy cry, so I went to my new little house to see whether Mr. Swierzbowski or Mr. Caminiti had come.

They had not, but Mr. Zoltan and Johnny were there sawing fretwork. When Mr. Zoltan saw me, he got down on his knees. When Johnny saw that, he did too. They begged me to let them use their truck again. If they had their truck, they could go to the dump and find things for me, and buy nails and shingles whenever they needed them, and bring them back here in their truck. It was hard for me to understand everything they said, Danny, because Mr. Zoltan's English is not even as good as Mr. Chen's (at the Post Office). And Johnny would not look at me, or talk very loud either. But that was what they wanted, and when I understood I said of course they could use their truck, go right ahead.

They started thanking me then, over and over, and crying. And while they were doing that, we heard a funny noise from the direction of my house. I did not know what it was. You will think it silly of me, Danny, I know. But I did not. Mr. Zoltan and Johnny knew at once and ran toward it. I worried for a minute that someone might come and take the saws and hammers and things they were leaving behind. And I thought, they are not my things, and Johnny and Mr. Zoltan ran right off and left them so why should not I! No one asked me to watch them while they were gone.

By that time even Mr. Zoltan was out of sight. Johnny was out of sight almost before he began to run, because Johnny can run very fast. I did not run. I walked, but I walked fast, carrying Pusson and petting him as I went along. He is very nice for a black cat, Danny, about as nice as any cat that is not calico can be.

When I got back to my big house, Mr. Zoltan's trailer was still there, but Mr. Zoltan's truck was gone. That was when I knew what the noise we heard had been. It was the noise of the engine starting. Mr. Zoltan and Johnny had heard it many times, so they knew what it was. I had not, so I did not know.

Marmar said Suzette (Yvonne) had taken it. She thought she had run away. I said I did not think so, because I think that she needed to visit her little store, and that if Johnny telephoned her there in a few minutes she would be there. Johnny did not think so. Marmar said we would never see her again and little Ivy cried. Zoltan said I could get her back, but he would not say how.

After that, I decided to telephone myself, but I did not tell them that because I did not want them to think I was interfering.

That was when Mr. Swierzbowski came to talk about plumbing for my new little stranger. I made Mr. Zoltan and Johnny go back to it with us, so they could show Mr. Swierzbowski what needed to be done. There were some trees that would have to be cut for the septic tank, and a lot more that would have to be cut so Mr. Swierzbowski could bring in his big digging machine. I do not like trees being cut, so I said Mr. Zoltan and Johnny would dig it with shovels. They looked very despondent when I said this, so I said that if they would I would get their truck back or get them a new one. I said it because I do not think Suzette (Yvonne) has really run away and left her baby.

After that I came back here and Pusson and I called (phoned) Yvonne's store. There was no answer, so I am writing this letter to you instead. As soon I sign it and address your envelope and find a stamp for it, I will try again.

Hugs,
Your cousin Ivy

Dear Cousin Danny:

I have been so busy these past few days that I have not written. I am terribly sorry, but I have not even had a chance to go to the post office to buy Mr. Chen's stamps. Little Ivy is sleeping now. I think that she is more used to me, or perhaps I am more used to her. But she is sleeping like a little angel, with Pusson curled up beside her. I would take a picture if I could only find my camera, which is not in the kitchen cabinet or the library or anywhere.

But I have stopped trying to remember where my camera might be, and started trying to remember what I have told you and what happened after that letter was out in the big tin box, with the flag up. You know that Suzette (Yvonne) took Mr. Zoltan's truck. He is angry about it and so is Johnny. Suzette is not even Mr. Zoltan's daughter, only his daughter-in-law. I have talked to them, and Marmar is Mr. Zoltan's wife, just like I thought. Suzette (Yvonne) is Johnny's wife. But Johnny says was, and says he will beat her for a week. I do not see how he can beat her if he is going to divorce her. He says he will go to the king and get a divorce. Do you think he means George III, Danny? George III is dead, but then you are dead too, so perhaps George III can still divorce people. Johnny is Mr. Zoltan's son, and Marmar's.

It is funny, sometimes, how these things work out. When I had called Suzette's (Yvonne's) store several times and gotten no answer, and talked to Marmar besides Mr. Zoltan and Johnny, and called the store twice more, I felt sure that Suzette had stolen Mr. Zoltan's truck and was not ever going to bring it back.

So she had really stolen my truck because I had promised Mr. Zoltan and Johnny that I would get them a new one if we could not get their old one back. Besides, their trailer was parked in my front yard, and it still is. I like them and they have never asked to use my bathroom, not even once. But I do not want them living in my front yard until I am old and gray, which is now.

So I called the police. I described my truck to the nice policeman, and when he asked about license plates I said it did not have any because I had noticed that before Suzette took it. I said it had just been parked on my property but I had gotten two men to work on it, and as soon as it would run Suzette had run off with it. You can see that I told the nice policeman nothing but the truth, Danny. All that was just as true as I could make it without getting all complicated. I spoke clearly and enunciated plainly, and the nice policeman never argued with me about a thing.

Then he asked me about Suzette. I told him how old she was, and pretty, and black hair. And I explained that she was the wife of one of the men who had been working on my truck and building a new little house for me. That was fine too, Danny, and perhaps I ought to have left it at that, but I did not, and that seemed like it might be a mistake for a while. I told him that her professional name was Yvonne. Which it was.

He became very interested and asked about her store, so I told him where it was and that I had never gone in there to buy anything. He said that there was a Mr. Bunco who would want to hear about Yvonne. I said Mr. Bunco could come out and talk to me anytime and I would tell him all I could, and I told him where I live.

After that I fixed dinner, which was macaroni-and-cheese and salad from my garden with canned salmon in it for me, and more salmon for Pusson. It was very good, too.

Pusson had only just finished saying thank you when we heard a police car. I went outside because I thought I ought to show the policemen where the truck had been, and I was just in time to see Mr. Zoltan and Marmar running into the woods. Johnny was gone already. I know he can run much faster. Little Ivy was crying, so I went into their trailer and picked her up. I rocked her, and she quieted down right away. She is such a good baby, Danny. You would never believe how good she is.

I told the lady who came with the policeman that I had been expecting Mr. Bunco. And she said she was Miz Bunco and that would have to do. But she gave me her card, and she was only fooling. Her name is really Sergeant Lois B. Anderson, unless it was someone else's card. She asked about little Ivy, and I explained that I was taking care of her while Suzette (Yvonne) was away stealing my truck. She said she would tell D.C. and F.S. and they would take her off my hands. I do not know who F.S. is, Danny, but D.C. is the District of Columbia which means the president. He looks like a very nice man, I know. Still, Danny, he is very busy and may not know how to take care of children. So I said that I did not want little Ivy taken off my hands, that I like her and she likes me, which is the truth. Then Miz Anderson said we ought to go inside where I could sit down, and perhaps little Ivy's diaper needed changing.

Miz Anderson held her while I put water on for tea and we had a nice talk. She said the president would put little Ivy in a faster home, and that might not be the best thing for her. Some faster homes were nice and some not so nice, she said. I did not like the idea of little Ivy living in another trailer, and it seems to me that one that went fast would be worse than Mr. Zoltan's, which does not move at all but is terribly crowded and smelly. So I said why not just let me keep her, she will be right here and perhaps Suzette will come back?

Miz Anderson and I agreed that might be better, and Miz Anderson took her card and wrote call at once if Yvonne returns for baby on the back of it.

So little Ivy is mine now, Danny. Another little stranger is what I said to Pusson, who is a little stranger himself and delighted. I have told Marmar that I have to keep her until Suzette (Yvonne) comes back for her. I do not think Marmar likes that very much, but Mr. Zoltan and Johnny are on my side.

Hugs,
Your cousin Ivy

Dear Cousin Danny:

It has been days and days since I wrote last. I have been so busy! My little house is finished now, and some nice children came to see me today. Their names are Hank and Greta, isn't that nice? They are *twins*, and their mother loves old movies. They are ever so cute, and we had a wonderful time together. They have promised to come back and see me again. I made them promise that before they left, Danny, and they did. I am so looking forward to it.

So that is what I wanted to write you about. But I should have written before, because I have ever so much wonderful news. My little house is finished! Isn't that nice? And little Ivy is still with me, which is even nicer. I will give my little stranger back to her mother, of course, if her mother (Suzette) ever comes back. I suppose I'll have to, but I won't like it.

I call her the little stranger, and then I have to remind myself there are really three. That is little Ivy, Pusson, and the first little stranger ever, my new little house. But, Cousin Danny, there are *five* now, because I must include Hank and Greta, who are such sweet little strangers. I could just eat them up!

After Ivy got settled down for her nap this morning, I went to my new little house (it has a name now and I will tell you in a minute) to see if the nice lady from the department store had brought my new furniture yet. And out in front of my new little house were the sweetest children you ever saw, little tow-heads about seven or eight. I said hello and they said hello, and I asked their names, and they wanted to know if my little house was made of gingerbread.

I explained that there was a lot of gingerbread on it, because that is what you call the lovely old-fashioned woodwork Mr. Zoltan and Johnny made for me. Danny, I had to hold each of them up so they could feel it and see it was not the kind of gingerbread you eat! Can you imagine?

After that we went inside, and I told them all about the nice big Navigator car you got for me from Mr. Cherigate, the building inspector. How hard it was to get him to stand up, and how I promised I would stop the bleeding and walk him out of my cute little Gingerbread House and never tell anyone what happened if he would give me his car for Mr. Zoltan. But I am not breaking my promise by talking about it to you in this letter, because you know already. He was so startled when you and that Hopkins girl joined us that he ran into the pantry and bumped his nose on a shelf trying to get out, remember? I still laugh when I think of it, but it was not really funny at all until I made it stop bleeding. Anyway Mr. Caminiti has come and fixed what he had put in wrong, and there are lights, ever so pretty when they shine out through all the trees.

But I just told Hank and Greta that a nice man had given me a big black car for what I did, bigger than Mr. Zoltan's truck had been. And I had given it to Mr. Zoltan and Johnny for building my house. It was too big for me anyway, and I have my own car. I do not think I could ever drive a big thing like that.

Hank and Greta liked my new little house so much that I have decided to call it Gingerbread House. Now I will never forget them, and I will find somebody to paint a sign saying that and put it on my little house, too.

But I was worried about little Ivy. I do not like to leave her alone for a long time, and the time was getting long. So I made Hank and Greta come back with me to this big house. I showed them little Ivy, and I showed them to little Ivy, too! She liked them and laughed and made all sorts of baby noises. Pusson told me her diaper needed changing, and Greta changed while

Hank and I helped. After that, we baked gingerbread men and played with little Ivy, and played checkers with our gingerbread men, too, breaking off heads and things to make them fit on the squares. You could eat the cookies you captured, but if you did you could not use them to crown your kings. Hank ate all his, so Greta beat him. I did too. By that time it was getting dark, so I showed them how I could make fire fly out of Pusson's fur.

Then we went back to Gingerbread House, and Miz Macy had brought the furniture and set it up like she promised, just like magic. The children were amazed and ever so pleased. Hank wanted to know if they could come back on Halloween, and Greta said no, she will be busy then.

So I said I hoped I would be very busy with little trick-or-treaters, but I would save special treats for them. Children never come, Danny, but I did not want Greta to feel badly. So perhaps she and Hank will come then. I hope so. Oh, I do! It has been ever so long since the children came here.

Hugs,
Your cousin Ivy

P.S. Brenda called while I was looking for your envelope. Hank and Greta are hers! And they had come home very late, she said, full of stories about baking cookies with a witch in the woods. Sally Cusick gave her my number and told her I might know something since I lived out this way. Of course I said my goodness there are no witches out here.

Only me.

2004

BENJAMIN PERCY

(b. 1979)

Dial Tone

A JOGGER spotted the body hanging from the cell tower. At first he thought it was a mannequin. That's what he told Z-21, the local NBC affiliate. The way the wind blew it, the way it flopped limply, made it appear insubstantial, maybe stuffed with straw. It couldn't be a body, he thought, not in a place like Redmond, Oregon, a nowhere town on the edge of a great wash of desert. But it was. It was the body of a man. He had a choke chain, the kind you buy at Pet Depot, wrapped around his neck and anchored to the steel ladder that rose twelve hundred feet in the air to the tip of the tower, where a red light blinked a warning.

Word spread quickly. And everyone, the whole town, it seemed, crowded around, some of them with binoculars and cameras, to watch three deputies, joined by a worker from Clark Tower Service, scale the tower and then descend with the body in a sling.

I was there. And from where I stood, the tower looked like a great spear thrust into the hilltop.

Yesterday—or maybe it was the day before—I went to work, like I always go to work, at West Teleservices Corporation, where, as a marketing associate, I go through the same motions every morning. I hit the power button on my computer and listen to it hum and mumble and blip to life. I settle my weight into my ergonomic chair. I fit the headset around my skull and into my ear and take a deep breath, and, with the pale light of the monitor washing over me, I dial the first number on the screen.

In this low-ceilinged fluorescent-lit room, there are twenty-four rows of cubicles, each ten deep. I am C5. When I take a break and stand up and peer into the cubicle to my right, C6, I find a Greg or a Josh or a Linda—every day a new name to remember, a new hand to shake, or so it seems, with the turnover rate so high. This is why I call everyone *you*.

"Hey, you," I say. "How's it going?"

A short, toad-like woman in a Looney Toons sweatshirt massages the bridge of her nose and sighs, "You know how it is."

In response I give her a sympathetic smile, before looking away, out over the vast hive of cubicles that surrounds us. The air is filled with so many voices, all of them coming together into one voice that reads the same script, trying to make a sale for AT&T, Visa, Northwest Airlines, Sandals Beach Resorts, among our many clients.

There are always three supervisors on duty, all of them beefy men with mustaches. Their bulging bellies remind me of feed sacks that might split open with one slit of a knife. They wear polo shirts with "West Teleservices" embroidered on the breast. They drink coffee from stainless-steel mugs. They never seem to sit down. Every few minutes I feel a rush of wind at the back of my neck as they hurry by, usually to heckle some associate who hasn't met the hourly quota.

"Back to work, C5," one of them tells me, and I roll my eyes at C6 and settle into my cubicle, where the noise all around me falls away into a vague murmur, like the distant drone of bees.

I'm having trouble remembering things. Small things, like where I put my keys, for instance. Whether or not I put on deodorant or took my daily vitamin or paid the cable bill. Big things, too. Like, getting up at 6 A.M. and driving to work on a Saturday, not realizing my mistake until I pull into the empty parking lot.

Sometimes I walk into a room or drive to the store and can't remember why. In this way I am like a ghost: someone who can travel through walls and find myself someplace else in the middle of a sentence or thought and not know what brought me there. The other night I woke up to discover I was walking down the driveway in my pajamas, my bare feet blue in the moonlight. I was carrying a shovel.

Today I'm calling on behalf of Capital One, pitching a mileage card. This is what I'm supposed to say: *Hello, is this _____? How are you doing today, sir/ma'am? That's* wonderful! *I'm calling with a **fantastic** offer from Capital One. Did you know that with our **no-annual-fee** No-Hassle Miles Visa Signature Card you can earn 25 **percent more** than regular mileage cards, with 1.25 miles for every $1 spent on purchases? **On top of that,** if you make just $3,000 in purchases a year, you'll earn 20,000 **bonus miles!***

And so on.

The computer tells me what to tell them. The bold sections indicate where I ought to raise my voice for emphasis. If the customer tries to say they aren't interested, I'm supposed to keep talking, to pretend I don't hear. If I stray too far from the script and if one of the supervisors is listening in, I will feel a hand on my shoulder and hear a voice whispering, "Stay on target. Don't lose sight of your primary objective."

The lights on the tops of cell towers are meant to warn pilots to stay away. But they have become a kind of beacon. Migratory birds mistake them for the stars they use to navigate, so they circle such towers in a trance, sometimes crashing into a structure, its steadying guy wires, or even into other birds. And sometimes they keep circling until they fall to the ground, dead from exhaustion. You can find them all around our cell tower: thousands of them, dotting the hilltop, caught in the sagebrush and pine boughs like ghostly ornaments. Their bones are picked clean by ants. Their feathers are dampened by the rain and bleached by the sun and ruffled and loosened and spread like spores by the wind.

In the sky, so many more circle, screeching their frustration as they try to find their way south. Of course they discovered the body. As he hung there, swinging slightly in the wind, they roosted on his shoulders. They pecked away his eyes, and they pecked away his cheeks, so that we could see all of his teeth when the deputies brought him down. He looked like he was grinning.

At night, from where I lie in bed, I can see the light of the cell tower—through the window, through the branches of a juniper tree, way off in the distance—like a winking red eye that assures me of the confidentiality of some terrible secret.

*

Midmorning, I pop my neck and crack my knuckles and prepare to make maybe my fortieth or sixtieth call of the day. "Pete Johnston" is the name on the screen. I say it aloud—twice—the second time as a question. I feel as though I have heard the name before, but really, that means nothing when you consider the hundreds of thousands of people I have called in my three years working here. I notice that his number, 503-531-1440, is local. Normally I pay no attention to the address listing unless the voice on the other end has a thick accent I can't quite decipher—New Jersey? Texas? Minnesota?—but in this case I look and see that he lives just outside of Redmond, in a new housing development only a few miles away.

"Yeah?" is how he answers the phone.

"Hello. Is this Pete Johnston?"

He clears his throat in a growl. "You a telemarketer?"

"How are you doing today, sir?"

"Bad."

"I'm calling on behalf of—"

"Look, cocksucker. How many times I got to tell you? Take me off your list."

"If you'll just hear me out, I want to tell you about a fantastic offer from—"

"You people are so fucking pathetic."

Now I remember him. He said the same thing before, a week or so ago, when I called him. "If you ever fucking call me again, you fucking worthless piece of shit," he said, "I'll reach through the phone and rip your tongue out."

He goes off on a similar rant now, asking me how can I live with myself, if every time I call someone they answer with hatred?

For a moment I forget about the script and answer him. "I don't know," I say.

"What the—?" he says, his voice somewhere between panicked and incensed. "What the hell are you doing in my house? I thought I told you to—"

There is a noise—the noise teeth might make biting hurriedly into melon—punctuated by a series of screams. It makes me want to tear the headset away from my ear.

And then I realize I am not alone. Someone is listening. I don't know how—a certain displacement of sound as the phone rises from the floor to an ear—but I can sense it.

"Hello?" I say.
The line goes dead.

Sometimes, when I go to work for yet another eight-hour shift or when I visit my parents for yet another casserole dinner, I want to be alone more than anything in the world. But once I'm alone, I feel I can't stand another second of it. Everything is mixed up.

This is why I pick up the phone sometimes and listen. There is something reassuring about a dial tone. That simple sound, a low purr, as constant and predictable as the sun's path across the sky. No matter if you are in Istanbul or London or Beijing or Redmond, you can bring your ear to the receiver and hear it.

Sometimes I pick up the phone and bring it to my ear for the same reason people raise their heads to peer at the moon when they're in a strange place. It makes them—it makes me —feel oriented, calmer than I was a moment before.

Perhaps this has something to do with why I drive to the top of the hill and park beneath the cell tower and climb onto the hood of my Neon and lean against the windshield with my hands folded behind my head to watch the red light blinking and the black shapes of birds swirling against the backdrop of an even blacker sky.

I am here to listen. The radio signals emanating from the tower sound like a blade hissing through the air or a glob of spit sizzling on a hot stove: something dangerous, about to draw blood or catch fire. It's nice.

I imagine I hear in it the thousands of voices channeling through the tower at any given moment, and I wonder what terrible things could be happening to these people that they want to tell the person on the other end of the line but don't.

A conversation overheard:
"Do you live here?"
"Yes."
"Are you Pete Johnston?"
"Yes. Who are you? What do you want?"
"To talk to you. Just to talk."

*

Noon, I take my lunch break. I remove my headset and lurch out of my chair with a groan and bring my fists to my back and push until I feel my vertebrae seperate and realign with a juicy series of pops. Then I wander along my row, moving past so many cubicles, each with a person hunched over inside it—and for a moment West Teleservices feels almost like a chapel, with everyone bowing their heads and murmuring together, as if exorcising some private pain.

I sign out with one of the managers and enter the break room, a forty-by-forty-foot room with white walls and a white dropped ceiling and a white linoleum floor. There are two sinks, two microwaves, two fridges, a Coke machine and a SNAX machine. In front of the SNAX machine stands C6, the woman stationed in the cubicle next to me. A Looney Toons theme apparently unifies her wardrobe, since today she wears a sweat-shirt with Sylvester on it. Below him, blocky black letters read, WITHCONTHIN. She stares with intense concentration at the candy bars and chip bags and gum packs, as if they hold some secret message she has yet to decode.

I go to the nearby water fountain and take a drink and dry my mouth with my sleeve, all the while watching C6, who hardly seems to breathe. "Hey, you," I say, moving to within a few steps of her. "Doing all right there?"

She looks at me, her face creased with puzzlement. Then she shakes her head, and a fog seems to lift, and for the first time she sees me and says, "Been better."

"I know how you feel."

She looks again to the SNAX machine, where her reflection hovers like a ghost. "Nobody knows how I feel."

"No. You're wrong. I know."

At first C6 seems to get angry, her face cragging up, but then I say, "You feel like you would feel if you were hurrying along and smacked your shin against the corner of the coffee table. You feel like you want to yell a lot. The pain hasn't completely arrived, but you can see it coming, and you want to yell at it, scare it off." I go to the fridge labeled *A-K* and remove from it my sack lunch and sit down at one of the five tables staggered throughout the room. "Something like that, anyway."

An awkward silence follows, in which I eat my ham sandwich and C6 studies me closely, no doubt recognizing in me some common damage, some likeness of herself.

Then C6 says, "Can't seem to figure out what I want," nodding at the vending machine. "I've been staring at all these goodies for twenty minutes, and I'll be darned if I know what I want." She forces a laugh and then says with some curiosity in her voice, "Hey, what's with your eye?"

I cup a hand to my ear like a seashell, like: Say again?

"Your eyeball." She points and then draws her finger back as if she might catch something from me. "It's really red."

"Huh," I say and knuckle the corner of my eye as if to nudge away a loose eyelash. "Maybe I've got pinkeye. Must have picked it up off a doorknob."

"It's not pink. It's red. It's really, really red."

The nearest reflective surface is the SNAX machine. And she's right. My eye is red. The dark luscious red of an apple. I at once want to scream and pluck it out and suck on it.

"I think you should see somebody," C6 says.

"Maybe I should." I comb a hand back through my hair and feel a vaguely pleasant release as several dozen hairs come out by the roots, just like that, with hardly any effort. I hold my hand out before me and study the clump of hairs woven in between the fingers and the fresh scabs jewelling my knuckles and say to no one in particular, "Looks like I'm falling apart."

Have you ever been on the phone, canceling a credit card or talking to your mother, when all of a sudden—with a pop of static—another conversation bleeds into yours? Probably. It happens a lot, with so many radio signals hissing through the air. What you might not know is, what you're hearing might have been said a minute ago or a day ago or a week ago or a month ago. Years ago.

When you speak into the receiver, your words are compressed into an electronic signal that bounces from phone to tower to satellite to phone, traveling thousands of miles, even if you're talking to your next-door neighbor, Joe. Which means there's plenty of room for a signal to ricochet or duplicate or get lost. Which means there are so many words—the ghosts of old conversations—floating all around us.

Consider this possibility. You pick up your phone and hear a voice—your voice—engaged in some ancient conversation, like that time in high school when you asked Natasha Flatt out for coffee and she made an excuse about her cat being sick. It's like a conversation shouted into a canyon, its words bouncing off walls to eventually come fluttering back to you, warped and soft and sounding like somebody else.

Sometimes this is what my memory feels like. An image or a conversation or a place will rise to the surface of my mind, and I'll recognize it vaguely, not knowing if I experienced it or saw it on television or invented it altogether.

Whenever I try to fix my attention on something, a red light goes on in my head, and I'm like a bird circling in confusion.

I find myself on the sidewalk of a new hillside development called Bear Brook. Here all the streets have names like Kodiak and Grizzly. All around me are two-story houses of a similar design, with freshly painted gray siding and river-rock entryways and cathedral windows rising above their front doors to reveal chandeliers in the foyer of each. Each home has a sizable lot that runs up against pine forest. And each costs more than I would make in twenty years with West Teleservices.

A garbage truck rushes past me, raising tiny tornadoes of dust and trash, and I raise my hand to shield my face and notice a number written on the back of it, just below my knuckles —13743—and though I am sure it will occur to me later, for the moment I can't for the life of me remember what it means.

At that moment a bird swoops toward a nearby house. Mistaking the window for a piece of sky, it strikes the glass with a thud and falls into the rose garden beneath it, absently fluttering its wings; soon it goes still. I rush across the lawn and into the garden and bend over to get a better look at it. A bubble of blood grows from its beak and pops. I do not know why, but I reach through the thorns and pick up the bird and stroke its cool, reddish feathers. Its complete lack of weight and its stillness overwhelm me.

When the bird fell, something fell off a shelf inside me—a nice, gold-framed picture of my life, what I dreamed it would be, full of sunshine and ice cream and go-go dancers. It tumbled down and shattered, and my smiling face dissolved into the distressed expression reflected in the living room window before me.

I look alarmingly ugly. My eyes are black-bagged. My skin is yellow. My upper lip is raised to reveal long, thin teeth. Mine is the sort of face that belongs to someone who bites the heads off chickens in a carnival pit, not the sort that belongs to a man who cradles in his hands a tiny red-winged blackbird. The vision of me, coupled with the vision of what I once dreamed I would be—handsome, wealthy, feared by men and cherished by women—assaults me, the ridiculousness of it and also the terror, the realization that I have crept to the edge of a void and am on the verge of falling in, barely balanced.

And then my eyes refocus, concentrating on a farther distance, where through the window I see a man rising from a couch and approaching me. He is tall and square-shouldered. His hair is the color of dried blood on a bandage. He looks at me with derision, saying through the glass, "The hell do you think you're doing on my property?" without saying a word.

I drop the bird and raise my hand, not quite waving, the gesture more like holding up something dark to the light. He does not move except to narrow his eyes further. There's a stone pagoda at the edge of the garden, and when I take several steps back my heel catches against it. I stumble and then lose my balance entirely, falling hard, sprawling out on the lawn. The gray expanse of the sky fills my vision. Moisture from the grass seeps into my jeans and dampens my underwear. My testicles tighten like a fist.

In the window the man continues to watch me. He has a little red mustache, and he fingers it. Then he disappears from sight, moving away from the window and toward the front door.

Just before I stagger off the lawn and hurry along the sidewalk and retreat from this place, my eyes zero in on the porch, waiting for the man to appear there, and I catch sight of the address: 13743.

And then I am off and running. A siren announces itself nearby. The air seems to vibrate with its noise. It is a police cruiser, I'm certain, though how I can tell the difference between it and an ambulance, I don't know. Either way, someone is in trouble.

*

The body was blackened by its lengthy exposure to radio frequency fields. Cooked. Like a marshmallow left too long over flame. This is why the deputies shut off the transmitters, when they climbed the tower.

Z-21 interviewed Jack Millhouse, a professor of radiation biology at Oregon State. He had a beard, and he stroked it thoughtfully. He said that climbing the tower would expose a person to radio frequencies so powerful they would cook the skin. "I'd ask around at the ER," he said. "See if somebody has come in with radiation burns."

Then they interviewed a woman in a yellow, too-large T-shirt and purple stretch pants. She lived nearby and had seen the commotion from her living room window. She thought a man was preparing to jump, she said. So she came running in the hopes of praying him down. She had a blank, round face no one would ever call beautiful. "It's just awful," she said, her lips disappearing as she tightened her mouth. "It's the most horrible thing in the world, and it's right here, and we don't know why."

I know I am not the only one who has been cut off by a swerving car in traffic or yelled at by a teacher in a classroom or laughed at by a woman in a bar. I am not the only one who has wished someone dead and imagined how it might happen, pleasuring in the goriest details.

Here is how it might happen:

I am in a kitchen with duck-patterned wallpaper. I stand over a man with a Gerber hunting knife in my hand. There is blood dripping off the knife, and there is blood coming out of the man. Gouts of it. It matches the color of his hair. A forked vein rises on his forehead to reveal the panicked beating of his heart. A gray string of saliva webs the corner of his mouth. He holds his hands out, waving me away, and I cut my way through them.

A dog barks from the hallway, and the man screams a repulsive scream, a girlish scream, and all this noise sounds to me far away, like a conversation overheard between pops of static.

I am aware of my muscles and their purpose as never before,

using them to place the knife, putting it finally to the man's chest, where it will make the most difference.

At first the blade won't budge, caught on a rib, and then it slips past the bone and into the soft red interior, deeper and then deeper still, with the same feeling you get when you break through that final restraining grip and enter a woman fully. The response is just as cathartic: a shriek, a gasp, a stiffening of the limbs followed by a terrible shivering that eventually gives way to a great, calming release.

There is blood everywhere—on the knife, on the floor, gurgling from the newly rendered wound that looks so much like a mouth—and the man's eyes are open and empty, and his sharp pink tongue lolls out the side of his mouth. I am amazed at the thrill I feel.

When I surprised him, only a few minutes ago, he was on the phone. I spot it now, on the shale floor, with a halo of blood around it. I pick it up and bring it to my ear and hope for the familiar, calming murmur of the dial tone.

Instead I hear a voice. "Hello?" it says.

One day, I think, maybe I'll write a story about all of this. Something permanent. So that I can trace every sentence and find my way to the end and back to the beginning without worrying about losing my way.

The telling would be complicated.

To write a story like this you would have to talk about what it means to speak into a headset all day, reading from a script you don't believe in, conversing with bodiless voices that snarl with hatred, voices that want to claw out your eyes and scissor off your tongue. And you would have to show what that does to a person, experiencing such a routine day after day, with no relief except for the occasional coffee break where you talk about the television show you watched last night.

And you would have to explain how the man named Pete Johnston sort of leaned and sort of collapsed against the fridge, how a magnet fell to the linoleum with a *clack* after you flashed the knife in a silvery arc across his face and then his outstretched hand and then into that soft basin behind the collarbone. After that came blood. And screaming. Again you stabbed the body, in the thigh, the belly, your muscles pulsing with a red electricity. Something inside you, some internal switch, had been triggered, filling you with an unthinking adrenaline that made you feel capable of turning over Volkswagens, punching through concrete, tearing phone books in half.

And you would have to end this story by explaining what it felt like to pull the body from the trunk of your car and hoist it to your shoulder and begin to climb the tower—one rung, then another—going slowly. You breathed raggedly. The dampness of your sweat mingled with the dampness of blood. From here—thirty, then forty, then fifty feet off the ground—you could see the chains of light on Route 97 and Highway 100, each bright link belonging to a machine that carried inside it a man who could lose control in an instant, distracted by the radio or startled by a deer or overwhelmed by tiredness, careening off the asphalt and into the surrounding woods. It could happen to anyone.

Your thighs trembled. You were weary, dizzy. Your fillings tingled, and a funny baked taste filled your mouth. The edges of your eyes went white and then crazy with streaks of color. But you continued climbing, with the wind tugging at your body, with the blackness of the night and the black shapes of birds all around you, the birds swirling through the air like ashes thrown from a fire. And let's not forget the sound—the sound of the tower—how it sounded almost like words. The hissing of radio frequencies, the voices of so many others coming together into one voice that coursed through you in dark conversation.

2007

BIOGRAPHICAL NOTES

NOTE ON THE TEXTS

NOTES

Biographical Notes

Charles Beaumont (January 2, 1929–February 21, 1967) b. Charles Leroy Nutt in Chicago, Illinois. At the age of 12 Beaumont left school after being diagnosed with spinal meningitis. He became absorbed in the world of science fiction and fantasy, editing his own fan magazine, *Utopia*, at 16. After working with limited success as a radio and screen actor, he found work inking cartoons for MGM and wrote in his spare time, living on the edge of poverty with his family. In the mid-1950s he began to achieve recognition after the publication of some stories in *Playboy* ("Black Country" was the first work of short fiction to appear in that magazine); subsequently published the collections *Hunger* (1957), *Yonder* (1958), and *Night Ride* (1960). He also wrote episodes for the TV series *The Twilight Zone* and movie screenplays including *The Intruder* (1962), *The 7 Faces of Dr. Lao* (1964), and *The Masque of the Red Death* (1964). In 1964, Beaumont began suffering from a mysterious brain disease that may have been related to the spinal meningitis he'd contracted as a boy, and his condition degenerated rapidly until his death three years later.

Jerome Bixby (January 11, 1923–April 28, 1998) b. Los Angeles. Best known for writing the *Star Trek* episode "Mirror, Mirror" (1967) and the short story "It's a Good Life" (1953), which was later adapted into a *Twilight Zone* episode. His science fiction stories were collected in two volumes: *The Devil's Scrapbook* (1964) and *Space by the Tale* (1964). He also wrote numerous westerns under various pseudonyms. His last work, *The Man from Earth*, was filmed in 2007, produced by his son Emerson Bixby.

Anthony Boucher (August 21, 1911–April 29, 1968) b. William Anthony Parker White in Oakland, California. Earned B.A. from the University of Southern California in 1932, and an M.A. from the University of California, Berkeley, in 1934. Published a number of detective novels—including *The Case of the Seven of Calvary* (1937), *The Case of the Crumpled Knave* (1939), and *Rocket to the Morgue* (1942, as H. H. Holmes)—and reviewed crime, fantasy, and science fiction novels for the *Chicago Sun-Times, New York Times* and *San Francisco Chronicle*. His own fantasy and science fiction stories were collected in *Far and Away; Eleven Fantasy and SF Stories* (1955) and

The Compleat Werewolf and Other Stories of Fantasy and SF (1969). Also wrote radio scripts for programs including *The New Adventures of Sherlock Holmes, The Adventures of Ellery Queen,* and *The Casebook of Gregory Hood* (which he created). He was the first English translator of Jorge Luis Borges; his version of "The Garden of Forking Paths" appeared in *Ellery Queen's Mystery Magazine* in 1941. He was a founder of the Mystery Writers of America in 1946; co-founded *The Magazine of Fantasy & Science Fiction* with J. Francis McComas in 1949, and edited it until 1958, when poor health forced him to quit.

Paul Bowles (December 30, 1910–November 18, 1999) b. Paul Frederick Bowles in Jamaica, New York. Introduced to classical music at eight, and composed his first piece of music a year later. Two of his poems, written when he was 16, were published in the Paris literary magazine *transition.* Left University of Virginia during his first semester to go to Paris, where he befriended Aaron Copland and Gertrude Stein. Traveled in Europe and North Africa; returned to the U.S. in 1937 and for the next ten years devoted himself to composing music. Wrote scores for over a dozen films and several plays produced by the Federal Theater, along with numerous Broadway shows including William Saroyan's *My Heart's in the Highlands* and Lillian Hellman's *Watch on the Rhine.* In 1947, moved to Tangier and with the encouragement of his wife, Jane Auer, began writing a novel, published two years later as *The Sheltering Sky.* (As Jane Bowles, his wife published the novel *Two Serious Ladies* and the play *In the Summer House.*) The story collection *The Delicate Prey* appeared in 1950. He resided in Tangier for the rest of his life, publishing the novel *Let It Come Down* (1952), *The Spider's House* (1955), and *Up Above the World* (1966) as well as other works including stories, travel writing, poems, and the autobiography *Without Stopping* (1972). He also translated works by Moroccan authors including Driss ben Hamed Charhadi and Mohammed Mrabet. He continued to compose music and made extensive field recordings of traditional Moroccan music for the Library of Congress. He died of heart failure in Tangier and was buried in Lakemont, New York.

Ray Bradbury (b. August 20, 1922) b. Ray Douglas Bradbury in Waukegan, Illinois. Started reading comics at six and within two years was engrossed in pulp magazines such as *Amazing Stories* and later Jules Verne, H. G. Wells, Edgar Rice Burroughs, and the *Oz* books of Frank L. Baum. Claimed he was inspired to begin writing when his parents took him to see a magician called Mr. Electrico, who knighted him with an electrified sword, shouting "Live forever!" In 1934, the family moved to Los Angeles, where Bradbury attended a writing class taught by Robert Heinlein. Graduated from high school in 1938, and in the same year his first published story, "Hollerbachen's Dilemma," appeared in the fan magazine *Imagination!* He started his own fan magazine, *Futuria Fantasia*, a year later. After "Pendulum" was published in *Super Science Stories* in 1941, began writing full time; first story collection, *Dark Carnival*, was published by Arkham House in 1947. The story cycle *The Martian Chronicles* (1950) secured Bradbury's reputation as a fantasist, and was followed by the story collections *The Illustrated Man* (1951) and *The Golden Apples of the Sun* in 1953. The science fiction novel *Fahrenheit 451* (1953) was followed by other novels and story collections in a range of genres, including *The October Country* (1955), *Dandelion Wine* (1957), *Something Wicked This Way Comes* (1962), *The Halloween Tree* (1972), and *Death Is a Lonely Business* (1985). Along with novels, poetry, and children's books, Bradbury has written screenplays, including *It Came From Outer Space* (1953) and *Moby Dick* (1956), and teleplays for programs including *Alfred Hitchcock Presents*, *The Twilight Zone*, and a series based on his own works, *The Ray Bradbury Television Theater* (1985–90). In 2004, he was awarded the National Medal of Arts by George W. Bush.

Poppy Z. Brite (b. May 25, 1967) b. Melissa Ann Brite in New Orleans. Grew up with her mother in Chapel Hill, North Carolina. Started writing at 12 and sold her first story, "Optional Music for Voice and Piano," to *The Horror Show* at 18. Awarded a three-book contract by Dell in 1991 for the novels *Lost Souls* (1992), *Drawing Blood* (1993), and *Exquisite Corpse* (1996). In recent years, Brite has moved away from horror, as in the Liquor series, comprising the dark comedies *Liquor* (2004), *Prime* (2005), and *Soul Kitchen* (2006) and set within the New Orleans restaurant world.

Truman Capote (September 30, 1924–August 25, 1984) b. Truman Streckfus Persons in New Orleans to Arch Persons, a salesman, and 16-year-old Lili Mae "Nina" Faulk. Parents divorced when Capote was six, after which he lived with his mother's cousins in Monroeville, Alabama. He became interested in writing at an early age and in 1934 his story "Old Mr. Busybody" appeared in the *Mobile Press Register*. Adopted the name Truman Capote in 1935 when his parents' custody battle ended and he was legally adopted by his mother and her new husband, Joseph Capote, a Cuban-American textile broker. He went to live with them in New York and attended various schools, including a military academy, before family relocated to Greenwich, Connecticut. After graduating from high school, began working as a copyboy for *The New Yorker*. Began publishing stories regularly, including "Miriam," which won the O. Henry Memorial award in 1946. Spent time at Yaddo in Saratoga Springs, where he worked on novel *Other Voices, Other Rooms* (1948), which was published by Random House and brought him national attention. Subsequently published story collection *A Tree of Night* (1949), novel *The Grass Harp* (1951), journalistic account *The Muses Are Heard* (1956), and novella *Breakfast at Tiffany's* (1958). *In Cold Blood* (1966), his "nonfiction novel" dealing with a multiple murder in Kansas, was tremendously successful. Drug and alcohol abuse diminished his output in later years; he published the nonfiction collections *The Dogs Bark* (1973) and *Music for Chameleons* (1980), and worked on a novel that was published in unfinished form as *Answered Prayers* in 1986.

Jonathan Carroll (b. January 26, 1949) b. New York City to Sidney Carroll, a screenwriter, and June Carroll, an actress. Attended boarding school in Connecticut. Graduated from Rutgers University in 1971; earned an M.A. in English at the University of Virginia two years later. Moved to Vienna (where he continues to live) to teach English at the American International School. His first novel, *The Land of Laughs*, was followed by 15 others to date, including *Sleeping in Flame* (1988), *Kissing the Beehive* (1997), *White Apples* (2002), *Glass Soup* (2005), and *The Ghost in Love* (2008). His short fiction has been collected in *The Panic Hand* (1995).

Michael Chabon (b. May 24, 1963) b. Washington, D.C. Parents divorced when he was 11; he grew up in Columbia, Maryland. Earned a B.A. from the University of Pittsburgh and an M.F.A. in creative writing from the University of California–Irvine. His master's thesis became his first published novel, *The Mysteries of Pittsburgh* (1988), which was a bestseller, as was his next novel, *Wonder Boys* (1995). The story collection *Werewolves in Their Youth* (1999) contained the horror story "In the Black Mill." *The Amazing Adventures of Kavalier & Clay* (2000) won the Pulitzer Prize for Fiction. His interest in genre fiction has been reflected in *Summerland* (2002), a fantasy book for children; *The Final Solution* (2004), whose protagonist is Sherlock Holmes; *The Yiddish Policemen's Union* (2007), a novel of alternate history; and *Gentlemen of the Road* (2007), a swashbuckling adventure.

Fred Chappell (b. May 28, 1936) b. Canton, North Carolina. Received B.A. (1961) and M.A. (1963) from Duke University in 18th-century literature; taught various courses at the University of

North Carolina at Greensboro for 40 years. His published novels include *Dagon* (1968), *I Am One of You Forever* (1985), and *Brighten the Corner Where You Are* (1989). His poetry has been collected in *Midquest* (1981), *Source* (1985), *Spring Garden* (1995), *Shadow Box* (2009), and other volumes. His latest volume of short fiction is *Ancestors and Others* (2009). He has been awarded, among other honors, the Bollingen Prize in 1985, the T. S. Eliot Prize in 2003, and the Thomas Wolfe Award in 2006.

John Cheever (May 27, 1912–June 18, 1982) b. John William Cheever in Quincy, Massachusetts, to Frederick Lincoln Cheever, a shoe salesman, and Mary Liley, a gift-shop operator. Expelled from Thayer Academy in South Braintree at 17 for smoking, an incident forming the basis for his first published story, "Expelled," which appeared in *The New Republic* in 1930. Moved to New York in 1934 where he supported himself by writing novel synopses for MGM. Married Mary Winternitz, daughter of the dean of the Yale Medical School, in 1941. Published story collection *The Way Some People Live* (1943). After serving in the army during World War II, devoted himself to a career as a writer. Awarded a Guggenheim fellowship in 1951; moved with his family to Westchester County, New York. In addition to story collections, including *The Enormous Radio* (1953), *The Housebreaker of Shady Hill* (1958), and *Some People, Places and Things That Will Not Appear in My Next Novel* (1961), published novels *The Wapshot Chronicle* (1957), *The Wapshot Scandal* (1964), *Bullet Park* (1969), and *Falconer* (1977). Alcohol abuse led to hospitalization; he stopped drinking in 1975. His novel *Falconer* (1977) and his *Collected Stories* (1978) were bestsellers, and for the latter he won the Pulitzer Prize for Fiction.

John Collier (May 3, 1901–April 6, 1980) b. London to John George Collier and Emily Mary Noyes Collier. His interest in fantasy writing was sparked by childhood reading of Hans Christian Andersen's fairy tales. He was educated at home by his uncle, Vincent Collier, a novelist. With an allowance from his father, set himself up in London as a journalist and fiction writer in the early 1920s. Became poetry editor for *Time and Tide* and won a poetry award from *The Quarter* for his collection *Gemini* (1931). Published the novels *His Monkey Wife; or, Married to a Chimp* (1930), *Tom's A-Cold: A Tale* (1933), and *Defy the Foul Fiend; or, The Misadventures of a Heart* (1934). Moved to Hollywood and began writing scripts; collaborated on *The Elephant Boy* (1937), *Her Cardboard Lover* (1942), *The African Queen* (1951), and *The War Lord* (1965). His short fiction, which appeared frequently in *The New Yorker*, was collected in *Presenting Moonshine*

(1941), *The Touch of Nutmeg Makes It* (1943), and *Fancies and Good-nights* (1951), the last of which won both the International Fantasy Award and the Mystery Writers of America's Edgar Award. A number of his stories were adapted for television, notably "Back for Christmas" and "Wet Saturday" by Alfred Hitchcock. Collier moved back to Europe in the early 1950s, first to London and eventually to Grasse, France. In 1973 he published a screenplay based on *Paradise Lost*. He returned to California in 1979 and died of a stroke in Pacific Palisades a year later.

John Crowley (b. December 1, 1942) b. Presque Isle, Maine; grew up in Vermont, Kentucky, and Indiana, where he attended Indiana University (B.A., 1964). Lived in New York City, writing scripts for documentary films; his first novel, *The Deep*, appeared in 1975, followed by *Beasts* (1976) and *Engine Summer* (1979). Subsequent novels included *Little, Big* (1981) and the *Aegypt* tetralogy, consisting of *Aegypt* (retitled *The Solitudes*, 1987), *Love & Sleep* (1994), *Dæmonomania* (2000), and *Endless Things* (2007). His short fiction has been collected in *Novelties and Souvenirs* (2004). Corresponded with literary critic Harold Bloom, who admired his fiction, and in 1993 he became a professor at Yale. Received Award in Literature from the American Academy and Institute of Arts and Letters in 1992.

Harlan Ellison (b. May 27, 1934) b. in Cleveland, Ohio. He has written or edited 76 books and more than 1700 stories, essays, articles, and newspaper columns, as well two dozen teleplays (for programs including *The Outer Limits* and the 1985 revival of *The Twilight Zone*) and a dozen movies. He has won many awards including multiple Edgar, Hugo, and Bram Stoker awards; a Lifetime Achievement Award from the Horror Writers' Association; a World Convention Achievement Award from the Science Fiction Writers of America; and the Silver Pen for Journalism from P.E.N. In 2006 he was named Grand Master of the Science Fiction/Fantasy Writers of America. His best-known works include *Web of the City* (1958), *Memos from Purgatory* (1961), *Ellison Wonderland* (1962), *I Have No Mouth, and I Must Scream* (1967), *Love Ain't Nothing but Sex Misspelled* (1968), *Approaching Oblivion* (1974), *Deathbird Stories* (1975), *Strange Wine* (1978), *All the Lies That Are My Life* (1980), *Shatterday* (1980), *Stalking the Nightmare* (1982), *An Edge in My Voice* (1985), *Angry Candy* (1988), *Mind Fields* (1994), and *Slippage* (1997). He edited the influential anthologies *Dangerous Visions* (1967) and *Again, Dangerous Visions* (1972), and his work has been featured in *The Best American Short Stories*. A retrospective of his work has been published as *The Essential Ellison* (1987; expanded edition, 1998). He has been actively engaged with such issues as First Amendment rights, censorship, and global Internet piracy of writers' work. *Dreams with Sharp Teeth*, an award-winning documentary on his life, was released in 2008.

Brian Evenson (b. August 12, 1966) b. Ames, Iowa, to William Edwin Evenson, a physicist, and Nancy Ann Evenson, an architect. Began to write seriously in college under the mentorship of Welsh poet Leslie Norris. Received Ph.D. from University of Washington, then returned to Brigham Young University, where he had studied as an undergraduate, to teach. The gruesome subject matter of the stories in his first collection, *Altmann's Tongue* (1994), caused dissension with fellow Mormons, and he was obliged to leave both the school and the church. Became Chair of the Literary Arts Program at Brown University. Later books include *Prophets and Brothers* (1997), *Father of Lies* (1998), *Dark Property: An Affliction* (2002), *The Wavering Knife* (2004), *The Open Curtain* (2006), *Last Days* (2009), and *Fugue State* (2009).

Jack Finney (October 2, 1911–November 14, 1995) b. John Finney in Milwaukee, Wisconsin. Graduated from Knox College in Galesburg, Illinois. Married Marguerite Guest in 1934 and moved to New York City where he wrote advertising jingles. His first story, "The Widow's Walk" (1946), won a prize from *Ellery Queen's Mystery Magazine*. A crime novel, *Five Against the House* (1954), was followed by *The Body Snatchers*, filmed in 1956 by Don Siegel as *Invasion of the Body Snatchers* (Finney worked on the screenplay). Other novels included *The House of Numbers* (1957), *Assault on a Queen* (1959), *Good Neighbor Sam* (1963), *The Woodrow Wilson Dime* (1968), and *Time and Again* (1970), a novel of time travel for which he meticulously recreated late-19th-century New York and which enjoyed wide success. He was awarded the World Fantasy Award for Life Achievement in 1987. His last book was *From Time to Time* (1995), a sequel to *Time and Again*.

Davis Grubb (July 23, 1919–July 24, 1980) b. Davis Alexander Grubb in Moundsville, West Virginia. His family's roots in the region went back several centuries. He was interested in writing and painting from an early age. Studied art at the Carnegie Institute of Technology in Pittsburgh (1938–39), but after finding that he was color-blind devoted his energies to writing. Moved around 1941 to New York City, where he wrote copy for NBC. Subsequently worked in radio and advertising in Florida and Philadelphia. His first story, published in *Good Housekeeping* in 1944, was followed by many others in *Collier's*, *Ellery Queen's Mystery Magazine,* and *American*

Magazine. His first novel, *The Night of the Hunter* (1955), was a finalist for the National Book Award, and was filmed in 1957 by Charles Laughton, with a screenplay by Laughton and James Agee. Grubb's later novels included *A Dream of Kings* (1955), *The Watchman* (1961), *A Tree Full of Stars* (1965), *Fools' Parade* (1969), and *Ancient Lights* (1982).

Joe Hill (b. June 4, 1972) b. Joseph Hillstrom King, to Stephen King and Tabitha King in Bangor, Maine. Began publishing stories in 1997 under the pen name Joe Hill. His story collection *20th Century Ghosts* (2005), which won the Bram Stoker Award, the British Fantasy Award, and the International Horror Guild Award, was followed by the novel *Heart-Shaped Box* (2007). He has also written the comic book series Locke & Key, beginning in 2008.

Shirley Jackson (December 14, 1916–August 8, 1965) b. Shirley Hardie Jackson in San Francisco, California. Moved with family to Rochester, New York, while in high school. Attended Rochester University, 1934–36, and Syracuse University, where she founded and edited literary magazine *The Spectre* with Stanley Edgar Hyman whom she subsequently married, and received a B.A. in English (1940). Began to publish in magazines including *The New Republic* and *The New Yorker*. Moved to Vermont in 1945 when her husband joined faculty of Bennington College. Published novel *The Road Through the Wall* (1948); in the same year "The Lottery" appeared in the June 26 issue of *The New Yorker*. It had great impact and was collected the next year in *The Lottery; or, the Adventures of James Harris*. Her later books include the novels *Hangsaman* (1951), *The Bird's Nest* (1954), *The Sundial* (1958), *The Haunting of Hill House* (1959), and *We Have Always Lived in the Castle* (1962), the humorous memoirs *Life Among the Savages* (1953) and *Raising Demons* (1957), and a history book for children, *The Witchcraft of Salem Village* (1956). She died of a heart attack.

Caitlín R. Kiernan (b. May 26, 1964) b. in Skerries, Ireland. Moved to Leeds, Alabama, with her family when she was a child. Developed early interest in writing and paleontology. While in high school spent summers on archaeological digs; earned B.S. from University of Colorado at Boulder, studying geology and vertebrate paleontology. Her first published novel, *Silk*, appeared in 1998, followed by *Threshold* (2001), *The Five of Cups* (2003, but written a decade earlier), *Low Red Moon* (2003), *Murder of Angels* (2004), and *Daughter of Hounds* (2007). Her short fiction has been collected in volumes including *Tales of Pain and Wonder* (2000), *From Weird and Distant Shores*

(2002), and *Tales from the Woeful Platypus* (2007). She has also contributed scholarly articles to paleontology journals, such as an examination of the biostratigraphy of Alabama mosasaurs for the *Journal of Vertebrate Paleontology* (2002). She lives in Providence, Rhode Island.

Stephen King (b. September 21, 1947) b. Portland, Maine, second son of Donald Edwin King, a master mariner in the U.S. Merchant Marine, and Nellie Ruth Pillsbury King. When he was two, his father abandoned the family, and over the next nine years his mother moved with him and his older brother from town to town across the northern United States, staying with relatives and working sporadically. They settled in Durham, Maine, in 1958. In high school, published his first story, "I Was a Teenage Grave-Robber," in *Comics Review*, a fan magazine, and wrote a book-length manuscript, a post-apocalyptic story called "The Aftermath." Attended University of Maine at Orono on a scholarship; wrote steadily throughout college. Published "The Glass Floor" in *Startling Mystery Stories* (1967), was active in student politics and the anti-war movement, and taught a seminar on "Popular Literature and Culture." Married Tabitha Spruce in 1971; began teaching at the Hampden Academy in Hampden, Maine. His first novel, *Carrie* (1973), enjoyed great success when published in paperback, and was followed by many novels —over 40 to date—that made him the most widely known writer of fantasy and horror, including *Salem's Lot* (1975), *The Shining* (1977), *The Stand* (1978; expanded version, 1990), *The Dead Zone* (1979), *Cujo* (1981), *Pet Sematary* (1983), *Misery* (1987), *The Dark Half* (1989), *Gerald's Game* (1992), *Dolores Claiborne* (1993), *The Green Mile* (1996), and *Lisey's Story* (2006). He also published a number of novels under the pseudonym Richard Bachman. His short fiction has been collected in *Night Shift* (1978), *Different Seasons* (1982), *Skeleton Crew* (1985), *Nightmares & Dreamscapes* (1993), *Everything's Eventual* (2002), and other volumes. Many of his works have been filmed and he has received numerous awards throughout his career.

T.E.D. Klein (b. July 15, 1947) b. Theodore Donald Klein in New York City. Graduated from Brown, 1969; wrote honors thesis on H. P. Lovecraft. Studied film history at Columbia, receiving M.F.A. in 1972. Worked as a reader for Paramount Pictures. Edited magazines *The Twilight Zone* (1981–85) and *CrimeBeat* (1991–93). His novel *The Ceremonies* (1984), for which he won the British Fantasy Society Award, was an expansion of his 1972 novella "The Events at Poroth Farm" (subsequently published in revised versions). Published story collections *The Dark Gods* (1985) and *Reassuring Tales*

(2006). He wrote the screenplay for Dario Argento's *Trauma* (1993) and two critical essays on the weird fiction genre, *Dr Van Helsing's Handy Guide to Ghost Stories* (1981) and *Raising Goosebumps for Fun and Profit* (1988).

Fritz Leiber (December 24, 1910–September 5, 1992) b. in Chicago, Illinois, to Fritz Leiber and Virginia Bronson Leiber, both Shakespearean actors. After graduating with a B.A. in psychology from the University of Chicago in 1932, studied at the Episcopal General Theological Seminary in New York. Returned to the University of Chicago to study philosophy; after a year, dropped out and went on tour with his parents' theater troupe. Attempted to find work in Hollywood; returned to Chicago, where he worked as staff writer for the *Standard American Encyclopedia*. Married Jonquil Stephens in 1936; their son Justin was born two years later. Began writing stories with encouragement of H. P. Lovecraft. Sold fantasy story "Two Sought Adventure" to *Unknown* in 1939. Relocated to Los Angeles with family; taught drama and speech at Occidental College; subsequently took a job with Douglas Aircraft. From 1946 worked for 11 years on editorial staff of *Science Digest* in Chicago. Published novels including *Conjure Wife* (1943), *The Green Millennium* (1953), *The Wanderer* (1964), and *Our Lady of Darkness* (1977); stories collected in *Shadows with Eyes* (1962) and *The Secret Songs* (1968). The sword and sorcery tales involving Fafhrd and the Gray Mouser were collected in numerous volumes including *Swords in the Mist* (1968), *Swords and Deviltry* (1970), and *Swords and Ice Magic* (1977). The increasing popularity of his science fiction and fantasy stories enabled him to move back to Los Angeles and support his family through writing. His first wife died in 1969; he died of a brain disease not long after his second marriage.

Thomas Ligotti (b. July 9, 1953) b. in Detroit, Michigan. After receiving B.A. from Wayne State University in 1977, worked for many years at Gale Research Company as associate editor; left in 2001 to move to south Florida where he currently lives. He began publishing horror stories in small press magazines in the early 1980s. Story collections include *Songs of a Dead Dreamer* (1986), *The Nightmare Factory* (1996), *My Work Is Not Yet Done* (2002), *Sideshow, and Other Stories* (2003), and *The Shadow at the Bottom of the World* (2005). He has also collaborated on albums with the musical group Current 93.

Kelly Link (b. July 19, 1969) b. in Miami, Florida; moved with her family to Greensboro, North Carolina. Received B.A. from Columbia and M.F.A from University of North Carolina at Greensboro.

Her short fiction has been collected in *Stranger Things Happen* (2001) and *Magic for Beginners* (2006). She lives in Northampton, Massachusetts, where with her husband, Gavin Grant, she operates Small Beer Press and co-edits, with Grant and Ellen Datlow, the *Year's Best Fantasy and Horror* anthology series. She has taught in writing programs at Smith College, Bard College, the University of Massachusetts, and other schools.

Richard Matheson (b. February 20, 1926) b. in Allendale, New Jersey. Raised in Brooklyn and attended Brooklyn Technical High School. Served in the infantry during World War II. Earned B.A. in journalism from the University of Missouri in 1949. Moved to California; married Ruth Ann Woodson, with whom he had four children. His story "Born of Man and Woman" appeared in *The Magazine of Fantasy and Science Fiction* in 1950 and was collected in a volume of the same name published four years later. Published many novels including *I Am Legend* (1954), which has been filmed three times; *The Shrinking Man* (1956), filmed, with a script by Matheson, as *The Incredible Shrinking Man*; *A Stir of Echoes* (1958); *Hell House* (1917); and *Bid Time Return* (1975). He also published numerous collections of short stories including *The Shores of Space* (1957), *Shock!* (1961), *Shock 2* (1964), *Shock 3* (1966), and *Nightmare at 20,000 Feet* (2000). He wrote a number of screenplays and also television scripts for programs including *The Twilight Zone* and *Star Trek*; he adapted his story "Duel" for Steven Spielberg's film of the same name, and won an Edgar for his script for the television film *The Night Stalker*.

Steven Millhauser (b. August 3, 1943) b. in New York City. He grew up in Connecticut, where his father, Milton Millhauser, taught English at the University of Bridgeport. Received B.A. from Columbia University (1965) and did graduate studies at Brown. His first novel, *Edwin Mullhouse: The Life and Death of an American Writer 1943–1954* (1972), was followed by *Portrait of a Romantic* (1977) and a number of story collections including *In the Penny Arcade* (1986), *The Barnum Museum* (1990), and *Little Kingdoms* (1993). He won the Pulitzer Prize for his novel *Martin Dressler: The Tale of an American Dreamer* (1996). His subsequent books include *The Knife Thrower* (1998), *Enchanted Night* (1999), and *Dangerous Laughter* (2008). He teaches at Skidmore College.

Vladimir Nabokov (April 23, 1899–July 2, 1977) b. in St. Petersburg, Russia, to Vladimir Dmitrievich Nabokov, a jurist and statesman, and Elena Ivanovna Nabokov; he was the eldest of five children of a wealthy and aristocratic family. He was educated by a private tutor, and learned to read and write English before Russian. After the Bolshevik Revolution, the family fled first to the Crimea, and then to England. Nabokov enrolled in Trinity College, Cambridge, where he studied Slavic and Romance languages. The rest of his family moved in 1920 to Berlin, where his father helped set up the émigré newspaper *Rul* and was assassinated two years later by Russian monarchists. After graduating with honors from Cambridge, Nabokov moved to Berlin, where he wrote for his father's newspaper under the pen name V. Sirin. Married Vera Evseyevna Slonim in 1925; his first novel, *Mashen'ka* (*Mary*, 1925), was followed by others, as well as poems and plays. Fled with Vera and their son, Dmitri, to France in 1937, then came to the United States in 1940. Began writing only in English; published novels *The Real Life of Sebastian Knight* (1941) and *Bend Sinister* (1947) and memoir *Conclusive Evidence* (1950, later retitled *Speak, Memory*). Met and befriended Edmund Wilson. Taught comparative literature at Wellesley College. Curated lepidoptery department at Harvard's Comparative Zoology Museum. After teaching at Cornell, the Nabokovs moved to Ashland, Oregon, where he finished writing *Lolita*, which was published in France in 1955 but not in the United States until 1958; its success made him a celebrity. Moved in 1961 to Montreux, Switzerland. Translation of Pushkin's *Eugene Onegin* published in 1964. Later books included *Pale Fire* (1962), *Ada* (1969), and *Look at the Harlequins!* (1974).

Joyce Carol Oates (b. June 16, 1938) b. Lockport, New York, to Frederic James Oates, a tool and die designer, and Caroline Bush Oates. Began writing stories in elementary school and at 15 submitted a novel to a publisher that was rejected as "too depressing." Began writing novels (which remained unpublished) at a rapid rate while studying at Syracuse University, majoring in English and minoring in philosophy. Received graduate degree in English from the University of Wisconsin in 1961. Married fellow student Raymond Joseph Smith and moved with him to Beaumont, Texas, to teach. After several years teaching in Detroit and Canada, became creative writing professor at Princeton, where she continues to live. Her first published novel, *With Shuddering Fall*, appeared in 1964, followed by *A Garden of Earthly Delights* (1967) and *Expensive People* (1968); *them* (1970) received the National Book Award. Among her many other novels—she has published an average of two books a year—are *Wonderland* (1971), *Childwold* (1976), *Bellefleur* (1980), *Black Water* (1992), *Zombie* (1995), *Blonde* (2000), *The Falls* (2004), *The Gravedigger's Daughter* (2007), and *A Fair Maiden* (2009). She has also published collections of short stories including *Dear Husband*

(2009), poetry, essay collections, and novels under the pseudonyms Rosamond Smith and Lauren Kelly.

Benjamin Percy (b. March 28, 1979) b. Eugene, Oregon; lived briefly in Hawaii as a child; family moved back to Oregon, where he attended a private school in Bend. Attended Brown University, studying archeology. Received B.A. with honors and went to Southern Illinois University for M.F.A. in creative writing. First story collection, *The Language of Elk*, appeared in 2006. "Refresh, Refresh," published in *The Paris Review*, won George Plimpton Prize and Pushcart Prize, and became title story of his next collection, published in 2007. Joined the faculty of Iowa State University. In 2009 he received a Whiting Writers' Award.

Tim Powers (b. February 29, 1952) b. in Buffalo, New York. Grew up in California, where his family moved in 1959. Studied English literature at Cal State–Fullerton; earned his B.A. in 1976. Befriended Philip K. Dick, who based the character of "David" in his novel *VALIS* on him. Powers has won several awards for his novels, many of which deal with time travel, among them *The Anubis Gates* (1984) and *Dinner at Deviant's Palace* (1985). His other novels include *Last Call* (1993) and *Declare* (2001). Powers also teaches part-time as writer-in-residence for the Orange County High School of the Arts.

Jane Rice (April 30, 1913–March 2, 2003) Beginning in the early 1940s, Rice was a prolific contributor of short fiction to periodicals such as *Unknown*, *The Magazine of Fantasy & Science Fiction*, and *Charm*. She sometimes collaborated with Ruth Allison under the name Allison Rice. Her stories were first collected in *The Idol of the Flies and Other Stories* (2003). She died in Greensboro, North Carolina.

M. Rickert (b. December 11, 1959) b. Mary Rickert in Port Washington, Wisconsin, and grew up in Fredonia, Wisconsin. Moved to California at age 18, worked a series of odd jobs to support herself, and taught kindergarten at a small private school for ten years. Her first collection of stories, *Map of Dreams* (2006), won the 2007 World Fantasy Award for Best Collection and the 2007 Crawford Award. She lives with her husband in Cedarburg, Wisconsin, not far from where she grew up.

George Saunders (b. December 2, 1958) b. in Amarillo, Texas and grew up in Chicago; in 1981 graduated from the Colorado School of

Mines with a B.Sc. in geophysical engineering. Went on to earn his M.A. in creative writing from Syracuse University. Worked for Radian International, an environmental engineering firm, as a technical writer and geophysical engineer. Since 1996, has been on the faculty of Syracuse University, teaching creative writing in its M.F.A. program. His five collections of short stories and novellas have won many awards including four National Magazine Awards, an O. Henry for *Pastoralia* (2000), and the 2006 World Fantasy Award for Best Short Fiction for his story "CommComm." In 2006, he was named a MacArthur Fellow. He contributes a weekly column, *American Psyche*, to the weekend magazine of *The Guardian*'s Saturday edition.

Isaac Bashevis Singer (c. November 1904–July 24, 1991) b. Yitskhok Zynger in Leoncin, a Polish village northeast of Warsaw (then part of the Russian Empire). His father was a Hasidic rabbi and his mother the daughter of the rabbi of Bilgoraj, in the province of Lublin. Family moved to Warsaw in 1908, where father presided over a rabbinical court in the family home at 10 Krochmalna Street. Went to live with mother in Bilgoraj; studied Talmud, philosophy, and literature. Older brother Israel Joshua Singer began to achieve prominence as a writer in the early 1920s, and Singer, who had moved to Warsaw, soon began publishing stories and literary translations. Novel *Satan in Goray* published in 1933. Moved to the United States in 1935, joining his brother who was already living in New York. Wrote many stories and sketches, mostly for publication in the Yiddish paper *Forverts*. Married Alma Wassermann in 1940; became American citizen in 1943. Brother Israel Joshua died in 1944. Published novel *The Family Moskat* as magazine serial (1945–48); English translation appeared in 1950. His story "Gimpel the Fool," translated by Saul Bellow, was published in *Partisan Review* in 1953. Beginning with *Gimpel the Fool and Other Stories* (1957), English-language collections of Singer's stories began to appear, including *The Spinoza of Market Street* (1961), *Short Friday* (1964), *The Seance* (1968), *A Friend of Kafka* (1970), and *A Crown of Feathers* (1973), as well as the novels *The Magician of Lublin* (1960), *The Slave* (1962), and *Enemies, a Love Story* (1972). Also published stories for children and memoirs. Died in Surfside, Florida.

Jack Snow (August 15, 1907–July 13, 1956) b. John Frederick Snow in Piqua, Ohio. Began to work as a journalist while in high school; later worked in radio, including seven years at WNBC in New York. Published a number of stories in *Weird Tales*; short fiction collected in *Dark Music and Other Spectral Tales* (1947). He wrote two sequels to the Oz novels of L. Frank Baum—*The Magical Mimics in Oz*

(1946) and *The Shaggy Man of Oz* (1949)—and a study of Baum, *Who's Who in Oz* (1954).

Peter Straub (b. March 2, 1943) is the author of 17 novels, which have been translated into more than 20 languages. They include *Julia* (1975), *Ghost Story* (1977), *Koko* (1988), *Mr. X* (1999), *In the Night Room* (2004), and two collaborations with Stephen King, *The Talisman* (1984) and *Black House* (2001). He has written two volumes of poetry and two collections of short fiction, and he edited The Library of America edition of H. P. Lovecraft's *Tales* (2005). He has won many awards including the British Fantasy Award, eight Bram Stoker awards, two International Horror Guild awards, and two World Fantasy awards, and in 1998 was named Grand Master at the World Horror Convention. In 2006, he was given the Horror Writers Association's Life Achievement Award.

Thomas Tessier (b. May 10, 1947) b. Waterbury, Connecticut. Studied at University College, Dublin. His novels include *The Fates* (1978), *The Nightwalker* (1979), *Shockwaves* (1982), *Phantom* (1982), *Rapture* (1987), *Secret Strangers* (1990), *Fog Heart* (1997), *Father Panic's Opera Macabre* (2001), and *Wicked Things* (2007). His fantastic short fiction has been collected in *Ghost Music and Other Tales* (2000). He has also published three collections of poetry.

Jeff VanderMeer (b. July 7, 1968) b. Jeffrey Scott VanderMeer in Bellafonte, Pennsylvania; spent part of childhood in the Fiji Islands, where his parents worked for the Peace Corps. A two-time winner of the World Fantasy Award, his novels include *City of Saints and Madmen* (2001), *Veniss Underground* (2003), *Shriek: An Afterword* (2006), and *Finch* (2009). He is also the author of *Booklife: Strategies and Survival Tips for 21st-Century Writers* (2009) and has edited several anthologies with his wife, Ann VanderMeer, including *Best American Fantasy* (2007), *The New Weird* (2008), and *Steampunk* (2008). His nonfiction has appeared in the *New York Times Book Review*, and elsewhere.

Donald Wandrei (April 20, 1908–October 15, 1987) b. St. Paul, Minnesota. Graduated from the University in Minnesota in 1928; later worked in public relations. He contributed prolifically to pulp magazines and corresponded extensively with H. P. Lovecraft, whose Cthulhu Mythos he explored in several of his own stories. With August Derleth, he co-founded Arkham House, dedicated to the publication of Lovecraft's work; later edited Lovecraft's selected letters (1971–76). Served in the army during World War II. Published novel

The Web of Easter Island in 1948. His stories were collected in *The Eye and the Finger* (1944) and *Strange Harvest* (1965).

Tennessee Williams (March 6, 1911–February 24, 1983) b. Thomas Lanier Williams III in Columbus, Mississippi. Father worked as a traveling salesman. Ill as a child with diphtheria and Bright's disease. Family moved in 1918 to St. Louis, where father had a job as shoe company branch manager. Began writing in junior high school; while in high school published "The Vengeance of Nitocris" in *Weird Tales*. Studied at University of Missouri School of Journalism at Columbia. Began writing plays and studied playwriting at the University of Iowa. His play *Battle of Angels* was produced unsuccessfully by the Theatre Guild in 1940. Spent much time in New Orleans, Key West, and New Mexico. *The Glass Menagerie* opened on Broadway in 1945 and won New York Drama Critics Circle award. Success of *A Streetcar Named Desire* (1947) followed by New York productions of *Summer and Smoke* (1948), *The Rose Tattoo* (1951), and *Camino Real* (1953). Short story collection *Hard Candy* published in 1954. Later plays included *Cat on a Hot Tin Roof* (1955), *Orpheus Descending* (1957), *Suddenly Last Summer* (1958), *Sweet Bird of Youth* (1959), *The Night of the Iguana* (1961), and *The Milk Train Doesn't Stop Here Anymore* (1962). Subsequent plays, including *Kingdom of Earth* (1968), *In the Bar of a Tokyo Hotel* (1969), and *Small Craft Warnings* (1972), found less critical favor than his earlier work.

Gene Wolfe (b. May 7, 1931) b. New York City. Attended Texas A&M University where he began to publish speculative fiction in a student literary magazine. After serving in the Korean War, earned a degree in industrial engineering from the University of Houston. Had long career as industrial engineer and edited technical journal *Plant Engineering*. Since 1970 he has published many novels and stories, many of them honored by awards, and won particular acclaim for the tetralogy *The Book of the New Sun*, consisting of the novels *The Shadow of the Torturer* (1980), *The Claw of the Conciliator* (1981), *The Sword of the Lictor* (1982), and *The Citadel of the Autarch* (1983). Two related cycles, *The Book of the Long Sun* and *The Book of the Short Sun*, appeared in multiple volumes between 1993 and 2001. His later books include *The Wizard Knight* (2004), *Pirate Freedom* (2007), and *An Evil Guest* (2008). Thomas Disch once described him as the "most underrated" author in his field.

Note on the Texts

This volume contains 41 fantastic tales by American writers originally published between 1941 and 2007 and presents them in the order of their original publication. In the case of stories not yet collected in book form, or that were not collected in book form during the author's lifetime, the texts are taken from periodical versions.

The following is a list of the sources of the texts included in this volume, listed in the order of their appearance in this volume.

John Collier: Evening Primrose; *Presenting Moonshine* (New York: Viking Press, 1941), 1–15. Copyright © 1941 by John Collier, renewed © 1969 by John Collier. Permission to reprint granted by Harold Matson Co, Inc.

Fritz Leiber: Smoke Ghost; *Unknown*, October 1941. Copyright © 1948 by the University of the South. Reprinted by permission of New Directions Publishing Corp.

Tennessee Williams: The Mysteries of the Joy Rio, *Hard Candy* (New York: New Directions, 1954), 203–20. Written c. 1941. Copyright © 1948 by the University of the South. Reprinted by permission of New Directions Publishing Corp.

Jane Rice: The Refugee, *Unknown*, October 1943, 111–20.

Anthony Boucher: Mr. Lupescu, *Weird Tales*, September, 1945, 74–76. Reprinted in *The Compleat Werewolf* (New York: Simon & Schuster, 1969). Copyright © 1945 by Anthony Boucher. Reprinted by permission of Curtis Brown, Ltd.

Truman Capote: Miriam, *A Tree of Night* (New York, Random House, 1945), 115–34. First published in *Mademoiselle*, June 1945. Copyright © 1945, 1946, 1947, 1948, 1949 by Truman Capote. Used by permission of Random House, Inc.

Jack Snow: Midnight; *Midnight* (New York: J. Little and Ives Co., 1947), 200–8. First published in *Weird Tales*, May 1946.

John Cheever: Torch Song; *John Cheever: Stories*, Blake Bailey, ed. (New York, Library of America, 2009), 109–25. First published in *The New Yorker*, October 4, 1947; collected in *The Enormous Radio* (New York: Funk & Wagnalls, 1953) and *The Stories of John Cheever* (New York: Alfred A. Knopf, 1978). Copyright © 1978 by John Cheever. Used by permission of Alfred A. Knopf, a division of Random House, Inc.

Shirley Jackson: The Daemon Lover; *The Lottery: Adventures of the Daemon Lover* (New York: Farrar, Straus and Cudahy, 1949). First published (as "The Phantom Lover") in *Woman's Home Companion*, February 1949. Copyright © 1948, 1949 by Shirley Jackson. Copyright renewed 1976, 1977 by Laurence Hyman, Barry Hyman, Mrs. Sarah Webster and Mrs. Joanne Schurer. Reprinted by permission of Farrar, Straus & Giroux, LLC.

Paul Bowles: The Circular Valley; *Paul Bowles: Complete Stories & Later Writings*, Daniel Halpern, ed. (New York: Library of America, 2002), 90–99. First published in *The Delicate Prey and Other Stories* (New York: Random House, 1950); collected in *The Stories of Paul Bowles* (New York: HarperCollins, 2006). Copyright © 2001 by the Estate of Paul Bowles. Reprinted by permission of HarperCollins Publishers.

Jack Finney: I'm Scared; *The Clock of Time* (London: Eyre & Spottiswoode, 1958), 43–63. First published in *Collier's*, September 1951; collected in *About Time* (New York: Simon & Schuster, 1998). Copyright © 1951 by Crowell Collier Publishing Co., © renewed by Jack Finney. Reprinted by permission of Simon & Schuster, Inc. All rights reserved.

Vladimir Nabokov: The Vane Sisters; *Nabokov's Quartet* (New York: Phaedra Publishers, 1966), 75–90. First published in *The Hudson Review*, Winter 1959. Written 1951. Copyright © 1959, renewed © 1987 by Vera Nabokov and Dmitri Nabokov. Used by permission of Alfred A. Knopf, a division of Random House, Inc.

Ray Bradbury: The April Witch, *The Golden Apples of the Sun* (New York: Doubleday & Co., 1953), 31–43. First published in *The Saturday Evening Post*, April 5, 1952. Copyright © 1952 by the Curtis Publishing Company, renewed 1980 by Ray Bradbury. Reprinted by permission of Don Congdon Associates, Inc.

Charles Beaumont: Black Country; *The Hunger and Other Stories* (New York: G. P. Putnam's Sons, 1958), 213–34. First published in *Playboy*, September 1954. Copyright © 1957 by Charles Beaumont, renewed 1985 by Christopher Beaumont. Reprinted by permission of Don Congdon Associates, Inc.

Jerome Bixby: Trace; *Space by the Tale* (New York: Ballantine Books, 1964), 91–94.

Davis Grubb: Where the Woodbine Twineth; *Twelve Tales of Suspense and the Supernatural* (New York: Scribner, 1964), 161–75. First published (as "You Never Believe Me") in *Esquire*, February 1964; collected in *You Never Believe Me and Other Stories* (New York: St. Martin's, 1989). Copyright © 1964 by Davis Grubb.

Donald Wandrei: Nightmare; *Strange Harvest* (Sauk City, WI: Arkham House, 1965), 284–89. Copyright ©1965 by Donald Wandrei for *Strange Harvest*. Reprinted by permission of Harold Hughesdon.

Harlan Ellison®: I Have No Mouth, and I Must Scream; *Essential Ellison* (Beverly Hills, CA: Morpheus International, 1991). First published in *IF: World of Science Fiction*, March 1967. Copyright © 1967 by Harlan Ellison®. Renewed 1995 by The Kilimanjaro Corporation. Reprinted by arrangement with, and permission of, the Author and the Author's agent, Richard Curtis Associates, Inc., New York. All rights reserved. Harlan Ellison® is a registered trademark of The Kilimanjaro Corporation.

Richard Matheson: Prey; *Nightmare at 20,000 Feet* (New York: TOR Books, 2002), 321–35. First published in *Playboy*, April 1969. Copyright © 1969 by HMH Publishing Company, Inc., renewed 1997 by Richard Matheson. Reprinted by permission of Don Congdon Associates, Inc.

T.E.D. Klein: The Events at Poroth Farm; *Reassuring Tales*, (Burton, MI: Subterranean Press, 2006), 121–67. First published in *From Beyond the Dark Gateway* #2, December 1972. Copyright © 1972 by T.E.D. Klein. Reprinted by permission of the author.

Isaac Bashevis Singer: Hanka; *Singer: Collected Stories: A Friend of Kafka to Passions*, Ilan Stavans, ed. (New York: Library of America, 2004), 567–83. First published in Yiddish in *Di goldene keyt 83*, 1974, and in English in *The New Yorker*, February 4, 1974; collected in *Passions and Other Stories* (New York: Farrar, Straus & Giroux, 1975). Copyright © 1975 by Isaac Bashevis Singer. Reprinted by permission of Farrar, Straus & Giroux, LLC.

Fred Chappell: Linnaeus Forgets; *More Shapes Than One* (New York: St. Martin's Press, 1991), 1–18. First published in *American Review*, November 1977. Copyright © 1991 by Fred Chappell. Reprinted by permission of St. Martin's Press, LLC.

John Crowley: Novelty; *Novelties and Souvenirs: Collected Short Fiction* (New York: HarperCollins, 2004), 38–58. First published in *Interzone*, Autumn 1983. Copyright © 1983 by John Crowley. Reprinted by permission of the author and his agent, Ralph M. Vicinanza, Ltd.

Jonathan Carroll: Mr Fiddlehead; *The Panic Hand* (London: HarperCollins UK, 1995), 9–22. First published in *Omni*, February 1989. Copyright © 1989 by Jonathan Carroll. Reprinted by permission of The Richard Parks Agency.

Joyce Carol Oates: Family; *Omni*, December 1989, 75–87. Copyright © 1989 Ontario Review. Reprinted by permission of John Hawkins & Associates, Inc.

Thomas Ligotti: The Last Feast of Harlequin; *Shadow at the Bottom of the World*, (Cold Spring Press, 2005), 195–228. First published in *The Magazine of Fantasy and Science Fiction*, April 1990.

Copyright © 1991 by Thomas Ligotti. All rights reserved. Reprinted by permission of the author.

Peter Straub: A Short Guide to the City; *Houses Without Doors* (New York: Dutton, 1990), 95–105. Copyright © by Peter Straub. Reprinted by arrangement with the Genert Company.

Jeff VanderMeer: The General Who Is Dead, *Secret Life* (Prime Books, 2004), 80–83. First published in *Freezer Burn Magazine 5*, 1996. Copyright © 1996 by Jeff VanderMeer. Reprinted by permission of the author.

Stephen King: That Feeling, You Can Only Say What It Is in French; *Everything's Eventual: 14 Dark Tales* (New York: Scribner, 2002) 347–64. First published in *The New Yorker*, June 22, 1998. Copyright © 2002 by Stephen King. Reprinted with the permission of Scribner, a Division of Simon & Schuster, Inc.

George Saunders: Sea Oak; *Pastoralia* (New York: Riverhead Books, 2000), 91–125. First published in *The New Yorker*, December 28, 1998. Copyright © 2000 by George Saunders. Used by permission of Riverhead Books, an imprint of Penguin Group (USA) Inc.

Caitlín R. Kiernan: The Long Hall on the Top Floor; author's typescript. First published in *Carpe Noctem 16*, 1999. Reprinted in *Tales of Pain and Wonder* (Springfield, PA: Gauntlet Publications, 2000; Burton, MI: Subterranean Press, 2008). Copyright © Caitlín R. Kiernan. Reprinted by permission of the author.

Thomas Tessier: Nocturne; *Ghost Music and Other Tales* (Abingdon, MD: Cemetery Dance Publications, 2000), 293–96. Copyright © 2000 by Thomas Tessier. Reprinted by permission of the author.

Michael Chabon: The God of Dark Laughter; *The New Yorker*, April 9, 2001, 116–28. Copyright © 2001 by Michael Chabon. All rights reserved. Reprinted by arrangement with Mary Evans Inc.

Joe Hill: Pop Art; *20th-Century Ghosts* (UK: PS Publishing, 2005), 51–74. First published in *With Signs & Wonders*, edited by Daniel M. Jaffe (Montpelier, VT: Invisible Cities Press, 2001). Reprinted in *20th-Century Ghosts* (New York: William Morrow, 2007). Copyright © 2001, 2005, 2007 by Joe Hill. Published in the U.S. in 2007 by William Morrow, an imprint of HarperCollins Publishers.

Poppy Z. Brite: Pansu; *The Devil You Know* (Burton, MI: Subterranean Press, 2003), 99–109. First published as a Camelot Books chapbook in 2001. Copyright © Poppy Z. Brite. Reprinted by permission of the author.

Steven Millhauser: Dangerous Laughter; *Dangerous Laughter* (New York: Alfred A. Knopf, 2008), 75–93. First published in *Tin House* #17, Fall 2003. Copyright © 2008 by Steven Millhauser. Used by permission of Alfred A. Knopf, a division of Random House, Inc.

M. Rickert: The Chambered Fruit; *Map of Dreams* (Urbana, IL:

Golden Gryphon Press, 2006), 278–308. First published in *The Magazine of Fantasy and Science Fiction*, August 2003. Copyright © 2003 by M. Rickert. Reprinted by permission of the author.

Brian Evenson: The Wavering Knife; *The Wavering Knife* (Tallahassee, FL: Fiction Collective Two, 2004), 81–97. Copyright © 1998 by Brian Evenson. Reprinted by permission.

Kelly Link: Stone Animals; *Magic for Beginners* (Northhampton, MA,: Small Beer Press, 2005), 67–112. First published in *Conjunctions #43*, Fall 2004. Copyright © 2004. Reprinted by permission of the author c/o the Renee Zuckerbrot Literary Agency.

Tim Powers: Pat Moore; *Strange Itineraries* (San Francisco, Calif.: Tachyon Publications, 2005), 41–77. First published in *Flights: Extreme Visions of Fantasy*, edited by Al Sarrantonio (New York: Roc, 2004). Copyright © 2004 Tim Powers. Reprinted with permission of the author.

Gene Wolfe: The Little Stranger; *The Magazine of Fantasy and Science Fiction*, October/November, 2004, 184–201. Copyright © 2004 by Gene Wolfe. Reprinted by permission of the author and the author's agents, the Virginia Kidd Agency Inc.

Benjamin Percy: Dial Tone; *Missouri Review*, Summer, 2007, 97–108. Copyright © 2007 by Benjamin Percy. Reprinted by permission of Curtis Brown, Ltd.

This volume presents the texts listed here without change except for the correction of typographical errors, but it does not attempt to reproduce features of their typographic design. The following is a list of typographical errors, cited by page and line number: 13.15, vicious,; 14.5, diaphram; 25.23, to Millick; 40.8, hurt-/ting; 41.29, it's; 57.1, Lupescue; 74.14, abhorently; 122.21, singing,; 146.1, fate; 150.3, name"; 156.6, Town Illinois; 183.13, Brother; 255.23, Walden; 297.23, oppossums; 318.33, said.; 338.4, capitol; 368.19, thought; 379.24, the,; 425.39, weren't we were her; 447.15, drier; 456.22, It; 463.4, circus; 585.11, grass,".

Notes

In the notes below, the reference numbers refer to page and line of this volume (the line count includes titles and headings). The editor wishes to thank Stefan Dziemianowicz for his expert and deeply knowledgeable assistance in the preparation for these volumes and the selection of their contents.

2.10   Piranesi] Giovanni Battista Piranesi (1720–1778), Italian artist known for his elaborate depictions of labyrinthine imaginary prisons (*Carceri d'Invenzione*).

41.16   Maginot Line] System of defensive fortifications along the French border, constructed during the 1930s; it was successfully circumvented by German forces in 1940.

54.38–39   "The Werewolf of Paris"] Popular horror novel (1933) by Guy Endore (1900–1970).

84.40   Mitropa] German-Austrian catering company founded in 1916.

87.19   Marion Harris] Jazz singer (1896–1944) whose hits included "After You've Gone" (1918), "A Good Man Is Hard to Find" (1919), and "I Ain't Got Nobody" (1920).

91.11   Saranac] The Adirondack Cottage Sanitarium for the treatment of tuberculosis was established in 1885 in Saranac Lake, New York.

96.3   *The Daemon Lover*] Traditional British ballad, also known as "James Harris," in which a woman is tempted to her doom.

122.2   Major Bowes] Edward Bowes (1874–1946), host of the radio series *Major Bowes Amateur Hour* (1934–46).

122.4   "La Paloma."] Song composed by Sebastián Iradier in the early 1860s and widely recorded throughout the 20th century.

122.21   "You Butterfly,"] "Butterfly" (1957), song by Kal Mann and Bernie Lowe.

122.32   Moran and Mack] George Moran (1881–1949) and Charles Mack (1888–1934), known for their blackface comedy act Two Black Crows.

122.34   Floyd Gibbons] War correspondent (1887–1949) who covered World War I for the *Chicago Tribune* and was later known as a radio and newsreel commentator.

137.20–21   *Cette examain . . . jeunes filles!*]   The faulty French can be translated: This test is over and so is my life. Goodbye, girls!

142.21   "Alph"]   See Samuel Taylor Coleridge, "Kubla Khan."

142.22   Anna Livia Plurabelle]   Female figure associated with the River Liffey in James Joyce's *Finnegans Wake* (1939).

146.29   the Fox sisters]   Three sisters from Hydeville, New York, who beginning in the late 1840s acquired a reputation for mediumistic abilities manifested through mysterious rappings. At the height of their celebrity they attracted support from many prominent figures, notably Horace Greeley. In 1888 Margaret Fox published a confession (later recanted) that the rappings had been faked.

146.38   Alfred Russel Wallace]   British naturalist (1823–1913) who developed a theory of natural selection independently of Charles Darwin; he later became an advocate of Spiritualism.

153.16   "Beautiful Ohio."]   Ohio state song, written by Ballard Mac-Donald and Mary Earl.

162.17–18   Jelly Roll's]   Jelly Roll Morton (1890–1941), pianist and composer whose works included "Wolverine Blues," "New Orleans Bump," and "Shreveport Stomp."

165.25   Muggsy Spanier's]   Cornet player (1906–1967) active on the Chicago jazz scene from the 1920s on.

180.9   *Mephisto Waltz*]   One of four waltzes composed by Franz Liszt between 1859 and 1885.

225.33   Bruno Hauptmann]   Hauptmann (1899–1936) was executed for the abduction and murder of Charles Lindbergh Jr.

233.5   *Vathek*]   Oriental romance written in French by William Beckford (1759–1844), and first published (in English translation) in 1786.

233.21   *The Mysteries of Udolpho*]   Enormously popular novel published in 1794 by Ann Radcliffe (1764–1823).

233.26   Montoni]   Villain who passes himself off as an Italian nobleman in *The Mysteries of Udolpho*.

234.27   Maturin]   Charles Robert Maturin (1782–1824), Irish novelist best known for *Melmoth the Wanderer* (1820).

235.3–4   Arthur Machen]   Welsh novelist (1863–1947) whose many works of fantastic fiction included *The Great God Pan* (1894), *The Three Imposters* (1895), *The House of Souls* (1906), *The Hill of Dreams* (1907), and *The Terror* (1917).

236.12   Algernon Blackwood's] English writer (1869–1951) best known for supernatural stories.

237.16   *Otranto*] *The Castle of Otranto* (1765), prototypical Gothic novel by Horace Walpole (1717–1797).

238.8   *The Monk*] Novel (1795) by Matthew Gregory Lewis (1775–1818).

238.37   Brother Ambrosio] The malevolent protagonist of Lewis's *The Monk*.

239.3   *The Thief of Baghdad*] *The Thief of Bagdad* (1940), film produced by Alexander Korda and directed by a team including Michael Powell and Ludwig Berger; the title role was played by Sabu.

244.26   LeFanu] Joseph Sheridan Le Fanu (1814–1873), writer known for his stories of terror and the supernatural; his novels include *The House by the Churchyard* (1863) and *Uncle Silas* (1864).

245.12   "The Uninhabited House" . . . "Monsieur Maurice,"] Novel by Mrs. J. H. Riddell (1832–1906); novella (1873) by Amelia Ann Blandford Edwards (1831–1892).

245.14   "The Amber Witch,"] German novel (1845) by Wilhelm Meinhold (1797–1851), originally presented by the author as an authentic historical document; in a subsequent edition Meinhold admitted the hoax. An English translation appeared in 1861.

246.39–247.1   *American Scholar*] Magazine of the Phi Beta Kappa Society, published since 1932.

246.13   A. E. Coppard] Short story writer (1878–1957) whose collections included *Adam and Eve and Pinch Me* (1921), *The Black Dog* (1923), and *Fearful Pleasures* (1946).

249.9   Barbara Byfield's *Glass Harmonica*] Byfield's book, published in 1967, is subtitled *A Lexicon of the Fantastical*.

249.14–15   Maria Ouspenskaya] Russian actress (1876–1949) who came to the U.S. as a member of the Moscow Art Theater and went on to appear in Hollywood films such as *Dodsworth* (1936), *The Wolf Man* (1941), and *The Shanghai Gesture* (1942).

249.17–18   Marryat . . . Endore] Frederick Marryat, English writer of nautical novels (1792–1848); Guy Endore, see note 54.38–39.

251.28   Shirley Jackson] American writer (1916–1965) whose works include *The Lottery and Other Stories* (1949) and *The Haunting of Hill House* (1959).

251.30   Aleister Crowley] British occultist (1875–1945), author of *Magick* (1912-13) and other works.

255.6   Ruthven Todd's *Lost Traveller*]   *The Lost Traveller* (1943), novel by the Scottish poet Ruthven Todd (1914–1978).

255.11–12   Lafcadio Hearn . . . "Gaki,"]   See Hearn's 1923 collection *Kottô: Being Japanese Curios, with Sundry Webs*: "The belief in a mysterious relation between ghosts and insects, or rather between spirits and insects, is a very ancient belief in the East, where it now assumes innumerable forms,— some unspeakably horrible, others full of weird beauty."

259.10   *The King in Yellow*]   Collection of short stories (1895) by Robert W. Chambers; the first four all deal in different ways with the evil influence of the fictional play "The King in Yellow."

260.6   M. R. James]   Montagu Rhodes James (1862–1936), antiquarian and author of ghost stories collected in *Ghost Stories of an Antiquary* (1905–11).

262.7   Lovecraft's essay . . . Literature."]   Pioneering survey by H. P. Lovecraft (1890–1937), first published in *The Recluse* in 1927 and reprinted after Lovecraft's death in *The Outsider and Others* (1939).

262.29   John Christopher's *The Possessors*]   Science fiction novel (1965) written by Samuel Youd (b. 1922) under the pseudonym John Christopher.

280.2   Pavlova . . . Isadora Duncan]   Anna Pavlova (1881–1931), Russian ballerina celebrated for her performance as "The Dying Swan"; Duncan (1877–1927), American pioneer of modern dance.

284.15   Marranos]   Sephardic Jews threatened with expulsion from Spain who converted to Christianity under duress, but continued to practice Judaism in secret.

289.5   Carl Linnaeus]   Swedish botanist (1707–1778), pioneer of modern systems of taxonomy.

289.30–31   Albrecht von Haller]   Swiss physiologist and anatomist (1708–1777).

290.8   Siegesbeck]   Johann Georg Siegesbeck (1686–1755), German botanist who engaged in bitter polemics against the Linnean system of classification.

303.38   Andromeda]   In Greek mythology, daughter of Cepheus and Cassiopeia, rulers of Ethiopia; she was chained to a rock and offered in sacrifice to a sea monster who had been sent to punish her mother's pride.

307.12   *Euphues*]   *Euphues, the Anatomy of Wit* (1579), romance by John Lyly (?1554–1606), who followed it with *Euphues and his England* (1580); the ornately allusive and circuitous wordplay of these works were for a time greatly influential among English writers.

315.23   Murillo]   Bartolomé Esteban Murillo (1617–1682), Spanish painter who specialized in religious subjects.

326.30–31   Antonio Sant' Elia]   Italian architect (1888–1916) associated with Futurism.

333.2   Scott Joplin]   American composer (?1867–1917) known for his ragtime pieces and for the opera *Treemonisha*.

358.34   "The Conqueror Worm,"]   Poem by Edgar Allan Poe, collected in *The Raven and Other Poems* (1849).

385.22   *O carne vale!*]   O farewell to flesh (or meat)!

402.14   Inchon]   Decisive battle (1950) of the Korean War, won by United Nations forces.

414.33   *Let the wild rumpus start*]   See Maurice Sendak, *Where the Wild Things Are* (1963).

420.38   "In-A-Gadda-Da-Vida"]   The 1968 hit by the psychedelic rock group Iron Butterfly ran 17 minutes and took up one side of the album named for it.

421.22   Jerry Lee Lewis]   Rock and country performer (b. 1935) whose recordings include "Great Balls of Fire," "Lewis Boogie," and "High School Confidential."

422.25   *The hard days are coming.*]   In the collection *Everything's Eventual*, Stephen King added the following commentary to this story: "I think this story is about Hell. A version of it where you are condemned to do the same thing over and over again. Existentialism, baby, what a concept; paging Albert Camus. There's an idea that Hell is other people. My idea is that it might be repetition."

441.2   *The Prophet*]   Perennially popular collection of prose poems (1923) by the Lebanese-American writer Khalil Gibran (1883–1931).

447.20   Herman and Lily Munster]   Central characters of the television comedy series *The Munsters* (1964–66), played by Fred Gwynne and Yvonne De Carlo.

447.35   Randy Newman]   Singer, songwriter, and composer (b. 1943); his albums include *12 Songs* (1970), *Sail Away* (1972), and *Good Old Boys* (1974).

448.27   *The Martian Chronicles*]   Collection of linked stories (1950) detailing the colonization of Mars by humans.

449.34   Beastie Boys]   American hip hop group known for the albums *Licensed to Ill* (1986) and *Paul's Boutique* (1988).

451.3–4   George Romero]   American filmmaker (b. 1940) best known for his series of zombie movies beginning with *Night of the Living Dead* (1968) and also including *Dawn of the Dead* (1978) and *Day of the Dead* (1985).

471.26–27   Poe's story . . . rampaging orang]   "The Murders in the Rue Morgue" (1841).

475.10   Madame Blavatsky]   Helena Petrovna Blavatsky (1831–1891), born in Russia, came to the U.S. in 1873 and founded the Theosophical Society; author of *The Secret Doctrine* (1888).

481.23   Occam's razor]   Dictum of the English philosopher William of Occam (?1290–1349): "Entities are not to be unnecessarily multiplied," or the simplest explanation is most likely correct.

485.31   Bernard Malamud]   Novelist (1914–1986) whose works include *The Natural* (1952), *The Assistant* (1957), and *The Fixer* (1966).

529.28   Grandma Moses]   Anna Mary Robertson Moses (1860–1961), American folk artist who began to paint in her seventies.

581.23   *The Velveteen Rabbit*]   Novel for children (1922), subtitled *How Toys Become Real*, by Margery Williams (1881–1944).

595.2   *Fight Club*]   Novel (1996) by Chuck Palhniuk.

600.19   Jane Goodall]   English primatologist (b. 1934) known for her studies of the social life of chimpanzees.

607.32   *A Curtain of Green*]   Story collection (1941) by Eudora Welty.

630.17–18   Frost . . . *back*]   See Robert Frost "Two Witches: The Witch of Coös" (collected in *New Hampshire*, 1923), lines 16–18: "Don't that make you suspicious / That there's something the dead are keeping back? / Yes, there's something the dead are keeping back."

THE LIBRARY OF AMERICA SERIES

The Library of America fosters appreciation and pride in America's literary heritage by publishing, and keeping permanently in print, authoritative editions of America's best and most significant writing. An independent nonprofit organization, it was founded in 1979 with seed money from the National Endowment for the Humanities and the Ford Foundation.

To subscribe to the series or to order individual copies,
please visit www.loa.org or call (800) 964.5778.

*This book is set in 10 point Linotron Galliard,
a face designed for photocomposition by Matthew Carter
and based on the sixteenth-century face Granjon. The paper
is acid-free lightweight opaque and meets the requirements
for permanence of the American National Standards Institute.
The binding material is Brillianta, a woven rayon cloth made
by Van Heek-Scholco Textielfabrieken, Holland. Compo-
sition by Dedicated Business Services. Printing by
Malloy Incorporated. Binding by Dekker Book-
binding. Designed by Bruce Campbell.*

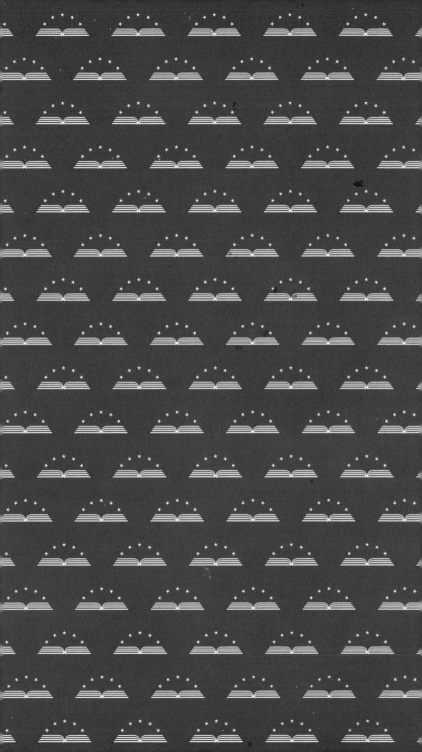